A DAZZLING REVENGE

Matthew caught his breath as he gazed upon the glittering gems nestling on a cushion of blue velvet. This was even lovelier than he had imagined, more magnificent than he had ever dreamed, flashing a flawless fire, a brilliance, a radiance beyond compare.

Each worker, each link in the human chain, had carried out his appointed task to perfection. Yet Matthew had the satisfaction of knowing that he was the chief architect of that glowing perfection. It was his choice of stones which had made it possible.

'It is a triumph,' said the manager quietly.

Matthew nodded. Excitement and anticipation were mounting within him as he prepared to put his plans into action. He held the jewels in his long sensitive fingers, savouring this long-awaited contact with the instrument of his revenge. 'The Bright necklace,' he murmured. 'At last!'

King of Diamonds

CAROLYN TERRY

SPHERE BOOKS LIMITED
London and Sydney

First published in Great Britain by
Century Publishing Co. Ltd. 1983

Published by Sphere Books Ltd 1984
30–32 Gray's Inn Road, London WC1X 8JL

Publisher's Note

This novel is a work of fiction. Names, characters, places and incidents are either the product of the author's imagination or are used fictitiously, and any resemblance to actual persons, living or dead, events, or locales is entirely coincidental.

TRADE
MARK

Set in 9/11 Compugraphic Cheltenham Book

Printed and bound in Great Britain by
Collins, Glasgow

To Roy

PROLOGUE

ENGLAND 1866

The first diamond to attract the attention of Matthew Harcourt-Bright nestled in the pale bosom of the Comtesse de Gravigny, the hard coldness of the stone warmed by her soft flesh and by the drowsy heat of Matthew's sixteenth summer.

Invited to spend the school holidays at Desborough Park with his friend, Lord Nicholas Grafton, a carriage had collected the two boys from Eton and conveyed them briskly along the leafy lanes and shaded byways of Berkshire, through Reading to the western end of the Royal County. Part of Matthew enjoyed the journey, revelling not only in the comfort of the carriage and the status bestowed by its splendour and the coat-of-arms upon the door, but also in the deference they were accorded along the way. Another part of him was nevertheless apprehensive and ill-at-ease, unsure of the warmth of the Duke of Desborough's welcome.

Matthew's uncle was the Earl of Highclere whose lands adjoined the Desborough estate, but his father was a country parson and he was painfully aware of the contrast between the ducal mansion and his own more humble home. Moreover, the Highcleres were not numbered among England's wealthiest landowners and the system of primogeniture ensured that the family's limited fortune was bestowed in its entirety upon the eldest son. Matthew's father, the Honourable Peregrine, was a gentleman but an impoverished one, and Matthew and his siblings dwelt on the shadowy fringe of society.

However, no one could have detected Matthew's inner uncertainty: his composure appeared complete as he lounged gracefully in one corner of the carriage, his blue eyes surveying the procession of rolling Berkshire downs with the utmost self-possession. Long, well-muscled legs and broad strong shoulders enhanced his air of maturity and he could have passed for eighteen at least – Lord Nicholas at his side looking a mere boy by comparison. Not that anyone noticed Nicholas when his friend was present, for there was a natural magnetism about Matthew. Without any conscious effort he drew the gaze of every eye and those eyes feasted on the haunting beauty of his face, on the lean curve of his cheek, thick golden hair and clear blue eyes, and the chin which already revealed a jutting determination. Only the wide thin lips betrayed his sensitivity, lips which compressed slightly as the equipage swept through Desborough's handsome gates and up the long drive to the imposing façade of the great house.

'They'll be in the garden,' Nicholas announced, jumping down from the carriage the instant it drew up at the main door and dashing up the steps.

Matthew followed at a more leisurely pace, to allow his friend some privacy for the family reunion. Slowly he walked through the cool corridors to the terrace at the back of the mansion and descended the steps to the smooth lawns. The scent of roses drifted on the light breeze and the hum of insects floated on the air, ebbing and flowing in insistent waves against his senses. The Desboroughs and their daughters were sitting in the shade of a cedar tree beside a laden tea-table. The pale colours of the dresses, the pure white of the tablecloth and the glow of the silver seemed to sparkle and then shimmer out of focus as Matthew crossed the lawn in the full glare of the sun.

The bulky figure of the Duke of Desborough advanced a couple of courteous steps to meet him. From beneath beetling eyebrows a pair of pale blue eyes transfixed him with a haughty stare and the heavily-bewhiskered face of his host seemed set in lines of contempt and disapproval.

'Your Grace.' Matthew bowed.

He was slightly taller than the Duke and resolutely tried to hold his head high. But although pride caused Matthew's back to stiffen and his shoulders to straighten, the innate sense of inferiority he always felt here forced his gaze to the ground as the Duke grunted and turned away.

Fortunately Matthew did not encounter the same problem

with his hostess; already his effect on women was markedly different from the reaction he sparked in men.

'Matthew, my dear boy!' The Duchess rose to envelop him in a rustling taffeta embrace. 'We are so pleased to see you.'

'It is awfully good of you to have me.'

'Not at all. We have plenty of room!' responded the Duchess as she waved a casual hand in the direction of the massive walls and countless windows of the house. 'I do hope that your sister is getting better.'

'I believe so.' Matthew hesitated. 'I'm afraid,' he continued apologetically, 'that they don't want me home for some weeks.'

'I should think not!' The Duchess looked horrified. 'Mumps can be a most difficult ailment and under no circumstances must you be exposed to it. You must stay here, my boy, for as long as you like.'

'Thank you, ma'am. My parents and I are much obliged.' And Matthew bowed again.

She looked at him, aware that being a mother of six children did not render her immune to his attraction. He had always been a boy of charm and character, she thought, but now there was a fresh force and strength about him and his astounding good looks had chiselled into an adult masculinity.

'How you have grown,' she said slowly.

At that moment Matthew heard a sharp intake of breath and was astonished to see an unfamiliarly mellow expression settle on the Duke's features as the forbidding gaze softened and the tight lips relaxed into the semblance of a smile.

The Duchess was looking in the same direction as her husband. 'Ah, here comes the Comtesse,' she said with satisfaction. 'Now we can start tea.'

She was walking across the lawn towards them, her wide skirts swaying and a parasol shielding her from the sun. Her dress of white silk was striped with silver and lavishly trimmed with lace. It covered her with due propriety from her long neck to her slender wrists, down to the tips of her dainty slippers. Yet it somehow served to emphasise the allure of her figure, with its tiny waist and swelling bosom, and her graceful walk.

It was only when she came closer that Matthew saw she was no longer young. But he did not try to reckon her years. Her face was heart-shaped and her skin was pale and translucent as fine porcelain. Her eyes were deep-set, and of a mysterious green flecked with gold, and her lips wide and sensuous. She wore a small hat of white straw trimmed with white and yellow flowers, tied with white satin ribbon. The hat was tipped forward over her luxuriant chestnut hair, which was combed high to cascade into shining ringlets at her neck. As she greeted the Duchess, she presented Matthew with a profile made perfect by an upturned retroussé nose.

Never had Matthew felt more shy and gauche or more conscious of his mere sixteen years.

'You have already met Matthew's uncle,' the Duchess commented after the introductions had been completed. 'The Earl of Highclere.'

'Yes, of course.' The Comtesse spoke perfect English with a delightful French accent, her voice low and husky. 'I see the resemblance, I think.' And she appraised Matthew from under long dark lashes before allowing the Duke to lead her to a chair.

'Oh, Matthew is the image of his father,' the Duchess declared. 'Peregrine was by far the better looking of the two boys. Being the younger son he had to choose between the army and the church, and he chose the church – he was, I recall, always a trifle on the pious side.' And she gave a small sigh of regret.

'And you, Matthew, are *you* pious?' inquired the Comtesse.

She is laughing at me, he thought, and fought back the flush which threatened to stain his cheeks. 'Not particularly,' he replied indifferently.

'Good!' And again she cast him a lingering sideways glance, while the Duke hovered attentively behind her.

Matthew politely began to hand round cups of tea and plates of cake and sandwiches, while the Duchess beamed approval on him.

'Such a good friend for Nicholas,' she said softly, leaning confidentially towards the Frenchwoman. 'And his elder brother Frederick is at Oxford with Lambourne.'

The Duke snorted, partly at the reference to his own eldest son, Hugh, Marquess of Lambourne, and partly at mention of the

Harcourt-Bright brothers. 'Useless young puppies, both of 'em!' he muttered. 'Can't see why Lambourne and Nicholas cultivate their acquaintance so assiduously. Their cousin Swanley is a much more suitable companion, being heir to the Highclere estate and title; a connection with that branch of the family would bring considerable advantages,' and his prominent eyes rested speculatively on his four daughters who were clustered round Nicholas.

'My dear, he'll *hear* you!' hissed the Duchess, giving her husband a reproachful look. Raising her voice, she called to Matthew, 'Is Freddy going to Cowes?'

Matthew *had* heard and, although he managed to conceal his shame, his hand shook and the cup rattled dangerously in its saucer at the mention of his elder brother.

'Yes, ma'am.'

'And you wish you were going too!' The Duchess smiled as Matthew opened his mouth to protest. 'Yes, of course you do, so does Nicholas. Much more fun than boating on the Desborough lake! But you are still young – you have many Cowes weeks ahead of you. And you are not alone in your exile from the festivities.' She laid a plump hand on the slender white fingers of the Comtesse. 'The Comtesse and her husband visited London for the Season and were intending to go to Cowes before returning to Paris. Now the Comte is ill and confined to bed. My dear Comtesse, we will do our best to amuse you, but I fear you may find us dull indeed in August in the country.'

Matthew stood up to offer the Duke a tray of iced cakes and the sun, filtering through the thick foliage of the cedar tree, gleamed on his golden hair. The neat grey worsted suit he wore was a trifle on the small side, stretching tight across his shoulders and accentuating the length of his legs and the narrowness of his hips.

'We shall contrive,' murmured the Comtesse.

During the first weeks of August the weather continued fine and hot. In the mornings the two boys walked with the dogs, fished in the river or rode; in the afternoons they repaired to the lake for boating and swimming. They saw little of the young girls. The two middle sisters, Jane and Elizabeth, hung back shyly in the presence of their elder brother and his friend, but the eldest and the youngest – Isobel and Anne – were more forward. At thirteen Isobel directed sly slanting glances at Matthew, greeting him with unconscious natural coquetry, while seven-year-old Anne ran to meet her brother with sunny smiles of spontaneous pleasure.

One morning about two weeks after Matthew's arrival, he and Nicholas descended the stairs en route for the stables to find that Isobel had stationed herself in the hall. She was wearing her riding habit.

'I thought I would ride with you this morning,' she announced airily.

'Did you? Then you will be disappointed!' retorted Nicholas. 'Matthew and I have better things to do than bother with little girls.'

'I'm not a little girl, I'm thirteen.'

'Run away and play with your sisters, Isobel, and leave us alone.'

'My sisters are boring.' Her voice was petulant and her pretty mouth set in ugly lines of sulkiness. 'And I don't like girls; I much prefer being with boys.' Out of the corner of her eye she watched Matthew, who was standing a little apart while brother and sister settled their family differences.

'You have never wanted to ride with me before,' Nicholas stared at Isobel suspiciously as he spoke. 'Usually you're fawning over Lambourne and even though he's away at Cowes . . .' His voice trailed away as he followed the direction of Isobel's artless gaze. 'Oh, so that's it!' and he seized his sister's arm and pushed her towards the stairs. 'Go back to the nursery, you ninny!' he hissed under his breath. 'I'll not stand for you making a fool of yourself in front of my friends.'

But Isobel stubbornly stood her ground, eyes fixed on Matthew's expressionless face.

'I'll put a frog down your back,' threatened Nicholas as he plunged a hand into his pocket, cupped the other hand over it and reached towards her.

With a shriek, Isobel fled up the stairs, Nicholas following and gaining on her with every stride. Then from high above on the curve of the stairs came a peal of infectious laughter – the merry face of Anne was peering through the banisters and she clapped her little hands excitedly.

'Faster, Nicholas, faster!'

Nicholas pounced on Isobel, but as she began to shriek again he opened his hands to reveal that they held . . . nothing.

'Fooled you that time, stupid!' he taunted.

Anne was giggling helplessly. 'Isobel, you did look silly.'

Isobel glared furiously at them both, then looked down into the hall and saw the amusement on Matthew's face. Gathering together the remnants of her wounded pride, she turned and continued up the stairs with as much dignity as she could muster.

'I think,' she said coldly over her shoulder, 'that you are all exceedingly childish.' And she swiped at Anne with her riding crop as she passed, viciously but unsuccessfully.

Nicholas rejoined Matthew and hastily propelled him out of the house. 'The noise might have annoyed Papa,' he explained, 'and so far we have succeeded very well in keeping out of his way, except in the evenings.'

Matthew nodded slowly. The evenings! This was the time of day that he had come both to love and to dread. Moments of sweet torture.

It was at the lake that afternoon that Matthew began to admit to himself that something was wrong. He no longer felt the complete satisfaction in Nicholas's companionship of which he had always previously been conscious. There was a strange restlessness within him, a yearning, a frustration, that he had not experienced before. At first he attributed his unease to an exceptionally virulent reaction to the life, habits and general existence of his elder brother.

'Nicky,' he said suddenly, 'do you get along all right with Lambourne?'

They were lying face downwards on towels, naked after a swim, screened from public view by the dense bushes bordering the lake. The sun was warm on their backs and already their bodies were tanned a deep golden brown.

Nicholas considered the question carefully. 'I don't see him often; he doesn't come home unless he has to – doesn't see eye to eye with His Grace.'

This was something Matthew could well believe. 'But *when* you do see him,' he persisted, 'is he civil?'

'Of course,' said Nicholas in astonishment. 'A bit damn superior, but that's because he's older. Why? Isn't Freddy civil?'

Matthew rolled over on to his back and stared up at the sky, shielding his eyes with his right hand. Suddenly he regretted raising the subject. Not to anyone, even Nicholas, could he describe his relationship with Freddy.

As a small child Matthew had adored his brother, trotting trustingly after him and copying his every word and move. Freddy had responded with cruelty, bullying and acts of calculated meanness which had hurt Matthew in mind as well as body. The young Matthew had endured. The growing Matthew fought back. There now existed a bitter enmity between the Harcourt-Bright brothers which no longer had its roots in any particular deed or episode. The hatred simply *was*: the detestation as much a part of them as any of their physical characteristics. It was there, and it was there to stay.

Matthew could voice none of this since his pride recoiled from seeking sympathy, but he had to give Nicholas some form of answer.

'Freddy's a bit odd. As soon as I show a liking or preference for something, it either disappears or is destroyed. For instance, he hates water and loathes boats – all our family do except me – but Uncle Gervase told Papa that either Freddy or I could go to Cowes with his party. So Freddy insisted on going simply because he knew *I* wanted to go. Not,' added Matthew hastily, 'that I'm not just as happy here but Freddy did that out of spite.'

'He is older,' Nicholas pointed out.

'Don't I know it! Seniority is something of which Freddy takes full advantage. He never ceases to remind me that I am merely the second son of a second son.'

'You are too sensitive about that. Nobody else takes the least notice.'

'Freddy does. And I suppose he's right. Mama is always saying that second sons are worthless and destined to be paupers.'

'Hey, wait a minute!' protested Nicholas. '*I'm* a second son, too.'

'Yes, but your father wasn't and your family is richer than ours. The Earls of Highclere have never been very wealthy. Which reminds me: Freddy said the most incredible thing during the Easter hols. He said to me, "If both Uncle Gervase and cousin Aubrey die, and then Papa dies, I shall inherit the title." '

'So he would. But I do agree that it's not exactly an acceptable topic of conversation.'

'I wish,' said Matthew slowly, 'that I knew why he hates me.'

'That's obvious. He's jealous.'

'Jealous? Of what?'

Nicholas raised himself on one elbow and stared incredulously at his friend. The sun had bleached Matthew's hair several shades lighter and the blue eyes were startling sapphires in his bronzed face. His long lithe body lay relaxed on the white towel.

'Modesty!' mocked Nicholas. 'Or perhaps you genuinely haven't looked in a mirror lately! Now, I haven't seen Freddy for several years but I doubt he's changed much. He was five feet six inches tall, with mousy hair, a most unbecoming moustache and a squeaky voice. And he was also very fat.'

'You're right,' said Matthew, grinning. 'He hasn't changed much.'

'There you are, then. What Freddy needs,' opined the infant philosopher, 'is the love of a good woman, and then he can stop worrying about your devastating effect on the fair sex. I'm going for another swim. Are you coming?'

Nicholas ran into the water. He, too, had experienced a sudden stab of jealousy – towards the girls Matthew would attract, dreading any rift in their friendship. Also he instinctively felt the need to pull away from Matthew's powerful physical presence, before he succumbed to the urge to reach out and stroke his friend's smooth skin. Nicholas and Matthew both knew of the relationships between some of the boys at school and of fumblings in the night in dark dormitories. He had rebuffed several such approaches and, while Matthew's almost aggressive masculinity deterred advances, Nicholas was aware that his friend's lack of interest in these activities caused disappointment among their schoolmates. Nicholas was vaguely disappointed himself, but goodnaturedly drew satisfaction and comfort from the strong deep ties of friendship which bound him and Matthew together. In the lake he splashed noisily to cover his emotion.

Matthew, feeling too warm and lazy to swim, rolled over on to his belly and buried his face in the towel. Soon it would be time to return to the house to dress for dinner. The Desborough dinners were formal affairs, even in August in the country. There had been other house guests since his arrival – friends and relatives breaking their journey as they travelled south to the coast and the Isle of Wight. The evening gatherings had been gay and glittering, a pageant of colourful crinolines and fairy-tale jewels. And at the centre, each evening, was the Comtesse de Gravigny – most beautiful of the women – most sought after by the men. She held the company in thrall and even the unfathomable gaze of the Duke himself reflected an unfamiliar longing as his eyes rested on her exquisite face.

As if gracing the opulent court of the Second Empire, the Comtesse descended each night in a fresh creation by M. Worth and a different set of blazing jewels. Matthew could not decide which *ensemble* had been the most ravishing: the lilac gauze, perhaps, with the jewelled lilac blossom; the maize silk scattered with diamond ears of corn; or the white tulle with its lily-of-the-valley, the heavy ropes of pearls at her neck enhancing her bare shoulders.

But last night – and Matthew's throat constricted at the recollection – last night she had looked the most beautiful of all. As she entertained the company with stories of Napoleon and Eugenie's court Matthew had hardly listened, beyond being aware of the enchanting cadence of her voice. Her gown was of a clear green, the green of water meadows on a summer day, the green of her eyes. The lovely Lyons silk was spangled with gold, just as her eyes were flecked, and she had sprinkled gold dust on her shining hair. Long diamond and emerald earrings flashed at her ears, but it was to her bosom that Matthew's eyes were drawn, over and over again.

The gown displayed the gleaming white perfection of her shoulders and was cut extremely low over the marble mounds of her breasts. And there, nestling in the cleavage between those breasts, blazed the largest and most brilliant diamond that

Matthew had ever seen. It was a pear-shaped pendant, hung on a simple gold thread, flashing a fire and radiating an iridescent light that dazzled Matthew's bemused eye. He was hypnotised by the jewel, like a moth before a flame, yet he knew not whether it was the bauble or the setting which attracted him most.

He had gazed upon that diamond on the backdrop of lustrous flesh, pondered on it and dreamed of it; seeing in his mind's eye her lovely body naked except for the jewel. Even at the dinner table these images had crowded his mind and his body had stirred to a painful bulge in his trousers; in his embarrassment he was certain that everyone noticed, everyone knew the reason for his arousal and could read his thoughts.

Now, in the warm afternoon sun, Matthew's body responded again to his fantasies and he groaned aloud and dug his fingers into the soft earth. She haunted his dreams and his waking moments, too. He gloried in her beauty and her nearness, but plumbed the depths of despair in his knowledge of her inaccessibility. Of the ailing Comte there was no sign, but Matthew had no doubt that every man at dinner last night had shared his own feelings. So what chance did a raw youth of sixteen have in competition with those witty and sophisticated men of the world? And yet . . . and yet. . . . She had a way of looking at him, a sideways glance that seemed full of promise. Sometimes he would catch her watching him, moistening her lips with her sharp pink tongue. But then, as his hopes began to rise, she would address him as '*mon petit*' or casually refer to him and Nicholas as '*les enfants*' and he would consider himself relegated to the schoolroom again.

Suddenly Matthew's head jerked up as he heard a noise like a twig snapping. He listened intently for several minutes but nothing more disturbed the silence. About to return to his reverie, he heard another sound, like the swish of a skirt in the long grass, and caught a flash of yellow beyond the bushes. With thumping heart he watched it disappear. *She* was wearing yellow today. But why was she watching them at the lake? Matthew squirmed to think of her green gold-flecked eyes watching his nakedness. But what did she want? His confusion returned in full measure and he was possessed by an ache which cried out for fulfilment.

* * *

The Comtesse joined the Duchess in the shade of the terrace and sat down, arranging her yellow skirts around her. Casually she raised the subject of Matthew.

'*Les enfants* are swimming in the lake.'

'Thank heaven the weather is fine, otherwise I do not know how we would keep them occupied.' The Duchess paused: 'Matthew is beautiful, isn't he!'

'An Adonis indeed,' the Comtesse agreed lightly.

'Everyone thinks so. Everyone turns to stare. Everyone, that is, except his own family.'

'That is natural.'

The Duchess shook her head. 'No, the way that Matthew's family ignore him isn't natural. Let me tell you something of his history. As you know his father, Peregrine, is the younger brother of our neighbour, the Earl of Highclere. He entered the church not only out of necessity but also from genuine vocation. He married Louisa, who was dark-haired and very lovely but penniless and not quite *comme il faut*. It was supposed to be a love-match and I'm sure that for Peregrine it was. He is a vague idealistic fellow and he drifted helplessly into the relationship, unable and unwilling to withstand the allure of Louisa's beauty or the greater strength of her character.'

There was something in the way the Duchess emphasised the last few words which caused the Comtesse's sensual lips to curve in understanding. 'But Louisa did not marry for love? She married an earl's son because she thought he was rich and enjoyed a high position in society?'

'Exactly so. Nobody knows what she said when she discovered her mistake, but her vituperations have reverberated round the county ever since. Louisa is a shrew, grown fat and plain, forever bewailing her lack of position and fortune. Now Peregrine and Louisa Harcourt-Bright are shunned, except for duty visits, but the only reason for their isolation is Louisa's lack of breeding and unfortunate personality.'

'An unhappy home indeed. I am sorry for her husband and children.'

'One need feel no sympathy for Peregrine. Louisa's complaints pass serenely over his saintly head and he finds a lot of work to do among his parishioners which keeps him out of the house. But I do feel, don't you agree, that Louisa's discontent must be absorbed by the children?'

'They will see things through their mother's eyes, most assuredly,' agreed the Comtesse, a troubled frown furrowing the smooth perfection of her brow.

'Louisa dotes on Freddy and pushes him constantly into the lime-light. Peregrine gravitates towards gentle, docile Mary. It is noticeable, sometimes, how lonely Matthew appears: a circumstance I have observed in other "middle" children.'

'I still cannot understand how Louisa could ignore her little Greek god.'

'There is often a special bond between a mother and her first-born son. And in this case Freddy takes after Louisa's family, while Matthew has inherited the splendid good looks of the Harcourt-Brights. However,' and the Duchess smiled confidently, 'I don't really think we need worry about Matthew. With his looks and self-assurance, he can take care of himself.'

The Comtesse smiled back but an observant eye would have seen that her expression was enigmatic and that the smile did not reach her eyes. She possessed an instinctive understanding of men, an effortless rapport which enabled her to penetrate their outward masks and expose the vulnerability beneath. Far from his being self-assured, she perceived that Matthew lacked confidence in himself; that he was sensitive and easily hurt; but that he was proud and concealed his emotions.

But, most importantly, the Comtesse sensed that Matthew was growing up without love and unconsciously was looking for love. A sharp pain pierced the Comtesse's heart as she contemplated Matthew's beauty and the power which lay dormant within him. *Mon Dieu*, if only she were younger, what a pair they could have made! A soft sigh escaped her as she accepted the sad fact that she could not provide the love which Matthew sought. However, another gift did lie within her power.

When the boys returned to the house, Nicholas complained of a headache and of feeling unwell. 'Too much sun!' exclaimed the Duchess and packed him off to bed. The Desboroughs and their guests were dining with neighbours and a disconsolate Matthew ate his dinner off a tray in Nicholas's room. He was anguished at missing all the fun but incapable of abandoning his duty to his sick friend. As he looked at the fair head on the pillow he was overwhelmed by a protective urge and aware of how much he owed to Nicholas. He could have had any friend he wanted, Matthew thought, but he chose me, even though I have nothing to offer but myself. I have no money and no grand home in which to entertain him during the holidays. He even faces his father's disapproval of our friendship. There was strength and constancy in Nicholas and yet a defencelessness, too, which aroused a great rush of tenderness in Matthew's heart. He sat by the bed until a sleeping draught finally brought some relief to his friend's feverish tossing and Nicholas slept. Quietly Matthew rose and padded down the deserted passage to his own room.

It was eight o'clock. The sun was still shining, low in the sky, and his room was suffocatingly hot. He stood for a moment by the window staring out at the empty gardens and listening to the unusual hush which had fallen over the house. The ducal party had left for their dinner engagement, the young ladies were in the nursery wing, and no doubt the servants were enjoying a leisurely and convivial meal below stairs. Matthew suddenly felt lonely and depressed. He stripped off his clothes and cast himself dejectedly upon the bed, covering his body loosely with a thin sheet. He picked up a book but deciding that he did not feel much like reading he put it down and lay flat on his back, contemplating the ceiling.

He must have dozed off, then a light tap on the door jerked him back into consciousness. As he raised himself on one elbow and struggled to clear his mind and eyes of the enveloping fog of sleep, he became aware of a white figure gliding towards him. It was the Comtesse. Incredulously Matthew lay transfixed as she crossed the room and sat on the bed beside him.

'Nicholas is asleep,' she said. 'I thought I should make sure that you were all right. *Pauvre petit*, what a miserable evening you have endured.'

She was wrapped loosely in a flimsy white silk robe. As she leaned over him the folds fell away from her body and there, in the luscious valley between her breasts, lay the diamond. The sun was setting in a riot of crimson and gold and the rays which streamed through the window brought alive the dazzling fire within the gem. As Matthew stared, mesmerised by the beauty of breast and brilliant, a droplet of sweat formed in the cleft and remained suspended over the stone. To Matthew it was as if everything hung in limbo – the stifling heat, the strange silence, even the birds did not sing, and his very heart seemed to have stopped. Every instinct urged him to reach out to grasp those breasts and to lick the sweat from her flesh. As his body responded to those instincts, so his erection tented the pale sheet.

In a horror of humiliation, Matthew turned his face away. The Comtesse stared at the tell-tale shape beneath the sheet before slowly drawing back the cover to expose his nakedness.

'I see that you are indeed feeling all right,' she said in her low seductive voice, 'and I shall no longer call you "*petit*".'

Her hand hovered over him and for one magic moment Matthew thought she was going to hold his hot, throbbing body. Instead the Comtesse laid a cool hand on his thigh and gazed upon his beauty, glorying in his youth, feasting her eyes on the glowing health and purity of his unblemished body.

'I thought you had gone out with the others,' he stammered.

'I made an excuse. My husband is not well. But now he sleeps and we . . .' she paused, 'we are alone.'

He said nothing but lay tense, his hands clenched tightly by his sides.

'Don't you want to touch me?' she asked gently.

'You know I do,' he whispered, 'but . . .'

'You think I am playing with you, teasing you, that I will lead you on and then slap you as you stretch out a hand. No, *cherie*. I came here tonight to love you. I am not a clever woman but I have one great gift – I am well versed in the ways of love. And I have chosen you as a recipient of that gift.'

'Why me?'

'Because you are beautiful and I desire you. And because I see in you the promise of great passion, a subject worthy of my art.' Her hand was still resting on his thigh but then she began to stroke his leg, moving slowly closer to his groin. 'Not for you the clumsy fumblings with an innocent or prudish bride, the arid encounter with a paid courtesan, or the crude act in a back-street bordello. Come . . .' and she guided his hand to her breast.

At the touch of the cool smooth flesh, all reason fled. She was naked beneath the robe and impatiently Matthew pulled aside the flimsy material and fastened his lips to her breasts. His mouth and tongue were rough and the rosy nipples hardened and stiffened under his urgent touch.

'You are a virgin,' the Comtesse murmured, 'and so we will slake your passion first,' and she drew his lips to hers and sent fresh shock waves of desire through him as her slender fingers grasped his penis. She caressed him slowly and deliberately, gradually increasing the pace, and then pulled him hard towards her so that he thrust eagerly into her and spent himself in a few ecstatic strokes.

Matthew rolled away to lie sweat-soaked and panting in the gathering dusk.

'And now,' said the Comtesse, 'we will show you how to prolong your performance. And how to pleasure a woman.'

She guided his hands and lips over her satin curves, to the silken skin inside her thighs and the damp musky sweetness between her legs, teaching him the gentle art of arousal. He grew hard again but entered more confidently and moved with patient, measured strokes until her breath quickened and she clung to him as a shuddering series of convulsions shook her. The diamond pressed hard into his chest and he tugged it aside, vaguely aware of the snapping of the chain. The gem remained clasped in his left hand as he drove on, bringing her to a triumphant climax a second time before he was spent.

As she was leaving, the Comtesse held out a hand.

'My diamond, please, Matthew,' she said.

With a start of surprise, he realised that he was still clutching the diamond tightly in his fist. In some mysterious fashion the jewel seemed to stick to his fingers and he had to make a conscious effort to wrench himself free. He relinquished the stone reluctantly.

The Comtesse took it from him and looked, rather sadly, into his eyes. The boy he had been before she came to him would have apologised for damaging the chain.

'Tomorrow!' he said. It was a statement, not a question, spoken with new-found confidence.

Fate played into their hands, enabling them to meet not only the next day but for many days thereafter. Nicholas was not suffering from sunstroke but from typhoid fever, a comparatively mild attack which nevertheless confined him to his room for a fortnight. The Comte, too, progressed slowly so Matthew and the Comtesse tended their invalids, took decorous walks together, talked vivaciously at dinner and lived every hour for the moments when they could be alone. Most nights she glided silently to his room, but sometimes Matthew crept to the chamber she occupied adjacent to that of her husband.

Only the jealous eyes of Isobel detected anything untoward about Matthew's friendship with the Comtesse and eventually, artlessly, she whispered her puzzlement into her father's ear. That night, as Matthew emerged cautiously from the Comtesse's room, the sound of footsteps froze him in his tracks and he dodged back through the door as the unmistakable figure of the Duke rounded the corner of the corridor.

'I don't think he saw me,' Matthew whispered. 'Do you suppose he was intending to visit your husband?'

'At this hour of night?' The Comtesse raised her eyebrows sceptically. 'No, I do not think it was the *Comte* de Gravigny he wished to see.'

Whatever his mission, the Duke did not approach her door. But by the time his footsteps had faded into the distance, Matthew no longer wished to leave. As she submitted again to the dominance of his demanding embrace, the Comtesse wondered what sort of devil she had unleashed.

Part One

ENGLAND AND SOUTHERN AFRICA 1869–1877

CHAPTER ONE

Three and a half years passed after that idyllic summer before Matthew visited Desborough again. By this time he had left Eton for Oxford and Nicholas was still chief among his friends. They moved in a circle of hot-blooded young aristocrats who took their studies lightly and their pleasures freely: life was a combination of drinking, gambling, sport and women. Fresh variations on these well-worn themes were always welcome and it was Matthew who regularly produced the best and most outrageous ideas for new entertainment.

No one realised that Matthew's heart and mind were not totally engaged in these superficial pursuits. For one thing, the younger son of a clergyman – even if his grandfather was an earl – did not have access to the kind of funds needed to support such a lifestyle. Matthew ensured that his presence was considered indispensable to the success of the festivities by organising parties for cards, horse-racing, cock-fights and ratting matches, and so disguising the fact that he wagered little or seldom because he could not afford to lose. But there were other reasons for his disaffection and as usual it was Nicholas who probed his defences.

They were sitting in Matthew's rooms after a particularly convivial evening and Nicholas was gazing glumly at a sheaf of IOUs. He sighed heavily.

'You're a lucky fellow, Matt. I've never known you to be in debt.'

Matthew laughed. 'I don't run up debts because I could never repay them. And I want to be accepted by society, not drummed out of it.'

Nicholas looked surprised at such an original philosophy, and he groaned deeply and pushed the IOUs out of sight. 'Well, I still say you are fortunate.' He brightened suddenly. 'At least we are *all* short of money and there's no disgrace in it.'

Matthew refilled their glasses and leaned back in his chair, stretching out his long legs before the dying embers of the fire. He smiled compassionately at the innocent face of his friend, reluctant to invade Nicholas's cosy world with a lecture on the difference between being short of money because one spends a lot or being short of money because one has none to spend in the first place. He said nothing and in the silence Nicholas's drink-hazed mind wandered back to Matthew's last remark.

'You're a clever chap as well, you know. More intelligent than the rest of us. There's something different about you.'

Matthew raised a quizzical eyebrow and was about to dismiss the statement with a jest, but then he decided to treat it seriously.

'I fancy that it is more a matter of ambition than intelligence.' He rose and began pacing round the room. 'I feel a kind of restless energy within me,' he said at last, 'driving me on, but it is a frustrated urge because it has no direction. I know that I must make my mark in this world but I don't know how. Our present existence is all very well for you and the others, just as it served for our Regency forebears, but I don't fit in. Besides, on a practical level, I must earn a living eventually. Papa wants me to enter the church.'

'With the best will in the world, I don't see you in a cassock.'

'Neither do I.'

'The Army?'

'Insufficient prospects.'

'Parliament? Now there's a distinct possibility! Plenty of outlets for that energy you were describing.'

'Dearest Freddy has been chosen to carry the family banner into Parliament,' said Matthew with a mocking smile, 'although fortunately for England he is displaying no sense of urgency in the matter. Freddy at Westminster is likely to prove the death of democracy.'

Nicholas grinned. 'You'll think of something,' he said comfortably, 'and the difficulties are probably a good thing. You're so damned stubborn that whenever an obstacle is placed in your path, you push all the harder towards your goal. Not that you meet many obstacles in your pursuit of the fair sex. I never knew anyone who was so irresistible to the ladies!'

And Nicholas shook his head enviously. Any thoughts of a physical relationship with Matthew had been nebulous at best and had long since faded from Nicholas's mind. Yet, as the bond of friendship grew stronger with the passing of the years, Nicholas knew that he would never love anyone as much as he loved this enigmatic and often exasperating young man.

'Incidentally,' Nicholas asked, 'what are you doing for Christmas?'

'I shall go home, I suppose.'

'Come to Desborough. Perhaps there will be a young lady of the county who might prove more elusive than usual and you can work off some of that excess energy in the chase.'

Matthew arrived at Desborough in the early afternoon of Christmas Eve. After freshening up in his room, he went in search of Nicholas who was, he understood, in the smoking-room. He strolled slowly through the deserted hall, trying to remember which room this might be. Flinging open a door, he found that it led to the Blue Salon and was about to retreat when a movement outside the window caught his eye. He crossed the room and looked out to see the four Desborough daughters standing on the terrace, well wrapped up against the winter chill and having evidently returned from a post-prandial walk. They stood motionless for a moment – even the little dog at their feet pausing in his play – in a group which was natural and spontaneous and yet so perfect in its composition that it might have been posed by a portrait painter. But the image was fleeting and dissolved in a second as the girls swung apart and Isobel raised her hands to untie her bonnet. Bareheaded, her resemblance to Nicholas was startling and a muscle twitched in Matthew's cheek.

They were coming indoors – the youngest girl, Anne, trailing behind with the dog. Matthew turned away abruptly and resumed his search for Nicholas. He found the smoking-room at his next attempt; although it was empty, a tray of decanters and glasses advertised Nicholas's recent presence and Matthew eyed the spirits longingly. This house was oppressive with its memories and reminders of youthful insecurities, and he was unexpectedly shaken by the revelation of Isobel on the terrace. Boldly he poured himself a generous measure of whisky and was drinking it gratefully when he became aware of a scuffling noise behind him and a sudden sharp pain in his ankle.

'What the hell . . . !'

A small dog had attached itself to his foot. Mercifully it had abandoned his ankle but was tugging determinedly at his trouser leg.

'Scruff! Come here, you naughty dog!'

Breathlessly Anne gathered the animal into her arms and faced Matthew.

'I'm sorry. Did he give you a nip on the ankle?' Her laughing eyes slid towards the glass in his hand. 'And I see you have had one already!'

Matthew's eyebrows rose in surprise that the child should be familiar with such new-fangled and undoubtedly masculine expressions.

'You're a bit young for such tap-room talk,' he observed drily, discomfited that his unauthorised imbibing had been discovered.

Anne was disappointed at such dull reception of her wit. 'I shall be ten next birthday, but Nicholas says I'm precocious,' she remarked candidly. 'He says it's because I am the youngest of six and pick up too many expressions from my elders and betters. But *I* don't see why they're better just because they're elder, do you?'

Matthew drained his glass and turned to replace it on the tray, so Anne did not see the gleam of amusement in his eyes.

'Indeed I don't,' he agreed gravely, 'although I'm sure that Nicholas is the best of brothers.'

'Oh, he is!' She was smiling again. 'When I grow up I shall marry someone exactly like Nicholas. Or, better still, neither of us will marry and we can live together instead.'

'You are very like Nicholas,' said Matthew. 'And,' he added thoughtfully, 'very like Isobel.'

Anne's expression changed to one of watchful wariness at this, but Matthew failed to notice. 'Tell me,' he coaxed, 'about Isobel.'

But there was a world of difference between Anne's favourite and least favourite topics of conversation. 'You must be Matthew,' she said suddenly. 'Now that you're here, Nicholas won't have time for me.'

And, still carrying the little dog, she left the room.

The house was filled with guests and more visitors arrived during the course of the evening. Because it was Christmas the two older Desborough girls were allowed to put in a brief appearance while Elizabeth and Anne sat wistfully on the stairs peering at the company through the banisters. The room was full of pretty girls but they ceased to exist for Matthew when Isobel entered.

She was tiny and fragile, dainty as a Dresden figurine, Nicholas in female form. Her delicate features were dominated by huge eyes of cornflower blue, and her pink lips held the suggestion of a pout. Her hair was so fair that it shone silver in the lamplight; her demure blue dress matched her eyes, its modest neckline revealing only a hint of her developing figure.

'How old is your eldest sister?' Matthew asked his friend.

'Sixteen,' replied Nicholas vaguely, 'or it might be seventeen.'

The child had a quality of purity and innocence, like a butterfly which had emerged from its chrysalis and hesitantly dried its wings in the sun, but was not quite ready to launch itself in flight. So Isobel was poised on the brink of womanhood, while retaining one last tenuous hold on childish things. And Matthew felt the desire rising in him as it had not done for years. Not since he had encountered the Comtesse in this very house had he experienced that almost tangible attraction reaching out to him from across a room.

'Perhaps,' he suggested, 'we could speak to her?'

'Speak to Isobel?' Nicholas was patently astonished. 'Don't be ridiculous, Matthew. What on earth would we talk about?'

He was right, of course. Matthew knew that he and Isobel could have nothing in common, that her experience of life was so limited; she was not yet seventeen, not yet 'out'. His reaction to her was ridiculous, he told himself – possibly caused by memories of the Comtesse which wafted to him from every corner of the house. Deliberately Matthew turned his back on the girl and followed his friend to the card-room.

But her fresh young beauty exerted a powerful influence over him and his retreat was only temporary. After Christmas the weather became bitter and Matthew began to store up pictures of her in his mind – Isobel in a red coat and bonnet skating on the frozen lake and shyly accepting his arm as they twirled together on the ice; Isobel walking beside him in the park, the snow falling on her fur-trimmed bonnet and fluttering on the rosebud of her mouth; Isobel at the piano in the drawing-room, singing in a clear sweet voice, while a fire blazed in the massive hearth.

His partiality was noticed. It was not, after all, Matthew's style to throw snowballs with the children while his friends lounged in the smoking-room or the young ladies of the county paid their morning calls.

An embarrassed Nicholas broached the subject as they sat alone over a drink one bright and frosty morning, coughing and clearing his throat before he spoke. 'Awfully good of you to spend so much time with my sisters,' he said awkwardly, 'but please don't feel under any obligation to do so.'

'Your sisters are charming. I enjoy their company.'

'Don't they bore you?'

'Certainly not.'

'What I can't understand,' said Nicholas earnestly, 'is why you seek out Isobel so much. The silly ninny hasn't a thought in her head beyond the next pretty dress and her coming-out party. I can't see how you endure it.'

It was true, thought Matthew, that Isobel was a little short on intellectual conversation or indeed conversation of any kind, but her blue eyes and the curve of that young bosom more than compensated.

'I find her company extremely stimulating,' he replied sincerely.

'Now, if you wanted some childish amusement, you'd be better off with Jane. She's only fourteen but she reads widely, is well-informed and has a ready wit. She isn't as pretty as Isobel, of course. Mind you, Mama believes that Anne will be the beauty of the family – the infant is very like Isobel at the same age.'

'I like Isobel,' said Matthew stubbornly, staring out of the window at the gaunt outlines of the winter trees. He felt a tremor of apprehension at the direction the conversation was taking.

There was a long pause before Nicholas spoke again. 'Fact is, old man, that His Grace don't like it. Asked me to mention the matter. Sorry.'

The Duke had, reflected Matthew, barely acknowledged his presence since he had arrived. Evidently, however, His Grace had been taking an interest in his guest's activities. Matthew's customary self-control snapped.

'Doesn't *like* it?' he inquired angrily. 'Doesn't like it! What exactly is it that His Grace doesn't like? Interest being shown in Isobel or the fact that it is *me* taking the interest?'

Nicholas looked flustered. 'Calm down,' he begged. 'Matthew, Isobel is very young and . . . '

'No, it isn't that. His Grace would not countenance a match between Isobel and me because I have neither title nor fortune!'

'Good God, it isn't a matter of a *match*, surely!'

'Yes, it is,' said Matthew impulsively, although he had not given it a thought until that moment. 'I want to marry Isobel so I would like to know if the Desboroughs object to my family and connections.'

Lord!' Nicholas stared at his friend in dismay. 'There's no one I'd rather have as a brother-in-law, Matt, but you're mad, quite mad! Isobel! I told you, the girl's a fool. And don't look at me as though you would like to call me out. I'm her brother and I'm entitled to say what I like about her. She's had her head turned completely by your attention and is queening it over the entire household in her triumph over her first beau. And I assure you that His Grace has never mentioned your family or connections, although,' and Nicholas frowned slightly, 'he did say something about family traits.'

Matthew remained unconvinced. His deep-seated sense of inferiority, so carelessly implanted by his mother and so cleverly nurtured by Freddy, nagged him into continued belief that the second son of a second son was unacceptable as a husband for a duke's daughter. His regard for Isobel blossomed in exact ratio to the ducal disapproval. Following his conversation with Nicholas, he observed greater caution in public but pressed his attentions more ardently upon her in private.

But Isobel, well aware that by some miracle her suitor was the most handsome man in Berkshire, made sure that there were not many private moments. She paraded her conquest as often as possible and, while casting Matthew adoring glances, was between times ensuring that her success was noticed and envied.

Among her siblings, however, she did not achieve the level of respect and envy which she considered her due. On the last day of the Christmas festivities, the four sisters had been walking in the garden. Jane, Elizabeth and Anne returned to the nursery rosy-cheeked and laughing, pulling off their coats and bonnets. They had left Isobel loitering on the terrace with Matthew.

'Oh, but they are so funny!' exclaimed Anne, collapsing on to the hearthrug before the blazing fire. 'I cannot understand what Isobel sees in that man.'

'He's very good-looking,' observed Elizabeth.

'But he's so pompous,' Anne objected. 'He hardly ever smiles or says anything amusing.'

'He smiles when he's with Nicholas,' said Jane. 'But I do agree he takes himself very seriously. Come to think of it, though, Isobel takes herself very seriously, so perhaps they are suited after all!'

They broke into giggles again and Anne jumped to her feet. 'They don't even talk to each other,' she announced. 'The atmosphere is always very *intense*. Have you noticed that Isobel has affected a new, grown-up walk? Like this,' and mischievously Anne peacocked down the room with a mincing step, head tilted arrogantly and a most superior expression on her face. 'Mr Harcourt-Bright strides slowly beside her, like this.' Now Anne took enormous exaggerated steps, hands clasped behind her back, head inclined deferentially towards her shorter, imaginary companion.

Jane and Elizabeth were convulsed with laughter. 'Anne, stop it! You're incorrigible, you really are,' gasped Jane.

But Anne had not finished. 'All they do is look at each other and sigh.' She was Isobel again, hand clasped to her heart, gazing up into the burning eyes of her suitor, and she heaved a deep dramatic sigh. 'Oh, Matthew!' she intoned soulfully.

'You little beast!' Unnoticed, Isobel had entered the room and witnessed the conclusion of Anne's performance. She dived towards her youngest sister, ready to pinch or pummel her into submission, but Anne expertly evaded those clawing fingers. Isobel turned to Jane and Elizabeth. 'And what do you two find so funny?'

'Nothing.' Elizabeth opened her eyes wide. 'And Papa certainly doesn't find your behaviour amusing. You must have noticed how he glowers at Mr Harcourt-Bright.'

'Papa will have to become accustomed to the attentions I receive,' replied Isobel loftily. 'Men are greatly attracted to my beauty.'

'Isobel, you really are very vain,' said Jane indignantly.

'You're just jealous, because you're so plain and uninteresting that you will never find a husband,' snapped Isobel.

Tears sprang into Jane's brown eyes and Anne turned angrily on Isobel. 'Oh, you are horrid and unkind! And I don't see why anyone wants a beau anyway, because being in love doesn't seem to be much fun.'

'It is Matthew who is in love, not I.'

The three younger girls stared at her in open-mouthed astonishment. 'But last week you said you did love him. You said that he was the most handsome and attractive man in the whole of England,' objected Anne.

'So he is. But that doesn't mean that I love him or would marry him,' said Isobel calmly.

'You're only saying that because he will leave Desborough tomorrow without asking you to marry him,' said Anne scornfully.

'He will ask for my hand.' Isobel felt a faint flutter of apprehension as she said this; the situation was getting quite out of control but to save face she must continue. 'More than that,' and she paused impressively, 'I shall allow him to kiss me.'

Now horror replaced astonishment on her sisters' stupefied faces. 'You wouldn't dare!' breathed Anne.

'I would dare, and I shall.' A superior smile settled on Isobel's lips, disguising her inward trepidation. 'Then he will be bound to ask for my hand. But, of course, I may not accept him.'

'You don't show any consideration for his feelings.'

'I do not see,' said Isobel, preparing to make a dramatic exit, 'that Matthew's feelings have got anything to do with it.'

By the evening Isobel's confidence had returned. She chose the same blue dress that she had worn on Christmas Eve, but now she tugged at the neckline in fruitless attempts to expose a bit more bosom. Her eyes were shining with excitement – she was looking forward to testing her power.

In the crush of people in the drawing-room, she was able to whisper to Matthew: 'I must speak to you. The library. In ten minutes.' He was there first and stood with his back to the fire, anxiously awaiting her arrival, as she slipped through the door and ran towards him, Matthew took her hands in his and held them tightly against his chest. Her head did not reach his shoulder and he bent to rest his cheek against her hair.

'I had to speak to you alone, just once more,' Isobel said, 'before you leave tomorrow. And they will send me away to bed soon.'

Involuntarily Matthew's hands tightened on hers at the thought of her innocent slumbers. 'I love you and want you so much,' he murmured and unconsciously went on to talk to Isobel as though she was Nicholas because in his mind they were one and the same person. 'And you love me. You don't mind that I have neither title nor fortune.'

A tiny frown appeared momentarily between Isobel's fine brows as for the first time she contemplated this disadvantage to his splendid good looks. She was saved from replying because Matthew was looking down into her upturned face, feeling her fragility so close to him. He let go of her hands, put his arms around her and crushed her to him, pushing her against the tall shelves of books. Eagerly his lips sought hers.

At first, having achieved her aim, Isobel stood in stunned clumsy compliance but then the sensation of his mouth and hands drowned all other considerations and she clung to him, returning his kiss with an ardour beyond her years. They failed to see or hear the library door open and Matthew's first indication of an intruder on the scene was when a fist caught him on the side of the face and sent him reeling. He landed in a crumpled heap on the carpet and looked up to see the Duke of Desborough pushing his daughter towards the door.

'I shall speak to you later, Isobel!' the Duke thundered. 'As for you, sir, if it was not for the scandal which would surround her name, I would expose you to the world for the seducer that you are.'

Matthew had risen cautiously to his feet, feeling his jaw tenderly.

'Seducer!' he said. 'I never seduced anyone in my life!'

Nicholas came into the room just then, closing the door behind him. He had met a sobbing Isobel in the hall and now leaned against the door with folded arms while awaiting developments.

'Indeed?' The Duke bristled visibly. 'I recall a certain situation in this very house, under my very roof, when you were only sixteen!'

Nicholas's eyes widened and he looked at Matthew with a new respect.

'So you did see me that night,' said Matthew softly, his old fear of the Duke gone forever. 'It was not I who did the seducing, Your Grace, of that I do assure you. The lady preferred me to any other available alternatives.'

The Duke spluttered furiously and Nicholas suppressed a smile.

'Get out of my house,' the Duke roared, 'and never . . .'

'. . . darken your doors again!' Matthew smiled sardonically. 'As Your Grace wishes. But I will still marry your daughter.'

'Out! Tonight!'

'Matthew cannot go now, sir,' interposed Nicholas. 'It is late, and the snow is deep. First thing in the morning would be a reasonable compromise, surely?

'Very well. Out of consideration for your father and uncle, you may sleep here tonight. But I never wish to see you again and I forbid you to have any contact with my daughter.' And with a final glare at Matthew, the Duke left the room.

'Phew! Matthew, honestly, old man, I did ask you to take it quietly.'

Matthew cast himself into the depths of a large armchair, fingered his jaw again and stared gloomily into the heart of the fire.

'Anyone would think I was trying to rape the girl,' he complained. 'I want to marry her, damn it!'

'That was your first mistake,' said Nicholas drily. 'Letting His Grace find you in here with the child was the second. What, incidentally, did he mean about your previous visit here?'

Matthew explained. 'And I never suspected a thing,' Nicholas shook his head ruefully. 'You might have confided in me before.'

'I do not,' said Matthew reprovingly, 'tell tales about a lady.'

'Will you go home tomorrow?'

'Yes,' Matthew grimaced. 'I will go home and contemplate how to make enough money to maintain a wife. Things have come to a head, Nicholas, and decisions must be made. It's probably just as well, for I could not continue to act as court jester.'

'Well,' Nicholas said judiciously, 'making money fast is not an easy proposition, particularly if you have no capital to invest. There is only one thing for it,' he grinned, 'you'd best join the diamond rush.'

'The diamond rush!' Matthew lifted his head with an expression of dawning hope. 'Of course! That's it! Nicholas, you're a genius!'

'I was only joking,' protested Nicholas feebly.

'Why didn't I think of it before?' Matthew rose and began pacing the floor. 'There was an article in *The Times* only the other day about the big finds being made at the Vaal River in Griqualand in southern Africa. Just think of it, Nicholas! The joy of digging diamonds out of the soil! The satisfaction of creating wealth by honest labour with one's bare hands.' And Matthew spread out his own large hands and gazed at them triumphantly.

'It all sounds very romantic, but it might not be quite as easy as that,' Nicholas warned.

'Prospectors are converging on the Cape from all over the world. The newspaper report described men "of every pursuit and profession forming a straggling procession to the diamond fields". Butchers, bakers, sailors, tailors, lawyers, blacksmiths, masons, doctors . . .' Matthew's voice trailed off. 'I must go to Griqualand, Nicholas, I *must*!'

'Then go quickly, because the supply of diamonds may not last!'

Matthew ceased his pacing and resumed his position in front of the fire. He looked seriously at his friend.

'I haven't the money for the fare,' he said at last. 'I don't suppose you could . . . ?'

Nicholas shook his head decisively. 'Afraid not, old chap. His Grace is keeping me on a pretty tight rein just at present. There is, you see, another reason for his shortness of temper this season; Lambourne has piled up a pretty penny in gambling debts. And, frankly, I've more owing than I can meet.'

'No use asking Papa, he will be furious that I'm not returning to Oxford. I shall have to hope Uncle Gervase will oblige.'

But it transpired that the Earl of Highclere would not oblige, even when offered a part share in Matthew's as yet mythical diamond mine. As usual in the face of opposition, Matthew's determination increased. After days of unsuccessful canvassing among his friends and acquaintances, however, feeling angry and humiliated, he was forced to take the distasteful step of approaching his brother.

Frederick Harcourt-Bright still looked as Nicholas Grafton had described him more than three years previously. His only generous feature was his girth, otherwise the Fates had been niggardly in his design: his stature was short, his hair thin and his eyes narrow. His demeanour was one of contemptuous disdain and this was never more in evidence or more sincere than when he confronted his younger brother.

Freddy, too, was a product of his mother's neuroses and had inherited many of her bad qualities. Louisa had instilled a sense of superiority and self-importance in Freddy; told him he had been cheated out of something which was rightfully his; told him she expected him to achieve all the things Peregrine had not achieved, to succeed where his father had failed.

The only person Freddy could dominate was his younger brother. He had bullied Matthew, ridiculed and taunted him, and experienced fulfilment and satisfaction in so doing. Freddy was not yet lord of the manor but he had one serf at his command. Then Matthew's beauty began to blossom as he grew taller and his ash-blond hair turned to the gold of ripe corn. Freddy was consumed by a jealousy so fierce that he trembled. Enraged, he saw how other people stared at Matthew, and for the first time became aware of his own ugliness and feared losing his pre-eminent position in the family.

Freddy could no longer bully Matthew physically because Matthew was now bigger, so his attacks became more subtle and yet more vicious as he indulged a naturally cruel streak. He mocked and denigrated Matthew in order to prove to himself his own superiority, and he made sure that he acquired anything – absolutely anything – which his younger brother wanted.

Now, when he heard Matthew's stiff request for funds, Freddy laughed incredulously.

'*I* haven't the money to spare. And if I had, it would not be coming your way for such a harebrained scheme.'

'It is an investment,' insisted Matthew. 'Our arrangement could include a share in the profits.'

'Profits? Profits in what? You haven't the faintest idea what you're talking about,' scoffed Freddy. 'For a start, you are thinking in terms of money for a steamer passage and for food and hotels in the Cape. You will need much more than that. For one thing, you will have to buy a diamond claim – or did you think that you would simply arrive on the diamond fields, pitch your tent where you pleased and start lifting diamonds out of the ground?'

Matthew flushed. To his chagrin Freddy had given an extremely accurate account of how he pictured the scene.

'There is more to this than a sudden desire for adventure,' speculated Freddy, watching Matthew carefully. 'You are not one to leave Oxford and London and your rich friends without good reason. Is it gambling? Or a scandal, perhaps?'

'Certainly not.'

'A woman, then? Yes, it must be a woman. You have allowed one of your soiled doves to embroil you . . .'

'She is no soiled dove,' interrupted Matthew furiously. 'I intend to marry and need money with which to maintain a wife.'

'Do you indeed! And who, might I ask, is the fortunate young lady?'

Matthew hesitated. 'Her father does not want the matter aired about.'

'You may rely on my discretion. Or perhaps it is really *you* who does not want it aired about. Perhaps the lady ain't quite up to scratch?'

'How dare you!' shouted Matthew. 'She is a daughter of the Duke of Desborough.'

Frederick smiled with satisfaction; his taunts had had the desired effect. 'Indeed? I thought they were all in the schoolroom still.'

'Isobel is nearly seventeen.'

'Ah, almost antique.' Frederick surveyed his brother in silence for a few moments. 'So, you are a true Harcourt-Bright. You have inherited one of the family characteristics after all.'

'What on earth do you mean?'

'The Harcourt-Brights,' explained Freddy smoothly, 'have a penchant for young – and I mean *young* – ladies. Or haven't you noticed how Papa fusses over the juvenile females in his congregation and how Uncle Gervase pets our little sister?'

'I had not noticed.' So that was what the Duke of Desborough had meant by 'family traits'. 'For the last time, Freddy, will you lend me the money?'

'No.' Freddy's tone was contemptuously final and dismissive.

After Matthew had gone, Frederick poured himself a drink and carried it to the window where he contemplated the bleak winter landscape.

'So,' he said softly to himself, 'it's Isobel, is it! We shall see, little brother, we shall see.'

It was a black day for Matthew, who seemed to have exhausted all the possibilities for raising a loan. Gloomily he surveyed his worldly possessions – rings, cuff-links, tie-pins, a gold watch and some shirt studs and buttons set with pearls. Not enough . . . not nearly enough. He wandered into his father's study and idly picked up a copy of *The Times*.

A short paragraph conveyed the information that the Comtesse de Gravigny was in town.

Immediately there materialised in Matthew's mind the memory of that superb diamond: the beautiful stone which had nestled at her breast and which he had touched in circumstances which would live forever in his recollection. The more he thought about it, the more significance it assumed. It seemed such perfect symbolism that a diamond should provide the means to acquire the vast hordes of gems of which he now dreamed.

However, the step from an honest life to theft was not easy. Matthew lay on his bed and struggled with his conscience. He knew Freddy would take the diamond in his situation – Freddy took all sorts of things and Mama did not think the less of him. However, that argument was insufficiently convincing; already Matthew associated his brother with a darker side of life, a world which he was not yet prepared to enter.

The Comtesse, he maintained to himself, was a wealthy woman who would not be devastated by the loss of a single gem. He remembered how the diamond had clung to his hand like a leech, seemingly reluctant to leave him. It was fate, Matthew argued, it was meant to be.

But still he could not bring himself to decide on such a drastic step. He must visit the Comtesse and see what transpired. If he was right, he would be led to the diamond.

Thus already the glittering prizes of the diamond fields began to dazzle him. Matthew had compared the diamond with a leech in his hand and failed to comprehend that it could indeed suck his life's blood.

The Comtesse was staying at her sister's house in Eaton Square where Matthew waited in the tastefully appointed salon with thudding heart and dry throat, certain that guilt was written all over his face. But when the Comtesse entered they moved eargerly and instinctively towards each other.

'You are as beautiful as ever,' said Matthew sincerely, as he bent over her hand.

'You have altered a little,' she asserted in that well-remembered seductive voice. 'You are a little taller, a little broader, and much more handsome. Yes, you have fulfilled your promise.'

'I came as soon as I heard you were here. I couldn't wait to see you again.' Boldly he retained her hand.

She was flattered and allowed it to show. 'I have often thought about you and wondered if you remembered me.'

'Remember you!' he exclaimed. 'Comtesse, you are constantly in my thoughts.' His words rang hollow and false in his ears, but to his surprise the Comtesse seemed to notice nothing.

'It is said one always remembers the first time and the first woman.' She smiled. 'My favourite pupil!'

He kissed her hand, his lips burning into her palm. She was wearing a high-necked dress of deep claret velvet which accentuated the lights in her chestnut hair. Her only jewellery was a pearl pin. Perhaps the diamond lay underneath, resting on her satin skin. Slowly Matthew drew her closer and kissed her lingeringly on the lips.

'Is there not somewhere more private,' he whispered, 'where we could conduct our reunion?'

'The bedroom,' said the Comtesse with admirable bluntness.

'The servants . . . ?'

'. . . are discreet.'

Later they lay side by side on the bed. The Comtesse's even breathing indicated that she slept and cautiously Matthew extricated his arm from beneath her shoulders and raised himself on one elbow to peer about the room. The removal of the claret-coloured gown had not revealed the diamond, but he saw that on a table by the window was what appeared to be a trinket box. Carefully he eased himself out of bed and crept across the room.

It had grown dark and the lamps were unlit, the only illumination being the flickering flames of the fire. As Matthew raised the lid of the box, the jewels within caught the meagre rays and reflected the light in glowing radiance. Trembling, he lifted the diamond pendant from its velvet embrace and clutched the gem, fiercely and possessively.

Then his excitement ebbed and he faced cold reality. He was desperate for money, but he could not steal. Slowly he lowered the diamond back into the box, the gold chain trickling tantalisingly through his fingers.

'Have you found what you were looking for, Matthew?'

He spun round to see the Comtesse sitting up in bed.

'I was only looking at the jewels.'

'I think not. You were taking the diamond. So that is why you remembered your old teacher.' Her voice was flat and hard.

'I was putting it back.' He paused and then said softly, 'But you're right. I do need money desperately. I have only fifty guineas to my name.'

She seemed not to have heard him. 'How beautiful diamonds are,' she mused. 'Such symbols of wealth and status . . . such symbols of love. But they are also the hardest substance known to man and they call forth all the hardness in man's nature. Diamonds breed jealousy, greed and hate and in their light lurks the darkness of death. That stone,' and she pointed to the pendant, 'is an excellent example. It formed part of the Peacock Throne of the Great Moguls but its story is blood and butchery, treachery and evil. And now you want it.'

She paused. Matthew no longer tried to deny her allegations but waited to see what she would do.

'Take it!' she said suddenly. 'Take it, but remember my warning. I do not know why you want the stone, but I know you are setting out on a dangerous path. Already you have diminished yourself by your actions tonight. The diamond will undermine you, eat into your heart and soul and subvert you to the ways of desperate men. Ultimately it will destroy you.'

'It did not destroy you,' he countered.

'You think not? You are wrong; it has brought me no happiness and much pain. Take it now and go.' Her face was suddenly tired and older in the dim light. 'The diamond is not all you have taken from me today. And my illusions were one of the few things left to me.'

CHAPTER TWO

Matthew had no difficulty in selling the diamond. It was not unusual for a young nobleman to part with valuable heirlooms in order to placate his creditors and he could offer the stone openly on the market. Even so, he did not wish to approach the fashionable jewellers of the West End and felt nervous and guilty when he entered the dark unprepossessing premises to which he had been directed in the back streets of Soho. As he watched the diamond buyer examining the jewel, Matthew thought a flicker of recognition crossed the man's face. Certainly he showed no surprise at being offered a stone of such quality.

'Five thousand. Take it or leave it.'

It was worth far more than that, Matthew was sure. He did not know how much, but was certain that five thousand pounds was only a fraction of the diamond's value. However, he did not wish to argue. The gem was sufficiently unusual to be recognised as the property of the Comtesse and five thousand pounds was ample for his needs, a much larger sum than he could ever have hoped to borrow.

Matthew took the money and went immediately to the offices of the Union Line where he booked a passage on the next mail-ship to the Cape.

His mother appeared indifferent to the venture and not sorry to see him go, but the Honourable Peregrine Harcourt-Bright viewed his son's action as indicating a blatant disregard for duty and responsibility and a foolhardiness bordering on insanity. Freddy was not at home to air his opinion but their sister Mary, a plain dumpy girl of fourteen with a strong physical resemblance to Freddy, seemed to have no comprehension of Matthew's plans. For all the interest she displayed, he might have been travelling to Bath to take the waters rather than crossing seven thousand miles of ocean. Matthew thankfully escaped to London once more where, flushed with his new-found affluence, he entertained his friends royally at a farewell banquet.

'At last,' he said to Nicholas afterwards, 'I have been able to repay hospitality and meet my friends on equal terms. This project of the diamond fields is good for me – already!'

'To me,' Nicholas murmured, 'you were never the court jester. You know that, don't you?'

Matthew smiled and placed a companionable arm around Nicholas's shoulders. 'You said you were a bit short of cash – would this help to settle your outstandings?' He held out a money bag.

His friend's eyes widened. 'There must be a thousand here,' he exclaimed as he opened the bag and gazed at the coin.

'About that,' said Matthew offhandedly.

'I couldn't possibly take it. And how on earth did you come by it? You were so desperate . . .' A worried look came over Nicholas's face.

'I came by it honestly,' snapped Matthew. 'A loan from a friend. What do you think I did? Steal it?'

'Of course not,' Nicholas protested. Wistfully he caressed the bag of coins. 'Could you really spare it?' When Matthew nodded, he breathed a huge sigh of relief. 'I could use it. *How* I could use it! His Grace is in such a pet over Lambourne's debts that I haven't dared mention mine. Thank you, Matthew.' He reached out and shook Matthew's hand warmly and affectionately. 'I shall miss you, old chap. Very much. And if there's anything I can do . . .'

'There is. Tell Isobel what I'm doing. And why.'

Matthew had insisted that Nicholas should not see him off. However, when he saw the SS *Briton* through the murk and drizzle of the winter's day, he rather regretted his solitary state. Painted all in black, with only a flesh-coloured funnel with black top to lighten the funereal aspect, the ship depressed him. He had spent thirty-five guineas to secure the best accommodation but his cabin seemed poky and dark and he shuddered at the prospect of thirty-odd days' confinement in this 'hell-hole' as he described it to himself with considerable exaggeration. His depression deepened as the ship sailed into Southampton Water, then out into the Channel and wallowed in the mid-winter miseries of the Bay of Biscay. However, Matthew discovered he was an excellent sailor and buoyantly attributed his depression to the English weather, experiencing a resurgence of hope and spirits as they approached the sunshine and blue skies of the Canaries.

His thirty-five guineas provided eveything he required on the voyage – bedding, cabin fittings and four meals a day. The only extra expense incurred by passengers was for alcohol and mineral waters and in this respect Matthew spent freely. His time was divided principally between strolling on the deck and sitting in his cabin with a whisky in one hand and a book in the other. Sounds of merriment penetrated from the second- and third-class decks, where exuberant young men bound for the diamond fields gave vent to their high spirits and optimistic outlook. But Matthew felt no urge to join them; his voyage, he considered, was not a light-hearted adventure but a mission to prove himself worthy of the Lady Isobel. The fact that at night in his bunk he dreamed only of diamonds and riches, and not of his lady, did not strike him as significant.

Only one man dared to penetrate Matthew's invisible shield. Mr Thomas Reynolds was, he decided, an enigma: neat and dapper in appearance, he managed to be both faceless and without personality. Even after talking to him for an hour or more, one could neither recall his features nor feel that one had learned anything at all of his history. Yet he persisted in seeking out Matthew and it would have been churlish to discourage him.

'You take your quest for diamonds more seriously than our compatriots on the other decks,' Reynolds remarked one morning when he discovered Matthew on deck reading Tavernier's *Six Journeys*.

'One ought to learn as much as possible about the occurrence of diamonds,' Matthew rejoined. 'It is encouraging that the finds in South Africa seem to confirm the theories originated in India – that diamonds are alluvial, forming part of the deposit in a river bed.'

'Not being a geologist, I would hesitate to give an opinion. However, I do recall Tavernier describing his visit to the banks of the Kistna river, where sixty thousand workers slaved in the scorching heat for a mere pittance. I always wonder what those poor peasants thought of that stylish French gentleman, but,' and here Reynolds smiled cynically, 'diamonds are a commodity which accentuate the divisions among people.'

'It is incredible really how few sources of diamonds there are in the world,' said Matthew, not noticing the other man's note of censure. 'India, Borneo, Brazil . . .'

'. . . also using slave labour,' interpolated Reynolds. 'The history of the Brazilian mines does not make pretty reading. The slaves – men and women, black and white – toiled under the lash of their master in an unhealthy climate, and died like flies in order that the nobility of Europe might deck itself in sparklers.'

'I was going to say,' continued Matthew firmly, 'that the South African discoveries might well be the best of all. One day the diggings at the Vaal might produce great gems to rank alongside the Koh-i-Noor.'

'The Koh-i-Noor, of course, belonged to the Mogul emperors who sat upon the Peacock Throne.' Reynolds paused and Matthew's face flamed at the memory of another diamond of similar parentage. 'When the Persians conquered the Moguls, they only managed to acquire the fabulous gem by further treachery and intrigue. Since then, one owner had boiling oil poured on his shaven head, another was blinded by his brother, and a third was imprisoned and starved – all in various attempts to obtain the diamond. I wonder if these lurid tales trouble our noble Queen when the stone adorns her gracious person.'

'It is said that the Koh-i-Noor never brings bad luck to a woman,' observed Matthew. 'Incidentally, I believe that in olden times diamonds were so rare that they were worn only by kings?'

'That is correct. Then in about 1430 a certain French lady, Agnes Sorel, wore diamonds at the French Court and started a fashion which has never faltered. The French have a flair for these things, don't you agree?' Reynolds cast a lingering look at Matthew's flushed face and continued imperturbably on his constitutional round the deck.

When Matthew set unsteady feet on the rickety planks of the Central Jetty in Cape Town, Reynolds appeared at his elbow and fell into step beside him.

'Let us share a hansom,' he suggested, 'if you are not overburdened with baggage.'

'I only brought a couple of boxes,' answered Matthew. 'It seemed more sensible to acquire here the equipment I need. By all means, let us travel together.'

A crowd of people had gathered at the end of the pier to welcome friends and stare at new arrivals. Coloured porters carried luggage, an excited hubbub filled the air, the sun blazed in a cloudless sky – and the stench from the nearby fish market was so overpowering as to make Matthew wrinkle his nose in disgust.

'There is worse to come, I fear,' smiled Reynolds, as they settled into a cab driven by a small and wrinkled Malay coachman and moved up a broad street opposite the jetty. 'Look!'

Matthew followed the direction of his companion's pointing finger and saw the open drain at the side of the road, a foetid stream of black mud in which floated the dead bodies of cats, rats and dogs. The smell was unspeakable. 'Perhaps it will improve when we reach the main street?' he suggested.

Reynolds laughed. 'My dear sir, this *is* the main street. They call it Adderley Street.'

It was long and fairly wide, but to Matthew seemed less imposing than a provincial thoroughfare, let alone the chief highway of a capital city, although Table Mountain provided a majestic backdrop. He gazed curiously at the cosmopolitan population – the white men and women dressed in fashions very similar to those of London and Europe; the Malay women in innumerable petticoats with silk kerchiefs on their black polished hair and the Malay men wearing wide, pointed straw hats; the bizarre costumes of the yellow-skinned Hottentots and black-skinned Africans. Private carriages, carts, hansom cabs, even ox-wagons, all jostled for position in the roadway. A particularly bright blaze of colour caught Matthew's attention and he leaned forward eagerly to feast his eyes on the wares of the flower sellers, grateful for the glimpse of the blooms after more than a month at sea.

'Adderley Street,' Matthew repeated. 'I seem to know that name.'

'No doubt you do. Charles Adderley is the member of Parliament for Staffordshire. He steered through the Act which created the Dominion of Canada, but in about 1850 he took up the cause of the Cape colonists who opposed settlement here by convicts. The convict ships were not allowed to put in and sailed on to Australia. Everyone was very happy about it,' Reynolds smiled crookedly. 'I wonder if they will continue to be so satisfied.'

'It seems the best thing to me,' said Matthew. '*I* wouldn't want convicts dumped on my doorstep.'

'There is bound to be a rough and rowdy element among them, but most will settle down to build a prosperous new life. The point is that they were English-speaking settlers. This could prove important later on, for the British here are still greatly outnumbered by the Dutch.'

'The Dutch can learn English.'

Reynolds laughed. 'Of course the Dutch *could* learn English, but they don't *want* to. Remember that the Dutch were masters here for about 150 years. The British have ruled for only 70 years. The Boers have a bitter hatred of the British and some years ago many trekked out of the Cape to establish their own states in the Transvaal and the Orange Free State. They love their language, which is a sort of pidgin Dutch, and their religion – a particularly puritanical Calvinist form of Protestant worship. Yet for all their religion, they believe the coloured people to be inferior and deeply resent the laws of equality introduced by us. Yes, the time may come when the British regret that their numbers are not greater and rue the day the convict ships landed at Botany Bay instead of Table Bay. Ah, here we are at the hotel. Pray keep your seat, Mr Harcourt-Bright, and I will secure the accommodation.'

However, within a few minutes Reynolds returned, shaking his head sadly.

'The place is full,' he announced, 'due to the crowds heading for the diamond fields. We must try elsewhere.'

At their next stop Reynolds reported the same state of affairs, but at the third attempt accommodation was found at the Masonic Hotel.

'Unfortunately there is only one room available,' said Reynolds apologetically, 'albeit with two beds. Do you object to sharing?'

'Of course not,' Matthew assured him.

After depositing his bags in their room, Matthew wasted no time in inquiring the quickest route to the diamond fields. His face blanched when he heard what lay before him, for they were six hundred miles away in an area called Griqualand, to the north of the Cape Colony, west of the Orange Free State and south of Bechuanaland. Between Cape Town and this land of promise lay fertile valleys, high mountain ridges and the immense desert of the Great Karoo where the dry heat sears the scrub-covered veld and withers all vegetation except the hardy thorns and aloes.

The train, he discovered, went only as far as Wellington, fifty-eight miles from Cape Town. From there, there were four ways of reaching the diggings – by cart, quickest but most expensive; by horse- or mule-drawn coach; by ox-wagon; or to walk.

Matthew patted his money-belt reassuringly and bought a railway ticket to Wellington, secure in the knowledge that he could easily afford a cart to cover the tiresome distance in the shortest possible time.

Then he entered the bar of the Masonic Hotel, ordered a drink and sat down to listen to the talk of diamonds which came from every corner of the crowded room.

The first stone to be identified as a diamond in South Africa was discovered in 1866 but, surprisingly, there was no great rush at that time. The 'Eureka', as that first diamond was named, was considered a freak and it was not until March 1869 that the great white diamond called the 'Star of South Africa' was found and subsequently fetched £30,000 in London. Now the flood-gates opened and from all over the world the treasure hunters poured in. More diamonds were found and more men swarmed to aptly-named Hopetown and to the banks of the Vaal River where the best finds were made.

Matthew looked at the excited faces about him and listened to the talk which swirled around the room in a variety of accents. What, he wondered, was driving these men to the fields? Hope or despair? Boredom or love of adventure? Or perhaps it was the fever – the fever which grips men who search the soil for the Earth's treasures. The fever which forces them on, even when success eludes them, to suffer privations or endure great hardships and dangers, because the next sod lifted by the spade, the next blow from the pick, or swirl of a sieve, may bring the glint of gold or the dazzling fire of a diamond.

Matthew could feel that fever taking control of him, luring him on, showing him visions of great riches. Already he envisaged piles of diamonds far in excess of his requirements for maintaining a wife and a position in society. Already there was a danger that the diamonds could become an end in themselves and that the desire for them could never be satiated. A sudden surge of confidence engulfed him. He would succeed here in this new country, a land of opportunity where antecedents were irrelevant. He would find the wealth which would bring the power and position he wanted.

He went happily to bed to dream of El Dorado. Reynolds had not yet come in and Matthew stripped off his clothes and slept.

He awoke, refreshed, to another blazing day. Before pulling back the curtains he lay in the cool darkness, savouring the tranquillity of the moment. He had slept soundly, the floor had stopped heaving under his feet as though it were the deck of a ship and he felt ready to face the next part of his journey. When he opened the curtains and let in the light, he saw that the other bed had not been slept in and that the small valise which Reynolds had placed at its foot had disappeared. Odd, thought Matthew. He had not heard the man come in during the night and the chap must have crept about as stealthily as a cat. Confound it, Matthew said to himself, I hope the blighter hasn't made off without paying his share of the bill.

He reached for his money-belt in order to strap it next to his skin, but as soon as he picked it up he knew something was wrong . . . very wrong. The belt felt light enough to be empty: frantic investigation soon revealed that it *was* empty.

He had carried some spare cash in the smallest of his travelling bags. Now he flung the bag on the bed and sank to his knees beside it, clawing feverishly at the fastenings. That cache had gone, too: it was all gone.

Panic set in. He was thousands of miles from home, in a strange country where he knew no one. He had to find the money! Matthew began to tear the room apart – it must be here somewhere.

Otherwise he would have to call in the police. That bastard Reynolds had stolen it – there must still be time to catch him before he left Cape Town.

Then Matthew saw the small money-bag on the floor beside the bed-head. He seized it and gazed incredulously at the bright stream of coins which poured on to the bed. There was exactly fifty guineas: precisely the amount he had possessed before he acquired the diamond. It could not be a coincidence that this was exactly the sum he had told the Comtesse he possessed.

He sat down on the bed as the first feeling of blind panic abated. Reynolds had taken the money, of that there was no doubt, but what information could he give the police? He would have to admit that he could not describe Reynolds – the face was elusive, difficult to recall, it slipped away every time he tried to bring it to mind. He would have to admit that he knew nothing about the man and had been sufficiently trusting to share a room without checking for himself whether other accommodation was available. Also, he would have to confess that he had been naïve enough to carry all his cash on his person instead of inquiring about the banking system in these parts.

He had been a fool and the blow to his pride was almost as severe as that to his pocket. But there was another reason why Matthew decided against calling the police.

Reynolds must have been working for the Comtesse; it was the only possible explanation. Not only did the fifty guineas he had left in the money-bag tally exactly with the amount Matthew had told the Comtesse was all he possessed, but those allusions on the ship to certain diamonds and French ladies had not been coincidental either. The Comtesse had allowed him to reach the Cape but had decided that now he must learn the hard way. No doubt Reynolds had also followed him to the diamond dealer in Soho and re-purchased the gem. Matthew wondered what they would make of the shortfall of one thousand pounds – the money he had given to Nicholas.

As he faced up to his own stupidity and the seriousness of his situation, the memory of the Comtesse and her lessons loomed large in his mind. An appreciative smile curved Matthew's taut mouth as he realised that her teaching days were not over. She was still hardening his manhood, testing him, probing his strengths and his weaknesses. She wanted to know if he was man enough to persevere. Matthew threw back his head and laughed aloud and then, briskly, began to dress. He repacked his meagre possessions, placing in the small bag several changes of linen and other essentials. The rest he packed in the large portmanteau: it would have to be sold. Once again he surveyed his watch and jewelled rings, tie-pins and studs. He would keep the watch but the rest would have to go.

In his pocket he found the railway ticket to Wellington and some loose change. He walked downstairs to pay the hotel bill and ask where he could sell his things. Then he went to the railway station. He did not have enough money for a cart or even a seat on a coach – not if he was to have funds to buy a diamond claim and equipment. He might not even be able to afford a ride on an ox-wagon. Well, by God, he would damn well walk!

CHAPTER THREE

Two weeks later Matthew was still walking. For much of the time he had been plodding but now he was stumbling.

He had enjoyed the first stage of his journey, for the air was warm and balmy in the luxuriant valleys of the fertile Cape. He had bought food and filled his water flask before he left Wellington, a sleepy little town with broad empty streets and quiet slow-moving people. There was other traffic on the road – vehicles belonging to the local populace, carts and coaches dashing towards the diamond fields and lumbering ox-wagons of supplies. Matthew strode out with good heart and confident determination, feeling young and strong and proudly independent.

The land was more beautiful than he had dreamed. Even though it was late summer, there were still grapes on the vine and fruit on the trees at the prosperous farms with their thatched and gabled homesteads. He crossed mountain passes over grim gorges and canyons and descended through wild and romantic scenery to river banks lined with willow and graceful karee trees. He was up early each morning, to see the rising sun gilding the mountain tops while dusky twilight still glimmered mistily in the valleys.

Then he entered the burning heat, the silence and the solitude of the seemingly limitless Karoo. The barren plateau stretched before him to the shimmering horizon in endless desolation, with not even a tree to break the flat grey-brown monotony of the landscape. The road was only a rough brown track, scored by the wheels of heavy wagons; its course was haphazard, running in a winding ribbon across the sandy, scrub-covered veld, crossing dry river beds and deep dongas.

Yet at first the Karoo had its own beauty. Its austerity cleansed and purified; its dawns were immaculate and its sunsets wicked in their rapturous perfection. Here and there amid the dry stunted bushes were yellow-flowered mimosa and red aloes, and an alert pair of eyes could spot animal life such as the meerkats which fled at Matthew's approach. But his pleasure in the novelty of his surroundings was short-lived, obliterated by the searing sun.

The heat was overwhelming, its intensity greater than anything he had ever envisaged. The sun was brilliant in a cloudless sky and beat down on him in unrelenting savagery, dazzling his eyes and scorching his skin. In the furnace devil-devil dust clouds, or miniature whirl-winds, spiralled skywards and grey-white rocks grew too hot to touch.

Matthew's clothes were torn and caked with dust. His bowler hat had gone, living up to its name by spinning merrily over a mountain pass and leaving his gold head bare to the sun. His stiff boots were broken and he limped because of huge blisters on his feet. Midges buzzed in a cloud around his head, flying into his eyes which streamed incessantly as he struggled vainly to remove the irritating insects. Sometimes he blundered into swarms of horse-flies which stung his exposed flesh and clung tenaciously to his skin, leaving festering sores.

The only sound was the sighing of the wind, interspersed infrequently by the scream of devil-devils, and the only smell was the pungent aroma of the sparse shrubs. While the sun scorched and seared through the day, the nights grew crisp and cold and Matthew huddled in a blanket under the clear sky where stars twinkled like the diamonds he sought.

The road was nearly always empty now. Only an occasional coach thundered past carrying its fortunate passengers towards the Vaal, smothering Matthew in dust and leaving him coughing and humiliated by the side of the track. The staging posts of the coach company were spaced far apart and often the stores were empty of goods and awaiting fresh supplies. The Boer homesteads were few, standing stark against the desert on which sheep and scrawny goats tried to feed. Matthew pleaded for water and, while no Boer would refuse him, his tattered and disreputable appearance roused suspicions and he was soon hustled on his way. At times he saw pools of water ahead and in a renewed burst of energy and hope lurched towards them – but the closer he came the further they receded and with a groan of despair he realised they were mirages. Matthew grew hungrier, thirstier and weaker but never once did he even think of giving up.

His thoughts became more and more confused as the sun and lack of sustenance muddled his brain. He wished that Nicholas was by his side. He dreamed of Isobel, bestowing on her attributes and qualities no earthly woman could possibly possess. He gloated over Freddy's chagrin when he became the wealthiest man in the world. In time his memories of home so seethed and twisted and hammered in his head that they tormented him as much as the discomfort of the present.

And always overhead wheeled the great vultures which seemed to be watching him as he staggered through the dust and heat, waiting for him to drop, waiting, waiting . . . He had never imagined a country so vast, or heat so great, or a loneliness and silence so intense.

At last he realised that it was wiser to travel at night and sleep while the sun was high. Thereafter he made good progress until the day he lost his way.

He had trudged on as soon as the sun sank from sight. This was the best part of the day; the air was cool but not cold and the vivid colours of the sunset, pink, rose, orange and scarlet, flamed against the deepening purple of the sombre landscape. As he walked he tried to calculate how far he had come. The distance from Wellington to the diamond fields was about 550 miles and he had been walking for seventeen days. Suppose, he mused, he had walked about twenty miles a day? This would mean he had covered about 340 miles and that left about 200 to go. So he was well over half-way there. Matthew attempted to smile but his lips were too dry and cracked and he tried to moisten them with his tongue. He quickened his pace, but pulled up sharply as the blisters chafed against his broken shoes.

The sky was cloudless but the moon was in its last quarter and shed little light on the path he was struggling to follow. Several times Matthew stopped and peered at the ground to make sure he was still on the cart track. The last store, some ten miles back, had been empty and he had not passed a farm for several days. Since he lost his hat he had suffered continuously from headaches. There was a pain in his head now, magnified by hunger and thirst.

He was suddenly aware of his own footsteps on the hard sun-baked ground. He stopped. The silence was eerie, surrounding him with a weird ghostly pressure that was almost tangible. He strained his ears into the void but could hear nothing. He was alone in the blackness, utterly alone in the vast emptiness of the African desert. For the first time Matthew felt afraid.

Now his footsteps sounded even louder than before. The fear was rising within him and he took to glancing nervously over his shoulders as he walked. Yet he did not know of what he was afraid.

Then he became aware that he had left the path and blundered into the undergrowth at the side of the road. Even as he cursed and hesitated slightly in his stride, his foot caught on something and he fell headlong to the ground, twisting his ankle under him.

His fingers scrabbled for a hold in the pile of stones beneath him as he tried to pull himself to his feet, red-hot pain stabbing in his ankle. Touching something cold and unfamiliar, he peered closer and a strangled gasp escaped his lips. It was a hand, a human hand, sticking up out of the pile of stones. For a few moments he gazed at the macabre object, transfixed, as he realised that the cairn of stones covered a body and he had tripped over a grave. The horror of it was too much for him. Gooseflesh rose on his skin, he broke out in cold sweat and gave a great bellow of fright as he stumbled away as fast as his injury would allow.

On and on he crashed in his headlong flight until his ankle would carry him no further and he collapsed, panting, half-sobbing with pain and cursing himself for his foolishness. It would be impossible to find the road again in the dark and almost impossible to walk. The agony in his ankle gradually subsided, however, and eventually he slept.

Matthew woke to a daze of heat and pain. The sun seemed to be directly over him, in a haze of white light, and the ache in his head was excruciating. His leg felt numb but the ankle was hugely swollen and it would be torture to put his weight on it.

'But I must,' he muttered aloud. 'I must get back to the road, or I will die.' Involuntarily his dazed eyes lifted to the sky and he saw the vultures hovering above. They would not get him – they would *not*.

He looked about him for something from which he could fashion a crutch but there was nothing. Groggily he struggled to his feet, the sharp pain stabbing through him. Helplessly he sought a landmark which would show him the road, for he had no idea what direction he had taken in his panic-stricken flight from the shallow grave. But there was nothing to tell him whether to move to left or right: he must strike out blindly.

After a couple of faltering, agonised steps he sank to the ground again. It was no good, he could not walk but would have to crawl. Slowly he dragged himself over the ground, suddenly realising that at some stage he had dropped his bag.

Matthew gritted his teeth. He would not give up. He would not die. He would not give Freddy the satisfaction of hearing of his death nor the Duke of Desborough the relief of his permanent absence. 'I'll show them,' he muttered through parched, cracked lips. 'I'll show them all.'

For what seemed like hours Matthew inched painfully over the veld, only semi-conscious as the heat, hunger and thirst took their toll. He did not find the road and there were no other travellers on the horizon. What has happened, he thought in one of his rare lucid moments, to that procession of men making for the diamond fields?

He was growing weaker. It became more difficult to move and his rest periods became longer and more frequent. Once he saw a mottled branch lying in his path and stretched for it eagerly in the belief that he had found a crutch. But just as his hand reached out the 'branch' moved and slithered into the scrub. Matthew lay face downwards on the earth and began to laugh, hysterical laughter of pain, anger, fear and frustration.

No doubt the snake was still near, but Matthew was too exhausted to care. He turned on to his back and as he looked up at the sky he glimpsed something he had not seen for weeks. Clouds were gathering, boiling on the horizon and billowing across the sky. Slate-grey they were and as Matthew strained to focus his weary eyes, he saw the vivid flashes of lightning and heard in the distance the rumble of thunder. He smiled because he believed this to be his deliverance: rain, life-giving rain, which would cleanse him, refresh him, soothe his injured foot and moisten his parched throat.

As the storm drew nearer he watched in awe the brilliance of the lightning, covered his ears against the deafening roar of the thunder and trembled at the violence the elements unleashed about him. Thunderstorms in England were never like this, not on a scale so majestic and amazing, so daunting and terrifying. Crouched beneath the seething cauldron of cloud, Matthew felt utterly exposed and defenceless, a small and insignificant flame which Nature could extinguish with one casual puff.

Then the rains fell. Not the soft, soaking, soothing droplets he had imagined but lancing rods of rain which stung and lashed him into submission. Matthew lay in a pool of water, drifting in and out of consciousness, and stayed there still when the storm had passed. Once he managed to open his eyes and saw a vulture land nearby and begin to waddle towards him. Feebly Matthew shook a fist at the horrid bird and it took off with a wild flapping of wings as his lips moved faintly in a curse. Again he lapsed into blackness, but was vaguely aware of a voice and could almost have believed that strong arms were lifting him. But perhaps it was only a dream . . .

The dream persisted however. Sometimes he thought he was in a tent where flickering light formed dark shadows on white canvas. At other times he shivered with cold and a pale face seemed to appear over him while kind hands wrapped him in blankets. These periods of intense cold alternated with such burning heat that he was convinced he was indeed dead and roasting in the fires of hell. From time to time he was aware of the low murmur of voices in a language he did not understand. But most of the time was blank and black.

Then came the day when Matthew opened his eyes and was himself again. He tried to sit up, but fell back weakly against the pillows. He could see enough, however, to know that it was not a tent which sheltered him but a tented wagon, before he slipped again into healing sleep.

When he awoke, a woman was sitting in the wagon, her head bent over a piece of mending. Matthew lay still, watching her. She was dressed in a simple frock of blue and white cotton and her head was covered by a white linen sunbonnet. She had turned back the brim and Matthew could see a glimpse of brown hair beneath the cap, brushed back severely from a centre parting.

She became aware of his eyes upon her and came swiftly to his side. Laying a hand on his forehead, she nodded with satisfaction when she found his skin was cool and the fever had passed. Her face was broad and plain, with small dark eyes and a tight mouth – an honest face, thought Matthew, but dour and unsmiling.

The woman did not speak to him but went to the rear of the wagon and called loudly. A man appeared, a giant of a man with brown hair and beard flecked with grey, and leathery sunburned skin. He wore brown trousers, a brown-and-white checked shirt with a yellow waistcoat and a wide-brimmed brown felt hat.

'Good. You are better.'

'You speak English,' said Matthew thankfully.

'A little,' the man answered brusquely. 'Now rest again. If you are well enough, we will travel on tomorrow.'

'How long is it since you found me?'

'Five days.'

'So long!' exclaimed Matthew.

'You had a fever. And your ankle was badly twisted.'

Gingerly Matthew moved his bandaged foot under the blanket. There was no pain. 'It feels much better.'

'You go to the diamond fields?' asked the man in his deep guttural voice. Matthew nodded and the man continued: 'Then we travel together. You are not strong enough yet to walk.'

'Are you going to the diamond fields too?' asked Matthew, hardly daring to believe his luck.

'Ja. I am a farmer, but here in the Karoo,' and the man shrugged, 'there is not much luck in farming. I have no money to buy more stock, so hope to find diamonds which will provide the sheep.'

'What else should I want? I have land with a house upon it. All I need is stock to graze upon that land and bring money for our daily bread. What else does a man need? Except, if the good Lord had seen fit to bless us with children . . .' He sighed, leaving the sentence unfinished, and glanced at the stolid figure of his wife who was sitting, hands folded in her lap, staring out of the open flap of the wagon.

'How did you find me?' Matthew asked.

'We were trekking to the road and sheltered by a *wag-'n-bietje* thicket for the storm to pass. We moved on slowly, the ground being heavy and wet, and I saw a vulture come down from the sky, only to flap into the air again almost immediately. I knew then that its prey was not quite dead so went to look.'

'Lucky for me that you did,' said Matthew fervently, with a shudder at the memory of the ghastly bird and the horrible lonely death and unmarked grave which he had escaped so narrowly. 'You saved my life.' He stretched out limp fingers to grasp the other man's sunburned hand. 'Thank you! And I don't even know your name?'

'Jacobs. Willem Jacobs.' He pronounced it with a 'y' and a short 'a', like 'Yakkobs'. 'My wife is called Martha. And you?'

'Bright,' said Matthew after a moment's hesitation. 'Matthew Bright.' He never used any other name again.

Willem inspanned the oxen and, as they lumbered across the veld to the road, Matthew gazed in astonishment at the transformation wrought by the rain. Miraculously the once-parched earth had burst into flower. Purple, white, carmine and yellow blooms glowed upon a carpet of brilliant green and the scented air smelled fresh, like new-mown hay.

In the days that followed Matthew gradually regained his strength, riding at first upon the wagon until he was able to walk alongside, eating lightly until his appetite was fully restored. The Boer fare was simple, mainly stews of hares or small antelope which Willem shot, washed down by strong black coffee, but it was infinitely more sustaining than Matthew's previous diet. Willem also introduced Matthew to biltong, the coarse dried antelope meat which at first had the appearance, flavour and texture of shoe leather but for which Matthew soon acquired a taste. And at night, before he retired to a makeshift bed beneath the wagon, there was a tot of fiery brandy to warm his stomach and relax his mind and limbs.

One night they outspanned at a waterhole beside three other wagons. A fire was already blazing and while Willem watered the oxen Martha brought food to add to the stewpot. Ten sat round the fire that night, the brandy bottle was passed from hand to hand and the lilt of a concertina blended with the throb of a guitar.

They spoke the *taal*, thus excluding Matthew from their comradeship, but he was still too grateful to be alive to feel resentment. At least there was no evidence of the 'bitter hatred' between Boer and Briton which Reynolds had described. He sat within the circle, accepting their hospitality and enjoying the warmth of the fire beneath the vast bowl of the star-studded sky. London seemed a very long way away.

There was one interruption when a wagon passed near and made camp a few hundred yards away. In the darkness the group at Matthew's fire turned to stare and strained their eyes to identify the newcomer who spurned their company. One man rose and walked softly into the night. He returned within a few minutes and threw himself down again in his place.

'Steyn,' he announced, and spat loudly. '*Daai bliksem!*'

The following morning was clear as crystal, fresh and sparkling as champagne. Matthew caught a glimpse of his reflection in the still surface of the waterhole, and grinned. No one at home would recognise him. His skin was deeply tanned and his face, dominated by bright blue eyes, was protected from the sun by a thick golden beard. He was thinner, moving with a lean grace and purpose over the veld and, thanks to Willem and Martha, fitter than he had ever been. Martha had burned his filthy London suit and he was dressed in brown trousers, blue shirt and waistcoat, and big slouch hat belonging to Willem. His feet were encased in soft, comfortable *veldschoen*.

They set off in convoy, the fifth wagon of the unfriendly stranger keeping its distance from the main group. The nearer they drew to the Vaal River the busier the road became. Other tracks converged with the main thoroughfare to the diggings, bringing men, carts and animals from all corners of the country. When night fell men and women stretched aching bodies, fires were lit and thirsty oxen led to water. There were some days when water was scarce, when spruits were dry and dams empty. It was at one such dam that the first piece of unpleasantness occurred.

The atmosphere on the convoy had been remarkably friendly and easy-going, considering the varied nationalities, professions and characters of the men. Recently there had been a bit of barging as drivers fought for position, resulting in collisions with teams and whips entangled.

It was the unfriendly stranger, Steyn, who started the fracas. Matthew had taken a strong dislike to the man, a feeling he knew was shared by his companions. Steyn had taken up a position in the convoy and had been responsible for much of the barging and jostling, wielding his whip a great deal more than was necessary on his poor, struggling oxen. His ugly face wore a surly look, his body was short and thickset while his hair and beard were black and bushy. He always outspanned well away from everyone else, with the wagon between his fire and the rest of the encampment. Once Matthew thought he saw a movement like the billow of a woman's skirt, but presumed he had been mistaken.

The dam where they stopped that night was very low. The water was muddy and shallow and the men were worried lest there should be insufficient for all the animals. The line of men and patient oxen were waiting their turn at the water's edge when Steyn pushed past the queue and bent to drink.

A growl went up from the men. It was an unwritten law of the veld that animals drank first. Not only had Steyn broken that tradition but had selfishly left his poor beasts yoked to the wagon where they bellowed thirstily as they smelled the water.

Matthew stepped forward, put a firm hand on Steyn's collar and booted him head-first into the dam.

'You wanted water, you bastard!' he shouted. 'Well, you've got it! But you'll stay there until I let you out.'

The men cheered, Steyn glowered, and Matthew stood guard

until every animal and every digger had drunk their fill. Willem led Steyn's oxen to the water, his smile of approval at Matthew's action fading from his eyes as he inspected the lacerations Steyn's lash had imprinted on their backs and thin flanks.

'Who is he?' Matthew asked Willem when at last he allowed a dripping Steyn out of the water.

Willem shrugged. 'I don't know him. I only know what others have told me. Johannes,' and he pointed at the man who had identified Steyn originally, 'met him before. Steyn was married then, but it's said his wife died from the treatment he meted out to her.'

To Matthew's fury, Steyn's ducking did not teach him a lesson. If anything, his aggression increased and the murmurings of resentment among the other travellers grew. Matters came to a head one morning when the wagons waited to cross a deep drift.

At least, thought Matthew, there was shade from the sun here. They were less than twenty miles from the Vaal and trees had become more numerous. He drowsed peacefully as they waited their turn to cross.

'*Ag*, now there will be trouble!' muttered Willem at his side, and Matthew opened his eyes to see Steyn pushing his team past the wagons ahead.

'Damn him!' Matthew exclaimed. 'If he's so anxious to reach the fields first, why doesn't he get up earlier and start off at the head of the queue?'

Willem did not reply but made a gesture of drinking from an imaginary flask.

Steyn drew up at the drift, alongside the lead wagon. As Matthew watched, two figures dropped off another vehicle and ran silently to the left rear wheel of Steyn's wagon. After a few minutes they moved to the right-hand wheel and then raced back to their own wagon.

No one else moved, but every eye watched as Steyn drove his team into the water. The entry to the drift was steep, the oxen slipping and sliding on the rocks in the river bed. The water was deep, muddy and fast-flowing. Suddenly the left rear wheel of the wagon dropped off its axle and the vehicle tilted. Steyn cursed and 'sjambokked' his straining oxen but as the wagon jolted forward the right rear wheel also fell away. Cheers rang out from the river bank.

'What a splendid idea,' grinned Matthew, 'but I feel sorry for the oxen. Knowing that bastard, he'll whip them till they're raw.'

'No. He'll have to get off his backside and replace the locking pins. The wagon is too far off-balance to move.'

Indeed the wagon was tilting dangerously, settling back into the water, and its load was sliding to the rear. The flaps of the wagon were closed but the pressure from within forced the canvas to give way and a case of brandy crashed into the water.

'He's not likely to get drunk tonight,' laughed Matthew. 'Shall we fish it out and have a drink ourselves?' He swung his long legs off the seat and walked to the bank. Several others had had the same idea and the case of liquor was quickly recovered.

Then Matthew's blood froze and he stared at the torn canvas of Steyn's wagon. A small hand was gripping the rent, as though its owner was hanging on for dear life to avoid being swept away in the water, and two frightened little faces appeared in the opening.

'Children!' shouted Matthew. 'Quick! Who has the locking pins for the wheels?'

'*Kinders!*' The shout went up. The two men who had removed the pins which connected the wheels to the axle ran forward and Matthew led the group which jumped into the water. Setting their shoulders to the wheels, they raised the wagon and inserted the pins, struggling to stay upright in the swift current. When the wagon was on an even keel, the men helped to push it through the drift. On the other side, Matthew pulled open the canvas and lifted down the two shivering children. Their eyes had remained fixed on him during the rescue operation and now they gazed up at his tall golden figure speechlessly.

He had never seen two such woebegone creatures. Wet tattered clothes clung to pathetically thin bodies, dark hair was plastered to their scalps and their pale faces were dominated by huge grey-green eyes. The girl would be about eleven or twelve, Matthew estimated, and the boy probably five.

'What is your name?' Matthew asked, but they stared at him uncomprehendingly.

'*Wat is jou naam?*' prompted one of the other diggers.

'Alida,' answered the girl, '*en* Daniel.'

There were bruises on her arm and a scar on her cheek which Matthew did not believe had been caused by the tilting of the wagon in the river. His lips compressed. So Steyn not only kept his children virtual prisoners in the suffocating heat of the wagon but he knocked them about as well.

At that moment Steyn walked up. '*Klim in die wa!*' he ordered, and hurriedly Alida and Daniel climbed back to their accustomed place.

Steyn's small dark eyes bored into Matthew's face with a look of intense hatred.

'*Verdomde Engelsman!*' he spat. 'I'll not forget I have a score to settle with you. Meantime, keep away from me and from my *kinders*.'

'He seems to think *I* removed the locking pins,' said Matthew to Willem later.

'He's not worth worrying about,' soothed Willem. 'Forget him!'

'You're right,' said Matthew softly, 'but Alida and Daniel are not so easily forgotten.'

His eyes rested on Martha who was standing on the fringe of the firelight, staring at the distant shape of Steyn's wagon. As usual, however, nothing could be seen of his bivouac.

The anguish in Martha's eyes cast a gloom over what should have been a joyous night. For this was their last camp – tomorrow they would reach the Vaal.

CHAPTER FOUR

The road ran up a kopje which blocked the vista beyond. Matthew could contain his excitement no longer but leaped from the wagon and raced to the crest of the hill for his first view of the diamond fields.

Below him was the wide, sluggish, chocolate-brown river with tents and wagons and flimsy structures of galvanised iron strewn on either bank. The scene was one of indescribable confusion: there were ten thousand men at the river diggings and it seemed as if they were all in Pniel that day. In his bewilderment Matthew was aware only of continuous movement, noise and dust as men and animals hurried by, carting gravel to and from the stream, carrying buckets of water or transporting supplies. Men shouted, dogs barked, oxen bellowed while from the claims near the river came the noise of spades and picks and barrows and, above all, the shaking of the sieves. The water was nearly as busy as the land, crowded with natives working in the riverside claims, washing clothes or bathing.

'It looks as though we are in time,' Matthew shouted happily to Willem. 'There are still diamonds here!'

'Ja,' agreed Willem, somewhat doubtfully. He was staring at a group of shabby diggers whose tattered clothes and air of disillusion indicated a certain lack of prospecting success. 'But *they* didn't find any.'

'They probably wouldn't know a diamond from a dandelion,' scoffed Matthew, happy in what he believed to be his superior knowledge of such things as he gazed eagerly about him. He was here, actually here, after weary months of travelling, and was impatient to start digging. He felt as if the very ground beneath his feet was stuffed with diamonds, just waiting for him to pull them out. And yet he was disconcerted by the chaos – there appeared to be no centre to the activities, no town or official organisation. 'Where do we go, Willem? What do we do? How do we buy a claim and get started?'

But Willem, accustomed to the silence and space of his remote farm, was even more confused than Matthew. He shook his head wordlessly and concentrated on controlling his team.

'Pniel and Klipdrift are said to be the richest diggings,' Matthew announced. 'We must settle for one of them. But which?' Again he surveyed the teeming mass of people and the bemused expressions of his companions. 'Klipdrift!' he decided. 'It might be quieter, at least it couldn't be more crowded!'

In fact Klipdrift was indistinguishable from its sister camp across the river and the precarious crossing on the pont seemed hardly worthwhile. But Matthew did obtain directions to a small shack where prospecting licences were sold.

'They are only valid for one month,' he informed Willem, 'but the diamonds we find will pay for the next, and with plenty to spare!'

Willem was looking longingly at the line of wagons which stood at the rear of the camp. 'I think,' he said, 'I will join my people there and learn from them what I should do.'

'Good idea! And I shall go down to the river bank to buy a claim.'

But he soon found that buying a claim was not so easy. All afternoon Matthew trudged from claim to claim and camp to camp. Weird names they had, like Gong Gong, Waldeck's Plant, Poormans Kopje and Moonlight Rush. Not only were no claims for sale but to his astonishment he was greeted with a torrent of abuse; later he realised that when he came so close the diggers thought he wanted to steal their diamonds.

He was retracing his steps to Klipdrift in the early evening when he heard someone call.

'Hey you, Englishman! You want to buy a claim?' Two young men were waving at him from the river bank and Matthew hurried towards them.

'We have a claim for sale.' They were both blond, with long stringy beards and moustaches and spoke with guttural German accents.

'How much do you want for it?'

'Fifty pounds.'

Matthew was crestfallen. 'I don't have that much. I started off with fifty guineas but had to buy food along the way and licences. I have only forty pounds left.'

'We'll settle for forty pounds,' said one man quickly. 'And you can have the spade and the bucket. We'll lend you the sieve. You'll soon pay for it out of your first diamond.'

His willingness to compromise had been too swift; Matthew's eyes narrowed and he stared at the man suspiciously.

'How kind,' he said at last. 'But how do I know there are diamonds here?'

'Look for yourself before you buy. That's fair, isn't it?'

'Yes.' Matthew did not miss the derisory smile the two men exchanged but continued to feign innocence. 'What do I do?'

'Take this spade and this bucket and dig . . . let me see, try here. This is a standard size claim, thirty-one feet square, and there could be diamonds anywhere but something tells me you should try here.'

Matthew took the spade and dug his first sod of Griqualand soil. He filled the bucket and carried it to the now deserted river. The two Germans showed him how to wash the earth by swirling it in a sieve and then they tossed the residue on to the sorting table and began combing through the debris with an iron scraper. Matthew watched, a sardonic gleam lurking in his bright blue eyes.

'Ah, you are lucky, my friend!' Triumphantly one of the men held up a stone in his hand.

'It's not a very big diamond,' observed Matthew.

'What do you expect? The Koh-i-Noor, the first time you look?'

'I'll tell you what I expect,' snapped Matthew. 'An honest deal, not two cheating bastards trying to palm me off with a salted claim.'

Furious at being taken for a fool and frustrated at not finding a claim, he stepped forward and punched the man on the jaw, sending him reeling into the river. The German surfaced, gasping, but still clutching the diamond while with a bellow of rage, the second man lunged at Matthew who sidestepped neatly. The man turned and pulled a knife from his belt and he and Matthew circled warily.

Matthew watched the man's eyes, trying to anticipate his next move and waiting for an opportunity to strike. He saw the eyes widen in sudden surprise and the concentration waver for one vital second, whereupon he moved instantly, grabbing his opponent's wrist and forcing him to drop the weapon. As he pinioned the man's arms in a vice-like grip, Matthew turned and saw what had distracted the man's attention: the first German, dripping and bedraggled, was standing a few feet away, firmly held by a tall stranger in the act of wrenching the spade from his hand.

'He was about to crack you over the head with it,' the stranger commented, 'and that could have been messy.' He released his captive and motioned Matthew to do the same. Reluctantly Matthew complied and the two Germans hurried away.

'I can't let them go,' Matthew protested indignantly. 'They tried to sell me a salted claim and then they tried to kill me! They can't do that to me!'

'They didn't do it to you,' the stranger reminded him calmly. 'So forget about it! They aren't such bad lots. Something must have upset them – I've never known them get into a fight before. The diggings are very peaceful and orderly. Surprisingly so, in fact. Although,' and he sighed, 'I guess it won't stay that way for long.'

He spoke with an unfamiliar accent and Matthew frowned as he tried to identify it.

'Are you American?'

'John Court from Lynn, Massachusetts,' and he held out his hand.

The American was even taller than Matthew, and broader in the shoulder. He had brown hair, the inevitable beard to shield his face from sun and wind, and gentle hazel eyes. He was wearing a black shirt and pair of brown trousers made of strong-smelling corduroy, and high boots.

'Come with me,' Court said. 'I have a suggestion to make.'

He led the way down the river bank to a shady spot beneath a clump of trees. The foliage was a picturesque oasis in the dusty desert around them, casting pleasant leafy shade over the sorting table and assorted implements. It was dusk and quiet had fallen over the formerly frenetic diggings. Matthew could hear the river sounds: the light chatter of the flowing stream, the splash of a leaping fish, the squeak of oars from a boat crossing to Pniel. He sat down and waited to hear what Court had to say.

The American was pouring coffee from a blue enamel billy-can. 'Black, I'm afraid,' he said, handing the mug to Matthew. 'Milk is scarce and expensive.'

'That's fine. Thank you.'

'Like I said, I've a proposition for you. This is my claim, I've had fair success with it. Nothing spectacular, but enough to keep going. I suggest we go into partnership.'

'Partnership?' Not unnaturally, Matthew was cautious.

'It has advantages for both of us. We will share the proceeds equally. For you, this means that you have a half-share in a diamond claim without any capital outlay, and you will have all the equipment you need – except a tent, there isn't room for two in mine and besides I may need it as you will see.'

'What is the advantage to you?'

'I don't really want a diamond claim,' said Court simply.

'What!' Matthew stared at him in amazement. 'So why are you here?'

'I am a seeker after knowledge, rather than wealth,' the American explained. 'I am a geologist, interested in the origin of diamonds.'

'Why then did you acquire a claim?'

'Unfortunately, even geologists have to eat. I was running out of money – fast! Food is very expensive here because it has to be transported many miles, so I bought this claim cheaply and have been trying to make enough to stake me in supplies.'

'I still don't see why you need a partner,' objected Matthew suspiciously. 'You can return from a prospecting trip when your food runs out and then dig for more diamonds.'

'That is exactly what I *cannot* do, and why I need you. There is little administration here, but a Diggers Committee has made some rules and regulations. For instance, one rule states that a man may own only one claim. Another, the one that affects me, states that if a claim is not worked for three successive days, it is automatically forfeit.'

Matthew nodded, as he began to see the logic of Court's plan and to analyse the advantages to himself. He had nothing to lose and everything to gain.

'I will teach you all I know about diamonds,' said Court, rising to his feet, 'because, believe me, diamonds in the river bed do not remotely resemble the gems that adorn the lovely necks of the London beauties. But first we must buy you a tent, a billy-can and some food.'

To his chagrin Matthew found that he could not even pitch a tent correctly. Court showed him how to position it with its flap away from the prevailing wind so that dust and refuse would not blow in, and to place a bottle on the tent-pole as a lightning conductor. Matthew invested a precious fifteen shillings in a coir mattress and twelve shillings and sixpence in a blanket – money well spent, Court assured him, because a digger needs a good night's sleep as well as food in his belly.

Then Court produced a cooking pot and a pile of firewood from his tent.

'You will learn to guard your firewood almost as carefully as your diamonds,' he said cheerfully, 'because it is even more scarce. And if you see any dung lying about, pick it up and bring it here. The locals call it "mis" and it makes damned good fuel.'

They piled some vegetables and a scrawny chicken into the pot and huddled over the welcome warmth of the flames while waiting for the food to cook. All over the tent town fires were flickering. The smell of woodsmoke mingled with the scent of the bushveld and with the aroma rising from cooking pots and freshly roasted coffee. Voices were loud but less strident than during the day, laughter sounded more frequently and the concertinas, mandolines and guitars wove a thread of melody which bound the scattered groups into one harmonious whole.

'How long have you been on the diamond fields?' asked Matthew.

'Four months.'

'Did you come all the way from America to Griqualand just because you are interested in the origin of diamonds?'

'I did, but such a bald statement of fact does not perhaps reflect the true position.' Court smiled, the wide, slow, generous smile that Matthew was to know so well. 'For a start, I had a somewhat unconventional unbringing and, second, my family has had connections with Africa for several generations.'

Court leaned forward and threw another handful of wood on the fire, sending up a shower of sparks into the black velvet night. He opened the tobacco pouch at his belt and began filling a carved wooden pipe.

'The Court family came from Rockingham Country, New Hampshire, but then settled in Lynn, a small port north of Boston in Massachusetts. They were an enterprising bunch and pretty soon they were the best known merchants, the biggest ship-owners and the most respected bankers in town. They were the leading lights in most of the town's activities from the Nahant Bank to spice and coffee mills and a whaling company. The business soon expanded to Long Wharf in Boston and about forty years ago, when American merchants were permitted to re-open commercial relations with the Cape Colony, my grandfather began trading with Cape Town.'

Court paused to puff industriously at his pipe and succeeded in summoning up a steady spiral of smoke.

'My uncle Henry became American consul in Cape Town. His chief concern was the whalers, but the job is unpaid and so he set up as an agent and merchant. However, my father was a very different character. He was a maverick, unable to settle down, forever searching for something new. After a brief improvement at the time he met and married my mother – she was descended from Puritans who came to America on the *Mayflower* – Father embarked on his last and greatest adventure. In December 1848 he travelled to the gold fields of California.'

'Was it like this? asked Matthew curiously, gesticulating at the serried rows of tents, the flames of the camp fires, the dark shapes of men and dogs moving in and out of the light.

'In some ways,' Court answered. 'I was only three years old when we left Boston, so my memories are hazy. The money was better than here and there were more people – one hundred thousand men in 1852, who found gold worth eighty one million dollars.'

Matthew's eyes gleamed. 'I wonder if we can make that much money out of diamonds.'

'If my theories are correct, there could be diamonds in this part of Africa which could make more money than all the gold found in California! But is that all this means to you? Money?'

'Yes, of course,' Matthew was surprised at such a question. 'What else should it mean?'

Court poked the fire and gave the stewpot a vigorous stir. 'There is a charm to this life,' he said slowly, 'particularly here beside the river. There is a communion with nature and a kinship with one's fellow man. It brings a contentment which is not related to the quantity of diamonds found. Men stay on and dig on whether they find diamonds or no. Money does not buy happiness.'

'It will buy my happiness,' said Matthew firmly and told Court about Isobel.

Court was silent for a long time after Matthew had finished. 'Perhaps,' he said at last. 'Perhaps it will work out as you wish. I can only tell you that for my father the gold fields of California proved to be the road to ruin. He found gold, a great deal of it, but as fast as he made money he spent it – he drank and gambled away a fortune. At last my mother could stand it no longer and she took me home, a long hazardous journey back east to live on the charity of our relations.' Court smiled sadly. 'She stuck it for seven years, until I was fifteen, and then she died. My uncles sent me to school, and to Harvard, and now here I am.'

'What happened to your father?'

'I don't rightly know. We heard that he was dead, but we never knew how he died.'

'But you must be like him. You're here, on the diamond fields, thousands of miles from home, so how can you say that his philosophy or way of life was wrong?'

'I am not like him – I don't think so anyway. I don't remember him too well. I believe, though, that there is a basic difference between us – I have a greater respect for convention than he had. I may be here now, doing what I want to do, but I accept that the time will come for me to go home and to take on the responsibilities that homecoming will bring.'

And Court sniffed at the stewpot and gave the chicken an experimental prod. 'Let's eat.'

Matthew did not want the enchanted evening ever to end. After Court retired, he lingered in the open and reviewed the day's events. The fire turned from yellow to red and still he sat by the glowing embers. Only when the blue of the dying flame had changed to soft grey ash did tiredness finally overwhelm him and he stumbled to his bed.

'Matt, you sluggard, wake up!'

Groaning, Matthew emerged into bright sunlight. Wisps of blue smoke from the camp fires wafted on the slight breeze while the smell of woodsmoke and 'mis' and coffee penetrated his sleepy senses.

'You sit up half the night and then waste the best part of the day!' chided Court. 'Get up early and work while it is cool. You can take an hour's rest after lunch.'

After a quick breakfast of mealie-meal porridge and coffee, they went immediately to the claim. Already the noise was mounting towards the crescendo which had greeted Matthew the previous day.

'The methods of recovering diamonds vary according to the position of the claim. The chief advantage of our riverside position is the proximity of water in which to wash the gravel. The main disadvantage is that claim walls can subside and the claim can be flooded. I've dug down to the pay dirt which is level with the bed of the river and dumped the debris in the stream.' Court pointed to the rough earthen wall, studded with stones, which stood like a dam in the river. 'It's nearly finished. Soon it will be safe enough for us to dig down to the bedrock below water level.'

'Good God!'

'As I mentioned, methods of recovery vary. Some diggers do not possess equipment for washing or transporting gravel so they merely sieve it on site. Others, who have African labour, use a more elaborate method involving troughs. I have water but no labour . . . '

'Why not?' interrupted Matthew.

'They steal,' explained Court simply. 'One cannot blame the poor fellows. The white men who buy the stolen stones are responsible. Now, I use a three-tiered sieve for recovering diamonds. The top sieve has a coarse mesh, the middle a medium and the bottom layer a fine mesh. We call the system "cradling". After rocking the cradle, the deposit in the first and second layers is examined for large diamonds and discarded. The deposit in the third sieve is washed to flush away fine sand and dirt and the residue is placed on the sorting table for careful scrutiny. Come, I'll show you.'

Fascinated, Matthew helped with the spadework, 'rocking the cradle' and washing the gravel. Then came the big moment when they sat down at the sorting table. Bursting with excitement Matthew gazed at the heap of 'stuff', as Court called it, which was lying there. Lovingly he ran his fingers through it, certain in his surge of confidence and optimism that it was full of precious stones.

Court picked up a flat piece of metal and swept a small section of the 'stuff' towards him.

'These are only crystals,' he said, 'for all their beautiful shapes and colours. And these are agates, cornelians and jasper.' He pushed the pretty pebbles across the table to Matthew. 'What do you think this is?'

'A ruby!' exclaimed Matthew, holding the glowing red stone up to the light.

'Wrong! It's a garnet and there are so many of them here that they are practically valueless. There are a few rubies, however, and I will teach you how to tell the difference.'

But there were no diamonds. They searched on, interrupted frequently by a constant stream of diggers who brought stones to Court for identification. Patiently he answered each inquiry in his kindly good-humoured way.

'Geologists,' he remarked with a smile, 'are in remarkably short supply around here. Ah, what's this?'

'Well, what *is* it?' asked Matthew rather impatiently, viewing the small pebble with some disdain.

'It's a diamond, of course.'

'A diamond? That?' Matthew stared at the stone in disbelief. 'But it's such an irregular shape, and it's so dull and smoky.'

'I told you that rough diamonds from the river do not look like the diamonds you have seen before,' chuckled Court. 'That's why it is important I teach you all I know, and why I try to help the other diggers. Like you, these fellows don't really know what they are looking for. Many of them are throwing away good diamonds with the debris they discard,' and he pointed to the rubbish tip along the perimeter of the claims.

'Why do the diamonds I have seen sparkle so much more?'

'Because they have been cut and polished. What a pity, this stone isn't much good, I'm afraid. See here, it has a blackish blemish in the centre. It is a shame, because otherwise it was very promising, having an almost colourless blue-white light.'

'Is colour more important than size?'

'Colour and quality are the most important factors. The clear blue-white are highly prized, while yellow-tinged stones are numerous and considered inferior – it is said they are used to decorate the horses of Indian princes and women in Turkish seraglios! Some brown diamonds, if flawless and a good shape, can fetch a fair price. Pink, green and blue are extremely rare and very valuable.'

An hour later they were separating a pile of moonstones, garnets, agate and quartz when Court let out another shout.

'This is more like it! Oh yes, my beauty, you'll do very nicely, very nicely indeed. Take a look at this, Matthew, as a small but perfect example of a river diamond, while I fetch my gun.'

'Why on earth,' said Matthew when Court returned with a firearm, 'do you need a gun?'

'To announce our find. Yahoo!' yelled Court and fired the pistol into the air. There was an immediate stampede of diggers to the claim, all eager to inspect the new find, see how it had been recovered, learn what kind of equipment had been used and in what type of gravel it had been found. Again Court answered their questions with infinite care and patience while Matthew stood by, trying to conceal his pride in ownership of the gem. But his pleasure faded when he saw the stocky figure of Steyn elbowing his way through the crowd, greedy eyes fixed on the diamond. Alida followed hesitantly, holding Daniel by one hand and casting scared looks at the big men towering above her. The diamond was being passed from hand to hand and when it came to Steyn's turn he peered at it for a long time, looking at it from every angle and – to Matthew's surprise – handed it to the children. Such an interest in the education of the children, thought Matthew, seemed out of character.

As soon as the crowd had dispersed, returning with renewed zeal to their claims, Court and Matthew walked to the diamond dealer's hut to sell the stone. They received fifty pounds for it.

'Make it last,' Court advised as he handed Matthew twenty-five pounds. 'It may be days, or even weeks, before we find another.'

Court was right. After several days of fruitless labour a dirty, tired Matthew, stiff and sore and with aching muscles, decided that this diamond digging was both back-breaking and heart-breaking. The mosquitoes buzzed ceaselessly, scorpions scuttled underfoot and he was pestered by ticks. Leaning on his spade, he paused to wipe the sweat from his eyes; in the distance diggers were tramping to and from the rubbish heap where they piled the sorted stuff.

Then Matthew's sharp eyes detected a movement at the far end of the discard pile. It was Alida. She was crouching beside the dump, sorting through it with her bare hands, the sleeves of her thin cotton dress rolled high above the elbows exposing the bony wrists and forearms. She did not look up and Matthew returned to his own work. All afternoon she sifted industriously through the discarded soil, often pausing to inspect a stone more closely and lay it carefully to one side.

So that was why Steyn had showed her the diamond, thought Matthew grimly.

At last she rose and hurried to the river. She did not see Matthew and he watched her as she washed her hands in the stream, noticing that the skin was broken and bleeding. She returned to the rubbish heap and piled a collection of stones into the folds of her skirt before setting off towards the row of wagons against the hillside.

The wagons reminded Matthew that he had not yet inquired how Willem and Martha were faring and he wondered if they had found any diamonds and if Willem could add anything to his ever-increasing knowledge. He called on them that evening.

'I hope, my friend,' said Willem, 'that you have found more diamonds than I.'

'Not many,' admitted Matthew. 'And you? Do you have a claim?'

'Of a sort. I could not buy a riverside claim but obtained ground here upon the kopje.' Willem shook his head. 'A few diamonds are found but it is not promising.' He stared down into the valley, at the grazing herds of cattle and flocks of sheep. 'I would have done better to stay a farmer,' he said wryly. 'There is more money to be made in supplying produce to the diggers than in digging oneself.'

'It is early days yet.'

'You are right. I will persevere. After all, Steyn finds diamonds, so why shouldn't I?'

Immediately Matthew was alert and interested. 'I have seen Alida at the debris dump. Is that the source of the stones?'

'He says he finds them in his claim. So that is where Alida goes in the afternoons! I have noticed her absence from the claim. The little boy is there all day, wielding a spade many sizes too big for him in trying to fill the buckets for his father. Slave labour!'

The success of Steyn's prospecting aroused Matthew's curiosity. He continued to look out for Alida, watching her brave little figure toiling in the sun, battling tenaciously with heat, flies and exhaustion. Several times he strolled past Steyn's claim and saw little Daniel staggering with buckets of sand, receiving a curse from his father in return. One night soon afterwards Matthew passed near Steyn's lonely wagon and saw him sitting by the fire, a brandy bottle upright on the sand beside him. Alida was tending the cooking pot and little Daniel was playing, making patterns in the sand with a handful of pretty pebbles. As Matthew watched, the boy strayed closer to his father. Alida realised this and stretched out an arm to pull the child away but too late; the boy's foot caught the brandy bottle and toppled it into the dirt. With an oath, Steyn picked it up and pointed furiously to the spilled liquid which was spreading in a damp stain on the dry earth. He emptied the remaining contents of the bottle down his throat and cuffed the boy so hard across the head that the child was sent sprawling in the dust. Daniel began to cry and as a torrent of abuse came from Steyn's lips, Alida moved between her father and brother. Her protective gesture was of no avail, however, because a slap across the cheek knocked her to her knees. Steyn stepped forward, his arm raised, when mercifully there was an interruption as a native stepped from the darkness into the circle of firelight. Steyn stared at the man and then beckoned him away to the shadows behind the wagon. Stealthily Matthew crept forward to watch. The African held out his hand, palm spread upwards and even in the poor light Matthew could see the faint gleam of the stones. This was followed by the clink of coins as the stones changed hands and the African disappeared again.

So that was how Steyn 'found' diamonds in his claim! Illicit diamond buying. And what could be easier than to purchase the stolen stones cheaply, plant them in one's own claim, dig them up next day and sell them on the legitimate market at a good profit!

When Steyn lurched away into the darkness. Matthew rose and stretched his aching limbs, pausing once more before the tableau by the fire where Alida was comforting the sobbing Daniel. He became aware of someone by his side and had the feeling she had been there for some time, watching the children.

'Nooit al die blink-klippies in die wêreld nie . . .' she murmured slowly and, as the tears brimmed over, Martha left her sentence unfinished and walked quickly away.

Matthew's Dutch was still sketchy but he understood her meaning. All the diamonds, or glittering pebbles in the world, were as nothing compared with those children.

CHAPTER FIVE

In June, Court decreed that Matthew now knew enough to be entrusted with the claim while he embarked on his geological expedition. The claim had yielded few diamonds, only enough to pay expenses.

'Willem Jacobs is right,' Matthew complained. 'There is more money to be made in supplying the diggers' wants than in digging for diamonds.'

'There are some storekeepers who wouldn't agree with you,' observed Court. 'The Klipdrift and Pniel camps are fairly stable but further up river the merest rumour can empty a camp overnight as men go in search of richer ground. The shopkeepers then face a dilemma – to serve the remaining handful of men or to pack up and follow the rush.'

'It's is by no means certain that diamonds are alluvial,' Court asserted. 'Remember, Matthew, that the "Star of South Africa" was not found by a river. Even if diamonds are alluvial in origin, they could be lying in the dried-up beds of rivers that vanished millions of years ago.'

'Well, I wish you luck, but it's bloody inhospitable country out there. Griqualand is nothing but a miserable treeless desert, yet everyone is squabbling over it.'

'The squabbling only started when diamonds were found. The Griquas maintain that the land belongs to them; the two Boer republics of the Transvaal and Orange Free State are laying claim to it, and Britain is trying to arbitrate and will probably end up annexing it for herself.'

'The diggers are talking about forming our own republic and electing a president.'

Court shot Matthew a sharp glance. 'Stay out of politics, Matt,' he warned. 'Let others run the place while you concentrate on making money. The diamond fields have not yet reached a state of development where power is synonymous with wealth. And business and politics don't mix.'

Matthew nodded but heaved a silent sigh of regret. It would have been wonderful to write home that he was president of the republic – how the Duke of Desborough would have goggled when he read the news in *The Times*!

Without the protective presence of the greatly respected Court, Matthew was very much alone. His isolation increased because, in his preoccupation with his own affairs, he afforded scant time and courtesy to the diggers who approached him for advice. The diggers, who correctly assumed that Matthew had inherited Court's knowledge of stones, trudged sadly but indignantly back to their claims to wrestle with problems Matthew could have solved easily and quickly.

The only person to whom Matthew gave any thought was Steyn, partly out of hatred for the man and partly out of jealousy of his growing wealth. He had told no one of his discovery of Steyn's illicit diamond deals; first, he could prove nothing and second, a nagging voice at the back of his mind told him that Steyn's way was the path to riches.

Late one afternoon in July Matthew happened to follow Alida from the river. She was staggering under the weight of a dripping bucket as she made her way up the kopje and passed her father's claim. The area was deserted, the diggers having finished work for the day and there was no sign of Steyn. Only little Daniel was still toiling, his small begrimed figure trotting staunchly back and forth carrying tiny loads of excavated stuff from the edge of the claim to where the sieve and sorting table stood. Alida called out to him and continued on her way to the wagon.

Darkness falls fast in Griqualand and the gloom was gathering now, so Matthew had to strain his eyes to see Alida's disappearing figure. Then he heard Daniel give a small cry. The boy tripped over a pick handle and fell, dangerously close to the edge of the claim. There was a faint groaning sound as the earth subsided and in an avalanche of sand and stones, Daniel disappeared into the depths of the hole.

Matthew sprinted to the spot and gazed into the pit. Twenty

feet down Daniel was flailing desperately as the wall continued to collapse and the deluge of rocks and earth crashed upon him in a smothering blanket. The rough steps that Steyn had hewn in one corner of the pit were disintegrating. Matthew launched himself into the abyss, slipping and sliding down the steep sides. Frantically he began scraping and digging with his hands at the spot where Daniel had disappeared and uncovered the gasping, semi-conscious child. Rocks and earth were still pouring from above, cutting and bruising their flesh, but then, to Matthew's intense relief, the bombardment ceased and he was able to draw breath.

Matthew stood in the blackness of the pit and gazed upward at the dark night sky. The walls of the claim towered sheer above him, the soft earth and lack of footholds offering no opportunity for escape. An eerie quiet had fallen over the fields and Matthew knew there was little likelihood of people passing by – the danger of tumbling into deserted claims was too great. He called loudly, but was not surprised to receive no response.

Cautiously Matthew edged his way round the perimeter of the pit, peering into the darkness and feeling with his hands in an effort to find an escape route. He discovered that the ground at one corner, where the rough steps had been situated, had subsided into a reasonable slope. Or so it appeared. Matthew groaned aloud and swore that never again would he venture out at dusk without a light. He decided, however, that this uncertain slope offered the only possible route to safety and he had no choice but to give it a try.

Matthew lifted Daniel over his shoulder and, very slowly, started the ascent. Several times he failed to find sufficient leverage or his footholds slipped and he began a perilous slide into the chasm, one hand groping desperately for support while the other steadied the limp body of the child. Then he resumed the climb and doggedly inched his way upwards. At last he reached the top, stumbling away from any danger of further subsidence before stretching full length on the ground to draw deep shuddering breaths of relief. His whole body was shaking and aching from the effort and from the child's weight. His clothes were dirty and torn and he was bleeding from cuts on his face and arms.

When, after some minutes, the trembling of his limbs had

ceased, Matthew stood and carried the unconscious Daniel towards Steyn's wagon.

Alida had the fire going and the flames illuminated a bright circle in the camp. Immediately Matthew could see why Steyn was not concerned about his son. The man was roaring drunk and, as Matthew approached, struck Alida on the cheek and sent her reeling towards the fire. In trying to save herself from the flames, the girl fell against the pail of water and the bucket tipped over her dress. With a growl of anger Steyn pulled her to her feet and there was a loud tearing sound as the bodice of her dress ripped open. Matthew saw the expression on Steyn's face change. One white, gently-rounded breast was exposed in the jagged tear of the material while the other was clearly outlined against the wet clinging cotton. As Steyn reached out a lascivious hand towards the gleaming flesh and Alida cringed away, Matthew dumped Daniel on the ground and ran. He ran straight to Steyn and hit him hard on the head. Alida screamed and it was only afterwards that Matthew realised what a terrifying sight he must have been, caked in mud and blood from his ordeal in the claim.

Steyn was back on his feet and blundering towards him in wild drunken blindness. Matthew stepped aside and dealt another blow to Steyn's posterior as the man staggered past.

'Find out if Daniel is all right!' Matthew shouted to Alida. 'Daniel, *Daniel*!' he repeated, pointing to where the boy lay and not knowing how much English the girl understood. But Alida did not move. Instead she stood as if frozen to the spot, her great grey-green eyes fixed wide in horror, staring at something behind Matthew's back. He swung round in time to see Steyn weaving an erratic but determined path to where a rifle stood against the wagon.

Matthew covered the ground between them in a couple of giant leaps and brought down Steyn with a flying tackle just as his hand closed on the rifle butt. They wrestled in the dust, desperately trying to gain possession of the firearm. Now Steyn had it again and Matthew tried to use his superior size to wrest it from him but the Boer was remarkably strong and hung on grimly, gradually forcing the barrel of the rifle against Matthew's head. If he fires that thing now, thought Matthew, he'll blow my bloody brains out.

Then a shot rang out and involuntarily Matthew flinched. He must have closed his eyes momentarily, too, because when he opened them again he saw, in slow motion, Steyn dropping the rifle and crumpling to the ground. He had been shot through the head. As Matthew straightened up, he saw the folds of a blue skirt disappear into the darkness behind the wagon.

Alida screamed again and instantly there came the sound of running feet and shouting and a horde of diggers burst into the camp. They were chiefly Boers from nearby wagons and they closed fiercely round Matthew, rifles at the ready. The Boers disliked Steyn but he was one of them, their brother and compatriot, while Matthew was the *uitlander*, the stranger who could not be trusted. They saw not only Steyn's lifeless body but Alida's torn dress and frightened face and the battered Daniel who was sitting up and watching the proceedings with a bewildered expression. And they came to the wrong conclusions.

The Boers were normally stolid folk, not quick to anger, and would undoubtedly have given Matthew a chance to defend himself had not a crowd of more unruly elements appeared. A group of extremely inebriated Australians arrived and, by banging tins together, advertised to the entire diggings that an unusual event was taking place. An excited crowd gathered and a babble of different languages debated Matthew's fate. Certainly it was the rowdy newcomers who began the chant of 'Lynch! Lynch!'

Matthew was feeling sick and giddy. He tried to clear his head and control his spinning senses, but the whole scene had taken on the aspect of a ghastly, garish nightmare. The people were pressing tightly around him, pushing, poking and prodding with rifles, elbows and hands. He felt as if he was suffocating, choking in the heat of emotions and the rank stench of unwashed bodies, gasping as surely as if the rope were already tightening around his neck. He struggled to find his voice.

'I didn't kill him,' he shouted desperately. 'I was trying to help.'

But no one listened and the chanting grew louder and more insistent. 'Lynch him! Lynch him!' until even the equable law-abiding Boers seemed unable or unwilling to resist and were swept along with the tide.

'You must listen to me.' Matthew's voice was cracking in fear and desperation. 'Alida, Daniel, tell them what really happened.'

But the two children were too numb and shocked to do anything. They clung to each other in the midst of the mass of people and stared at him in terrified silence.

'We'll need a tree to hang him on.'

'There are trees by the river. Take him there!'

Wildly Matthew searched the crowd for a friend, an ally, someone who would speak up for him. He saw several familiar faces, men who had come to him with stones for identification and whom he had turned away.

'Help me!' he pleaded. 'I didn't kill Steyn. He was trying to kill me.'

But they said nothing and Matthew was pushed roughly out of the circle of firelight into the darkness and the faces around him became a blur. 'Is this the end?' he asked himself as he lurched down the kopje to the river with the barrel of a rifle in his back. 'A makeshift gallows in the middle of nowhere?' Damn it, he did not want to die! And regardless of the rifles, Matthew lashed out at his captors and sent two of them reeling to the ground. Immediately his hands were seized and bound behind him.

'I demand a fair trial!' he shouted.

But they only laughed and jeered. Their breath smelled of cheap brandy and the noise rose to a crescendo which confused and disoriented him, sending harsh discordant vibrations hammering through his head. The mob halted in front of the tallest tree where several men were already knotting a loop into a long length of rope which they tossed over a branch. In a daze Matthew saw an agitated Willem pleading with the ringleaders, but no one was taking any notice of him.

'You must listen to me,' Matthew shouted, as they slipped the noose over his head. 'I didn't kill Steyn. You must listen to me!'

'Quite so!' A cool voice came out of the darkness. 'Cut him loose.'

The crowd swung round to see who spoke. It was Court, sitting astride his big raw-boned horse, complete calm and utter authority exuding from his large square frame.

'Cut him loose,' he repeated. *'Now!'*

Hurriedly one of the lynch party untied Matthew's hands and removed the noose. Matthew swallowed hard and rubbed his neck to take away the choking sensation.

'Sit down, all of you!' commanded Court.

Like a bunch of burst balloons, the diggers subsided to the ground. Court towered above them on his horse.

'Is this the sort of justice dispensed by the Diggers' Republic?' he thundered. 'Where are the officials of the Committee or our new police force? How dare you think you can take the law into your hands and condemn a man without a fair hearing!' His eyes raked the crowd. 'You, Jones, are an American,' he roared at one man, 'and as an American you should be ashamed of being party to such a despicable scene. Weren't the lynchings on the Californian gold fields enough for you? Roberts, as an Australian you may have indulged in such shenanigans at Ballarat . . . ' and Court went on to pick out half a dozen men and berate them while the rest of the mob gradually fell silent. As soon as Court had achieved complete quiet he turned to Matthew.

'Matt, tell us what happened.'

Matthew took a deep breath and stared at the faces in the crowd, playing for time while he planned what he would say. Then he spoke of the scenes in the claim and at Steyn's camp, but he confined his description to the blow Steyn had given Alida and did not mention the man's abuse of his daughter's body.

'We fought for possession of the rifle,' he continued. 'Suddenly the gun went off and Steyn fell dead. It was an accident; I swear that *he* was trying to kill *me*.'

Alida and Daniel were propelled gently into the centre of the throng. Court dismounted and walked towards them. He saw Alida's torn dress and took off his coat to wrap round her. Then he asked Willem to tell the children, in the *taal*, what Matthew had said.

As Willem spoke, the two children seemed to come slowly to life. They glanced repeatedly to Matthew and Alida nodded several times. She gasped, however, when Willem spoke of Daniel's fall into the claim.

'We must check the facts,' Court announced.

Matthew tensed. Had either of the children seen the flash of blue behind the wagon? Would Court examine Steyn's rifle to see if it had been fired?

'Check if there has been a subsidence in Steyn's claim,' Court commanded, and Matthew breathed again.

After the men returned, it was agreed that a report would be handed to the police the next day. The abject diggers drifted away to their camp fires.

'We must bury Steyn,' said Court, 'and, my God, what are we going to do with these children?'

Suddenly Alida began to shake from head to foot and flung herself at Matthew. He put his arms around her while appealing mutely for help. Alida was sobbing and trying to speak.

'She says,' interpreted one of the Boers, 'that she wants to stay with him.'

'I can't look after them,' said Matthew quietly, 'but I think I know who could. Willem? Would you?'

'Ja, of course, *Kom, kinders*. We will go to Martha.'

'We will all go,' said Court.

Martha was sitting by the fire, her blue dress trailing in the dust as she stared vacantly into the embers. She seemed oblivious of their approach. Matthew saw that Willem's rifle was standing by the wagon where it always stood.

'Martha,' he said, 'we have brought the children.'

She raised her head slightly but did not look at them, and Matthew walked up to her, holding Alida by the hand. 'It's all right, Martha,' he whispered. Without saying any more he placed Alida's hand in hers and as Willem came up with the sleeping Daniel in his arms, Martha began to cry.

But it was on Matthew's face that the eyes of Alida lingered.

Court was refreshed and invigorated after his expedition. He brought back a small bag of diamonds which he had found away from the river, on the bleak kopjes and windswept hills, in gritty soil, fissures and sandy gullies. He had followed chalk seams, dug round barriers of rock and climbed into crevices.

He soon settled down by the river again, but in August came the news of two new discoveries – at Koffiefontien and Jagersfontein in the Orange Free State – and his restlessness increased.

Matthew was tired but optimistic. He still hoped each day would be the day he would find the gigantic diamond which would make his fortune. The diggings were yielding about three million pounds annually – surely the time must come when he would receive his share?

He had now succeeded in making his tent into a cosy retreat. The mattress and bedding took up most of the floor space but he had utilised packing cases as shelf-units and a table top. In addition to the billy-can, he had acquired a paraffin lamp and two grey enamel plates and the rough shelves usually held candles and matches, and tins of mealie-meal, sugar and coffee. If he was in funds, a demi-john of wine would be wedged securely into a corner. His spare clothes were suspended from the tent-pole in what was usually a vain attempt to keep them dry.

Also strapped to the tent-pole were Matthew's fishing rods. Several billiard saloons had opened at Klipdrift, but apart from them and the bars there was little in the way of entertainment. Matthew and Court found fishing a pleasant pastime and it provided a good meal into the bargain. Alida and Daniel watched so wistfully that Matthew allowed them to join in and they passed beguiling hours by the river in that African spring of 1870.

These were idyllic days in seemingly Elysian fields. In fact, it was all too good to last.

The end of the river dream for Matthew and Court, and for a number of others, came one afternoon at the beginning of September.

They were standing in the claim, the high walls of the breakwater looming over them as they worked below the river level. They were struggling to move a large boulder which obstructed their progress, when suddenly Matthew paused.

'What's that noise?' he asked.

It was a roaring sound, growing louder by the second, augmented by shouts and then, horribly, an anguished scream.

'Out!' yelled Matthew. 'Get out of here, as quickly as you can!'

He dived for the rope which dangled down the wall of the claim nearest to the river bank and shinned up it expertly. Court made slower progress and had not reached the top when cascades of flood water broke down the dam walls and poured over him. The current was so powerful that it nearly swept Court away and he clung on grimly until he felt Matthew's strong arms pulling him to safety. They lay gasping on the bank while the torrent surged past, carrying forlorn flotsam of sieves, cradles, timber, hats and shirts, and a grisly cargo of dead animals and several dead diggers.

'There must have been a storm up-country,' said Court. He stared at the lowering clouds that were gathering on the horizon. 'And by the look of things, it's coming this way.'

All night the wind howled, the rain deluged and the camps were battered by hailstones so large that they ripped open tents and even killed a man. It was impossible to sleep. Matthew huddled in his leaking tent, wrapped in a sodden blanket, while the water dripped down his neck and the rough floor turned into a quagmire. But as the miserable night wore on, it was not his personal discomfort which preyed on his mind and caused the ache of apprehension in his heart. He was listening to the roar of the river and visualising the damage to the precious claim.

When morning came Matthew and all his possessions were soaked and he wallowed ankle-deep in mud. Shivering and with chattering teeth he hurried to the river and surveyed the devastation.

For a moment Matthew wavered. Wet, cold and depressed after the terrible night, he almost gave up. He nearly said farewell to fame and fortune, accepting that since the claim was flooded, the dream of diamonds must be over. Then, his determination reasserting itself, Matthew turned to Court.

'We must start all over again,' he said.

CHAPTER SIX

A benign sun beamed down from a mellow September sky and bathed the trim lawns and late summer roses of Harcourt Hall in gentle golden light. On the Continent, the Empire of Napoleon III had collapsed after the defeat of French troops at Sedan and there was upheaval in Italy over the annexation of Rome and the Papal States, but nothing disturbed the peace and tranquillity of the ancestral home of the Earls of Highclere. In particular, nothing marred the untroubled countenance of Frederick Harcourt-Bright who was on the point of delivering the *coup de grâce* in a little campaign he had been conducting.

For Freddy this was a duty visit to Uncle Gervase and cousin Aubrey and he had not expected to enjoy himself. But he was ever on the lookout for any situation which might further his interests and at last his patience had been rewarded.

Freddy had entertained high hopes of cousin Aubrey for a long time – there was something in the carriage and demeanour of the young Viscount Swanley which aroused his suspicions. Swanley had the blond good looks of the Harcourt-Brights and indeed bore a strong resemblance to Matthew. But while Matthew's fierce pride, forceful manner and strong physique were immediately discernible, Swanley bore himself with a lazy languid grace, spoke softly and preferred horticulture to hunting. However, it was his other preferences which interested Freddy as he withdrew from the buzzing warmth of the terrace in the early afternoon, mounted the staircase and tapped lightly on his cousin's bedroom door. He found Swanley sitting at a writing desk, wrapped in a blue silk robe.

'You're not dressed,' said Freddy, affecting surprise. 'Have you forgotten that we are invited to Desborough for tea?'

'I have not forgotten, but I do not intend to go. The

Desboroughs, and your friend Lambourne in particular, are not my favourite company. All those daughters!' Swanley shuddered. 'And the dear Duchess angling for me as a son-in-law!'

'Quite.' Freddy sat down and smiled: a cold, sinister smile, oddly out of place on his plump features. His eyes glittered dangerously. 'And you and I both know that the Duchess's hopes are entirely misplaced,' he said softly.

Swanley swung round and faced him. 'What do you mean?'

'I refer to the procession of young men which wends its way in and out of your rooms, and in and out of your bed.'

Swanley turned pale. 'You're talking nonsense,' he said thickly.

'Oh, no. I never talk nonsense, dear cousin Aubrey. Never. And, equally, I never make statements unless I am absolutely sure of my facts. Let me see, it's that young footman at the moment, isn't it? Harold? I have been observing him most carefully for the past few days.'

'What do you intend to do about it?' Swanley had abandoned pretence of innocence.

'Do? Nothing.' Once again Freddy showed exaggerated surprise. 'Your private life is not my concern, and I certainly did not come here this afternoon to talk about it. I came to put a proposition to you.'

Swanley stared at his cousin with the utmost dislike and dawning comprehension. 'How much is it likely to cost me?'

'Only a few thousand.'

'A few *thousand*! Good God, Freddy . . . '

'He has been good to you, hasn't he, Aubrey! Surely you can spare a little for those less fortunate than yourself? Only a loan, of course.'

'Of course,' echoed Swanley drily.

'I want to buy a yacht.'

'A *boat*! You cannot mean it! One of the few characteristics you have inherited from the Harcourt-Brights is an intense hatred of water. It is something we all have – Papa, myself, your father – only Matthew seems to be immune.'

A muscle twitched in Freddy's cheek. 'It is a ridiculous fear which I am determined to overcome. Besides, I have no intention of sailing the yacht myself. It is a business venture.'

'A yacht requires more than a few thousand.'

'Mine will be a half-share. Lambourne is putting up the other half.'

'Blackmail!' whispered the Viscount, desperately searching his mind for a way out.

'Of course. But someone is bound to blackmail you sooner or later and it might as well be me; keeps it in the family, don't you know?' And again Freddy smiled that grotesque smile.

An hour later he was taking tea with the Desboroughs. He was at his most charming, paying compliments to his hostess and acting the gallant with the girls. He was particularly attentive to Isobel. She was seventeen now and had matured much this summer. Already it was forecast that she would be the great success of next Season when she came out. She was prettier than ever, but Freddy was not deceived by her air of delicate fragility. He sensed the steel beneath the gentle blush of her English rose complexion, the selfishness which caused the pout in those tempting pink lips, the calculating appraisal behind the vacuous gaze and the emptiness in that pretty head.

Freddy knew that Isobel's sisters were more worthy than she: Jane had a better brain than either of her brothers; Elizabeth was sweet and gentle; and Anne, at eleven, bade fair to combine these merits with Isobel's beauty. But for Freddy, only Isobel would do.

Also present was the Desboroughs' eldest son Hugh, Marquess of Lambourne and after tea Freddy suggested that the two of them should take a brief constitutional. The Duchess returned to the house and the sisters were left alone on the lawn, the three younger girls eyeing Isobel's discontented expression and exchanging knowing glances.

'She's upset because he didn't come to tea,' said Anne to Elizabeth in a piercing whisper.

'Who didn't come to tea?' Elizabeth, too, pitched her voice just loud enough for Isobel to hear.

'Swanley. Isobel likes him, but he doesn't pay her any attention.' Anne turned and smiled seraphically at Isobel's irritated face. 'Never mind, Isobel,' she said consolingly, 'you'll get over it.

After all, you soon forgot Matthew. And then there was Arthur, and John, and . . . '

'The only thing,' said Isobel icily, 'which keeps me sane is the knowledge that by this time next year I shall be married, or engaged to be married, and with any luck I'll never have to see you again!'

'I wonder who the lucky man will be?' Elizabeth clasped her hands together and feigned intense interest. 'Perhaps Matthew will return with a fortune in diamonds.'

'The chances of that happening are rather remote,' said Jane seriously. 'But *Frederick* Harcourt-Bright makes no secret of his infatuation.'

Elizabeth and Anne giggled and made a great show of screwing up their faces and shuddering.

'Imagine,' exclaimed Elizabeth, 'being married to Freddy!'

'It is something,' agreed Isobel, 'which I prefer not to contemplate.'

'I should think not,' said Anne. 'He's really horrible, isn't he! Rolls of fat everywhere. And did you see how much he ate at tea? Even Matthew or Swanley would be better than him.'

'*Anyone* would be better than Freddy,' retorted Elizabeth. 'And Matthew was rather nice in a way. Aloof. Remote and romantic.'

'Yes,' said Isobel, 'he was.' There was such a dreamy expression on her face and such unusual emotion in her voice that her sisters stared at her in surprise. Matthew had been her first love and sometimes she could recall his attraction for her. But Isobel was by nature fickle and Matthew's image had been unable to survive her sisters' teasing, her father's strictures or her brothers' advice. 'But he is not eligible.'

'Fortunately, neither is Freddy,' said Anne.

'But suppose he was eligible,' pondered Jane. 'Suppose he was the heir to the Highclere earldom instead of Swanley. What would one do then?'

'Under those circumstances,' replied Isobel in bored, world-weary tones, 'one would have to reconsider the matter.'

While the sisters were discussing him so disrespectfully, Freddy was standing on the bank of the Desborough lake with his friend

Lambourne, gazing with distaste at the placid water.

'I can raise the cash for my share of the yacht.'

'Good show! I do hope though, Freddy, that you know what you are doing. You are quite sure we'll win back all the money?'

'Of course,' said Freddy confidently. 'Leave it to me. I'll ensure that no one knows her capabilities and we'll win every wager at Cowes. The chaps will queue up to bet that we can't even float and then she'll win every race by a streak.'

'I hope you don't expect me to help? I know absolutely nothing about boats.'

'Neither do I, but I intend to learn. Basically it's a matter of finding the right crew. All the same . . . ' A faint breeze stirred the still surface and Freddy shuddered. Then, in a sudden gesture of defiance, he bent down and hurled a stone into the water as hard as he could. It hit the surface with a loud splash and sent a ring of ripples scurrying to the bank. 'Do you think you could teach me to swim?'

Lambourne stared at him in astonishment. 'Of course, with pleasure. But, Freddy, you've always hated the water – even at Oxford there was no way you could be persuaded into a punt.'

'A foolish fear, a childish thing.' Freddy spoke with difficulty and clenched sweaty palms. 'Perhaps we could begin with a small boating trip?' he suggested, pointing to a light skiff tied up at the water's edge.

Lambourne clambered into the boat, helped Freddy in and unshipped the oars. He looked at Freddy's rigid figure and taut white face.

'You must be jolly keen to win those wagers,' Lambourne remarked. 'Isn't there an easier way to make a fortune?'

'I cannot think of one and, believe me, I have tried.'

'We still have these,' and Court spread out a handful of diamonds on a blanket beside the wreckage of his tent. 'So we are not entirely without capital. The question is: how do we invest it?'

'The only alternatives are trying to rescue this claim or else buying another claim in this area,' Matthew asserted.

'We could buy Steyn's wagon and go prospecting,' suggested Court wistfully.

'Is the wagon still for sale?'

'As far as I know. But we shall have to hurry. We're not the only ones left homeless after the storm.'

'Then let us secure the wagon and sleep in the dry tonight.' Matthew hesitated; he sensed the hopelessness of trying to salvage their river claim, but felt a strong reluctance to leave the area where diamonds were known to exist. 'We'll make up our minds about the future tomorrow.'

That decision never had to be made, because in the morning came news of a fresh diamond discovery.

'Diamonds have been found on a farm at Dorstfontein,' Matthew informed Court as they hurriedly inspanned the oxen. 'Word is spreading rapidly, so we must move quickly if we want to obtain a good claim.'

'I know that farm,' said Court eagerly. 'It's about twenty-five miles to the south.'

'Tell Willem to follow us as soon as he can.'

Court handled the oxen, so the journey provided Matthew with unaccustomed leisure time to look about him. The land no longer held any terrors for him; he respected its extremes of climate and varied animal and plant life, but had acquired the knowledge needed to survive in the veld.

Now he could appreciate the beauty of the thousands of stately aloes with their huge flower stems, ten to fifteen feet high and as thick as broomsticks, tapering gradually to the top where they burst into red or yellow blooms. He recognised the mimosas – the camel-thorn with its spreading umbrella-shaped crown, feathery leaves and deep yellow flowers, and its smaller sister the sweet-thorn. He knew the prickly pears, the bracken of the Karoo, and how to skin the edible fruit without piercing his finger on the thorns.

Matthew had learned to identify the venomous snakes, the puff-adder, the cobra and the boomslang, and the secretary birds which abounded in the Karoo and preyed on reptiles. There was a blue-headed lizard which was said to gaze steadfastly to the north when rain was near; Cape hares, porcupines and squirrels; a wide range of antelope, from the tiny grey duiker to the proud kudu; black-backed jackals, baboons, polecats and aardvarks or antbears.

To Matthew, however, the strangest feature of the Karoo was the silence. He missed the song of the birds. Here there was only the harsh, grating 'kruk-kruk-kruk' of the korhaan or scolding cock as it used its ventriloquist powers to warn all creatures that danger approached.

But mostly the Karoo belonged to the ants and the meerkats. Matthew loved to watch the mongoose-like meerkat as it sat beside an anthill, its bushy reddish-brown tail shading its head parasol-style. The little animal would sit bolt upright, its small paws hanging loosely against its stomach, two wide eyes ringed with black fur watching from an inquisitive snouted face. As the wagon drew level, the meerkat flashed back into its burrow, only to re-emerge after they had passed with all its friends and relations, gossiping, chattering and staring like a Boer family on a stoep.

The 'rush' to Dorstfontein was more surreptitious, more gradual and haphazard than the big rushes which were yet to come. Men slipped away from the river in wagons, on horseback or on foot and descended on the formerly remote and solitary farm. As the weeks passed, those latecomers who failed to find room on Dorstfontein moved to the adjoining farm of Bultfontein.

Matthew and Court were in the van of the exodus from the Vaal. They staked a good claim in a prime position on Dorstfontein and pegged an adjoining claim for Willem. Then they made camp together, with their wagons side by side, and fell into an easy routine of eating together around the same fire. At night when Matthew and Court fell exhausted into bed, it was in a wagon tidied and freshened by Alida and with a pile of clean clothes to wear the next day.

For Alida the new arrangement was heaven. She had adored Matthew ever since he had jumped into the drift to save her from the sinking wagon and his subsequent rescue of Daniel from the claim had increased her devotion. With his tall figure and golden hair he looked like . . . like . . . Alida did not have much means of comparison. She had no knowledge of knights or gods or heroes – the only book which had been read to her was the Bible. Matthew looked to her like an angel, she decided – no, an archangel. He and Daniel were the only people whom she truly loved. She was very fond of Martha and Willem and grateful for the way they looked after her and Daniel, and she felt safe and happy with Court, but Matthew she worshipped.

She moved like a shadow around him, anticipating his every need, running errands, taking immense pains that each detail should be perfect, striving anxiously to please. To Alida it was a privilege to wait upon him and she took great joy in the rare smile or quiet 'dankie' with which Matthew rewarded her efforts. Not only was Alida accustomed to undemonstrative people, but also she was only fourteen years old and it never occurred to her that the chasm between a simple Boer girl and an archangel could ever be bridged.

The worst aspect of the new diggings – which came to be called Dutoitspan – was the shortage of water for washing gravel and for washing clothes and bodies. The wind stirred a red dust from the veld while a constant cloud of grey hung over the claims, caused by the constant inroads of picks and shovels in the parched earth and the shaking of countless sieves. The dust covered men's faces and arms, coated their clothes and so penetrated hair and skin that it caused sickness, sores and eye infections. Digging was somewhat less strenuous than at the Vaal, however, for the ground was softer and boulders were fewer. Even the diamonds themselves seemed different at the dry diggings, having an oily film on the surface and a cold, greasy touch.

There was no doubt that diamonds were more plentiful here than at the river. Matthew admitted that he had been mistaken in his ardent adherence to the alluvial theory and listened with more respect to Court's conviction that diamonds were volcanic in origin, formed deep in the bowels of the earth in cataclysmic upheavals and burning heat.

Matthew and Court worked their claim with moderate success, but were unable to make a profit. Food prices continued to rise and in addition to feeding themselves they had to buy fodder for Court's horse and the team of oxen because the veld had been grazed bare of grass. Also they found that they could not manage the work unaided and the hire of a Griqua labourer at two shillings a day plus food was a further drain on their resources.

They liked to talk to the labourer and his friends and learn about their homes and customs, and it was around the camp-fire one night at the beginning of May 1871 that the natives began talking of the white man who worked alone in the veld and found many diamonds.

'Where?' asked Matthew. The man pointed north-west and indicated that the place lay between the Dorstfontein-Bultfontein diggings and the Vaal River.

'I've heard that story before,' Court said.

Thoughtfully Matthew looked at his friend and then gazed into the distant north-west. In the past year he had come to know Court well and had learned how to make the most of his strengths and to compensate for his weaknesses. Court was kind and clever but unambitious – he dreamed not of power and riches but of a great diamond mine which would reveal Nature's secrets and provide the answers to the questions which haunted him. More and more Matthew took the initiative in business matters while making use of Court's geological expertise.

Now he asked his friend, 'You want to take a look?'

Court's face shone with happiness. 'You bet! I'll leave first thing in the morning.'

He was gone for only four days, galloping back into the camp in the middle of the night and shaking Matthew awake.

'I found it! Matt, I found it!'

'Huh?' Matthew struggled into wakefulness.

'I found diamonds, Matt. Look!' And into Matthew's hand Court pushed a massive stone which even in its rough unpolished state gleamed in the muted light of the lamp.

Matthew stared into its clear, blue-white depths and drew in a shuddering breath of excitement and satisfaction. 'This is finer than anything we have found here. How far away is the place?'

'Less than five miles to the north-west, on a farm called Vooruitzicht. But the old man who has been prospecting there told me that men from the river camp at Hebron had discovered it and pegged claims. They will be returning from the river very soon.'

'Then we must return before they do.' Swiftly Matthew began

to dress. He paused for a moment. 'We're taking a chance, you know,' he said quietly. 'It's a hell of a gamble to abandon a good claim here and stake everything on untried ground. But I'm sure it's the right thing to do.'

'So am I,' Court agreed simply.

'Good! Now, hitch up those oxen as quietly as you possibly can while I persuade Willem to join us.'

The two wagons rolled out of Dutoitspan as dawn broke. After several hours' travelling they crested a small rise to look down on the rolling veld down.

'There it is! You can just see the small homestead and the prospector's tent.'

'Who owns the farm?' Matthew asked.

'Two brothers called De Beer.'

They ambled on, enjoying the pleasant day and savouring the anticipation of new diggings, new experiences and in Matthew's case the hope of new riches.

'What is all that dust in the distance?' asked Matthew suddenly.

'I'm not quite sure; it looks like the dust stirred up by an army on the march. My God, the secret of Vooruitzicht must have leaked out already! The rush is on!' With this Court leaned forward and lashed the oxen with his whip, urging on the faithful beasts to a faster pace while Matthew craned round the side of the wagon to look back the way they had come.

'There's no one behind us.'

'The rush will come from the river,' said Court, 'from the men who returned there when they could not find room at Dutoitspan or Bultfontein. That is why the dust is spread so far, they are coming from all directions.'

Now it was a race between their little party and the advancing army from the Vaal. Breathlessly they abandoned their wagon by the old prospector's tent and raced to the spot which Court had marked. Frantically Matthew and Willem hammered in pegs in the places Court had measured out.

'Sit down in the claims,' ordered Matthew, 'and stay there, no matter what happens. Possession is about to be the only law on Vooruitzicht.'

As the approaching hordes drew nearer, they saw that another race was in progress. One wagon seemed to be slightly ahead of the rest and discharged several diggers who raced to a ready-pegged area nearby; these were the men who had discovered the diggings and only just beaten the rush in time to preserve a small share of the find. Within minutes the entire area was inundated with shouting, scrambling, swearing diggers who pushed and shoved and fought for a piece of the precious land. Within hours not a square inch of unclaimed ground could be found and within days a new tent town had erupted on the farm, while in Pniel and Klipdrift the wind sighed in the empty shells of shops and hotels and rattled the doors swinging on unoiled hinges.

As Matthew set to work in the new claim and began unearthing the finest gems yet discovered in South Africa, he believed his travels had come to an end. He had endured the bewilderment of his introduction to the diamond fields at Klipdrift, his first experience of the dry diggings at Dutoitspan, and now the rush to De Beers. He did not intend, he told Court firmly, to dig for diamonds all over Africa.

Yet, less than two months after their arrival at De Beers, he and Court took part in another rush: the greatest rush of all to the greatest diamond mine of all. On July 17 1871 came news that diamonds had been discovered at Colesberg Kopje, only a short distance from De Beers. This time, however, they did not abandon their previous claim but staked another at the New Rush which was worked by Matthew while Court continued to work at De Beers.

Matthew Bright and John Court had founded their fortune and the city of Kimberley had been born.

CHAPTER SEVEN

On the Isle of Wight preparations were being made for the annual Cowes Week of yacht racing. With the money provided by Viscount Swanley and the Marquess of Lambourne, Freddy had purchased a sleek boat, renamed her *Highclere* and after some refitting had ordered sea trials in the Solent. His kinsman, the Viscount, informed him curtly that the less he heard about the matter the better but Lambourne did express an interest in his investment. Had Lambourne been rather better informed on matters nautical or taken the trouble to make an on-the-spot inspection, he might have queried Freddy's account of his expenditure. To a more experienced eye it would have been obvious that Freddy's 'refit' consisted merely of painting over the defects rather than remedying the boat's numerous shortcomings.

Neither was there any sign of the expert crew of whom Freddy had talked so glibly. In fact he had found a former naval officer who had fallen on hard times and hired him to supervise the work and the farce of the sea trials. Throughout the spring and early summer of 1871 Freddy forced himself to board the yacht and sail in the Solent on calm days. By the end of July he had mastered his phobia to the extent that he could go on the water, if not without a shudder at least without *appearing* to tremble.

In London during the Season, Lambourne's enthusiastic prattle about *Highclere* was having the desired effect – much good-natured chaffing and a host of bets that 'that tub of yours' would not even make it across the starting line. Such was the interest that, when the family gathered at Cowes, Freddy had no difficulty in persuading them that the Prince of Wales himself intended to honour *Highclere* with a visit.

'You really ought to be aboard to receive him, Uncle,' Freddy asserted.

'Don't try to tell me my duty, young man,' growled the Earl. 'I know what I ought to do. The point is that the bloody boat is out there on the water and as far as I can see the only way of reaching it is by an even smaller boat.'

Cousin Aubrey paled. 'You and your bright ideas,' he muttered vindictively to Freddy.

'Well, I'm certainly not going,' declared Freddy's father, the Honourable Peregrine. 'The journey from Southampton to the island is bad enough.'

'You must come, all of you,' insisted Freddy, 'HRH would never forgive us and, besides, think of the disgrace when the reason for the discourtesy becomes known.'

'I thought that *you* didn't like the water any more than the rest of us,' said Aubrey.

A smug expression now settled on Freddy's face. 'That used to be so. But now I have conquered my fear and I can assure you that there is absolutely nothing to it. Once one has overcome the initial hurdle, the experience becomes most enjoyable. But, of course, if you are too scared . . . '

'I'll go,' said Aubrey abruptly, and turned away to conceal the terror and tension on his handsome features.

The Earl stood biting his lip in an agony of indecision, torn between his duty to his Prince and his horror of water. 'I must try,' he said at last. 'If you can do it, I suppose I can. But let me warn you, Freddy, that next time you want to use the family name in one of your schemes, you will ask my permission first. What with your bloody boat and Matthew on the damn diamond fields, you are both a positive disgrace.'

'Yes, Uncle,' said Freddie meekly. 'Sorry, Uncle.'

'Oh dear!' twittered Peregrine, running his hand uneasily round his collar, 'I cannot be outdone. Let us go out to the yacht this afternoon and see how we get on. And,' he added piously, 'let us commend ourselves to the mercy of the Lord.'

'Yes, Papa,' agreed Freddy. 'That is one thing you really should do.'

Later that day they stood in a miserable little group, eyeing the dinghy in horror and dismay. 'Freddy, are you sure this is the way it's done?' asked Peregrine, aghast.

'Quite sure,' said Freddy firmly. 'I will show you how to step in without upsetting the boat. Then Wilson,' and he pointed to the ex-naval man who was seated athwartships, 'and I will row you out to the yacht.'

Carefully Freddy and Wilson helped the other three to negotiate the ordeal of stepping into the dinghy, where they sat trembling and clutching the side of the boat with shaking hands. They watched with awe as Freddy nonchalantly unshipped his pair of oars and began rowing in time to Wilson's stroke.

'It only takes a couple of minutes,' shouted Freddy reassuringly, 'but unfortunately the wind is getting up a bit.'

Indeed, it was not a pleasant afternoon for an introduction to nautical life. The sky was overcast and threatening and a stiff breeze was blowing across the harbour, ruffling the sea into humps and hollows. The faces of Freddy's passengers turned from pink to white to pale green.

'Not long now!' Freddy managed to say – he was not feeling too well himself.

At last the dinghy was alongside *Highclere*. 'Now,' said Freddy cheerfully, 'comes the tricky bit. Don't move until I tell you. Wilson will go first.'

Swiftly and efficiently Wilson boarded the yacht while Freddy held the dinghy steady alongside. But somehow, before Wilson could secure the dinghy's painter, Freddy's hold slipped and the dinghy drifted away, the gap between the two boats rapidly widening. Freddy assessed the size of his relations and decided his Uncle Gervase was the heaviest.

'Quick, Uncle, move to my side of the boat!' he called, and as the Earl blindly obeyed Freddy himself also stood up. The sudden movements and the combined weights of the two largest members of the party on one side of the boat had the inevitable result – the dinghy capsized, spilling its occupants into the sea.

The swift current and strong breeze had already carried them some distance from the yacht and was rapidly pulling the struggling figures still further out to sea. Wilson dived into the water and swam hard for the spot, but by the time he reached them only Freddy was clinging to the upturned dinghy and three bright fair heads had disappeared forever beneath the waves.

Wilson helped Freddy back to *Highclere* and pulled him aboard. 'Wilson,' gasped Freddy, 'they couldn't swim! Why didn't they tell me? I would never have brought them out here if I had known they couldn't swim!'

Then Freddy's hard-won victory against the water wavered and was lost. He stood, dripping and shivering, on the deck of the *Highclere*, saw the heaving grey water around him and felt the unsteady boat beneath his feet.

The new Earl of Highclere fell in a dead faint on the deck.

As expected, Lady Isobel Grafton had enjoyed an extremely successful Season. Her classic English beauty had been much admired and if her conversation was found a trifle wanting and her manner was cold and proud, it was no more than was to be expected from a lady of her impeccable connections. No ball was considered a success unless she graced it with her presence; the Prince of Wales was seen to favour her above all other débutantes, and her own coming-out ball at her parents' London home was the high spot of the calendar.

At the outset Isobel, radiant in silks and satins, coquettish in velvet and alluring in muslin, was in danger of having her giddy head turned by the attention and acclaim. Her eldest brother took her aside and offered her a few words of serious advice and for once Isobel listened. She knew that Lambourne was especially well placed to guide her, for as a veteran of seven Seasons and a notorious player of the field in the matrimonial stakes, he knew exactly what was what.

'Remember,' said Lambourne now, 'it is vital that you make a good match at the end of your first Season. However sound your reasons for refusing offers, if you remain unwed it will seem as if your early promise faded and was lost. In assessing your suitors, personal appearance is nothing; fortune and position everything. After a decent interval that fortune and position, coupled with discretion, will enable you to lead whatever life you choose.'

Isobel conceded that Lambourne was right. Unlike Nicholas, who made no secret of his dislike for her, Lambourne had her best interests at heart. Her outlook became more objective; a pair of flashing eyes assumed less importance than a bank balance, and fine broad shoulders made less impression than a title. As the Season drew to a close, it was evident that Isobel could have whom she chose but among the throng of viscounts, marquesses, lords and baronets there was no one outstanding man.

Then she heard the news of the Highclere tragedy and her pink lips pursed into a thoughtful pout.

The Highclere connection would be perfect – she had always known that. The two families were neighbours and the estates were only half-an-hour's ride apart. As her sisters had perceived, Isobel had found Swanley attractive and had been disconcerted to discover that her provocative glances were not appreciated. Now Freddy, the new Earl, was one of the most eligible bachelors in Britain.

She wondered how long it would be before he came to her.

In fact, Freddy called at Desborough with indecent haste. Hardly had the obituaries been written and the obsequies spoken than he rode in and requested an interview with her.

'You know why I am here, Isobel.' Freddy saw no reason to disguise his intentions. 'May I speak to your father?'

'You may,' she replied with perfect composure.

'I have always admired you, Isobel,' said Freddy, kissing her hand, 'and I believe that you and I can have a most satisfactory relationship.'

There was no declaration of love by either of them. It was not necessary. Isobel and Freddy perfectly understood – and indeed deserved – each other.

They were married at St Margaret's, Westminster, in the spring of 1872. That night Isobel suffered Freddy's fat fingers on her fair flesh and while she cringed from his repulsive touch she thought of the few years of duty she owed him and her family and of the pleasure she would take thereafter.

Not one of her thoughts was of Matthew, that first fleeting love whom she had forgotten so quickly so long ago.

Alida watched Matthew open the first letter as he sank down by the camp fire at the end of the day's work. She was curious about the letter because Matthew had never received one before, and she was sure that he was the loneliest person at the diggings. He never mentioned family or friends or joined in any social activities. Apart from their own small circle he seemed to live only for his work, driving himself to a state of exhaustion day after day.

Matthew tore open the envelope. Alida envied people who could read, for the Boer *volk* had little education. Neither her true parents nor Willem and Martha could read and write and there was no school on the diamond fields. She stirred the stewpot and heaped more 'mis' on the fire, lingering over her duties longer than was necessary so that she could remain near him.

She glanced across at him and saw that he had finished reading the letter and was sitting perfectly still, staring into the fire. He held the crumpled letter in one hand and then, to Alida's puzzlement, he began beating the ground with the other fist, striking strongly and rhythmically at the hard ground.

'The bastard!' he choked. 'The murdering, lying bastard!'

As soon as Matthew saw the letter and recognised his mother's handwriting, he knew it must contain important news, otherwise she would not write to him. He did not expect to receive letters because he had written none, not even to Nicholas, apart from a short note to his father advising him of his address.

At first he was numbed by the shock of his mother's account of the Cowes tragedy. Then the pain hit him – pain of grief for his family and the powerful all-consuming fury and hatred of his brother. The red tide of hate swamped him, twisting his heart and stomach, closing his eyes; in his agony of frustration Matthew hammered his fist on the ground as though it was Freddy whom he thus punched and pulverised.

To Alida's relief, Court appeared as Matthew sprang to his feet, flung down the letter and shouted: 'He murdered them! He murdered them all!'

'Matt, what on earth is the matter?' asked Court anxiously. 'Who has murdered who?'

Speechlessly, Matthew gestured towards the letter and Court picked it up and smoothed out the crumpled pages.

'It was an accident,' Court protested. 'No one was murdered, your mother says quite clearly here that it was an accident.'

'Freddy,' and Matthew spoke the name with difficulty, 'knew

perfectly well that none of them could swim. Do you hear me, John? He *knew* that neither my father, my uncle nor my cousin could swim. He murdered them so that he could succeed to the title.'

'Surely someone would suspect? Your mother – surely she would suspect?'

'My mother is a most estimable woman in many ways but she dotes on Freddy and can see no wrong in him. Even the tone of her letter shows that her grief for my father is tempered by her pleasure at Freddy's elevation. As far as others are concerned, the very flamboyance and incredibility of the deed acts as a smokescreen, diverting attention from Freddy's evil intent.'

'You cannot be absolutely sure he did such a dreadful thing,' protested Court unhappily.

'I *am* absolutely sure. But he will not get away with it! I will avenge those murders,' Matthew vowed, 'and I will have my own revenge for Isobel.'

'Isobel?'

'Oh, Isobel will be Freddy's next move. As you see, my mother's letter says nothing of her, but I know Freddy. My God, *do* I know Freddy. He will marry Isobel and he will marry her for only one reason – because he knows I wanted her.'

Court was completely out of his depth in such troubled waters and like Alida, could only stand helplessly by and wish there was some comfort he could offer.

'I need a drink,' and Matthew turned on his heel and strode away.

Alida had understood. There were so many Americans, Englishmen, Australians and Canadians at the diamond fields that her English was greatly improved. Now she thought she knew why Matthew had never sought the company of the girls in town: he was in love with a girl called Isobel. Not, thought Alida sadly, that it would make much difference; he had never taken much notice of her and there was no reason why he should start to do so now. Unhappiness gripped her like a physical pain as she watched Matthew's retreating figure.

'It must be nice,' she said wistfully, touching the letter which Court still held, 'to be able to read.'

'You poor child!' Court stared at her remorsefully. 'You ought to be at school instead of here on the diamond fields, rubbing shoulders with the world's riff-raff. Would you really like to learn to read?'

'Yes, please,' she said eagerly, 'and to write, too.'

'I can teach you to read and write English, and to do sums, but you will have to find another teacher for your own language. I'm afraid.'

'Can we start soon?'

'Yes, of course.' And Court laughed as he read the unspoken question in her eyes. 'And Daniel, too,' he promised, 'but not right now. I must go after Matthew, for in his present state he's likely to get into a fight tonight.'

Alida was fifteen when the second letter came. In the six months which had elapsed since the first, she had grown taller and now topped Martha by several inches. She seemed older than her years, her maturity hastened not only by her experiences but also by the unconventional life she led and the ever-increasing measure of her education.

When the letter arrived, she turned it over and over in her hands with growing apprehension in her heart. She felt a strange reluctance to give it to Matthew and to know what news it contained, and handed the envelope to him with considerable trepidation.

Matthew sat in his accustomed place by the camp fire. He stared at the envelope for a long time before opening it to read the single sheet of paper it contained.

Alida watched the dancing patterns the fire cast upon his face, turning his hair to red-gold flame. Her eyes rested longingly on his broad shoulders and strong arms and she remembered the one time he had touched her. He had only leaned casually against her but she had felt the hardness of his lean body on hers and the warmth of his breath on her cheek. That fleeting moment had left her with a hammering heart and a strange sweet ache in her breast. The hero-worship of the young girl had been replaced by a more adult emotion which she did not yet fully comprehend.

Court watched Matthew, too, and both he and Alida started

with surprise when Matthew flung the letter into the fire and roared with laughter – harsh, discordant laughter.

'It is just as I said it would be,' he cried. 'Isobel is now Countess of Highclere. Have we any brandy or wine? Let us drink a toast to the happy bride and groom!'

Obediently Alida fetched a fat jar of Tulbagh wine and poured generous tots into thick enamel mugs. Matthew drank deeply and then smiled at Court.

'So, John, you once told me that money did not buy happiness. Yet Isobel sold herself to the highest bidder and has lain in bed with fat Freddy because he gave her a fortune and a title. What do you say now?'

'My opinion has not changed.'

Matthew's eyes glittered and his teeth flashed white as he smiled again. 'Well, whatever the case, I tell you now that I will never be without money again. I will never be without the power to acquire whatever – and *whoever* – I want!'

'But that is why you came here in the first place,' said Court calmly. 'Money. It had nothing to do with Isobel. Pride sent you to the diamond fields, not love, not true, long-lasting love.' He watched his friend's face, trying to fathom Matthew's real mood and feelings without success. 'Will you revenge yourself on Isobel as well as Freddy?'

There was a long silence as Matthew considered his answer. 'No,' he whispered at last, 'Isobel is not to blame. She is the victim of her own nature and the tool of the marriage system among the English upper classes. No, my quarrel is not with Isobel but with her father, and the Duke of Desborough will rue the day when he humiliated me.' And at the thought of the Desboroughs, the germ of an idea was planted in Matthew's mind. 'The Duke of Desborough,' Matthew said, with that same air of false gaiety, 'sells his daughters, but I will buy me another woman tonight.' And he disappeared into the darkness, heading towards the marquee tents and shabby shacks which housed the hotels, bars, beer halls and canteens.

Conflicting emotions had torn at Alida as she witnessed the scene – sorrow for Matthew's pain, anger at his brother's betrayal, a guilty joy at the rebirth of her own hopes and still a pang of jealousy for the fickle Isobel who could hurt him so. She longed to put her arms around him and comfort him, and she watched his departure with a heavy heart.

'I wish he wouldn't go to those women,' she said sadly.

'Do him a power of good,' replied Court absently, and then his head jerked towards her in surprise. 'Hey, young lady, just what do you know about "those women"?'

'I know about them,' she said simply.

'Do you, indeed! And do you know why Matthew goes to see them and what he will do when he gets there?'

'Yes.' She lowered her eyes and a blush spread slowly over her cheeks.

Court's breath caught in his throat and he swallowed hard. She was so exquisitely beautiful. Her face was heart-shaped, with strong, well-defined features. Her skin was clear and glowing, sun-tanned to dark honey and suffused now by a becoming rosy blush. Her pink lips were wide and sensuous, parted to reveal white even teeth. Lids, lowered so that long dark lashes brushed her cheek, covered huge luminous grey-green eyes. She flouted Boer custom and went bareheaded, her shining dark hair rippling round her shoulders and cascading down her back.

But it was her body which drew every eye. She was tall and slender, with graceful shoulders and arms and a tiny waist which accentuated the generous curve of her breasts. She moved with an unconsciously alluring sway and Court knew that this woman's body and girlish innocence were a dangerously captivating combination.

Court had seen the men look at her as she went about her daily tasks. It was no longer safe for her to go out alone after dark; he must speak to Willem about it.

Fifty thousand men had swarmed to the dry diggings. They were packed together in an area only three miles in diameter, a small circle containing four diamond mines. The tent towns of De Beers and the Kopje, which became the town of Kimberley, adjoined on the rough road between the two mines but as yet no buildings of consequence had been put up. It was still a transit camp, each man intending to make his fortune and move on. Iron shacks and canvas tents were stifling in summer and cold in winter. Flies were a plague during the day and fleas were torment at night.

At the outset the Kopje diggings covered about 250 acres, but the diamond-rich area was subsequently found to be much smaller. Within the enchanted circle, claims changed hands for £2,000, then £4,000, and were shared by more and more men. At De Beers problems had arisen as men dug deeper, for some claimholders excavated more quickly than others so that pits were at different levels; it became equally impossible to remove ground from the deepest mines or to prevent walls collapsing into adjacent claims. So at the Kopje, roadways – fifteen feet wide – separated the claims in order to provide access for everyone. However, the diggings went deeper than anyone had originally anticipated and diggers nibbled away at the walls with their picks to extract the diamonds concealed there. The tall narrow walls were undermined and became crumbling, unsafe bridges between the chasms.

Added to all their physical dangers and discomforts, Illicit Diamond Buying was rampant. Matthew was impatient of the system. 'The regulations don't give enough scope for expansion,' he protested to Court. 'Only two claims each, and no blocks of claims allowed. Do you realise how much money we're losing? We cannot even take advantage of our full claim allowance, because without eyes in the backs of our heads we cannot supervise the working of more than one claim.'

'What do you want to do, then? Give up one of the mines so that we can both work at the same place?'

'No.' Matthew was emphatic. He sat, deep in thought, for several minutes. 'The answer is to find other partners. Junior partners, of course,' he added hastily, 'who preferably should own claims adjacent to ours. The claims would remain registered in their names, to circumvent the regulations, and their owners would stay on in a managerial capacity.'

'If a claim is worth having, the owner is bound to be making sufficient money to work it himself,' Court pointed out.

'Something,' said Matthew, and there was a peculiar light in his eyes, 'may happen soon which will persuade a few people to sell.'

It was a Saturday night, Court went to bed early and was only vaguely aware of Matthew returning. Therefore he did not see Matthew and several of their native labourers creeping to the mine with picks and ropes in order to demolish the last vestiges of the roadways, and was merely surprised that Matthew slept next morning until the sun was high. In fact his friend was still asleep when a labourer brought news that the few remaining portions of the roadways had collapsed at the Kopje, and some diggers were lamenting that they could never afford to clear up the mess in their claims.

'Fortunately,' said Court, 'it happened on a Sunday and no one was hurt. How lucky!'

'Yes,' Matthew said innocently, 'very lucky.'

Next day he bought two adjoining claims from diggers who had insufficient capital to go on working, and installed the men as managers of the operation.

With the collapse of the roadways, mining methods changed and tall timber platforms or 'staging' were now erected round the perimeter of the Great Hole; from these, ropes and buckets were lowered to each claim, so that the massive crater was criss-crossed with fibre like a gigantic spider's web. The early workings had descended unevenly, so that massive columns of hard ground protruded above the deeper claims on either side. As the pit deepened, so its sides sloped inwards like a funnel and landslides cascaded down these slopes, flinging earth and rocks on the men who swarmed like black ants in the depths below.

Opportunities for illicit diamond buying remained, and it was said that about one-third of the diamonds found were stolen. Matthew caught one of his labourers pocketing a stone at the sorting table and angrily raised his hand to strike the man; then he lowered his arm and stared at the miscreant consideringly.

'You know what I could do to you for this?'

'Yes, baas.'

'Instead I will make a deal with you. But if you steal from me again, you will go to prison and I will make sure that the warders throw away the key.'

'What do you want me to do?'

'Doubtless your friends are stealing from their masters just as you have been stealing from me. I want to buy the stones they steal and then plant them in my own "stuff".' Matthew smiled as he recollected the lesson he had learned from Steyn more than two years ago. 'You will act as go-between and bring the stones to me. Also, I will appoint you boss-boy of my claims, and you will make sure that my other workers do not steal. Finally, under no circumstances is Boss Court to know about this.'

With the genuine richness of Matthew's claims at the Kopje, the extra diamonds passed unnoticed and there was merely widespread envy of his good fortune. His illegal activities enabled him to buy even more claims at the Kopje, or Kimberley Mine as it was now called, while Court enlarged their interests at De Beers by more conventional methods.

'We are not the only ones thinking in terms of partnerships and syndicates,' Court reported. 'At De Beers, Charles Rudd and Cecil Rhodes have evolved a mutually satisfactory working relationship and are talking in terms of amalgamating the entire mine.'

Matthew frowned, jealous of the competition. 'We must make sure we are on equal terms with them,' he declared, 'and that we are vital to any of their plans for consolidation. Which involves our buying as many claims as possible. Damn it, the Council must lift the two-claim restriction!'

This soon happened. The limit was raised to ten claims per person and the Bright–Court partnership flourished. In addition Matthew opened an office and set up as a diamond buyer; dressed in his breeches, clean shirt and top boots, he supervised his business interests from a hut in Main Street. Never again would Matthew Bright need to dirty his own hands in the soil of Griqualand West.

Court was almost incredulous at the growth of the enterprise and the size of their balance in the Standard Bank. He would have been even more amazed had he known of Matthew's private horde, of his secret cache of the biggest and most beautiful diamonds he had found, which he hid and gloated over when he was alone. To Matthew these were very special stones, tangible evidence of his success and the means of his revenge.

CHAPTER EIGHT

Alida had an appointment at Clarke's clothing store and was beside herself with excitement. In a few days it would be her sixteenth birthday and when Willem and Martha had asked her what she would like as a present, she had answered without hesitation: 'A dress! If we can afford it.' Willem could well afford it, for he possessed a fruitful claim at De Beers and was prospering. The dress was ordered from Cape Town and Alida was in a fever of anticipation and at the same time filled with dread lest the garment should arrive too late for her birthday party.

Now she waited for John Court to escort her into town and sighed with resentment at not being allowed out on her own. When a figure emerged from their neighbours' wagon and came towards her, Alida's heart quickened to see that it was Matthew, but her pleasure turned to nervousness as he drew near. To her relief, he smiled.

'John has asked me to go with you tonight. Are you ready?' She nodded shyly and they set off, Matthew adjusting his long stride to her shorter step.

'I am sorry to put you to this trouble, Matthew.'

'I was going into town anyway,' he replied casually. 'Someone has a diamond for sale weighing 500 carats, and I want to look at it.'

'Why do they weigh diamonds in carats?' she asked.

'The term originated in the East,' he explained patiently, 'where the carat gets its name from the carob tree whose seeds are of equal weight. The seeds are used to balance the scales in the bazaars and were particularly useful for weighing diamonds, some of which are very small. There are 142 carats to the ounce.'

'I wonder why there are so many diamonds in this place?'

Matthew smiled indulgently and decided that a folk-tale was a more suitable answer for the child than the geological details. 'The natives say that a spirit, who was sorry about the poverty of the land, flew down to earth with a huge basket of diamonds. The spirit scattered gems along the Vaal River and then flew away from the river towards Kimberley. It grew tired and flew close to the ground so that the basket bumped into trees and tipped out diamonds in large quantities on the farms which are now the mines here.'

'What a lovely story! I wonder if . . .' But she thought she might be talking too much and dared ask no more questions.

They reached the town as darkness was falling. Diggers were so busy in the claims during the day that most shopping was done in the evening and crowds packed the narrow roadway outside the trading stores. Matthew halted outside Clarke's.

'I'm going to my office. Wait for me here and I'll come for you when I've finished.'

Alida entered the store and waited anxiously to find out if the dress had arrived. She gave a sigh of relief when told it was ready and a murmur of disbelief when she saw it for the first time. It was, without a doubt, the most beautiful dress she had ever seen. She touched the shining folds with awe, imagining its softness next to her skin and Matthew's eyes upon her when she wore it. She raised such a radiant face, alight with happiness, that even Mr Clarke – hot, tired and bad-tempered at the end of a busy day – felt his heart soften.

'Your birthday, is it? Here, take this for your bonny hair,' and he wrapped up a length of satin ribbon which exactly matched the dress.

Alida gabbled excited thanks and then stood in the shop, holding the parcel and considering what she should do next. Matthew had told her to wait here, but she was tired of being treated like a child. She was almost sixteen and quite old enough to look after herself. Besides, she did not want to be a nuisance to Matthew and by meeting him at his office she might save him valuable time.

She turned and ran out of the shop, but in her haste cannoned into a group of men who were strolling past on their way to the saloon. From the smell on their breath and their lurching walk, they had visited one such establishment already. Alida's only concern, however, was for the precious parcel which flew out of her hands into the dust.

'My dress!' she cried in anguish, but as she bent to retrieve it, she felt an iron grip on her arm.

'Want your parcel, do you, darlin'? Is it worth a kiss?' and the man holding her arm tried to twist her towards him while his companions laughed.

Frantically Alida lunged for the packet and there was a dreadful ripping sound as the man clutched at her sleeve and the bodice of her dress tore open. She grabbed the parcel and held it against her chest, backing away from her tormentors as, eyes glittering at the beauty of their prize, the diggers advanced towards her. Fortunately Mr Clarke appeared in the doorway of his shop, having heard the scuffle and sized up the situation. He quickly pulled Alida into the safety of the store and sent the drunken group packing.

Matthew was explaining to a disappointed and disbelieving digger that his huge diamond was virtually worthless due to its poor colour, when the boy from Clarke's ran in to tell that 'the young lady' had met with an accident.

'What on earth has happened to the child?' he asked Mr Clarke when he hurried into the shop.

'She was molested outside the store by drunks,' replied the shopkeeper severely, 'and you, sir, ought to be horse-whipped for allowing so beautiful a young lady to wander about unprotected.'

Matthew cast him an incredulous glance. Beautiful? Alida? 'Where is she?' he asked impatiently.

'In the store-room over there, but you can't go in. She's mending her . . .' But Matthew already had his hand on the door and was pushing it open.

Alida was standing in one corner of the room, holding up her blue dress to the light of a dim lamp, dressed only in a white cambric chemise and petticoat. The chemise was narrow and shaped to her figure, the neckline cut low over her bosom. Matthew could see the fullness of her voluptuous breasts straining against the thin material and the outline of the large nipples showed clearly. The petticoat hinted at the long shapely legs beneath and allowed a tantalising glimpse of slender ankles and dainty feet. As if seeing her for the first time, Matthew drank in every detail of the delicate heart-shaped face and tumbling dark hair.

Suddenly she became aware of him and automatically covered her breasts with the dress. As she saw his eyes darken and the expression on his face grow taut and intense, she knew that nothing could ever be the same again.

A sound from the shop broke the spell. 'I will be waiting outside,' Matthew said abruptly and closed the door.

When she emerged wearing the mended dress, he took the packet in one hand and her arm in the other and almost pushed her out of the town towards the wagons. In complete silence, he propelled her along at a fast pace, delivered her to Martha and then flung himself into his own wagon. There he lay face downwards on his mattress and endured the hot waves of desire which engulfed him and the throbbing of an erection he knew no saloon girl could assuage.

From then, Alida haunted Matthew. From barely noticing her existence, he now lived for the sight and sound and scent of her. He was aware of every movement of her rippling hair, of the soft flutter of her eyelashes and the curve of her cheek. He watched the sensuous sway of her beautiful body and yearned to cast aside the demure high-necked dress and reveal her in all her perfection. His hands burned to touch and caress her until passion banished the candid innocence from her eyes.

His desire for her was all-powerful, dominating his every thought and action, but he seemed unable to catch her alone. He groaned at the thought of the countless hours he had wasted through his blindness to her attraction. Perhaps at her birthday party he would be able to touch her at last.

Willem and Martha were sparing no expense to give their adopted daughter a memorable day. Willem had hired a small marquee which stood next to an hotel in the main street; for days Martha, Alida and the hotel-keeper's wife bustled about preparing mountains of food. They heaped the tables with roast joints, pies, curries and *bredies*, and with plum puddings and fruit tarts, while Willem laid in Cape wines and brandy plus a few more expensive wines from abroad for special guests.

Matthew and Court arrived together and Matthew's eyes immediately sought Alida. The muscles in his cheek tightened when the saw her.

She was wearing a gown of pale celadon green, made of a textured silk and cotton mixture and trimmed with satin piping. It had short sleeves but the daringly low neckline was masked by a chemisette. The dress was high-waisted, its full skirt flaring from just below the bosom and draping seductively over her slender hips. Alida, in her pride and joy at her new acquisition, was not to know that the gown was sadly out of fashion; the style and shade were no longer in vogue among the young ladies of Cape Town, where bright colours and crinolines were now all the rage. The Cape Town shopkeeper had unloaded an item of unwanted merchandise on unsophisticated diamond fields society – but he could not have chosen anything more suitable for Alida. It matched her grey-green eyes, accentuated the perfect lines of her tall slim figure and gave her a natural elegance which set her apart from other women. Even her hair, tied with the matching satin ribbon and cascading down her back like dark velvet, balanced the overall effect.

All this was meant for Matthew: every swish of her skirt, every wave of her hair and all the dreams she had dreamed as she dressed that night, were for him alone. As he came into the tent her heart quailed within her – surely she must have mistaken the look in his eyes at Mr Clarke's store; no one so magnificent as he could possibly notice her, and he seemed to be glaring at her so severely. Nevertheless, she could see that he had gone to some trouble with his attire. He wore a cream and blue striped shirt with a blue silk scarf tucked into the neck, well-cut cream breeches secured by a wide brown leather belt at the waist and high shining brown leather boots. The breeches hugged his narrow hips and long legs, his golden hair and beard had been trimmed and his blue eyes glittered brightly in his tanned face.

John Court reached her first and bent to kiss her chastely on the cheek. 'Happy birthday!' he said softly. 'To the most beautiful girl in Kimberley.'

She opened the packet he handed her and gave a cry of delight. 'A book of Shakespeare's plays,' she gasped. 'Oh, John, how wonderful! Now my English will really improve.'

'That isn't all Shakespeare will teach you,' Court laughed, and smiled with pleasure as Alida flung her arms round his neck.

Her nervousness returned as Matthew approached and her heart beat faster and faster in her breast. He did not smile and seemed to hesitate slightly before following Court's example and kissing her swiftly on the cheek. His lips were cold and hard on her flaming skin, but she felt as if the spot had been burned and marked indelibly on her forever. With trembling fingers she unwrapped the small parcel he gave her and stood staring incredulously at the gift in her hand – a golden locket, heart-shaped, on a slender gold chain.

She looked up at him, her lips curving into a smile, all her emotion showing naked in her eyes. Matthew did not smile back but as he gazed at her, Alida felt she was drowning in the intensity of his stare. For a brief magic moment, it was as if no one else existed.

'Would you like to wear it?' Matthew asked.

She nodded eagerly, but her hands were shaking too much to undo the clasp. He took the locket and moved behind her and while she lifted the mane of shining hair he fastened the chain around her long neck. Alida quivered at the touch of his fingers on her bare skin, while Matthew's every instinct was to press his lips to the golden satin-smooth perfection of her sun-kissed flesh.

The moment they shared was brief and noticed by no one. But throughout the evening Court saw how her hand moved constantly to the jewel at her neck, while the book he had given her lay seemingly forgotten on a chair. He experienced a pang of hurt, but chided himself for becoming a sentimental old fool. How could be have expected that a young girl would treasure a work of genius and a key to learning more than a pretty bauble? Alida was not to know that Matthew had paid a quick visit to the store for the locket that morning, while the book was Court's own copy – lovingly handled, often read, and precious companion of his lonely hours.

Court drew some small comfort from the fact that the book was joined by another present later in the evening. A young man sat in a corner, quietly sketching a head-and-shoulders portrait of Alida. With a few deft strokes of his pen he captured not only the individuality of her facial contours but the animation and innocence of her expression. Alida was so enraptured with the gift that the artist promised to retrieve the picture the next day, in order to colour and frame it for her.

Matthew only managed to touch Alida once again that night and that was in full view of the company. An impromptu band formed – a fiddle, a concertina and a guitar – and the guests eagerly seized the opportunity to dance. But men heavily outnumbered women on the diamond fields in 1873 and Alida was much in demand as a partner. She could spare him only one dance, an emotionally-charged, body-tingling waltz, and then they parted, she to worry over his stern unsmiling expression, he to meditate on the message he had seen in her eyes.

Several weeks after Alida's birthday party, Court disappeared into the veld for one of his occasional periods of solitude. The atmosphere in the little camp was at a low ebb. Matthew returned home each night weary from the extra work, Willem was not well and Martha, too, looked tired and ill.

'Is Willem no better?' asked Matthew when only Martha appeared to serve his supper.

Martha sighed. Her broad face was pale and she had to drag her unwilling body from one task to the next. 'No. They say it is dysentery. The camps are unhealthy.'

Matthew nodded. 'There is not enough water and the sanitary arrangements are appalling. Conditions here breed dysentery, diarrhoea, fever and scurvy.'

'We have friends who are going to the river for a few days. It is believed to be more healthy there.'

Matthew said nothing. He knew that not everyone recovered their health at Klipdrift and there were said to be more graves than claims.

'We would like to go with them,' Martha continued, 'but Willem is too weak to drive the wagon. Our friends say we could ride with them but . . .' She hesitated and looked at Matthew for encouragement but his face remained impassive. 'There is not room for all of us – they could take Daniel, but not Alida.'

'Oh.'

Martha drew a deep breath and summoned up all her courage. There was something about this man which frightened her and usually she avoided being alone with him. The events of that dreadful night hung between them like a thick dark veil and, although they had never spoken of it, Martha was overwhelmed by guilt and terror in Matthew's presence. Now she had to ask him a favour and the words were sticking in her throat.

'Matthew, would you look after Alida for a few days? I know you are busy and I do not like to burden you, but Willem is very sick,' Martha pleaded.

'It would be no trouble.' The muttered words were barely audible.

'Thank you, Matthew. Thank you a thousand times! With John away, you are the only person I could trust to protect her.'

Smiling and relieved, Martha turned away and did not see how Matthew gazed at her with troubled eyes nor how he bowed his head and buried his face in his hands.

Willem, Martha and Daniel left the next morning, so Matthew and Alida were alone in the two wagons resting side by side in the encampment. Alida spent the afternoon at Willem's claim attempting to supervise the labourers, for the natives must continue working during Willem's absence or else he would forfeit the claim. They would steal most of the diamonds, of course, but the loss of revenue was preferable to loss of health or life or the claim itself. She turned to the camp well before dusk to change her dress and brush her hair before preparing Matthew's favourite supper.

But as the meal progressed Alida became nervous and self conscious, because Matthew scarcely spoke and even seemed to avoid looking at her. He ate slowly and without appetite and although she was accustomed to his taciturn and preoccupied manner, she had never known him to be so very distant and withdrawn. She became anxious that she had displeased him in some way.

'Is something wrong with the food?' she ventured timidly at last.

'Not at all,' Matthew assured her gravely, keeping his face averted. 'It's very good, thank you.'

'But something is wrong,' Alida persisted.

'I'm just a little tired, that's all.' He pushed back his plate and rose to his feet. 'I think I will go to bed early. Good night, Alida.'

Alida was engulfed in a wave of disappointment. All day she had been looking forward to this time alone with him. She had imagined that they would sit and talk together: perhaps she might even be able to break through the impenetrable barriers of his reserve and perhaps that special look would burn in his eyes again. Now he was gone, none of those dreams had come true and she felt miserably empty and unhappy.

As she rinsed the plates, she saw that a light still glowed in his wagon. Suppose he was not tired but ill? There was so much sickness in Kimberley at the moment that it could easily be so. Alida bit her lip in an agony of indecision; she did not wish to annoy Matthew by intruding on his privacy, but if he was ill it was her duty and responsibility to help. She hesitated a while longer, wondering if she should seek advice, then she straightened her shoulders and her lips set in firm line of determination and resolve. If she was sufficiently grown-up to be left in charge of the camp while Martha was away, she was adult enough to take the necessary steps to save Matthew's health. Alida found a bottle of the medicine Willem had been taking for his illness and walked to Matthew's wagon.

'Matthew?'

'What is it?'

'I thought you might be feeling unwell and I have brought some of Willem's medicine. Would you like to take some?' She listened intently for his reply.

'Yes, that's a good idea. Thank you, Alida . . . leave it on the step.'

'Do not get out of bed. I will carry it to you if you like.'

There was a long pause and then Alida was horrified to hear

what sounded like a low groan. Hurriedly she clambered into the wagon, expecting to find a prostrate invalid, but to her astonishment Matthew was not even in bed. He was sitting on the mattress, stripped to the waist, his head hidden in his hands. She carried the medicine to the bedside and placed it beside the small paraffin lamp.

'Shall I pour it for you?' she asked solicitously.

He raised his head and looked at her for the first time that evening. His expression was very strange, as if he was struggling with some inner conflict, and Alida's heart began to beat faster.

'Tell me, Alida, are you wearing the locket?'

She blushed and nodded, puzzled at his question and not daring to admit that it had never left her neck since he put it there.

'Show me,' he said softly.

She hesitated, a flicker of uncertainty crossing her face, but slowly lifted her hands to undo several buttons at the neck of her gown. The locket gleamed dully in the dim light against the triangle of exposed skin.

Matthew stood up, the rays of the lamp catching the golden hairs on his sunburned chest and the muscles rippling in the firm flesh of his broad shoulders and strong arms. He stared down at her and his hands moved to the remaining buttons of her dress. Slowly he began to undo them one by one, until the dress was unbottoned to the waist. Alida stood like an ice maiden, her eyes locked into his but then his mouth met hers and at the same moment his hand slid inside the dress to grasp her breast. Roughly he parted her lips and as his tongue probed her mouth she felt an ecstatic fusion of their two beings and clung to his lips as though she drank thirstily from the very well of life.

Suddenly she realised that he was pulling the dress from her shoulders. 'No,' she protested faintly, 'no, Matthew!'

But giving no sign that he had heard, he bared her to the waist, caressing the magnificent mounds of her full breasts until the big brown nipples were erect and firm. He held her tightly against his chest, the softness of her breasts crushed against his hard body while his hands stroked her back. She was growing dizzy from his caresses, the impact of his body against hers, the feel of his skin under her fingers and the rough male smell of him.

'I want you!' he was murmuring. 'I want you so much. Alida, beautiful Alida.'

Her dress was round her ankles. On such a warm day she had worn neither chemise nor petticoat, and now she stood trembling in her drawers. He pulled her down on to the bed and held her close, smothering her face and breasts with kisses. Then she felt his hands tugging at the drawers and pulling them down over her legs.

'No!' she cried again. 'No, you mustn't. It's wrong.'

In reply he closed her mouth with his and she could not find the will-power to break away. Shutting her eyes, she heard him give a deep sigh as she lay before him in her nakedness. She was aware of him moving slightly and when he held her again she realised he had removed his breeches and was naked also. His hands and lips were everywhere, teasing, cajoling and exciting, but Alida remained rigid and tense.

'I want you,' he said again. 'Feel how much I want you,' and he moved against her so that his penis pressed into her leg. Lightly he laid a hand on her silken thigh and began stroking her, smoothly and sensuously. Alida held her breath and quivered as the desire rose in her, longing for his touch and yet terrified that he would try to take her.

Then Matthew's fingers touched her between the legs and Alida let out a cry of anguish and delight. As he caressed her and the aching void deepened inside her, she melted and was lost. The tension vanished and she wrapped her arms around him, urging him silently to come closer. As he drove his body into hers and entered her she gave a sharp cry of pain, then she was aware only of a mounting spiral of delight, sent ever higher by the strength and penetration of his repeated thrusts until the wave crashed and broke, leaving her shuddering and shaking in his grip.

Afterwards, when they lay quietly, Alida pushed back her sweat-soaked hair and turned to him to say how much she loved him. But Matthew was already asleep.

The week passed in a daze of happiness for Alida, but when Willem and Martha returned from the river the dream became a nightmare. The holiday at Klipdrift had restored Willem's health, but Martha was far from well. She lay, grey-faced, while alternating attacks of fever and lassitude assailed her wasted body. In her delirium she babbled incoherently and terrified young Daniel by pulling him close and moaning: 'It's a judgment on me. May the Lord have mercy on me!'

Naturally it fell to Alida to nurse the invalid, look after Daniel and cheer Willem who was only too well aware of the large number of camp fever victims who had been laid in the cemetery. Overwhelmed by exhaustion, numb from anxiety and strain, she moved like a sleepwalker in her efforts to satisfy everyone's demands.

Matthew stood beside her in the early evening as she leaned against the wagon, drinking in welcome breaths of fresh air.

'Shall I see you tonight?' she whispered, forcing a smile.

'You look too tired.'

'No! No, I'm not tired.' She gripped his arm and fixed beseeching eyes on his lean face, terrified of losing him and certain that another woman would take her place in his bed.

'Martha might wake and miss you,' he demurred.

'I'll be very careful. Matthew, John will return soon and our opportunities to be alone will be even fewer.'

'Get some sleep, Alida.' His lips brushed her cheek and he walked away into the darkness.'

Nonetheless she came to him later that night. She slipped into bed beside him and he held her tight in a comforting embrace. He made love to her gently, coaxing and cajoling her to her release, soothing her and relaxing her until she fell into blissful sleep. She awoke reluctantly, aware that he was shaking her arm.

'Alida, you must wake up! You must go home before Willem or Martha notice your absence.'

She stared at him dully, nodded and dragged herself out of bed. 'Martha has been asking to see you,' she said.

'Did she say why?' Matthew's tone was wary.

'No, but she calls your name constantly and asks for you most urgently. I know this will sound strange, but at times her life seems to hang by a thread and only her determination to see you keeps her alive.'

'Why the devil didn't you say so before?'

Alida hung her head. She could not tell Matthew how he awed them, or explain how grateful they were for all the favours they had received from him and that therefore they avoided troubling him whenever possible. Willem had decided that Martha's delirious ramblings were not to be taken seriously.

'I will come tomorrow,' he promised.

He had business appointments next morning, however, and it turned out that Court, who rode in at noon, saw Martha first, He took one horrified look at the sick woman and went straight to Matthew's office.

'She's dying!' he announced bluntly. 'Why in heaven's name haven't you been to see her?'

'I'm going tonight.'

'Now!' said Court emphatically. 'Tonight might be too late.'

The wagon was dark and stuffy, and Martha's hand felt dry and hot. Matthew clasped the hand firmly and waited for her to open her eyes. When she did see him it was evident that she recognised him and that this was to be one of her rare lucid moments.

'I want to speak to Matthew alone,' she said faintly.

Everyone else left the wagon – everyone, that is, except Daniel who crouched in a corner at the front, forgotten and unnoticed.

'It is a judgment on me,' Martha whispered. 'I had to speak to you about it. Do you think God will forgive me?'

'Martha,' said Matthew gently, 'you don't need me for that. You need a priest.'

'No. Only you know the whole story. Your fate is inextricably bound up with the children. I am paying the penalty for freeing them from their father's tyranny. I don't regret killing Steyn but I must seek God's forgiveness . . . and yours.'

'Mine? Why do you need my forgiveness?'

'Because,' and he had to lean very close to hear what she said, 'I let the lynch party take you away.'

Involuntarily Matthew's free hand flew to his throat. With vivid clarity he could feel again the ghastly choking sensation of the rope round his neck and he remembered his horrible helplessness amid the howling mob.

'I assumed that you did not know about the lynching. I thought you were in a state of shock.'

'I did know about it but I was too frightened to come forward. Too frightened. And I wanted the children too much.' Tears spilled down her gaunt cheeks.

'Martha, Martha . . .'

'My conscience has troubled me all these years . . . it seems a whole lifetime and yet the years have been few . . . too few to raise and love the children as they deserve.' She was finding it more and more difficult to speak. 'I wanted to ask for your forgiveness before I died, because I thought that if you could forgive me, so could the Lord.'

A heavy silence hung between them and Matthew's face was shadowy and blurred in the dim light. He was reliving the night of the lynching, but a part of his memories was the sensation of Steyn's rifle against his head. *If he fires that thing now, he'll blow my bloody brains out!* Matthew's eyes wandered round the familiar interior of the wagon. He had lain where Martha now lay and opened his eyes to see her sitting beside him, watching over him, tending him after his ordeal in the Karoo. A vision of the vulture rose in his mind and Matthew shuddered, while Martha sensed his revulsion and cried aloud because she thought he shrank from her.

'There is nothing to forgive, Martha,' Matthew said at last, softly and gently. 'And I'm sure the Lord will remember, as I do, that by killing Steyn you saved my life. *Twice* you saved my life.'

A smile lit her ravaged features briefly. 'You are a good and merciful man, Matthew.'

'Am I?' he murmured, more to himself than Martha. 'I think not. And there will be others who will think not too.'

'Dare I ask for more? Will you promise me something?'

'Gladly!'

'Promise that you will never tell anyone what happened that night? I could not bear the children to think ill of me after I am gone.'

'I promise.'

'And . . .' Martha paused, fighting desperately for breath, '. . . look after the children . . . Willem will do his best, but he is not as strong and clever as you . . . Alida needs you . . .'

'I will see that they are provided for.'

'Not just money, *you*, yourself, your strength . . . marry Alida, please . . .' Martha was trying to raise herself in the bed, clutching wildy at Matthew in her desperation.

'I cannot promise to marry Alida.' The words were wrung from him.

'You must . . . please.'

'I cannot make a promise that I cannot keep. I'm sorry, Martha, I'm so terribly sorry.'

The dying woman stared at him with glazed, beseeching eyes and tried to speak again but the effort was too much for her. Her grip on Matthew's arm weakened and with a sobbing sigh she fell back on the pillows and lay still. Martha Jacobs was dead.

And to Daniel Steyn, aged eight, it seemed as if Matthew Bright had killed her, just as surely as he had killed Daniel's father all those years ago. Matthew and Martha had spoken so quietly that Daniel had been unable to hear what passed between them and had only seen the expressions on Martha's face. Matthew might be an archangel to Alida, but to her little brother he was the angel of death.

CHAPTER NINE

The sprawling brash settlement at Kimberley was now beginning to take on a more organised and lasting appearance. The tents and wagons were giving way to more solid structures, although the little shacks of timber, iron or wattle and daub were not intended to be permanent. Matthew bought one of the most expensive houses, built of timber imported from Sweden, comprising one large room with a door and two windows.

'We can divide the room with a curtain,' he suggested to Court, surveying their new domain with satisfaction, 'and then you can entertain your lady friends in peace.'

'Which means that there is a lady *you* wish to bring here,' interpreted Court, 'though the term "lady" is questionable. Come to think of it, I haven't see you walking in the direction of the saloons lately.'

'Let us just say that I have made more satisfactory arrangements. The girls will be missing me, though.' Matthew cocked an impish eye at Court. 'Why don't you take my place? I'm sure they would welcome you as a worthy substitute. Not quite up to my standard of performance, perhaps,' he boasted with a grin, 'but I was priviledged to have an exceptional tutor.'

'No, thanks.' Court's tone was dismissive but Matthew ignored his reticence and persisted with questions.

'You lead the pure unsullied life of a celibate priest. Don't you like making love?'

'Yes, of course, but I don't find pleasure in the mechanical physical act in the same way that you appear to do. I need to care for someone. And I am afraid I do not experience any mental rapport with a barmaid who auctions herself every night to the highest bidder.'

'So there is no woman on all the diamond fields whom you

fancy?' Matthew's eyes were alight with tolerant amusement.

'I didn't say that. I am merely biding my time.'

Although Court's tone was casual enough, Matthew shot a quick glance at his friend and the expression on his face indicated that this information was unwelcome and disturbing. When Matthew spoke, however, he chose to pursue another interpretation of Court's comment.

'I'm pleased to hear that apparently you intend staying in Kimberley. Recently I have wondered about the extent of your commitment to our enterprise.'

'I'm bored to death,' said Court passionately. 'Seeking diamonds is one thing, but toiling every day in the dust and heat to pull the bloody things out of the earth is another!'

Matthew laughed. 'What a contrary fellow you are, John! Lifting diamonds out of the earth would be most men's idea of heaven, particularly when the proceeds lift their bank balances to the levels our accounts have achieved!' He leaned forward and gazed intently at Court, his piercing blue eyes burning with deep conviction. 'You cannot leave yet, John. You must *not*!'

'The decision will be made for me soon. We have dug so deep that there cannot be many diamonds left.'

'Maybe, but somehow I don't think Kimberley has finished with us yet. This strange, unique, wonderful place still has a few surprises in store. You wouldn't want to miss those surprises, John! And we need each other. We have the perfect partnership: the combination of your geological knowledge and my business instinct has kept us one step ahead of the rest from the beginning. It is imperative we maintain our advantage. Please don't turn your back on all we have built up together.'

'All right. I will give it a while longer.'

Matthew grinned in triumph and relief to think that he had succeeded in rejuvenating Court's interest in the mines, but neither of them realised the extent of his dominance. It was not yet apparent that Court's will and ability to act and think for himself were being slowly eroded.

It was soon after they moved into the house that the mongrel adopted them.

Dogs were something of a problem on the diamond fields; they were too numerous, barked without ceasing and were too often abandoned to fend and forage for themselves. Many were reduced to mere bags of bone, skulking among the refuse heaps and stealing scraps from empty tents.

At first Matthew and Court tried to ignore the scruffy yellow dog which trotted trustingly at their heels and waited wistfully for any meagre scraps of food. Once Matthew threw a stone at it, but although the dog's ears went flat and it cowered to the ground, it did not go away.

'Miserable cur!' said Matthew with exasperation. 'Can't it see that it's not wanted?'

'One has to admire its persistence. The animal has a blind optimism which believes that if it stays close enough and hangs on sufficiently tightly, it will win us over in the end.' Court watched the dog with growing affection, never dreaming of the circumstances in which he would remember that remark.

The dog took to sleeping outside their door, shivering on cold frosty nights but still greeting them ecstatically with wildly wagging tail when they emerged in the morning. One particularly cold night Court could not sleep for thinking about him and eventually got out of his warm bed and opened the door. A full moon shone brightly in the cloudless sky, showing the dog lying in the dust of the dirty street. It raised its head and looked at Court inquiringly.

'Come on.' The dog did not hesitate. He was over the threshold in one incredulous bound and ran round the room, sniffing eagerly at everything within reach.

'Quiet!' begged Court. 'If you wake Matthew, he will throw you out faster than you could eat a steak.'

In the moonlight he could see the dog gazing longingly at Matthew's bed. 'Over here,' Court whispered, placing a blanket on the floor next to his own bed. Gratefully the dog sank down into the unaccustomed warmth and resumed its slumbers.

The next morning Court was woken by a furious roar from Matthew. 'That goddam dog woke me up, licking my face,' he spluttered indignantly. 'It can't stay here, it's probably full of fleas!'

'If it was cleaned up a bit, I reckon it would be quite a decent sort of dog,' Court suggested. The animal pushed a wet cold nose into Matthew's hand and its tail beat a tattoo on the floorboards as if in agreement.

'I suppose it can stay for a while,' said Matthew grudgingly, 'while the nights are cold. And as long as you clean it up.'

Court gave the dog a bath, amid derisive remarks from fellow diggers about the shocking waste of water, and brushed his coat till it shone. After several weeks of regular meals, he was hardly recognisable as the beggarly cur which had haunted the street corners. He trotted proudly beside his new masters, lorded it over his peers and fiercely protected his preserves.

'You're proud, strong and independent, aren't you?' said Court, giving the gleaming yellow coat a loving pat. 'Just like Uncle Sam.'

So Sam he became.

The odd thing was that while Court fed and cared for him, Sam gave his greatest love to Matthew. It was for Matthew's step he waited, Matthew on whom his faithful brown eyes rested. Gradually Matthew came to look for Sam, to talk to him when they were alone, to miss him when he was not there and to depend on his companionship.

On Sundays Court usually gave Daniel his lessons, sitting in the shade outside the little house occupied by Willem and the two children. The old wagon stood behind, like a memorial to a former way of life, and Willem always kept it clean and travel-ready. Daniel was a bright intelligent boy and was becoming a better scholar than his sister whose interest in education had waned. His temperament, however, was less sound; he had become nervous and insecure, terrified of being alone. Even on a sunny Sunday afternoon, his fear was obvious from the moment he realised that Willem and Alida were not in the house.

'Where are they? Have they gone away?' he asked.

'Of course not,' said Court reassuringly.

'I expect Willem has gone to see Martha,' observed Daniel, turning to stare in the direction of the cemetery, 'but where is Alida?'

'I don't know, but she won't be long. Let's go for a walk.'

There was not much to interest to boy in Kimberley in 1873. There were certainly no places of entertainment suitable for an eight-year-old and Court thought longingly of the river and the fishing expeditions they had enjoyed. He also began to long for his own bed and a lazy afternoon's rest. However he could not abandon Daniel and, besides, Matthew had shown particular interest in his friend's activities today. Court smiled to himself. So far there had been no evidence of a visit to the house by any of the town girls, but perhaps today was the day.

'Are you having lessons in your own language, Daniel?'

'Yes. The dominie is teaching me and some of the other boys. We go to the church in the mornings.'

'Good. What does he teach you?'

'To read and write in the *taal*, to learn the Bible and to know the history of my people.'

'A fine education, indeed! And have you decided yet what you want to do with your life when you grow up?'

The boy regarded him with steady grey-green eyes, his black hair ruffled by the breeze.

'I shall dig for diamonds with Willem. When the diamonds are finished, I shall go to the Transvaal or the Free State.'

'I haven't visited the Transvaal, but I have travelled in the Free State a little. It seems to me that the land in the Cape is richer and more fertile.'

'It is British land! I will not go there! The British treat us no better than kaffirs. They try to make the kaffirs equal to the white man, whereas everyone knows they are inferior. And the British take our land. This country belongs to us. It was given to us by God; to us, His chosen people, He gave the promised land.'

The words poured out in a passionate torrent, leaving Court astonished and disconcerted.

'Is *this* what they teach you at school?'

'Yes. And my father told me, too. Our family trekked from the Cape to find freedom. I will go to the Transvaal or the Free State, where Boers rule. Willem thinks the same as I do.'

'Willem!' exclaimed Court. 'I have never heard him say such things.'

The boy gave him a sly, sideways glance. 'You do not understand what Willem says when he speaks the *taal*.'

'But you have British friends. Matthew is English, and I am an American.'

'Willem says Americans are different, so I guess you are all right,' the boy admitted grudgingly.

'Thank you very much,' said Court drily. 'Though you must try, Daniel, to see things from the other person's point of view. There are always at least two sides to every question and tolerance is very important. The Boers, the British and the natives should all work together to develop this country.'

Daniel did not reply, but the baleful look on his face made his feelings perfectly clear.

When they returned to the house, there was still no sign of Willem or Alida.

'May I play with Sam?' asked Daniel.

Court smiled with relief at the boy's calmer acceptance of his relatives' absence and at the return to more boylike pursuits.

'Sure,' he said. 'He's probably at home with Matthew. Come on, we will find him.'

Court put his fingers to his lips when they reached the door. 'Matthew may be sleeping,' he whispered.

Cautiously he opened the door an inch and peered inside for Sam. The curtain which separated his bed from Matthew's had been closed so that Matthew's corner of the room was not visible from the doorway, but Court could hear movement and saw that a dress was lying on the floor at the end of Matthew's bed. Suddenly Court remembered that he had suspected Matthew was expecting company and was about to back away when a naked arm appeared behind the curtain and picked up the dress. A moment later the slender figure of a girl stepped into sight. It was Alida.

Ashen-faced, Court watched in frozen horror as Alida began to button the dress, only for the naked figure of Matthew to appear beside her and push his hands roughly inside the bodice and bruise her lips with his.

'Come back to bed,' Court heard Matthew say and the two figures disappeared again behind the curtain.

Daniel, he thought – Daniel must not see! He turned hurriedly, but it was too late. A small curious face was fixed on the curtain. Fortunately at that moment Sam emerged from under Court's bed and bounded happily towards them and Court was able to shut the door and make his escape.

He walked quickly. He was trembling, his stomach churned and waves of nausea engulfed him. Daniel was running to keep up.

'Was Matthew hurting Alida?' the boy panted anxiously.

Court slowed his pace and tried to regain control of himself so that he could smooth over the crisis for the boy.

'Of course not. Matthew would never hurt Alida.'

'He pushed her over, though. On the bed. I saw him.'

'No, no, he didn't push her,' Court insisted. 'I expect she tripped. Anyway, do you think I would stand and do nothing if he was hurting her?'

'Matthew is your friend.' Daniel still sounded doubtful.

'Yes.' Court swallowed hard. 'Yes, he is.' As the initial shock began to abate, Court could not blame Matthew for what he had done. He could only feel a deep disappointment. 'But Alida is my friend, too. I would let no one hurt her.'

Yes, Court said to himself, as Daniel romped with Sam. Alida is my friend. And now that is all she will ever be. So much for biding my time. So much for waiting. What a fool I have been!

In his pain Court knew a great loneliness and a great homesickness for America. He looked around him at the ugly diggings, the cheap shacks, the raw red earth and the dust clouds under the harsh blue sky. He felt a great longing for the sea, for the rollers off the Massachusetts coast, for the fresh salt breeze and the wheeling of the gulls. He wanted the trim ships and busy wharves of Boston harbour and the elegant houses in the city's gracious tree-lined streets.

He had once dreamed of taking Alida there. Now there were times when he wondered if he would ever see his homeland again.

'Alida,' said Daniel that night, as she tucked him into bed, 'you won't ever leave me, will you?'

'What a peculiar thing to say! Why should I leave you? Or Willem, either.'

'Shall we always be together, the three of us?'

'Circumstances may change as time passes, Daniel. You must not be afraid of change. One day I shall get married, but you can still live with me, although we ought not to leave Willem on his own.'

'The man you marry might not want me.'

'I know who I am going to marry,' said Alida firmly, 'and of course he wants you.'

'Is it Matthew?'

Alida smiled. 'You are a clever boy! Yes, it is Matthew. We shall be married very soon, so you see that it need change nothing. But it is a secret for now, Daniel. You must tell no one.'

'All right, but Pa would not have wanted you to marry Matthew.'

She laughed. 'Good heavens, do you remember how he used to call Matthew "*verdomde Engelsman*"! Forget about that, Daniel. Pa did not know Matthew like I do.'

At Harcourt Hall the Countess of Highclere reclined on a sofa before the fire. Outside the wind blew dead leaves from the trees and autumn rains lashed the windows, but inside Isobel was warm and snug, wrapped in bronze velvet and cocooned in luxury.

With her fair hair piled high on her head and her cheeks bare of rouge, Isobel looked pale and delicate. In fact she had adopted a deliberate air of fragility since the birth of her son three months ago. It was a double-pronged subterfuge, enabling her to entertain her admirers who called to inquire after her health, while banning Freddy from her bed until she was stronger. Isobel reflected sourly that she could not hold him at arms' length for much longer, since another baby would be required of her soon. She possessed a well-developed sense of duty, but the prospect of submitting once more to Freddy's embrace caused her frown to deepen and she glared at her youngest sister who sat opposite.

Not that the child had done anything wrong, but her mere presence was an irritation. Anne was not Isobel's favourite company, showing far too much spirit and perception for the Countess's liking, also far too much promise of great beauty.

However, her constant requests to see the baby had not improved the fraught atmosphere at Desborough, where Lady Jane's first Season had been so disastrous that even the placid Duchess had been reduced to tears. Much against her will, Isobel had been prevailed upon to allow Anne to visit.

The girl was staring into the fire with a faraway look on her face.

'Day-dreaming again?' snapped Isobel tartly. 'Mama said that sampler was to be finished before you went home.'

With a sigh, Anne picked up the square of linen and resumed her painstaking stitchery. Isobel craned her neck to see the embroidery and sniffed loudly.

'What a mess! Even Jane could do better than that.'

'What do you mean, "even Jane"? Poor Jane! Everyone is being horrid to her because she didn't receive an offer during the Season and I'm sure it wasn't her fault.'

'Of course it was her fault,' asserted Isobel. 'When a girl has such poor looks as Jane, she must compensate by being especially interesting and amusing. But Jane stammered and blushed every time a man spoke to her and gave the impression that she would prefer to be at home with a book.'

'She's shy,' said Anne defensively, 'and she can't help it. Besides, she *would* have preferred a book and I don't blame her if the men were anything like Lambourne or Freddy or some of *your* beaux.'

Isobel's cheeks flushed pink. 'Anne! You must not speak of my husband in that manner. And I do not have beaux,' she added hastily.

'Yes, you do. The Honourable George *lives* on your doorstep and hangs on your every word. But I don't blame you; if I were married to Freddy, I'd have beaux as well. Which is why I intend to marry for love.'

'Have you been reading those dreadful books from the lending library again?' asked Isobel suspiciously. 'Mama said you were much too young for such nonsense. You are far too romantic, Anne, and I am only thankful that you have time to grow out of it. Eventually you will marry sensibly and do your duty, as I did.'

'I won't! I shall marry the man I love, and our love will last forever and ever. Mama and Papa won't mind if he is not particularly eligible, because I'm only the youngest.'

'At the rate Lambourne is squandering his inheritance, Papa is likely to take a very close interest in your marriage plans,' said Isobel drily. 'Our beloved brother is going to need all the wealthy brothers-in-law he can find in order to keep Desborough intact.'

Anne hesitated. She respected the sharpness of Isobel's tongue and did not want to provoke a family quarrel. 'Mama says that Freddy leads him on and they are both a very bad influence on Nicholas.'

Isobel's lips tightened, for truth to tell she was becoming increasingly concerned over her husband's behaviour. She had no objection to his drinking, gambling and wenching as long as the activities were discreet and comparatively inexpensive. Freddy, however, had thrown himself into the pursuit of pleasure with a determination bordering on dissipation. It was as though something drove him to a pitch of frantic activity in which he found oblivion and an escape from reality.

'Freddy is being extravagant,' acknowledged Isobel reluctantly. 'Fortunately we can afford it – at the moment, anyway.'

Emboldened by the restraint of Isobel's answer, Anne pursued a topic which had been concerning her for some time. 'Nicholas hardly ever comes home any more. And when he is at Desborough he talks only of gambling and parties.'

'He is twenty-three years old. How else do you expect him to fill his time?'

'He never used to be so wild. And when he came home he always found time to play and be pleasant.' Anne's voice was low and her face was sad. She adored Nicholas and had always felt closer to him than to the rest of her family. 'I'm so afraid that he will fall into bad company and that some harm will come to him.'

'Extremely unlikely,' said Isobel decidedly, 'but if Nicholas should come to harm, the remedy will not lie in your hands, so there is no point in your worrying about it. Ah, here comes Nanny with Swanley!' and in her relief at being able to change the subject, Isobel greeted her offspring with more than her customary enthusiasm. Even so, she expressed no wish to touch him but merley gazed at him from a discreet distance.

'Isn't he absolutely adorable!' exclaimed Anne. 'Please may I hold him for a few minutes?' And she took the baby and settled him carefully in her arms. 'Is he any better in his bath, Nanny?'

'I'm afraid not, Lady Anne.'

'Isobel, he's afraid of the water, really he is. It seems to be a sort of curse on Freddy's family. Nicholas once told me that years ago Freddy's brother said that all the Harcourt-Brights were terrified of water.'

'Freddy has never mentioned it to me. And don't talk about curses, Anne. It might bring bad luck.'

'And with Freddy for a father and Lambourne for a godfather, this little angel is going to need all the luck he can get,' murmured Anne naughtily as she returned the baby to the nurse.

Isobel did not hear. Her fertile brain was busy assimilating the import of the information Anne had unwittingly provided.

CHAPTER TEN

Matthew's prophecy of change came true a year later.

At Kimberley a vast amount of surplus red topsoil had been lifted from the claims. Next was a layer of barren limestone which varied in thickness and which also had to be penetrated and removed. Below this was the diamond-bearing yellow ground. Then one terrible day in 1874, about sixty feet down, the picks struck solid rock. The yellow ground was gone and the supply of diamonds was exhausted – or so it seemed.

A mood of despondency settled on the camp. In their heart of hearts, the diggers said, they always knew it had to end but equally they had hoped the dream would last forever.

'I refuse to believe that Kimberley is finished.' Matthew was striding up and down in the limited confines of the cabin. 'Come on, John, you're the expert. What's your opinion?'

'Haven't you made enough money?' asked Court with a smile.

'Good Lord, no!' snapped Matthew impatiently. 'I've only just begun.' He stopped suddenly and eyed Court consideringly. There was a calmness, almost a smugness about the other man's demeanour which aroused Matthew's suspicions – and his hopes. 'What do you know that I don't know?'

'It isn't only the claimholders who will suffer if the diamonds have run out,' Court continued, with maddening deliberation. 'An entire infrastructure has developed round the diggings – traders, farmers, transporters and native labourers. Unemployment will be a serious problem.'

'And unemployment will be nothing compared with the serious problem *you'll* have unless you tell me why you are sitting there so bloody calmly!'

'I am calm because I don't believe the mines will cease to exist. I don't believe that the diamonds are finished. In other words,

Matt, I don't believe the blue ground is solid rock.'

'Ah!' The tension eased out of Matthew's body and he sat down to listen.

'All along,' Court explained, 'I have disagreed with the generally held theories about the origin of diamonds. These theories differed in certain respects but they all had one thing in common – they presupposed that diamonds were deposited *on top* of the ground. I maintain that diamonds are volcanic – that they come from *under* the ground, spewed to the surface by intense pressure. Therefore it follows that the deeper one digs, the more diamonds one will find.'

'I can understand that, but why has the ground changed its nature?'

'It is the same ground. What we call "yellow ground" is merely weathered "blue". All that should be required is to weather the blue ground by exposing it to the atmosphere.'

Matthew had accepted Court's theory and his brain was clicking into another gear. As each year passed he was becoming quicker to see and seize his opportunities and more ruthless in their execution. Now he realised that there was a fortune to be made by anyone who held the secret of the blue ground. All he had to do, he thought, was fuel the belief that the ground was worthless and acquire the claims of the faint-hearted at appropriately 'rock-bottom' prices.

Speculatively, Matthew took a look at the honest face and clear hazel eyes of his partner and sighed inwardly. Court would never countenance such an idea.

'You're looking tired, John,' he said solicitously. 'You need a holiday.'

Court blinked. 'I'm not tired.'

'A proper holiday,' Matthew continued persuasively, 'not one of your geological expeditions. I have been on the diamond fields for four years and to my certain knowledge you haven't had a holiday in all that time. Come on, man, we can afford to indulge ourselves a little.'

Court considered the matter for a moment. He had a sudden, almost painful, vision of the sea.

'A trip to the coast might be refreshing,' he said slowly.

'The very thing,' Matthew exclaimed. 'Cape Town! Tavern of the seas! There might be some errands you could do for our friends,' he suggested slyly, 'or your family in Boston might like an up-to-date trade report.'

'Yes,' said Court. 'I shall go.'

Hardly had Court climbed aboard the Cape Town coach when Matthew's demeanour underwent a radical change. His face grew long, his expression doleful and his shoulders drooped.

'This is a bad business,' he groaned to everyone he met. 'A bad business indeed. Whatever will become of us all?'

Matthew's depression and the absence of Court in Cape Town caused a number of waverers to make up their minds. They sold their claims while, through the subordinate members of his syndicate, Matthew bought as many as he could.

Only to Willem did he whisper 'Buy'. Willem's claims were adjacent to the block belonging to Matthew and Court at De Beers Mine. While the ten-claim restriction continued, it suited Matthew's purpose that Willem should increase his holding. In this instance, Matthew's business interests coincided with sentiment.

The advent of blue ground brought about the final demise of the small claimowner and ushered in an era of different mining methods and the formation of syndicates. Matthew was in his element in the increasing sophistication of the industry, but his absorption in the affairs of his syndicate left him little time for other pursuits or other people. Inevitably he saw less and less of Alida.

At first Alida believed he had fallen in love with someone else. Careful observation, however, seemed to indicate that this was not the case and she had to battle harder for an explanation as to why he never mentioned marriage.

The strict Calvinist traditions of her people made it unthinkable that seduction should not lead to matrimony. Only the unconventional freedom of the diamond fields and Willem's preoccupation with his own problems had enabled her to carry on the affair. She never doubted, however, that Matthew intended to marry her. To Alida – without mother, friend or confidante – the fact that Matthew had taken her to his bed proved that he loved her.

What distressed her was the manner of his loving: he was rough with her or gentle with her according to his mood; he rarely spoke to her and then only in the most superficial terms. He never asked her how she was feeling or what she was thinking or what in life was precious to her. Sometimes she thought he knew nothing about her except her body.

Her confidence ebbed and her natural spontaneity drooped and died. Only when they were making love were her fears allayed. Then she felt close to him, with a communication based on touch. In his arms she felt warm and safe and loved, and could ignore the growing apprehension in her heart and forget the bleakness of the outside world. But even in his arms, sometimes, she thought he looked at her with troubled compassion in his eyes.

And then, at Christmas in 1875, Alida's spirits soared when she realised she was pregnant. Now Matthew would certainly marry her! Impatiently she sought an opportunity to give him the good news, but he was so busy that it was impossible to speak to him in private. At last, when walking home through the town one evening, she saw John Court entering a store and in the hope that Matthew might be alone, she hurried to his cabin. However, as she reached the door she heard voices inside. With sinking heart, she could not find the courage to enter but instead tiptoed to the window and peered inside.

Matthew was talking to Tom, his boss-boy. The matter must be important because their faces were grave. Then Tom produced a small leather bag from his pocket and handed it to Matthew. It was not the transaction itself which alerted Alida to its significance but something furtive and secretive in the African's gesture. Matthew opened the bag and poured out a stream of diamonds; he nodded, replaced the stones in the bag and in turn passed a handful of coins to Tom. Alida's eyes widened. Gold coins. *Gold* coins for an African labourer! That fistful of money represented about six months' pay to a worker on the diamond fields.

Suddenly Alida was desperately afraid about what would happen if Matthew found out she was here or discovered what she had seen. Swiftly she fled into the darkness and the sanctuary of her own bed. Matthew must have a good reason for such dealings, she told herself loyally, and she would not betray him. But she lay awake for a long time that night. She had been bewailing his lack of understanding, but now it dawned on her how little *she* knew about Matthew or the devils which drove him.

'You understand, don't you, Tom? I want everything strictly legal until I get back from Natal. And don't be tempted to set up in the IDB business for yourself while I'm away!'

'Yes, Baas Matthew. I mean, no, baas.' Tom's big white teeth flashed in his ebony face.

'I want you to do something else for me. Boss Court will be in charge of the mines in my absence. Now, as you know, Boss Court is a very nice man. The trouble is, Tom, that he's *too* nice, and all sorts of unpleasant characters will try to take advantage of him. Keep your eyes and ears open. If you get wind of any dirty dealings, don't take direct action but make sure you remember everything and tell me.'

'Yes, baas.'

'Good. There will be a bonus for you if you look after the mines and the boys well for me while I'm away.' Matthew grinned. 'And now, Tom, what would you like me to bring you as a present from Durban?'

'A bottle of sea water, baas.'

'A *what*! You must be joking!'

'A bottle of sea water,' Tom insisted.

'Why, for God's sake?'

'Sea water is good medicine, baas. It is good for stomach ache and to sprinkle on the garden to help the plants grow.'

'Do you really believe that? Do *all* your people believe that?'

'Of course.'

'Well, well. I'll bring you a bottle of sea water, Tom, only with pleasure. In fact, I may bring more than one. You have just given me an idea for a whole new industry!'

After Tom had left, Matthew sat down and yawned. He was tired out and had to be up at dawn for an early departure the next morning. Damn the flooding in the mines which necessitated this trip in search of pumping machinery. He was likely to be away for months, agitating constantly about affairs in Kimberley. But the journey was unavoidable. Although Cecil Rhodes had acquired the valuable contract for water-pumping, his machinery was out of action. If Matthew could be first to replace the pumps, he might gain the advantage over his adversary – because Matthew had recognised Rhodes, for all his prolonged absences at Oxford, as his chief rival for supreme power on the diamond fields.

Oh, and damn it again, he had not been to see Willem or Alida to tell them about his journey. It was too late now – they would be in bed. Alida . . . Alida . . . Matthew sighed wearily and shook his head.

His chaotic thoughts returned to business. He had told Tom to quit IDB temporarily, but in fact the time might have come to quit altogether. Increased security, policing and legislation were bound to come soon. Matthew had no intention of entering the political or civic arena, but he did wish to be seen as a prominent and respected member of the Kimberley community, in the forefront of moves to aid the diamond industry. All things considered . . . yes, it was probably time to stop illegal activities.

Matthew paused to stretch out a hand and stroke Sam's head and ruffle the dog's velvet ears. Then he finished sorting the batch of stones which Tom had brought before hiding them away; there was one very fine diamond which warranted addition to his personal horde. Lovingly he tipped out the gems in a sparkling stream of fire and light and caressed them with his long fingers. He knew every stone individually. Sometimes he felt he knew them so well that were they mixed with others he could have recognised and singled out his own with easy familiarity. He rubbed them between his fingers, feeling their coldness beneath his touch. His bride price! It would not be long now.

In June the heaviest snow in memory fell on Kimberley, cloaking the ugly shanty town in frosted white beauty. Alida and Daniel had never seen anything like it before and stood entranced at the window of their little home, peering through the delicate tracery on the window pane at the white crystal mantle covering the customary eyesores of the mining camp.

With the snow had come Matthew, after the long overland trek from Natal. John Court brought the news of his return. Dear John, thought Alida, as she smiled her joy and gratitude, always so kind and courteous, and who had tried to woo her in such gentlemanly fashion while Matthew was away. But John Court never would, never could, take Matthew's place in her heart.

'Come and play with me in the snow, Alida,' Daniel urged, but his sister shook her head. Today she would tell Matthew about the baby and nothing, absolutely nothing, would distract her from that resolve. She felt nervous but full of purpose, and any sensation was preferable to the sickening shock which had jolted her when she heard Matthew had gone away.

'I'm going to see Matthew,' she said, wrapping herself in a thick blanket. Her anxiety had not affected her looks. On the contrary, her cheeks glowed with colour, her eyes sparkled and her thick hair seemed more lustrous and shining than ever. She was confident, too, that she had concealed her pregnancy, with the aid of a tight corset and voluminous winter clothes.

'Can I come with you?' asked Daniel.

Alida started to refuse, but realised that Daniel could assist in removing Court from the house if he were home. So they set off together, making slow progress through the deep drifts. Daniel delayed them further by pausing to play. Alida was rehearsing, over and over in her mind, what she intended to say.

Once again, however, her plans met with a setback. The snow had brought diamond production to a halt and diggers were meandering about town in search of entertainment. The galvanised iron huts were freezing in such weather and a large group of men had congregated in the greater warmth of Matthew's timber home. As Alida and Daniel sidled through the door, their presence passed unnoticed among the press of people and the stench of unwashed bodies, rough tobacco and coffee.

'What price J. B. Robinson's brick house today?' bellowed one of the diggers, stamping his feet and rubbing his hands to restore life to his frozen extremities. 'I'll bet he's the warmest man in Kimberley!'

'In more ways than one,' laughed Matthew. 'But I think the time has come for more substantial and permanent buildings. I have ordered some bricks from the coast to be delivered in the spring.'

'For a house?' Court swung round in surprise.

'Yes. I can hardly expect my bride to live in this hovel, can I?'

Standing at the back of the crowd, Alida's heart lurched and she clutched Daniel's hand tightly. The boy looked up and saw his sister's face radiant with joy.

'I wouldn't mind living here,' she murmured. 'I'd live anywhere in the world with him.'

Matthew was receiving a lot of good-natured comment and advice.

'Who's the lucky lady?' asked one man.

It was at that moment that Court saw Alida, her beautiful face alight and smiling, at the far side of the room.

'I can't tell you her name,' said Matthew, 'because I haven't yet asked for her hand.'

'She might turn you down,' jeered another man.

'Oh no, she won't do that,' said Matthew confidently. 'I shall go to London for my bride after Christmas and marry at St Margaret's, Westminster, in the English summer.'

The wave of shock hit Alida like a sledgehammer. The blow sent her reeling against the wall and she pressed herself against it, grateful for its support. Every fibre of her being shrieked 'No!' Every particle of her brain cried out that he could not mean it, that he could not possibly *do* this to her. Bitter bile was rising in her throat and she wanted to vomit. Somehow she managed to stagger to the door, to step through it into the street and to collapse in the snow. She crouched, holding her churning stomach, but found that she could not vomit after all. The horror and the pain stayed in her throat and no matter how she heaved and retched she could not expel it from her body.

Court had seen, however. As the conversation in the cabin turned to Matthew's failure to beat Rhodes in the contest for the water-pumping contract, he had watched the colour drain from her face at Matthew's shock announcement and had witnessed her precipitate exit from the gathering. He pushed through the throng, out into the cold air to the huddled, heaving figure of Alida in the snow. Daniel was standing beside her, tugging at her sleeve. The boy's small swarthy face lit up with relief when he saw Court.

'Please, John, I think Alida isn't feeling very well.'

Alida started to struggle to her feet and Court hurried to help her, but she wrenched herself out of his protective grasp.

'Leave me alone!' she gasped and stumbled away into the snow.

As Court and Daniel watched her retreating figure, Matthew appeared in the doorway. 'She heard,' said Court abruptly. 'Alida heard you announce your forthcoming nuptials.'

The smile faded from Matthew's face and he stood as if turned to stone. Oh no, he thought, dear God, no.

'You never had any intention of marrying her, did you?' Court swung round to face him. 'You used her! You used that sweet, beautiful girl for your selfish pleasure! A man of your pride and position, with your smart friends in London society, would not deign to marry a simple Boer girl like her. Did it never occur to you that she loved you?'

'Stop it!' Matthew's voice was harsh and grating. 'You know nothing,' he said in anguish.

'Come, Daniel, I'll take you home.' And Court turned away.

After they had gone, Matthew continued to stand in the porch motionless. Then he leaned back against the doorpost and closed his eyes, his features contorted in a spasm of pain and remorse.

By early afternoon Alida had still not returned. Matthew joined Court at Willem's house.

'We must start to search,' he said, 'before it grows dark.'

They gathered together a search party of some twenty men and fanned out from the place where she was last seen. They combed the streets and inquired of her whereabouts from passers-by, moving ever outward until they reached the very last vestige of human habitation and confronted the snow-covered vastness of the veld.

It was Matthew who finally found her: Matthew and Sam. He was never able to say whether Sam guided him or whether it was instinct, luck or the Lord who led him. He found the footprints on the ground and followed them to where she lay in a warm, welcoming snowflake embrace.

And, he thought, he was in time. She lived: a faint heartbeat fluttered still. He tried to wake her but could not and when he started to lift her she moaned and hurriedly he set her down. It was dark and in the light of his lantern it began to snow.

Her groans were getting louder and in his ignorance Matthew thought that this might be a good sign, that she was rising to greater consciousness from the depths of her snow-induced sleep. Then he noticed the swollen shape of her body and with a horror such as he had never known, he realised she was giving birth to a baby – *his* baby.

His guilt and remorse were so overwhelming that Matthew had to battle for the composure and concentration he needed if he was to help her. He had failed her so often in so many ways, and he must not fail her now. But immediately he pulled up her skirt he could see it was already too late. The pains must have begun much earlier in the day. Probably it was these pangs which had forced her to lie down in the snow, so far away from help and comfort.

Matthew watched helplessly at the child was born. It was a boy, small and waxen and perfect, but quite dead.

Alida only outlived their son by a few minutes. In the swirling snow Matthew held her in his arms, pressing his lips constantly to her icy face. He continued to sit there, clutching her fiercely to him, long after he knew that she had died.

Finally he rose, placed the child against her breast, and wrapped them both tenderly in Alida's blanket. He lifted her from the blood-stained snow and, with Sam trotting beside him, set off slowly into the night.

Next day they buried Alida and the baby beside Martha. Matthew stared at the ground, avoiding the tragic faces of the other mourners. He had sat up all night, drinking, drinking, in an attempt to forget, but all he had achieved was nausea and a splitting head. Glancing up briefly, he saw that Daniel Steyn was standing opposite him on the other side of the grave and noticed abstractedly the strong resemblance Daniel bore to Gerrit, his father. He had the same stocky figure, swarthy complexion and dark hair, and the same malevolence lurked in his dark eyes. However, Matthew thought no more about it – then.

Daniel watched Matthew with a hate in his heart which was

never to lessen. The angel of death who had taken his father and Martha from him had become the devil incarnate who had killed his sister. Alida! Alida, who had promised never to leave him and who now lay cold in her coffin. In his grief and insecurity, as his little world rocked around him, Daniel could only remember one sentence that had been spoken that terrible day.

'You would not deign to marry a simple Boer girl like her.'

All his personal grief and grievances, and all the history he had learned from family and teachers, came together in a fusion of intense hatred and desire for revenge. To Daniel, Matthew Bright became the embodiment of the British oppression of the Boer people.

CHAPTER ELEVEN

In November the ten-claim restriction was abolished, opening up the path to further expansion for the syndicates. The dream of consolidating entire mines no longer appeared fanciful.

This seemed to place the final seal of success on Matthew's endeavours as, in the New Year of 1877, he prepared to travel to London. Seven years previously he had left England as a raw, penniless youth. He would return as a man of substance and experience, a formidable adversary and one whose opinion was worth obtaining and whose company was worth cultivating. He was looking forward to the impact he would make.

The house was finished: a single-storey ranch-style home, rambling over extensive grounds on the outskirts of the town. Brick-built and encircled by wide verandahs, it formed a welcome oasis of shade in the dust bowl that was Kimberley. But its empty shell stood stark against the red earth, bare of vegetation.

'You will live with us, of course,' Matthew said to Court as they gave the house a final inspection.

Court hesitated. 'Mrs Bright might not want a stranger in her home,' he said evasively.

'She won't be "Mrs Bright".' More than that Matthew would not say and even when he drove off in the Cape Town coach, Court had no notion of whom Matthew intended to marry. Uppermost in Court's mind, however, was a feeling of tremendous peace and anticipation of the coming months without Matthew's increasingly abrasive presence.

Matthew himself was aware that there was only one quarter in which he would be missed. 'I shall miss you too, old chap,' he said softly to Sam. The dog had sensed change in the atmosphere and had clung to Matthew's side for several weeks as if terrified of being abandoned. 'I'll be back as soon as I can.'

Matthew also remembered the lesson of his outward journey. This trip he transferred his money to London through the bank and hid the diamonds in a belt around his waist. The hard stones bored and bit into his flesh but the bruises and discomfort were a small price to pay for the safety of his fortune.

As soon as he reached England Matthew went straight to the plush premises of Garrards, the exclusive jewellers in London's West End. The doorman displayed some reluctance in admitting him and the supercilious assistant eyed his crumpled travel-stained clothes with disdain.

'Can I help you, sir?'

'I imagine so. I want these made up into a necklace.' And Matthew poured his gems on to the counter in a sparkling crystal stream.

There was a moment's stunned silence before the assistant found his voice again and called the manager. Another assistant brought Matthew a chair and placed it deferentially behind him as a symbol of his new status.

'These are magnificent diamonds,' said the manager in hushed tones, picking up gems at random and examining them carefully.

'They are the very best of all the output of my mine.'

'*Your* mine?'

'*My* diamond mine. In Kimberley.'

The assistant who had brought the chair now dusted the seat with his handkerchief and Matthew sat down.

'I would like to see designs for the necklace in a week,' he said. 'The necklace itself must be ready within the month.'

The jeweller gasped. 'But the stones must be cut and polished,' he protested.

'It can be done if everyone works hard enough,' said Matthew coolly. 'I am prepared to pay handsomely for good workmanship and efficient service.'

'I must make an inventory of the stones,' said the man distractedly. But Matthew pulled a sheet of paper from his pocket. 'I have already listed them,' he said.

'Come through to my office, sir. This will take some time. There are too many diamonds here for a necklace only. Perhaps a tiara, sir, or a bracelet . . .'

'And a ring.' Matthew leaned over the counter and picked up one of the stones. 'This one is for a ring.'

He paused before following the manager to the inner sanctum. He looked round the elegantly furnished, discreetly lit salon, at the gold and silver shimmering in alcoves; at rubies, diamonds and pearls glowing against shining satin folds, while emeralds, topazes and sapphires nestled on velvet cushions. A beautiful, exquisitely dressed woman swept into the room in a rustle of silk and an aura of expensive perfume.

This was the culmination of all his hopes. This is why he had sweated in the dust and dirt and heat of Kimberley for seven years. This is what money could buy. Beauty and power. Beautiful women, beautiful clothes, beautiful jewels, beautiful houses. And power – power over other people. Look how the man's attitude had changed when he saw the stones! There were those who would say that money did not buy happiness but to Matthew, aged twenty-seven and in the prime of his health and confidence, happiness *was* beauty and power.

He left Garrards with an appointment to return in a week and the address of Mr Poole, tailor to the Prince of Wales.

'We are wearing trousers rather wider this year,' Mr Poole informed him as he measured for day suits and evening wear.

'I do not like baggy trousers.'

'But the Prince of Wales has set the fashion!'

'The Prince of Wales has bandy legs – I don't! You will please provide me with trousers of a slim and narrow cut.'

Mr Poole pursed his lips disapprovingly but did not argue. A little while later he tried a different tactic.

'The tails of the coat are a little shorter this year. Will that be in order, sir?'

Matthew considered the matter and nodded. Emboldened, Mr Poole continued, 'And, of course, we do not fasten the frock coat.'

'Bloody silly! I shall fasten mine.'

'But the Prince of Wales . . .'

'. . . has a fat stomach which a fastened coat does not flatter. I am not a slavish follower of fashion, Mr Poole. Neither do I intend to run to flab. Kindly ensure that I can button my coats – with these.' He held out three large diamonds and laughed aloud at the tailor's outraged expression. 'You believe a diamond button to be vulgar! And so it might be, on some people. But not on me. These are for my wedding coat, Mr Poole. Have the buttons made for me and I'll guarantee it will not be the last time you will receive such a commission. The Prince of Wales isn't the only man in England to set a fashion.'

Matthew had told no one of his impending arrival in England and he contacted none of his family or friends until his first suit of clothes was ready. He stayed quietly in London and took long walks through the streets and parks, breathing in the bustle and vitality of the great capital. He had not realised until now how much he had missed it, how rustic and monotonous had been his daily routine in Kimberley, how much of a colonial he had become.

He experienced that strangest of all sensations for the returning exile – a sense of alienation from one's own people. He walked each street looking for signs of change and, seeing comparatively little alteration in the familiar scenes and surroundings, wondered why he should feel isolated from his fellows. He did not perceive that the change was within himself, that he had grown in another direction during his absence and was different from the other Englishmen around him. Neither did he realise that he always had been different and that was why he had left in the first place. The irony was that the first motivation Matthew could remember was the desire to be the same as his peers – to live as they did, spend as they did and to be accepted as their equal. He had achieved the means to obtain that equality but in so doing had exposed himself to other experiences and influences which separated him further from the friends of his youth than ever his poverty had done.

Having previously had his hair cut and beard trimmed, Matthew emerged from Mr Poole's establishment dressed in grey striped trousers, a dove-grey frock coat, grey brocade waistcoat and a grey top hat. The effect on his tall, broad-shouldered figure and against the deeply tanned face, fair beard and blue eyes was devastating. He had confined his accessories to a diamond tie-pin, knowing that the elegant cut of his clothes sufficiently advertised his wealth.

Fully aware of the admiring glances in his direction, Matthew went in search of Nicholas. But finding his old friend turned out to be far more difficult than he had imagined. He was not at his Club, neither was he to be found at his rooms. Assured that Nicholas was definitely in town, Matthew left messages and returned to his hotel to await a call. Nothing happened. Two days later, Matthew returned to Nicholas's rooms in the evening and demanded an explanation from the manservant, Preston.

'You must know where he is!' he urged.

'It is not in my power to say, sir.'

'In other words, you do know where he is but he ordered you not to tell anyone.'

Matthew studied the man's face. Preston's loyalty was something he could understand and applaud, but he discerned unhappiness and concern beneath the servant's polite mask.

'He has not been back here or he would have got in touch with me, of that I am sure. Does he often disappear for days on end?'

'I wouldn't like to say, sir.'

'So obviously he does. A girl? No, he wouldn't need to be so secretive. Is he drunk? No, he would return here to sleep it off. For heaven's sake, man, you must tell me – he might be in trouble.'

'That is what I am afraid of,' groaned Preston. 'But it is more than my job is worth to break his Lordship's confidence. If the Duke was to find out . . .'

'Tell me!' thundered Matthew.

'Lord Nicholas will be at The Golden Pagoda, sir.'

'Where and what the hell is that?'

'It is an opium den in the City.'

'Opium!' Matthew seized the man's shoulders and shook him until his teeth rattled. 'That vile stuff! And you did nothing about it? Couldn't you at least have informed his brother?'

'The Marquess of Lambourne is aware of the facts, sir.' Preston paused. 'So,' he added, 'is the Earl of Highclere.'

'Damn them for selfish indolent fools,' swore Matthew. 'Get your coat, Preston! We must bring him home.'

The hansom rattled east, through the dark streets of the City, to the wharves of the London docks. They left behind even the brothels and cockpits and entered narrow stinking alleys where every shadow bore a hint of menace. Outside The Golden Pagoda the clash of steel upon steel and the grunts of contestants attracted Matthew's attention to a drunken brawl at the end of the lane, a timely reminder of the danger which lurked in these festering alleys.

'Drive on,' Matthew instructed the cab driver. 'It's too dangerous to wait here. Keep moving and return in ten minutes.' Squaring his shoulders, and followed by the petrified Preston, Matthew strode purposefully down the stone steps to the Hades below.

At first the sight and sound and smell of the place reminded him of the early days on the diamond fields. It was hot, the warmth wafting from braziers standing about the room, and there was the rancid stench of sweat and a pall of thick smoke. But as his eyes grew accustomed to the gloom, he perceived little resemblance between the opium den and the diamond mines. At Kimberley the scene was one of continual, frenzied movement, while here bodies were draped in heedless lassitude or lay crumpled in an unconscious trance. At Kimberley came the cacophony of picks and shovels, buckets and pulleys, horses and men. Here was silence, broken only by the semi-conscious mutterings and mumblings of the opium-smokers. At Kimberley the cloudy atmosphere emanated from the dust of a thousand sieves. Here the air was thick with the poisonous fumes of the drug.

A small Chinese bowed low and beckoned them to a vacant place.

'I am looking for a friend of mine,' said Matthew loudly. 'Lord Nicholas Grafton.'

The Chinese lifted his hands apologetically and no one spoke.

'Preston, start searching!' commanded Matthew as he dived into the gloom, staring into ravaged faces and turning over recumbent bodies. Preston nervously did the same at the other side of the room.

Nicholas was slumped on one of the wooden bunks against the wall and opened glazed eyes as Matthew and Preston bent over him.

'Another pipe,' he babbled, 'another pipe and then I must go home. I have been here several hours.'

'You have been here several *days*, Nicky. Time to go home. Come on, old chap.'

'Who are you?' cried Nicholas in a high tremulous voice. 'You look like a friend I once had, but he's far away and I shall never see him again.' He began to cry.

'It's me. Matthew. Come home, now.'

'Don't want to go home. Nothing to go home *for*.'

But he allowed them to lift him from the bunk and stood swaying as Matthew and Preston supported him on either side. Matthew summoned the Chinese, settled what Nicholas owed and, breathing shallowly to avoid inhaling the noxious drug, he and Preston half carried Nicholas out into the fresh night air where they shuffled up the steps and stood in a huddled group in the lane.

The hansom cab was not in sight but the welcome sound of hooves was soon heard. As the cab appeared a bunch of sailors materialised from the shadows; recognising the quality of the gentlemen and believing them all to be under the influence of opium, the sailors reckoned the group to be easy pickings but had reckoned without Matthew, however. As four of them came in slowly and confidently, laughing at their prey, Matthew quickly assessed the situation and heaved the limp form of Nicholas to Preston.

'Get him inside the cab!'

Freed of his burden, Matthew swung a swift right jab at the first sailor and a sharp left hook at the second. They crashed to the ground and as the two astonished faces of their companions gaped at their assailant, Matthew stretched out both arms and banged their heads together with a resounding crack. They joined their comrades in the gutter and Matthew, dusting his hands with some satisfaction, climbed into the cab. Not for nothing had he sorted out drunken brawls between the natives in Kimberley.

Later, as Nicholas slept, Matthew sat by the bed and watched the pale haggard face on the pillow. Far away in Kimberley, immersed in his own activities, he had not thought of Nicholas as often as he ought. He should have come home sooner, or at the very least kept in touch by letter. Matthew cursed his poor performance as a correspondent and cursed too the indifference of Hugh, Marquess of Lambourne, to his brother's plight.

'How I have missed you,' Nicholas said when he woke and they exchanged news. 'How little I have achieved in this time and how well you have done for yourself.'

'Oh, that's nothing,' said Matthew impatiently. 'What I don't understand is how you were ensnared by the opium dealers. You always swore you wouldn't touch the stuff.'

Nicholas sighed and tried to sit up a little higher in the bed. He looked better than when they had found him the previous night, but was still a far cry from the healthy young man Matthew remembered.

'It's a very strange thing,' said Nicholas thoughtfully, 'but really the whole sequence of events can be traced back to the time you left England and the £1,000 you gave me.'

'Good God!' exclaimed Matthew. 'You haven't been smoking opium for seven years I hope!'

'No, no, but the chain of circumstances started them. You gave me £1,000 to pay my gambling debts, but I didn't use it for that. I decided to put the whole lot on a horse. That way I could pay my debts and still have some over.'

Matthew groaned.

'It worked,' Nicholas told him triumphantly. 'Your money brought me luck and the horse won. And so did the next, and the next. I hit a winning streak. For years I was wealthy and successful. I became confident that I could win any bet, so I accepted a challenge that I could smoke opium and never want to do so again. It was a bet that I lost. I smoked the opium and found it heavenly and wanted more. And so my decline began, because not only was I unable to stay away from the drug but I began to lose other bets as well. Your gift, Matthew, was my undoing. It would have been better to have been unable to pay my debts and therefore been unable to gamble more without my father knowing. As it was, your money brought me years of heaven, but then the luck changed and it has led me into hell.'

'Why didn't Lambourne stop you?'

Nicholas shrugged. 'He tried, after a fashion, but he and I have never been close. He and Isobel are chums and they have never cared for me. About Isobel – Matt, I am so sorry.'

'I'm not,' said Matthew brusquely. 'I have other marriage plans, as you will see.'

'So has Lambourne. But he's in debt as usual and Papa is at his wits' end to know what to do. My poor Papa and Mama. Six children and only one married!'

'So Lambourne wants to marry!' There was a predatory gleam in Matthew's eye which might have served as a warning signal to anyone with more recent knowledge of the man and his methods. 'Thank you for the information. Now, a doctor is what you need. Under no circumstances must you go anywhere near opium again.'

'It is not easy to give it up,' Nicholas said. 'I have tried.'

'But now you will have me to help you,' Matthew promised, 'and I know you will be able to get well.'

After placing Nicholas in a doctor's care. Matthew returned to his hotel and thought seriously about his next move. The more he considered Nicholas and his own business interests in England, the more he concluded that he needed an agent he could trust. He had to find a completely honest man who would look after his London affairs. Matthew smiled cynically to himself. Honest men were rarer than rubies. Where would he find such a treasure, who would guard his interests even in absentia? Then Matthew remembered something. Attiring himself in his splendid new clothes, he checked his appearance in the looking-glass and set off to call on the Comtesse de Gravigny.

He had been quick to note that the widowed Comtesse now resided permanently at the house in Eaton Square where he had visited her all those years ago. He was also aware that she might not wish to receive him, but decided to risk a rebuff. In the event she welcomed him coolly in that same salon and they chatted politely while she appraised his expensive dress and he tried not to notice how she had aged; there were flecks of grey in that glorious chestnut hair and lines now puckered the porcelain skin.

'You have prospered,' she said at last.

'Thanks to your teaching and your generosity,' returned Matthew. 'The lessons you taught me at out last encounter were even more valuable than those of our first meeting. Tell me,

Comtesse, did you recover your diamond at a reasonable cost?'

'I did. I was not much out of pocket on your enterprise, Matthew.'

'But you lost more money than you had expected.'

The Comtesse tilted her head sideways and gave him a speculative look. 'Yes. About a thousand pounds more.'

'The exact sum,' agreed Matthew, 'and the reason for my visit today. Allow me, my dear Comtesse, to repay the debt,' and with a flourish he laid a cheque for the sum on the table.

The Comtesse's eyebrows shot up in astonishment. 'You are full of surprises, Matthew. What has prompted this sudden attack of remorse?'

'I gave the money to Nicholas, but it brought him unhappiness, disappointment and despair.' Matthew then recounted what had happened to his friend. 'Not only do I feel a moral obligation to you, Comtesse, to settle the debt but I hope to break the spell it indirectly cast on Nicholas.'

The Comtesse's eyebrows twitched again. 'Morals? Spells? This does not sound like the Matthew I knew – or thought I knew.' She stared at the cheque in silence for a few moments. 'And yet,' she said slowly, 'you were always very fond of Nicholas, and to have spared him one-fifth of the diamond price was a generous gesture.'

She transferred her gaze to Matthew's enigmatic, hooded face and, although she doubted his repentance, her lips curved in a reluctant smile. 'You are a rogue, Matthew,' she said, 'but a charming one. Women will always find a reason for your shortcomings and an excuse to continue caring for you. Men, however, may not be so forgiving!'

Matthew grinned and for a moment there was a flash of the adorable boy who had attracted her eleven years ago. 'Incidentally, when you missed the thousand pounds, did it not occur to you that Reynolds might have taken it? After he retrieved the money from me in Cape Town, he could have set aside a portion for himself.'

'Never,' said the Comtesse emphatically. 'Reynolds is an honest man.'

'Ah, I thought as much. I am in need of just such a man to keep an eye on Nicholas when I return to Kimberley. Does he still work for you?'

'Mr Reynolds has never been in my full-time employ; he is an agent who accepts various commissions. I can give you his address and I'm sure he will be pleased to do your bidding – as long as the work is honest and honourable.'

Matthew pocketed the address and left so precipitately that the Comtesse was left wondering if, for all his courtesy to her and concern for Nicholas, that information had been the real purpose of his visit.

She moved awkwardly in her chair and grimaced with pain. Matthew had noticed nothing, but the crippling disease was steadily engulfing her. Widowed and childless, her beauty fading, with over-whelming sadness the Comtesse de Gravigny looked back upon a wasted life. Under her gown, cold and hard against her ageing flesh; was the pear-shaped diamond. She wore it always; hating it, loathing it, fearing its aura of evil, yet still she wore it. There was no escape from the diamond and today it seemed heavier and more ominous than usual, pressing relentlessly into her breastbone.

The Comtesse was sure that Matthew could not escape either – the diamonds had him in their grip, controlling him, directing him. Yet perhaps there remained an innate spark of goodness in him which would triumph over the vile corruption of the gems.

'Mr Reynolds?' For the life of him Matthew could not remember what the man looked like and he tried again to recall the face of the man he had last seen in the Cape Town hotel seven years before.

'Mr Harcourt-Bright.' They shook hands.

'You have an excellent memory,' said Matthew wryly.

'A cultivated gift. It is of exceptional importance in my profession, but there are, however, some people who stand out readily in one's mind.'

Matthew bowed at the implied compliment and outlined the problem with Nicholas.

'A little drinking, a little gambling, a few women – these do not concern me. Moderation is the keynote, Mr Reynolds. And the most important task is to ensure he does not go near the opium dens.'

'I shall do my best, Mr Bright, with the co-operation of his lordship and the man Preston. What the young lord needs, if I may be permitted to say so, is useful employment.'

'You are right,' said Matthew thoughtfully. 'He must and will conquer the addiction, with the doctor's help, but his customary empty round of pleasure makes for poor self-discipline. There is the possibility that I may set up an office in London for diamond dealing and I was hoping that you could take charge of it for me. If and when that time comes, perhaps Lord Nicholas could be useful or *made to feel* useful.'

Reynolds smiled appreciatively at the subtle distinction and with equal tact guided the conversation to the mundane matter of remuneration for his services. When this was settled, Matthew rose to leave.

'There may be one other task you can perform for me. I will call again before I depart for the diamond fields.'

Matthew discharged another duty, and then stayed in Brighton for a few days with his mother and unmarried sister. He listened to Louisa's proud talk of Freddy, but noticed with mixed feelings that his own wealth made a favourable impression on her. She introduced him to her acquaintances and acted for all the world as if he was her beloved prodigal son. Matthew was satisfied to have gained some of her attention at last but not as happy as he had expected. There was something oddly demeaning about buying one's way into a mother's affections. As a child he had loved her and tried to please her in the hope that she would love him. Now he felt nothing – the opportunity for any real relationship between them had passed.

He returned to London to check on Nicholas and transact business with the Hatton Garden diamond merchants. In reality, however, he was waiting restlessly for the necklace to be finished so that he could pay his eagerly anticipated visit to Highclere.

Word came from Garrards at last. The tiara, bracelet and ring and his own accessories were not yet complete but the necklace, the centrepiece of the fabulous collection, was ready.

The box lay on the manager's desk. Reverently the jeweller opened the lid and Matthew caught his breath as he gazed upon the glittering gems nestling on a cushion of blue velvet. This was even lovelier than he had imagined, more magnificent than he had ever dreamed, flashing a flawless fire, a brilliance, a radiance beyond compare.

Each worker, each link in the human chain, had carried out his appointed task to perfection. The cutters and polishers had brought out the full beauty of each stone, but the designer had surpassed himself. He had set the stones in gold but the delicate tracery was inconspicuous, allowing the diamonds to dominate. In its simplicity the design was far ahead of its time and possessed a unique sophistication.

Yet Matthew had the satisfaction of knowing that he was the chief architect of that glowing perfection. It was his choice of stones which had made it possible. Not only had he picked the purest gems but had selected stones which matched and could be cut to identical shapes and size and symmetry.

'It is a triumph,' said the manager quietly.

Matthew nodded. Excitement and anticipation were mounting within him as he prepared to put his plans into action. He held the jewels in his long sensitive fingers, savouring this long-awaited contact with the instrument of his revenge. 'The Bright necklace,' he murmured. 'At last!'

CHAPTER TWELVE

When Matthew arrived at Highclere the next day, Freddy waddled out to greet him. On the one hand this was the moment Freddy had waited for – the moment when he flaunted his status, castle and Countess. But he was also apprehensive, because Matthew might want to discuss the 'accident' at Cowes. Freddy had decided that when Matthew requested a loan, as he was bound to do, the money would be handed over on the strict understanding that Matthew returned to South Africa by the next steamer and stayed there.

Only when he saw the splendid stranger step from the carriage did Freddy remember how much he detested his brother. Matthew was more handsome than ever and, judging by the arrogance of his bearing and the elegance of his attire, he had not brought a begging bowl. Even before they spoke a word to each other, Freddy's throat was dry and constricted and the familiar fury and envy were pulsating through him.

To Matthew, Freddy had not changed one bit. He was as repulsive, as fat and flaccid as ever, and his complexion was if anything more florid than before. Revenge, thought Matthew, was going to be sweet.

'Freddy!' he cried. 'My dear brother, how good it is to see you,' and Matthew clasped him in an affectionate embrace.

'Yes . . . of course,' Freddy stared at Matthew suspiciously.

'You know, Freddy, only when one is far from home does one realise how dear the family is. And after our tragic loss, you and I should be even closer than before.'

'Quite.'

Totally eclipsed by the size, splendour and ebullience of his brother, Freddy puffed up the steps with the uncomfortable feeling that things were not going quite as planned. However, he still had a trump card to play. 'Come and meet Isobel.'

'Ah, Isobel!' Matthew paused and stared intently into Freddy's small pig-like eyes. 'I had hopes there myself at one time, as you may recall.' He heaved a deep sigh. 'But I have persuaded myself that it was for the best. Isobel was born to be a countess and to grace the magnificence of such a home as Harcourt Hall. I do realise that I aspired too high.'

Baffled, and sensing that he had lost the second round of the contest as well as the first, Freddy led Matthew into the drawing-room.

Isobel was reclining on the sofa, her face set in pouting lines of boredom. The visit of Freddy's brother was an awful inconvenience – not only had it occasioned Freddy's return to Highclere, but she had been forced to cancel several *intimate* engagements. She sighed with irritation and tried to remember what Matthew looked like, but it was too long ago to recall any detail of that brief flirtation.

She looked up petulantly as she heard Freddy's voice and with a jolt of surprise saw the handsome man in the doorway. Now she remembered Matthew and the impact he had made on her. As he crossed the room his magnetism was powerful, and aggressive strength and intense virility emanated from him like a pungent odour. There was undisguised admiration on his face and as he bent over her hand he looked up at her from beneath long dark lashes. The message which smouldered in his blue eyes was definitely not one of fraternal affection.

Isobel smiled and preened herself confidently. This brother-in-law was an unexpected bonus. How right she had been to marry Freddy – this way she could be a countess and enjoy a few family fringe benefits as well.

Matthew saw an undeniably beautiful woman. His frank gaze travelled over the fine blonde hair, periwinkle blue eyes and creamy skin, down to the swelling bosom and handspan waist unspoiled by childbearing. His scrutiny brought a flush of anticipation to Isobel's cheeks and she felt the fire flare within her. But today Matthew saw what he had overlooked before – the hard calculating selfishness in her eyes and mouth.

'Isobel! My dear sister – if you will permit me to call you that!'

He held her hand a fraction longer than was necessary and the slight pressure of his fingers was not obligatory.

Freddy frowned. He had not missed Isobel's reaction to Matthew's overpowering presence. He was well aware that his wife had lovers and he considered this to be perfectly normal. She could bed with every man in England for all he cared – except Matthew. Any man but him.

The rage inside Freddy triggered off a sudden upsurge of emotions and memories. Matthew reminded him of childhood and youth, of family, of fathers, uncles and cousins . . . Freddy swallowed hard and fought off the panic which threatened to overwhelm him. One thing was certain – Matthew's stay must be short. Very short.

However, Freddy could not fault his brother's behaviour during the next few days. Matthew was fervent in his admiration of the Highclere house and estate and played the fond uncle to perfection with four-year-old Charles and two-year-old Julia. If he was a trifle too attentive to Isobel, even those gallantries were paid with such simple courtesy and transparent devotion that it was impossible to take offence.

Two things puzzled Freddy. First, Matthew never spoke of Cowes. Second, he was singularly unforthcoming about his success or otherwise at the diamond fields.

Four days after his arrival at Highclere, Matthew rode over to Desborough. As he rode, his penetrating gaze took in the signs of neglect on the Desborough estate, the untilled fields and crumbling cottages, and evidence of decay at the great house itself. Obviously the Duke of Desborough was much in need of funds.

Matthew walked through the doorway which, seven years ago, had been forbidden him and handed his card to the footman. On it he had written: 'I have urgent news of Nicholas.' Left alone in the Hall, he strode to the door of the Blue Salon and flung it open. The room was empty. Swiftly he crossed to the window and looked out on to the terrace. Three girls were walking there: two of them dark-haired like Lambourne and the youngest fair like Isobel and Nicholas. His curiosity satisfied, Matthew returned to the Hall.

The Duke greeted him with a glare but Matthew bowed with studied politeness.

'I am aware, Your Grace, that you ordered me never to darken your doors again. I trust, however, that you will not regret admitting me to your house today.'

'What is the problem with Nicholas?' snapped the Duke without preamble.

'Nicholas is unwell. I am hoping it is nothing serious, but have taken it upon myself to place him in the care of a doctor. I shall call on him again as soon as I return to town.'

'Most civil,' acknowledged the Duke grudgingly. 'Is that all?'

'No,' Matthew laid the box he was carrying on the table and opened it with a theatrical flourish. 'Is this enough, sir, to buy your youngest daughter?'

The Duke leaped angrily to his feet but the protest died on his lips as he saw the beautiful necklace. He gaped at the gems with bulging eyes, gulping and gasping like a landed fish, while Matthew sat down and waited.

'You insult me, sir!' roared the Duke when he regained his breath and his equilibrium. 'Nobody *buys* my daughters.'

'Oh, do forgive me,' said Matthew in apparent surprise. 'I assumed that my brother had acquired Isobel with his newly-found fortune and title.'

The Duke spluttered again and Matthew took advantage of his temporary indisposition to continue.

'Naturally the necklace is not all I have to offer – it is what you might term a sample. Garrards are making up the other pieces with stones from my diamond mines.'

'Diamond *mines*,' exclaimed the Duke, emphasising the plural. 'Just how many mines do you have?'

'I really don't know, I haven't counted them,' smiled Matthew with disarming frankness. 'However, the income from them is quite sufficient, I assure you, to keep my wife in considerable comfort.'

Against his will the Duke's eyes were drawn back to the magnificent diamonds in the velvet box. 'Really?' he said faintly; he could feel he was weakening.

'As a wedding present to my bride's family, I shall be delighted to settle Lambourne's debts. I believe such a release might open the way for his own betrothal?'

The Duke swallowed hard. 'Yes.'

'And I shall make myself responsible for Nicholas who also has, should we say, a few financial obligations. What he needs,' said Matthew sententiously, 'is useful employment.'

'Quite,' whispered the Duke, closing his eyes. He loathed the sight of Matthew and was hating him more with every word he uttered. But the temptation was growing too great . . .

'So that settles the matter of Lambourne, Nicholas and, of course, Anne. Three children off your hands at one fell swoop, Your Grace! Surely that should make for an improvement in your finances? Though, of course, should my father-in-law find himself a little pressed for cash, I would consider it my duty and my pleasure to oblige him.'

A strangled groan erupted from the Duke's throat and the noble peer buried his face in his hands.

Matthew smiled. It was just as he had known it would be – his offer was simply too good to refuse.

'But not Anne,' said the Duke. 'She has two elder sisters who are unmarried. It would be more seemly . . .'

'Anne.'

'My daughter Jane was many fine qual . . .'

'*Anne.*'

The Duke gave way before the finality in Matthew's voice and the ruthless expression in his eyes. 'You might not like her,' he said lamely.

'I do not ask to *like* her. I wish to *marry* her.'

'She is a pretty girl,' the Duke said distractedly, wondering how he would break the news to his wife and family.

'I know. She has a great look of Isobel at the same age.'

And Matthew's eyes locked into the bulbous blue eyes of the Duke with a message that was as clear as day. The Duke understood – he realised that Matthew sought revenge, hated him for it and yet knew he was powerless to prevent it. By God, he thought, if only I didn't need the money so badly and if Lambourne and Nicholas were not such problems to me . . . then I could send him packing. But he knew this was only a dream and that his need for

Matthew was inescapable – so Matthew would marry Anne. Poor little Anne.

She had escaped from her sisters and was strolling alone in the kitchen garden, revelling in her own company and the signs of spring. Tender young green shoots were pushing through the moist earth, giving promise of a fruitful season, and the aromatic scent of herbs drifted on the slight breeze. Anne walked through the archway in the old wall and crossed the velvet lawns to the bubbling stream which had gurgled and laughed its way across the rolling acres of the Desborough estate for a thousand years or more. A few late daffodils and crocuses bloomed beneath the willows and combined with the clear fresh water and verdant green lawns to perfectly illustrate the English spring. Anne sighed as she surveyed the beauty around her. She loved the countryside, the trees and birds and flowers, and other years at this time she had been happy. This year, however, her moods were variable, at one moment ecstatic and the next melancholy. Anne was seventeen and in love for the very first time.

If only, thought Anne, she could know what his feelings were towards her. He had said nothing but the way he looked at her turned her stomach to jelly and surely he did not need to press so close while she sat at the piano. She had told no one of her infatuation, because she knew people would laugh and say that every girl fell in love with her music master. This was different, though – Paul was so sensitive; even the curve of his cheek was pure and aesthetic and their love was on an altogether higher plane than the mundane emotions of more worldly beings.

It was ironic, she thought, that the previous music master had been sent away because it was feared he was too fond of Jane. Anyone could see that Jane was madly in love with the schoolteacher in the village and he with her. The affair had no future, though. The Duke would never countenance such a match even if Jane or her teacher did pluck up courage to speak to him – which they would not.

Then the servant came to say that her father wished to see her. The summons being unusual, Anne searched her mind for any sins she might have committed. Her parents looked stern and her trepidation increased.

The Duke was not a man noted for subtlety or tact.

'I have received an offer for your hand in marriage,' he said bluntly.

Anne's heart lurched and she caught hold of a chair for support. Paul! So he did love her!

'The offer comes from Matthew Harcourt-Bright, Freddy's brother. Naturally you will accept.'

For a moment Anne stood in numb, stunned disbelief. The room reeled around her and the shock was like a kick in the stomach. But she did not question the statement; if her father said something, she knew it to be true. He was not looking at her but addressed his remarks over her head in the direction of the window. There was compassion in her mother's eyes but also an inflexibility about her mouth.

'Freddy's brother! He's the last man on earth I'll marry!'

'He is entirely suitable.'

'You mean that he's rich. So he did make a fortune on the diamond fields?'

'Yes, he is a wealthy man. But that is not all. He is, I assure you, the catch of the Season.'

'Why should the so-called "catch of the Season" want *me*?' Anne stared at her father with flushed cheeks and rebellious eyes.

The Duke continued to gaze out of the window. 'It is a long story, but I promise you that it is you he wants.'

'Not Jane? Not Elizabeth? They are older than me. Surely it would be better to marry off your elder daughters first!'

'Anne!' Her mother spoke for the first time. 'That is no way to address your father. Matthew wants you – not Jane, not Elizabeth. You are extremely fortunate.'

'Fortunate! To be fobbed off with fat Freddy's brother!' Anne's wail of despair contained all the agony of her broken dreams and expressed the emptiness of the wasted life which stretched before her.

'Matthew is not one bit like Freddy,' said her mother gently. 'You met him years ago. Don't you remember him?'

'Yes, I do. I remember that he was dull and serious and, most of all, I remember that he was in love with Isobel. A man who cared for Isobel is not likely to love me, or be loved *by* me. I will *not* marry him!'

'It is your duty to marry whoever I wish you to marry,' growled the Duke.

'Why? Is that how people like us justify our existence? We set an example to the lower classes by saying: "Oh yes, we have all these advantages, but look at the awful things we have to endure in the name of duty"? Well, I won't do it! When I marry, it will be for love.'

And she ran from the room.

The Duke swore under his breath and the Duchess tried to refrain from commenting that he had handled the interview badly.

'She ought to meet Matthew as soon as possible. He was always a most attractive young man. Perhaps he could persuade her.'

'He did not ask to see her. He has no intention of pleading his case or begging her to marry him,' said the Duke grimly. 'She is to be served up to him as the willing sacrifice.'

The Duchess hesitated unhappily. 'My dear, you are quite certain that this marriage is the only course open to us?'

'Quite sure.'

'Then I will speak to her again when she has had time to grow accustomed to the idea. I will explain how necessary the marriage is to the family, and to Lambourne and Nicholas in particular. Anne has always been very fond of Nicholas.'

Matthew returned to Highclere in time for a light luncheon. Ostentatiously he placed the jewel box on the table and Isobel glanced at it curiously.

'What a fascinating box! May we see inside or is it a secret?'

'Of course you may see.' He passed the box to her. 'Just a few stones from my diamond mines.'

Isobel lifted the lid and gasped audibly, then took out the necklace and let the shimmering fire ripple through her fingers. She pictured the necklace round the proud column of her alabaster neck and coveted it more than anything she had ever seen.

'Your diamond mines?' queried Freddy, in a passable imitation of his father-in-law.

Matthew gave a graphic account of his career in Kimberley and an optimistic estimate of the future revenues from the mines. With infinite pleasure he watched the reactions of his companions, Freddy chastened and envious while Isobel licked her lips with greed. Once Matthew had felt the urge to smash his fist into Freddy's face and hit him until he begged for mercy and confessed his sins. Now he had decided on a slower form of torture and was tightening the screw.

'I am going to Desborough,' said Freddy to Isobel after luncheon. 'Your father has a hunter for sale.'

Not any more, thought Matthew. The Duke no longer needs to sell his horse; he has sold a daughter instead. However, he said nothing and watched Freddy ride off to what should prove an enlightening encounter.

He turned to Isobel with his most seductive smile.

'It looks like rain and we are all alone. How should we wile away the afternoon?'

He reached out and stroked her cheek. Isobel caught hold of his hand and pressed it against her skin.

'Isn't this the moment we have been waiting for ever since you arrived and we saw each other for the first time?' she asked huskily.

'Not quite for the first time, Isobel. We did have a slight acquaintance before, or perhaps you have forgotten.'

'Of course I haven't forgotten, but then I was only a child. Now I am a woman, with a woman's desires and a woman's body which I know how to use.'

She swayed towards him and he caught her savagely in his arms, kissing her long and hard.

'Dismiss your maid,' he whispered against her lips. 'I will come to your room in ten minutes. First I must put away the necklace.'

'For whom is the necklace intended?'

He kissed her again, a series of short intense burning kisses. 'The lady of my choice,' he said, and looked at her with love, desire, passion and promise in his eyes.

Isobel hurried to her bedroom and undressed feverishly. She inspected her naked body in the looking-glass – Matthew must not find a flaw – and wrapped herself in a black role of sheer silk which clung to her curves. Then the door opened and he was there, closing the door behind him and leaning against it with arms folded across his chest.

His slow lazy glance took in everything in the room, lingered deliberately on the massive four-poster bed with its pale blue hangings, before coming to rest on her. His narrowed, half-hooded eyes sent such a shaft of sexual magnetism through her that Isobel began to tremble. She flung her arms round him and pressed herself against his body, trying to get closer, ever closer, to him. His hands moved over her, feeling her body through the thin silk, caressing her breasts, back and buttocks until the ache of desire inside her was almost unbearable. He pulled aside the robe and laid his hand on the inside of her thigh and she clung to him in an agony of anticipation.

He stepped back. 'Take off your robe,' he said, 'and turn round, slowly, in a full circle. I want to look at you.'

Proudly, provocatively, Isobel did as she was bid. The black silk tumbled to the floor, revealing the marble perfection of her white body. She raised her arms and, as she pivoted, loosened the shining coils of hair to cascade about her shoulders. When she faced him again, she stretched out her arms to lead him to the bed.

But his expression had changed. There was boredom in his eyes and a cynical curl to his mouth.

'Thank you for the offer, Isobel,' he said with a yawn, 'but I don't think I'll bother today. Somehow I can't seem to raise the necessary . . . enthusiasm.'

Humiliation, disappointment and frustration raged in her. Suddenly she felt foolish in her nakedness and grabbed the robe.

'How dare you!' she snarled. 'How dare you lead me on and cast me aside so lightly!'

'How indeed!' And he laughed. 'Why, Isobel, surely you know that *you* showed me how.'

'And the necklace, you were going to give me the necklace!'

'Certainly not. The necklace is for the lady of my choice, for my bride.' He paused significantly. 'For your sister. Anne.'

'*Anne*!' Isobel shrieked. 'You're going to marry Anne!' Jealousy shot through her as she thought of her little sister wearing that necklace and going to bed with this gorgeous, mocking man. She flew at him with raised fists but Matthew was already disappearing through the door.

'The marriage must be stopped!' Isobel stormed at Freddy after he had returned from Desborough with the news. 'He simply cannot marry that chit of a girl.'

'You wanted the necklace for yourself, didn't you!'

'Of course not.'

'Yes, you did, and I don't really blame you. A very pretty trinket, very pretty indeed. And I would not be averse to receiving the other fruits of the diamond mines. The thought occurs to me that while Matthew has no wife and no heir, I am his next of kin.'

Isobel ceased her restless pacing about the room and stared at her husband scornfully.

'And you are rather good at arranging family affairs to your satisfaction!'

Freddy's face grew pale and still. 'What do you mean by that remark?'

'Merely that the deaths of your uncle, father and cousin did prove to be awfully convenient. Remarkable, really, that you should have been the only survivor.'

Freddy crossed the room, seized her by the shoulders and shook her hard. 'Don't ever say that again! Don't even think it!'

'I've known for a long time,' said Isobel softly, 'that all your family were frightened of water and could not swim.'

'Who told you?'

'Matthew,' she lied, watching him through narrowed eyes.

'*Matthew*!' Freddy's voice cracked. Fear replaced the anger on his face and he leaned against the table for support, making a conscious effort to recover his poise. 'The idea is ridiculous. I don't want to hear it mentioned again.'

'You will not hear it mentioned by me, anyway, so long as I don't hear any more complaints about George.'

Freddy waved a hand wearily. 'George or Tom or Dick or Harry, it's all the same to me. And to you, too, I gather.'

'And remove your brother from this house immediately.'

'I can't do that – it would look extremely odd.' Freddy surveyed his wife sardonically. 'Have you two fallen out?'

'He made extremely unwelcome advances to me which, naturally, I spurned.'

Freddy gave a bark of sarcastic laughter. 'The other way round more likely! So Matthew managed to resist your charms, did he! He goes up in my estimation. Perhaps he is saving himself for the reluctant bride.'

Isobel pricked up her ears. '*Reluctant* bride? Doesn't Anne want to marry him?'

'Your father was loathe to discuss it in detail but I did gain the impression that matters were far from finalised.'

'That stupid child,' spat Isobel. 'Too romantic by half. She imagines herself in love with the music master and moons over him all day, while fondly imagining that no one has noticed.'

'Does she? Does she indeed?' Freddy digested the information thoughtfully.

'The marriage must be stopped,' Isobel repeated. 'I'll deal with Anne while you do something about Matthew. But no more drownings, Freddy. I won't stand for that.'

Isobel left the room and Freddy turned back to the table to pour himself a glass of wine. His hand was shaking and he spilled a pool of red burgundy on the cloth. Matthew! Why hadn't Matthew asked questions about Cowes? His silence on the subject was somehow more menacing and unnerving than any confrontation. Freddy stared at the crimson stain on the table, watched its widening blood-like rim, spreading, oozing, over the snowy cloth. With an oath, he raised a trembling hand and swept both glass and bottle splintering to the floor.

That evening he started to sleep badly, to wake in the night and find that further slumber eluded him, and to hear Isobel pacing restlessly in the room next door.

And in his own quarters Matthew smiled. He was savouring every step of the way, every turn of the screw, along the path towards the pinnacle of his revenge.

CHAPTER THIRTEEN

Isobel lost no time in visiting Desborough and suggesting that she should speak to Anne.

'After all, Mama,' she declared, 'no one is better placed than I to persuade Anne of the advantages of the match, and of the necessity of being sensible and doing one's duty.'

With her parents' blessing, Isobel rustled upstairs and entered her sister's room. Anne was standing by the window, her fingers beating a restless tattoo on the sill while wild plans for escape seethed in her head. She glared at Isobel.

'I suppose you've come to gloat and say "I told you so",' she snapped.

Isobel smiled and summoned all her subtlety and guile to her aid. 'You and I have never been the best of friends, Anne,' she said, sitting down and arranging her skirts with care, 'but I do assure you that on this occasion I came to offer you my profound sympathy.'

'I thought,' said Anne acidly, 'that Matthew Harcourt-Bright was supposed to be "the catch of the Season" and that I was being stupid in refusing him. Why should I need your sympathy?'

Isobel was taken aback by this sharp rejoinder. 'Oh, Matthew is good-looking and very rich but, well, you must remember that I know him much better than most people do and of course I know things about his family which . . .' Isobel floundered, obviously searching desperately for words. 'Oh dear,' she sighed, 'I didn't intend to say that. All I wanted, Anne, was to tell you that you must do your duty and marry Matthew, but that I do know how much you wanted to marry for love, and I feel so sorry that now you will never experience such happiness.'

'What do you know about Matthew and his family?' Anne demanded.

'I cannot tell you, much though I would like to warn you. Loyalty to my husband forbids it.'

'And why shouldn't I experience love?' The fact that it was Isobel who was voicing these opinions prompted Anne to take a contrary point of view. 'Matthew has asked to marry me. Why do you assume that he doesn't love me?'

Isobel rose and paced agitatedly up and down the room. Surreptitiously she watched her sister and did not fail to notice the gleam of suspicion which shone in Anne's eyes. When Isobel spoke again it was more in the manner Anne was accustomed to hear from her. 'You little fool! I've done my best to spare your feelings and to hint at the true state of affairs. Must I spell it out for you!'

'Yes, please.' Anne stood perfectly still and watched Isobel's face.

'Matthew loves *me*. He always has and he always will. After all these years he has still not recovered from the anguish he suffered when I married Freddy. He has asked for your hand because you look like me – not as pretty as me, of course, but fairly like – and you are the nearest substitute he could find for his true love.' Isobel could not realise how close her fantasy came to the truth, nor how subtly she had distorted that truth.

Anne was icy cold and yet for some strange reason perspiration beaded her brow. 'How do you know this?'

'Matthew told me, of course.' Isobel laughed. 'He has declared his passion for me constantly since he arrived at Highclere. And, while Freddy is out of the house, he has pressed his attentions upon me most ardently . . . *most* ardently . . .' Isobel allowed her voice to trail off significantly. 'I think I had best say no more,' she murmured. 'As an unmarried girl, you have no notion what takes place between a man and a woman in the privacy of the bedroom.'

Indeed, Anne was ignorant of the mysteries to which Isobel referred, but to her it was enough that Matthew had apparently rejoined the ranks of Isobel's much ridiculed beaux. Anne did not want to believe her sister, but somehow Isobel's words reverberated with an undoubted ring of truth.

'It makes no difference to me what motives prompted Mr Harcourt-Bright to ask for my hand,' Anne said proudly, turning back to the window. 'You and Mama and Papa can preach to me about duty from now until the end of time, but I shall not change my mind. I will *not* marry him.'

Isobel smiled inwardly and returned to her parents, to wring her hands and complain of Anne's obduracy.

Anne meanwhile was left feeling even more wretched than before. The one saving grace of her tragic situation, she had decided that morning, was to be loved by the 'catch of the Season'. Those circumstances contained an element of romance. But now even that consolation had been taken from her.

Yet there had been something odd about Isobel's behaviour. Why, wondered Anne, could she not shake off the nagging persistent belief that Isobel did not want her to marry Matthew?

During Isobel's absence at Desborough, Freddy buttonholed Matthew in the morning room at Highclere.

'I am delighted that you should choose one of Isobel's sisters for your wife,' Freddy said, with a clumsy attempt at suavity, 'but I must confess to being a trifle surprised that you should pick Anne.'

'And no doubt you will proceed to expound your reasons for that surprise.' Matthew remained standing, staring down sardonically at his brother from his superior height.

'Anne has been a cause for concern for some time,' Freddy confided. 'Of course, all the Desborough girls attract attention. At one time, in her extreme youth, even my dear Isobel was said to encourage her admirers more than was proper. Then there was the scandal of Jane and the former music master. But these slight aberrations are as nothing when compared with Anne's behaviour.'

Matthew's expression betrayed not a flicker of emotion. He had expected Freddy and Isobel to make some attempt to prevent the marriage and he was ready to ascribe this 'information' to just such a move. But, quite suddenly, Matthew realised that it could be true. With a jolt, he realised that he was linking his life to that of a girl with whom he was barely acquainted and about whom he knew nothing. She might be sinner or saint – she might be like Isobel or, God forbid, worse than Isobel.

'I think I should warn you,' Freddy continued in the same confidential manner, 'that it is rumoured that Anne is no longer *virgo intacta*.'

'Well,' drawled Matthew, 'I shall soon find out, shall I not!'

'You mean that you would marry soiled goods?'

'I strongly doubt whether the Lady Anne and her paramours – if any – would escape the eagle eye of her sainted father in order to commit such an indiscretion. But even if they did, nothing would deflect me from my purpose.'

'It's your decision, of course.' Freddy shrugged and tried to appear indifferent. 'But when you speak to her, ask her about the present music master. His name is Venables. I should be most interested to learn how Anne reacts. Now, how about some exercise this morning? I thought we might . . .'

'Thank you, no.' Matthew's voice cut in on Freddy with the decisiveness of cold steel. 'I shall not be hunting with you, Freddy, or walking. I shall certainly not be joining a shooting party of which you are a member – you were *such* a bad shot, were you not, and we wouldn't want any more accidents, would we? And I do assure you that a boating trip is the last thing I have in mind.' He paused. 'What I intend to do is marry Anne and have lots and lots of children – heirs, Freddy, who will inherit my vast fortune.'

Matthew stalked out of the room as Freddy collapsed on to a chair, raising a clammy hand to his forehead to wipe away the sweat. No matter what he tried to do, Matthew was always one step ahead of him. And, to make matters worse, his brain was refusing to function properly; he could not think of a way in which to dispose of Matthew – permanently. Matthew had become too formidable, almost invincible, and Freddy was frightened of him – frightened of his power and his quick brain; frightened of what he knew and the grudges he might bear. Shivering, Freddy cowered in his chair, terrified of what the future held, appalled by his growing, fumbling impotence and haunted by the ghosts of the past.

The Duchess had decided that the last course open to them was to appeal to Anne's sweet nature. Once again she was summoned to the library, but this time the Duchess did the talking while the Duke stood by with averted eyes.

'We have concluded we must be blunt with you, my dear,' the Duchess said quietly. 'In fact, your father and I have the unwelcome task of throwing ourselves on your mercy.'

Anne was startled and puzzled. With a frown of concern, she noticed that her father looked hunched and old. His shoulders were stooped and his expression, usually so haughty and proud, was humbled and unhappy.

'We are not *asking* you to marry Matthew,' the Duchess continued, 'but begging you. Your sacrifice – and I do believe, most truly, that sacrifice is too strong a word – would be the salvation of the entire family.'

Anne felt sick. 'The money, I suppose?' she said.

'Yes. You are the youngest in the family, Anne, and we have tried to shield you from our problems. The fact is, however, that Lambourne and Nicholas have placed us in desperate straits and in addition Nicholas is not at all well.'

'What's the matter with him?' Anne cried anxiously.

The Duchess patted her reassuringly on the shoulder, displaying more calmness than in fact she felt. Matthew had not explained the nature of Nicholas's malady, but Lambourne had been prevailed upon to do so.

'It's nothing to worry about; given time, he will make a complete recovery. The point is that Matthew has offered to pay all our debts. This will enable Lambourne to marry the Pendleton girl and at last he may settle down and provide an heir. In addition, Matthew will furnish money to improve the estate, which means we can also improve the living accommodation and livelihoods of the estate workers. And, perhaps most important to you, Matthew will ensure that Nicholas is cured, his debts paid and that he will be kept occupied.'

Anne closed her eyes. She had come to this interview full of the utmost determination to fight to the last breath for the right to choose her husband. Now that battle would never take place. How could she set her personal happiness above the united welfare of the whole family? If this was what was meant by duty, then she would be dutiful – not out of meekness but out of love, and in particular for love of Nicholas. As Anne sat and fought back the tears, she remembered one member of the family who had not been mentioned specifically. And Anne set her teeth and determined that one of her family should marry for love, even if that person was not herself.

'You leave me no choice, Mama.'

The Duchess uttered a sob of relief and thankfulness. 'Then you agree to marry Matthew?'

Anne stared at her mother and then at the silent figure of her father, so crumpled and deflated and ashamed. She was aware of feeling much older than when she had entered the room; aware that these once formidable parents had forfeited her full respect.

'I agree,' Anne said, and her chin tilted proudly. 'But I want to tell him so myself. Alone.'

As Matthew arrived at Desborough for his meeting with Anne it chanced that Venables, the music master, was just leaving. Matthew watched him don his hat and walk away up the drive towards the road which led to the village. Contemptuously he took in the detail of the young man's graceful walk and dark, romantic looks. He knew the type – flirtation was part of Venables's stock-in-trade, as much a part of his repertoire as the scales and songs. It was important that the young ladies should like him because it was necessary that he kept his job. If Anne was involved with him, then she was a fool.

Anne was waiting for him in the library. She stood with her back to the door and did not turn round when he entered.

'Good morning,' said Matthew courteously.

His voice was beautiful. Somehow she had not expected this, and it caught her slightly off-guard. It was a deep voice, vibrant yet intensely masculine, a voice which should read poetry aloud and murmur endearments into one's ear. Except, she reminded herself that *this* voice murmured endearments into Isobel's ear! Anne stiffened and slowly turned round.

They stared at each other.

Oh yes, but he was handsome. Anne hated him but her heart fluttered a little as, in spite of herself, she responded to his attraction. Those blue eyes in that lean tanned face seemed to pierce her defences. He stood so still, yet the air in the room seemed to pulse with life and vitality, drawing her towards him. And yes, he was accustomed to having his way with women. Well, he would not gain ascendancy over her so easily!

Matthew saw an enchanting face, with angular aristocratic

bones and huge violet eyes, framed by smooth, shining silver-gilt hair. She was small, barely reaching to his shoulder, but her body was exquisitely curved. She was totally alluring while remaining absolutely a lady, an ice-cold exterior with a smouldering fire within.

His mouth relaxed appreciatively, 'Lady Anne, you are even more beautiful than I imagined,' he murmured softly. 'More beautiful than your sisters. More beautiful than any . . .'

'More beautiful than Isobel?' Anne said scornfully.

'Why yes,' and Matthew, puzzled, 'but I was going to say . . .'

'Are you pleased with your purchase, Mr Harcourt-Bright?' she interrupted, twirling in a mocking pirouette. 'Shouldn't you be inspecting my teeth or something? Isn't that what people do when they buy a horse?'

Matthew had started to walk towards her, to kiss her hand. Now he halted abruptly and a wary expression settled on his face. 'What do you mean by that remark?' he demanded. 'Are you telling me that you are a spirited filly which needs breaking in?'

'What I am telling you,' flashed Anne, 'is that I am not horseflesh to be bought or sold. I have agreed to marry you for the sake of my family, not of my own free will. Your wealth may have influenced my father, sir, but it does not impress me!'

Matthew's face hardened and the sparkle in his blue eyes turned to ice. 'Is that so!'

'Yes. I would like you to know that you are the last man on earth I would marry, given any freedom of choice.'

'But,' said Matthew, his voice dangerously quiet, 'you know nothing about me.'

'Oh, but I do. I remember you, Mr Harcourt-Bright . . .'

'Bright,' interrupted Matthew. 'Matthew Bright. You had best get used to it.'

'Oh.' Anne was momentarily disconcerted, but not for long. 'I remember that Christmas when you were in love with Isobel. How ridiculous you were! How we all laughed at you!'

'Did you indeed!' His features were like granite and he seemed to control himself with difficulty. 'I believe, however, that you do not laugh at the music master. Mr Venables arouses something more than amusement in your breast, Lady Anne?'

'How do you know about that?' Anne gasped. She looked at him and flinched before his steely gaze. 'Mr Venables,' she said, recovering her composure, 'has more breeding in his little finger than you have in your whole body, Mr Bright, even though he has no money.' Anne was aware that this was not true, but also knew instinctively that it would wound him.

In a single stride Matthew reached her and his hands grasped her shoulders roughly. 'How much is Venables to you? How close did he come? This close?' and Matthew pulled her against his chest and bent his head until his lips were only inches from hers.

Anne's heart somersaulted as, against her will, the magnetism of his body exercised its magic over her. Inexplicably she wanted to relax in his arms and to feel his mouth, hard and demanding, on hers. But reason reasserted itself and she jerked away.

'Closer,' she said defiantly. 'Much closer.' And then she remembered what Isobel had said. 'Although,' and here Anne copied Isobel's tone and Isobel's sly, seductive look, 'I am supposed to have no notion of what takes place between a man and a woman in the privacy of the bedroom.'

With an exclamation, Matthew dropped his hands and stepped backwards. His expression was so fierce and so disgusted that Anne was at first afraid and then full of hope.

'After what I have said, perhaps you don't want to marry me any more?' she suggested.

'I will marry you, Anne, for many reasons,' he replied grimly, 'not least to teach you some manners, and how a lady should behave. Will the beginning of June suit you?'

'Is it not a little soon?'

'I have to return to Kimberley as soon as possible.'

'Kimberley!' This was an aspect of the marriage which had not occurred to Anne; she had not realised she would have to travel so far away from home. 'I don't think I will go with you immediately. I will wait until you have acquired a house for us.'

Matthew smiled. His eyes flicked round the luxurious room and then glanced out of the window at the beautiful English gardens, and he recalled the ugly squat house in the dust of the Karoo. 'I have already acquired a house.'

'But we will need servants – lots of servants,' said Anne, desperately seeking a reprieve.

'There is no shortage of labour in Kimberley.' And again Matthew smiled an almost satanic smile.

'Oh. Well, in that case there is nothing else to discuss.' Imperiously Anne rang the bell and at this prearranged signal the Duke and Duchess entered.

'The wedding will take place on June sixth,' Matthew informed them. 'I will meet all the expenses and,' and here Matthew's eyes gleamed strangely, 'I wish to arrange the reception.'

'As you wish.' How very odd, thought the Duchess. Matthew really could be remarkably unconventional at times. Why on earth would he want to bother about the reception?

'I will call on you in London,' said Matthew but as he took his leave Anne spoke again.

'I have agreed to marry Matthew, Papa, but there is one condition.'

Matthew and the Duke and Duchess stared at her in silence. Anne experienced a qualm of trepidation at her audacity but was determined to take advantage of this unique opportunity, her one real moment of power.

'I will only marry Matthew if you allow Jane to marry Mr Bruce.'

'Bruce! That piffling schoolmaster!'

'Jane loves him and he need not be a village schoolmaster all his life. You could use your influence to help him to a more important position. And,' here Anne shot Matthew a sarcastic look, 'use some of Mr Bright's money to pay Jane a reasonable allowance.'

'What will people say?' groaned the Duke.

'We *could* hold a quiet wedding here later in the year,' suggested the Duchess. 'No one will take much notice after the fuss over Anne.'

'Very well,' agreed the Duke reluctantly.

Anne's smile of happiness transfigured her face, while Matthew stared at her thoughtfully. This little bride was showing more spirit than he had bargained for.

CHAPTER FOURTEEN

The Desboroughs moved to London within the week and for Anne life became a hectic round of dress fittings, making and receiving calls, and endless conferences on hairstyles, guest lists and menus. Matthew called at the house regularly, usually with her brother Nicholas who was recovering from his mysterious illness. However, he rarely sought Anne's company. She told herself that she was glad not to have to endure the tedium and unpleasantness of his presence, but in fact she was piqued by his indifference. Occasionally – and just out of curiosity, of course – she hid on the balcony above the ballroom and watched his preparations for the wedding reception.

He had a positive fixation about a fountain he was installing. The ballroom at the Desborough town house was vast and Matthew placed the fountain against the far wall, directly opposite the main table where its shimmering waterfalls would be seen by the maximum number of guests. Anne reflected that Matthew seemed to do everything on a grand scale; the fountain was huge, with a deep carved stone trough and high jets of water. The project fascinated him, he spent hours supervising the work and when it was completed he would turn it on and sit watching the cascades, a strange smile playing round his lips.

The amount of time he devoted to the reception, and to the fountain in particular, was astonishing. The event seemed to be imbued with an almost mystical significance, as though it were the culmination of a lifetime's ambition. Yet, Anne thought, his marriage to her could not be the reason for his intensity of feeling. The only time she had noticed any warmth on his face was when he smiled at Nicholas and Anne wondered if he smiled at Isobel like that.

A few days after their arrival in London, Matthew had delivered the engagement ring; he organised a peculiarly official ceremony and placed it on her finger in the presence of the entire family. There was a sharp intake of breath, followed by a stunned silence, as everyone stared at the ring. Anne moved her hand so that the massive central stone caught the light and the incomparable fire of the crystal-clear white diamond flashed the rainbow colours of the spectrum.

Out of the corner of her eye, Anne noticed Isobel's face contort briefly in a sudden spasm of jealousy. So her belief that Isobel did not want her to marry Matthew was correct. In which case, Anne decided, it would be best to put on a public display of affianced bliss. She turned to Matthew with her most charming smile, but he was not looking at her – he was covertly watching the reactions of the other people in the room.

He watched the Duke of Desborough, who shifted from foot to foot and avoided Matthew's eyes, and knew that His Grace was as uncomfortable and humiliated now as ever Matthew had been at Desborough in his youth.

He had also seen and relished Isobel's jealousy, but most of all Matthew watched Freddy. His brother was tense and nervous, pale and tired, jumping at shadows as if he expected some ghastly event or ghostly visitation. Matthew smiled. Freddy had not long to wait. The wedding day would also be a day of retribution.

At last the day came. Anne's trunks were packed with a trousseau fit for a princess; day dresses and evening dresses, ball gowns and riding habits, travelling clothes, shoes and slippers, hats and bonnets, underwear – all had been ordered in profusion. Her new maid, Henriette, came to dress her for the wedding – Henriette whom she barely knew, but who would be the only person from home to accompany her to the diamond fields. In white stockings and a pair of the latest combinations – a combined chemise and drawers which preserved the smooth line of her close-fitting dress – Anne stood obediently as the white silk gown was fastened about her.

Anne had not seen the necklace or the other jewellery but, as ordained by Matthew, the gown had been designed to show off the diamonds. The bodice was very simple but, instead of the customary high neck of a bridal gown, the material was cut wide at the shoulders and deep at the breast, to display the necklace to full advantage. The front of the skirt was plain, the only decoration being a rich flounce of antique lace. At the back, however, the silk was draped over a bustle and cascaded into a flowing train.

As Henriette began to coil the shining fair hair into a high smooth chignon, she glanced at the clock. The coiffure could not be finished or the veil fixed in place until the tiara arrived. Then came a knock at the door and Nicholas hurried in.

'Matt sent me over with the baubles. I say, Anne, you do look topping.'

'Thank you, Nickly.' She smiled in real gratitude for his presence and air of normality. She was feeling numb and detached from everything that was happening, as though she were outside her own body, watching from somewhere up on the ceiling. 'I wish you were coming to Kimberley with me,' she said forlornly.

'Matt will look after you,' her brother comforted, 'and I shall visit. Come on, open the box.'

Dazed, she lifted the fabulous gems from the casket. The necklace first while Nicholas, crowing with delight at his favourite sister's amazement, fastened the clasp around her slender neck. The bracelet Anne managed for herself and a wide-eyed Henriette took the dazzling tiara and settled it on the gleaming hair, anchoring the white cloud of the veil and pulling down the gauze to cover Anne's face. Veiled in mystery, the face of the beautiful bride and the secret of her gems would not be fully revealed until after the service.

She drove with her father through the early summer sunshine to the ancient church of St Margaret's and walked up the aisle to where Matthew waited, her long train whispering behind her. Her dreamlike state persisted. The pageantry of the service eddied around her in hazy images of colour, sound and movement; she made her responses mechanically and afterwards could remember nothing.

After signing the register, Matthew lifted the veil and bestowed a chaste kiss on her cheek. Then he gazed at his new wife for a long time.

'Wonderful!' he said.

But Anne only stared at him coldly. She knew that he referred to the jewels.

Impatiently Matthew seized Anne's arm and led her to the head of the aisle where, with a superb sense of theatre, he paused. The congregation gasped. It was not only Anne's beauty in the deceptive simplicity of her white gown and the dazzling fire of the fabulous gems which attracted their attention. Beside her was the splendid figure of Matthew, resplendent in his immaculate clothes, the ornate diamond buttons on his coat and massive diamond tie-pin drawing incredulous looks. On anyone else such ornaments might have appeared vulgar, but not on him. There was something about Matthew which was larger than life; he seemed taller and broader than other men, the golden mane of his hair thicker and more shining, the glance of his blue eyes more piercing. As he paused momentarily on the steps, the power and magnetism of the man seemed to pulse through the church. And when he saw their faces, particularly the frozen cold fury of Isobel and Freddy, he smiled. This was it, the moment he had waited for, his victory parade.

Matthew pulled Anne forward again and the movement called forth a fresh shimmer and sparkle from the gems which adorned them both. It was then that Matthew was given his nickname: Diamond Bright, they called him, and Diamond Bright he remained until he died.

To Anne the reception was as much a blur as the ceremony. She knew that it was a triumph, that she was admired and envied beyond her wildest dreams, yet she could feel nothing. What a waste of what should have been her finest hour!

For Matthew this was the supreme moment, the culmination of months of planning and years of hate. He raised his hand and signalled to the group of young men whom he had hired and who now hovered on the fringe of the festivities. They moved closer, until they were immediately behind Freddy's chair.

'How splendid the fountain looks,' declared Matthew in a loud voice. 'Have you seen it, Freddy? Go and look more closely.'

'No, I can see it well enough from here.'

'Go closer, Freddy,' said Matthew in a light voice, but with undertones of steel, 'or someone may think you are afraid of the water.'

The moment was masked by the young men who, apparently already drunk and waving bottles of champagne, bundled Freddy across the room to the fountain. Amid loud cheers from the assembled guests, who enjoyed a bit of horseplay with their entertainment, Freddy was tipped head first into the fountain. With shrieks of mirth the young men pushed him back under the water each time he surfaced, while Freddy thrashed furiously in the water and made ghastly gurgling sounds each time he was able to drawn breath.

Matthew clenched his hands, while in his mind it was he who thrust Freddy beneath the water. Then he rose and strolled over to the fountain, laughing genially at the joke on his brother.

'Enough!' he said.

They fished Freddy out and he lay gasping on the floor. He started to scream and he screamed until Matthew signalled for him to be carried out.

'I'm afraid our young friends rather overdid it,' he apologised, with apparent remorse. 'It's not at all like Freddy to take a ducking so badly.'

Around him the chatter of the guests was rising again and Matthew slipped out to the adjoining room where a wet and shaking Freddy was lying on a sofa wrapped in blankets.

'Murder,' Matthew said, 'is so crude, Freddy! There are more subtle ways of achieving one's ends.'

Convulsed by terror, Freddy stared at him. Then, in his mind, the water closed over his head again and he flailed with his arms to fend it off, and screamed and screamed.

Matthew returned to his guests, feeling strangely lightened and cleansed as if a burden had been lifted from his shoulders and some devil laid to rest. He had settled his old score and avenged the murders of his family – but even Matthew could not know the extent of the damage he had done.

In her smart travelling dress of violet silk and matching velvet hat with sweeping ostrich feathers, Anne took a tearful farewell of friends and family. Two of the Desborough carriages had been placed at their disposal and Henriette and their luggage waited in the second equipage. The bulk of their trunks and cases had been forwarded separately to Southampton for loading aboard the steamer. While Anne was saying her goodbyes, Matthew sought out Reynolds.

'I want my brother watched. And that wife of his. If possible, have your man appointed to the staff of Highclere, preferably inside the house. The way Freddy and Isobel treat their servants, staff are always wanted there.'

Then Matthew said goodbye to his mother and sister, but it was Nicholas whom he embraced most warmly.

'Damn it, Matt,' said his friend ruefully, 'do you have to go away? Haven't you made enough momey? Couldn't you stay in London and manage the business from here?'

'One glorious day I will be able to do that, but not just yet. There is still a lot to do on the diamond fields. And no, I haven't yet made enough money. Long ago I realised that money buys power and beauty, but in fact it buys something else as well – freedom. Freedom to do what you want *when* you want.'

'I see. Or rather, I don't see. What sort of freedom is it that forces you back to Kimberley when you would prefer to stay here? You are money's slave, not its master.'

But Matthew only laughed and clapped him on the shoulder. 'Now, behave yourself while I'm gone and remember that Reynolds is your friend. Go to him if you need anything.'

They were alone, sitting stiffly side by side as the carriage jolted its way through the London streets. A kaleidoscope of memories and impressions danced in Anne's weary mind as she stole a glance at Matthew's impassive profile. Who was he, this man she had married? What was he thinking and what was he feeling? She looked out of the window for a while and then risked another peep at her husband. His eyes were closed and he seemed to be asleep. After that, Anne refused to look at him again, in case he might catch her doing so and interpret it as weakness. She folded her hands in her lap and gave herself up to her thoughts.

Since the engagement she had forced herself to take one step at a time and had not allowed herself to gaze into the deep, dark abyss of the future. Now the wedding and the painful farewells were over and she was faced with the fearful reality of the long sea voyage and overland trek to the diamond fields. But before that journey, there was another obstacle to be overcome. Tonight, presumably, she would have to share a bedroom with Matthew. Inside her elegant gloves, Anne's knuckles whitened. Anything, she thought, would be better than this ignorance of what he was going to do to her.

Rooms had been reserved at an inn and at bedtime an expressionless Henriette helped Anne into the luxurious white silk nightgown and brushed her hair. Anne climbed into bed and waited, with wildly beating heart, for her bridegroom.

She had felt sure that whatever happened, whatever he did to her, it would be done in the dark. Such a thought did not apparently cross Matthew's mind, however. He strode into the room, stared at her in the bed, grunted and immediately began stripping off his clothes. She tried not to watch, but his actions seemed to have a fatal fascination for her. Wearing only his trousers, he washed his face in the bowl of water on the table while Anne watched the rippling muscles in his bare back still tanned by the African sun.

She was terrified, but refused to give him the satisfaction of seeing she was afraid. All the same, she went rigid and clenched her hands tightly under the sheets as, casually, he tore off his trousers and walked naked towards her. Steadfastly she kept her huge violet eyes fixed on his face as he sat down on the edge of the bed and cupped her face in his hand.

'So,' he said, 'the moment you have been dreading has arrived.'

'I am not dreading anything,' she replied defiantly.

Matthew's eyebrows rose. 'Really? Ah, but of course, Mr Venables initiated you into the mysteries of the bedroom, did he not!'

His smile mocked her and Anne was sure he did not believe it. 'Yes,' she lied desperately.

'And did your music master make love to you like this?' He bent his head and kissed her hard on the lips, probing passionately with his tongue while his fingers felt for the laces at her gown.

'The light!' she gasped when his mouth left hers. 'Turn out the light!'

'No,' he said, 'I want to see you. As you are so fond of pointing out, I have paid a lot of money for you.'

'While the only thing you are fond of is flaunting your beastly money in everyone's face!'

Had she not been so sure that he despised her, Anne could almost have believed that he looked at her with dawning respect in his eyes. But angrily she turned her head away and the next thing she knew he was pulling the nightgown over her head. He ran his bronzed hands slowly but firmly over the white smoothness of her body and in panic Anne struggled to free herself. He let go and she lay still, with her face averted.

'Anne,' – and to her surprise his voice was gentle – 'I will not take you by force, but it is something you must face in the end. You want children, don't you? And, who knows, my lovemaking may not be so terrible as you imagine.'

He took her silence as acquiescence and kissed her again. 'Relax,' he ordered. 'There will be less pain for you and more pleasure for us both if you can relax.' He eased the tension out of her terrified body, running his fingers down her slender back, caressing her breasts and teasing the nipples with his tongue. Then he moved his hands along her narrow hips and slim legs, and held them tightly against the hardness of his own body.

And Anne began to feel sensations such as she had never known or dreamed of and she wrapped her arms round his neck and returned his kisses. Matthew felt the moistness come between her legs and judged the time to be right. As he thrust into her, she cried out with pain and shock and Matthew knew there could be no pleasure for her this first time. He climaxed quickly and withdrew, leaving Anne quivering and unfulfilled but not knowing why she was left wanting.

He reached for her again. 'Hold me,' he commanded. 'Here!' And he guided her hands to his penis, which began to grow under her touch and she stared at it in such wonderment that Matthew laughed. He entered her again and this time made love to her easily and slowly and then with increasing violence as if timing every movement purely for her pleasure and deliberately creating the crescendo within her like a master musician on a treasured violin.

Afterwards, the rapture dead but not forgotten, Anne lay awake in the darkness while Matthew slept. She had felt instinctively that she wanted to be held in his arms after the storm had broken around her, that she craved tenderness and words of love. But he had said nothing. He had been gentle with her, but he did not love her.

Well, Anne reminded herself fiercely, she did not love him! She hated him. Perversely, the fact that his lovemaking had been wonderful and that she had responded to it only made her hate him more. He had broken through the defences of her body, but he would not dominate her in any other way.

They arrived in Kimberley at the beginning of August and Matthew was in high spirits. It gave him intense pleasure to compare his present circumstances with his first arrival at the Cape. Then it had been a room at an hotel and a long hard slog to the diamond fields. Now, with money in his pocket and a Duke's daughter for his wife, he stayed at Government House as the guest of the Governor of the Cape and purchased his own carriage and horses to transport him from the railhead to Kimberley.

Court was waiting for them at the house and opened the carriage door to help Anne alight. She was wearing the violet dress and hat of her wedding day and Court's first impression was that they exactly matched her eyes.

Anne was in a state of shock. She had been charmed by the grace of Cape Town and awed by the vastness of the southern African landscape. From afar, Kimberley had sparkled and shimmered in the sun and Anne received an image of a magical city built of diamonds, a fairy-tale place of glass and gems. She was devastated when the carriage entered the shabby shanty town and she discovered that the sparkle was only the reflection of the sun on a myriad of corrugated iron roofs. The noise of the mining-gear, the clamour of the people and animals in the narrow streets, the half-naked natives, filled her with horror. Dazedly she alighted from the carriage and was enormously relieved to be greeted by this tall man with the gentle smile and kind eyes.

'Here we are, Anne. Home!' Matthew gestured to the house and, with narrowed eyes, flashed her a wicked smile.

She stared at the place in stunned disbelief. By nature of her background and upbringing, Anne's idea of home was a mansion such as Desborough or Highclere, set in a softly undulating landscape of trees and lawns and streams. Before her she saw an ugly red-brick shack, in which she would not have housed the most humble retainer. There was no garden, not a blade of grass or a shrub or tree, just bare rust-coloured earth.

Anne was seventeen and never had England, Desborough and her family seemed so far away. Despair and loneliness threatened to engulf her but she fought them off, refusing to let Matthew see her dismay. She tilted her chin resolutely.

'Just exactly the kind of taste I expected you to display, Matthew. Where are the servants?'

Matthew looked inquiringly at Court who indicated two natives standing sheepishly by the door. 'A cook and a houseboy,' said Court.

Anne swallowed. She had a sudden vision of the dignified butler at Desborough, of the regiment of footmen, cooks, kitchen-maids, scullery-maids and upstairs maids, all working to keep the establishment in order.

'I hope they will be satisfactory,' said Court anxiously, realising something of what she was feeling. 'I sent them to the hotel for a training course.'

Anne laid a reassuring hand on his arm. He had obviously tried so hard to please her. 'Thank you,' she said softly. 'I do hope you will dine with us, Mr Court, and that you will consider this as your home.'

Matthew was involved in his reunion with Sam, revelling in the renewal of their mutual adoration, and for him the brief exchange passed unheeded. But from that moment John Court was Anne's slave.

Part Two

ENGLAND AND SOUTHERN AFRICA 1883–1894

CHAPTER ONE

Six years later, in the Cape spring of 1883, the Bright house looked very different. The stark outline of its brick walls had been softened by shrubs and plants and, with assiduous care and watering, the trees which Anne had planted would soon cast a welcome shade. Other magnates followed Matthew's example and moved out of the cramped ramshackle town into well-built houses adorned with turrets and pillars, balustrades and wide verandahs. Yet even this select neighbourhood was pervaded with that air of impermanence which was as much a part of Kimberley as the 'diamondiferous blue'.

Griqualand West had been annexed to the Cape Colony and, by and large, the tumultuous events in neighbouring states left Kimberley untouched. The Zulu Rebellion of 1879 and the Anglo-Boer War of 1880–1881 caused barely a ripple in the diamond stream. Kimberley was strictly commercial – except for its most prominent citizen, Cecil Rhodes, who viewed diamonds as a means to an end. Like Matthew, Rhodes recognised that wealth bestowed power. Unlike Matthew, he was possessed by an idealistic dream of nationalism and he intended that his money and its power should be used to extend and glorify the British Empire.

Several other men were also emerging as leaders of the industry. Charles Rudd had been Rhodes's partner at De Beers from the start and they had been joined by the astute and refined Alfred Beit. Barney Barnato, a flamboyant Cockney from the slums of Whitechapel, was in competition with pith-helmeted J. B. Robinson for supremacy at the Kimberley Mine. The leading actors in the diamond drama were assembled and vying for the starring role.

Matthew was playing his cards very close to his chest. In 1880 Rhodes had formed the De Beers Mining Company which combined the holdings of the Rhodes–Rudd partnership with other syndicates; he continued to make overtures to Matthew to merge his holdings in the company and the latter was inclined to agree but could afford to hold out for the best possible terms. Like Robinson and Barnato, his claims in the Kimberley Mine had been affected by landslides but he had sufficient capital to carry on. He was confident that he could ride out the current recession and come out of it stronger than before. As in previous crisis periods, Matthew knew that less fortunate diggers would be forced to sell, and sell cheaply. There were some small claim-holders left, clinging on stubbornly like old Willem Jacobs and his adopted son, Daniel Steyn, and Matthew intended to swallow them up in his syndicate before merging with Rhodes. The more claims he possessed, the greater the influence he could wield in the company. Matthew did not object to playing second fiddle to Rhodes, but he was damned if he would be subordinate to anyone else.

Matthew lunched with Court at the Kimberley Club, where one could watch one's rivals and gauge the mood of the industry. One could, if one wished, manipulate that mood and send rumour flying by one's demeanour or even choice of companion. It was an atmosphere in which Matthew thrived but which left Court uncomfortable and isolated.

They had spent the morning supervising the daily 'wash-up'. The blue ground, or 'kimberlite', was taken to the company's sorting grounds, spread out, wetted periodically and left to disintegrate. African labourers hastened the process by breaking up the largest lumps with picks and each day some of the crumbled soil was treated by special washing machinery. Matthew and Court had reliable management but occasionally they liked to appear at the wash-ups, particularly at times like the present when there was so much unrest.

'Though God knows why we bother,' said Court, 'with diamonds the price they are.'

'The recession cannot last much longer. Rhodes is right when he says that every man who becomes engaged wants a diamond for his bride. How many stones he will buy depends on the market – if diamonds are expensive, he will buy few; if they are cheap he will buy more. However, the amount of money he will spend remains the same. Rhodes estimates annual demand at four million pounds.'

'Then he is not only advocating amalgamation of the mines but regulation of output as well.'

'The two are inseparable, because the value of a diamond depends upon its scarcity. Ten years ago an expert said that diamonds require the most delicate manipulation; they need a hand to hold them back or loose them as the occasion asks. What I intend, John, is that it shall be my hand on the tiller.'

'Right now the work-force's hand is on the tiller,' Court reminded him. 'The white overseers are striking again because they will not submit to the searchers. "Who will search the searchers?", they demand, and I can see their point of view.'

'We all know that the Diamond Trade Act of 1882 left some loop-holes in its measures to combat IDB,' Matthew retorted. 'Even so, it is a piece of the most stringent legislation ever passed in British territory, because basically an accused is guilty unless proved innocent.'

'IDB is the curse of our industry, I agree, but even I sometimes feel that police methods for trapping suspects and the searching of employees goes too far. As for the compounds, well, you will never convince me of the necessity for keeping African workers locked up behind a barbed-wire fence for the duration of their six-month contract.'

'It *is* necessary,' Matthew insisted. 'And what's more, those Africans are better housed and better fed than formerly, and they will come out of there considerably healthier than when they went in.'

'Your paternalism disguises the fact that your primary aim is to stop IDB, not improve the lot of the worker. However, do you think our men will strike against the search laws?'

'I believe our men are loyal,' said Matthew thoughtfully, 'and if the overseers stay away from work – and I often wish Connor and Brown would do just that, they're up to their necks in IDB – we have enough junior partners with vested interests to enable us to carry on. Nothing – and I mean nothing – must halt production.'

'I doubt that Nicholas would agree with you. Sales in London have been low.'

'Nevertheless, we're doing better than anyone else.' Matthew's tone was sharp. He was sensitive to charges of nepotism in putting Nicholas in charge of Bright Diamonds in Hatton Garden. 'And I still maintain we should open an office in New York. "Court Diamonds, New York". Doesn't that sound good to you?'

'Sure. But when the time comes, I want to run that operation myself, and I'm not yet ready to leave Kimberley.'

'Why not? Don't misunderstand me, I'd hate to lose you, we've been together a long time. But an American business is important to our future. Look how successful you were with the Tiffany diamond.'

There was a pause as the two men remembered the yellow-gold stone which they had found in the Kimberley mine: the largest golden diamond in the world which Court had sold to Charles Tiffany at the famous New York store.

'One day,' said Court, 'but not yet.' He could hardly tell Matthew that he could not find the will-power to leave Anne.

'I see. You want to stay here to guard your interests,' Matthew teased. 'You don't trust me to keep your bank balance growing, although you must have the healthiest account in Kimberley. Apart from your trip to America in '79, you don't spend anything.'

'I've nothing and nobody to spend money on.' Court smiled, but the pain twisted deep inside him. Apart from many inconspicuous acts of kindness, he might as well have been on a desert island with a chest full of gold for all the use his wealth was to him. To enjoy his money he needed a family and a home in his own country. The irony was that he seemed destined to fall for Matthew's women and to continue to amass these arid riches.

Right now the hurt was greater than before: Anne was pregnant at last.

Anne had almost begun to give up hope of ever having a baby. More than anything in the world she wanted a child and her failure to conceive had threatened to darken even her brave spirit. She consulted doctors: it was the climate, she was told; her health was poor; there was an erratic history of fertility in her family. Anne was left with a stabbing jealousy of Isobel who had meanwhile borne another son and a deep sympathy for Jane who was also childless.

During these six hard and lonely years Anne had furnished the house, tamed the garden and trained the half-dozen servants. To Matthew, and to Court who lived with them, the house was a home but Anne would never find peace here.

She loathed Kimberley. She hated the dust which crept into every corner and through every crack, the heat which sapped her energy, the harsh dry winds which weathered her hair and skin, and the flies which swarmed in clouds everywhere she walked. She detested the ugly town and had little respect for the majority of its cosmopolitan, brash population, most of whom were intent only on making as much money as possible in the shortest possible time.

However, no one knew of her unhappiness. Like Matthew, Anne was proud and masked her true feelings. And she strove constantly to take a positive approach and to make the best of things.

In the matter of the servants, Henriette had proved helpful and supportive. The maid had a distant relative who was an accomplished chef and she had lured Pierre from France to the diamond fields with promises of great wealth, and promptly married him. Anne was grateful on two counts – she gained an excellent chef and she retained the services of Henriette. Kimberley was no more stimulating to a refined lady's maid than it was to the refined lady herself.

The garden proved a genuine source of pleasure. Anne planted flowers which reminded her of home – roses, daffodils, marigolds, dahlias and carnations – but she also became fascinated by South African varieties which she brought up from the Cape and Natal. Under her careful supervision and constant watering, the flowers flourished – aloes or 'red-hot pokers'; yellow and white arum lilies; agapanthus, sometimes called the African lily, whose flowers reminded her of bluebells; strelitzia, the exotic crane flower with its bird-like blue and yellow blooms; delicate, creamy-white chincherinchees; multi-coloured gladioli; and, Anne's special favourite, huge banks of massive-headed proteas.

Conscious of her position in the community, Anne undertook

various charitable duties but ill-health restricted her activities. The climate, with its hot humid days followed by frosty nights, drained her strength. Although she avoided the epidemics of typhoid and pneumonia, she was laid low by a fever which wasted her slender frame and she remained thin and delicate.

Life was not all gloom, of course. There were concerts and soirées to attend, as well as performances by the Kimberley Dramatic Society. However, Anne's life was pervaded with an overwhelming sense of loneliness. None of the ladies in town matched her social status and this set her apart. Almost as much as she longed for a child, Anne longed for a friend. As it was, the nearest thing she had to a real friend was John Court.

Anne's lips curved in an ironic smile when she looked back over the barren years. It would have been more logical for her to have filled the nursery by now because the bedroom was the only place – and making love the only time – she had any real communication with Matthew. Outside the bedroom they were rarely alone. Court, of course, was nearly always present at meals and sometimes guests were entertained. Frequently Matthew was out, so Anne spent many evenings alone or with Court for company. She often felt almost as if John Court was her husband and Matthew her lover.

Anne never asked Matthew where he went. If she asked, he might think she cared and she would not wish to give him such a false impression! She assumed that much of his time was taken up with his precious diamonds and that the rest was spent with his mistress – or mistresses, she snorted to herself, since he probably had more than one.

As she strolled in the garden one afternoon with Sam, Anne's thoughts were of the child, due to be born four months from now, and of the difference it would make to her life. And because of the baby, she must get Matthew on his own tonight and speak to him about something important.

A hoopoe darted across the garden and Anne paused to watch the flash of its exotic red feathers and to push away the churlish wish that she could exchange its brilliance for the sombre plumage of an English blackbird. Then she caught sight of a movement by the fence. It was him – that boy – again.

She had seen the boy at odd times, hanging about the house, ever since she came to Kimberley. He would be, she judged, about seventeen now and was rather ugly with his black hair and swarthy complexion. The peculiar thing about these encounters was that no one else ever mentioned seeing him and that Sam never barked at him. On the contrary Sam often ran to meet him, tail wagging and with joyous yelps of welcome. But the boy threw stones at the dog, which ran back to Anne's side and whined sadly, beseeching her to explain what it had done wrong.

He had been here more often these past few months, Anne reflected. She noticed it because she was self-conscious about the visible evidence of her pregnancy and, silly though it might seem, it was almost as if the boy came to stare at her expanding waistline.

She reached the house and glanced again towards the fence, but the boy had gone. Anne laughed aloud at her fanciful imaginings and went to change her gown. Matthew insisted that they dressed for dinner every night whether or not they had company and tonight she wanted to look her best.

Daniel walked slowly home.

Home for him was still the shack which he had shared with Willem since the deaths of Martha and Alida. A native woman kept house for them and the two men, one forty years older than the other, lived together in grubby bachelor disarray and usually in silence. Willem was not a great one for talking and had become even more monosyllabic after Martha died. So Daniel sat alone and brooded.

Mostly he brooded about Matthew. He had begun visiting the big house as soon as Matthew's wife arrived. Curiosity had driven him there to see the Englishwoman, to see what sort of woman Matthew had preferred to Alida. She was beautiful, Daniel had to acknowledge that. She looked at him with kindness in her eyes and several times she had smiled at him when Sam wagged his tail. For a moment Daniel had felt himself softening, then he was angry at himself for the moment of weakness and threw the stones at Sam and ran away.

Now he had no difficulty in maintaining the hatred in his heart because he saw that she was expecting a baby. Engraved on Daniel's memory was a picture of Alida as she lay in her coffin with the tiny waxen child in her arms. His bitterness and his jealousy doubled, directed at the unborn child and its mother.

At the moment Daniel's anger was passive and he was content to watch and wait and allow the canker to grow within him. It would not take much, however, to push him over the edge into active vengeance.

Anne fastened the clasp of the diamond necklace and stared at her reflection in the looking-glass. One needed to take a lot of trouble with one's appearance when one wore the necklace; its magnificence, its sparkle and its fire were such that the diamonds outshone the wearer instead of enhancing her beauty. In fact the necklace was rather like Matthew, Anne thought idly as she confirmed to herself that she could hold her own against its glitter. His personality was so overpowering that he dominated everyone around him – even John Court. At the beginning of their relationship Anne had thought Court was weak. Then she had realised that it was not Court who was weak but Matthew who was strong and eclipsed the other man's more kindly light.

She waited until after dinner to broach the matter on her mind.

'Matthew, I know how reluctant you are to be involved in affairs outside your direct mining interests, but there is a matter which I believe is your concern and it is your duty to speak out.'

'What is it?' His tone was hardly encouraging.

'Smallpox.'

Matthew set down his brandy glass with a clatter. 'There isn't any smallpox. You have been talking to that blasted Boer doctor again.'

'Hans Sauer may have been born in the Orange Free State, but he did his medical training in Edinburgh and is a highly skilled physician.'

'Sauer is a trouble maker. There is no smallpox, I tell you.'

'Yes,' insisted Anne, 'there is. You know as well as I do that the threat has been there for over a year, ever since the outbreak in the Cape Peninsula. Hans has established a quarantine camp on the main road from Cape Town where he vaccinates every traveller, but the disease has somehow slipped through the net.'

'Is he still challenging the doctors' report? You know perfectly well that gang of black labourers from Portuguese East Africa was isolated and examined by every doctor in Kimberley. The report states clearly that the labourers do not have smallpox but a bulbous disease of the skin allied to pemphigus. The report is signed by Dr Mathews, Dr Murphy, Dr Leander Starr Jameson and others, but your dear Dr Sauer is still not satisfied!'

'Hans has experience of smallpox, and is absolutely certain that the labourers carry the disease. The outbreak is being hushed up because the other native labourers would leave town if they heard about an epidemic.'

'Stuff and nonsense!' scoffed Matthew. 'But even if it was true, what do you expect me to do about it? I may have some influence in the mining community, but the entire population is affected by this. If the mines shut down, the whole town will suffer and every type of business will lose trade.'

Anne clenched her fists. 'Someone has to make a stand – someone has to make a start. You are a respected member of the community; if you say that you believe something ought to be done, people will listen to you.'

'But I don't believe that anything ought to be done,' he responded calmly.

She stared at him, white-faced and trembling. 'Even on something as vital as this, you put your diamonds first! Nothing must come between you and the increase of your wealth, not even the spectre of death.'

'You exaggerate.'

'Matthew, have I ever asked you to do something for me?'

Rather reluctantly, he shook his head.

'I am asking this favour now. I want you to talk with Hans Sauer and to recommend that the mines close until the epidemic is checked. It is the only way to prevent the disease spreading.'

'No.' His tone was final.

Anne rose in a rustle of silk and faced him with angry spots of colour in her pale cheeks. 'There will be death in this town,' she said, in a low voice filled with desperate conviction. 'The men, the women, the children and the children yet unborn will curse the day that greed came before humanity. Let that be on your conscience, Matthew Bright – except that I cannot believe that you have one!'

She swept out of the room and for the first time in their married life Matthew found the bedroom door barred against him that night.

CHAPTER TWO

At about the same hour of the evening as Anne was putting on the necklace, Isobel also sat before her looking-glass and admired her reflection. At thirty she was at the height of her beauty. The perfection of her figure was unmarred and the glory of her eyes and hair undimmed, but her skin remained her chief asset. It glowed with health and clarity and gleamed with such creamy satin smoothness that every man longed to touch it, to stroke it with his fingers or caress it with his lips. Tonight Isobel was radiant; she had a new lover and she wore the special sheen of a woman who knows she is admired.

A noise in the corridor outside her room caused a frown to crease her white brow. Freddy! The large fat fly in her otherwise admirable ointment.

His attacks were growing more frequent. At night he could be heard screaming in his room and she had arranged for his valet to sleep next door. The nightmares were always the same: he believed that water was closing over his head and he fought for breath and tried to rise to the surface of this imaginary inundation. Not only was it extremely disturbing for everyone, but the condition meant that Freddy was often at home. Tonight they would be dining alone and she did hope he would behave.

Isobel finished twisting the rope of pearls around her neck and pattered swiftly to the nursery wing to say good night to the children. The newest arrival, four-year-old Edward, was already asleep, chubby cheeks and curly brown hair nestling on the pillow and hazel eyes closed. Julia, aged eight and showing promise of her mother's fair beauty, was lying in bed waiting for her mother's visit. Isobel kissed her perfunctorily and hurried out, leaving the little girl sad-eyed and wistful. Charles, Viscount

Swanley, was standing by the window of his bedroom, gazing out at the setting sun. School resumed next week and he was making the most of his last hours of freedom. Like his sister, he received a token brush of his mother's cold lips.

Dinner was dreadful. Freddy's fear of water had extended to almost anything liquid. He would stare wild-eyed into a bowl of soup and push it roughly aside and one had to be extremely careful with jugs of water or milk, tureens of gravy or bottles of wine. The latter he would drink, but sometimes hysteria would mount as he twirled the white or blood-red wine in his glass and he would mutter incoherently under his breath. Unfortunately, however, it was not possible for Freddy to wash in wine and he was beginning to smell rather strongly.

Tonight he was at least a little more lucid than usual. He ate his dinner with some measure of enjoyment and in total silence. Isobel lapsed into a dream world where there was a complete absence of Freddies and children and instead a long procession of handsome enamoured young men.

'Been to see your bastard tonight?'

Isobel's thoughts had been far away and she was startled by the sound of his voice. 'What did you say?'

'Your bastard son – how is the dear little chap?'

'All our children are well, Freddy, I am glad to say.'

'*Our* children! *Our* children!' cackled Freddy as he took a long draught of wine. 'Edward is no son of mine. His brown hair and hazel eyes are irrefutable proof of that. He belongs to the Honourable, or not so honourable, George.'

'He most certainly does not! How dare you impugn my honour in this way!'

Freddy threw back his head and laughed. 'Impugn your honour! Coming from you, my dear Isobel, that is priceless, it really is. How old is Edward now? Four, I think. And I know for a fact that I have not been in your bed since Julia was conceived.'

Isobel glared. She almost preferred his raving fits of madness to this active animosity. 'Yes, you have. Anyway, such suggestions come distinctly amiss from you. I could make a few accusations myself.'

'Such as what?'

'At least if Edward was George's son, he would not be afraid of water,' said Isobel tartly.

Freddy growled deep in his throat and clutched the wine glass convulsively. 'Don't say that. I will not have that matter referred to.'

'I will say what I wish to say. Look at you, you're a pathetic wreck! Your precious brother did this to you – Matthew arranged it all, out of revenge, because you . . .'

Freddy had risen from his chair and dragged her to her feet, his hands gripping her arm so tightly that he left marks on her white flesh, and his face so close to hers that his stinking breath was hot in her face.

'Dangerous words, my lady, dangerous words!'

Isobel broke free and ran to the door. As she opened it. Freddy yelled after her, 'I will shut your mouth for you, my lady. Aye, and your legs as well. Edward is your bastard and I will make sure you do not have another.'

He lurched back to the table to pour more wine while Isobel fled up the staircase to her room. She did not notice the frightened face of her eldest son as he hid behind the tapestry in the passage, covering his ears against what he had heard.

Finally Isobel slept, but awoke to a confusion of strange sounds and sensations. She was hot, gasping for breath and the room was filled with a loud crackling noise. As she sat upright in bed, her sleepy eyes focused on the bright flames leaping around her: the bed hangings were on fire! With a scream she ran towards the door, but the flames formed a barrier between her and freedom. Choking, and beaten back by the smoke and heat, Isobel groped for the window. The cool night air which rushed in only served to fan the flames, and the ground was too far below for her to jump. Summoning what breath she could muster, Isobel screamed and screamed. The flames crept nearer. Her nightgown caught fire and as the pain seared her flesh she pulled off the garment and backed further into the corner. She stared, terrified, at the raging inferno and decided that she would risk death by jumping from the window rather than be burned alive. But as she tried to reach the window again, she was overcome by smoke and her naked unconscious body pitched forward into the flames.

* * *

The next thing she knew was pain: fierce, all-consuming pain. For an interminable period it was all she sensed: she could neither see nor hear; nor feel anything but the pain which raged through her body when she was roused from black periods of blessed unconsciousness.

Gradually, however, the pain abated and her awareness increased, enough to realise that she was entirely wrapped in bandages and to shudder when these bandages were changed. She knew that her head was bandaged and that this was why she could neither see nor hear. But *was* that the reason? Or had the fire rendered her blind and deaf? Isobel, in her cocoon, began to improve sufficiently to worry about the future.

Then came the day when they peeled off her head bandages in daylight and, her heart hammering in her ribs, Isobel forced open her eyes. Dazzled by the brightness after so long, she closed them again. But she could see, she could hear and her faculties were unimpaired. They tied a white linen mask around her face, with holes cut for her eyes and nose, which she thought was to protect her from infection.

Soon she was able to speak and to recognise people. Her parents came to visit with her unmarried sister, Elizabeth. Freddy's mother was there and also his sister Mary. Even Nicholas came down from London. The children were allowed only a quick glimpse of her in the darkened room in case they were frightened by the bandages. Only Freddy did not call and was never mentioned.

In the end Isobel asked about Freddy. At first they told her only that he was confined to his room, but eventually she learned the truth: he *was* confined to his room, but that room was in the remote West Wing where he was guarded day and night. There was no doubt that he had set fire to Isobel's bed and now that the madness had finally overtaken him, he would remain a prisoner.

A prisoner herself within her bandages and weak unwilling flesh, Isobel waited impatiently to regain the use of her limbs. They let her see her hands first.

Afterwards she realised that they were trying to break it to her gently and that the sight of her hands should have prepared her for what was to come. But at the time she could only gaze in speechless horror at the misshapen lumps of flesh and red puckered skin that once had been her delicate, shapely hands.

They covered her hands in white linen gloves and slowly Isobel raised them to touch the mask that covered her face. What did that mask conceal?

Now each day held fresh revelations of the injuries she had received, as she was unwrapped carefully and considerately, one limb at a time. At first she was barely able to look at herself but turned her eyes away, revolted at the ugliness she saw. Gently they told her that time would bring some improvement, but that she must not hope for too much. Gone forever was the creamy perfection of her lustrous flesh, to be replaced by hideously scarred and puckered scarlet skin. One side had been more affected than the other and Isobel would never recover the full use of her crippled right arm nor lose the limp in her right leg.

She sat in a chair and demanded a looking-glass.

'I would not advise it,' said the doctor.

'I must know the worst.' She steeled herself.

They brought the glass and she sat for a moment. How very odd she looked, Isobel thought, in that weird white mask and with the uneven strands of hair sticking out in all directions. The hair was growing again, still golden but heavily streaked with silver. She motioned for the mask to be removed, while her maid stood holding the glass, hands trembling, eyes terrified.

Slowly the doctor untied the cords, and a strangled scream rose in Isobel's throat as she gazed on the mangled mess which had been her face. She had expected scarring and red withered skin, but nothing had prepared her for the ghastly disfigurement she now beheld. The left side of her face had come off best and there was even a tantalising patch of white skin near her ear to serve as a reminder of former glories. The right side had borne the full brunt of the flames and as the puce-coloured skin had healed so it had tightened, pulling her eye and mouth hideously awry.

Isobel gagged and retched and finally vomited over her gown. The vomit dribbled down her chin and scalding tears ran down her cheeks while she sat rigid with horror.

'You clean it up!' she cried to her maid. 'I cannot bear to touch myself.'

In fresh clothes and with the mask back in place, she regained some measure of control.

'Who discovered the fire and pulled me out?' she demanded.

'Your husband's valet, madam.'

'I should like to speak to him.'

Isobel dressed carefully for the occasion. Stiffly she was eased into a severe black dress which covered her from neck to ankles. Instead of the mask, she wore a black cap on her head with a thick veil over her face. Her hands were encased in black gloves and there were velvet slippers on her swollen feet. Not a square inch of flesh could be seen.

The valet was ushered in and stood awkwardly prepared to receive the thanks of the lady whose life he had saved.

'You expect me to thank you, do you not?'

'No, my lady,' he lied.

'Probably you even expect a reward?'

'No.' With more conviction.

'Or at least a commendation. Let me see, it was my brother Lord Nicholas who found you, was it not? Through his colleague, Mr Reynolds? So they will know of your bravery already.'

The man said nothing. The atmosphere in the room was so charged with bitterness that he longed to escape.

'I shall do none of the things which are expected of me,' said Isobel, 'because I wish most heartily that you had not saved my life. It were better I were dead. Look upon my face, young man, and you will understand why!'

She suddenly flung back the veil and glared at him malevolently. Involuntarily he recoiled from the sight of her ghastly twisted face.

'You see? I am repulsive to you. Yet I was beautiful. Now I will never again know the touch of a man's fingers nor see admiration in a man's eyes. The rest of my life is meaningless. Look well upon my face, because you are the last man on this earth who will see it!'

The veil dropped again, cloaking her features in thankful obscurity. The valet bowed and left while bitter, scarred Isobel sat on. From that day she wore only black, shrouded always in that thick veil. Even her children never looked on her face again.

She became a complete recluse, leaving the running of the household to Freddy's mother and sister who came to live at Highclere. Something prompted them to wear black, too, and with the mad Earl shut up in the West Wing, this sombre crêpe-draped house was a gloomy place for three children to grow up in.

CHAPTER THREE

Time and distance diluted the impact of the tragedy for Matthew and Anne, but the news still came as a devastating shock. Anne was not fond of Freddy or Isobel, but she was appalled at such macabre misfortune and deeply concerned about its effect on the children.

Matthew shut himself in his study with only Sam's soothing presence for company. He leaned back in his chair, closed his eyes and allowed the import of the news to sink in. Certainly he had not planned or ever envisaged such a development, but there was a sense of inevitability about the justice of it, as though Fate had taken belated control and meted out to Freddy his just deserts. Matthew had no pity for his brother but he felt some compassion for Isobel as he contemplated what the disfigurement would mean to her. Freddy had been evil, a triple murderer in fact, but Isobel had only been stupid and shallow and did not deserve a punishment so severe. And the children . . . There was guilt when he thought about the children.

Even so, Matthew could not restrain a slight feeling of satisfaction as he realised he was now head of the family, with authority over Freddy. He wasted no time in claiming legal guardianship and in placing Reynolds in charge of the Highclere estate and finances.

That done, his attention returned to an obstacle which was blocking his relentless drive towards his goal of controlling the diamond fields. He wanted to buy the claims owned by Willem Jacobs at the De Beers Mine. The parcel of claims was adjacent to those owned by the Bright–Court syndicate and was the ideal acquisition to strengthen Matthew's position before he came to terms with Rhodes over the merger.

He had spoken to Willem about it only last week when, having watched for the right opportunity, he had seen him enter a bar in town while Daniel went off towards the shops.

'Willem! I haven't seen you for weeks. What are you drinking?' and Matthew signalled to the barman to replenish Willem's brandy. 'How's business?'

'Well enough,' said Willem cautiously and, Matthew thought, without enthusiasm. 'I needn't ask you that question,' and Willem eyed Matthew's clothes which, without being smart, nevertheless advertised his executive status by being clean.

Matthew smiled. 'The recession is serious, Willem, for all of us. But I have much to be grateful for. We little dreamed, did we, you and I, when we entered Pniel that day in 1870, what the future held in store?'

'No,' said Willem heavily, 'we did not.'

'I'm sorry, Willem. It has not all been good for you, has it?' Matthew said contritely. 'And now you, like all the small claimholders, are struggling to keep going.'

Willem started to protest that this was not true, but then shook his head and sighed. 'You are right, of course you are right. I hardly know which way to turn. And frankly, Matthew, my heart isn't in it any more.'

'What do you mean?'

'I am tired of it all – the noise and the dirt and the heat. What for? A fortune? I am not making a fortune, but even if I was, that is not why I came here. I never intended to stay; I only wanted enough money to buy my sheep.' Willem slammed his hand on the bar counter in an agony of frustration. 'Diamond mining is a disease. It wriggles under your skin and perverts you. Sometimes I long for the peace and quiet of the farm.'

'Then why don't you go back to your old farm?'

'*Ag*, I sold it years ago at a time when I was short of capital.'

'I will buy your claims, Willem, and give you a good price for them. You can buy a new farm with the proceeds.'

'*Ja*. I know you would. So would others. Matthew, I am tempted – very, very tempted. But I cannot sell the claims; Daniel would not hear of it.'

'Ah, I see. Daniel has joined the ranks of the fortune seekers.'

Willem nodded. 'You see, Matthew, he says that it is the

uitlanders who find the diamonds and make the money. And he says that the earth is South African earth, that it belongs to the Boers and we should have our share of its riches.'

'Does he indeed!' Matthew frowned. 'So you won't sell, Willem? I will give you three times the market price.'

'I cannot, Matthew.'

'But you would like to leave here?'

'Yes,' Willem admitted, sighing heavily.

So, pondered Matthew, how could he persuade the old man to sell?

Willem was the last of the old farmer diggers and he worked his claims on old-fashioned principles and out-of-date methods. Since he did not understand the complexities of forming companies and issuing shares to obtain working capital, there was no sophisticated method of forcing his hand. Willem still dug out his diamonds and used the direct proceeds of the sale for living and mining expenses. Matthew grimaced: it followed therefore that it would be necessary to deprive Willem of the diamonds.

Matthew trapped Connor and Brown, the two overseers whom he suspected of illicit diamond buying, by the well-established method used by the police. Tom, the boss-boy who had aided Matthew's operations years ago, acted as bait and as Connor and Brown examined the stones offered by the African, Matthew stepped from the shadows and confronted them.

'Of course, I should call the police,' said Matthew. 'I have known about your activities for a long time. But perhaps you would rather do me a favour than serve a jail sentence?'

'It depends,' said Connor.

'Oh, what I suggest is right up your street! I want you to collect some diamonds for me. In return I will forget about the IDB *and* I will give you a percentage of the diamonds, enough to provide you with a fresh start well away from here.'

The two men looked at one another doubtfully.

'I don't think,' said Matthew gently, 'that you really have any choice in the matter, do you?'

A mental picture of hard labour on the Cape Town breakwater swam before their eyes. 'What exactly is it you want us to do?'

* * *

Willem took his weekly output to the diamond buyer on Fridays. The buyer's office was a mile or so from Willem's house and he and Daniel usually walked there, stopping for a drink and a meal at the hotel afterwards. Darkness falls early in Kimberley, but Matthew decided to play for safety and delay their departure somewhat. It was simple for the boss-boy to slip a bottle of gin to Willem's native servant so that she was in a state of happy inebriation and the house not cleaned when Willem and Daniel came in from the mine. They had to sober her up and eject her from the house before they could unearth the other diamonds from their secret hiding place and add that day's output. Then they set off together in the darkness.

So indignant were they at the lapse from grace of their servant girl, and so intensely did they discuss the matter and berate her, that they were easy prey. Willem was a big man but he was growing older and slower, while Daniel had strength and youth but was short in stature and taken by surprise. Brown dealt with Daniel while the boss-boy gripped Willem with one arm and clamped his other hand across Willem's mouth. Connor swiftly located the diamonds and winded Willem with a sharp blow to the solar plexus so that they made their escape before the alarm could be raised.

Matthew was pleased. The plan had worked with the minimum of fuss and the minimum physical hurt to Willem and Daniel. He paid off Connor and Brown and sent them packing to Natal.

'Remember,' he warned, 'that it would not pay to be clever with me. Don't think you could ever blackmail me because of my part in tonight's work. It would be your word against mine. John Court knows nothing of this matter, but he knows plenty about your IDB activities. And who in Kimberley would doubt the word of John Court?'

He tipped the boss-boy handsomely and hid the diamonds under the piles of Anne's underwear in the bedroom.

'This is the end of diamond mining for us,' said Willem. 'There is no money left; those diamonds represented the last cash I had.'

'Wouldn't the bank lend some money?' asked Daniel. 'We could pay it back from the next batch of stones.'

Willem shook his head. 'No. In better times they might have done so, but the recession in the industry is making them cautious. The bank manager told me that they have lost a lot of money this year in bad debts, caused by the drop in share prices of the mining companies. He said we were not a viable proposition, that the days of the small digger were ended and the future lay with syndicates, joint stock companies and foreign investment. What do I know about obtaining capital from overseas? No, Daniel, we must go elsewhere and start again.'

Daniel looked at Willem's tired, lined face. 'What will you do with the claims?'

'Sell them to the highest bidder.'

'I know who that will be: Matthew Bright. He wants to buy the claims, doesn't he?'

'He has already spoken to me about them,' Willem admitted. 'He is offering an excellent price.'

'He can afford to pay a good price,' said Daniel bitterly. 'I am sure he was behind the robbery. I got a fairly good look at one of those men and I'm positive it was one of his overseers.'

'Matthew agrees with you. Two of his men have left town. He came to offer his apologies if they had been involved in the attack upon us and to propose paying four times the market price of the claims by way of compensation.'

'I hope you refused. It should be against your principles to accept money from that man.'

'I accepted,' said Willem quietly. 'I cannot afford principles.'

'So he's won,' Daniel hissed. 'As usual!'

His latent hate, which had lain dormant for so long, erupted in an uncontrollable burst of fury. The rage seemed to spill out and swirl about him as he ran through the town in the direction of the Bright house. He would not wreak his vengeance on Matthew directly but would aim his attack at the two beings whom he believed Matthew valued most: his wife and unborn child.

Anne's day had started badly. To begin with, she was now eight months pregnant and most of the time felt cumbersome and depressed. Then it transpired that Henriette, who had been ill for several days, was still not well enough to leave her bed. Anne did not hurry the unaccustomed task of dressing herself. She laid out a clean cotton dress of dove grey trimmed with white and reached for fresh underwear.

Then she saw the unfamiliar leather bag. Puzzled, she lifted it from the drawer but even before opening it she had guessed its contents by their weight and hard chunkiness. She took a quick peep inside the bag before pushing it back among the snowy petticoats, and sat down on the bed to think. Why on earth would Matthew hide diamonds in the house?

She did not have to wait long to find out, for at mid-morning the police called.

'Sorry to trouble you, Lady Anne,' the Sergeant apologised, 'but is Mr Bright at home?'

'At this time of day? Certainly not. Why do you want him?'

'There has been a diamond robbery. We tried to find Mr Bright at his office, but he is not there.'

'A robbery!' Anne's stomach lurched sickeningly. 'Surely you cannot think my husband committed a robbery!'

'No, of course not. Are you all right, ma'am?'

Anne had suddenly sat down on a chair, pale and shaking, but she forced herself to compose her features and managed a wan smile. 'It's the heat, Sergeant. I'll be better after the baby . . . soon. How can Mr Bright assist with your inquiries?'

'We wish to question him about two of his overseers who were seen near the scene of the crime. I don't suppose you would know anything about them, Lady Anne? Their names are Connor and Brown.'

'I'm afraid I have never met them. Mr Bright discourages my presence at the mine or the sorting grounds. And I am absolutely certain they have never been to the house. I am so sorry I cannot help you.'

'I quite understand. Would you have any objection if we questioned the servants, ma'am, and searched their rooms? They might know something.'

'By all means.' Anne's entire attention was focused on protecting Matthew. 'Perhaps you would like to search the entire house, Sergeant,' she suggested boldly, 'just to be on the safe side?'

'Oh, gracious no, ma'am. No need for that.'

As soon as they had left the property, Anne called Sam and hurried out into the garden. Her head was aching, but she had to escape from the claustrophobic heat of the house.

Why did Matthew need to steal diamonds? It made no sense. But she had to admit that he had picked the perfect hiding place. With Henriette in bed, no one else was likely to find them, and if the police had searched the house they would not have rummaged amongst her clothes. No, Matthew could have counted on the fact that only she would have found the stones and that her innocence and status in the community would have prevented a police search. Which is exactly what had happened, Anne thought bitterly. How very sure he was of her!

From his vantage point behind the garden wall, Daniel watched her slow progress across the lawn. He cursed the blind fury which had propelled him here without his gun, but his hand confidently caressed the shining blade of his hunting knife. It would suffice, but he would have to come close to her. He moved in a low crouching run behind the wall, wary eyes watching for the servants, his silent stealth part of every Boer boy's training for hunting the wild-life which teemed in the African veld.

Anne reached her favourite part of the garden, where the shrubs were high and thick and the trees were growing tall. Here she could gain some illusion of home and England and the gentle landscapes of her childhood. She entered the grove with a sigh of thankfulnss and did not notice the dark figure slipping ever closer.

Matthew . . . robberies . . . violence . . . such ugly reminders of the unsavoury undercurrents which ran beneath the crystal stream of the diamond mines . . . Anne watched Sam dart off in the opposite direction, eagerly following some scent, and she suddenly remembered the way Matthew had smiled at Nicholas. Here in Kimberley, the only time she had seen that smile was when he played with Sam. Most people, Anne thought, would assume that she headed the list of Matthew's priorities, particularly now that she was with child, but she had no doubt at all that Nicholas and Sam were what Matthew loved best.

Daniel stood poised with the knife in his hand, waiting to strike. The Englishwoman paused and stood still, head bent, staring at the ground. When she raised her head again, her expression was sad and she seemed weighed down with care. Daniel fixed his eyes on the rippling golden hair and crept forward, blind to everything but his desire to revenge himself on Matthew through this woman.

Matthew didn't even care about the baby, Anne was thinking. He had displayed no interest in his unborn child. All the infant would be to him was an heir to inherit his diamonds. No doubt he wanted a boy who . . .

Suddenly Daniel's hand clamped across her mouth and as she tried to scream she felt the cold touch of steel against her throat. With a strength born of panic she managed to wriggle free and scream once before Daniel stifled her cries again and his knife caught her a glancing blow on the breast. The hurt took her by surprise, but the next blow in the shoulder went deeper and as the man pulled out the blood-spattered knife the pain was excruciating. My throat, she thought vaguely, he's trying to cut my throat . . . he must not hurt my throat or my baby . . . and she pulled away again as best her bulk would allow. Someone must have heard me scream, she thought frantically.

Only Sam had heard. He dashed into the small clearing and stopped, his tail giving a hesitant wag as he recognised Daniel. Then Daniel raised his hand against Sam's mistress and with a growl the dog flung himself at Daniel's back.

With an oath Daniel was forced to let go of Anne who sagged to the ground, fighting for breath. Sam hung on grimly to Daniel's shirt, but with a deft twist Daniel reached round and savagely slashed the dog's throat. As the blood spurted, the dog crumpled to the reddening earth and Anne began to scream afresh as she saw Sam's last seconds of agony. Hurriedly Daniel grabbed a stick and clubbed her hard across the back of the head. She collapsed unconscious while Daniel fled silently the way he had come.

The servants found her and carried her to the house, where Henriette struggled from her sick-bed to bathe the wounds and send for Matthew and the doctor. It was several hours before Matthew could be found. He listened, stony-faced, to Henriette's incoherent and incomplete account of the accident.

'And Sam?' he asked, when she had finished.

'Dead.'

'Where is he?'

Henriette looked puzzled. 'I don't know, sir. In the garden, I suppose.'

In the bedroom Anne lay, very white and still. They had staunched the flow of blood from her wounds but her breathing was shallow. Her life, and that of her unborn child, hung in the balance. Matthew sat by the bed and waited, his face grim and his eyes thoughtful. When the doctor came again, Matthew left the room and walked into the garden in search of Sam.

The pathetic bundle of yellow fur, matted with blood, was lying forgotten in the copse, covered in flies. Matthew knelt beside the dog and stroked his head. He tried to swat away the flies, but they were too numerous so he pulled off his coat and laid it over the body. He stayed there for a long time, thinking of Sam and how the dog had chosen him from all the men in Kimberley. He thought of Sam's unquestioning love, of the brown eyes which watched him with such devotion, of the cold wet nose and warm pink tongue that thrust against his hand and the tattoo of the wagging tail.

Matthew closed his eyes, trying with the limited information at his disposal to reconstruct the scene of Sam's defence of Anne. Clenching his teeth, he rose and fetched a spade. Alone, in the gathering darkness, he began to dig Sam's grave.

When Daniel reached home, he found that Willem was piling their household goods into the old trek-wagon which had stood at the back of the house for so many years. Willem had maintained it lovingly and for all its age it would continue to serve them well.

'We leave now,' Willem said, 'and make camp in the veld tonight.'

'It will be dark in a few hours,' Daniel protested.

'I want to go tonight, after I have said goodbye to Martha.'

The packing did not take long since the two men had few personal possessions. The only items which Daniel cherished were the picture of Alida which had been painted on her sixteenth birthday, the golden locket which she had worn at her neck and the volume of Shakespeare plays which she had read to him. When all was done and the oxen were inspanned, Willem led Daniel swiftly to the small cemetery nearby where Martha and Alida lay side by side. They removed their hats and stood in silence. Tears began to run down Willem's leathery cheeks.

'I hate to leave her here alone.'

An unwilling lump rose in Daniel's throat. 'She is not alone. She and Alida and the baby will keep each other company.'

The idea seemed to comfort the old man and he nodded slowly as he replaced his hat and moved away with many a backward glance.

'Where shall we go?' asked Daniel. 'To the Free State?'

'Further. To the Transvaal. I have great faith in Paul Kruger to keep the land for the Boers, while I have less confidence in President Brand of the Free State who flirts with the British.'

'How shall we live?'

'We will return to our roots, Daniel, back to the land. We have enough money to buy a sizeable farm and we will head for Pretoria.'

For days Anne lay suspended between life and death, but finally the tide began to turn and she struggled back to consciousness. A week after her eyelids fluttered open and she first gazed about her with some semblance of recognition, she went into labour and gave birth to a daughter. After that her improvement was rapid and they dared to ask her about the attack. She described her assailant well enough for Matthew and Court to identify him, but by that time Willem and Daniel had disappeared from the district and were well over the border.

'Sam died, didn't he, Matthew?'

'Yes.'

'And I am alive. And you would have preferred it to be the other way round.'

He was standing by the window but now he turned round and stared at her. 'Why do you say that?' He crossed the room, sat on the bed and placed his hand on her forehead. 'You're very hot,' he said gently. 'Perhaps I should call the doctor again.'

'No, I'm all right. Did you find the diamonds, Matthew? The

police came that morning, but I made sure they would not find them.'

'You did that for me?' He sounded surprised.

'I have found out more about it since then; John told me you had bought the old man's claims. Is that the only way you could force him to sell? By theft and violence?'

Matthew stared at her. 'You always think the worst of me, don't you, Anne?' he said slowly.

'What do you expect? You bought *me*. You think you can buy anything and if someone refuses your money, then you resort to other methods in order to get what you want!'

'Things are not always exactly what they seem.' Matthew reached for her hand, but she snatched it away. 'Perhaps I did marry you for the wrong reasons,' he continued gravely, 'but I never intended we should live together in such . . . such *conflict*! Could we not try to achieve a better understanding, if only for the baby's sake?'

Anne glanced down at her tiny daughter, asleep in the crib beside the bed. 'Yes,' she whispered, 'we could try.'

Matthew leaned forward and pulled her into his arms. 'Thank you,' he said softly, 'for protecting me from the police. You are right – I did steal the diamonds – but my reasons are not what you think. Believe me, Anne, the old man is much happier without his claims.'

He released her and walked to the door. Anne watched him go with dawning hope and happiness in her heart.

CHAPTER FOUR

During the first few months of 1884, Matthew made a fresh discovery. Not a new mine or a particularly fine diamond or a way of increasing his influence but the source of a different kind of riches: his baby daughter.

Unlike Anne, Matthew had not longed for a child nor felt deprived during the barren years. Even his natural wish for an heir had abated as soon as distance was put between him and Freddy. After the birth, he took a mild interest in the infant when he visited Anne, but kept her at arms' length. Then the child was moved from Anne's bedroom to the nursery and into the care of a nanny. Now it required a special effort on Matthew's part to see her, and it was an effort which apparently he could not find the time or inclination to make.

One evening, however, he came home late from a business meeting and walked past Anne's closed door to his own bedroom. A faint cry came from the nursery along the passage and Matthew paused. Slowly he approached the nursery door, which stood ajar, and peered inside. A dim lamp burned and the room was empty except for the baby in her crib. The nanny, he thought, must have gone to the kitchen for something.

Matthew stood on the threshold and hesitated. He felt a vague apprehension, as if he was entering some foreign environment over which he had insufficient control. Then the baby uttered another cry and a frown of concern creased his forehead. He tiptoed into the room and bent over the cot.

The baby was not crying, as he had feared. She was gurgling happily, waving tiny fists in the air and kicking her sturdy legs. She looked at Matthew and screwed up her face. Oh Lord, he thought, *now* she's going to cry. But instead the baby smiled and Matthew's reserve melted, along with the ice around his heart.

He knew that everyone else had always considered her adorable. Loyally named Victoria, her enchanting little face was framed with wisps of silver-fair hair and her blue eyes beamed at what was evidently a perfect world. Matthew felt that he was seeing her for the first time, communicating with her for the first time – and suddenly he realised that he had never been alone with her before.

Cautiously, in case he frightened her, Matthew bent closer and tentatively held out a finger. Victoria promptly clutched it tightly, surprising him with the amount of strength her plump fist contained. Gently he extricated the finger and tickled her under the chin. Sam, he remembered, had loved being tickled under the chin. So did Vicky; she chuckled and wriggled with delight and then reached up and grabbed Matthew's beard.

Matthew roared with laughter. '*Touché*,' he said admiringly, as he and his daughter shared the joke.

She possessed her mother's sweet expression and good looks, he decided, but definitely she had inherited his strength and disposition.

Matthew left a few minutes later, not wishing the nanny to find him there, but his visits became regular once he had discovered the nanny's routine. He was absolutely fascinated by this tiny being who had appeared in his life, as trusting and loving and dependent as Sam. She gave his life a new dimension and a deeper meaning; she made sense of everything he was trying to achieve. But the hours he spent with the child were their secret, hidden from everyone, even Anne and Court, for Matthew was still constrained to conceal his feelings.

He was angry, therefore, to be discovered by Anne in the nursery one evening and responded with defensive aggression in his embarrassment.

'I just happened to be passing,' he said curtly, in response to Anne's exclamation of surprise.

'Oh!' Disappointment dampened a quick flare of hope that Matthew might come to care for his family after all. 'Anyway, I am glad you are here. I must speak to you about something important and I haven't seen you for several days.'

'I'm very busy at present. Negotiations with Rhodes are at an extremely delicate state.'

'So I gathered.' Her tone was dry. 'Unfortunately another matter has also reached crisis point and can no longer be ignored – not even by you.'

Matthew knew what was coming and tensed.

'You cannot deny the presence of smallpox in this town, Matthew. Not any more. There is too much evidence against you.'

'You have been listening to gossip again.' But his tone lacked conviction.

'Certainly gossip is rife,' agreed Anne, determined not to lose her patience or her courage, 'but it is a fact that doctors are reporting smallpox as "Felstead's Disease" after the farm where that group of Moçambique Africans was held.'

'I am sure that the doctors have good reason for whatever they are doing.'

For once, however, Matthew did not deny the charge outright and Anne pressed home her advantage. 'There is a smallpox "war" being waged in this town, between Hans Sauer on the one side and Jameson and his cronies on the other. I know whose opinion I support and I intend to take action. I want Hans Sauer to vaccinate me.'

Matthew stared at her in silence. His expression was forbidding but his thoughts and emotions were more complex. Again he knew just what Anne was about to say and his gaze rested on Vicky in her cot. What was his reply to be?

'Not only me,' Anne continued, 'but Vicky, you, Henriette, Pierre and all the servants.'

'I'm not sure that you are well enough for such treatment.'

Anne's pale cheeks flushed rosy pink at this unexpected kindness. 'Of course I am well enough,' she said unsteadily. 'I'm a little tired, that's all.'

In fact her physical delicacy was becoming more and more apparent. After years of ill-health, the birth of Victoria and the wounds inflicted by Daniel had weakened her still further. Anne was determined, however, to regain her health. Her conviction that Matthew cared nothing for his daughter fuelled the belief that Victoria depended solely on her.

Matthew gazed down at his daughter as she lay on her back,

counting her toes and crowing with delight. As Matthew bent down the baby reached up and tried to tug at his watch chain. Still he hesitated. 'All right,' he said at last. Anne's breath exhaled in a long sigh of relief, but Matthew's was not to be a complete capitulation. 'But Jameson must do it,' he insisted.

'I don't care who does it as long as it is done, and quickly too! I will make the necessary arrangements.'

'Don't include me; I have a host of meetings over the next few days. I will ask Jameson to attend to me at the office.'

After he had gone Anne found she was shaking uncontrollably, a reaction due partly to the strain of tackling Matthew and partly to her physical weakness. It was all very well for him to say that they must try to achieve a better understanding but how did she get to know a husband whom she hardly saw? Matthew was more interested in building a diamond empire than a relationship.

Often, as she had lain in bed, Anne's thoughts had dwelled on Isobel and on Matthew's love for her sister. Looking at the situation logically and sensibly, surely Matthew's devotion to Isobel could not have survived the years of separation and Isobel's accident? Having decided that point to her satisfaction, Anne's mind roamed over the ladies of Kimberley. Even allowing for the fact that there was a certain type of woman whom she had never met, and never would meet socially, it was apparent that Kimberley offered Matthew opportunities for sexual adventure but not for long-lasting liaisons. Therefore, the path to Matthew's heart was open and the right person could find it.

Instinct told Anne that when Matthew did love, it would be with a passionate intensity and sincerity. Slowly she was admitting to herself that she wanted him to love her.

She would have to fight for his love and to do so she would need to push herself further into the ambience which his incandescent quality generated. At the moment she felt as if she stood in the shadows, on the periphery of his life, and although she was allowed brief flashes of illumination on his thoughts and feelings, for the most part she and Matthew existed on separate planes.

But such a fight required strength of both mind and body and Anne's debilitating illness had left her weak and tired. Somehow she must overcome this exhaustion and find enough energy for the struggle.

Just now, however, Vicky was her most important concern. Anne lifted the baby from the cot and hugged her close. Whatever else happened, nothing must ever hurt Vicky; Anne had waited so long for her and she was so precious. Tomorrow Dr Jameson must be asked to carry out the vaccinations. Anne braced herself to persuade or if necessary command the servants to submit to the procedure. She knew that John Court would help. Here Anne frowned, however, because she was worried about John.

The next day she marshalled the household in readiness for the doctor's arrival and then held Vicky while the baby was vaccinated. After she had also received her own injection, she returned to the nursery, leaving Henriette to supervise the servants – and without noticing the Frenchwoman's terrified eyes.

Matthew saw Jameson at the Club later the same day. The doctor was a friend of Rhodes and closely associated with the affairs of the diamond fields. The talk between him and Matthew, therefore, was of the health of the industry rather than that of the body. As they were parting, Matthew recalled the smallpox.

'Matt, I've no vaccine left,' Jameson apologised. 'I used the last batch at your home this morning. Fresh supplies will be available within a few days, but remind me about it, will you? The demand is so great that I cannot keep track of all the requests.'

Matthew nodded absently and, engrossed in the negotiations with Rhodes, the matter faded completely from his mind.

A week later Matthew agreed terms with Rhodes and merged his holdings in De Beers Mine with Rhodes's De Beers Mining Company. It was an important step towards consolidation of the entire mine and the principals – Cecil Rhodes, Alfred Beit, Matthew and Court – celebrated the event with real satisfaction.

Over all the company brooded the genius of Rhodes, his ruddy complexion concealing his delicate health and his shabby clothes belying his position as one of Kimberley's richest men, with an income of at least £50,000 a year. In March he had risen to Cabinet rank as Treasurer of the Cape Colony, but the Ministry had been short-lived. His political aspirations marched hand in hand with his diamond interests, his dream of a monolithic diamond empire matching his aim of changing the face of Africa.

Matthew still doubted the wisdom of dividing energy and resources between two such demanding mistresses. but dared not criticise Rhodes and inwardly hoped that one day this diversification of interests might work to his own advantage. Meanwhile he soaked up like a sponge everything that Rhodes and Beit could teach him and soon began to make useful contributions of his own. Court, on the other hand, seemed increasingly remote and isolated from the mainstream of affairs.

Even Anne noticed and grieved at Court's apparent ineptitude and lack of interest. One afternoon in May she was arranging flowers and sparse autumn leaves in the drawing-room when she heard Matthew and Court enter the study. As usual she placed some flowers carefully to one side and carried them to the garden door. She paused at the entrance to the study and looked in. Court was sitting in a deep armchair, a glass of wine in his hand, while Matthew paced restlessly up and down.

'You've got it all wrong, John,' Matthew was saying. 'You don't seem to have any grasp of these matters. The Kimberley Mine is the key to complete consolidation. At the . . .' Matthew paused. 'Damn it, man, you're not even listening,' he exploded.

Indeed Court was not listening. He tossed back the wine and looked at Anne as she stood framed in the doorway.

'What pretty flowers,' he said dreamily.

'They are for Sam.' Anne smiled at them both. 'I'll be back in a moment.'

She walked across the lawn to where Sam was buried in the little grove where he had died so valiantly. There she placed the flowers on the grave – a gesture of love for Sam's memory, gratitude for his sacrifice and atonement to Matthew for his loss. When she retraced her steps to the house, she found that only Court remained in the study.

'Matthew will not be in to dinner,' Court informed her. 'He is dining at the Club.'

'Then it will be just you and me again, John. You will be tired of my company soon, if you are not already bored.'

'Never,' he assured her. 'Never.'

He reached for the wine and poured another glass while Anne watched sadly; he never used to drink so much, she thought.

Court drank because his life was empty and meaningless, without present or future. He did not even dare to go alone into the veld any more, because he could not confront the void which was himself and his existence. He drank to forget – to forget his ever-growing sense of inferiority to Matthew, to forget Alida and Anne and the mess he had made of his life – but with little real hope of forgetting any of these things. He could not yet go home.

His eyes, blurring slightly from the wine, rested on the fragile form of Anne as she sat on the arm of the chair. How different she was from Alida! They were absolute opposites in appearance, of course, but the difference went deeper than that. Even as a girl Anne had possessed a greater sophistication, an assurance bestowed by her birth and breeding. Alida had been a wood-nymph, more naturally sensuous, closer to Nature and the warm fertile soil. Court had wanted to protect Alida but he had desired her too, hungrily and fervently, and the shock of her seduction by Matthew was with him still. He admired and respected Anne and had given her a devotion more chivalrous than sexual. Now, however, his awareness of her seemed heightened and, while he wanted to smooth away the hurt from her brow, he also wanted to hold her tight in his arms and feel her slender body against his. Court gripped the wine glass and took another draught.

To Anne his face wore a defeated look and she noticed that there were flecks of grey in his brown hair. She knew that Matthew was responsible – unintentionally perhaps, but destroying him nonetheless. Court's quiet integrity and inner strength were being eroded and eclipsed by the greater brilliance of his partner.

'Why do you let him speak to you like that?' she asked gently. 'He treats you like a little boy who doesn't understand what the grown-ups are doing. Sometimes he is positively rude. Why, John? Why don't you stand up to him?'

'Why should I bother?' Court returned question for question. 'I have no relish for fights or quarrels, Anne, particularly when there is no advantage in winning.'

'Matthew ought to be grateful to you.' Anne sat down in the chair and faced him earnestly. 'You intervened over that salted claim; you saved him from the lynch party; you had faith in the blue ground when everyone else was giving up. *You* ought to be running the partnership, not Matthew.'

'No, his contribution has been bigger than mine. Besides, he has the inclination to manage things and I have not. I guess I must be a simple country boy at heart and I'm out of my depth in the sphere of big business. I should have stuck to prospecting. As for gratitude . . .' Court shrugged. 'One doesn't do something to win thanks but because it is the right thing to do at the time.'

'And do you really believe that you are doing the right thing now?'

Court was silent for a few moments. 'No,' he said truthfully, 'no, I cannot honestly say that I do believe that. In a way I feel as though I am waiting for something, a sign which will tell me when I can go home.'

'Back to Boston,' said Anne softly, 'where the sea is clear, the air is fresh and the people are free.'

He looked at her in surprise. 'Strange that you should say that. Freedom is so important to Americans that I thought perhaps only I had noticed it. The people here are not free, are they? The mines are like open prisons and each of us is bound by invisible chains of avarice.'

'Except for you and me. I am bound to Matthew, but you, John? What keeps you here?'

'I told you. I'm waiting for a sign.' He smiled at her over the rim of his glass as he raised the wine to his lips. He could admit to no one, especially not to himself, that he too was bound to Matthew and could not break those bonds. 'But as we're talking so personally, I would like to tell you a story. I'm drunk enough to tell you this story! You see, Anne, you put up a first-class front to everyone else but I live here, and you cannot fool me.'

Anne frowned, watchful and wary while she waited for him to continue.

Court swallowed another gulp of wine. He knew how much Anne loved Matthew; she tried to hide it, but he had glimpsed the fleeting expressions on her face and seen the movements of her hands and body. He knew this, but he was unaware of her inner conflict.

'I remember what happened when Sam adopted us. Matthew didn't want the dog but Sam persisted. Sam believed that if he stayed close and hung on grimly enough, he would win Matthew's love in the end. How right he was!'

The silence seemed endless but eventually Anne reached for his hand and held it tightly between her own. 'What a good friend you are!' She could not insult his friendship by denying his assumption. 'You have given me hope and that is worth a dozen diamonds.'

'And your brother's visit is worth another dozen.'

'Didn't Matthew tell you? He has written to Nicholas telling him not to come.' Anne's disappointment was obvious.

'Why? You were looking forward to it so much. And I want to meet this paragon of brotherly virtues.'

'The smallpox!' said Anne bitterly.

'Ah!' Court digested the information. 'So Matthew acknowledges the extent of the epidemic?'

'Yes. Unfortunately, like the majority of the citizens, he has acknowledged it far too late. What is the latest tally? An estimated 1200 cases and 350 deaths?

Court nodded. 'And it's only the start.'

'If only Matthew had listened to me!' Anne burst out.

He looked startled. 'Surely you don't blame Matthew? He only did what he thought was right. Anne, you must realise that Matthew is a born businessman and manager. When his own knowledge is inadequate, he takes the advice of specialists – as when he used my geological training in the early days. Now, in the matter of the smallpox, Matthew looked at the evidence and weighed up the opinions of the medical profession. A majority of doctors declared there was no smallpox. As it happens, they were wrong, but it was natural for Matthew to side with that majority.'

'I see.' Anne considered the matter carefully. 'I must admit that I had not looked at it in that light before. However, recriminations will not help now. John, you must be very careful – they say the disease is raging in the compounds and you visit there so frequently.'

'I cannot stop visiting the compounds. It is my duty to make sure the men have good food and decent living conditions. Besides, I've been vaccinated. But I will try to be particularly careful,' Court promised. 'Will you do the same?'

'Perhaps I ought to stop going to the hospital,' said Anne slowly. 'There has been a serious outbreak there and one cannot be too careful.'

Anne's remark was prophetic, for the next day Henriette complained of a headache and a stiff back, as though she was sickening for a cold. She went to lie down but her feeling of malaise increased and by nightfall she was vomiting and running a high fever. Before long the pustules appeared and a frantic Anne sent for the doctor.

'But she was vaccinated,' wailed Anne. 'How *could* it be smallpox?'

Henriette's weeping husband choked violently on his sobs, but he could be heard saying, 'Non! Non!' over and over again.

'Pierre, why do you say no?'

'She pretended to go away and come back later for the vaccination, but she did not return. She was too frightened of it.'

'You should have told me!' Anne buried her face in her hands. 'Or she should have told me! Pierre, did you . . .?'

'Oui, my lady,' he gulped hastily.

'Thank heavens! I want you to check immediately that everyone else in the house had their vaccination, then you can help me to make up a bed for Henriette in the spare room at the far end of the stableyard, beyond the servants' quarters.'

Pierre gaped at her, but Matthew sprang up with a roar. 'Henriette will be moved from this house immediately. She is going to the hospital.'

'No!'

'She is not staying here to infect the entire household.' Vicky, Matthew was thinking. *Vicky.*

'She *is* staying here and she will infect nobody because everyone has been vaccinated.'

Matthew turned away and stared out at the garden so that no one should see the anguish in his eyes. He could not bring himself to admit that he had not been vaccinated, that he had been so busy he had forgotten all about it. He calmed down as he reminded himself that Vicky had been vaccinated – she would be all right. She had to be. However, whether Henriette remained or went to the hospital, the infection was in the house. Matthew could not stay here.

'Who do you expect to nurse her?' Matthew would still feel happier if Henriette was removed.

'I will,' said Anne resolutely.

'You must be mad. Absolutely mad!'

'I brought Henriette to Kimberley,' said Anne calmly. 'She is my responsibility and I will look after her.'

'Well, I'm not staying here. I shall go to the Club.'

'Naturally you may go where you please,' retorted Anne, 'but you will not deter me from doing what I know to be right.'

Matthew slammed out of the room and Pierre scuttled after him. In the bedroom Matthew wiped the perspiration from his forehead. His absence would appear to be the result of bad temper and stubbornness and no one need suspect the truth. He ordered some clothes to be packed and delivered to the Club; then he walked to the nursery to say goodbye to Vicky but, with his hand on the door handle, he paused. He had not seen Henriette for days and was fairly certain that he had not been in any other contact with the disease. In any case, Vicky should be immune. Even so, Matthew dared not take the risk. His hand fell back to his side and with a heavy heart he left the house and rode to Jameson's surgery for belated inoculation.

In the drawing-room Anne turned to Court with a wan smile. 'And where will you go, John?'

'I shall stay here, of course. Perhaps there is something I can do to help.'

'Oh, there is! Would you keep an eye on Vicky for me? I shall isolate myself with Henriette and one of the hardest things to bear will be worry about Vicky.'

Court nodded and patted her shoulder reassuringly.

'It would have been nice,' Anne said, 'if Matthew could have worried about Vicky and tried to help.'

The house was roughly T-shaped, the reception rooms forming the stem and the bedrooms forming the crossbar. The black servants slept in accommodation on one side of the stableyard. There was a vacant room at the far end of the stable row and it was here that Anne installed Henriette. She managed to squeeze two beds into the tiny space and set up a strict isolation routine. Only Pierre was permitted to approach the room and then only to set down food and water before the door.

Henriette tossed on the narrow bed, muttering incoherently in her delirium. Her body, face and neck were covered with pustules so that soon her skin was one mass of huge suppurating sores. Shivering fits wracked her and she cried out for water. Four days after the blisters broke, the pustules crusted over and the scabs itched abominably. Anne tried, unsuccessfully, to prevent the girl from scratching but in her agony Henriette tore off large areas of scab, leaving vivid pink scars on her battered face. Then the fever ebbed and died and as soon as all the scabs had been scratched off or had come off naturally, Anne knew the danger of contagion was past. Even so, they stayed in isolation for several more days – days when Anne had the time to worry about Vicky and Matthew and the household, and Henriette sat dully before the looking-glass gazing in black horror at her face. The Frenchwoman's skin was hard and lumpy like the crust of a bread-loaf and was coloured a bright pink.

'Pierre,' she said. 'How can I face Pierre?'

'There will always be pockmarks, I'm afraid,' said Anne gently, 'but the vivid colour and the scars will fade. Pierre loves you and I am quite sure it is not only your face that he loves.'

'I do not see how he will bear to come near me. Who could force themselves to touch me?' and Henriette's tears rained down her ravaged cheeks.

'Of course Pierre will want to touch you,' chided Anne. 'Come, look in the mirror again. Your eyes are the same, aren't they? Beautiful eyes, Henriette, big and dark, and they will soon regain their sparkle. Your hair is lovely, although it does not look at its best because you've been ill and I am not clever at combing it. Now, stay there while I call Pierre.'

'No!' begged Henriette. 'Not yet. Please, my lady, I don't want to see anyone yet.'

'You must,' said Anne firmly.

She left the room and walked across the stableyard to the back door of the house, enjoying the warmth of the sun to her pale cheeks. The past three weeks had taken more out of her than she realised. Her dress hung loosely on her frame and her eyes were dull and tired in her sallow face.

The house seemed large, cool and spacious after the cramped sick-room. Pierre was not in the kitchen, so Anne succumbed to temptation and crept into the nursery. Victoria was asleep, curled contentedly in her crib, one minute thumb stuck into her tiny rosebud mouth. She looked so adorable that Anne could not help but break one of her own rules; she picked up the baby and woke her from her sleep. The child made no protest but opened sleepy eyes and then beamed approval at her mother's reappearance. Tears blinded Anne's eyes momentarily as she hugged the small body and smelled the sweet baby smell and she thought what a good-natured child this was – she really could not remember the sound of Victoria crying.

Hurriedly recollecting her duty, Anne laid down the baby again and continued on her way to the study. To her surprise she found both Matthew and Court there; evidently Matthew's self-imposed exile was over.

Court greeted her warmly but Matthew eyed her warily.

'Are you sure all danger of contagion is past?' he demanded.

'Quite sure,' said Anne coolly, 'and anyway I haven't had small-pox. I wish to speak to Pierre. John, do you think you could find him?'

She and Matthew waited in silence. Matthew never did tell Anne that he had returned to the house as soon as Jameson said it was safe to do so and that he had kept constant watch over the child.

When Court reappeared with Pierre, Anne explained briefly about Henriette's disfigurement.

'You must help her, Pierre. If she sees that you are horrified at her appearance, she will never face anyone again. Go to her now and prove that you still love her. Otherwise you can start looking for another job.'

Her small figure succeeded in appearing so angry and indomitable that Court hid a smile as Pierre backed hastily out of the room, virtually bowing to the floor in his desire to please 'my lady'.

Suddenly Anne was overcome by a wave of tiredness and utter exhaustion as the full impact of the burden and stress of the past few weeks struck home. Thankfully she sought the peace of her own room and slept.

She was woken in the night by an unusual sound – so unfamiliar to her that she lay for several minutes, hovering in and out of sleep, trying to identify it. Then with a gasp, she sprang out of bed and fled along the passage. It was Victoria. Crying the helpless bewildered sobs of a child who has never experienced pain.

In the nursery the nanny was kneeling by the crib. She turned, wild-eyed, to stare at Anne and began to scream hysterically, pointing towards the baby.

Anne placed a trembling hand on the child's forehead which was burning hot. Vicky wailed again.

Then, by the light of the lamp, Anne saw the small red dots on Victoria's neck. 'No!' she cried. 'It isn't possible! She was vaccinated. I watched the doctor do it.'

Anne seized the child from the cot and held her as if she would never let her go. Tension was building up inside her to unbearable heights and she opened her mouth to let out one terrible scream. The effort left her shuddering and gasping but the tightness within her had broken and by the time Matthew and Court rushed into the room, she was in control of herself again.

'Get her away from here!' she said, pointing at the hysterical nanny. 'Obviously she is not going to be the slightest help. Fetch Henriette.'

But Henriette had already appeared and together the two women began nursing the sick child.

The fever was fierce. They tried to keep her cool by sponging her and by placing ice packs round her hot body. The pocks itched and itched and Vicky wailed piteously as Anne clung to her flailing fists to try to prevent her from scratching.

Matthew and Court hardly left the house. In their helplessness and anguish they took refuge in the bottle and drank steadily, long into the night. But the alcohol had little effect on Matthew; his senses remained alert, focused on the nursery.

One day became two, became three and then four, and still the two women did not sleep. Or, thought Anne dully as she sat in a chair while Henriette tended the child, it seemed as though they did not sleep, but in fact they must have dozed a little from time to time. As if in confirmation, her head grew heavy and she lapsed into a dream state of semi-consciousness. In the white mist which swirled about her she saw John Court's face clearly several times, bent anxiously over her, and she could almost have believed that she saw Matthew walking up and down the room with Vicky in his arms. But surely she must have imagined that?

She awoke with a start as she heard Henriette say: 'The fever is rising again.'

'Oh, no!' Anne was immediately wide awake. 'She is weakening. I don't know that she can survive another attack.'

The little one was soaked with sweat, her hair darkened and her face bright red, almost concealing the pustules which showed more vividly on her neck and body. Anne lifted her and felt the small body go rigid and start convulsing. Then Victoria gave one last desperate shudder and lay still.

Anne's heart thudded uncomfortably. She closed her eyes. Either the fever had broken or . . . She stood, still holding the motionless form of her baby daughter and even before she opened her eyes she knew that the child was dead.

Henriette began to weep.

Anne sat down, clutching her daughter's dead body and staring blankly into space. In a state of complete shock she could not speak or weep or even move. Matthew and Court came at once and tried to take the child from her, but her hands seemed to take on a life of their own and to clutch the body more tightly. It took an hour or more to prise Victoria loose from Anne's desperate grasp and then Matthew lifted her limp form from the chair and carried her to bed. She was aware that it was night, that time before dawn when life and hope are at their lowest ebb, and that Matthew stayed with her until the sun rose.

Then Henriette was there and later Matthew again. It was as though they dared not leave her alone. Numbly Anne obeyed their orders and somehow stumbled through the days until she took faltering steps to the carriage and down the cemetery's winding path. Her gaze was riveted on the small white coffin. Victoria, so fair and bright, so good and happy and loving. How could it be that she was never to grow up, never to walk or talk, never to dance in the sunshine or kiss a man's lips? It wasn't fair! Anger began to burn in her. God was so cruel – why should He have taken her? Victoria, for whom she had waited so many years and whom she had enjoyed for so few months. Still Anne could not weep – the pain and the anger seethed inside her but she remained dry-eyed. Because with the pain and the anger was guilt; guilt which she could not yet acknowledge and which locked her emotions tightly within her.

Matthew, too, stared at the coffin and a layer of ice closed again around his heart, so recently and so briefly thawed. He glanced sideways at Anne's white face, feeling deep compassion for her pain and unaccustomed comfort for himself in the fact that they shared the guilt and grief. As Victoria was laid to rest, Matthew put his arm round Anne's shoulders and a shuddering sigh shook him. He knew the path along which their grief must lead them. But could he, dare he, ever love a child so much again?

Anne remained dry-eyed and a week passed before her tears were released. Each night Matthew came to her room and slept beside her, but he made no move to touch her. Every night Anne lay tense and wakeful in the bed until at last she found that she could speak to him.

'How could it happen? She was vaccinated.'

'Jameson says the vaccine must have been bad. Probably it was exposed to sun and heat. It was incredible that only Vicky was affected.'

'But they checked her arm to ensure that it had taken,' Anne insisted.

'Perhaps her arm was inflamed by the heat and this misled them.'

Matthew's voice was flat and heavy and Anne sensed a dark world of unspoken thoughts between them.

'You blame me, don't you?' At last she could put it into words.

'I believed that it was foolish of you to nurse Henriette and increase the risk of infection in the house,' he said carefully.

'So you do think that is how Vicky caught smallpox? From Henriette?'

'Not necessarily. Please don't let us argue about it, Anne. It cannot bring Vicky back.'

But for once it was Anne who wanted to argue. Anne who had to purge her soul of the torment within her.

'But in your heart of hearts you blame me, just as I blame you. If you had listened to me last year this epidemic might have been averted. You and your precious mining friends endangered this entire community. You . . .'

'Stop it, Anne!' Matthew cut in roughly. 'You will achieve nothing by this talk. Try to get some sleep.'

'It's your fault! You killed my baby. Oh, it's all right for you, you didn't love her, just as you never loved me . . . Oh!'

A stinging slap had caught her full across the face. Matthew was leaning over her, his face livid with anger.

'How dare you say I didn't love her! She was my daughter too and I loved her more than you will ever know. I have suffered more this past week than you will ever realise, because you have given no thought to anyone but yourself!'

Anne stared at him in horror. He was right – she had not for a moment considered the grief of others.

'Secretly you are blaming yourself for Vicky's death. You did wrong in nursing Henriette here, although everyone who knows you understands that you did it for the best motives. I do *not* believe that Victoria caught smallpox from Henriette. Do you hear me, Anne? I do *not* believe that and therefore I do not think you killed her. If *you* can believe that, it is the first step on your road to recovery. The second step will be to indulge in a good cry – your dry eyes are unhealthy. And there is a third step, too . . .' He paused.

'What is that?' Anne whispered.

'To have another child.'

She felt his lips on hers, stabbing her with short sweet kisses and while she felt no passion she welcomed his presence and his nearness. He seemed to sense her mood and did not try to arouse her but entered her swiftly, moving with gentle firmness and familiarity within her. Anne lay beneath his thrusting body and closed her eyes, seeing the moving pictures against her eyelids – pictures of her baby daughter. And as Matthew drove on, more savagely now, to his climax, Anne experienced a new fulfilment of her own. Instead of shuddering sexual satisfaction she found the sobs rising in her throat and the tears brought a welcome release greater than anything she had ever known.

For the first time Matthew did not turn away from her afterwards to his own sleep, but held her in his arms and comforted her. It was his way of sharing her grief and saying that he was sorry.

Anne did not conceive that night and it was three months before the new baby came into being. Philip was born in June 1885, a year after the death of Victoria. Matthew was pleased to have a son to whom he could bequeath his fortune and who would continue the diamond dynasty. But he did not unbend to Philip as he had to Victoria. He dared not risk his emotions again so soon.

CHAPTER FIVE

The following year Nicholas made his long-awaited visit to Kimberley. He was now plump and prosperous. Life as a diamond dealer suited him well, providing occupation and an income commensurate with his needs. He was not weighed down with the burden of business because Reynolds carried the major share of the responsibility. His private life was also untroubled; Nicholas showed no inclination to marry and was not deeply disturbed by family upheavals. At thirty-six he already wore the smooth youthful look of the committed bachelor and exuded the cheerful good humour of everyone's favourite uncle.

The threads of his relationship with Matthew and Anne were picked up as if they had never been apart. He brought the same comfort and relaxation as a well-worn shoe. Moreover he was the perfect guest. Nicholas genuinely found everything so novel, exciting and interesting that he could not contain his enthusiasm until Matthew had shown him every corner of this strange diamond city. He gaped in astonishment at the massive 'Big Hole' of the Kimberley Mine. Nearly a mile in circumference and occupying an area of about thirty-eight acres, the pit had not reached its ultimate depth but nevertheless plunged six hundred feet below ground level.

'Good Lord!' exclaimed Nicholas. 'Do you realise that one could stand three Nelson's Columns one on top of the other and they would not reach the surface? How can the men work down there? It looks absolutely terrifying.'

'Open-cast mining will come to an end soon – if the diamonds don't run out first!' Matthew answered. 'A system of underground mining, of shafts and tunnels, will be introduced. Rhodes knows an American engineer at the gold mines in the Eastern Transvaal who might effect the changeover. But first, we must consolidate the mines.'

'Will consolidation affect my side of the business?' inquired Nicholas, a touch importantly.

'Most decidedly. At the moment each link in the selling chain – from the mining companies to the diamond merchants to the jewellers – is trying to make as much profit as possible for itself, regardless of the state of the market. What is needed is a central selling agency through which every diamond can be channelled and the sales controlled.'

'In that case, surely you can come back to London soon?'

'The time may not be too far distant,' answered Matthew cautiously. 'The consolidation of the mines is all-important at present. After that – well, we'll see.'

Naturally Nicholas brought first-hand news of home but the situation at Highclere did not make for pleasant hearing. He reported that Freddy's condition had not improved and that the Earl was confined permanently to the West Wing, visited only by his mother. Isobel refused to see anyone except her personal servants. However, Nicholas had caught an occasional glimpse of her as she hobbled about the house and said that despite the thick black clothing she wore he could see that her body was bent and angular.

Charles was at Eton, a dull and rather surly lad, and developing into an unremarkable scholar; the best one could hope for was that ultimately he would make a responsible landowner and peer of the realm. The boy had a few youthful characteristics which Nicholas hoped he would outgrow – chiefly a tendency to bully his little brother. Charles was never unkind to Julia, it appeared, only to Edward.

Edward himself was a beautiful child with thick brown hair, plump pink cheeks, warm hazel eyes and a mouth which was always smiling; he had a sunny disposition which, amid the funereal atmosphere of Highclere, was little short of miraculous.

It was Julia who apparently gave real cause for concern. She was withdrawn and unresponsive – probably because, of the three children, she missed her mother the most. All the family had tried to penetrate the girl's reserve and Lady Jane, in particular, had given Julia a lot of time and attention before she and her husband Bruce left the district. But Julia had remained cold and aloof.

'Elizabeth, who looks like joining me as another unwed member of the family, has a theory about Julia,' said Nicholas. 'She says that Julia is extremely sensitive and will not give her affection because she is afraid that either it will be rejected or it will culminate in tragedy.'

Anne shivered. There was something ominous about Nicholas's casual choice of words.

The visit of Nicholas proved to be a turning point. Each of them – Matthew, Anne and Court – enjoyed his company. Matthew relaxed visibly, taking more time away from the office and spending that time at home. Court developed an instant rapport with the friendly unassuming Englishman, and abandoned his solitary drinking habits to join Nicholas on a few bachelor forays into the town.

Anne abandoned herself completely to the sunshine of these days, happier than she had been since Victoria died, happier perhaps than she had ever been. Apart from her pleasure in Nicholas's company, she saw much more of Matthew now. She revelled in the informal, friendly, family atmosphere and yet she dared to hope that Matthew's attitude towards her was rather more than merely friendly. Those brief flashes of illumination were becoming more frequent and once or twice she had seen him looking at her with unfamiliar tenderness in his eyes, veiled still, but there nonetheless.

Then the day of Nicholas's departure crept closer and Anne became afraid that the bubble would burst after he had gone. She became obsessed with the idea that if she and Matthew could return to London, life would always be like this.

'I hate this place,' she said vehemently to Nicholas a few days before he was due to leave.

'Great fun for a visit,' Nicholas agreed, 'but I shouldn't want to live here.'

'I have lived here for nearly nine years. Nine years of dust and heat, illness and death, in a social desert, where any individual comes a very poor second to those nasty little pieces of rock which, for reasons which escape me, are so highly prized.'

'Oh, that's coming a bit strong, old thing,' Nicholas protested. 'Those rocks as you call them have transformed the fortunes of Desborough and Highclere, you know.'

'Have they? I wonder. Oh, Nicky, I wish you could stay! Or, even better, I wish we could come home with you.'

'No reason why you shouldn't come, just for a visit, even if Matthew is too busy to tear himself away. You could travel with me and bring young Philip. This place don't seem to agree with him, either. Always crying, isn't he!'

Anne sighed but shook her head resolutely. 'I cannot leave Matthew.' *Dare* not leave Matthew, her inner voice advised, for fear she might lose what little ground she had gained. She tried to adopt a lighter tone. 'I would like to come home permanently. I find I like having a brother around me.'

'You always have John.'

'John? Yes, he is like a brother to me, but I prefer you.'

'Matthew did tell me that the time for going home was not too far away,' said Nicholas.

'Did he? Did he really? Oh, that's *wonderful*!' Anne flung her arms round his neck, 'Then I can begin to plan a whole new life!'

But after Nicholas had gone home, in the June of 1886, it was just as Anne had feared. He had provided a catalyst to the complex personal relationships in the Bright household and now they relapsed into their former ways. Worse than that, the tensions and divisions became even sharper. He had opened their eyes once more to the outside world, reminded them of the limitations of their everyday existence, and they became edgy, restless and dissatisfied. Automatically Matthew immersed himself in business, keenly interested in the rumours that gold had been found near Pretoria in the Transvaal. Court sought the familiar bottle. Anne alternated between attacks of sharp-tongued anger and bouts of deep depression, as she watched the happy days drift away and could find no means to recall them.

Not even her baby son could lift her spirits. Most of the time she thought more about the dead Victoria than the living Philip, who did not have Victoria's open and affectionate nature. As Nicholas had noticed, he cried frequently, but he found greater comfort with his nanny than with his mother. Not even Philip, Anne told herself bitterly, would miss her if she was gone.

As July drew to a close she grew thin and pale, inclined to sudden fits of weeping and uncharacteristic outbursts of temper over matters of trifling importance. Things came to a head when Matthew stalked into the house and announced elatedly that he was leaving immediately for the Transvaal.

Anne was lunching with Court. 'What's the hurry?' asked Court, his speech slightly slurred.

'Rhodes and Rudd have decided to take a look at the gold fields. We are leaving on today's stage.' Matthew laughed. 'There's no stopping Rhodes once he has made up his mind.'

'Why do you have to go?' Anne demanded angrily. If she had known Matthew was going away, she could have gone to England with Nicholas.

Matthew looked at her in astonishment. '*Why?* Because if these gold discoveries are as good as people say, I want a piece.'

'I thought you were in the diamond business.'

'I am.'

'And I thought you were making a lot of money?'

'I am. Just what are you trying to say, Anne?'

'That we don't need any more money, that we don't need to involve ourselves any further in the affairs of this God-forsaken country, that it is time we went home!'

Anne's voice rose shrilly as the torrent of words poured out – words that she had always sworn she would never speak, but which could be dammed inside her no longer.

Her tone irritated Matthew unbearably. He was hot, tired and exceedingly busy and had neither time nor patience for domestic drama. 'Do you want to return home so badly?'

'Yes!'

'Then go home! I shall not stand in your way.' Chafing to be off, he walked to the door and bellowed for Amos, his valet, to pack his valise.

Anne was shaking as his cruel words hammered in her tormented brain. 'So you want to be rid of me! Well, it certainly would make no difference to you whether or not I was here, since you find no time for your family at all. You could do without me very well.'

Matthew's lips tightened in annoyance. 'I can certainly do without scenes like this when I have business to attend to. However, I have no wish to "be rid of you" as you put it. I simply wish you to do whatever will make you happy. If going to England will achieve that, then you must go.' He shrugged impatiently and approached Court who was still sitting at table with the inevitable glass of wine in his hand. Matthew's progress was impeded, however, by the small furious figure of Anne whose pent-up emotions were being released in one almighty flood.

'You're tired of me, aren't you! Although "tired" is probably the wrong word, because you never really wanted me in the first place. You have never loved me.' In her distress Anne not only voiced her deepest fears but began saying things which in her heart she knew were untrue. 'I suppose you have a lover, and she is the reason you are rarely at home and even more rarely in my bed. Well, perhaps I will take a lover and you will know how humiliation feels!'

'My dear Anne,' snapped Matthew, by now thoroughly exasperated. 'Take a lover by all means. In fact, take as many as you want! But do remember what I indicated on the memorable occasion of our first meeting – that I expect my wife to behave like a lady.' He turned to speak to Court. 'John, I don't know how long I'll be away but either Rhodes or myself will be in constant touch. Send Amos to the coach station with the valise.' And he strode out of the room without another word. A moment later his horse could be heard clattering down the drive.

Anne was weeping hysterically. Court drained his glass and watched her uncomfortably. The face of Alida swam irresistibly into his mind and when Anne groped blindly for the door he stood up and barred her path. He had let Alida run away into the snow to assuage her sorrow alone, but Anne must not be allowed the same opportunty to harm herself.

'Don't go!' he said. 'I hate to see you so unhappy.'

Spontaneously he held out his arms and Anne went into them as though it was the most natural thing in the world. She buried her face in his broad chest and cried and cried while Court rocked her gently and laid his cheek against her hair.

'I know I said a lot of silly things, but he doesn't love me, John. He never has.'

'I love you,' Court murmured. 'I have always loved you, from the moment I first saw you.' He held her so tightly against him that Anne could feel the breath being squeezed from her body and hear his heart hammering in his chest. She could not absorb the implication of his words but only felt the healing balm of the warmth of his regard. She needed to be loved by someone and his arms were so safe and comforting.

But then his lips met hers and safety fled, and what had started out as comfort turned to passion.

The effect of the wine and the feel of Anne in his arms, after so many years of dreaming, drove all sense from Court's mind. His kisses grew ever more demanding and his hands explored her body urgently. Yet there was still a gentleness beneath his desire and Anne knew that one word or one move from her would be enough to stop him. But she did not say that word. Neither did she break free from his grasp. As his strong tanned hands moved to her breast she knew that she did not desire him, but she did want to stay close to him and immerse herself in the reassurance of his presence. And, above all, instead of being consumed with passion, she was consumed with hate for Matthew – smarting from the hurt he caused her and seeking a means to strike back.

She made no demur therefore when Court swept her into his arms and carried her down the corridor to his bedroom.

When Matthew left the house he rode hard for several minutes. Lovers indeed, he muttered angrily, I have been faithful to her from the day we were married. Then the tension and irritation in him eased and he reined in his horse and trotted more sedately along the road into town.

The violence of Anne's outburst had taken him by surprise. Usually she was cool and calm, coping admirably with everything, the perfect wife. Perhaps, he thought, he had been a trifle tactless. He should have broached the subject of the Transvaal trip more diplomatically and more apologetically.

Was it possible that Anne did not want him to go away because she would miss him? Was it possible that beneath that icy, proud exterior she cared just a little for him? Surely not, and yet . . .

His horse, as if sensing Matthew's indecision, walked still more slowly and finally came to a complete halt. Matthew sat in the saddle at the side of the road and stared into space.

Matthew did not know what constituted the perfect wife, but he did face up to the fact that Anne was the only wife he wanted. He discovered that he admired and respected her and that he was even proud of her. He found her body pleasing and her presence enjoyable. Most of all, he did not want to lose her. He did not care to examine how closely his feelings resembled love, but did decide that it had been a stupid quarrel about nothing and that he could not journey to the Transvaal without making his peace with her. And perhaps he might find out if she did care for him . . . a little . . .

Matthew turned his horse and galloped home.

In the drive he dismounted and handed the horse's reins to a stableboy before running lightly across the remaining few yards to the door and entering the house. He looked first in the drawing-room, but it was empty. The door leading to the dining-room was ajar and, thinking he heard a sound, he crossed the salon noiselessly and looked into the next room.

He saw Anne and Court in a passionate embrace, their lips meeting hungrily and Court's hand on Anne's breast. He watched as Court lifted Anne and carried her through the opposite doorway in the direction of the bedrooms.

For a moment Matthew was motionless, white-faced and shocked. Then his eyes blazed and his features twisted, and he took several strides down the passage after them, before stopping once more. He swung on his heel and walked to the drinks cabinet to pour a stiff brandy. He drained the glass and threw it hard against the wall, watching it shatter along with his marriage.

The noise brought Amos running and the valet stared in consternation at the broken glass but made no comment.

'The valise is ready, boss.'

'Thank you. I'm leaving now. I assume Boss Court did not give you a message?'

'No, boss.'

'I thought he would not have found the time.' Matthew smiled crookedly. 'Be sure to tell him, Amos, that I returned for the valise. That is most important.'

He strode out of the house, head held high and back straight as a ramrod, swung himself into the saddle and cantered off briskly without a backward glance.

When Anne and Court emerged from the bedroom an hour or so later, they returned to the drawing-room. There was an uncomfortable silence. They could not meet each other's eyes and guilt hung like an invisible curtain between them.

Anne rang for some tea. She was already wondering if Henriette had been searching for her. The houseboy brought the tea and then began sweeping up slivers of glass from the carpet by the far wall.

'What happened?' asked Anne.

'I don't know, my lady. Amos told me to clean it up.'

'Ask Amos to come here.'

But Amos had not witnessed the accident either. 'The boss might have broken it,' he volunteered.

'Matthew? But he didn't have a drink before he left.'

'I think he did, my lady. Just before I gave him the valise.'

The teacup rattled in the saucer as Anne's hands shook and she replaced it hurriedly on the table.

'Amos, I was supposed to give you a message about the valise. I'm sorry, but I forgot.' Court's voice was cracked.

'No matter, Boss Court. I had finished packing it before Boss Matthew left. He told me to tell you that he returned for it.'

Anne rose and, without speaking to Court, ran to her room and locked the door.

Court stayed on in the drawing-room, ignoring the tea but staring fixedly at the drinks cabinet. He knew that he had loved her and lost her all in one day. He had known a fleeting moment of paradise and now . . . But had it been paradise? Or had he felt bad and guilty all along? And how much did the wine allow him to remember anyway?

The wine! The damn drink! That was to blame. Even now his head ached and his mouth tasted stale. And he had lost her – lost not only her body and the remote dreams of everlasting happiness, but lost her friendship too, because she would hate him for what he had done today.

The wine! He would never touch the stuff again as long as he lived. Court stood up and, standing almost exactly where Matthew had stood earlier, he threw a bottle of wine at the wall. And another. And another. And the brandy and the rest of the bottles too.

The noise was deafening. The mess was appalling. The stench was nauseating. But it was worth it. At least, John Court said to himself, when one had money one could let off steam in style!

Anne lay wakeful throughout the long night. That Matthew had seen them, she had no doubt. This realisation was bad enough, but in addition she tormented herself with theories about why he had returned. Could it have been that he came to say he was sorry? She pressed her burning cheeks and sore eyes into the pillow to blot out the possibilities that this thought conjured up. Then another and even more terrible possibility came to haunt her. What if she conceived a child? Matthew had not slept with her for weeks, even months; he would know the child could not possibly be his. Panic started to engulf her. She clenched her hands and reminded herself that it had taken six *years* for Victoria to come into being and three months for Philip. It could not possibly happen the first time with John. It simply could not happen.

CHAPTER SIX

The little landlocked republic of the Transvaal had a small rural population of Dutch-speaking burghers, most of whom were of Trek Boer stock. They were a simple people, isolated and mostly uneducated; even the President was semi-illiterate. They measured wealth in terms of land and oxen, but by any standards the country was bankrupt. The dour Transvaalers resented, and resisted, any system of taxation.

This was the land to which Willem and Daniel trekked when they left the diamond fields. To the wild free land of the Highveld, with its vistas of rolling plains and tall grasses under a clear blue sky; with its herds of game and thin sparkling air as invigorating as champagne in the brilliance of each new day. This was a land of few towns and tiny communities, and of tough hard men who lived in the saddle with their rifles at their sides. A land which nobody but the Boers wanted, because it contained nothing of value.

So thought Willem and Daniel as they shook off the red dust and cosmopolitan furore of Kimberley and returned to their own people.

They bought a farm some five miles south of Pretoria. Sewefontein it was called, 'Seven Fountains', and while the wells were not abundant the water supply was adequate and Willem settled contentedly into a quiet pastoral life. But Daniel, or Danie as he became known, could not find peace of mind. There still burned within him a deep resentment against injustice and oppression which the attack on Anne had not assuaged. He did not know the result of his attack, did not know whether Anne had lived or died, but he was coming to the realisation that the job he had begun was far from being finished.

For Danie the first warning bells jangled when the news filtered through of gold discoveries in Barberton, in the north-east of the Transvaal. The search for gold was nothing new and Willem and his friends and neighbours shook their heads and shrugged their shoulders at these latest rumours. This time, however, there was gold and in payable quantities, but Barberton was far enough away for these men to remain unperturbed. 'It won't last,' they said about the Barberton boom, and they were right.

But the gold-seekers were busy closer to home. Mining concessions were granted and gold-ore-crushing batteries sprouted in the veld. Then a neighbour came to tell Willem and Danie that gold had been found only a few miles away, on the farm Langlaagte which belonged to the widow Oosthuizen. She had sold the property for six thousand pounds to a stranger. The description of the stranger was instantly recognisable to Danie: it was J. B. Robinson, and Danie's eyes glittered as he realised that the Kimberley diamond magnates had followed him to the Rand.

There was nothing Danie could do about the sale of the Oosthuizen farm, but he was determined to prevent others from making the same mistake. His difficulty lay in persuading the farmers that such deals *were* a mistake.

Danie soon found that he was a lone voice in the wilderness. Just as J. B. Robinson displayed rare genius in recognising the nature of the Reef – for he had no geological training – so Danie was motivated by an instinct which enabled him to foretell future developments on the Witwatersrand. He saddled his horse and rode from the farm to plead with his fellow Boers.

'I know these people from Kimberley,' he insisted. 'If J. B. Robinson offers £6,000 for a farm, it is more likely to be worth £60,000.'

The men laughed at such a ridiculous figure for a piece of bare Transvaal veld.

'Robinson is only the first,' Danie went on. 'Soon the other Kimberley diamond magnates will be here, and will use the money they have made from diamonds to buy our land.'

'Good! That means there will be competition for the land and prices will rise,' said one farmer, proud of his grasp of business affairs.

'Don't sell!' begged Danie. 'If there is gold, it should be ours. It belongs to us.'

'How do we dig the gold out of the ground?' asked another man with a practical turn of mind. 'Mining machinery is expensive and we might not even find enough gold to pay for it.'

'We can pay people from overseas to tell us about the gold. And the government should buy the machinery,' said Danie.

The group laughed again. 'Paul Kruger's coffers are empty. Everyone knows that.'

'Then he should borrow the money from other countries,' Danie asserted stubbornly, remembering the lessons which he and Willem had learned on the diamond fields.

But the Boers shook their heads. 'We will sell our farms here to the highest bidder,' they declared, 'and buy another farm elsewhere. We will make a handsome profit.'

'You do not understand,' said Danie slowly. 'You do not realise what the gold-mining will mean to you and to our land. The strangers will come, the *uitlanders* with their foreign habits and way of life. They will destroy us and the very fabric of our existence. I have seen it happen in Kimberley and it will happen again here.'

Danie followed Robinson like a shadow, riding at a safe distance, watching with an aching fury in his heart as property after property was sold. He traversed lonely miles across the stony kopjes and rocky outcrops of the Witwatersrand, 'Ridge of White Waters', in the desperate belief that he was the sole and seemingly impotent guardian of this land. He saw other Kimberley men, including Hans Sauer who was securing options for Rhodes. Then came the day that Danie had waited for: he saw Matthew.

When he spotted Sauer's familiar wagon in the veld on that particular day he could make out two figures in the cart. The second man was wearing a wide-brimmed hat and was unrecognisable from this distance, but Danie's heart beat faster and cautiously he rode closer. The wagon was descending into a shallow valley and by hugging the contours of the barren hills Danie could keep it in sight without revealing his own presence. When it stopped and the two men climbed out, Danie reined in his horse and watched. They seemed to be inspecting the ground minutely, crouching and bending, picking up samples of rock. Then the unknown man straightened and took off his hat and ran his fingers through his hair. The golden mane blazed bright in the sunlight and Danie gazed again on the unmistakable figure of his old enemy. He drew in his breath sharply and involuntarily his hand moved to his rifle and clasped the butt lovingly.

He could do it here and now. Kill Matthew. And get away with it, for Sauer's wagon would never catch him and he was too far away to be recognised.

Danie slipped from the saddle and tethered his horse. There was a piece of high ground to his right which would provide a clear view of the valley. Keeping low, Danie ran forward and quickly climbed the slope. At the summit he lay flat on his stomach and cautiously peered over the edge.

Matthew was still standing. He had his back to Danie and was examining a lump of rock in his hand. As Danie watched, Matthew shouted something to his companion and walked away from the cart towards a different patch of ground.

Wriggling on his stomach, Danie moved along the line of the ridge, inching towards a large boulder which would screen him for the shot – but, no, Matthew had changed direction again and, cursing silently, Danie was forced to follow suit.

Now Matthew stopped. Apparently he had found something which interested him because he picked up a rock specimen and turned to wave excitedly at Sauer; at that moment he was facing Danie full-square.

Danie lay motionless. It would be a long shot – literally. But Danie had the Boer's sharp eyes and steady rifle-hand which raked the herds of game and which had – and would again – decimate the ranks of British redcoats. He raised the rifle and took careful aim.

But just as he was about to squeeze the trigger, he heard the sound of hooves on the hard ground as two horsemen swept into the valley and pulled up beside the wagon. They were Boers and Danie did not doubt that they were the owners of the land, come to negotiate a selling price. Matthew hurried across to meet them. Angrily Danie lowered the rifle and retreated.

As he returned to the farm, he was considering his next move.

He was tempted to try another shot at Matthew, but common sense told him that this was a foolhardy course. He was mistaken in thinking he could get away with murder here: his links with Kimberley and his well-known opposition to the gold fields would make him an obvious suspect.

There had to be another way of fighting. His people needed capital, but Danie did not see how he could provide that commodity. The realisation of the role he had to play came gradually, like a great light spreading through the dark recesses of his struggling mind.

His people needed organisation. They needed a plan of action. Only by banding together could they defend their interests. They were losing ground and would probably lose more before the tide turned, but by a concerted effort they could win back that which they had lost. Danie knew that he must continue his campaign, continue to raise his voice in dissent until he had persuaded and influenced his people to follow him.

At present there was only one way in which he could do this. The dominie of the *Kerk* in Kimberley had taught him to read and write in Dutch; thanks to John Court, he had an equal facility in English. Armed with these rare accomplishments, Danie rode to Pretoria and presented himself at the offices of *De Volksstem*, the leading newspaper in the Transvaal. The editor hired him on sight and so, through *De Volksstem's* columns, Danie's burning nationalism began to reach a wider audience.

The first piece he wrote concerned the gold fields of the Witwatersrand which were officially proclaimed on 8 September 1886. 'A Township will be built at Ferreira's Camp where the miners have pitched their tents,' he wrote. 'The township will be called "Johannesburg" . . .'

Matthew stayed three months in the Transvaal, carving himself a sizeable share of the gold-bearing reef. He worked hard and played hard, flinging himself into a frenetic round of activity in order to forget the gnawing ache in his heart. When he returned to Kimberley at the beginning of November, he congratulated himself on controlling his emotions and on his ability to face the lovers with equanimity – a great deal more equanimity, he imagined, than they would feel in confronting him.

In that assumption Matthew was perfectly correct.

The disintegration of the Bright household had begun the day after he left. Anne and Court had been barely able to look each other in the face; they felt guilty, dirty and degraded. They had succumbed to a moment's passion, for all the wrong reasons, and jeopardised what should have been a sincere and lasting friendship. In addition, they faced the appalling prospect that Matthew knew what had taken place.

Court blessed the fact that for some unaccountable sentiment he had retained the old cabin where he and Matthew had first lived; even the sparse and shabby furniture still stood as they had left it. He despatched a servant to give the place a thorough clean and moved in with his few personal possessions the same day. The move caused no surprise or gossip. It was still quite normal for wealthy men to live in humble circumstances, and the propriety of Court leaving the Bright home during Matthew's prolonged absence was fully appreciated.

Anne was relieved when he went, but found the loneliness almost unbearable. There was no one in whom she could confide her fears and as the days became weeks, and the weeks became months, the tension mounted to such an extent that she could hardly eat and she suffered from blinding headaches. By the time Matthew returned, she was sure she was pregnant.

The pregnancy did not yet show and Matthew did not ask any questions. In fact, he hardly spoke to her at all. He neither mentioned the incident nor commented on Court's change of living quarters. He preserved a polite civility to her in front of other people and somehow contrived to ensure that they were never alone. If company was not expected for dinner, Matthew ate at the Club. As Anne sat alone at the vast dining-table on such evenings, she was aware of the sympathetic and worried looks of the servants, but she never allowed the calm mask of her features to crack. However, she could not disguise the great violet shadows under her eyes, the hollow cheeks and the gaunt boniness of arms and shoulders.

By Christmas she was nearly five months pregnant and she knew the time had come when she must tell Matthew. There had been guests at dinner that evening and after they had departed Matthew, as usual, coldly turned his back on Anne in order to go to his own room. But she called him back. He stared at her with ice-blue eyes and wordlessly led the way to the drawing-room, closing the door behind them. He did not sit down but stood in silence, waiting for her to speak.

Anne took a deep breath. Her heart was thudding and her throat was dry. The fact that Matthew was looking impossibly handsome in his evening clothes did not make it any easier for her to say what she had to say. She noticed that his coat bore the diamond buttons he had worn at their wedding.

Over and over again she had rehearsed her speech, but now that the moment was here she forgot all her fine phrases and the words tumbled out in a rush.

'I am expecting a child.'

Matthew's eyes narrowed and his gaze swept disdainfully over her body.

'My felicitations,' he said coldly. 'But why are you telling *me*? I would have thought that the news was of greater interest to the child's father.'

'I am telling you because you are my husband,' said Anne helplessly.

'A fact which you would have done well to bear in mind on other occasions.'

Anne drew herself up with as much dignity as she could muster. 'I realise that I can no longer continue to be your wife and that I must leave here to have my baby elsewhere.'

'You are certainly correct in your belief that I will not harbour a bastard under my roof,' agreed Matthew. 'However, I will not tolerate any kind of scandal; you are my wife and you will remain my wife.'

'I do not understand what you expect me to do.

'It is quite simple. You will leave here to have the baby in secret. After the birth you will make arrangements for the care of the child and then you will return here. The matter can be easily arranged. You have been looking unwell recently and it will seem perfectly natural for you to leave for the coast for a time to recover your health.'

'What,' said Anne unsteadily, 'do you mean by "arrangements" for the child?'

'I should have thought it was obvious. The child should be the responsibility of its father.'

'You expect me to part with my baby,' cried Anne. 'To give away my own flesh and blood and never see the child again?'

'If you wish to describe the event so dramatically, then yes, I do.'

Anne felt faint. Horrified as she was by Matthew's pronouncement, she knew she was powerless to argue. 'I assume you have no objection to Philip accompanying me to the coast.'

'Take the boy by all means,' said Matthew indifferently. 'His future is of little consequence to me, since I do not suppose he is any more my child than the bastard you are carrying now.'

A chill crept through Anne's bones which turned her body to stone. 'You surely do not think that John is Philip's father?' she gasped in horror. 'No, Matthew. Philip is your child. He is! He is! John and I only . . . it was only *once*, Matthew. Just that once because I was so upset with you and so unhappy.'

'You expect me to believe that? With all the opportunities you had for adultery?'

'Whose fault was it that we had so many opportunities?' flashed Anne. 'You should have been at home more often and cared more.'

'It ill becomes you, Anne, to blame others for the weakness of your own flesh.' Matthew walked to the door.

'You are not human,' said Anne brokenly. 'You are simply not human.'

Matthew paused with his hand on the door handle. 'On the contrary, Anne,' he said quietly, 'perhaps I am a lot more human than you have ever realised.'

In all these months Court had not once been back to the Bright house. Neither had he touched a drink. When he received Anne's note he felt stirrings of anxiety and was deeply tempted to seek the solace of wine. However, he resisted the urge and presented himself in Anne's drawing-room sober and grave-faced.

His reaction to the news was utterly different from what Anne had expected. 'Are you sure it is my child?' he asked, and his lean face broke into a joyous smile. 'That's the most wonderful thing I have ever heard!' Then the smile snapped off as suddenly as it had appeared. 'But it isn't wonderful for you,' he said slowly. 'Will Matthew accept the baby as his?'

Anne shook her head and explained the procedure Matthew had insisted she follow.

Court felt a growing excitement within him. It was as if all the paths he had trodden, all the self-doubt and frustrations of the past years had led him to this moment.

He seized Anne's hands and held them tightly. 'I will take the child,' he said. 'Please, Anne, please, let me take the child! If I am the father, then it is my duty and responsibility to do so.'

Anne looked at his transfigured face and her heavy spirits were lightened. The horror of parting with her child did not lessen, but there was enormous relief at finding a solution to the problem which wracked her day and night. How strange, she thought, as she saw the joy in his eyes, that the sinful act which had brought her such grim punishment should be his salvation.

'You can go to Cape Town,' Court was saying, 'and take a house there. I will pay all the expenses. Ask Jameson for the name of a good and discreet physician; you can trust him. Take only Philip and Henriette; hire any other servants you require when you reach the city. I will come to the Cape in April and stay near until the baby is born.'

'But John, how can you take care of a baby?' asked Anne in perplexity. 'You cannot conceal a child in your cabin or hide its existence from the society of Kimberley.'

'I have no intention of returning to Kimberley,' said Court softly. 'I shall take the baby home. To America.'

In so small a society as Cape Town it was impossible for a lady of Anne's standing to arrive unnoticed. She sent a note to the Governor announcing her arrival, but regretting that she was unable to call on him or receive visitors until her health had improved.

The dreary anxious days of waiting began, empty except for Philip and visits from the doctor. Matthew had observed the proprieties and dutifully seen her off on the train at Kimberley but otherwise he had not spoken to her and now no letter or message came.

Anne wrote letters and sewed and played with Philip and talked to Henriette. She sat in the privacy of the garden on warm summer days and when the wind blew from the south-east convinced herself that the breeze brought the fresh salt smell of the sea. Knowing what the future held, she could feel no joy in the movements of the baby within her and she worried that anxiety and lack of true maternal feelings might have an adverse effect on the unborn child. In her loneliness she was surprised by the surge of pleasure she felt when April came and brought Court to the Cape.

He slipped quietly into the house to visit her under cover of darkness. 'I know I should not have come,' he apologised, kissing her hand and looking intently at her strained face, 'but I had to see how you were.'

'I am very well, John, and so is your baby.' She smiled, trying to show more cheerfulness than she actually felt. 'I'm glad you are here, I am longing for news of Kimberley.'

'Of Matthew, you mean! He's fine. I have not spoken to him in private, of course, but in public he is polite and always careful to give everyone detailed accounts of your health.'

'He is as busy as always, I suppose.'

'Busier! There are negotiations in progress which could mean the final consolidation of all the claims in the De Beers Mine. If that is achieved, Rhodes and Matthew and the others will turn their attention to the Kimberley Mine.'

'I hope Matthew succeeds. He has worked very hard for this moment.'

'And I hope,' said Court gently, 'that our baby has your sweet forgiving nature. But I came to give you some good news. I have found a nurse for the child.'

'Oh!' Anne gritted her teeth. Such talk made the parting with the baby seem so near, so certain and so final.

'An Irishman was killed in an accident at the mine last week. His widow is only a young girl and to add to her troubles her newborn baby was at death's door. It died the day I left Kimberley. She readily agreed to nurse the child. She has a brother in America whom she would like to join, and she will be able to make a fresh start there.'

'That sounds splendid,' said Anne, attempting another brave smile. 'I hope you will not have long to wait.'

Anne's daughter was born on 6 May and was taken by Henriette to Court's lodgings. Before calling the nurse he stood alone, gazing down at the small bundle in his arms.

As he looked at the tiny crumpled face of his sleeping child, Court knew that he had received the sign for which he had waited so long. Now there was a reason for living and someone to benefit from the vast wealth he had accumulated from the Kimberley diamonds. Only one stone stood out in Court's mind from the thousands he had handled – the great yellow-gold diamond he had sold to the jewellers in New York.

And Court smiled. He would call his daughter Tiffany.

CHAPTER SEVEN

To Anne and Court 6 May 1887 was Tiffany's birthday, but to Matthew it had a very different significance. It was the day when De Beers became the first diamond mine in Kimberley to be consolidated. Within two years Rhodes had vanquished Barney Barnato in the battle for control of the Kimberley Mine and gained control of the diamond industry. The chief directors of the new Diamond Company were Rhodes, Beit, Barnato and Matthew Bright.

It was the end of an era. Gone was the colour, the life and vitality of Kimberley's early days. Gone were the fortune-seekers and the speculators. Gone too the rivalry and competition, the euphoria of success for some and the despair of failure for others.

In their place came the smooth grey efficiency of the great corporation. Soullessly, mechanically, the treasure was extracted from the blue ground, processed and shipped abroad. Underground mining was introduced and recovery methods improved. The marketing of the stones was refined by the formation of a syndicate of diamond merchants which co-ordinated sales at fixed prices.

For Matthew life settled into an almost monotonous routine of making money. Lots of money. His gold-mining interests in Johannesburg helped to swell the relentless growth of his bank balance, but the gold fields never held the same attraction for him as diamonds. The sparkle and glitter of beautiful stones fascinated him, providing the high points of his life and career and the pinnacles of his interest and achievement.

Nothing that Johannesburg produced ever quite matched that moment in July 1889 when the Diamond Company issued a cheque for Kimberley Central to finalise the consolidation of the mines. The cheque was for £5,338,650. When Matthew gazed at it, he knew that he had come a very long way in the twenty years since he had been hard pressed to find thirty-five guineas for his steamship passage to the Cape.

Through Matthew's mind marched a procession of memories, stepping-stones on the path to his success. The path led him from the Comtesse's diamond, through the vastness of the Great Karoo, to the river diggings and the excitement of his first diamond and his despair at the devastation of the river claim; on to the discovery of the dry diggings and the rushes to Dutoitspan, De Beers and Colesberg Kopje; IDB and the collapse of the roadways and the agony when the blueground seemed to be done; and finally to the steady expansion of his holdings which brought his reward.

Matthew was proud of his achievements and had conquered his innate sense of inferiority. Now he stood high in his own esteem and was ready to stand high in that of others.

The establishment of the giant corporation with its centralised systems and automatic procedures meant that Matthew's presence in Kimberley was no longer vital. Towards the end of 1889 he left for London to head the Company's operation there and to assume direct control of Bright Diamonds.

By 1893 he was well established in society. One of the hallmarks of the nineties was the interest shown by the Prince of Wales in self-made millionaires, among them the South African 'Randlords'. Robinson, Barnato and Beit were putting down roots in London, but of all the magnates Matthew was the most acceptable to the smart set. The label 'nouveau riche' could not be appended to him. People had not forgotten 'Diamond Bright' and now that he was among them with his stupendous wealth, he seemed to exude an aura of mystery and exoticism which set him apart and added to his fascination.

He bought a house in Park Lane from the Duke of Westminster. His own embellishments included a sweeping marble staircase, a vast ballroom, a billiard room and, since Anne felt the cold in winter after the heat of Kimberley, the entire house was heated by radiators. Matthew's favourite room became such a feature of the house that it was widely copied. Off the library he created a lush winter garden of brown rocks, green ferns and palms, mosaic pavements and exquisite fountains. In winter it had the soft moist warmth of a conservatory, while in summer it was a place of dim coolness and muffled silence, the muted murmur of London only vaguely audible.

In this Park Lane mansion Matthew entertained lavishly and threw himself into the smart lifestyle of the nobility, compensating for his youthful inadequacies and for the years in the 'wilderness' of Kimberley. He was careful, however, to conform and to ensure that his position in society was secure and soundly entrenched. He was particularly glad that liaisons with well-born ladies were both acceptable and prevalent.

For years Matthew had been faithful to Anne, not only out of duty or chivalry or propriety but because he directed his main energies into business activities. The bitter hurt of Anne's adultery with Court threw him into the arms of bought women in Johannesburg and Kimberley, but it was only when he came to London that he formed a lasting relationship.

The lady in question was Emma, Lady Longden. Matthew met her at a ball in the Season of 1890 and pursued her throughout the long hot summer, without any reward other than the encouragement which lay within her sensuous glance and the lingering touch of her hand. As tradition permitted, he began calling on her at tea-time. Every husband was expected to go out to tea and Lord Longden was no exception, sometimes taking tea at his club and sometimes with other men's wives. In the comparative privacy of the drawing-room, the affair progressed to passionate embraces and hungry kisses, with an ear cocked for the sound of a footfall at the door. But even if servants were trained not to enter a room unless summoned, the complicated tightly-laced clothes of the lady made further fulfilment impossible. Matthew and Emma had to wait for the autumn, when they received a mutual invitation to a house party in the country from an observant hostess who allocated them bedrooms in the same corridor. While Anne and Lord Longden slept unsuspectingly in their separate rooms, Matthew crept along the creaking corridor to his tryst, inexorably assailed by memories of the Comtesse and their assignations at Desborough nearly twenty-five years before.

There were echoes of the Comtesse too in Emma's chestnut hair and flawless skin, and in her maturity and worldliness. She had filled the Longden nursery with two sons and two daughters and society now permitted her a liaison, so long as the affair was totally discreet. That same society was merciless in its condemnation of the man and woman who relaxed this most rigid rule and committed the unpardonable offence of 'Being Found Out'.

Anne had been ill after Tiffany was born but it was a sickness of the mind rather than the body. She cared desperately that the child had been taken from her and was filled with despair at the knowledge that she would never see her daughter again. Gradually, however, she fought her way out of the black pit into which she had sunk, clawed her way up into the sunlight and regained her strength of mind and purpose. Eventually she accepted what she regarded as punishment for her sin and tried to consider the child as being dead – as dead as Victoria.

When she returned to London she was thirty years old and at the height of her beauty. Her good looks, impeccable lineage and prominent position as the wife of 'Diamond Bright' brought her instant success. But the long hard road to recovery had left its mark: although her expression was calm and serene, there was a sadness in the depths of her violet eyes which gave her a haunting ethereal air, an elusive quality which drove men mad. However, Matthew was not numbered among her admirers and without his approbation even the rich and varied life of London's high society seemed a desert.

Their marriage was a sham – a marriage in name only. In public they appeared to be the perfect couple – rich, well-born, handsome and happy: the people who had everything. In private they barely spoke to each other and occupied separate bedrooms. In the Park Lane house, or at Highclere or Desborough, it was easy to keep their distance from each other and to communicate by messages relayed by servants. So great was the gulf between them that Matthew had never once mentioned the child. Anne believed that he knew not if it was a girl or boy, whether it had lived or died, and obviously he did not care.

Apparently he did not care much for Philip either. He spent very little time with the boy and, on the rare occasions they were together, adopted an air of cold formality which even the autocratic Duke of Desborough would have deemed unnatural.

Anne tried to compensate for his lack of paternal affection, but gained little response. She had never felt close to her son and during her illness they had drifted even further apart. She did not find Philip a lovable boy. He was attractive to look at, the image of Anne with her silver-gilt hair and violet eyes, but he was lonely and withdrawn, wary of Anne's overtures and scared of Matthew's criticism. As he grew older, there developed in his eyes an expression of cynical assessment. This was a trait shared by his cousin Julia, who always exercised extreme caution in her personal relationships – or at least she had always done so until Matthew came home.

The children of Freddy and Isobel were a perennial source of anxiety to Anne.

Charles had been seventeen when his father died. At the time Freddy's health had seemed to be improving; his lucid periods were more prolonged and the imaginary torrents of water engulfed him less frequently. Security had been relaxed slightly, and during the summer of 1890 Freddy was allowed occasional walks in the Highclere grounds, although he was always accompanied by two guards. The children were not permitted to talk to him or to approach him in any way, and indeed were afraid to do so. They watched from a distance their father's short rotund figure trotting obediently between the two burly warders, and they kept their feelings to themselves.

One afternoon towards the end of the school holidays, Freddy requested a visit to the stables. A groom was leading out Charles's hunter, saddled and bridled for an afternoon ride, and with a whoop of joy Freddy broke free and sprinted across the yard. With remarkable athleticism he vaulted into the saddle and within seconds was galloping away.

Pandemonium broke out as Charles, the grooms and the guards dashed hither and thither, saddling horses for the pursuit. Freddy had a good start and the horse had taken a strong hold, so that at first it was all Charles and his companions could do to keep him in sight. He was taking a cross-country route in the direction of the Desborough estate, riding boldly at the gates and any other obstacles in his path. Gradually, however, the pursuers gained on him. Freddy's horse was tiring; he had always been a heavy man and years of inactivity had rendered him more corpulent still.

They were on Desborough land now and Freddy was lost from view on the other side of a copse. As they rounded the thicket and descended the gentle slope to the lake, their eyes searched the horizon for their quarry. But the landscape was bare – there was no one in sight.

It was Charles who saw the bay hunter, riderless, by the lake. He wheeled his horse, with a terrible premonition of what he would find. Freddy was lying face downwards in the shallow water at the edge of the lake. They pulled him out as quickly as they could, but he was dead.

Charles stood and stared down on the drowned body of the man who was his father – a man he hardly knew and barely remembered. Conscious of the sympathetic looks of his companions, he turned away and made an ostentatious examination of the hunter to ensure it had not been injured in the headlong flight from Highclere.

He did not want the grooms and guards to see his emotion, because he did not want them to recognise that emotion for what it was. Not grief for the father who was virtually a stranger. No, not grief but fear. Fear that he carried tainted blood. Fear that he, too, might go mad. Fear that he might pass on the taint to his children. Because Charles, like so many of his forebears, was afraid of the water.

It was for these reasons that Charles disliked Edward. In fact it was more a question of jealousy than dislike. Charles remembered vividly that dramatic scene between his parents on the evening of the fire, when he had heard Freddy refer to Edward as a bastard. Naturally Charles could not be sure of the facts, but the intensity of the scene he had witnessed inclined him to believe that the accusation was true. Whenever he looked at the sunny smiling countenance of the young Honourable Edward, a harsh bitter envy swept through him. 'It's all right for you,' Charles wanted to shout. 'It's easy for you to be happy and be liked by everyone. *Your* father didn't go mad.' Which was quite unjust, of course, since Edward believed his father had gone mad because he believed Freddy was his father. Edward coped with the situation better, that was all, and was puzzled (but not upset) by Charles's jibes and general lack of brotherly love.

Although they never discussed the subject, Charles was aware that Julia shared his fears. When she turned to Matthew for help he assumed that it was because – like himself – she welcomed Matthew as visible tangible evidence that not all Harcourt-Bright blood was bad.

However, Julia's relationship with Matthew was more complicated than that. Of necessity she had become a very cool, self-possessed young lady, cautious in what she gave and in what she accepted. The hurt in her ran deep and raw. Julia could remember that even before the accident her mother had been indifferent to her. When her father died Julia was fifteen and she examined her various male relations objectively to see if there was anyone on whom she could depend; she considered in turn her grandfather, her three uncles and her two brothers.

The first she rejected as being old and stuffy; Uncle Hugh was disinterested and preoccupied with his own affairs; Uncle Nicholas was nice, but weak; she shied away from Charles because he was beset with similar problems to her own; and Edward was too young. That left Matthew: Matthew of the splendid appearance, rapid stride, firm voice and unquestioned air of command.

At first he seemed to her cold and a little frightening but as the years passed and he made regular visits to Harcourt Hall to administer the estate until Charles should come of age, Julia's respect for him grew. His manner might be intimidating, but he could be relied upon to make decisions, solve problems and to mean what he said.

In 1893 Julia was eighteen and about to embark on her first Season. And eighteen is a dangerous age for a father fixation.

Anne had suggested that Julia should come to Park Lane and that the Brights should launch her into Society. Taking all the family circumstances into account, it seemed the sensible solution and, with no daugher of her own, Anne was sure she would enjoy the experience as much as Julia. Rather to Anne's surprise,

Matthew was entirely agreeable to the idea. He admired his niece: she was poised and sophisticated and, with the pale blonde beauty of Isobel and Anne, would be an ornament to the Season and a credit to his house. It was as if he had placed a diamond under a magnifying glass and found it to be flawless.

Unfortunately Julia also possessed the cold hardness of the gem. As Julia's partner escorted her back to Anne's side at the end of the dance, Anne saw with an inward sigh the haughty expression on the girl's face and the thankful way the young man escaped to a more lively rendezvous.

'You don't look as though you enjoyed that dance very much. Don't you like Alfred?'

'I find him extremely immature,' said Julia dismissively.

'He is in line to an ancient earldom and heir to a considerable fortune. And he will mature in time. I think he is a most charming young man.'

'Then *you* dance with him,' said Julia insolently.

Anne swallowed. For the past few weeks she seemed to have been constantly 'making allowances' for Julia's unnatural childhood, but even her endless patience was wearing thin.

'Have you no partner for this dance?' she asked as the music struck up again and Julia remained in her chair.

Julia's chin tilted in the manner of the Desborough girls. 'I received many offers,' she said proudly, 'but I do not wish to dance every dance.'

Rubbish! thought Anne. Every girl wants a partner for every dance. She had not been asked. Yet she looks so beautiful in her white dress, with her hair dressed high and the pearls glowing at her throat.

'Julia, please don't be upset by what I have to say. It is not your fault that you are unsure how to behave. Your upbringing has been different from that of other girls, and you have been too solitary. But you would be more popular and have more dancing partners if you could learn to smile. Look at the girls on the floor – watch how they smile and laugh. A man likes to be amused. Beauty and breeding are not enough.'

'Really?' Julia turned and stared at her with hard bright eyes. 'And you, of course, Aunt Anne, are an authority on how to win a man's heart – and keep it?'

Anne flinched and she could feel the colour drain from her face. 'What do you mean?' she whispered.

'From the first day I arrived at Park Lane it was obvious that Matthew does not care for you. So I do not believe you are qualified to give advice. In any case, these boys bore me.' Julia's eyes were searching the crowd and they sparkled into life as she found what she was looking for: Matthew's golden head and broad shoulders were pressing through the throng towards them. 'I prefer the company of older men,' said Julia softly.

'You do realise that I can send you home to Highclere at any time I choose.'

'No, that is just what you cannot do. It would cause gossip. Besides,' and already Julia was composing her features into an expression of artless innocence, 'Matthew would never believe you.'

'Not dancing, Julia? That will never do.' Matthew stood before them, bowing formally to Anne and smiling at his niece. 'Would you allow your old uncle the pleasure of your company?'

'Oh, I would like it more than anything!' and Julia was on her feet and into his arms in an instant.

Anne was left to fume in impotent solitude, watching Julia transformed into a gay bewitching creature who was smiling into Matthew's eyes.

What Anne could not understand was Julia's motive for such behaviour. She could not begin to fathom what Julia hoped to achieve.

The mind of every well-born Victorian girl was – or certainly should have been – firmly fixed on marriage. Not only was Matthew already married – and divorce was unacceptable to society – but also he was a close blood relation. It could not be that Julia was physically attracted to Matthew, reasoned Anne, because no Victorian girl had any inkling of sex. They were kept in ignorance until the wedding night. There must be a sadistic streak in men, thought Anne acidly, but the fact remained that Julia could have no thought of contact with a man beyond a kiss and an embrace. So what did she want of Matthew?

The last person who could have answered that question was Julia herself. Not that the question was ever put to her, nor did she ever consider it herself. She was impelled purely by a need to be close to Matthew and a desire to be the most important person in his life. Further than that she did not look. Sensing the weakness of Anne's position, Julia was determined to make the most of what seemed an advantageous situation.

The morning after the ball, she put on her most elegant riding habit and went in search of Matthew. He was sitting at his desk in a corner of the library, reading a letter from Emma. And he was smiling. Letters from Emma usually did put him in a good mood.

'The great thing about Emma,' he had confided to Nicholas recently, 'is that she is never a nuisance. She does not make demands and she does not put one under any obligation. She enjoys our relationship for what it is. A very relaxing attitude to adopt, I think you will agree?'

And Nicholas had agreed, albeit with a pang of concern for his sister and a touch of envy for Matthew's eternal good fortune with the ladies.

Now Matthew was smiling over a witty and amusing account of the entertainment Lady Longden had attended the previous night, but his eyes narrowed as he perused the closing paragraph.

'It seems so long since we were together,' she wrote, '*really* together. This interminable Season provides so few opportunities for us to be alone. How I long for the autumn and the house parties when I can look at you and know that night you will be mine. Will you come to tea today? Do, please, come. I shall leave instructions that I am at home to no one else and then if you come we can be alone together briefly and I can hold you and touch you a little.'

Matthew stared at the letter, written in Emma's round, feminine hand, in consternation. To have committed such emotions to paper was surprising enough, but he was much less troubled over what could be incriminating evidence than the fact that Emma was experiencing these feelings. As indicated in his conversation with Nicholas, her chief attraction for him was her undemanding nature. There were plenty of other ladies of equal good looks and background who were more than willing to be his mistress. Matthew stayed with Emma because her nature suited him. But what he had just read sounded horribly like a declaration of love – and involvement of that kind was exactly what Matthew did *not* want. It was messy and moreover it was dangerous. He did not love Emma and he never would love her but . . . Suddenly Matthew was aware of someone standing beside him and he swung round to look up into the fair face of Julia. She was staring at the letter.

Julia had crept into the library and stolen up behind him, intending to startle him as a game. She saw that he was reading a letter, but as he turned towards her she could tell by his expression that he did not consider her presence a joke. He was troubled, guilty rather than angry. Her eyes flicked back to the letter and registered a swift impression of it before Matthew thrust it into a drawer. Not a business letter, she thought, the handwriting was feminine. Could it be that Anne was not the only barrier between her and her goal?

She perched on the edge of the desk and smiled provocatively. She knew that she made a charming picture in the lavender-blue velvet riding habit and tall top hat.

'You will cause a riot in Rotten Row if you go out looking as beautiful as that.' Matthew had regained his composure and was eyeing her appreciatively.

Julia allowed the smile to fade sadly from her face. She stared at the floor. 'No one will notice me. They don't like me.'

'What nonsense, child! You are by far the most beautiful debutante of the year.' Matthew's voice was warm and sincere.

'Oh, Matthew, do you think so? Do you really believe I am beautiful?' Julia's voice shook and her huge blue eyes filled with tears which gradually spilled over and trickled artistically down her cheeks.

Matthew gazed at her in horror, leaning forward to take her hands in his. 'Whatever is the matter?'

'Nobody likes me,' she sobbed. 'Aunt Anne says it is because I am different from everyone else.'

'What!' Matthew was outraged. 'Anne said that? She had no right to hurt you so. I shall speak to her about it, and then she will tell you how sorry she is.'

Julia was shaking with sobs and Matthew rose to his feet in

order to comfort her. She rested her head against his shoulder and sighed deeply. To his great relief she stopped crying after a few moments and he sat down again with Julia on his knee and her arms wrapped tightly around him.

'Aunt Anne is right, you know. I am different. She says . . . No, it doesn't matter.' She paused, showing dutiful reluctance.

'Go on!' ordered Matthew grimly. 'Let me hear the rest of Anne's pearls of wisdom.'

'I'm afraid you will be cross with her,' demurred Julia hypocritically. 'And she has been so kind to me. I wouldn't like to cause trouble.'

'Tell me.'

'Well, she said that the Harcourt-Bright blood is tainted,' lied Julia, glibly putting her own fears into Anne's innocent mouth. 'And she's right – after all, my father did go mad. Is it any wonder that none of the men want to know me? They are afraid that I will pass on the bad blood to my children.'

'Anne said that?' Matthew repeated. 'Julia, she is wrong, quite wrong.' He hugged Julia more closely against him and buried his face in her neck. 'There is no tainted blood, as you call it, in our family. Your father suffered a grave misfortune, but that was an isolated incident. The Harcourt-Brights have no history of madness and, goodness knows, most of the noble families of England have an ancestor or two who were noted for their . . . well, *idiosyncracies*. However, there is one trait which crops up in some of our family and that is fear of water. Unfortunately your father was afflicted with this fear to a very great extent; I, on the other hand, do not suffer from it at all. Believe me, Julia, you have nothing to worry about. And I am absolutely certain that no one else ever gives the matter a single thought.'

'And that is the only characteristic prevalent in the family?'

Her face was so close to his that Matthew could smell the perfume of her skin; her body pressed so tightly against him that he could feel the thudding of her heart. As he gazed into the cornflower depths of her eyes, Matthew seemed to see two pictures and to hear a voice. The first picture was of Cousin Aubrey, associated with the homosexuality which Matthew had suspected he practised. The other picture was of the young Isobel. The voice was Freddy's: 'The Harcourt-Brights have a penchant for *young* ladies. Look how Uncle Gervase pets our little sister.'

Matthew closed his eyes and drew in his breath deeply. Then he firmly pushed Julia off his knee and stood up.

'Absolutely the only one,' he assured her.

'Thank you, Matthew. I feel better now.'

Matthew gave her a curious look. 'Tell me, Julia, why do you always refer to *Aunt* Anne but address me as "Matthew"?'

'You don't mind, do you?' she cried anxiously, and smiled prettily with relief when he shook his head. 'Somehow, you do not seem like an uncle. You weren't there when I was growing up and although I have seen you more often in the past few years, you could just as easily have been a friend of the family.' She hesitated. 'It's difficult to explain, but I don't feel you are like a close relation. Do you understand what I mean?'

'Yes, indeed,' said Matthew, passing a hand over his perspiring forehead. 'Now, run along.' After she had left the room, he stood for a while staring out of the library window. 'Yes,' he said again, 'God help me, I know exactly what you mean.'

When Julia returned from her ride in Rotten Row, she paused in the shadowy hall to inquire after her aunt and uncle. Mr Matthew and Lady Anne, she was told, were out.

Swiftly she ascended the stairs and went to the library on the first floor. She closed the door behind her and leaned against it staring at the desk in the corner with her heart leaping wildly. The desk top was bare. Her eyes travelled slowly to the drawer into which she had seen Matthew push the letter. Would it be locked? Setting her lips in a determined line she hurried across the room and pulled at the drawer handle.

The drawer opened easily and she saw that the letter was lying on top of a pile of papers, all covered in the same distinctive script. Rapidly Julia scanned it, impatiently searching for a clue to the real relationship between Matthew and this woman. When she reached the final paragraph, the red fire of jealousy shot through her. So pale, pathetic Anne was not the main threat. Emma Longden was the love of Matthew's life, the holder of his heart. Julia stood, clutching the letter tightly in one hand while she supported herself against the desk with the other. She had a mental picture of Emma – that tall woman with red-brown hair and hazel eyes. Not a bad figure, but she was old; she must be thirty at least. And Aunt Anne was thirty-four.

Julia glanced up and caught sight of her own reflection in the large mirror on the wall. She preened and smiled triumphantly at the vision of beauty which confronted her. These old ladies would be no match for her! She would soon oust them and then Matthew would belong to her, only to her!

In the meantime she would steal the letter. One never knew when it might come in useful.

Anne was dressing for a ball when Matthew came home that evening. She did so in silence and with a noticeable lack of enthusiasm. So sad and listless was she that Henriette was concerned that the depression might be descending on her again. And indeed she was right. As Anne wrapped her body in silk and draped herself in diamonds, she was struck afresh by the futility of it all. The only prospect the evening held was putting a polite public face on the sham which was her marriage and the dislike she was fast beginning to feel for Julia.

'All this glitter,' she said, half to herself and half to Henriette, 'conceals the sadness beneath and the emptiness within.'

Henriette did not reply, but brought the Bright necklace from its casket and fastened it round her mistress's neck. Anne stared at it with loathing. Like the necklace, she was only a symbol, to be displayed by Matthew on grand occasions. The ornament was like a slave collar round her neck: her purchase price, the heavy cold weight of the gold and diamonds pressing relentlessly against her bare flesh.

She was contemplating the necklace with distaste when the door opened abruptly and Matthew strode into the room. It had been so long since he had entered her bedroom that even Henriette gasped with astonishment and backed out hurriedly. Now he stood behind Anne as she sat before the looking-glass; their eyes locked in the mirror and their glance held.

She was still the loveliest woman he had ever seen, Matthew, thought, and she looked particularly beautiful tonight in grey silk, cut with the austerity and perfection of line which were the hallmarks of her taste. She was always immaculate, every gleaming blonde hair in its place, and the fine bones of her face enhanced her delicate aristocratic elegance. But during the long years of estrangement she had grown more and more remote, distant as an ice-maiden. It was an image emphasised now by the cold grey silk cut low over the snowy alabaster flesh, and the frosty sparkle of the superb gems in her pale hair and at her marble throat.

But appearances can be deceptive and Anne was far from feeling cool. A fierce flood of hope had coursed through her at the first sight of him, but it had been short-lived. She felt fear and apprehension as she saw the grim lines of his mouth and the anger in his stare.

'So madness runs in the Harcourt-Bright blood, does it?' he snapped. 'How dare you frighten that sweet child by telling such monstrous lies?'

Anne stared at him speechlessly for several moments. 'I really haven't the faintest idea what you are talking about,' she said at last.

'Don't play the innocent with me. Remember that I know what sort of woman lies beneath your guileless exterior. I had a long talk with Julia this morning. She was extremely upset, but eventually I persuaded her to tell me the whole story.'

'I can imagine,' said Anne, 'how much persuading she needed.'

'She did not wish to tell me; she did not want to cause trouble or put you in a bad light.'

Anne laughed, a high brittle sound. 'Is that what she said? Do go on.'

She listened while Matthew recounted his conversation with Julia and when he had finished two high spots of colour were burning in her cheeks as she rose and faced him.

'I did not say any of those things,' she said, as calmly as she could, but her whole body was tense and her hands were pleating the silk of her dress.

'Are you calling Julia a liar?'

'I suppose I am. In the circumstances, surely, one of us has to be.'

'So not content with frightening the girl out of her wits, and sapping her self-confidence at this most crucial time of her life, you are making her out to be untruthful. It is quite intolerable.'

'It is her word against mine. And it is even more intolerable that you should believe her and not me.'

'I know that you are capable of a great deal of deceit.'

'And that "sweet child" could never be deceitful? I never thought that you, Matthew Bright, could be such a fool. There is a side to our dear niece which you have not seen, although in your defence I will acknowledge that she has taken great care to keep it from you.'

'You are speaking of my niece, of my brother's child.'

'She is my niece too,' flared Anne. 'My sister's child. And Julia has a great look and a great *feel* of Isobel. Perhaps that is part of her hold over you, her resemblance to Isobel and me and Nicholas when we were young. Or is it guilt, Matthew? How much responsibility do you feel for Julia's unhappy childhood? How strong is your need to atone for it now?'

'That is enough,' shouted Matthew as her words struck home. 'I came here to tell you that you will apologise to Julia for your unkindness and that you will watch most carefully what you say to her in future. Any guidance she needs will come from me.'

'I will not apologise for what I did not say,' replied Anne flatly. 'And if I am to guard my tongue so carefully, I suggest that she and I do not attend the ball tonight. Who knows what "unkind" words might fall from my tongue during the long evening when she and I sit together because her unpleasant manner frightens the young men away!'

'*I* will take Julia to the ball. And she will dance every dance because *I* will be her partner if she has no other.'

And Matthew slammed out of the room.

Anne sank back on to the stool and remained motionless for what seemed a long time. The next thing she knew, Matthew was standing beside her again, having changed into his evening clothes. He looked handsome and debonair, and far younger than his forty-three years.

'Julia and I are ready to leave. I shall present your apologies to our hostess and inform her that you are indisposed.'

Anne nodded slightly.

'There is one other thing,' Matthew continued. 'I wish to make it clear to society that Julia has my backing. Her marriage prospects will be enhanced if it is recognised that she enjoys the position and therefore the dowry of a daughter of my own. That is why I wish her to wear the necklace tonight.' And he stretched out his hand to receive it.

Anne stared at him in horrified silence. She loathed the necklace, but it was a symbol of her position, outward proof that she was the wife of 'Diamond Bright' and as much a part of her public regalia as her wedding ring. She felt as though Matthew had slapped her in the face, that she had been supplanted and the necklace was being given to the new favourite. She opened her mouth to protest against the insult and to add that the necklace was an unsuitable ornament for a young unmarried girl. But her protest was still-born. Julia was their niece, so society would not divine any insult. And the necklace was cursed, Anne was sure of it. It had brought her no happiness and it would bring none to Julia. Let her wear it and be damned to all of them.

'Take it,' she said. She would not hand it to him. He had given it to her, let him take it away. She felt Matthew's fingers fumbling with the clasp and then followed him to the door.

Julia was standing at the head of the stairs, her white dress in startling contrast to the rich crimson of the carpets. She stood demurely with downcast eyes as Matthew fastened the necklace round her neck and then took his arm and glided down the stairs. As she reached the foot she turned to look upwards at Anne's motionless figure and to give a mocking smile of triumph.

It was, Julia told herself several hours later, the happiest night of her life. Not only did she have the handsomest man in the room as her escort, but the Prince of Wales had also singled her out for special favour. His Royal Highness had talked with Matthew and Julia for some time, had been lyrical in his praise of her beauty and had led her out to dance. Julia's stock had risen to dizzy heights and she sparkled into life in the glow of all the attention. As she twirled round the dance floor in the arms of young Lord Alfred, who was unable to understand how he could have previously overlooked her fine qualities, she was blissfully aware that

Matthew and the Prince were still watching her and smiled ever more bewitchingly into Lord Alfred's brown eyes.

The Prince and Matthew were certainly watching her but they were discussing the increasing price of 'Kaffirs', as the South African gold shares were termed. When the Prince moved on, Matthew checked that Julia was safely occupied on the dance floor while the Prince's place at his side was seized by Emma. She had been watching for her opportunity and hurried towards him with loud inquiries about the health of Lady Anne. What she really wanted was to know why he had not come to tea. Matthew groaned inwardly, while maintaining a polite expression. If Emma was starting to expect explanations, she would have to be quietly dropped.

However, all Julia saw was the presence of the stately Lady Longden, her chestnut head bent close to Matthew's fair hair. That spurt of jealousy ran through her again – she must somehow regain his attention. She began to flirt outrageously with Lord Alfred and danced several consecutive dances with him – enough to cause the old dowagers to whisper of forthcoming nuptials. Out of the corner of her eye she watched Matthew and Emma, while Matthew covertly watched Julia with mounting concern for her behaviour, and consumed by a strange tormented jealousy which he refused to acknowledge.

'I am quite exhausted,' Julia declared at the end of the next waltz. 'I must take a rest and have some air.'

Lord Alfred glowed at the prospects this statement presented.

'Let us go to the conservatory,' he said eagerly. 'It is cooler there and we can relax away from all these people.'

Julia hesitated and pretended to demur. 'I'm not quite sure that I ought to do that. My uncle would not approve.'

'He need never know,' Lord Alfred assured her. 'There are so many people here that we cannot possibly be missed. Do come!'

He edged her towards the door, anxious that they should slip away quickly and unobserved. But to be unobserved was the last thing Julia wanted, so she lingered deliberately in the doorway until she was sure that Matthew had located her before allowing Lord Alfred to lead her from the room. They hurried along several brightly-lit corridors and into the soft green gloom of the conservatory.

The transition from light to dark rendered Julia temporarily sightless and for a moment she was conscious only of the overpowering perfume of the flowers. Gradually her eyes grew accustomed to the dark and she made her way past the dim outlines of plants, flowers and miniature trees to the window. The conservatory overlooked the garden and a full moon was shining from a cloudless sky. The moonlight fell brightly on the window and was enough, Julia knew, to illumine her pale hair and white dress. Lord Alfred was standing very close, gazing at her raptly and murmuring praises of her beauty. Julia smiled modestly, straining her ears for the footfall she was expecting. Now the young man was leaning forward, placing his hands on her shoulders, and drawing her closer to him. In a second his lips would be on hers, and still Matthew had not come.

At the last moment Julia heard the sound she had awaited and spun out of Lord Alfred's arms in the nick of time with a startled, but suitably muffled, shriek.

The moonbeams played on Matthew's bright hair and lit the murderous expression on his face as he held Julia's arm in an iron grip.

'I ought to knock your teeth in,' he rasped at Lord Alfred, 'but the satisfaction it would give me is not worth the scandal. There is a chair in the corridor, Julia. Sit on it and try to look as wan as possible. Lord Alfred, fetch our hostess. We shall tell her that Julia has been taken ill as suddenly as my wife was struck down earlier tonight. Then we are going home.'

Minutes later they were in a carriage, bowling towards Park Lane. Matthew did not speak. When they reached home, he pushed her firmly up the steps into the hall and up the main staircase into the library. Julia, however, preferred to pick her own battle ground and she walked through the library into the winter garden, taking up a position which gave her a becoming background of trailing leaves and blossoms.

'Why were you kissing that idiot?' he demanded.

'I was not kissing him, he was kissing me. Except that he did not get that far.'

'He would have done had I not found you. And don't evade the question. Had he asked you to marry him?'

'No. But I am sure he was about to do so.' Julia's lip began to tremble as she judged it time to turn on the tears.

'And then again, he might not. Do you know no better than to go into conservatories and allow young men to kiss you before any declaration of marriage?' Matthew seized her shoulders and glared fiercely into her swimming eyes. 'You stupid girl, reputation is everything in our society!'

'It would have been my first kiss,' she whispered. 'No one has ever kissed me on the lips in my whole life.'

Involuntarily Matthew's hands tightened on her soft flesh. Against his will, desire was rising in him; he was longing to caress that white virginal body and to crush those sweet lips with his. He stood looking down at her, the struggle naked in his eyes. The temptation was so great. Almost he yielded to it . . . Almost. But not quite.

With a shuddering sigh he pushed her away. 'You will have to wait a little longer for that experience,' he said coldly. 'As your legal guardian, I am warning you to behave more circumspectly in future.'

Matthew was trembling as he turned away to hide the perspiration on his brow, his one aim being to conceal his feelings from Julia. On no account must she sense the terrible thoughts which had assailed him or know how nearly he had kissed her. He turned again to Julia.

'The necklace?' he said.

Her hands flew to the precious stones at her neck. 'I thought it was mine now.'

'Certainly not,' said Matthew impatiently.

'Couldn't I have it?'

'Of course not.' Unconsciously Matthew used the same words which he had spoken to Isobel many years ago. 'It belongs to the lady of my choice.'

Julia froze. 'You mean it belongs to the most important woman in your life?'

'That's right. To my wife.'

He unclasped the necklace while Julia stood as still as stone

'Good night, Matthew.'

'Good night, *Uncle*,' he corrected, and left the room.

Julia stood alone in the winter garden, the strange unnatural love she had for Matthew split by pulsating waves of hate. He had rejected her and for a moment she was swamped by humiliation and despair. But as the hurricane of emotions buffeted her, one desire surfaced above the rest. Revenge.

CHAPTER EIGHT

Matthew was appeased by a visit from Lord Alfred, who apologised for his behaviour and declared his intentions were entirely honourable. A relieved Matthew indicated that Lord Alfred's suit was approved, this encouragement being as much for his own benefit as Julia's. Matthew genuinely horrified at the physical attraction he had felt for his niece – it filled him with guilt, merging with the muddy waters of his disgust for the 'family traits' and the lingering suspicion that his revenge on Freddy and Isobel had gone too far. A marriage for Julia was essential for everyone's peace of mind and would remove temptation.

Julia appeared meek and malleable, apparently striving to make amends for her indiscretion, but her agile brain was occupied with plans for Matthew's downfall.

She bided her time, reflecting bitterly on the strait-jacket into which an unmarried girl was laced. Not only was her body surrounded by chaperones and propelled along the undeviating rails of society, but her mind was deprived of knowledge and expression. She would marry, she vowed, to escape these limitations and to escape from Highclere, Desborough and Park Lane to a home of her own. Alfred was doubtless as good a proposition as any. Julia redoubled her smiles in his direction and pondered on the means to hurt Matthew.

She could think of only two ways of ruining Matthew's reputation, two foolproof methods of drumming a man out of society: illicit love affairs and cheating at cards.

Julia knew little about card games and moreover had no intention of letting her reputation disappear with Matthew's. Her first action, therefore, was to protect her own interests. Once again, therefore, she allowed Lord Alfred to lure her into the conservatory where she accepted his proposal of marriage and received that first kiss. The experience left her unmoved – she closed her eyes and found that she was thinking of Matthew. Well, Alfred was stuck with her, no matter what happened. She opened her eyes and suggested that they go to the card-room. Clinging guilelessly to his arm, she chattered innocently about the games and remorselessly extracted the relevant information from him.

It quickly became apparent that she had a problem, for Matthew's favourite game was baccarat and the more Julia watched the play the less chance she saw of setting up Matthew as a cheat. His other favourite game was roulette, which left no scope for her activities either. It would have to be whist, but Matthew played it so seldom. However, if at a party at Park Lane to celebrate Julia's engagement, her fiancé particularly requested a hand of whist, Matthew could hardly refuse. Julia knew the matter was as good as settled and the night before the party she made her preparations.

The household retired early in order to be rested for the long and important day ahead. When she was sure everyone else was in bed, Julia tiptoed down the stairs to the ballroom. Silently she opened the door and stole through the vast room, past the tables and chairs covered with dust sheets, to the salon which opened off the ballroom and which would be used for cards the next evening. She dared not turn up the light, but crept across the room in the dark to the cabinet at the far end. The ormolu clock on the mantelpiece struck twelve and, startled, she gasped and froze in her tracks, glancing nervously over her shoulder. Then she moved forward again and, having reached the cabinet, groped over the heavily inlaid surface for the drawer handles. When she pulled open the drawer, piles of fresh unopened packs of cards were revealed, all with the same distinctive pattern on the reverse. Reaching carefully to the back of the drawer, she removed one pack, leaving the neat piles at the front untouched. Closing the drawer, she crept back the way she had come.

There was one more move she had to make the following evening. She dressed for the party early, dismissed her maid and hung about the bedroom floor watching for her opportunity. At last she saw Matthew's valet leave, holding a pair of black leather pumps, whereupon – taking a deep breath to strengthen her resolve – she ran along the corridor and entered Matthew's room. As she had expected, his evening dress suit was laid out ready: the short, well-fitting jacket with tails, black trousers, white waistcoat, white shirt with wing collar and white evening tie, and black silk socks. Swiftly Julia withdrew the handkerchief from the trouser pocket, wrapped it round a handful of carefully selected cards and thrust it back into place. She returned to her room and smiled. Everything was going perfectly.

The same could be said of the party itself. The arrangements were superb and the cream of society was present to enjoy the Bright hospitality. The family had turned out in force and only Isobel was missing.

To Julia the time dragged endlessly until the card tables were set out. Then she approached Alfred with her most winning smile and tapped him flirtatiously on the arm with her folded fan.

'I want you to do something for me.'

'Anything!'

'Ask Uncle Matthew to play whist. He loves a wager and I would adore watching you play together. Whist is much more fun to watch than baccarat.'

The card tables were filling rapidly. After a moment's hesitation, Matthew sat down with Alfred, Lord Ambleside and the Duke of Fontwell. Julia positioned herself strategically behind Matthew's chair. She was not carrying a reticule, but the flounced hem of her dress concealed a pocket which contained a handkerchief – and a single playing card. She watched several hands and then, with a quick glance around, bent down, removed the card from its hiding place and dropped it on the floor beside Matthew's chair. In a moment, in just a moment, she would give a cry of surprise and innocently inform Matthew that he had dropped a card. Then cards would be counted and, with luck, Matthew would be asked to turn out his pockets. Consternation! Julia smiled. Her eyes slid to the card on the floor and she opened her mouth to speak.

But the words died on her lips. All that she could see was a foot – a dainty foot in a blue satin slipper which was descending firmly on to the playing card and covering it from sight.

Anne had been in the ballroom when with a flash of annoyance she realised that Julia had stayed in the card-room instead of mingling properly with her guests. Her irritation increased when she saw that Julia was standing close behind Matthew's chair. Then she saw her bend down and drop the card and watched as the smug smile spread over the girl's face. She had no idea what Julia was doing but she smelled danger – danger to Matthew. In a few strides she was between Matthew and Julia and was standing on the incriminating card.

A servant passed with a tray of champagne glasses and thankfully Anne grabbed one, picking it up carelessly so that the contents spilled over Matthew, his coat, the table and the cards in his hand. He sprang to his feet, dropping the cards, and swore loudly.

'Oh, I'm so sorry,' Anne cried, 'How clumsy of me, Matthew! I've spoiled your game!' She crouched down and gathered up all the cards on the floor. 'They're ruined, I'm afraid. Do forgive me! Can you bear to start this hand again after Matthew has changed his coat? Thank you so much. Alfred, as you are nearly in the family, will you entertain Lord Ambleside and His Grace while we are gone? Bless you!' and Anne steered Matthew firmly from the room.

'What the hell is going on? How could you be so stupid? And I was winning, too!'

Anne said nothing until they reached his room, then she spread out the cards she was holding. 'You will do well to lose tonight – just in case anyone was watching. There is an extra card here.'

Matthew stared at her. 'I don't understand.'

'It was lying beside your chair. That was why I caused a diversion.'

Matthew stood in stunned silence. Anne came to him and started patting his pockets.

'Ah!' And she pulled out the handkerchief so that the cards cascaded to the floor.

'I don't believe it,' Matthew said at last. '*Who? Who* would do such a thing to me?'

'Julia would.'

'Don't be so ridiculous!'

'Matthew, I *saw* her drop the card.'

'Why on earth would she do a thing like that?'

'I don't know, I really don't know.'

'Well, I simply don't believe it. There's no possible reason for her to do such a thing. Either you're having hallucinations or you are deliberately trying to make trouble for Julia.'

Angrily Matthew changed his jacket while Anne tried not to lose her temper.

'If it was not Julia, perhaps you have a suggestion as to who else it could have been.'

'I haven't the faintest idea. It could have been anyone. Perhaps it was you.'

'Now *you* are being ridiculous.'

Matthew did not believe for a moment that Anne was guilty, but equally he refused to accept that the culprit was Julia. The fact that Anne was Julia's accuser only increased his stubbornness.

'I must go back. And I will take your advice and try to lose.' He paused at the door. 'Apart from the identity of the person who is trying to disgrace me, there is one other aspect of this business which is puzzling. Why are you so sure I wasn't cheating?'

Anne looked him straight in the eyes. 'Because you wouldn't do anything like that.'

'No,' said Matthew. 'No, I wouldn't.' But as he returned to the card room he remembered some of his dealings in his early days on the diamond fields and had the grace to feel just a little ashamed.

After a long and intense struggle with herself, Anne decided to say nothing to Julia about the incident. The girl would only deny the charge, a denial likely to be accompanied by one of those infuriating smiles. Now if Matthew was to tackle her on the subject, that might be different – he might possibly achieve something. But Matthew was completely taken in by Julia's wiles and his gullibility increased Anne's helplessness and frustration.

Julia waited for Anne's accusations and was rather disappointed when the confrontation never came. A week later the atmosphere still remained calm and she decided to proceed with her next move. Thereupon she sat down to write a letter; it was only a short letter, but it took a long time to execute as she disguised her script by writing laboriously with her left hand.

There was a moment of crisis when Anne paid a rare visit to her room, but Julia quickly leaned forward over the desk in order to cover the note and the other document which lay open beside her.

'I came to remind you that you have a dress fitting this afternoon.'

'I had not forgotten.'

'You have a very becoming flush.' Anne regarded her niece suspiciously. Her glance fell to the papers on the table. 'Good heavens, are you actually writing a letter?'

'I don't know why you should sound so surprised.'

'As I have never known you to write a letter before, my surprise will be as nothing compared with that of your fortunate correspondent,' said Anne drily. 'Ah, but I suppose that you write to Alfred?'

'Yes.'

'Please try to find time to drop a line to your mother. I am sure she would welcome news of you.'

'My mother does not care about my activities or my marriage or indeed anything about me.'

'That is not true,' said Anne firmly, although secretly she felt Julia might be right. 'We must all try harder to include Isobel in family affairs. Please write to her, Julia, and give her a pleasant surprise.'

'Oh, my letter will be a surprise all right,' murmured Julia when she was alone again, and sighed with relief that her purpose remained undetected.

Julia's industry reminded Anne of a note she must send herself. She wrote it quickly and then rang for the butler about half an hour after leaving Julia's room.

'Please ask Stephen to deliver this note.'

'My apologies, my lady, but Stephen has just gone out with a letter for Lady Julia.'

'What a nuisance!' exclaimed Anne. 'My note is to Lady Ambleside and since she lives almost next door to Lord Alfred, he could easily have taken both letters together.'

The butler looked puzzled. 'Lady Julia's letter was not addressed to Lord Alfred, my lady. It was for Lord Longden.'

'Are you quite sure?'

'Quite sure, my lady. Stephen remarked on it most particularly.'

'Why on earth,' Anne said slowly, half to herself, 'is Julia writing to Lord Longden? I am not even sure that she has ever spoken to him, except to welcome him here.' Once more she felt a constriction in her chest as apprehension clutched her, and was assailed by a sudden conviction that there had been something odd and ill-at-ease about Julia as she had sat at her writing desk. 'How long ago did Stephen leave?'

'Not more than ten minutes, my lady.'

'Order the carriage for me immediately. I will deliver my own letter.'

She directed the coachman to drive to Berkeley Square where the Longdens lived. On the way she sat stiffly upright in the carriage, watching anxiously for the figure of the footman in his familiar livery. Probably this was a wild goose chase, she told herself above the hammering of her heart. There was doubtless a perfectly innocent explanation. But no, Anne decided, nothing about Julia is innocent, and she knew she must be guided again by the instinctive feeling of danger which had saved the situation in the card room.

Suppose she did not catch up with Stephen? The length of Park Lane to Mount Street had never seemed so long and the traffic had never seemed so thick or so slow-moving. Here was Mount Street at last, but still no sign of Stephen. The footman was a good and conscientious servant who would undoubtedly carry out his task as quickly and efficiently as he could. For the first time in her life Anne wished she had a servant who would dawdle on the way. Her agitation was so great that she felt she could run along the street faster than the carriage was moving.

And what would she do if she did catch up with Stephen? It was hardly the action of a lady to intercept her niece's private mail. Anne decided to cross that bridge when she came to it – the first priority was to find the footman and intercept him.

As the carriage approached the junction of Davies Street and

Berkeley Square, Anne leaned forward and craned her head out of the window. There, walking briskly round the Square, was a man and surely it was Stephen?

'Call to him!' she shouted to the coachman. 'Stop him!'

The coachman complied, but Stephen did not hear. He was drawing perilously close to the steps of the Longden mansion and Anne's heart began to sink. But then to her vast relief, the coachman shouted again and at last Stephen turned, recognised the carriage and waited as they drew alongside.

'Get in,' Anne commanded him. She saw that he was holding the letter and imperiously held out her hand to indicate that he was to give her the envelope. She sat and stared in horror: it was not Julia's handwriting.

Dumbfounded, she tried to collect her whirling thoughts. She could not possibly intercept someone else's letter. Yet the butler had distinctly said that Stephen was on an errand for Julia. He must have been mistaken. She was on the verge of handing back the letter to the footman when something clicked into place in her mind. She knew there had been a jarring note about the way Julia had been sitting at her desk: Julia had been holding the pen in her left hand!

The discovery overruled what remained of Anne's scruples; swiftly she ripped open the envelope and read the short note. Then, with shaking hand, she slowly read the enclosure: the letter from Emma to Matthew. She laid down the papers in her lap and sat very still, eventually becoming aware of the curious stare of the footman.

'Are you all right, my lady?' he ventured anxiously.

'Perfectly, thank you, Stephen.' Anne pulled herself together and folded the letters briskly. 'Return to Park Lane,' she ordered the coachman, and to the footman: 'Stephen, I want you to say absolutely nothing about this to anymore. And I would like to assure you that however strange my actions might appear, it is in the best interests of everyone that this letter should not be delivered.'

'I quite understand, my lady. You may rely on me.' Stephen hesitated and coughed politely. 'May I be permitted to say, my lady, that we in the servants' hall have been concerned for some time over Lady Julia's . . . attitude towards you?'

Anne smiled wanly. 'You may be permitted to say that, Stephen, just this once. But I would not advise you to say it again, and particularly not in the presence of Mr Bright.' Her fingers tightened on the letters. 'But thank you, Stephen ,' she said softly. 'You have no idea what a comfort it is to know that I am not completely alone.'

At home she went straight to her room and gave orders that she should not be disturbed. She remained there throughout the long summer day, locked into her own private hell.

She had realised that it was inevitable that Matthew would take a mistress, but that realisation did not prevent its confirmation from causing her terrible hurt. If it had been an actress or a professional houri, it might not have been so serious. But Emma Longden! Anne clenched her hands and stared at the ceiling as she lay on her bed: her face hot, dry and burning, her eyes bright with unshed tears. Emma, whom she had welcomed as a guest in her house; Emma, whose hand she had taken, whose cheek she had kissed, when all the time . . . Anne groaned aloud, tortured by the memories of Matthew's sweet love-making and tormented by the vision of his body pressed against Emma's creamy flesh.

How widespread was knowledge of the affair, she asked herself. What were people thinking? Were they laughing behind her back? Was she the last to know?

The nightmare continued through the long day until, as the sun sank low, Anne made a conscious effort to bring matters into perspective.

Probably some people did know, she reasoned. But they were unlikely to be laughing at her and indeed the affair was likely to cause little comment. It was all too commonplace – there were so many similar liaisons. The affair would only cause gossip if the unforgivable happened and they committed the cardinal sin of being 'Found Out'. And Anne had already prevented that catastrophe: Lord Longden had not received the letters and would not feel obliged to take action.

The injustice lay, Anne agonised, in society's acceptance of such a relationship between Matthew and Emma, a relationship which could have been going on for years, while Matthew self-righteously banished her to the wilderness of his life for one hour's indiscretion. How many babies were there, she asked herself, in the noble nurseries of England, with blue eyes instead of brown, with brown hair instead of blonde, with features which found no precedent in the portraits on the walls? Such babies brought vital fresh blood to the tired genes of the aristocracy, but her baby – her daughter – had been wrenched away and Anne would never know what became of her.

The tears came then, in a healing flood, and when they were done Anne felt calmer. She rose, bathed her face and summoned Henriette, although she gave the maid no explanation for the day's seclusion. It was now evening and of course there was yet another entertainment which must be attended. Anne felt that she was hanging on to her sanity by a mere thread. She was exhausted, mentally and physically, and could endure the social round no longer. The Season ended in two weeks and somehow she would keep going until then. Tonight she must speak to Matthew before leaving for the ball; she might pretend to the world that nothing ailed her, but she could not pretend to him.

She dressed with care in a gown of turquoise green satin. It had only a suggestion of a bustle at the back, but the rounded skirt flowed into a graceful train. The bodice was sleeveless, with velvet straps supporting the low heart-shaped neckline. At first Anne rebelled against wearing the Bright necklace and ordered Henriette to bring her emeralds, but changed her mind and wore the diamonds as a reminder of her authority over Julia and her partnership with Matthew.

When she was quite ready, she went to find Matthew in the library. In silence she handed him the letters and watched the expression on his face as he read. The muscles in his cheek tightened and his lips compressed into a grim thin line.

'How did you come by these papers?'

'I intercepted their delivery to Lord Longden. As to how I knew of their existence, you would not believe me if I told you'

'At least you cannot try to put the blame on Julia this time; this is not her handwriting.' Matthew's antagonism was an attempt to cover his acute embarrassment.

'I thought you would say that and I shall pursue the matter no further. I brought the letters to you for several reasons, however. First, you must endeavour to conduct your affair with Emma Longden with greater discretion.'

'You need have no fears on that score,' replied Matthew stiffly. 'I shall not see her – in that way – again.'

'That is your decision entirely. The matter is immaterial to me. Second, someone – and you will not acknowledge who – is trying to ruin you. You must be on your guard, Matthew, because that person may try again.'

Matthew nodded.

'And this is the third reason.' She walked to the grate where, despite the summer heat, a fire burned brightly. Casting the papers into the flames, she watched as they flared and burned to ash. 'Doubtless there are other letters,' she commented as she returned to Matthew's side. 'I should burn those as well if I were you.'

He was staring at the fire as the final vestiges of the letters disappeared. Then his gaze travelled slowly to Anne's face. 'No recriminations, Anne? No hysteria? No shouting or screaming? Are you not supposed to ask how I could do such a thing to you? That is how most women would react.'

'And most men would deny the charge. They would talk of misunderstanding and exaggerations and idle gossip.'

Matthew smiled appreciatively. 'You are right. So you and I are not like most people! Why did you intercept the letter?'

Anne was astonished. 'What a foolish question! I could not stand idly by and see your reputation ruined!'

'Why not? I am not so unperceptive that I do not realise how unsatisfying our marriage has been for you in recent years. My downfall could be to your advantage – your connections are good enough to withstand the storm. Perhaps my mysterious enemy hoped that I would behave like an officer and a gentleman and blow my brains out. Then you would be free to marry again.'

'You would not shoot yourself,' said Anne decisively. 'You are not an officer and I have a shrewd idea that there have been times in your life when you have not acted like a gentleman.'

'Once again I have to admit that you are right, but then you usually are. So why, Anne? Why did you save me?'

She turned away so that he could not see her face and did not reply.

'Could it be,' he said quietly, 'that you care for me? Just a little? In spite of everything?'

Anne closed her eyes in anguish. She longed to say 'Yes' and throw herself into his arms, but the fear of disappointment and rejection was too great. 'I acted instinctively,' she replied stiffly. 'There is Philip to consider.'

'Of course. Do you know that for a moment I had completely forgotten Philip?' Matthew came to stand beside her and they both stared down into the darkening shadows of Park Lane. 'Perhaps there have been other moments in my life when I ought to have remembered him. Perhaps he would have liked a little sister.'

Anne gasped. 'You knew it was a girl?' She clutched his arm fiercely. 'Do you know anything about her? Is she all right?'

'I don't know very much, but I can tell you that the child is well. She is healthy and pretty and living with John in New York. Her name is Tiffany and I am told John dotes on her.'

'Tiffany,' Anne repeated. Her eyes glowed but soon dimmed again. 'How I wish I could see her! How I wish everything had been different. If only Victoria had not died. If only Philip was easier to know. If only . . .'

' "If only",' mocked Matthew. 'Those are the saddest words in the world. Don't waste your sympathy on Philip, he will settle down as soon as he goes to his prep. school in the autumn. It will be the making of him, just as it is for most boys.'

Anne's heart ached at the thought of the boarding school to which her son must be sent at the tender age of eight. 'I hope so.' She looked up into Matthew's face. 'It has been a long time since we talked like this.'

'It has been a long time since we did anything meaningful together. You have shown tonight that you have a more forgiving nature than I – I still cannot forget John Court.' His eyes travelled slowly over the curves of her body. 'How long is it since we slept together?'

'Seven years.'

'As long as that?' he murmured, stretching out a hand to stroke her cheek. 'Thank you for what you did. Even if it was only for Philip.'

They stared at each other, poised on the brink of reconciliation, but neither could bring themselves to make the first move. Slowly Anne left the room, while a disturbed and oddly humbled Matthew opened the desk drawer, removed a pile of letters and heaped them on the fire.

CHAPTER NINE

The end of the Season did not after all bring an end to the undercurrents of hostility and disturbance in the Bright household. It was Nicholas who brought the news which changed their plans – Nicholas, the catalyst, who so often caused events merely by being there, by existing, by being the unwitting point of contact.

'Papa is ill,' he told Matthew and Anne. 'Mama says that he cannot last much longer and she has asked me to go to Desborough.'

'He looked unwell when he came to Julia's engagement party,' said Anne slowly, 'but I never realised that he might be seriously ill.'

'He is seventy-eight,' Nicholas pointed out, 'and he can't last forever. But he will not admit that the outlook is bad and is complaining that Desborough is too quiet. Wants a house party, in fact. I hoped you might come down and bring Philip and Julia to liven the place up a bit. Would you?'

'Of course,' said Anne warmly. 'We were going to the Amblesides – really, Matthew, we ought to buy a country house of our own – but I am sure they will understand.'

So once again Matthew found himself at Desborough in August. With Nicholas he rode round the estate and inspected the improvements his money had financed. However much the old Duke might have resented Matthew's charity, he had put the money to good use. The buildings were in good repair, the fields and lanes were tidy and well-cared for, the stock was sleek and well-fed and the tenants and estate workers went about their business with a cheerful air. The scene was idyllic – rural England at its very best – and Matthew felt no small satisfaction and pride in his contribution. He wondered, however, how long it would last. There was no question but that his financial aid would cease with the old Duke's death, for he would not lift a finger to help Hugh. Matthew had neither forgotten Hugh's close friendship with Freddy nor forgiven Hugh's cavalier attitude to Nicholas during the opium affair. As he rode through the serene landscape in the bright summer sunlight, he was sure that Desborough must inevitably decline.

August wore on, while the Duchess put a brave face on her misfortune and filled the house with family and friends. The Duke was failing visibly and kept more and more to his room. He seemed to take particular pleasure in the company of Philip and Julia, but the two young people avoided him if they could. Philip was frightened of the old man and disliked the sick-room atmosphere. Julia was bored by him and could not be bothered to devote time which could be more enjoyably spent elsewhere.

Of all the people at Desborough that summer, probably Philip was the most miserable. Life in London was bad enough, secluded in his nursery but he felt even more alone and different in the country. His impressionable years in Kimberley, cut off from others of his own age with none of the traditional pursuits of the typical young English gentleman, had set him apart from his peers. Philip carried in his mind confused memories of Kimberley. Not of the diamonds – gems had no interest for him – but of the fascinating, whirring clanking machinery which operated at the mines.

At night he lay in bed, sick with dread at the prospect of the schooldays which lay before him at the end of the summer. In the morning he rose, sick with apprehension at the ordeal he must inevitably face: the riding lesson. For Philip hated horses. This was in itself a trait which placed him on a different planet from that of his contemporaries. In the shafts of a carriage or a plough, horses were fine but he was terrified the moment he had to ride one of the huge animals. The anathema had been there from the start; he had screamed with terror the very first time they had set him on a pony, and in those early days had taken several bad falls which did nothing to boost his confidence.

This particular morning in early September Philip stomped down to the stableyard with his customary pale face and resigned expression. A group of guests was setting off on their morning ride and the cavalcade clattered briskly past him. To Philip's horror, his cousin Julia reined in beside him and gazed at Philip's abject figure with contempt.

'Do stand up straight, Philip! You look positively pathetic. What will our guests think of you?'

Obediently Philip straightened his back and lifted his head to glare rebelliously at her.

'What a face! Anyone would think you were being led out to your execution rather than merely taking a riding lesson. But then we all know what a coward you are.'

'I am not a coward.'

'You are, too. I've watched you, quaking every time you so much as see a horse.' Julia edged her hunter closer to the boy and gave a tinkling laugh of triumph as Philip backed nervously away. 'You see? Coward!'

Tears sprang into Philip's eyes. 'I'm not! I'm *not*!'

'You're not what?' Matthew appeared unexpectedly round the corner of the stables and joined them.

Julia flashed him an angelic smile. 'Philip isn't looking forward to his riding lesson.' She sighed. 'It never ceases to surprise me, Uncle Matthew, that a son of yours could be so nervous of horses.'

She spurred after her companions, taking a short cut across the fields to catch up with them, making a superb figure as she flew stylishly over a five-barred gate. Matthew watched her admiringly and then glared down at his downcast scrap of a son. Julia's parting words rankled unbearably, for he still had his doubts over Philip's paternity. He spoke abruptly.

'You should model yourself on your cousin Julia. She has an excellent seat.'

'Yes, sir.'

'I am riding to Highclere, but I'll wait a moment and watch the beginning of your lesson.'

Riding a horse was frightful, but riding a horse in front of Papa was the ultimate torture, Philip was numb, his arms and legs felt wooden and did not seem disposed to obey the impulses from his brain. Automatically he climbed into the saddle on the small black pony and rode slowly into the paddock. Blindly he obeyed the commands: trot, canter, trot, walk, aware only of Matthew's penetrating stare. Now for the worst part. Now for the jumps. Desperately, and in the certain knowledge that he would fall, Philip blundered up to the low rail, misjudged it completely and shot straight over the pony's head. He lay in a confused, humiliated heap while his riding master bent over him anxiously. Trying to salvage his dignity, Philip struggled to his feet.

'He's all right, sir!' the instructor shouted to Matthew, who had not even moved from his position at the paddock gate.

And Philip heard quite clearly his father's exclamation of disgust at his performance and watched as Matthew mounted his own horse and rode away.

I'm not a coward, Philip said to himself desperately. I'm not! I'll show them one day. I'll show them all!

However, the incident had its compensations. Although Philip had to remount and do a circuit of the paddock, his lesson was curtailed. Gratefully he relinquished the pony to a groom, who regarded him thoughtfully.

'You don't much like horses, do you, Master Philip?'

'I *hate* them,' said Philip passionately, 'but I seem to be the only person in the whole world who does.'

'Oh no, not at all. Lots of people don't like horses,' replied the youth cheerfully, leading the pony into the stable. 'Big brutes, some of them. Oh no, you're not alone.'

Instead of returning to the house, Philip lingered with this comforting stranger. 'I thought I was the only one,' he said.

'We can't all like the same things, can we? People are made different.'

'I like machinery,' confided Philip shyly, and he told his new friend about Kimberley and the machinery at the diamond mines. 'I was only little,' he said, with all the gravity of his eight years, 'but I remember I liked it more than anything.'

'Now that's very interesting.' The stableboy had unsaddled the pony and was rubbing it down. 'One of these days, Master Philip, machinery will take the place of horses.'

Philip's big blue eyes grew round with astonishment.

'Horseless carriages,' continued the youth, whose name was Williams, 'are the transport of the future.'

Philip stared at him doubtfully. 'I have seen the steam coaches,' he ventured, 'but they seem to go very slowly.'

Williams snorted. 'That's because the law says steam vehicles are not allowed to go faster than four miles per hour in the country and two miles per hour in the town. And that a man must always walk ahead, carrying a red flag. The coaches could go much faster than that if they were allowed.'

'It seems a very silly law.'

'There are people who don't want self-propelled vehicles – people who want to preserve horse-drawn transport. Mind you,' and Williams patted the pony affectionately, 'I love horses myself but, like my uncle says, one must move with the times.'

'Does your uncle know a lot about horseless carriages?'

'A lot? He *drives* one,' said Williams impressively.

'Do tell me about it!'

'How old are you, Master Philip?'

'Eight.'

'Then according to my uncle, the real story of the horseless carriage began in the year you were born. In 1885, Karl Benz made his first machine in Germany.'

'Not in England!' said Philip in patriotic disappointment.

Williams snorted again. 'This red flag law is holding us back. No, the main developments are taking place abroad: Benz and Daimler in Germany; Peugeot and Panhard-Levassor in France.'

'I wonder if I could ever ride in a car.' Philip was absolutely fascinated.

'My uncle says that one day everyone will have a car of their own.'

'Surely not! Anyway,' and Philip looked glum, 'Papa would never buy one. He won't even let me have a bicycle.'

'I've got a bicycle. You could come and have a ride on it, on my day off, if you like.'

'Could I really?'

'We could take it to pieces and put it together again.'

'That would be marvellous.' Philip rose to return to the house. He stretched out his hand in an oddly formal and adult gesture. 'Thank you very much.'

Williams shook the hand and watched with a mixture of

sympathy and amusement as the little figure trudged slowly back across the stableyard.

Matthew had ridden to Highclere in a very bad humour. He was irritated by Philip's lack of prowess in the saddle, but that was not the only problem on his mind. He was edgy from constant pondering on the identity of his mystery adversary and taut from watching for another attack. None of it made any sense. Who could possibly hate him that much? Matthew's mind ranged over the list of his family, friends, acquaintances and servants. None seemed to be an enemy or even a potential enemy. In Kimberley he had been unpopular in certain quarters, but not with anyone who had access to his Park Lane home. Someone must have bribed a servant to plant the cards and steal the letter. But who?

At Highclere Matthew was met by his nephew, Charles. He scowled. A worthy fellow, Charles: built like a battleship, big and broad, but dull. Very, very dull. Only happy when he was pottering about his ancestral acres.

'We don't see much of you, Charles. You cannot have attended more than three balls all Season.'

'I had work to do here.'

'Work? Here? You?' Matthew fired off the three sharp words like bullets from a gun, as he pointed at a group of gardeners labouring in the flower beds. 'What are they for? And all the other servants? You are a belted Earl of Her Majesty's realm. You may administer a little but you don't *work*.'

'I like working the land,' said Charles obstinately, 'and besides, I detest the superficiality of the Season.'

'Nevertheless, it is an essential stage for the selection of a bride. A bit soon for you, of course, as you're only twenty. But you should start looking round and see what girls are coming up that might take your fancy.'

'I'm in no hurry.' Charles saw the dark shapes of his grandmother and aunt on the terrace and his glance was drawn inexorably to the West Wing where the burned and twisted figure of his mother hid herself from view. No use in trying to explain to Uncle Matthew that he could hardly introduce a young bride to this house.

'Your finances are not as sound as I would wish. Unfortunately your father frittered away a fortune in an orgy of extravagance after he inherited. You would do well to keep your eyes open for one of these American heiresses who are worth a mint of money in dowries. They are bringing in new blood, too – an excellent thing, fresh blood. Too much inbreeding in our families in the past.'

'Yes, Uncle.'

Charles left Matthew at the foot of the terrace steps and turned back to the garden. He did not waste words and had no intention of arguing with his uncle. Charles had decided long ago that he would marry whoever he wanted when he wanted, and 'when' was when he was old enough to act without his guardian's permission. Charles knew that an American heiress was unlikely to be suitable for him. She would exchange her father's wealth for an English title and a place in society, but he wanted a wife who would be content to stay at home. If he had his way he would never leave Highclere, never move beyond the great gates and the high walls which girdled the estate. He loved it. The land, the very earth of the estate, was the only security he had ever known.

As usual Matthew found conversation with his mother and sister tedious and dispiriting. As usual Isobel refused to see him. And as usual Reynolds' agent presented an immaculate set of accounts. Nothing at Highclere was any different from any other day. Despite family problems, the pattern of life seemed to go on and on as it had done for centuries and as it probably would continue for centuries more – golden and shining, founded on the firm unshaken confidence of the people in themselves, their country and their glorious Empire.

He took luncheon at Highclere and returned to Desborough to find that the Duke was having a bad day and had requested that Matthew and Nicholas join him for tea in his room. For some inexplicable reason Matthew had a sudden vision of Martha Jacobs and he grimaced.

The Duke lay, propped up with pillows, in an enormous canopied bed, the wooden posts elaborately carved and the hangings of rich gold damask. Because he found difficulty in negotiating the stairs, a bedroom had been prepared for him on the ground floor and outside the window he could see the emerald lawns, the colourful flower beds and that spreading cedar tree in whose ample shade Matthew had first encountered the Comtesse.

'There's nothing wrong with me, you know.' Even now the Duke managed to be bellicose and belligerent. 'Just a touch of old age, that's all. But this enforced inactivity makes one think; makes one look back and wish to tie up any loose ends. That's why I wanted to speak to you, Matthew. I owe you an apology.'

Nicholas cleared his throat in embarrassment, put down his tea cup and started to leave the room but the Duke waved him back into his chair impatiently.

'Stay where you are, Nicholas. Damn you, do you think I had forgotten you were there? I want you to hear this. You're a part of it, you see. You're his friend.'

The Duke paused, as if talking tired him and he had to gather his strength to continue. 'It was that friendship which started the whole thing, wasn't it? All that dreadful business with Isobel all those years ago. I have to admit that it was not only Isobel's youth which was a barrier to your marriage. I had decided that you were unsuitable as a son-in-law. I thought Isobel could do better.'

Matthew allowed a cynical smile to flicker across his countenance while Nicholas, who remembered his own assurances to Matthew at the time that this could not possibly be the case, looked acutely embarrassed.

'I was wrong about you, Matthew. And Nicholas was right, so my apology is partly directed to him. You, Matthew, are better than all the rest of us put together. You have made your own way in the world – you are a successful man and an honourable one.'

Matthew hooded his eyes and looked inscrutable.

'I realise now that you are a modern man, equipped to deal with this new-fangled world of weird inventions and changing customs.' The Duke was silent for a while. 'I was wrong about you,' he said again. 'That's all I wanted to say. I apologise. And I'm glad you married Anne.'

Nicholas blew his nose and his eyes looked suspiciously moist. Matthew stood up and looked down at the surprisingly shrunken figure of the Duke.

'Your apology is accepted, Your Grace, although I do assure you that none was necessary.' He hesitated for there was a mute appeal in the Duke's eyes. 'And I also assure you,' Matthew added quietly, 'that I, too, am glad I married Anne.'

The Duke sank back on to his pillows with a sigh of happiness and closed his eyes. Outside in the corridor Nicholas mopped his face furiously.

'Never saw eye-to-eye with His Grace,' he choked, 'but now I can't help feeling sorry for the old boy.'

'Quite.' Matthew waited for Nicholas to collect himself and then continued. 'It's disgusting, though. I'm sorry, Nicholas, I know he is your father but it is still disgusting. To be so pathetic on one's death-bed! To be so abject before one's former adversary! To go out with a whimper! I shall never do that, Nicholas. I will remain strong to the end. I could not bear anyone to feel sorry for *me*.'

Julia was in vivacious form at dinner that evening, basking in the admiration of the company. Only Anne recognised the spitefulness which underlay her witticisms and only she noticed how Julia directed her wiles at Matthew.

'Let's play hide-and-seek,' Julia suggested after dinner.

Alfred brightened. 'An excellent idea,' he enthused.

One of the anomalies of the age was the manner in which young ladies, so strictly chaperoned at all other times, were allowed to play hide-and-seek through the dimly-lit passages of the great houses. The game was, however, more an afternoon pastime than for the evening and now some of the ladies looked out at the summer night and shivered deliciously.

The Duchess was sitting with the Duke in his room and Anne was acting as hostess. She looked doubtfully at Matthew.

'I don't know . . .' she began.

'Oh, it's all right,' said Matthew breezily. 'We're mostly family here, anyway. I hardly think we need worry too much about any impropriety. It's either that or charades or cards.'

A groan went up. Everyone was heartily sick of charades.

'Then hide-and-seek it is,' Anne agreed hastily. She had been rather opposed to card games recently.

Julia began organising the party into pairs, leaving the family until last. 'Alfred and I will hide. Uncle Nicholas, you will hunt with Aunt Elizabeth, and of course Uncle Matthew with Aunt Anne. But you must give the others a start, because you have an unfair advantage through knowing the best places to hide.'

She ran lightly up the stairs and led Alfred through the maze of corridors in her grandfather's house, seeking the hiding places of her childhood. Alfred had soon lost his bearings entirely and, unknown to him, Julia doubled back to a small closet on the bedroom floor. The shelves were stacked with sheets and towels and tablecloths and Alfred looked sceptical.

'Isn't this a bit obvious?' he whispered.

'Exactly. Which is why they won't look here. They will go first to the attics.'

Alfred smiled admiringly. 'As long as it takes them all evening to find us,' he murmured and pulled her towards him. Julia allowed him to kiss her, wishing that his mouth was not so wet and his face so vacuous. She strained her ears and through the considerable thickness of the closed door heard the giggles and whispers as the seekers scurried past. While Alfred was occupied with kissing her, she removed one of her pearl earrings and concealed it in her hand. When Alfred let her go she bent in the darkness to hide the earring in the pocket of her dress before giving a loud gasp of dismay.

'Alfred! I have lost an earring!'

He swore under his breath. 'We can't look for it now, Julia. Don't worry about it, it will turn up.'

'No, I must find it! I remember hearing something drop on the staircase. You stay here, I won't be long.'

And before he could argue further, she had gone

She ran on tiptoe through the empty corridors towards the staircase. A door to a room at the end of the passage stood open and she slipped inside and pressed herself immediately behind it. Nicholas and Elizabeth were ascending the staircase.

'Damn silly business!' Nicholas grumbled. 'People of our age cavorting round the house at the dead of night.'

'Don't be such a spoil-sport, Nicholas. Just because you would have preferred to play cards, it doesn't mean everyone else wanted to do so.'

'Where are we going to look?'

'We are not looking anywhere at the moment. The whole point of the game is to give the young people a little time alone.'

'You mean we're going to tramp round the corridors indefinitely?' Nicholas sounded horrified.

'The exercise will do you good. You are growing much, much too fat.'

Their voices faded and cautiously Julia emerged. She reached the top of the stairs in time to catch a glimpse of Anne's pink dress at the far end of the hall and smiled to herself. They were taking the back stairs. Silently she floated down the main stairs and followed them.

Matthew and Anne were walking slowly. Like the rest of the seekers, they were in no hurry to locate their quarry. They walked in silence, unaware of the pale figure which followed them. They neither heard the whisper of Julia's skirt over the uncarpeted floors at the back of the house nor saw her shadow on the wall.

'I think I will look in on Philip,' Anne said suddenly as they reached the upper floor. 'I'm told he took a nasty fall today.'

'Go in if you want, but I shall not do so. You spoil the boy. Make a fuss of him because he falls off a horse and he'll be falling off more and more often, merely to gain attention.'

Perfect, thought Julia. Anne was playing right into her hands and presenting her with exactly the opportunity she needed. She followed them as far as Philip's room and shrank back into an alcove as Matthew and Anne paused outside the door before Anne entered. Matthew continued walking to the head of the main staircase and stood staring into the hall far below.

'Uncle Matthew!'

'Julia!' He swung round. 'Why aren't you hiding?'

'I lost an earring and came to look for it. And now I suddenly feel quite faint.'

Julia raised one hand delicately to her brow and dramatically staggered a few steps towards him.

'There's a chair on the far side of the stairs. Come on, let me help you.'

Matthew placed his arm around her and she drooped limply

against him. 'I don't want to sit down. If you can hold me up for a moment I will be better shortly. I must return to Alfred.'

'Would you like me to fetch some smelling salts or something?'

Julia's sharp ears caught the click as the nursery door closed and out of the corner of her eye she saw the rose-pink glow of Anne's gown advancing towards them. She recalled the struggle she had seen in Matthew's eyes that night in the winter garden when he had pushed her away. Any moment now, that meddling Aunt Anne would discover just who it was that Matthew loved best!

'Matthew,' she murmured and raised her face to his. As Matthew bent his head she wound her arms around his neck and pressed her lips firmly to his mouth.

He was numb and seemed to feel nothing at all. Certainly no desire coursed through his veins. He had lost all power over his body and could not move. As the shock faded, he was aware of being utterly appalled – at the same moment he heard a scream which came from behind him. Matthew turned to see Anne standing transfixed at the top of the stairs, staring at them with a wild anguish on her face. She lifted one hand in a gesture which might have been supplication or accusation, then pressed the hand against her eyes as if to block out the terrible sight she had seen, as she recoiled from them.

CHAPTER TEN

Matthew ignored the crumpled figure of Julia on the landing and leaped down the stairs to where Anne lay motionless, stretched out on the floor with one arm twisted awkwardly under her. Matthew knelt beside her and felt for her pulse. A flood of relief swept over him as he found a faint tremor and saw that she still breathed. Cradling her head against his chest, he looked up towards the head of the stairs. People were appearing from all directions in response to Anne's scream, the participants in the game of hide-and-seek bewildered at the sight of Matthew and Anne and at the prostrate figure of one of their quarry on the landing.

Ordering the butler to send for the doctor, Matthew lifted Anne and carried her back up the stairs to her room. Nicholas looked after Julia while the rest of the party milled about, half-excited, half-anxious, and eventually took themselves down to the drawing-room for a nerve-steadying drink.

The wait for the doctor seemed interminable. When he finally arrived, Matthew hovered in the background while the physician made a careful examination.

'Lady Anne is extremely lucky,' the doctor pronounced. 'She appears to have suffered nothing more than concussion, bruising and a sprained arm. However, she must be carefully watched. There might be some internal damage which will only manifest itself later.'

'I will watch,' said Matthew and sat down again to wait for the first sign of Anne regaining consciousness.

Julia had already come round and lay on her bed, shivering and trembling at the enormity of her sin. Nobody thought to tell her that Anne lived because no one knew that she believed Anne to have died.

'I am a murderess,' she thought. 'Will they take me to Newgate and hang me?' And she shrieked aloud as the doctor entered the room.

'Scream all you like, young lady,' said the doctor cheerfully. 'Perhaps the noise will wake your aunt.'

Julia flinched. 'Nothing will wake her,' she whispered hoarsely.

'Well, I agree that no outside noise will rouse her but I am hopeful the concussion is not too severe.'

'Concussion?' A faint ray of hope pierced the blackness of Julia's nightmare.

'Lady Anne should be up and about in a day or two. Well, there's nothing much the matter with you. I will leave you a sleeping draught, though. Good night.'

Julia began to sob with relief, but all too soon a new spectre rose to take the place of Newgate Gallows. Sooner or later, and probably sooner, she would have to face Matthew.

At midnight Matthew's patience was rewarded with the first flutter of Anne's eyelashes and a soft sigh. He sat on the bed and took her undamaged hand in his so that his face was the first thing she saw when she opened her eyes. As he leaned forward and kissed her on the cheek, Anne tried to smile but her brow puckered with pain.

'My head aches,' she murmured. She lay still, but from the desolation in her eyes Matthew could tell that memory was returning. She turned her head away. 'I saw, I saw . . .'

'You merely saw Julia's latest trick.'

'Matthew, do you see the truth at last?'

'I have been the biggest damn fool in England,' he said remorsefully, 'to be taken in by that deceitful chit. You were right and I was wrong and not for the first time. But you must rest now and try not to think harsh thoughts of me or of Julia. She meant to hurt you, but I am quite certain she did not intend that you should fall down the stairs and injure yourself.'

She slept then, but Matthew made no attempt to go to bed. He dozed fitfully in the chair beside her, refusing Henriette's offer to keep vigil. Despite his concern for Anne's health, he felt more at peace with himself than he had done for weeks. Furious though he was with Julia – and his anger was partly directed at himself for being so easily fooled – it was a relief to realise that she was the person behind the affairs of the the cards and the letters. Not knowing who the culprit was had nagged at him without ceasing. Now he could act.

How could he make amends to Anne? Unfortunately, Matthew thought only in terms of money and what it could buy. Jewellery, perhaps? New gowns? A visit to Paris? As dawn broke over the Berkshire vales, Matthew made his decision. He would give Anne a country house.

In his pleasure at this idea, and given the customary energy and enthusiasm with which he tackled any new project, his worry about Anne was completely swept away and he could hardly wait for her to wake so that he could tell her about it. The instant she opened her eyes, he bombarded her with his plans without even asking how she felt.

'Reynolds must find out what properties are on the market. I can't be bothered building because it will take too long and I want something we can move into very soon. Berkshire will be best – our family roots are here – but I would prefer to be nearer to Ascot than this side of the county. I'd like to buy some racehorses too.' Matthew briskly pulled back the curtains and did not notice how Anne winced as the bright light streamed into her eyes.

'Yes.' Anne tried to sit up and found difficulty in moving with only one arm.

'Are there any points you would like me to mention to Reynolds about the house?'

'No, nothing. Do you think you could help me up?'

He raised her shoulders and stuffed some extra pillows behind her back. 'Is the arm very painful?'

'A little.' It was not so much the arm, thought Anne, as her head. If this blinding headache did not recede, she felt she would go mad.

'I will be off then.' He stooped and kissed her cheek, 'And I'll send Henriette.'

It was very early and the house had not begun to stir, but Henriette was awake and awaiting a summons to Anne's side.

The bedroom seemed quiet and full of repose without Matthew's exuberant, overpowering presence.

'Would you like some breakfast?' asked Henriette. 'Or perhaps some tea?'

'Nothing,' said Anne faintly, 'but please pull the curtains closed again. And find out if the doctor is calling today. I must have something for this headache.'

Matthew slept for a couple of hours, awoke refreshed, partook of a late and hearty breakfast and then strode into Julia's room. She had slept well and was languishing decoratively in bed looking, she hoped, pale and interesting. She paled genuinely when she saw Matthew's face.

He scorched her with a blistering attack on her behaviour, couched in forthright language which he would not normally have used to a young lady.

'Why, Julia?' he asked at last. 'Why did you do it?'

'I don't know.' She gave him a chastened look. 'Yes, I do. I wanted you to love me best of all and when you did not I was angry and wanted to hit back.'

'Julia, I'm your *uncle*. It is Alfred who should love you best of all.'

'I wanted *you*. You are much more attractive than Alfred. You never seemed like an uncle and no one in the family was ever the least bit interested in me.'

'Nonsense. Your Uncle Nicholas . . .'

'Nicholas!' exclaimed Julia in tones of utter contempt. 'What use is Nicholas?'

'He is my best friend,' retorted Matthew sharply, 'and I will thank you to remember that.' He regarded her critically. 'That's something you have never had, isn't it? A friend? You will be married soon and able to build a new life for yourself. Then you will have family *and* friends.' He paused at the door. 'You are obviously a young lady of imagination and determination. I am half inclined to think that you are worth two of Charles and Edward, but I also see in you a most dangerous combination of your mother and father. Put your talents to good use, Julia, instead of bad. Find an outlet for your energies. Join the Women's Rights movement. Do something – anything – but stay out of my affairs in future or I will not answer for the consequences.'

Julia sank back on her pillows with relief as he left the room. The interview could have been very much worse, and she was thankful to get off comparatively lightly. She felt sincerely sorry for Anne's accident and chastened by Matthew's anger, but with the resilience of youth her spirits were already rising. Join the Women's Rights movement, he had suggested. Well, why not? She might just do that. She had felt miserably constricted and inadequate all summer, as she had tried to put her plans into practice. It was high time women had more scope, she considered. She rearranged the lace at her neck and inspected her face and hair carefully in the hand-mirror at her side. Alfred would be calling soon and she must look her best and make her peace with him. She had to get married – at the moment this was still the only path to some semblance of freedom for a woman.

Matthew was absent all that day and the following day and the next. Reynolds forwarded a list of suitable properties and Matthew made inquiries of friends and neighbours, travelling the length and breadth of the county in search of his Shangri-La.

Each night he returned to Desborough to give Anne vivid descriptions of the houses he had seen and each night she tried to conceal her illness and exhaustion so as not to spoil his happiness.

On the sixth day he burst into her room and stopped in disappointment.

'You're still in bed,' he said almost reproachfully.

'I am sorry, Matthew. I seem to have little strength.'

'But you must get up. You are better now except for your arm. You must dress and come out with me; there is a house I want you to see.'

'Matthew, I couldn't possibly . . .'

'Of course you can,' said Matthew roundly. 'You haven't tried. You must get up tomorrow and come to Reading with me.'

Anne swallowed at the thought of the effort this would entail and tried to take an interest. 'Is it a nice house?'

'*Nice!* Of course it's nice. What sort of question is that? Do you think I'd be interested in the house if it wasn't nice?'

'I'm sorry,' said Anne again. 'Tell me about it.'

'It is a bit ornate, but that's all I can find to criticise. The style is French Renaissance. It's like a bloody great château set in the Thames Valley instead of the Loire. The North and South fronts are massive, and there is an imposing portico as the main entrance. The most interesting features of the architecture are the East and West Wings, which are built in the form of towers with unusual spiral staircases. On the ground floor are a vestibute, two enormous galleries, three drawing-rooms, a breakfast room, a dining room, a morning room, a library, a study and a conservatory. The bedrooms and bathrooms are all on the first floor.'

'Are the grounds large enough for the racing stable?'

'Five hundred acres. Ample room! Yes, it's definitely the best proposition I have seen. We can take over most of the furniture and we won't have to wait long for possession. You must come and see it, Anne. You must!'

'I'll try, really I will.' How she wished he was not always in such a hurry! It would have been nice if he could have waited until she felt well enough to go with him to look at the houses – then they could have shared the decisions and the planning.

'You should be better by now.' He glared at her rather crossly, because he was disappointed she could not share fully in his new toy. Then, wonderingly, Anne saw the expression on his face change. His eyes darkened and his lips parted as he bent over her, slipping his hand inside her nightgown and caressing her breast. Anne was still black and blue from the fall and her sprained arm was torture, but she set her teeth in a determined effort so that he should not know how much he was hurting her.

'A new house, Anne,' he was saying. 'We should make it a symbol – a fresh start for you and me.'

His lips were on hers, hard and demanding, and he caressed her body more urgently. Then without more ado he thrust aside the sheets and pulled up her nightgown. Anne felt quite stunned but there could no longer be any doubt of his intentions. Not *now*, she groaned to herself, oh not now! Why couldn't he have made love to me in London after I burned the letters or . . . oh, on so many other occasions when I was well and wanted him so. Why must he choose now when I feel so weak and tired and ill? But I cannot refuse him or he might not come to me again.

So Anne suppressed all the pain she felt, and all thoughts of the pleasure she wanted so much to feel, and welcomed Matthew to her bed for the first time in seven years.

She was not well enough to go to Reading the next day so, rather huffily, Matthew went off with Nicholas. Reynolds met them at the house and the deal was concluded that afternoon. Matthew paid £200,000 for the house, furniture and estate. He would have prefered something a little plainer, a little more typically English, but few country houses of this size came on to the market. On the whole he was pleased with his purchase and it was arranged he could take possession in the New Year.

The house party at Desborough finally broke up. The Duke clung obstinately to life and cheated his guests of the privilege of providing him with a cheerful death-bed. Business called Matthew and Nicholas back to London. Philip went reluctantly to school. Julia returned sulkily to Highclere to prepare for her wedding. Only Anne lingered on at Desborough, unable to face the journey home. In October she managed to find the will-power to go, because she missed the rediscovered joy of Matthew's company, the new-found intimacy in bed, and the pleasure of participating in his life again. She had to be carried off the train at Paddington and taken straight to bed at Park Lane, but it was worth it. Or at least, it was for a little white. Matthew was so busy that she saw him seldom. He was either at the office or down at Brightwell, as he called the country estate, and she had not the heart to tell him that she would prefer to see more of him than to own a new house.

By November she suspected she was pregnant and by December, when Julia was married, she was sure. She was so delighted that her health improved greatly and she bloomed like a young girl. Even so, she could not undertake another journey so they spent an unconventional Christmas in London.

In the New Year Anne's health deteriorated again and the doctor ordered her to bed until the baby was born. She was as fragile and delicate as a bird. The long years in Kimberley in the dust and heat, the struggle with knife wounds, disease and childbearing had all worn out her slender frame long before time. The accident at Desborough had taken more out of her than anyone knew, and not even to the doctor could she fully describe the blinding headaches and the general feeling of ennui and lassitude which were her daily companions.

Because she could not travel to Brightwell, she asked Reynolds for plans of the house and spent hours in bed drawing pictures of the rooms and making little cut-outs of the furniture so that she could rearrange it to her liking. The Red Drawing Room, the Blue Drawing Room and the sunny Yellow Morning Room all took shape under her guidance. She had patterns of curtains, chair covers and bed covers brought to her and debated their respective merits with whoever called.

In April the old Duke died and was followed unexpectedly to the grave by Matthew's mother in May. A superstitious shiver ran through the members of the family as they feared these things ran in threes, and they cast their minds to crooked, black-robed Isobel in her tower and half-hoped she might obtain her deliverance.

Anne lay in her room and thought of the dead, wretched that she could not attend the funerals, and then tried to focus her mind on the living and in particular on the new life which she would bring into the world very soon.

The baby was due at the beginning of July, but one wet morning in early June Anne felt the first pains clutch at her body. She said nothing, hoping it might be a false alarm, but by nightfall she was groaning and sweating and Henriette sent for Matthew and for the doctor.

Matthew was at Brightwell, not having been there for several weeks due to pressure of work. The recession in the diamond industry was easing and also 'Kaffirs' continued to spiral, so business interests had required his full attention of late. He was putting the finishing touches to the house. There had been an important art sale in London and he had snapped up some prime exhibits; now he was supervising the hanging of his new collection – Canaletto and Guardi, Gainsborough and Reynolds, Murillo and Rembrandt.

There was also a surprise for Anne. During her period of

revived health at Christmas and in the New Year, Matthew had commissioned an artist to paint a secret portrait of her. The young man had made furtive drawings of her face and Henriette had provided one of Anne's favourite dresses – unworn now because she was confined to her room – so that the picture could be completed. It hung in the Blue Drawing Room, the silver of the dress and the shining coils of Anne's hair gleaming against the rich blue brocade which covered the walls. Matthew was standing before it, admiring the manner in which the artist had caught the serenity of Anne's expression and the deep tranquillity in her violet eyes, when they brought him the message.

He hurried to Park Lane at once but his haste was unnecessary. For three days Anne was in labour and with each hour she grew weaker.

'If there has to be a choice, save the mother,' Matthew commanded as he waited with Nicholas for news. 'Get as many doctors as you need. I will give anything, pay anything, to save her.' But the doctor looked at him pityingly. No amount of money could help Matthew now.

At last, at ten in the evening of June the tenth, Henriette came to tell him that a daughter had been born. Matthew knelt by Anne's bed as her painful breaths became fewer and more shallow. She became so still at one time that he was sure she had gone, but then the violet eyes opened again, as huge as a startled fawn's in her white wasted face. He buried his face in her breast and she managed to lift one hand and lay it on his head.

'I have always loved you.'

The faint words were barely audible even in the silence of the room where the ticking of the clock seemed to boom as loudly as the beating of Matthew's heart. He raised his head to tell her that he loved her too – words he had never spoken during the seventeen years of their marriage. But it was too late. Anne was dead.

Matthew stayed in his room for two days.

His marriage lay before him, and yet behind him, in a tangled web of misunderstandings and missed opportunities. He could see so much so clearly now. He could unravel the primary thread and follow the path of failure. Because he realised his marriage had been a failure and that it was largely his fault. Largely, but not completely.

He thought back to the clash and conflict of the early days when he and Anne had been prey to misconceptions about each other and too consumed with pride to overcome their difficulties. He had been busy as well as proud – utterly immersed in his business affairs, building a diamond empire instead of a relationship – and Anne became weakened by illness while his own strength grew.

The thread ran through the attack by Danie, the birth and death of Victoria and Anne's adultery with Court; times when nearly, oh so nearly, he and Anne had come together but always, at the last moment, something had happened to keep them apart. And after Court, he had not tried to close the gap, had not even *wanted* to do so.

Then had come Emma and Julia . . . but at least he had atoned for that. Emma and Julia did not burden his conscience and weigh him down with guilt. No, what haunted Matthew was the knowledge that he had not loved Anne. *He had not loved her*, and somehow this meant that her death was the only possible conclusion to their relationship, because he knew he would not have loved her had she lived.

Matthew could provide endless reasons and excuses. He had not been ready to love her, or to love anyone. She had been part of his life at a period when his time and attention were devoted to establishing his power-base. It might have been different if he met her now – now that he was rich, mature and confident, now that he could love anyone he chose, regardless of other considerations. But this introspection was immaterial. Anne was dead and while Matthew knew that he could not be blamed for not loving her, he had been guilty of marrying her for the wrong reasons and so poisoning her short life.

It occurred to him somewhat belatedly that he had never loved any woman. The only female being he had truly cared for was Victoria. And gradually, during those two days, Matthew's thoughts turned to the new baby and the belief was born within him that he possessed the courage, will and ability to love her.

On the third day, Matthew emerged from his seclusion and demanded his first sight of his daughter.

So great had seemed his grief for Anne that the family were afraid Matthew might reject the child and they watched apprehensively as he lifted the baby from the crib. The white bundle of the premature infant looked tiny and fragile against his massive chest and to Matthew his daughter seemed almost weightless.

'You will need someone to look after her,' his sister Mary said. 'Perhaps now that Mama is dead, and I am not needed at Highclere so much, I should . . .'

'No!' Matthew was seized with a sharp surge of possessiveness and his arms tightened fiercely round the baby. 'She is mine; no one shall take her from me.' The baby opened big blue eyes and stared solemnly into Matthew's excited face. 'I will have none of you women in my house, I will have none of you meddling in my affairs. *I* shall raise my daughter and I shall do it my way!'

His words were met by an embarrassed silence which was broken by Nicholas clearing his throat.

'What shall you call her?' Nicholas asked.

Matthew and the baby continued to stare unblinkingly at each other. Not Anne, he thought. There can only be one Anne in my life. But something which has the sound of Anne and yet a touch of me in it too. The name came to him then as easily as if Anne had breathed it in his ear.

'Miranda,' he said firmly.

He was equally emphatic over the arrangements for Anne's funeral. It had been assumed that Anne would be taken to lie in the family vault at Desborough, but Matthew would not hear of it.

'She will be buried at Brightwell,' he declared.

'But Anne never so much as set foot in the place,' Nicholas protested.

'I intend to be buried at Brightwell and therefore so will Anne.' And Matthew refused to discuss the matter further.

So instead of grand entertainments for the opening of the new house, it was Anne's funeral which brought the family – the Brights, the Harcourt-Brights and the Graftons – to Brightwell. After the service they walked to a part of the garden which had been set aside as a burial ground. In spring it would be sprinkled with crocuses, daffodils, primroses and violets but now the summer roses were in bloom, filling the air with heady fragrance.

Honeysuckle hugged the arbours and marigolds and marguerites formed a blazing carpet beneath the lilac and wild cherry trees.

Anne would have found it ironic that, Matthew apart, none of the group felt more stricken at her death than Julia.

Julia had now been married for six months. As required by convention, the wedding night had been a shock and Lord Alfred's actions had been as repulsive to her as any Victorian matron could have wished. She loathed Alfred's lovemaking, but also recognised that the act had possibilities. Possibilities, that is, if performed with the right person. Someone like Matthew, for example. Julia began to understand her feelings towards Matthew rather better and was not shocked by them. He still did not seem like an uncle to her.

She was shocked by Anne's death, however, because she felt partly responsible. It was obvious that the accident at Desborough had played a major part in finally undermining Anne's already precarious health. Julia lived in fear of Matthew's wrath, of the accusations he might make. Incredibly, though, and fortunately for her, any connection between the accident and Anne's death did not seem to have crossed Matthew's mind.

As they gathered at the graveside Julia found that she was standing next to Philip. He looked so lost and forlorn that Julia felt an unfamiliar pang of sympathy for the little boy. He should have been standing with Matthew but instead here he was, wedged into the mass of female relations, forgotten. Tentatively, Julia reached out to take his hand in hers and squeeze it comfortingly. But Philip snatched his hand away. She bit her lip and stared straight ahead, expressionless.

She called me a coward, Philip was thinking. I don't want any woman holding my hand, particularly not her. I am glad I am here where Papa can't see me. If he can't see me, he can't shout at me for doing something wrong. Philip watched the coffin being lowered into the grave. Mama was dead. He wondered if he would miss her; he hadn't so far, but then they had not been close. Philip wasn't close to anyone. Mama is dead, he said again to himself, and who wants a baby sister anyway?

Henriette had taken up a position slightly, decorously, apart from the family. Tears ran freely down her ugly pockmarked face. In spite of her loneliness, Anne had been too old-fashioned and too much a Duke's daughter to confide in her maid and make her a friend. But Henriette had watched over her mistress for seventeen years, and very little escaped her sharp eyes. Utterly devoted to Anne, especially since the smallpox, she suffered and shared silently in all Anne's misfortunes. Now she stared resentfully at Matthew's back, hating him as the source of all Anne's unhappiness. Henriette would stay on in the Bright household because her husband remained in his position as chief chef. She watched and waited, hugging to herself all her secret knowledge.

They stood, black crêpe billowing in the breeze, so different from the colour and gaiety of the Season a year ago. They stood as Anne was buried, to lie alone in the ground of the house she never saw and did not want, the house which took Matthew from her side when she would have given all her diamonds for an hour of his time.

Matthew stared blindly at the coffin. The scene had taken on an air of utter unreality. The vicar's voice droned on and on and Matthew wished the man would hurry because he wanted to spend some time with Miranda before lunch.

Part Three
NEW YORK, ENGLAND AND SOUTHERN AFRICA 1895–1899

CHAPTER ONE

When Court returned to the United States in 1887, he headed straight for Boston to show his daughter to his family, but he had no intention of staying there. His business interests dictated that he should settle in New York and, besides, Tiffany deserved the biggest and best stage in America.

The family had prospered, although not to the same extent as Court himself. Their import-export activities had expanded and in addition they had diversified into manufacturing. The family's traditional links with banking had also been maintained and Court was quick to note the standing this bestowed on them in the community. Banking, he decided, had the solidity and respectability which he required for Tiffany.

Perhaps unconsciously, Court was trying to compensate for Tiffany's illegitimacy, but he had no need. His story of a wife dead in childbirth in the wilds of Africa was believed by everyone. But from the start, Court geared his entire lifestyle and his every endeavour to providing Tiffany with all the accomplishments and accoutrements necessary for a leading position in New York society, which was at this time the most snobbish in the world.

He bought a house in Fifth Avenue at 56th Street, opposite William Vanderbilt's mansion. It was a white stone Renaissance palace and cost him a million dollars, plus another quarter of a million for the furniture. Like Matthew's Brightwell, Court's château was in the French style and the delicacy of furnishing and ornament formed an incongruous backcloth for his huge frame. He chose a colour scheme of various combinations of white and gold – white for the diamonds of Kimberley and gold for the Johannesburg Reef on which his fortune had been founded. In the reception rooms he perched on fragile chairs which could have graced the Petit Trianon and at night he lay in a white luxurious – if austere and uncluttered – room, utterly at variance with the basic simplicity of his nature. Gone now was the call of the wild, gone the restlessness and the wandering, gone the search for answers to so many questions. In their place had come Tiffany.

She bore little resemblance to Anne. Tiffany had inherited the dark hair, thick and curling, of Court's family. She was showing promise of height, too, and strength of limb. Only her eyes were Anne's; huge, violet and softly luminous in the pretty, pert face.

She reigned supreme in the sunny yellow nurseries adjoining Court's own suite. The original Irish nurse had been replaced by an English nanny – plain, middle-aged, extremely efficient and thoroughly disapproving of the constant capitulations to her charge's whims. Nanny foresaw trouble with this spoiled child. It's all very well giving her everything she wants, Nanny said to herself, but one day Miss Tiffany is going to learn a very hard lesson. One day there will be something she wants that she simply cannot have.

To Court's surprise, success in New York came quickly. He retained a large shareholding in the Diamond Company, but took no active part in the business. He opened the office of Court Diamonds on Wall Street and before long prestigious invitations came his way. For one thing, diamonds were not 'trade' and they carried a unique mystique. For another, he was rich, attractive and unmarried and therefore there could be not a shadow of doubt that he needed a wife.

Court himself was not averse to the idea of marrying. There were times when he considered it might be his duty to provide Tiffany with a mother. But none of the ladies he met appealed sufficently. None of them showed a genuine interest in Tiffany and not one was sufficiently like Anne or Alida. There was in Court an affinity for the vulnerable and the high society damsels, the daughters of the rich elite, were lacking in vulnerability. Unfortunately, Court did not realise that by the nature of things Tiffany would grow up the same way. He did realise, however, that he dared not look outside the top ranks for a bride, since society would not accept such a marriage and Tiffany would be cast out with him. So Court eluded the marriage brokers, although he never allowed them to give up hope, and concentrated on planning his daughter's life.

In those early years Court never parted from Tiffany, never slept under a different roof. Their first separation came in the New Year of 1896 when he received an unexpected summons to visit the President, Grover Cleveland, in Washington. The President needed advice and assistance from someone who knew South Africa well and had selected Court because of his well-known connection with the diamond and gold fields and the Court family's trading links with the region.

There was trouble in the Transvaal and an American citizen was apparently seriously implicated in the uprising.

'I told you so!' Danie Steyn pointed an accusing finger at his fellow burghers. 'If you had listened to me nine years ago, none of this would have happened.'

They listened now, in December 1895. Danie Steyn had acquired the status of a prophet among his own people, and all the things that he had predicted had come to pass.

At first glance Danie, at thirty years old, was not an impressive figure. He was short and stocky, like his father had been, and he had Gerrit Steyn's thick neck, black hair and heavy black beard. But closer inspection revealed that his unusual grey-green eyes burned with a fervent intensity and the expression on his swarthy features was intelligent and alert. For nine years he had expressed in the columns in *De Volksstem* his belief in the threat posed by the *uitlanders* to the Boer community. His forceful style and clarity of expression began to win adherents and he was aided by events. Gradually the British had fenced in the Boers, until neither the Transvaal nor the Orange Free State republics had access to the sea except through British or Portuguese land. The encirclement was complete when Rhodes's Pioneer Column hoisted the British flag at Fort Salisbury (which would become the capital of Rhodesia) and secured the Transvaal's northern border.

To Danie and his followers these moves were ominous but did not constitute the main danger. The Boers were accustomed to life in a *laager*; it was the enemy within their own camp which they feared the most: the thousands of men of many nationalities who swarmed in the gold mines of Johannesburg. The men who brought the ways of the city and the attitudes of big business to the little pastoral republic.

There were about eighty thousand foreigners in the Johannesburg area, nearly four times the number of Boers. They provided the brains and the money behind the fortunes of the country and had turned a bankrupt state into a prosperous nation. Yet these *uitlanders* had no electoral rights in the Transvaal nor any voice in Johannesburg, the city which they had built in the bare veld and in which they paid massive rates and taxes. These men were now demanding 'rights' in their adopted land.

'Some people feel the *uitlanders* should have the vote,' said someone diffidently. 'After all, they pay taxes.'

'They can vote, if they fulfil certain requirements.'

'But those requirements are virtually impossible for any *uitlander* to fulfil.'

'This is our country,' said Danie stonily. 'They will do things our way or not at all. Damn you, you'll be wanting to give the vote to the kaffirs next.'

The men laughed as the joke eased the tension, but the respite was brief.

'We need the strangers because we need the gold,' another man said. 'Revenue from the gold mines amounted to £4 million last year.'

'Gold is the curse, not the saviour of our people,' spat Danie, in the manner of his tirades in *De Volksstem*. 'It lies like a shadow over our sacred land. Every ounce of gold will be paid for in tears and rivers of blood which will flow in defence of our earth from the covetousness of others.'

Danie paused, but no one spoke.

'I saw Oom Paul today,' he said softly, 'and he sees things the way I do. They are up to something – Rhodes's friends in Johannesburg. Their speeches grow more inflammatory and their meetings more frequent. Yes, they are certainly up to something, but I do not know exactly what it is.'

Danie was right and he did not have to wait long for enlightenment.

Cecil Rhodes was Premier of the Cape Colony and he seized eagerly on the discontent of the *uitlanders* in Johannesburg. Keen to oust Kruger, as part of his imperialist expansion programme, he plotted an uprising in which the *uitlanders* would seize power. As well as conspirators in Johannesburg, who called themselves the Reform Committee, the plan involved British troops under the command of Dr Jameson, Rhodes's old friend and Matthew's doctor in Kimberley.

But the plot miscarried. President Kruger arrested the members of the Reform Committee and hurled them into Pretoria Jail. Jameson was returned to the British authorities for punishment but sixty-three of the Johannesburg conspirators were to be tried for their crime. Among the internees in Pretoria were a nephew of Barney Barnato, a brother of Cecil Rhodes and an American engineer called John Hays Hammond.

Cecil Rhodes had no choice but to resign as Premier of the Cape. His political career was ended.

'I don't see why you have to go to Africa, Papa,' Tiffany pouted sullenly.

'I am going because the President particularly asked me to go,' Court told her gently, ruffling the dark curls.

He did not want to visit Pretoria, but had agreed out of basic respect for America's first citizen. Cleveland was unpopular in many quarters, but Court admired the man's honesty and integrity. Possibly Court was influenced by the fact that Cleveland had an illegitimate son. When his political opponents had unearthed this information during the Presidential campaign of 1884, Cleveland's staff had asked what statement they should issue on the subject. Cleveland simply said: 'Tell the truth.' Such a man might Court have been if he had not fallen in with Matthew Bright.

'There is a man in Africa who needs help,' Court told Tiffany. 'An American, with children like you. You wouldn't want him to go without help so that I could stay here, would you?'

'I wouldn't mind,' said Tiffany candidly.

Court smiled indulgently. 'You are too young to understand. Now, be a brave girl. You will have a wonderful time while I am away. You and Nanny will stay with your Aunt Sarah in Boston and your cousin Randolph will be there too. You like Randolph, don't you?'

'Not very much. I don't want to go to Boston, I want to come with you.'

'Darling, you cannot possibly come with me,' said Court with a sigh. He was dreading the parting as much as if not more than his daughter, but was concerned that danger threatened foreigners in the Transvaal.

'I won't go to Boston,' screamed Tiffany, stamping her foot. 'I won't! I won't!'

'All right, all right.' Court bent and hugged her, to stem the flow of tears which he could never bear to see. 'You can come part of the way with me – to England, or even to Cape Town. But you cannot come to Pretoria, you must understand that.'

'Very well.' Having achieved her objective, Tiffany's tears ceased and the tantrum passed. She could argue about this Pretoria place at a later stage. Looking at her father's anxious face, Tiffany gauged that his mood was one of reconciliation and guilt at having upset her. 'Tell me about Mama,' she coaxed, with her most winning smile.

'You have already heard the story a thousand times,' exclaimed Court. 'There is nothing more to tell.'

'Tell me again, then,' Tiffany insisted.

Court sighed and sat down. His story was pure invention and his problem was that Tiffany remembered the details far better than he.

'Your mother was born in England,' Court began, 'into a great and noble family, one of the foremost in the land. They lived in a palace in the country. The palace had a moat with a drawbridge over it and inside it was filled with beautiful jewels and treasures and silken hangings.'

'Like a princess,' breathed Tiffany.

'Almost like a princess,' agreed Court cautiously. 'But then tragedy struck. There was a terrible quarrel in the family and your mother and her parents had to flee to a far and distant country, where they had to live very differently because they were very poor.'

'Where did they go?'

'To Africa, to a city called Cape Town.'

'And was Mama barefoot and dressed in rags?'

'Not quite, but her clothes were threadbare and shabby. Then another dreadful thing happened when her father and mother died very suddenly, leaving Mama alone and penniless.'

'What did they die of?' asked Tiffany, knowing the answer perfectly well.

'Smallpox.' With a faint smile Court recalled the first time Tiffany had asked that question and with what desperation he had cast round for an answer.

'And that was when you found her?'

'Yes. I was living in Kimberley, on the diamond fields, and I had to travel to Cape Town on business. I was riding up Adderley Street one lovely morning when I saw this beautiful girl standing alone at the corner of the street.'

'Describe what she looked like.' Tiffany's eyes moved worshipfully to the portrait which stood on the piano.

Court followed her gaze and his discomfort increased. The incredulity with which Tiffany had greeted the information that he possessed no likeness of her mother had prompted a diligent search in the galleries of New York for a picture which resembled his fictitious character.

'She was small and slender and she had long dark hair. When I came close, I could see that she had huge violet eyes and thick dark lashes.'

'Like mine?'

'Exactly like yours,' agreed Court. 'She was wearing a blue dress and she looked very sad.'

'Because she couldn't find any work and had no money to buy food,' cried Tiffany, 'but you took her up on your horse and rode off with her and gave her silks and furs and diamonds.'

'More or less.'

'I think it's the most romantic story I ever heard,' said Tiffany seriously. 'When we go to England, we could go to see Mama's relations.'

'Oh, no!' said Court hastily. 'I have no idea where they live.'

'You could ask, Papa.'

'I don't even know their name,' Court improvised desperately. 'Mama wouldn't tell me.'

'So you only knew her first name. It was a pretty name, wasn't it!'

'Yes,' said Court slowly. 'Very pretty.'

'What was it?'

'You know what . . .' Court began. He averted his eyes. 'Alida,' he said.

'Alida,' Tiffany repeated. She lifted down the picture and clasped it to her chest. 'If you don't mind, Papa, I shall take Mama to bed with me tonight and we will take the picture to England and Africa with us. Perhaps someone will remember her.'

As the door closed behind her, Court buried his face in his hands. He had meant no harm with his story, but he fervently hoped Tiffany would soon outgrow her childish curiosity about her mother, otherwise there would be even more awkward questions to answer when she grew up.

CHAPTER TWO

Court arrived in Cape Town at the end of March and to his astonishment one of the first people he met was the man he had come to help: the man whom he had thought was languishing in Pretoria Jail. John Hays Hammond.

It transpired that Hammond had been ill with dysentery and Barney Barnato had used his influence to have him released on bail. This was no mean feat, Hammond assured Court, because he was one of the four principal accused in the trial of the Reform Committee.

Furthermore, Hammond appeared quite unconcerned over his plight. Gaily he recounted how Nellie Joel, wife of Barney's nephew Solly, used to arrive at the jail with cigars under her hat and a brace of ducks in her bustle, while Natalie Hammond had smuggled in a long Bologna sausage wrapped around her waist.

Court felt foolish. Having come all this way to rescue his countryman, he was disconcerted to find Hammond sunning himself in Cape Town and talking in such jocular fashion of high jinks in Pretoria Jail.

The trial was due to start on April 27 and Hammond seemed confident that the defendants would be fined rather than imprisoned. So it was in sanguine mood that Court showed Tiffany the sights of Cape Town – the most important places being the spot where he had met 'Alida' and the house where Tiffany was born – and then they travelled to Pretoria. Tiffany had indulged in another fit of temper at the prospect of being left behind and Court had relented in view of Hammond's assurances that calm prevailed in the Transvaal.

Compared with New York, Pretoria was unbelievably small and sleepy. Already its upstart sister, Johannesburg, had outstripped the capital in size of population and growth of business and buildings. To Court's sophisticated eye, Pretoria seemed to consist only of Church Square, with the Raadzaal Building, and the broad long sweep of Church Street where the President's house stood.

He had originally intended to call on Paul Kruger in order to intercede on Hammond's behalf, but now this did not seem necessary. All the defendants were cheerful and optimistic and the substantial fines they were expecting to pay were not a problem to men of such means. It was only the night before the trial that Court began to have misgivings, when Barney Barnato informed him that the defendants had been persuaded to plead guilty.

Apparently a deal had been struck and the accused had been told that if they pleaded guilty, sentences would be lenient. This was fine on the face of it, Court and Barney agreed, except that the charges had been changed to treason and the punishment for high treason was death.

'Have a drink,' urged Barney, who was indulging freely.

'No,' said Court. 'No.'

The first day of the trial was incomprehensible to Court because the proceedings were conducted in Dutch and he shifted uneasily in his seat and glanced repeatedly round the courtroom. He worried about Hammond who looked ill and needed attention from a doctor several times; he worried about the judge, who was rumoured to have already asked for a black cap; he worried about the air of anticipation among the onlookers and particularly among the press representatives. One of the newspaper reporters looked faintly familiar to him but he was too agitated and preoccupied to ponder on the matter.

Proceedings were adjourned and it was announced that sentence would be delivered the next day.

'Have a drink!' Barney said again that night.

'No,' said Court, wavering. 'No.'

Next morning the judge stalked in and settled himself in his chair, laughing and chatting with officials. Then he suggested that women should leave the court. First he sentenced the main group of prisoners to two years' imprisonment, a fine of £2,000 and ultimate banishment from the Transvaal. In the stunned silence, the judge then donned the black cap and glared at the four ringleaders. Even the most limited linguist could understand the phrase '*Hangen bij den nek*'. Hammond and his three friends had been condemned to death.

The room was filled with hubbub and confusion. Court sat motionless, but he was vaguely aware that Barney had headed a stampede to the daïs and was yelling abuse at the judge. Court stumbled out into the street and stood blinking in the bright sunlight, until he was swept along to the Pretoria Club by Barney and his friends.

'We shall have them out in no time,' promised Barney. 'Have a drink?'

'Yes,' said Court. 'Thank you. I will.'

The first drink did not taste so good, not after all these years of abstinence, but the second tasted better and the third was nectar. Court stayed on at the Club; he even forgot Tiffany back at the hotel as he tried to lose an overwhelming sense of guilt at what he felt to be his neglect of his mission.

Suddenly he became conscious that he was being watched and realised that a man was standing at the far end of the bar, staring fixedly at him. It was the journalist he had seen at the trial, short and dark and familiar. Yes, definitely familiar. Now he was approaching and Court could see his eyes, those peculiarly grey-green eyes: Alida's eyes.

'Daniel!' he exclaimed. Instinctively he held out his hand, then let it drop back to his side as he remembered the circumstances of Daniel's departure from Kimberley. 'I never expected to see you again,' he said slowly.

'No? But I was sure I would see you. Or your friend Matthew Bright. You were bound to return to the gold mines of the Transvaal eventually.'

'I have not come to the gold mines,' Court said angrily. 'I came to see justice done. And I have formed a very poor opinion of justice in your country!'

'Why?' Danie saw a vacant table and led Court across to it so that they could sit down. He was uncomfortable talking to someone so much taller than himself. 'The sentences are quite legal. These men were trying to overthrow the State.'

'They were seeking political and municipal rights, a say in the running of the country and the city of Johannesburg which they have developed and made rich.'

Danie's eyes gleamed dangerously. 'They were the agents of British imperialism.'

'John Hays Hammond is an American citizen,' roared Court, 'and . . .'

'. . . he's in the pay of Rhodes,' interrupted Danie. 'He's as guilty as the rest.'

'I shall take up the matter with the President,' said Court. 'You will not get away with executing an American on such a flimsy trumped-up charge.'

'Won't we?' Danie settled back in his chair, folded his arms and grinned. 'And just what will you do about it? Join forces with the British and send in an army?' I tell you now, John Court, that the numbers of our burghers might be few but you would find us tough nuts to crack.'

'You wouldn't last a week,' said Court scornfully.

'Oh, but you are wrong. Very wrong. Look at it this way. What would you be fighting for? The life of one man? A point of principle? Moreover, you would be fighting in a land far distant from your own, which your soldiers had never seen before and probably would never see again. Whereas we would be fighting for the land we love. Our land. You *uitlanders* come here, to rape our country and pillage our riches, and then you go home. *This is our home.* Our families have lived in southern Africa for two and a half centuries. We have nowhere else to go.'

'Years ago, in Kimberley, I told you that your people should learn to live in peace with other nations.'

'We will live in peace with people here if they abide by *our* laws, *our* customs and speak *our* language.'

'Yet you are a minority,' Court pointed out.

Danie's eyes flashed. 'Only in Johannesburg. Throughout the states of southern Africa, Boers outnumber the rest.'

'I was thinking,' said Court, 'of the natives.'

'The *natives*.' Danie stared incredulously. 'Oh,' he said, with a dismissive wave of his hand, 'they don't count.'

'That,' said Court quietly, 'is what the people of the southern states of America thought before the Civil War. It is interesting how many similarities there are between your country and mine. We, too, are an immigrant people whose ancestors sought a new land – for religious freedom, perhaps, or political freedom; to escape economic or social vicissitudes, or simply for a hope of a better life. We, too, have seen the covered wagons set out across the great plains, beset by warring native tribes. And even in America, some men find riches while others remain poor. But we have something which you do not, something vital to the survival and progress of a great country: burning belief in the freedom and rights of the individual, whatever his race, colour or creed.'

Danie swore and banged down his glass loudly on the table. 'Perhaps you can afford such stupid notions. No one is trying to take America away from the Americans.'

'No one is trying to take your country away from you,' insisted Court. He watched the fanatical gleam in Danie's eyes. 'You want a fight,' he said suddenly. 'You want to dominate and beat and bully. Why?'

'To dominate, to be strong, is the only way to survive. To share, to give the slightest inch, is weakness and we will be swamped – by the British or else by the Blacks.'

'So this trial is a show of strength,' said Court. 'Now I understand – you believe that four executions will bring the entire population into line.'

Danie leaned forward. 'More than that,' he said softly. 'Our success will also prove to *our* people that we can fight and win.'

'Why did you attack Lady Anne?' asked Court suddenly.

Danie blinked, taken off guard. 'I don't know what you mean.'

'It was you, we were sure of that. Anne's description of you was unmistakable. By the way, where is Willem? How is he?'

'Willem died two years ago.'

'I am sorry,' said Court sincerely. 'He was a good and honest man. I am sure he did not know you had tried to kill Anne. And Sam! Daniel, you were always so fond of Sam.'

Danie said nothing and Court sighed. With a start he realised how late it was getting.

'Tiffany!' he exclaimed. 'Daniel, I must go. My daughter will be wondering where I am.'

'I will walk with you.' They stood up and moved out into the street. 'So you are married?'

'My wife is dead.'

'Ah.' They continued walking in silence. 'And what of Matthew Bright? He prospers in London, I believe.'

'I have not seen Matthew for nine years.'

'Really? You surprise me. I thought you were such good friends.'

'So we were.'

Court offered no explanation and seemed inclined to drop the subject.

'If you see Matthew, give him a message for me. Tell him that the punishment of the Reform Committee will seem as nothing compared with the justice I will mete out to him. Their swift execution will seem desirable indeed compared with the fate which will be his if he sets foot in South Africa again.'

Court stopped, aghast at the menace in Danie's voice. They were now a few feet from the entrance to the hotel.

'Why? Why do you hate him so much?'

'You know why. You, Court, of all people, should know why.'

Court stared at the vicious hatred in his companion's face. 'Alida,' he said.

At that moment the door of the hotel opened and Tiffany burst out into the street. She ran to Court and threw her arms round him, her Nanny in anxious pursuit.

'Hello, darling,' said Court, bending to kiss her. 'I'm sorry to be late.'

'Your breath smells funny,' she said, tossing her black curls. 'I've been waiting ages for you.'

'I am sorry,' said Court again.

Danie was gazing at the little girl curiously. Then he turned to Court again.

'Yes,' he said. 'Alida was one of the reasons. The main reason, in fact. There were others.'

'Daniel, Matthew saved your life. You would have suffocated in that claim pit if he hadn't . . .'

'My mother was called Alida.' Tiffany's clear childish voice cut across their conversation.

Danie stared at her, then at Court, and then at Tiffany again. 'Was she?' He frowned in puzzlement.

'Did you know her? Is she the same person as your Alida?'

'Alida was my sister. It could not be the same person.'

'It's an unusual name, though,' persisted Tiffany. 'It's a very big coincidence.'

'Yes.' Danie eyed her speculatively and took a long look at Court's embarrassed face. 'Quite a coincidence.'

Then he turned and walked across the street to the offices of *De Volksstem*, to finish his story on the trial. Court pulled Tiffany into the hotel, unaware that she was craning her head to see where Danie went.

To his surprise Court slept soundly. He woke elated to find that the alcohol had affected him so slightly and that evidently he could now control his drink problem. Later he had a long talk with Barney Barnato and between them they devised a plan to save the Reform Committee prisoners from the scaffold.

Dressed in black with a crêpe band round his hat, Barney obtained an audience with the President. If all the prisoners were not released within two weeks, he threatened to close down his entire business interests in the Transvaal and sell all his property. Not only would this entail crippling loss of revenue to the State, but 20,000 Whites and 100,000 Blacks would be out of work.

Next day it was announced that the death sentences had been commuted, but the prisoners stayed in jail.

At his desk in the office of *De Volksstem*, Danie Steyn seized a coffee mug and threw it violently against the wall.

Reinforced by cables from the American Secretary of State, several senators and the British government, Court and Barnato doggedly continued their campaign. On 30 May the minor offenders, including Barney's nephew, were released on payment of a £2,000 fine. Ten days later the four ringleaders were fined £25,000 each and set free. John Hays Hammond hastened to leave the Transvaal.

John Court, with the invaluable help of his old acquaintance from the diamond fields, had justified his President's choice of unofficial ambassador and succeeded in his mission. In so doing, he had perforce neglected his daughter – and he had also put Danie Steyn into a towering red rage. Cheated of an execution, Danie now raved at the indignity of setting the prisoners free in exchange for money. *De Volksstem* usually supported Kruger's policies, but now Danie's loyalty wavered. 'It is we, the burghers of the Transvaal, who will pay these fines,' he wrote darkly, 'who will pay for this weakness with our life's blood.'

And as if to illustrate his point, his temper exploded again; this time it was an inkwell which shattered against the wall, its blood-red contents dripping ominously on to the wooden floor.

Tiffany was bored. There was nowhere to go and nothing to do – if she had known it would be like this, she would have preferred to go to Boston after all. Papa, on the other hand, was always busy and to add insult to injury Nanny, who had hated Pretoria as much as Tiffany at the outset, had acquired a beau. Tiffany considered that Nanny was much too old to have beaux and she resented enduring the same walk day after day so that Nanny could meet her admirer. Indoors Tiffany stamped and screamed and outdoors she was sulky and surly. Nanny was at her wits' end and for once Court was too preoccupied to notice.

The only thought that relieved Tiffany's boredom was her determination to speak to the 'dark man' again. She remained convinced that his Alida and her Mama must be one and the same. Into the story her father had told her, she wove a romantic dream of a ne'er-do-well brother who had run away from home. She would not rest until she had spoken to him again.

Her problem was to find the opportunity. Nanny might be in love, but she did not relax her vigilance. Then came the day when Papa rushed into her bedroom and swung her round excitedly.

'Darling, it's all over! My business here is finished and we can go home. I'm going out to celebrate now and tomorrow I will book train tickets for Cape Town.'

It would have to be tonight or never. Tiffany sat so quietly and was so subdued that Nanny cast her an anxious look.

'Are you feeling all right, Tiffany?'

'No,' said Tiffany with a sigh. 'I feel as though I've got a cold coming on.'

'And us with a long journey ahead of us! You must go to bed immediately and get plenty of rest.'

'Yes,' agreed Tiffany, 'but I will be perfectly all right on my own, Nanny, if you want to say goodbye to your friend.'

Nanny hesitated. She ought not to leave Tiffany, who was looking very peaky and seemed unusually docile, but she succumbed to temptation. 'I won't be long,' she said as Tiffany lay down, fully dressed, and pulled the bedcovers over her. 'You ought to get properly undressed though.'

'Papa might come back early, or I might feel better.'

Tiffany allowed Nanny ten minutes' start and then slipped out into the street. It was late afternoon on a cold crisp Transvaal winter day and the sun was shining down out of a cloudless sky. She ran across the broad street to the building which she had seen the man enter on that first day and in which she had since glimpsed him several times. Standing outside, she pressed her nose against the glass, then sighed with relief. He was there! Sitting at a desk in the corner, writing. As she watched, he picked up something and threw it at the wall. Tiffany gazed with admiration as the ink ran down the wall and made a lovely pool on the floor. She had thrown a good many missiles in her short life, but never anything as messy and satisfying as that. She opened the door and went in.

Danie was alone. The newspaper was published in the afternoon, so its deadline was long past and already a good supply of copy had been prepared for the next day. Danie flung his pen in pursuit of the ink well and glared defiantly at the story he had just finished. Would the editor accept it? Or would he consider the piece contravened *De Volksstem*'s traditional role of government mouthpiece? He was considering the matter when the door opened and the child walked in. Danie scowled, waiting for John Court to follow: Court was not his favourite person at present. He suspected that the American had played a prominent part in the release of the Reform Committee and he also hated him for being a foreigner and an honest man. It was easy to hate Matthew and to count one's reasons for doing so, but harder to hate Court who was basically decent, who had been kind to little Daniel and who, as Danie now realised, had loved Alida. Nevertheless he was still a foreigner and he had interfered in Danie's affairs.

The child shut the door behind her and stood looking at him.

'Hello. I'm Tiffany Court.'

'I remember you. Where is your father?'

'He's celebrating.'

'I'll bet he is.' Danie's eyes narrowed and he glared at her, but Tiffany was unaccustomed to being glared at and did not take any notice. There was something familiar about her face, Danie thought: those violet eyes! Did Court have violet eyes? He thought not.

'I came to ask you about Alida,' said Tiffany.

The coincidence had been on Danie's mind, too. Only intermittently because the trial and imprisonment of the Reformers had claimed most of his attention, but it was there – that coincidence – nagging away at his subconscious.

'They are not the same person,' he said abruptly, 'your mother and my sister.'

'They might be,' she persisted.

'What do you know about your mother?'

Eagerly Tiffany related the story her father had told her, while Danie listened with growing cynicism. A likely tale! But what was it about Tiffany's mother or her birth which Court wanted to conceal? And why did those violet eyes seem so damned familiar?

'Do you have a picture of your mother?' Danie inquired.

'Yes but I've left it at the hotel. Shall I go and fetch it?'

'No, no, don't go. Tell me, does your father know where you are?'

Tiffany shook her head. 'I told you; he's celebrating, although exactly what he's celebrating I don't know. And Nanny went to meet her beau. She will miss me when she gets back, though.'

'Do you mind getting into trouble if you're late back?'

'Of course not,' she scoffed.

'I have a picture of Alida, my sister Alida, at my home. Come with me and you can look at it.'

'And then I shall know if they are the same person.' Tiffany's eyes sparkled, then she looked puzzled. 'But wouldn't it be quicker if you looked at *my* picture of Mama?'

'Don't you want to come with me? I live on a farm near here. You can ride on my horse and see the other animals – sheep, cows, chickens . . .'

'I'd love to come,' Tiffany breathed without waiting to hear any more.

Danie quickly steered her out of the office and along the street to the stable where he lifted her on to the horse and swung up behind her.

'This is so much fun!' said Tiffany. 'I do wish I had got to talk to you sooner. This is the most fun I've had since I arrived in this dreadful place.'

Danie's lips tightened at her disrespect for his beloved country. He urged his horse out of the stableyard into the gathering darkness and, taking care to avoid the main streets, he headed home.

At the hotel Court was trying to sober up and to calm a hysterical Nanny. The adjacent Pretoria streets had already been searched but revealed no trace of Tiffany. Then, in repeating his evidence, the desk clerk recalled that Tiffany had left the foyer, crossed the street and paused at the newspaper office. At that point his attention had been diverted by another guest and when he had looked again, Tiffany had gone.

'The newspaper office. Danie Steyn works there. That's it!' Court recalled Tiffany's intense interest in Danie's reference to Alida, but he also remembered with horror the attack on Anne and the murder of Sam. Without another word he raced across to the darkened offices of *De Volksstem* and tried the door. It opened readily and he stumbled inside, searching for a light. He found a lamp and lit it, holding it high as he gazed helplessly round the empty room. When he saw the red smears on the wall he gave a strangled gasp. Lurching towards the spot, he let out a sob of relief when the rays of the lamp illuminated the remains of the inkwell on the floor. He extinguished the lamp and ran back to the hotel.

'Danie Steyn,' he asked the desk clerk, 'where does he live?'

'Out of town,' replied the clerk doubtfully. 'You will never find it in the dark.'

'Can someone guide me there? I will pay well. It's urgent, man!'

'Go to the stables round the corner, ask for Jan Botha and tell him I sent you. He knows the way to Steyn's farm. But there's no need to worry, Mr Court. If the little girl is with Danie, she'll be fine. He may be a firebrand, but he'll not harm the child.'

Court swallowed and tried not to think of Anne's injuries and Sam's red blood on the green grass. Ten minutes later he was galloping through the clear night behind his guide.

Tiffany was enjoying herself enormously, although she was rather cold. She liked riding and the man held her firmly just as Papa did when he was with her. She wished that it was light so that she could see more of the countryside. The moon was up, but it was not full and only succeeded in making the trees and hills mysterious and menacing. She shivered, not entirely with cold.

'Nearly there,' said Danie.

'I didn't think it would be this far.'

'Sorry you came? Will Papa be angry?'

'Very! But it's his own fault, he shouldn't have left me alone so much. I've been very bored.'

'What a shame,' said Danie sarcastically. He smiled to himself. John Court would be a great deal more than angry – he would be beside himself with worry. Danie struck up a singularly tuneless whistle and kept it going until they reached the farm.

Even from the outside the farmhouse looked primitive and Tiffany, accustomed to the mansions of Fifth Avenue, stared round her with widening eyes. A black man came across and took the horse away while Danie led her into the house.

'Not quite what you're used to, I expect?'

'No.'

'Tell me about your house.'

Obligingly Tiffany described it as best she could, mentioning the servants and the carriages and the pretty stones which Papa said would be hers one day.

'So that is what the *uitlanders* do with the riches they wrest from our soil.' Danie looked round the simple bare living-room with its plain wooden furniture and uncarpeted floor, and he gave a sharp laugh. 'And if John Court lives in such style, I wonder what grandeur Matthew Bright adopts!'

'Can I see the picture now?' asked Tiffany. 'Please,' she added politely. She could be very polite when she wanted something.

Danie went to the bedroom and returned with the miniature of Alida. There she was, enshrined forever in the beauty of her sixteenth birthday, in the new grey-green dress, with Matthew's locket at her neck.

'It isn't Mama.' Disappointment overwhelmed Tiffany and unexpectedly her eyes filled with tears. She brushed them away angrily and swallowed hard. 'She was a very pretty lady, though. Nearly as pretty as Mama.' Again she choked back her sobs. 'I think I must go home now,' she managed to say.

'Oh, no.' Danie shook his head regretfuly. 'I am afraid you can't go home.'

'Why not?'

'Because I am not ready to take you.'

Tiffany's lower lip stuck out mutinously. 'But I *want* to go home.'

Danie merely stared at her.

'And I always get what I want!' Tiffany stamped her feet and turned on the tears, but the infuriating man took no notice. Watching for his reaction through her veil of tears, Tiffany saw his hands move to something at his waist.

'What's that?' she asked.

'A hunting knife.'

It lay between his hands: a plain knife, with no adornment on its handle and with death on its sharp blade. The knife that had slaughtered a thousand animals for the stewpot; the knife that had slashed Anne and slit Sam's throat. In Danie's hands it lay like a living thing, quiescent now but ready to burst into life.

He stared steadfastly at the girl. The knife was acting like a crystal ball and he saw the garden at Matthew's house and Lady Anne walking there with Sam. Now he was closer, arm raised to attack – now he was struggling with her and she looked up at him with huge frightened violet eyes. This girl's eyes!

And as Tiffany started to scream, Danie smiled.

The screams rang out clearly in the stillness of the night as Court and his companion galloped into the yard, the hooves of their horses thudding loudly on the rock-hard ground. In an instant Court had vaulted from the saddle, leaped up the steps to the stoep and crashed through the door.

The screams stopped abruptly. He saw Danie with the knife in his hand, smiling, and Tiffany standing several feet away, very red in the face.

Court ran to his daughter and caught her in his arms.

'Thank God you're safe!' He rounded on Danie. 'By the look of that knife, I am only just in time.'

Danie looked astonished. 'What are you talking about? Ah, Jan,' as the guide entered, '*Jan, my vriend, kom binne, kom binne.*' He turned back to Court. 'The only thing you are in time for, Court, is to prevent your daughter from bursting a blood vessel. She has a very nasty temper.'

'Did he hurt you, darling?' Court asked anxiously.

'Hurt me? Of course not. But I wanted to go home and he wouldn't take me.'

'As I tried to explain to the dear little girl, my horse had to rest.'

'What are you doing here, anyway, Tiffany? How could you go away on your own without telling anyone?'

'He showed me the picture of his Alida – oh Papa, she isn't the same person as our Alida.'

Slowly Court released Tiffany and his eyes rested on the miniature. A fleeting pattern of emotions played across his face as he remembered Alida and looked upon her features once again.

'Tell me, Daniel, did you ever find a book of Shakespeare's plays amongst Alida's things?'

'Yes.' Danie sounded surprised. 'I have it still. Why?'

'No reason. It doesn't matter.'

Court was trembling. He tried to control himself, but his eyes slid inexorably back to the knife which nestled once more in the belt at Danie's waist. Had Danie been about to use it? Had he wanted to hurt Tiffany as he had hurt Anne and Sam? Or had he merely wanted to frighten *him* to settle old scores and to ease his frustration at the release of the Reform Committee? Or could Court take Danie at face value – had he only wanted to show Tiffany the picture?

To his dying day Court would never be sure.

He put his arm round Tiffany and walked to the door. Danie

was chatting and laughing with Jan Botha, the guide, but he broke off as Court passed.

'I saw in the *Diamond Fields Advertiser* that Lady Anne had died,' he said. 'My condolences,' and with studied deliberation he looked straight at Tiffany's eyes.

Court shuddered and hurried through the door.

'I do realise,' Danie called after him, 'that you and Matthew are not such good friends as you were, but do remember to give him my message. I shall be waiting for him.'

CHAPTER THREE

In London one blazing afternoon in July Matthew sat in his Club and brooded on the day's events. He had just come from the court where Jameson had been sentenced to fifteen months' imprisonment for the abortive Raid into the Transvaal. Matthew felt no sympathy for his former friend. In fact he viewed the entire episode, and Jameson's role in particular, with utter incredulity and scorn. Anyway, his personal relations with Jameson had been strained for some years. Matthew still remembered the doctor's contribution to the Kimberley smallpox epidemic.

What interested Matthew, and sent an indescribable tremor of excitement through him, was the effect of the Jameson Raid on Rhodes. For the first time Matthew realised that Rhodes was not invincible – and for the first time also Matthew saw that *he* could become the dominant force in the Diamond Company.

It was like seeing a closed door open gently and stand slightly ajar, allowing a narrow shaft of light to penetrate the gloom. Matthew stared unseeingly into the haze of cigar smoke and felt the adrenaline pump through his body. He had been inactive for far too long. Since the consolidation of the Kimberley mines, diamond production had become a dull routine affair and Matthew was bored by it. His uninterest even extended to the social scene. He had emerged from a period of mourning to find himself the most eligible man in London – a situation which would have dazzled the young Matthew of twenty-five years ago and which for a while caused even the mature man to revel in the benefits and prestige of his position. After his narrow escape with Emma Longden, he had spread his favours over a selection of London's loveliest courtesans and married ladies. He rejected firmly, and not always courteously, the advances of the hopeful mamas and their blue-blooded daughters. Matthew Bright had not the slightest intention of marrying again. Miranda remained the axis of his existence and the only girl to hold his heart.

Now the glitter of London society had palled and he was once more restless for action. His discourtesies and eccentricities grew more apparent as he gained in confidence and stature. When he returned to London in 1889 he had been deferential and tentative in his approach, eager to conform and win the recognition he had lacked before his exodus to the diamond fields. Now he was sufficiently established to allow the inexorable imprint of his personality to dominate his words and actions. Gradually, during 1895 and 1896, he became again the man he had been in Kimberley, straddling his world with a colossal confidence which bordered on contempt; relentless and incisive in his relationships. Matthew was his own man again.

He stubbed out his cigar and rose to leave. Three men stood between him and the all-powerful position he sought in the Diamond Company: Rhodes, Barnato and Beit. Matthew frowned as he collected his gloves and cane. 'Little Alfred' was steady as a rock but Rhodes and Barnato were a different matter. Outwardly they were the Titans, the giants who fought for supremacy on the diamond fields. Inwardly they were crumbling. Rhodes was a spent force, his suspect health increasing his vulnerability. In many ways he had been Matthew's mentor, but Matthew had never condoned Rhodes's casual use of Diamond Company funds for financing imperialistic fantasies and still believed fervently that politics and business did not mix. All in all, Matthew considered that Rhodes had been the architect of his own downfall and that he was subsiding into impotence without any outside help. It was Barnato who needed a push in the right direction, Barnato who – and here Matthew's frown deepened – had connived with Court to interfere in the politics of the Transvaal. And who, moroever, according to recent reports from Johannesburg, was becoming increasingly neurotic and unstable.

Matthew descended the steps into Pall Mall and crossed the pavement towards his waiting carriage. So absorbed was he in his thoughts that he nearly collided with the man who stepped suddenly into his path. Matthew glowered angrily at this impediment to his progress and was about to walk on when the man spoke.

'Afternoon, Mr Bright!'

The voice was faintly familiar, but Matthew had to contemplate the man for several moments before recognition came.

'Connor,' he said. And the man grinned.

Connor, one of the overseers at the Kimberley claims who had dabbled in IDB; Connor who, on Matthew's instructions, had stolen Willem's diamonds and who, with his colleague Brown, had last been seen heading in the direction of Natal.

Apparently things had not gone well with him during the past thirteen years. His shabby suit made some effort towards respectability, but seemed sadly out of place in fashionable St James's and he was not at all the sort of person with whom Matthew wished to be seen. Matthew glanced round quickly to ensure that no one had noticed them and then motioned Connor towards the carriage. As they settled into their seats and the vehicle rolled off towards Park Lane, he surveyed his companion with distaste.

'Is this a coincidental meeting, or have you been watching me?'

'A bit of both, guv'nor.' Connor grinned again, no whit discomfited by Matthew's evident displeasure at their reunion. 'I chanced to see you today, but it has been in my mind to speak to you for some time.'

'Indeed?'

'When I saw you at the trial, I realised that the time was ripe. Ah, poor Jameson! To languish in Holloway Jail for fifteen months.'

'Bloody fool was lucky to get off so lightly.'

Connor blinked. 'Quite so, quite so,' he agreed hastily, but he seemed disconcerted by this unexpected reaction.

'I made it categorically clear to you and Brown that our association was at an end,' snapped Matthew. 'I told you not to blackmail me. That statement still stands – I bow to threats from *nobody*.'

'Guv'nor, guv'nor, nothing could be further from my mind.' Connor spread his hands wide, the picture of injured innocence. 'The fact is that I've a little proposition for you. After Jameson's conviction I thought . . . well . . .'

'You thought that I would be in a receptive mood,' Matthew concluded cynically. 'You thought that I would be aggrieved at

Jameson's imprisonment and disappointed at the failure of the Raid. So your proposition obviously concerns the Transvaal.'

'I have a friend who is willing to bring about the downfall of the government in the Transvaal – if he can find the right financial backing.'

Matthew laughed. 'A melodramatic scheme indeed! Though, admittedly, no more of a romantic nonsense than Jameson's ill-fated blunderings. No, Connor, you have without a doubt come to the wrong man. Incidentally, is Brown this "friend" of yours?'

'No, I haven't seen Brown for years. This is a German fellow of the very noblest connections.'

'I can quite imagine how noble he is,' said Matthew drily. 'Evidently he is at variance with the foreign policy of his own country. The Kaiser was quick to congratulate Kruger on the outcome of the Raid.'

Matthew's mind was racing. He was the last person to meddle in politics, but there was another family whose propensity for interfering in such affairs was well known. A family, moreover, who had been warned of serious repercussions if they dabbled in Transvaal politics again.

'Who is this German?' he asked.

Connor hesitated.

'His name, man!' said Matthew impatiently. 'I will not take part in your scheme myself, but I know someone who might be interested.'

'Von Veltheim,' said Connor. 'Baron von Veltheim. When can I meet this "someone"?'

Barnato was in Johannesburg, but was said to be sailing for England shortly. Matthew wanted to make a personal assessment of Barney's state of mind before putting Connor in touch with him.

'He isn't available at present,' said Matthew slowly. 'Come to my office three weeks from today, but come late and be discreet. We must not be seen together.'

'That's a very long time to wait.' Connor sounded doubtful and suspicious. 'Maybe Von Veltheim and me had better find someone else.'

Matthew pulled a bundle of banknotes from his pocket, peeled off a wad and handed it to Connor.

'Perhaps this will help to pass the time?'

Having dropped off Connor at Hyde Park, Matthew entered his home in high good humour. It felt good to be back in action again. That door which had swung slightly ajar with evidence of Rhodes's weakness, now stood well and truly open.

When Barney Barnato arrived in London, Matthew lost no time in evaluating his state of mind. In addition to the recent upheavals in the Transvaal, Barnato had business worries concerning the Barnato Bank and the continued drop in 'Kaffirs'. The self-made millionaire from the back-streets of Whitechapel was terrified of losing his money and his moods swung from aggression to despair and from the absent-minded to the impulsive. When Matthew questioned him about the trial in Pretoria of the 'Reformers', Barnato launched into such a vitriolic attack on Kruger and the Transvaal government that Matthew was certain he was ripe for Von Veltheim's pluckings. On the other hand, Barnato was so unstable that he might express totally different opinions on matters the next day. Matthew decided to risk it.

'The man you want is Barney Barnato,' he told Connor. 'I happen to know he will be in the smoke-room of the Hotel Metropole tonight. I advise you to approach him carefully, since his moods are volatile and unpredictable. But I want to make one thing clear: I am giving you Barnato's name on the understanding that this is a purely political plan. I trust that your friend Von Veltheim is not a violent man.'

'Gentle as a lamb,' Connor assured him.

'Make sure he stays that way,' Matthew emphasised. 'A conspiracy for the peaceful overthrow of the Transvaal regime is one thing, and I concede that Von Veltheim will find plenty of support among the Reformers whose grievances are still not settled. But assassinations are not to be contemplated.' Matthew paused. 'Another suggestion – let Von Veltheim persuade Barney not to tell his nephews, Solly and Woolf Joel, anything about the plan. I feel they may not be so enthusiastic about the idea as their uncle.'

Matthew wished only to discredit Barney, to have him ejected from the Transvaal in disgrace and to diminish his influence in the Diamond Company. Unfortunately, he forgot that sometimes – as with his revenge on Freddy – his schemes got out of hand. He did not realise that, unwittingly, he had a destructive effect on people and events.

Shaken by the perfidy of the Transvaal government in breaking its promise of leniency to the prisoners, and even more shaken by Tiffany's confrontation with Danie Steyn, Court vowed never to return to Africa. Before leaving Pretoria he fired the negligent Nanny, who opted to stay and marry her beau. Disinclined to hire a replacement in South Africa, on the voyage to Southampton he was therefore father, governess, nanny and even lady's maid. Fortunately Tiffany found the situation to her liking and behaved rather better than usual.

She was asleep now in the luxurious suite of their London hotel after a strenuous day's sightseeing. It was late and Court, too, was tired but still he paced the floor. While he was in England there were two duties he wished to fulfil, but both involved Matthew and Court could not find the courage to approach him. Then the solution to his problem came with such devastating clarity that he could not understand why it had not occurred to him before. He must get in touch with Nicholas.

In the sitting-room of Court's suite the two men greeted each other affectionately, both with happy memories of their comradeship in Kimberley. But the ghost of Anne came to stand between them, so vidid and overwhelming that sadness clouded their pleasure at meeting. They had been together so much in Anne's company that their reunion seemed to sharpen her loss and emphasise its finality. It was to Anne that the conversation inevitably turned after some discussion on the diamond business and the Transvaal.

'Her children must be a great comfort to you all,' said Court.

Nicholas sighed. 'Less of a comfort than you might imagine,' he admitted. 'Philip is exactly like Anne in appearance, but the resemblance is entirely superficial. He is a very withdrawn and secretive child. Still,' and here Nicholas brightened, 'my niece Julia was the same and she turned out all right,' and he beamed innocently at Court.

'And what of the baby?' Court tried to keep his tone casual and to conceal his eagerness to know how much Miranda resembled his beloved Tiffany.

'Hard to tell yet. She's only two. Actually,' Nicholas confessed, 'I hardly ever see her; Matthew guards her so jealously. But from the little I have seen, Miranda takes after Matthew, not Anne.'

'And Matthew himself? Is he well?'

Nicholas nodded vigorously. 'In the pink!' He eyed Court speculatively. 'I was wondering if you had seen him. Or if you planned to do so?'

'Such a meeting is extremely unlikely.'

'Why, John? It seems such a damned shame. I know there was a quarrel between you two but, whatever it was about, surely it cannot have been serious enough to keep you apart forever? And I'll tell you something else.' Nicholas leaned forward earnestly in his chair. 'I'm certain that Anne was unhappy about the rift. Couldn't you try to patch things up for her sake?'

Oh, Nicholas, thought Court sadly, if only you knew! If only I could tell you that it is precisely because of Anne that I can never speak to Matthew again.

'I wish it were possible but it is not. However, speaking of Matthew reminds me of two matters I wished to discuss with you. Nicholas, I need your help.'

'Only too glad to oblige,' beamed Nicholas, puffing out his chest importantly.

'I would very much like to visit Anne's grave.'

'Good of you. Anne would like that,' said Nicholas appreciatively. 'But it's such a simple matter. Why does it require my assistance?'

'I understand Anne is buried at Matthew's country house. I can hardly barge in on private property.'

'No one would bat an eyelid, old chap. Just ask the gardeners or any of the other servants in the vicinity to direct you to the spot. Matthew will not be there, if the possibility of meeting him is worrying you. He's at Park Lane at the moment.'

'I do not wish to creep about Matthew's property like a trespasser or a thief in the night,' said Court obstinately. 'I wondered if you could let them know I was coming?'

'Of course I can if it would make you happier. Look, Reynolds is sending down some supplies to Brightwell by rail on Friday. You could catch the train to Reading and then travel to Brightwell in the carriage which will collect the boxes.'

'Perfect! As I said, there are two matters in which I need your assistance but I fear that the second requires more direct intervention on your part.'

Swiftly Court gave Nicholas a summary of his dealings with Danie Steyn in Pretoria and of Danie's threat to Matthew.

'Surely you don't take it seriously?' exclaimed Nicholas.

'I'm afraid that I do,' returned Court. 'Remember that he attacked Anne and killed Sam, and his abduction of Tiffany still brings me out in a cold sweat. Tell Matthew what I have told you and tell him too that there is a dark menace about Danie which is very intense and very frightening. Tell him . . .' Court broke off as a door opened and a small dark head appeared. 'Tiffany! Go back to bed this instant.'

'I'm thirsty,' she complained.

'Then I will bring you something to drink in a minute. Now, back to bed!'

Tiffany was staring curiously at the fat man with the yellow hair and the red face. 'Hello,' she said, 'I'm Tiffany Court.'

'And I am Nicholas Grafton.' Nicholas shook the small hand solemnly and smiled. 'Sweet child,' he murmured sentimentally.

'I want an ice as well as a drink, Papa.'

'You have had far too many ices already today,' Court admonished, whereat the little face turned pink and the lower lip stuck out mutinously.

'All right,' said Court hastily, 'but I shall not order them until you're back in bed.'

Tiffany vanished, victory achieved.

'I spoil her,' said Court, a touch apologetically, 'but you see, she has no mother. I am determined that she shall want for nothing else, but there are times when perhaps I overcompensate for the loss.'

'Perfectly natural.'

'Where was I?' Court moved to the bell to ring for Tiffany's ice and another bottle of wine. 'Tell Matthew that Danie has not forgotten Alida. Memories of her have combined with Danie's hatred of everything British to make Matthew a bitter enemy. Tell Matthew that I believe the threat is real and under no circumstances should he go to South Africa.'

'I will try, I promise. But it would sound much better coming from you.'

'There is nothing in the world,' said Court slowly, 'that could be sufficiently serious to make me speak to Matthew Bright again.'

'I never heard such a load of poppycock in my life!'

'Matthew, John was very serious about the matter. He genuinely has your welfare at heart.'

'Like the good friend he is?' sneered Matthew sarcastically. Then he relented slightly. 'Anyway, I know *you* have my welfare at heart, but I can honestly say that even if the message came from someone other than Court, I would give it no credence. The incidents he mentions took place years ago and if anything *I* have a grudge against Danie, not the other way round.'

'I still wish you would agree not to go.'

'I am not planning a trip to either Kimberley or Johannesburg at the moment. There is nothing there which requires my attention, everything is going very smoothly.' Too smoothly, thought Matthew with an inward sigh. 'But,' he continued, 'if the need to visit South Africa does arise, you cannot seriously expect me to allow a mere Boer like Daniel Steyn to stand in my way.'

'What a beautiful house!' exclaimed Court.

'Not as nice as ours,' said Tiffany loyally.

In fact she was more impressed than she cared to admit by the grandeur of the mansion, the vast estate and the lush verdant beauty of the English countryside. Belligerently she glowered at the house.

'I still think America is best.'

'Of course it is,' Court agreed.

The carriage travelled up a long avenue of limes and deposited them in front of the portico, where a servant met them and led the way through the sweet-smelling rose gardens and past the herbaceous borders in the vicinity of the house. Beyond the formality of these carefully-laid out areas, the path wound through a casual tangle of hollyhocks, delphiniums and lilies before emerging on to smooth green lawns leading down to the serpentine lake. Two white swans rode majestically on the water, the purity of their plumage standing out in brilliant relief against the blue of the lake, the green of the graceful willows and the darker green of the tall Lombardy poplars bordering the water's edge.

It was a long walk and Tiffany felt hot and a bit cross.

'I still don't see why we have to come all this way just to see a silly old grave, Papa.'

It is your mother's grave, was what Court wanted to say. This is the closest you will ever come to your mother. But of course he said nothing and they walked on in silence round the lake, past huge banks of rhododendrons and over a gentle scattering of wild flowers – chicory and camomile, red campion and white dropwort and an occasional orchid. Ahead lay the woods and groves of oak, pines, silver birch and holly. As they moved into the shade of the lilac trees, their guide pointed to a clearing ahead and then tactfully left them. Court and Tiffany walked forward alone.

The sun filtered through the thick foliage, casting irregular patterns of light and shade on the neat grave. The inscription on the headstone read simply:

Anne 1859–1894
Beloved wife of Matthew Bright

Tiffany watched with detached curiosity as her father took off his hat and stood with bowed head.

'Say a prayer for her, Tiffany.'

She pulled a face and sighed. 'All right. Who did you say she was?'

'A friend I once knew in Kimberley.'

Tiffany half-closed her eyes and had begun to mumble, 'God bless Mrs Anne Bright who . . .' when she sensed a movement among the trees. Opening her eyes a fraction wider, she peered surreptitiously through her long dark eyelashes and caught a glimpse of a boy's head and shoulders as he watched them from behind a large oak. She looked again at her father; his eyes were shut and he seemed absorbed in silent contemplation. Tiffany, however, found the living much more interesting than the dead.

Quietly she stole from the graveside in the direction of the oak tree. The boy was walking swiftly through the woods ahead of her and Tiffany set off after him at a determined trot. When she considered they were sufficiently far away from her father, she called out:

'Hey, don't go! I want to talk to you.'

The boy stopped and turned reluctantly, watching her with a guarded expression on his face.

'Why did you run away?' demanded Tiffany as she caught up with him. 'Couldn't you see that I wanted to talk to you?'

'Well, *I* didn't want to talk to *you*.'

He walked on but still Tiffany kept pace beside him.

'I'm Tiffany Court,' she said in that imperious manner of hers, as if her identity explained everything.

'Philip Bright.'

'Bright? That's the name on the gravestone.'

'My mother. Who are you and what are you doing here?'

'My father knew your mother in Kimberley, at the diamond mines. His name is John Court – perhaps you remember him?'

But Philip had no recollection of the name or the man and shook his head. They had come to the lake and sat down there, watching the busy insect and marine life around them. Tiffany gazed with pleasure as a dragonfly zoomed low over the water, its iridescent wings shining in the sunlight. On the far side of the lake one of the swans raised itself and flapped its wings before settling back more comfortably into the water.

'You are lucky to live here,' she said impulsively. 'It's very nice.'

Philip's face remained impassive and he shrugged slightly. 'Everyone I know lives in a house like this. They're all the same really.'

'The houses or the people?'

A glimmer of a smile appeared on the boy's pale features. 'Both! Won't your father be wondering where you are?'

'He was saying a prayer for your mother, but when he finds I have gone he'll be real mad.'

'Don't get into any trouble on my account.'

Tiffany opened her eyes wide. 'Oh, I won't be in trouble; he'll be mad with *worry*. He'll think I have fallen in the lake or something.'

The half-smile faded from Philip's lips and his mouth set in a bitter line. 'Girls can get away with anything,' he complained. He picked up a stone and threw it into the water, causing the swans to bend their long necks in an arc of reproach. 'Fathers always like girls the best.'

'I'm an only child and my mother is dead. At the moment I haven't even got a nanny and it's *bliss*. Papa and I have been travelling for months. Do you travel with your father?'

'Good Lord, no! I haven't seen him since Easter. He's in London, with Miranda.' Philip paused. 'He's always with Miranda,' he added bitterly.

'Is Miranda your sister?'

'Yes. She's only two but she's going to be just like you. She gets away with anything, too.'

'Even if your father is not here, won't someone be wondering where you are?'

Philip shook his head. 'My nanny is old and falls asleep a lot. Still,' and he brightened, 'I'm going to Desborough next week. I have a friend there.'

'Do you go to school?'

'Of course.'

'Is it nice?'

'It's absolutely horrible!' Philip shuddered.

'Why?'

'Why? Don't you know *anything*?' Philip stared in amazement at her ignorance. 'At first it's horrible because one is away from home, but there are lots of other beastly things: the cane, for instance. The food is ghastly and there isn't nearly enough of it. We have to hope that one of the chaps will receive a hamper from home that we can share.'

'Your father obviously has a lot of money, like mine. He must send you a lot of hampers.'

Philip went very still. 'He has never, not once, sent me a single hamper,' he said in a choked voice.

'Perhaps he doesn't realise you need them? Haven't you asked him?'

'You don't know my father! One doesn't ask him for things. Or at least *I* don't. Miranda has anything she wants.'

'If she's only two, she's probably not needing very much yet,' Tiffany said sensibly. 'But I see what you mean. So what do you do for hampers? Can you share with the others if you never receive one of your own to offer them?'

'For a whole term I had to endure the humiliation of being offered the occasional morsel of charity.' Philip swallowed hard at the memory. 'I shall never forget it. *Never*. And I shall never forgive my father for the way the other chaps laughed at me and bullied me and the things they made me do for a mere piece of cake. Fortunately, Uncle Nicholas started sending me supplies after that.'

'Nicholas? Oh, I think I met him. A fat man, all pink and yellow.'

In the distance a voice was calling.

'That's Papa,' said Tiffany. 'I suppose I shall have to go. Good-bye, Philip. I'm going back to America soon and I don't suppose we will ever meet again.'

'No,' said Philip. 'I don't suppose we will.'

CHAPTER FOUR

A week later Philip was ensconced in his favourite place – the stables at Desborough – watching Williams groom the horses and listening to the latest information about the motor car. The smells and sounds of the stables held no terror for him now. He associated the place with Williams and with happiness and, because his mind was not concentrated on his fear, he had learned to ride tolerably well.

Philip listened eagerly as Williams told him that 1896 was a momentous year for motoring in Britain. A new Locomotives on the Highways Act was being introduced which increased the speed limit to fourteen miles per hour.

'So a man won't have to walk in front of the car any more?' cried Philip.

Williams laughed. 'Hardly! He'd have to skip along pretty sharpish, wouldn't he!'

'What else has been happening?'

'Panhard, Peugeot, De Dion and Bouton are the main manufacturers of cars in Europe now. Duryea are leading the field in America, but I hear that someone called Ford is starting up.'

'Have there been any more races?'

'Paris to Marseilles and back, a distance of 1,063 miles. It was won by a Panhard at an average speed of 15.7 mph.'

Philip clasped his knees and gazed into the distance, imagining the ecstasy of hurtling through the thick clouds of dust along the long straight roads of France, at the tiller of one's own motor car, at the unbelievable speed of fifteen miles per hour. He imagined passing town after town, reaching forward for the next goal, striving to go faster and faster down the never-ending road to the horizon.

'I can't think of anything more wonderful,' he said in a muffled voice. 'I can't imagine anything that would be more fun.'

'You're right, but it's more than fun. These races are vitally necessary to the development of the motor car. Not only do they help improve the design of the cars, but they prove to the public that cars are reliable and safe and can travel further and faster than horse-drawn vehicles.'

'Now that the Red Flag Act is being repealed, British car makers will be able to catch up with the French and the Germans, won't they?'

'You bet we will,' said Williams fervently, 'and we'll make better cars than the bloody foreigners if I have anything to do with it.' He laid down the harness he was polishing and confronted Philip with a serious air. 'I'm glad you mentioned that, Master Philip, because I've something to tell you. I'm afraid I won't be here when you come for the Christmas holidays.'

An expression of utter horror settled on Philip's face.

'What do you mean?' he gasped. 'Have you lost your job? I'll speak to Uncle Hugh about it, really I will. They shan't send you away. They *shan't*!'

'No, no, it's not like that,' said Williams gently. 'It's me that wants to leave. I've got another offer, you see, Master Philip, and you must understand that although everyone's very kind to me here, a job as a groom doesn't have a great future.'

'No, I understand that,' said Philip, trying manfully to hide his hurt at his friend's desertion.

'Don't you want to know about my new job?'

Politely Philip nodded.

'I'm going to Coventry – to build Daimlers.'

'What? Oh, Williams, you lucky, lucky thing! How marvellous!' Philip's sorrow was swamped in a flood of admiration and envy. 'That's what I want to do when I leave school.'

'Well now, I expect there are other plans for you. No doubt your father wants you to go into the diamond business. And very nice too, I should say.'

But Philip was hardly listening. 'You will write to me, won't you? To tell me all about it? And I will be able to see you again?'

'I'll try to write,' promised Williams, 'but I'm not much of a hand at it. I know how to read and write, of course. I was taught at the village school by Mr Bruce, who married your aunt Lady Jane. A real nice lady she was; used to help with the lessons herself sometimes. Yes, of course, I'll try to write, but don't worry if it's only a few lines.'

After Philip had gone, Williams resumed cleaning the harness. He felt oddly guilty, as if he was leaving the boy in the lurch. Philip Bright was, without a doubt, the saddest and loneliest young fellow that Williams had ever encountered and he wouldn't change places with him – no, not for all his father's millions.

It was not until November that Williams kept his promise and sent a letter to Philip at his preparatory school. To Philip, however, the contents were well worth all the waiting. He spent days in a state of suppressed excitement, unable to keep his mind on his Latin or his Greek, reading the letter over and over again whenever he was alone.

Apparently a Motor Car Club had been formed and its members were planning to celebrate 'Emancipation Day' with a Motor Tour from London to Brighton. The event would take place on 14 November, the day the new law came into force. Williams's employer would be driving a Daimler and had invited Williams to accompany him in case of mechanical trouble.

The Tour would be the biggest gathering of motor cars ever seen in Britain and Philip knew that he must be there. But how? Though 14 November was a Saturday, it was not a school holiday. It would be useless to ask either father or headmaster for permission to go to London. Scheme after scheme was considered and rejected; Philip could devise no foolproof plan. As Friday the 13th dawned, with desperation in his heart Philip decided to simply run away for the day. No punishment that he could imagine could be worse than missing the London to Brighton Run.

That night he was terrified to fall asleep in case he failed to wake in time. Several times he dozed, waking with a jolt, certain that it was morning and that he would be too late. At five o'clock he could bear it no longer: he got out of bed, grabbed his clothes and stole out of the dormitory. Dressing hurriedly in the corridor, he put on an extra jersey because the morning felt damp and cold and he dared not go downstairs for his coat. Then he opened a window on the landing and leaned out to grasp the drainpipe – a well-worn escape route trodden by many generations of truants. He landed with a thud on the soft ground and then ran as fast as he could for the school wall which he scaled easily with the help of a conveniently placed tree. He set off at a steady pace, through the darkness, for the railway station.

At the station he kept out of sight, knowing that a boy alone at this time of the morning would attract attention. Immediately he heard the train coming, he bought his ticket and was able to climb straight on board. He received some curious glances, but no one stopped him and the train pulled away into the darkness.

The journey seemed endless, since the train appeared to stop at every station and wayside halt and as they approached London fog began to thicken. Philip fidgeted and worried the whole way, in an agony of apprehension that the Run would start without him. But when the train pulled into Charing Cross station, he realised that his difficulties were by no means over. Williams had told him that the Run would start from the Hotel Metropole in London and finish at the Hotel Metropole in Brighton. Philip had no idea where the hotel was situated and was dismayed to realise that he had insufficient money for a cab. He stood in the entrance to the station, looking at the grey damp day, the trailing clouds of foul-smelling fog and the thousands of people, and wondered what on earth he should do.

He was scanning the surging crowds in search of a friendly face when he spotted a young man whom he instinctively felt might be sympathetic to his plight. The young man was walking rapidly out of the station as Philip ran across and caught hold of his arm.

'Excuse me, but can you tell me the way to the Hotel Metropole?'

The man stopped and grinned at him. 'Just follow the crowds, sonny. That's where everyone is heading.'

'Oh, is it near enough to walk?' Relief washed over him.

'Across Northumberland Avenue to Whitehall Place. Ten minutes at the most. Are you alone?'

'Yes, but I'm meeting a friend at the Start. He's driving a Daimler.' Philip felt inordinately proud of this personal link with the great event.

'Good. We will walk there together and perhaps you can introduce me to your friend. He might give me a story.'

'Are you a newspaper man?'

'*Daily News*,' replied the young man laconically and set off again at the same brisk pace.

Philip was very glad of the company, not only to show him the way but to act as a battering ram in forcing a path through the teeming crowds. At the young man's cries of 'Press' and '*Daily News*', the throng parted good-naturedly to let them through and Philip soon found himself at the very front of the rows of spectators. He gazed spellbound at the array of exquisite machinery assembled before him.

In the road outside the Hotel Metropole were forty-one vehicles. All the famous names were represented: Panhard, Daimler, Leon Bollée and Duryea; electric landaus and hansoms made by Bersey and De Dion tricycles; even an electric Bath-chair. Although the November day was so dismal the metalwork gleamed and shone and attracted Philip like a magnet. He edged forward, itching to touch one of the machines, but a policeman waved him back. There was no sign of Williams or any of the other drivers.

'They're all having breakfast,' said the journalist, 'and I must cover the speeches. Now stay here, young man, so I shall know where to find you when I come back.'

So enraptured was Philip with the scene that it seemed no time at all before his friend returned.

'Great copy,' said the journalist happily. 'The Earl of Winchilsea tore up a red flag. Look, they're coming out now! That's the Duke of Saxe-Weimar. There's the Earl, and Gottlieb Daimler, and behind him is Jerome K. Jerome, the famous author.'

'And there's my friend,' cried Philip excitedly and he broke through the cordon round the cars to fling himself at Williams.

'Master Philip! What on earth are you doing here?'

'I had to come to see the cars.' He literally danced with excitement.

'Does your father know you're here?' asked Williams suspiciously.

Philip shook his head.

'I should have known!' Williams groaned, as the journalist

joined them. 'It's all my fault. I should never have told you about it! Master Philip, you're a caution, that's what you are.'

'Truant, is he?' said the journalist. 'I thought so. Never mind, we'll keep an eye on him. Can you tell me about your car, for the *Daily News*?'

For a few moments no one took any more notice of Philip. Quietly he crept up to the Daimler, laid his hand reverently on the bonnet and caressed the shining mudguard. The ecstasy in his eyes was so touching that Williams, looking round quickly to ensure his manager was not watching, helped him to climb in. As Philip sat down he felt that nothing in his entire life could compare with this moment. The only possible thing which could add to his bliss would be an invitation to Brighton.

Williams read his thoughts and shook his head firmly. 'I'm very sorry, Master Philip, but I cannot possibly take you with me. What are you going to do? Go straight back to school?'

'I haven't enough money,' said Philip, feeling foolish. 'I haven't even enough for a cab. But it's all right,' he continued valiantly, 'I can go to my father's house or to my Uncle Nicholas.'

It was raining hard now and as he climbed reluctantly out of the Daimler and stood in the road, he made a pathetic little figure, his jacket hanging on him damply and his pale hair plastered wetly to his head.

'Take this.' Williams thrust some money into Philip's hand. 'When you leave here, call a cab to take you where you want to go. Don't hang about here all day in those wet clothes. Look, it's nearly time for the start now and I've got work to do.'

'Good luck, Williams! Write and tell me all about it.'

Williams watched him walk away with the journalist and again shook his head, though whether in exasperation or sympathy it was difficult to tell. What sort of millionaire's son was it who could not find a cab fare and talked of his 'father's house' instead of 'home'?

A horn blew, to warn that there were only ten minutes to go before starting time. Burners were lit and then the horn sounded again and promptly at 10.30 am the cars moved off in a cacophony of sound and clouds of smoke.

'Which way do they go?' asked Philip.

'Along the Embankment, over Westminster Bridge, past the Oval and up the Brixton Road. They're having lunch at the White Hart at Reigate – if they make it that far!'

'Williams will make it, I know he will!' Philip gave his friend a special wave as the Daimler trundled past and swelled with pride as Williams raised his hand in acknowledgement.

'Hey,' said the journalist after a while, 'if we're lucky we might even scrounge a cup of tea in the hotel before they clear away all the breakfast debris. Let's try, anyway.'

Waiters had started to remove the dirty crockery but at the sound of the magic words '*Daily News*' two cups of tea miraculously appeared. Philip gulped down his tea quickly, grateful for the hot drink and the shelter of the breakfast-room but unwilling to miss anything which might be happening outside.

Another man had been sitting at the far side of the room and now he walked across to them.

'Look,' he said, 'what I have found! The Red Flag that was torn up by the Earl of Winchilsea.' He held up the tattered remnants triumphantly. 'It's a symbol of emancipation and I shall keep it forever.'

Philip eyed the trophy enviously.

'No, young man, I'm afraid you can't have it,' the man laughed. He looked at his watch. 'The petrol should be here by now. My De Dion tricycle won't start,' he explained, 'and I'm waiting for new burner wicks and some decent fuel.' He paused and gave Philip an appraising look. 'So you're interested in motor cars, are you?'

'They're my whole life,' Philip breathed.

'Ah!' The man smiled at such intense enthusiasm. 'Here,' and he handed Philip a small object. 'A memento of the occasion.'

It was a small enamel badge of the Motor Car Club. Philip clutched it tightly as a joyous wave of possession gripped him. He remembered what the man had said about the flag. 'I shall keep it forever,' he vowed.

The last stragglers had started the Run and two participants had already given up the struggle and admitted defeat. Already some victims of mechanical failure were trailing back.

'I have to go now,' the journalist told Philip. 'There's a special train running to Brighton from Victoria, and I must be on it to report the finish. What will you do?'

Philip sighed at the prospect of the reckoning to come.

'I'll go to my Uncle Nicholas.'

'Make sure that you do. Goodbye!'

Philip watched him go with a sense of desolation. The day, this magic day, was coming to an end. I never even asked his name, he thought, and felt sad and guilty.

He took a cab to Nicholas's rooms and was greeted by his uncle with consternation. Philip did not dissemble, but flatly told Nicholas the true story.

'Good Lord! You *will* be in trouble. I hope it was worth it?'

'It was *marvellous*. I'm going to build cars and drive cars when I'm grown up.'

'I don't know about building cars,' said Nicholas doubtfully. 'You will be following your father into the diamond business.'

It was the second time someone had said that recently and Philip experienced a momentary qualm. Then he remembered how much his father disliked him and felt a certain relief. Surely it was highly unlikely his father would want him around the office every day?

'Have you eaten?'

Philip shook his head.

'Then have some luncheon and dry out before you face the music. Whose wrath would you prefer to confront – the headmaster's or your father's?'

'The head,' Philip replied without hesitation.

'Really? Yes, perhaps you're right. Come and have something to eat and then I'll take you back to school.'

The wrath of the headmaster was indeed impressive and the impressions his cane left on Philip's bottom were likewise painful and long-lasting. In addition to this corporal punishment, Philip was banished to the solitary confinement of the sanatorium for a week, allowed out for lessons but not permitted to speak to any of the boys. However, when he finally emerged from this enforced seclusion, he found that a transformation had taken place and his prestige and popularity had risen to unparalleled heights. His classmates were full of admiration for his daring exploit and he was accepted as the leading authority on motor cars.

He was wrong, however, in thinking that no punishment could be worse than missing the London to Brighton Run. His father's anger might have cooled by the time they eventually came face to face but it was still sharp and glacial. At the beginning of 1897 Matthew made his point. Having something to celebrate and having learned of the Prince of Wales's interest in motoring, he had bought a Daimler which was delivered to Brightwell one frosty day towards the end of January, just before Philip was due to return to school. Matthew had said nothing about the car, and when he heard the engine Philip immediately ran out to the drive. On hearing that the car belonged to his father, his face became one huge radiant smile of joy. At that moment Matthew appeared, carrying Miranda. He climbed into the vehicle and sat down beside the driver with Miranda on his lap, but as Philip prepared to follow, his father unbelievably barred his way.

Matthew had not always been so hard on his son. At the beginning it had been more that he could feel no warmth for the child. Raw and bleeding from the death of Victoria, he looked upon the pale, puling Philip from a distance, not daring to give his heart again so soon. But then came Anne's affair with Court and Tiffany's conception. Matthew never believed Anne's assertion that she and Court had bedded only once. He was certain they must have availed themselves of other opportunities for love-making and genuinely suspected that Philip was the result. Philip was so like Anne physically that his appearance gave no clue to his paternity – unlike Victoria and Miranda who, thank God, had 'Matthew Bright' imprinted on body and personality.

Now Matthew glared down at what he believed to be John Court's bastard: a bastard who perforce must masquerade as Matthew's son and inherit his diamond empire; a bastard who had not even the grace to behave himself.

'I doubt that our drive would be of interest to such an advanced motorist as yourself. We go only to the village, not to Brighton.'

An anguished Philip stood alone in the vast forecourt as the car rolled away down the long tree-lined avenue, the breeze ruffling the golden curls that peeped from beneath Miranda's bonnet.

CHAPTER FIVE

The event which Matthew celebrated with the purchase of the Daimler was a knighthood. The reason for this honour was never entirely clear, but was loosely supposed to be in recognition of services to the diamond industry. Why Matthew should have been singled out from all the other magnates was also a mystery, but this was not a matter which troubled him or his acquaintances. 'Sir Matthew' seemed so right and proper, sat so easily upon his broad shoulders, that it felt entirely natural to everyone. Moreover, it was appropriate that 'Diamond Bright' should be knighted in this year of 1897 – the year of Queen Victoria's Diamond Jubilee.

All in all, Matthew had every reason to be pleased with himself. The stock market was unstable, but Diamond Company shares held firm and City experts forecast an improvement in all share prices in the summer, when Jubilee celebrations would be at their height. And for Matthew the news from South Africa was good, although he was careful to conceal his elation.

Rhodes was still labouring under a burden of troubles, culminating in the destruction by fire of his beloved house, 'Groote Schuur', on the slopes of Table Mountain. Gone was the gracious homestead, the furniture, the priceless collection of glassware, porcelain and Dutch silver. Rhodes rose above the disaster and ordered the house to be rebuilt, but Matthew knew that slowly but surely he was being undermined.

Barney Barnato had sunk into a state of manic depression and was drinking heavily. He was reported to be obsessed with the political situation, and accused Kruger and the British Prime Minister of pushing the Transvaal into civil war. Kruger was introducing harsher measures against the *uitlanders* as part of his election programme but when he started fortifying Pretoria,

Barney's outbursts became dangerously vitriolic. Matthew was not in direct touch with Connor at this time, but it looked as though Von Veltheim's plans were working.

In the meantime, Britain was in the grip of Jubilee fever. The London Season seemed more splendid than ever, as each hostess tried to raise the standard of her entertainment to the level of this landmark in history. The high spot of the Season was to be the Duchess of Devonshire's fancy-dress ball, but excitement mounted among all classes as June arrived and decorations festooned the streets of London.

Then, in the week before the festivities were due to commence, the news came – news which struck a chill of horror and guilt into the depths of Matthew's very soul. Barney Barnato was dead and the circumstances of his death were suspicious and intriguing.

Barney had sailed from Cape Town on 2 June aboard the *Scot*, bound for Southampton. The salt air and sea breezes seemed to revive his spirits and except for a peculiar preoccupation with the date, his mood was buoyant. Yet on 14 June, at thirteen minutes past three in the afternoon, Barney Barnato apparently threw himself overboard and was drowned. It was then three weeks before his forty-fifth birthday.

'Suicide!' said Nicholas heavily, as he sat in the library at Matthew's Park Lane home. 'Who would have thought it?'

Matthew was quite stunned by the news. He had wanted Barney disgraced, not dead. Or, nagged a persistent voice inside his head, deep down had he really wished for Barney's death? It meant that he took a step up in the Company hierarchy; a new director would be appointed in Barney's stead, but he would be junior to Matthew. His attention had wandered, but he surfaced with a jolt as his mind registered a particular word which Nicholas uttered.

'Murder! What the hell do you mean, murder?'

'There is talk that Barney didn't jump but was pushed,' said Nicholas.

'Never!' Matthew's heart lurched as the insidiously creeping fear intensified inside him.

'Even in his most disturbed moments Barney never talked of

doing away with himself,' Nicholas asserted. 'The fourth officer of the *Scot* states that he heard a shout of "Murder! For God's sake, save him!" and saw Solly Joel's hand clutching Barney's trouser-leg before his uncle went into the water. Solly Joel himself is said to have talked mysteriously of "seeing a flash" before Barney went over, and it might have been the flash of a gun.'

'It was the fourth officer who jumped after Barney in an attempt to save him, wasn't it?' queried Matthew.

Nicholas nodded. 'And he says that Barney was swimming strongly.'

'I don't suppose we shall ever know the truth,' said Matthew, using prosaic words to preserve an outward calm.

'No,' agreed Nicholas, 'but rumours are flying. It is even being said that Solly pushed Barney, and that it was Barney himself who shouted "Murder". After all, Barney had become something of a liability and both Woolf and Solly Joel stand to gain from their uncle's death.'

'It's all nonsense.' Matthew stood up with a sudden angry decisiveness. 'Barney committed suicide – "while temporarily insane" is, I believe, the official phrase. I want to hear no more rumours. I have enough to worry about as it is. Diamond Company shares and gold shares have both been hit by a selling panic.'

In fact Matthew's next move was to try to get in touch with Connor. Rather reluctantly, Connor had given him an address – a public house in the East End – where he could be contacted. Matthew dared entrust no one else with the mission so, wrapping himself in a thick cloak and pulling a hat well down over his golden hair, he hired a hansom to take him there. He had not been in this part of London since rescuing Nicholas from the opium den, but the streets showed little sign of change. The public house was as sleazy, and its customers every bit as shady and dangerous looking, as Matthew had expected.

As it turned out, the effort and the danger were all for nothing. Connor, the landlord said, was out of town and not expected back for several weeks. Was there any message? Matthew hesitated, but dared not leave his name. Shaking his head, he returned to the waiting cab.

What would he have said to Connor anyway? Promised him more money to buy Von Veltheim's agreement to leave the Barnato family alone? Because not even to Connor would Matthew have been able to voice his chief concern: that Von Veltheim had been aboard the *Scot* and murdered Barney himself. Probably, Matthew thought as the hansom rattled west, the German was as mentally disturbed as Barney. It would not have taken much for them to fall out.

He tried to put the matter out of his mind and concentrate on his business affairs. But the name of Von Veltheim was to come to his attention again within a few months in even more suspicious and tragic circumstances.

On Tuesday 22 June Queen Victoria rode in a triumphant procession through the streets of London to celebrate her Diamond Jubilee. Never had the pageantry been more gorgeous as the crowned heads of Europe came to pay their respects to the greatest monarchy of them all. From the farthest outposts of the Empire came princes and potentates, chiefs and premiers, chanting tribesmen from Africa, slouch-hatted soldiers from Australia, Canadian Mounties and sepoys from India. At the centre of all the magnificence was the diminutive figure of the aged Queen. Before leaving the Palace she had telegraphed her Jubilee message to the Empire: 'From my heart, I thank my beloved people. May God bless them!' Then she rode out in an open carriage into the blazing sunshine – 'Queen's Weather', they called it – and to a rapturous reception from the people, who had deep affection for the venerable Queen and tremendous pride in her symbolic representation of a great country and an Empire on which the sun never set.

Matthew participated in another and sadder procession through the bedecked streets when Barney Barnato's funeral cortège left his sister's house at Marble Arch on the four-mile journey to the Jewish cemetery at Willesden. Two hundred carriages followed the coffin and the cab-drivers and bus-drivers in the Edgware Road saluted the hearse with whips tied with crêpe ribbons. Matthew travelled with Alfred Beit and together they mingled with the enormous crowd which waited at the cemetery.

The Lord Mayor of London was among the mourners, together with representatives from Rothschilds and other banks and finance houses. But there also gathered a great crowd of East Enders, come to pay tribute to generous warm-hearted Barney who had made a rags-to-riches story come true. And, perhaps for the first time, Matthew felt mortal and wondered what his own epitaph would be.

'Why are you rusticating here at Highclere instead of surveying the marriage market in London?'

'Lord, Julia, you sound exactly like Uncle Matthew!' Irritated, Charles turned away and leaned both arms on the stone balustrade of the terrace. It was a glorious afternoon and there were plenty of jobs to be done on the farm. He wished that Julia would go away and let him get on with his work.

'You are twenty-four years old, Charles, and every other young sprig of nobility is having the time of his life doing the Season. You're not really bad-looking, either. You could be quite handsome if you washed more frequently. But all you do is hang about the house and the fields like some clodhopping peasant.'

'Save your sermons for the good causes and lame ducks you embrace so enthusiastically, Julia. Better still, have some children of your own.'

Julia winced, for her childless state was painful to her. Don't worry about it, she told herself for the thousandth time. You are young and there is plenty of time.

'What do you do for sex, anyway?'

'Julia!'

'For heaven's sake, don't be such a prig! I am your sister, after all. If you cannot discuss the subject with me, who on earth can you discuss it with?'

Julia had become a leading light in the Women's Rights agitation. After Matthew's lecture, she had read Lady Florence Dixie's book *Gloriana; or, the Revolution of 1900* and had been so impressed with its views that she had sought out the author and joined in the activities of that rather eccentric daughter of the Marquess of Queensberry. In addition, Julia began subscribing to radical newspapers and was taking an increasing interest in the

Labour movement. In this area her model was Daisy, Lady Warwick, who combined the unlikely roles of mistress to the Prince of Wales and champion of the underprivileged. As a result, Julia had seen and heard a good deal in the past few years and was frequently, and embarrassingly, outspoken on delicate matters. Now she fixed her brother with a steely stare.

'I see there's another new parlourmaid!'

Charles flushed crimson.

'Yes, I thought so,' said Julia grimly. 'It's girls like that, poor souls, who turn up at my Relief Centres with the child in a shawl and no job and nowhere to go. I only hope that someone has told the new recruit about her unofficial duties. Judging by the scared expression on her face, I imagine she knows.'

'They like it. They come to me, panting for it.'

'Do they? I doubt that very much. But it is very difficult for a parlourmaid to refuse the attentions of an Earl, isn't it? Either way, she will lose her job in the end. It is a man's world all right, and particularly an upper-class man's world. If you enjoy producing children, why not marry a nice duke's daughter and sire some legitimate heirs?'

'I don't like duke's daughters. I prefer the company of working women – they don't expect so much of me.'

Unfortunately Julia did not take this statement seriously. It was an oversight which she would come to regret. She pursued her theme.

'In fact, you ought to marry money. It can hardly have escaped your notice that Highclere is looking distinctly run down.'

'It's not that bad. Desborough is a lot worse,' said Charles defensively.

Julia snorted. 'I do hope you're not modelling yourself on Desborough. Our dear Uncle Hugh can be held up only as an example of a dissolute spendthrift.'

'Highclere will survive without my marrying an heiress,' Charles asserted stubbornly.

'How? I trust you are not relying on Uncle Matthew to come to the rescue, because I don't think he's very interested.'

'Well, he ought to be interested. We are his closest family after Philip and Miranda. He's worth millions and millions – looking after Highclere is surely the very least he can do!'

'I don't see why he should give you a penny. There never has been much money in the family, you know, which is why Uncle Matthew took himself off to the diamond fields and made his fortune. *He* showed some initiative – plenty of it, in fact. I have a strong feeling,' and here Julia gave her brother a shrewd glance, 'that he will be well disposed to those who demonstrate the same resourcefulness.'

'You don't have to rub it in. I am well aware that he is pleased with Edward and is paying him an allowance to meet his mess bills. Edward is everyone's favourite! *I* can hardly join the army, can I? I am needed here.'

'It is not what you're doing so much as the way in which you're doing it.' Julia shook her bright curls in exasperation. Sometimes Charles was as slow and stolid as the great cart-horses which lumbered about the estate. Unfortunately he was less biddable. 'Actually, it's about Edward that I came. I do realise that he must carve a career for himself, but I am very worried about him choosing the army. If there is a war, he could be killed! And he is the only direct heir to the earldom.'

'Well, now, if Edward dies I have no doubt you will redouble your efforts for Women's Rights.' Charles's voice was heavy with sarcasm. 'I hear that you have been campaigning for sex equality and revision of the marriage service and divorce laws. You were quoted the other day on the subject of succession – both to the Throne and to the peerage – opining that this should be in favour of the eldest born and not the eldest son. If the law was changed, *you* would succeed to the Highclere title if I die without issue.'

'What an absolutely foul thing to say!' Julia was white with anger. 'How dare you insinuate that my campaign is prompted by self-interest! The last thing I want is to be Countess of Highclere. What I *do* want is to uproot from men's minds the idea that women are born to suffer and work for men, to hide all their natural gifts so that men may rule alone. Women are treated as inferior beings – here we are, on the brink of the twentieth century, while women have no more rights or a sense of their own identity than they did in the Middle Ages.'

'Enough!' pleaded Charles. 'This is not one of your political platforms. I know you think me a clod, but even I have managed to gather the general gist of your argument. So you came here today to persuade me to marry, so that there would be a legitimate heir in the event of Edward's glorious death in battle?'

'Yes.'

'What about Uncle Matthew and Philip? The title would go to them.'

'They don't want it, they're too busy with diamonds to worry about estates. The title must stay with our branch of the Harcourt-Brights.'

'Edward isn't a Harcourt-Bright.' The words were out before he could prevent them. And Charles was glad – he had been dying to tell someone for years.

'What on earth do you mean?' said his sister.

Charles explained. 'Rubbish.' Julia's tone was decisive.

'I heard Papa say it.'

'Our father,' said Julia, 'was insane.'

'Our mother,' replied Charles with a vindictiveness which surprised him, 'was a whore.'

Julia ignored the remark; it was not a subject on which she felt qualified to comment.

'I came here to remind you of your responsibilities. Having done so, I shall leave.'

'While on the subject of my responsibilities and our mother, are you not going to ask me how she is?'

'Oh . . .' Julia paused in the act of drawing on her gloves. 'How is she?'

'Why not visit her and ask her yourself?'

Julia cast an almost fearful glance up at the West Wing, into which Isobel had moved after Freddy's death.

'Well . . . yes, I'd like to, of course. Unfortunately I have a train to catch today. But next time . . . next time I come I will definitely see her.'

Charles's smile was sardonic. 'I understand perfectly.' He stepped forward and bent down so that his eyes were inches from his sister's. 'Do you really think,' he hissed, 'that I would bring a bride to Highclere while *she* is here, while her dark presence broods over the place?'

Julia shuddered. She felt an overwhelming urge to put a considerable distance between herself and Harcourt Hall. Having finished buttoning her gloves, she walked briskly to the door.

'Remember what I have said, Charles. And remember this, as well: I shall expect to see the same parlourmaid the next time I call – and without a bulge under her apron!'

Edward was lying on his back in the long grass on the hills above Highclere. His horse was tethered in the shade of a large oak tree, but his face was lifted to the sun which shone as warm and bright as Edward's own personality.

Miraculously untouched by the macabre history of the Harcourt-Brights, Edward walked serenely through each day in an aura of unassuming confidence that God was in His heaven and would always be good to him. He was unfailingly courteous, friendly and unruffled. His lack of intellectual ability was compensated by an eagerness to please and a strong sense of duty. Now that he was exchanging his Eton collar for cavalry boots, he looked forward to his new life in the calm knowledge that he would be as happy and popular at Sandhurst as he had been at school.

Edward had known for three years that he wanted a military career, ever since he had watched the cavalry manoeuvres in the Vale of the White Horse in the autumn of 1894. The dashing officers in their smart uniforms – among them Colonel John French and Major Robert Baden-Powell – the superb horses and the easy comradeship had captured Edward's heart and given him a sense of purpose which had never wavered. It was the Lancers or the Hussars for him and nothing else would do.

He never realised that there might be a barrier between him and his dream: that most sordid and widespread of all barriers – money. In choosing the cavalry, Edward had selected the most costly arm of the army where a private income was absolutely essential. A minimum of £500 a year was needed by a cavalry officer to supplement his pay and in some regiments a great deal more was required – the 8th Hussars, for instance, were notorious for expensive living and the officers of the 9th Lancers drank claret for breakfast. The Highclere estate had been neglected for years after Freddy inherited the title and its coffers were nearly empty.

But for Edward it had to be the cavalry. He loved horses, their power and their beauty. He loved to ride, and he rode well. He excelled at steeplechasing, and was bold in the hunting field, while the polo fields of the army beckoned irresistibly to his gregarious spirit.

Uncharacteristically it was Matthew who came to the rescue. Not because he was a victim of Edward's unconscious but compelling charm, but simply because he admired Edward's single-minded determination to achieve his ambition and was rather amused by the boy's simple faith that everything would be all right in the end. In this instance, Matthew played God and paid up.

Edward rose and stretched luxuriously. He had wavy brown hair, merry hazel eyes and a mouth which was always smiling. A little under six feet tall, his body was slim and light yet strong as steel and pliant as a willow to merge with the movements of his mount. His gaze swept over the tranquil valley below him, but his thoughts were not of peace. With any luck there will be a war, he said to himself as he untied his horse. There was already talk of trouble in the Transvaal; he did hope it would not start before he was ready.

Edward had 'For Queen and Country' emblazoned on his heart and he carried the motto with a purity and fervour which would not have been out of place at the Court of King Arthur.

CHAPTER SIX

Matthew disliked fancy-dress balls. He considered that they did not suit his style, for he cut enough of a dash without the aid of flamboyant costume. He was one of the few, therefore, who viewed the Duchess of Devonshire's ball with a certain lack of enthusiasm. For a time he was tempted to 'cheat' by donning corduroys, cotton shirt and polished high boots to appear as a diamond digger. After all, he was 'Diamond Bright' and the ball was being given in honour of the Queen's Diamond Jubilee. On second thoughts, however, he decided that such informal attire would be deemed an insult and not even Matthew wanted to upset the formidable Louisa, who had been Duchess of Manchester before she married her second Duke and was consequently known as 'The Double Duchess'. With a sigh he resigned himself to doing the thing properly and chose to go to the ball as Henry VIII.

The costume was very splendid. Blue velvet breeches ended at mid-thigh and were worn over stockings of ivory-white. The over-doublet of ivory satin was belted by a velvet band set with diamonds. Over the doublet Matthew put on a short blue velvet gown with enormous puff sleeves, slashed with ivory satin and gilt ribbon and jewels. His shoes were blue velvet and so was the flat cap on his head with its white plume.

With his golden hair and beard, his piercing blue eyes and tall figure, Matthew mirrored the popular conception of bluff King Hal. His valet was loud in his praise.

'Bloody good job it looks all right,' growled Matthew, 'because it *feels* dreadful. Too damn hot!'

He went to the nursery, since he had promised Miranda she could see his costume before he left for the ball.

'Sir Matthew,' said the nanny, with as much conviction as she could muster, 'it really does not *do* to disturb a little girl's rest at this time of night.'

'She won't be asleep. And if she is, wake her up.'

'It is very bad for her,' protested Nanny desperately. 'A little girl needs a routine. Miranda does not have a settled routine – you come in and out of the nursery whenever it suits you and . . .'

'You do not seriously expect me to come in and out when it suits *you*, do you!' roared Matthew. 'Of course I see Miranda when it suits me. It's my house and she's my daughter and she will adapt to *my* routine. Now, fetch her from bed immediately. I promised she would see the costume and I always keep my promises.'

Nanny scuttled away, feeling that King Henry himself could hardly have been more autocratic.

After Miranda had admired the costume and been prevented from doing irreparable harm to the plume in his cap, Matthew descended the staircase to the hall where Julia and her husband were waiting for him.

'You look extremely handsome, my dear,' Matthew congratulated her, kissing her lightly on the cheek. 'May I inquire whom you are supposed to represent?'

Julia's graceful figure was swathed in Grecian folds of white chiffon. The drapery left one white shoulder bare and clung to her breasts before gathering at her slender waist and flaring to the ground. Her silver-gilt hair was arranged in curls around her face and a long coil gleamed against the bare flesh of the exposed shoulder. As Julia settled into the carriage opposite Matthew, she was aware that she had never looked better.

'I'm Lysistrata.'

'Good God!'

'The name means "Dismisser of Armies" and it is the title of a play by Aristophanes. When the Athenian men failed to stop a particularly unpleasant war, Lysistrata suggested that the women should take over and force them to make peace. The women seized the Acropolis and stayed there so that the men had no access to the treasure. The main point was, however, that the women refused to go to bed with the men until peace was made. Good, isn't it? One of the first blows for female emancipation!'

'I know the story of Lysistrata,' said Matthew drily. 'I am merely surprised that your classical education was so comprehensive.'

'Oh, it wasn't. Aunt Jane told me the story.'

'Ah yes, of course. Dear Jane. Quite the blue-stocking of the family.' murmured Matthew.

'Don't be so patronising, Uncle Matthew. Daisy Warwick is quite right when she says that as a class we do not greatly admire brains.'

'With the hold she has over the affections of the Prince of Wales, Daisy Warwick is entitled to voice any opinion she chooses, however outrageous,' retorted Matthew. 'And I do admire brains – it is the use to which those brains are put that I do not always support.'

'Aunt Jane is using her intelligence to very good effect and now that she and Robert are living in London we are able to work more closely together on our projects. We are embarking on a new venture – a school for underprivileged girls.'

'Oh, good!' said Matthew sarcastically. 'So if they can't find work or a husband they will be able to find comfort in declining a Latin verb or reciting a Shakespeare sonnet?'

Julia's reply was drowned in the hubbub which engulfed the carriage as they approached Green Park. An enormous crowd had assembled in the warmth of the summer night to gape at the guests.

'Perhaps they have come to listen to the music,' suggested Lord Alfred.

'Or to contemplate the gulf which separates the rulers and the ruled,' muttered Julia under her breath, trying to avoid the gaze of the shabbily-dressed people who pushed and jostled each other in their attempts to obtain a better view of the splendid beings who were summoned to the ball.

Matthew suffered no such qualms, but threw back his head and shoulders and stalked into the mansion with a swaggering magnificence which drew cheers from the onlookers. Hands on hips, he made a grand entrance into the most spectacular and brilliant scene that London had ever witnessed.

Three thousand people attended the Duchess of Devonshire's fancy-dress ball. The Duke and Duchess themselves were attired as the Emperor Charles V and Zenobia, Queen of Palmyra. The

Prince and Princess of Wales attended as the Grand Prior of the Order of St John of Jerusalem and Marguerite de Valois. Notable also among the guests were Daisy, Lady Warwick, who was dressed as Marie Antoinette and the Duke of Marlborough as Louis XV. The Duke's costume had been made by Worth and was considered extraordinary even by that imperturbable establishment. It was made of straw-coloured velvet embroidered in silver, pearls and diamonds. The waistcoat was of white and gold damask, the material being an exact copy of an old pattern. Each jewel was sewn on by hand and it had taken several girls a month to carry out the jewelled embroidery.

'I am told it cost 5,000 francs,' commented Julia, eyeing the Duke with a mixture of fascination and disgust. 'That's nearly £300. Do you realise how long an ordinary family could live on that sum?'

'Julia, please, no more,' begged Matthew in tones of mock dismay. 'I have had more than enough socialism for one evening. We are here to enjoy ourselves and if you feel so strongly about these things I cannot imagine why you came.'

'I wouldn't miss it for the world,' said Julia frankly. 'My absence wouldn't help anyone and, besides, my dress cost nothing like three hundred pounds.'

'Neither did that one over there,' murmured Lord Alfred. 'It couldn't have, there simply isn't enough of it.'

There was such relish in his voice that Julia looked at him in surprise and turned to follow the direction of his gaze. Her attention was distracted, however, by the arrival of Nicholas, a plump and perspiring Nero in a white tunic and purple toga with a wreath of gilt laurel leaves adorning his thinning hair. Hot on his heels came the first of the hopeful mamas with a debutante daughter in tow.

'Sir Matthew, I'm *sure* you would like to meet my daughter!'

Matthew bowed. 'I am glad you are so sure, madam, because the strength of your belief will compensate for my own lack of certainty on the subject.'

He walked on, with Julia stifling giggles, leaving behind a thunder-struck lady who was trying to decide whether or not she had been insulted. The only disinterested party was Alfred, who was developing a crick in his neck through turning to watch a figure on the other side of the room.

Instantly another bejewelled dowager blocked their path.

'Sir Matthew, Lord Nicholas, you are precisely the people I wanted to see!' she gushed. 'Please be so kind as to give your opinion of my new necklace.'

Matthew glared but Nicholas obligingly made a show of studying the glittering diamonds at the lady's wrinkled neck.

'Very fine stones, Your Grace,' he proclaimed, enjoying his position as connoisseur. 'Very fine indeed.'

'Thank heavens, I am vastly relieved! We bought the piece privately, you see, and the price was so reasonable that I began to fear the stones might not be genuine.'

'They are genuine all right,' Nicholas assured her. 'If you didn't buy the necklace from a reputable jeweller, there might be an element of IDB involved and that would certainly bring down the price.'

'Really? Most interesting! Do tell me how the diamonds are smuggled out of the mine.'

Nicholas was about to talk soothingly of carrier pigeons, but Matthew leaned down and grinned wickedly into the old lady's face.

'The Kaffirs swallow them,' he said, with a devilish glint in his eye. 'The exact details of the procedure, I leave to your imagination.'

A look of absolute horror transfixed the lady's face and the fingers which had been toying coyly with the diamonds let go of the necklace as though it had suddenly become red hot.

Again Julia struggled for composure and a low musical laugh behind them revealed that the conversation had been overheard. Abruptly Matthew swung on his heel to face the newcomer, closely followed by Julia and Nicholas. Alfred did not need to turn; he was facing that way already with eyes bulging and mouth hanging open. It was the woman he had been watching ever since he arrived.

A moment's silence seemed to spread softly through the room and even Matthew was not impervious to a shock of emotion as he saw her.

She was probably the most beautiful woman he had even seen – and he had seen a great many. She was dark. Thick, shining black hair was brushed back from a perfect face and huge brown eyes stared haughtily ahead, disdaining to acknowledge the attention they were so accustomed to receive. Yet it was her body which drew the gaze of everyone present, attracting them in spite of themselves like a powerful magnet. It was an incredible body – olive-skinned, with magnificent high breasts, tiny waist and long slim legs. And indeed there was plenty of it on view. Dressed as Cleopatra, Queen of the Nile, her gauzy white gown left her back bare and plunged daringly low in front. Evidently she was a lady, Matthew thought as the dark beauty walked away, who did not greatly care for conventions. He was not sure, however, whether the term 'lady' applied, because flowing across the room was not so much femininity as utter animal sensuality. Probably there was no semblance of an intellectual thought or opinion in that beautiful head, but that was unimportant. This was not a woman to converse with, but a woman to love with, a woman to touch. To unfasten that dress and bare those breasts . . . Matthew blinked and swallowed hard to shake off the spell. Gradually the buzz of conversation was heard again and the atmosphere around them returned to normal.

Lord Alfred's mouth had dropped open to such an extent that his chin seemed almost to touch his chest, but he was brought back to earth by a sharp dig from his wife's elbow. Julia had noticed Matthew's reaction and was staring after the dark lady with ill-disguised venom in her eyes.

There was a dazed look on Nicholas's face. 'Isn't she . . . extraordinary?' he said, as if making a deliberate attempt at understatement.

'Who is she?' asked Matthew abruptly.

'Princess Raminska, newly arrived from St Petersburg and a most charming ornament to London society.'

'She is Russian?'

'Polish. Her father was an exiled Polish Count living in southern Russia. Good family, though: they were descended from the former kings of Poland, were mixed up in various revolutions and one of their ancestors married Louis XV.'

'If her father is a Count, how is it that she's a Princess?'

'She married Prince Raminska, another Polish exile who was living in Berlin.' Nicholas paused and mopped his perspiring forehead with a handkerchief produced from beneath the folds of his toga. 'They left Berlin several years later under rather mysterious circumstances. Officially, the Prince was said to be ill and in need of a warmer climate. Unofficially, the illness may have been diplomatic. Certainly the Princess had become *persona non grata* with the Empress. After wintering in Cairo they settled in St Petersburg, where the Princess enjoyed considerable success at the Russian Court. Now, though, she is said to be out of favour there as well.'

'I can understand her unpopularity with the German Empress,' said Matthew softly, his eyes riveted to the svelte figure of the Princess as she held court in the centre of the room, 'but I find it impossible to believe that she lost the favour of the Czar.'

'She indulges in intrigues.'

'I was rather hoping she would.'

'*Political* intrigues, Matt,' Nicholas emphasised. 'She is the type of woman who rifles writing desks and sews documents into her dresses.'

'There is no document sewn into that dress,' said Matthew with absolute conviction. 'There is nothing inside that dress which is not one hundred per cent natural.'

Nicholas was becoming more and more alarmed. He had seen that look on Matthew's face before, but this time it bore a passionate intensity that was entirely new.

'Matthew, please, leave the woman alone! The Princess is dangerous. What is anathema in Berlin and St Petersburg isn't likely to be acceptable at Buck House. Steer clear, my friend, steer clear!'

'Nicholas, look again at that beautiful face and that bewitching body. I must, and will, have her!'

He pursued her throughout the evening, through the rich colours and fantastic costumes, through the waltzes and the minuets and the champagne. But the Princess Raminska constantly eluded him, evading capture so skilfully that he became convinced that she was doing so on purpose. He would approach in order to ask her to dance and with a swift glance in his direction she would allow some other fortunate man to lead her on to the floor. Yet a short while later he would catch her looking at him. As she held a wine glass to her lips, her glance held his and did not waver as she drank. Then she lowered the glass to the table and her moist, sensuous lips parted in acknowledgement of interest, appreciation and mutual attraction. She had recognised him and singled him out for what he was – the most handsome man in the room.

Not even an introduction to the Princess by a mutual acquaintance was much help. She kept her eyes lowered as Matthew spoke.

'May I have the pleasure of the next dance, Your Highness?'

'Most kind of you, Sir Matthew.' She spoke perfect English in a sweet low voice. 'But I do not feel that Cleopatra would have been in sympathy with Henry VIII. No, I think she would have preferred Mark Antony.' She gave Nicholas a dazzling smile. 'That is who you represent, no?'

'Nero' gulped and his florid countenance blushed a deeper shade of puce. 'Oh yes. Rather!'

Matthew was left to seethe impotently as the Princess melted into her partner's arms and Nicholas's pudgy hand rested on the delectable flesh of her back. More than anything in the world, he wanted to touch her. While the other ladies were still encased in whalebone stays beneath their ornate costumes, it was obvious that the Princess wore nothing – or indeed very little – under her flimsy dress. Only Lily Langtry had previously had the courage to appear in society unlaced and now the proximity of the Princess's luscious curves sent the blood pounding through Matthew's veins. In his imagination he held her close and ran his hands over every inch of her body, until at last his fingers slid inside her gown to caress the cool white mounds of her breasts.

He was irritated to find that he was sweating – and not with the heat. 'We might as well take a turn round the floor,' he growled at Julia.

It was so obvious that she was second-best that Julia was half-inclined to refuse. As usual where Matthew was concerned, her baser instincts won the battle against her pride and she moved towards him. And, as usual, his touch sent shivers of longing through her and turned her knees to jelly.

'While you have been feasting your eyes all evening, I have been making a few inquiries. Uncle Nicholas is right: the Princess is a very strange lady.'

He made no reply, but she knew she had his attention.

'The story of the Princess's family is like something out of a tale by Mary Shelley. Her father sounds like the original Count Dracula and the entire family are said to be steeped in the occult and also reputed to possess second sight. Their ancient castle in Poland contains eerie garrets full of vampire bats, and sinister dungeons conjuring up creaking coffins and corpses with stakes through the heart. There is even a family curse, and the nearby forest is haunted by the gruesome ghosts of three hundred Cossacks who were supposed to have been put to death there in a single night.'

'Why, Julia, I had no idea you had such a taste for macabre, romantic rubbish.'

'They also say she is a witch.'

'She has certainly bewitched me.'

'Then she is as clever as she is beautiful. I thought you disliked intelligent women.'

'I never said that,' Matthew reminded her as he smiled lazily into his niece's blue eyes. 'You have encouraged candid speech lately, so let me see how you like a dose of your own medicine. I do not intend to cultivate her company for the pleasure of her conversation. In fact, I have no wish to speak to her at all. What I do want is to possess that beautiful body. I want to tear off her clothes, throw her on the bed and ravish her as no man has ever ravished a woman in the history of the human race.'

Julia closed her eyes in agony as bitterness and frustration gripped her and she sensed the intensity of Matthew's passionate desire for the other woman. She was consumed, too, by an overwhelming conviction that the Princess was not the right woman for Matthew. If only, Julia thought, he was not my uncle. How different things would be if he could have been mine.

Nicholas and the Princess glided past and again Matthew's gaze locked into hers. He was aware of nothing else, drowning in that sultry, languorous invitation and drawn irresistibly to the moist shining curve of her lips. Then suddenly the lips parted in an enigmatic smile and she was gone, twirling into the throng of dancers. He did not see her again that night.

After the ball, Matthew began to accept every invitation that came his way with uncharacteristic alacrity. For a few days he arrived at each function with heart thudding and throat dry from fear that she would not be there. He need not have worried: Princess Raminska was the rage and was invited everywhere. She dazzled with her dynamic personality, ready wit and persuasive charm as well as her outstanding beauty. She could hold an intelligent conversation on any subject and possessed an astonishing knowledge of English literature and history.

The Princess was not without critics – mostly women. Her separation from her husband was much talked about, but no one was sure whether or not she was actually divorced. It was certain, however, that she had three small children who were living with the Prince in Berlin and who did not feature unduly in the Princess's life or conversation. There were many pursed lips and disapproving frowns over such unnatural abandonment of maternal responsibilities, but Matthew's lips and forehead remained uncreased. The Princess's marital status and family life had no bearing on his plans.

Her moods were changeable. She could be haughty and every inch a Princess at one moment, flirtatious and alluring the next. To Matthew she seemed like a butterfly, gorgeously gowned in rainbow colours, forever fluttering just out of reach.

He watched, lynx-like, for an opportunity to speak to her alone. At last came the evening when he saw her slip through the french windows to escape the heat of the ballroom and seek the cool air of the terrace. She was easy to see in the darkness in her gleaming gown of rich ivory Duchesse satin trimmed with lace. Matthew followed at a discreet distance, glancing over his shoulder to make sure that no one had noticed their exodus from the festivities. The Princess descended the steps of the terrace to a small arbour, where she sat down and heaved a loud sigh. She gave a small shriek as Matthew appeared.

'Sir Matthew! How you startled me!'

'Really? I am so sorry. I could have sworn that you saw me by the window before you left the ballroom. You must have known that I would follow you.'

'No. I did not see you.'

Matthew sat down beside her. 'Obviously I flatter myself. No matter, I am extremely glad to catch you alone. Why do you avoid me so assiduously?'

'I have no idea what you mean.' She averted her face, presenting him with that perfect profile, and the movement caused the diamond coronet in her thick dark hair to take fire from the moonlight.

'My dear Princess, this naïvete ill becomes you. You know exactly what I mean – you will not even dance with me.'

She turned towards him again and the lovely oval of her face wore that same deeply sensual expression which Matthew had seen at their first meeting. Somehow she conveyed a secret promise of bliss and ecstasy. The message was there in the warmth of her eyes and the knowing curve of her mouth, yet belied by her next remark.

'I do not want you to touch me.'

'Why? We are made for one another!'

'I know too well the fire that will consume us once our bodies touch.'

Matthew leaned forward eagerly, sensing that she was yielding. 'Then what is stopping you? Ah, Katherine, what perfect bliss our bodies can know together!'

He reached for her hand, with a wild hope of kissing first her fingers and then that luscious mouth, but she brought down her jewelled fan in a stinging blow across his knuckles.

'No, you do not touch me! Neither did I give you permission to use my first name.' She was the Princess again, imperious and remote. 'However, I do congratulate you on your acting ability. Even in private you put on a frivolous front to cover your real designs.'

'Do I? I thought that I had made my real designs fairly obvious!'

'Earlier you accused me of naïvete. Now it is my turn to say that you do not fool me for one moment. I know the important matters which occupy your mind, and I would like you to feel that you can discuss them with me in complete confidence.'

'I can? How kind!' Matthew's face wore a bemused expression. 'What matters do you have in mind that are preoccupying me?'

The Princess leaned forward earnestly. 'The situation in South Africa is worsening and may lead to war. I realise that you are working behind the scenes with the British government and the Cape Parliament to maintain peace with the Transvaal. I am sure I can help. I have great experience in political affairs. Indeed,' and she lowered her voice conspiratorially, 'I undertook a number of missions on behalf of the Czar.'

She is serious, thought Matthew in amazement. She really is serious.

'If you were so important and useful to the Czar, why did you leave St Petersburg?' he asked shrewdly.

'I worked for the Czar Alexander. The new Czar, Nicholas, is not the same calibre of man at all,' she replied with a dismissive wave of her hand.

Also Czar Nicholas is much in love with his beautiful Czarina, Alix of Hesse, thought Matthew cynically.

'Why should such a lovely woman as yourself wish to concern herself with dull politics?'

'Pah! How like a man to be so condescending! You think it is enough to sit and be admired all day? Well, it is not enough for *me*. And politics are not dull. I have a gift for politics – a flair – it is my forte. I must put this talent to good use.'

'I am quite sure you are blessed with many talents . . . Kate.'

The low insistent timbre of his voice caused her indignation at the forbidden familiarity to die on her lips. Their eyes met and immediately the alchemy stirred between them, sending the shock of desire tingling through their bodies.

The Princess rose and in her rustling ivory dress flitted up the terrace steps to the lighted windows of the ballroom like a moth towards the candle flame.

There she mingled brightly with her fellow gue 's, while Matthew sat and smoked a cigar quietly in the warmth of the scented evening. Physically apart, each thought of the other. Both were planning a conquest and both were confident of success.

Katherine Raminska had been married at fifteen to her Prince. She did not know him and was given no choice of bridegroom. From a childhood just as weird and gloomy as Julia had described, she was pitchforked into marriage with a stranger and life at the prim and proper Prussian court.

She lived in the Raminska Palace with thirty Raminska relatives who gossiped, intrigued, quarrelled and indulged their various idiosyncrasies. The everyday routine of the Palace had been ordained by her husband's late father, and any attempt to diverge from it was considered an insult to his memory. Worse still, the Princesses Raminska were not permitted to venture on to the streets of Berlin without their hushands and – the Princes being home infrequently – walking was perforce confined to the gardens. The only outings allowed were specific social calls on a carefully vetted list of aristocratic ladies. Katherine began to feel that she was confined to a convent, a prison or at times even a lunatic asylum. Pregnant at sixteen and again at seventeen, it was extraordinary that she managed to survive the monotony which, however luxurious, dominated her lifestyle. But by her late teens Katherine's beauty had blossomed and her wit and intelligence catapulted her to the forefront of society.

It was inconceivable that so exotic a creature should ever be acceptable to Empress Augusta and her dabbling in socialism was the last straw. Forced into exile, Katherine and her long-suffering husband settled in St Petersburg and for a long time she was happy, enjoying considerable influence and importance. She had a genuine passion for politics and a genuine belief in her ability to manipulate affairs. When her star waned in Russia and her marriage broke down, she sought a new stage. She had chosen London and since her arrival she had selected Matthew Bright.

Princess Katherine Raminska was accustomed to the best and she calculated that Matthew could give her the best of everything – material goods, life at the centre of great events and, if she was any judge of men, sexual satisfaction. Perhaps his appearance as Henry VIII at the ball influenced her indirectly. Katherine knew her English history well and she had always admired Anne Boleyn's ensnaring of the King – despite the episode's tragic end. Black-haired, sloe-eyed Anne had enticed the King until he was mad with passion for her, but she remained adamant: no sex without marriage. The Princess was in daily expectation of her final divorce from Prince Raminska and was resolved to adopt the same tactics. She had decided to marry Matthew.

Matthew meanwhile smoked his cigar in the garden and contemplated the situation. Obviously she was feigning reluctance at this stage, but there was no denying their mutual attraction and he was certain the citadel would eventually fall to his assault. She believed, as did so many people, that his wealth and position automatically meant that he sought political power. Should he disillusion her? No, not yet, he concluded. Was she trying to lead him into some sort of trap? A trap is only effective if it is not divined, he reasoned. Besides, he wanted the bait.

CHAPTER SEVEN

'Aunt Jane, he is drooling over her, absolutely drooling. I only hope it is not as obvious to everyone else as it is to me.'

'I hear that she is very beautiful – Matthew is bound to be attracted to her. And really, Julia, it would be best for everyone if he married again.'

'Heavens, I hope he doesn't marry *her*.' Julia stared at her aunt in horror. 'The idea is impossible. However, I hardly think Matthew has marriage in mind. The Princess is a vastly intelligent woman, but Matthew made it quite clear that he is only interested in her body. Florence Dixie is quite right, you know, when she says that men have made women their playthings and slaves.'

'Quite so,' agreed Jane placatingly. She was more interested in the educational aspects of Women's Rights and tended to stand aside from Julia's militancy. Jane was one of the dark-haired Graftons and was taller and heavier than her sisters or niece. The dress she wore was of good quality silk poplin but had obviously seen better days. Certainly it was in startling contrast to Julia's modish gown. Julia might devote her time and energy to the poor, but she did not believe in being indistinguishable from the masses.

Jane finished hanging the cheerful chintz curtains and stepped down from the chair on which she had been standing.

'There! How does it look?'

'Marvellous!' Julia enthused, surveying the room with a satisfied air. 'The place is absolutely transformed.'

They were standing in a grimy, ramshackle house in London's East End and surveying one of the two downstairs rooms they had rented for their Girls' School. The room they were occupying was intended for the older girls and bore little resemblance to its former state. The floor had been scrubbed, the walls and ceiling painted and curtains hung at the sparkling windows. Rows of neat tables occupied the major portion of the floor space, while a desk and chair and blackboard for the teacher stood opposite the door. The second room was similar, but on a smaller scale, for the little ones.

Jane flopped down on to a chair.

'I think we are nearly ready to open, don't you?'

'Yes, except that I still believe we might need some assistance.'

'Another teacher, you mean?'

'Aunt Jane, I cannot be here every day. If the response to the school is good and we find we are using both rooms, you cannot supervise two classes simultaneously. And suppose one of us is ill?'

'A teacher ought to be paid – we cannot expect people to work for nothing.'

'A nominal salary will have to suffice. Leave the fund-raising to me. Now, let's decide on the duties and then we can obtain a clearer picture of the type of person we are seeking.'

'Reading, writing and arithmetic will be my province. Unfortunately you were never outstanding academically, Julia.'

'No, Aunt, I'm afraid that is true,' Julia agreed humbly. 'Naturally I shall address the older girls on the role of women in the modern world and I think some lessons in hygiene are essential. Otherwise, I shall devote my time to the younger ones. There is also something else we have to consider.'

Jane raised an inquiring eyebrow.

'They will need practical knowledge. We are not dealing with ladies. We shall not be turning out budding society hostesses, nor producing girls who will storm the walls of the universities or the medical profession. These are ordinary working-class girls who would not otherwise receive any education but who need to earn a living. Regrettably, at the outset reading and writing may not be the help we hope it will be.'

'So what do you suggest?'

'Sewing. Just as a start, of course. We may later think of something better.'

'What sort of sewing?'

'Dressmaking mainly, and lingerie – embroidered, of course. Daisy Warwick did it at Easton Lodge and the Duchess of York ordered her trousseau from them.'

'So she did,' said Jane thoughtfully.

'If the standard of work here is high enough, we could sell some of the garments, give the girls a percentage and keep the balance towards our overheads – cost of material and so on.'

Jane eyed her niece with growing respect. 'And to think that before you were married I was convinced that you were nothing but a flibbertigibbet and a cold-hearted one at that. Alfred has done wonders for you.'

'I don't think it was Alfred.'

'Who was it, then?'

'Let us just say that I learned a lot from Uncle Matthew. Now, to summarise the talents our teacher must possess! She must be an expert needlewoman, be good with girls of all ages and atrocious backgrounds, be able to teach the three Rs and perhaps progress to some English and history, and also be willing to work for a pittance.' Julia began to laugh. 'Where can this paragon be hiding herself?'

'Number 10 Princes Terrace,' said Jane unexpectedly.

'What!'

'Julia, I know the very girl.' Jane's face was flushed with excitement. 'It came to me when you said "expert needlewoman". The other day, I met a girl who was wearing the most fashionable coat and skirt, exquisitely cut. I admired it and, knowing she hasn't much money, asked where she shopped. She confessed that she had made it herself. Julia, I promise you, those clothes could have come from Paris, from the Rue de la Paix itself.'

'Yes, yes,' said Julia impatiently, 'but who is she?'

'Her name is Laura Vaughan. Her father is Classics master at Robert's school – a brilliant man, quite brilliant, but lacking in ambition. The mother is dead and Laura is an only child, so she spends a great deal of time with her father and is very well educated and informed.'

'Do you think she would come?'

'I can certainly ask her.'

'Do so at the first opportunity,' said Julia firmly. 'Tomorrow, in fact. No, tomorrow we have the fund-raising meeting for the Seaside Holiday Camps for Underprivileged Children. The day after, then.' And Julia shook her head in disbelief. 'Laura Vaughan,' she observed, 'sounds too good to be true.'

When Julia met the young lady several days later, she had no cause to change that opinion. Laura Vaughan was perfect. Lower middle-class she might be, but she had an indefinable air of gentility. Her voice was low but clear and sweet and Julia had the feeling that when necessary it would command attention from the unruliest of pupils. She was of medium height and had a neat figure under the demure grey dress. Her hair was brown, worn with a centre parting and scraped severely back into a bun, and a large pair of spectacles almost covered her face. Oh yes, Laura Vaughan was perfect and furthermore she had agreed to come.

After the interview, Lady Julia hurried off to change for a ball and Lady Jane went home to speak to her cook about dinner. Laura Vaughan made her way slowly back to Princes Terrace, where she climbed the stairs to her small bedroom and took off her hat. Then she removed the spectacles and smiled mischievously at her reflection in the mirror; the spectacles were of plain glass and she had never worn them before in her life.

'It was a good idea,' she said to her reflection. 'The image definitely impressed Lady Julia.'

Next she released her hair from its restraining bun and shook it loose. It hung in luxuriant gleaming folds about her shoulders and no longer seemed a dull brown but a rich chestnut shot with red and gold lights. The face that now looked back at her was heart-shaped with a clear translucent skin, a wide gentle mouth and the biggest and most brilliant emerald eyes in England. Not at all the eyes a school-teacher was supposed to possess, so Laura had acquired the spectacles to disguise and soften the impact.

Then she began to unbutton the dress and what had seemed to be a long-sleeved gown was revealed to be a short-sleeved garment topped by a cunningly-designed, tight-fitting jacket. Laura sighed with relief as she removed the hot jacket and stretched her slender arms luxuriously. If Julia could have seen her now – the shapely shoulders, full bosom and handspan waist – she might have had second thoughts about Laura's suitability for the post. But Laura was determined that her disguise would never be penetrated because she desperately needed the work. She was being underpaid, of course, but there was little she could do about that. The money was better than nothing and it hardly seemed genteel to haggle. She hoped her father would not raise objections; she could not seem to make him understand how short of money they really were. If she stressed the charitable nature of the enterprise and the association with aristocratic do-gooders, then he would not consider her position demeaning. Humming happily to herself, Laura went downstairs to the kitchen and began peeling the potatoes for supper.

The Princess laid down the letter and smiled wryly.

She was free. But she had to pay the price.

The letter contained notification of her final divorce from Prince Raminska. It also stated that the Prince would not pay her an allowance, neither would he be responsible for any expenses incurred by her since their parting. These conditions, the letter continued, had been made quite clear to her from the start of the divorce proceedings.

But she had not thought that he meant it. She had believed the Raminskas would pay her a pension to preserve her position in society for the good of the family name. A faint frown now puckered her brow. Was it possible that her judgment of men was not infallible?

Well, she did not care about the money. She would rather be a pauper and be free than live with that man and his odious relations in the vacuum of the prison Palace. Katherine was not a woman to bemoan what could not be changed – resolutely she looked to the future and set her mind to plans for survival.

A sheaf of unpaid bills lay on the desk – rent for the elegant house she occupied, dressmakers' and milliners' accounts, servants' wages, butchers' and grocery bills. Somehow she had to find the wherewithal to pay them. It was a great deal of money. The cost of maintaining a style fitting for a Princess was exorbitant.

Matthew! Matthew could pay those bills and never notice the difference to his bank balance. Marriage to him was now more important than ever.

At the thought of him Katherine's stomach constricted and her skin tingled. Here in the privacy of her own drawing-room the mask slipped from her face and desire burned in the beautiful brown eyes. Matthew was keeping her awake at night, but it was neither dreams of political machinations nor greed for worldly goods which drove sleep from her. She was consumed with a primitive lust for the sexual power of his body.

Masculinity emanated from him like a strong animal scent, and she could sense it seeping from him whenever he was near. She lived on a knife-edge of excitement, aware of every muscle in his broad chest and shoulders and every movement of his slim hips. She was haunted by the sensual stride of his long legs. At night she tossed beneath her satin sheets, unable to satisfy the aching void within her which craved to be filled. Again and again she fantasised the moment when he would assault her with that blend of brutality and tenderness which his hooded glance promised.

Several times recently she had nearly succumbed. Several times, when the invisible line of contact between them had been unbearably taut and almost tangible, she had nearly swayed towards the magnet of that cool hard mouth and those strong arms and allowed the glorious tide to sweep her away. On each occasion common sense had prevailed. 'Keep a cool head,' her inner voice advised. 'You are playing for high stakes. He is strong but you are stronger. Make him marry you for it.'

But I want it, the woman in Katherine wailed, and *am* I stronger? There were moments when the penetrating glance of his narrowed eyes seemed to bore right through her façade and expose her innermost thoughts. It made Katherine squirm. She was accustomed to being in command of the situation and was not prepared to be outwitted. His air was insolent. 'You will come to me,' he telegraphed. 'They always do. And I will give it to you – on my own terms.'

Yes, that was what held her back and determined her to continue the seduction to the marriage bed. Matthew Bright was a rock. He would hold steady in a storm and keep his head. He would catch you in those strong arms and never let you fall – but only if he wanted. If he did not care, he would pass by while you tumbled in the mud and never give you a backward glance.

Katherine drew a deep breath. What a man! What an adversary!

And what a mating it would be when it finally took place! In the meantime, her immediate financial requirements must be met from another source. Unlocking a drawer in the desk, she drew out a box and opened the lid. In the velvet-lined depths sparkled the diamond coronet, the ornate diamond necklace, the rubies and emeralds and sapphires.

The Princess eyed them dispassionately. It was a pity they were paste: the originals had gone long ago, before she left St Petersburg. In this hour of real need she regretted her former extravagances, but did not dwell on the past and what could not be remedied. As things stood, she must collect the insurance. She spread a cloth on the desk, fumbled in another drawer for a sharp letter-opener and methodically began to demolish the expert fakes. When the pieces had been reduced to rubble her hand strayed to the pearl choker at her neck. No, she would keep that. One could not, after all, appear in public mother-naked. One must have *some* jewels.

The hiding place for the incriminating fragments was ready and waiting. That night the Princess stole silently up to the attic where the travelling trunks were stored and by the light of her lamp located the piece of luggage she sought. Many years ago this willing spy had purchased a case with a false bottom which she had even used for its intended purpose. Now she secreted the small lumps of paste in the narrow aperture. If the house were to be searched, which was unlikely, no one would look here – the hidden space was designed for documents, not coronets.

The next evening the Princess dressed for a soirée and called for the diamonds. When the ashen-faced maid returned empty-handed, Katherine threw a memorable fit of hysterics and then called the police.

The story shot round London in a flash. After a busy morning with the police and the insurance company officials, Katherine dressed with particular care for afternoon tea. She chose a tea-gown of delicate sea-green silk with floating sleeves and a full skirt. As usual she went unlaced and the thin material stretched tightly over her firm, high breasts before curving in to her minuscule waist. Her ebony hair was dressed in a graceful Grecian knot. Skilfully she powerdered her face to achieve a heart-wrenching pallor and made no attempt to hide the violet shadows beneath her eyes caused in fact by her nightly yearning for Matthew.

As she had hoped, he was her first visitor.

She instructed the footman that she was not at home to other callers and prepared to meet him, remaining seated on the sofa, her pale face and misty green dress a cool oasis in the heat of the summer afternoon. The instant he entered the room, the atmosphere became charged. As he strode towards her the air seemed to move in pulsating currents like the bow-wave of a ship. He sank to one knee before her and kissed her hand, retaining it in his powerful grip.

'Kate!' he said.

There was such tender sympathy in his voice that she almost believed her jewels had been stolen and nearly cast herself upon his breast for comfort. Hazily she allowed him to retain her hand, the first time he had touched her, and as the throbs of passion began drumming through her senses, she raised tragic eyes to his. Matthew's face was only inches away, his eyes holding hers, his lips pulling hers, willing her towards him. With a superhuman effort, Katherine withdrew her hand and managed a broken smile.

'Thank you for calling, Sir Matthew, but as you see I am perfectly recovered from the shock.'

'Do the police have any clues?' He sat down beside her and crossed his long legs with easy grace.

'No. They think one of the servants must be responsible, but I do not believe that.' She smiled again, more readily this time, because she genuinely had no conception of the ordeal the servants were enduring.

'I am glad you still have your pearls.'

'Fortunately I was wearing them all day; for the past few days, in fact. I too am glad. They are now my only link with the past.'

'The stolen items were insured, I hope?'

'Of course, but it is not only the money which is important. The jewels were of great sentimental value to me.'

Like hell, thought Matthew, detecting a false note. You are composed of a rare mixture of components and emotions, Princess, but sentiment certainly isn't one of them!

'So they are irreplaceable,' he said smoothly.

'I'm afraid so. You see, Sir Matthew, my divorce from Prince Raminska is now final. I am alone in the world and trying to build a new life. The jewels were a reminder of former, happier times before things began to go so terribly wrong.'

A great light began to dawn and Matthew suppressed a smile of sheer delight.

'I would have thought your children represented a stronger tie with the past,' he observed wickedly.

'Oh, they do! But the Prince will not allow me to see them. I can only comfort myself with the knowledge that one day they will grow up and then they will learn the facts and understand the unhappiness I have suffered.'

'Do you know what I think?' Matthew edged closer to her. 'I think you are lacking in maternal feelings.'

His tone of voice and his nearness were lowering her resistance. Katherine's body was throbbing and she could feel the dampness spreading between her legs. Her nipples hardened to sharp peaks and pushed so hard against the bodice of her dress that she was sure he could see their outline through the thin silk. The realisation that his hard body was only inches from her flesh made her feel dizzy.

'I think your instincts lie in quite another direction,' he went on. 'You have the body of Aphrodite and were made for love. Stop fighting it, Kate, and stop fighting me. I want you. You cannot know how much. And you want me. I can see it.'

'No!' Katherine wrenched herself free from his compelling eyes and jumped to her feet.

He rose slowly and faced her. 'There is a very unpleasant name for women like you, but I still believe you will surrender.' He bent his head and pressed his mouth firmly to the inside of her wrist. 'The jewel robbery has obviously been a shock,' he added casually. 'You have a very rapid pulse.'

Nicholas gave Matthew the clue he lacked. They were enjoying brandy and cigars after dinner, sitting in comfortable companionship, when Nicholas raised the subject of the jewel robbery.

'The Princess should receive a tidy sum from the insurers,' he remarked, 'and I have a feeling she may need it.'

'What makes you say that?'

'I met Prince Raminska once,' said Nicholas slowly. 'The Princess was not with him – off on one of her jaunts, I suppose. He struck me as being a typical Prussian – a case of environment prevailing over inherited traits! He's narrow-minded and tight-fisted. If his separation from the Princess goes on much longer, he won't be sending any fat cheques to her bank account.'

'She says they are divorced.' Matthew's eyes had narrowed and somehow brightened.

'Well, there you are, then.' Nicholas paused and gave one of his embarrassed little coughs which always preceded an awkward statement. 'Matt, fact is, there's something I have been wanting to mention. I know how keen you are on the Princess but there is no one else I dare confide in.'

'Go on.'

'I think her jewels were fakes! Not all of them, necessarily, but some at least. There was one piece, a diamond necklace, which particularly attracted my attention. If the stones were paste they were excellently done, but they were not perfect and the workmanship of the necklace was not up to the standard warranted by genuine stones.'

'You're very observant,' said Matthew.

'I like to think I have become something of an expert.' Nicholas looked modest and sipped his brandy thoughtfully. 'But if they were fakes, I'm surprised you didn't notice.'

'When I'm with the Princess I don't look at her jewels. I have eyes only for the abundance of her natural beauty.' Matthew's voice was rueful. 'Nicky, you may be right. But for God's sake, say nothing to anyone else about it.'

'If she collects the insurance money, she's stealing,' said his friend indignantly.

'Insurance companies, like the tax-man and the banks, are fair game,' said Matthew firmly. 'Anyway, we cannot prove a thing. She would soon have you in court for libel and collect another packet from you. Leave it alone.'

Matthew himself had no intention of leaving it alone, however. The Princess's plans were now an open book and her fatal weakness had been revealed. Matthew poised himself for the kill.

CHAPTER EIGHT

The laughter of the children faded into the distance and a blessed hush floated softly over the classroom. Gratefully, Laura sank on to a chair and closed her eyes. She was dead tired. Lady Julia had not been at school at all today and Lady Jane had a headache. Laura had coped virtually single-handed with both groups of girls and, as luck would have it, the classes had been full and the pupils in particularly vociferous and active mood. Weariness seeped into her bones and blanketed her mind. She tried to relax, willing the weariness to flow through her body and be absorbed by the chair on which she sat. It was several minutes before she realised she was not alone. And she knew before she opened her eyes that her quiet companion would be Maggie Green.

The girl sat in the shadows at one corner of the room, head bent over a scrap of material which she was stitching diligently.

'Maggie, that's enough for one day. You will hurt your eyes in this poor light.'

Reluctantly Maggie laid down the needlework. Her sewing was excellent and she was far and away Laura's star pupil. In addition, she had uncommon aptitude for other subjects. Now she continued to sit and look wistfully at Laura. But for what was she hoping? What hope was there, thought Laura in a sudden fit of despair, for girls like Maggie Green?

'As you're here, Maggie, you might as well help me to clear up.'

Instantly the girl sprang to her feet and eagerly collected books from the tables, stacking them neatly on a shelf. She wiped the blackboard and polished every desk and table till they shone. She was neat, quick and efficient. Even her shabby dress and her brown hair were cleaner than those of the other girls and Laura was certain this was due to the efforts of Maggie herself. Her slut of a mother would not care tuppence how the child looked.

Laura pinned her hat on the severe coils of her hair and adjusted the spectacles. She shivered as she reached for her coat. Autumn was drawing in. She must speak to Lady Julia about the possibility of buying a small stove to provide heating. At the moment the only thing which warmed Laura was the pay packet in her bag, which, meagre though it was, would settle the grocery bill.

'I'm going your way, Maggie. We'll walk together, shall we?'

The girl's footsteps dragged as they walked along the darkening street. 'What's the matter? Don't you want to go home?' Laura kept her voice light but she was dreading the reply.

Maggie shook her head.

'Why not?' asked Laura automatically, although she was sure she knew the answer.

They had reached the door of Maggie's terraced home. The girl turned and the expression on her pale plain face was serious and sad.

'It's difficult to explain, miss. School is nice. It's clean and bright and the lessons are interesting. Home is . . . different. And Ma and Pa don't know what I'm talking about when I try to tell them what I've learned.'

She disappeared into the house without waiting for a reply and Laura was glad. She was in no mood to offer comfort and felt incapable of giving advice. Maggie confirmed Laura's worst fears. She had seen inside homes like that of the Greens. She knew that Mr Green was a drunkard and strongly suspected Mrs Green was supplementing the family income in an ancient and time-honoured way. What use was education in such an environment? Already Maggie was being alienated from her background, yet her chances of escape were slim. With her fastidious nature and newly-aroused intelligence, would she be able to live happily in these surroundings? Could she marry someone of her own class, a man like her father, with whom it was unlikely she would be able to communicate? For all the sterling work of the Women's Rights movements, it would be some time before opportunity for advancement came the way of the Maggies of this world.

Laura sat in the omnibus feeling drained and desolate. She was honest enough to know that her concern for Maggie was partly personal, because she saw in Maggie a magnification of her own problems. Highly intelligent and given an excellent education by a father brilliant enough to have been a university don, Laura too found herself in limbo. She came into contact with few eligible men, and those whom she did meet were either impoverished or impossible. With no money of her own, her choice was necessarily limited. She might not care about status and material possessions, but her experience was that most men did. The attractive young teacher who had spent two terms at her father's school had made it quite clear that he desired her and equally clear that he could not afford to marry her. The curate who gazed at her longingly and the rich factory-owner who leered lasciviously were out of the question on a different count. Laura could never have endured them to touch her. A classical education and books left lying around the house by an absent-minded parent had ensured that she was fully *au fait* with the facts of life. The marriage bed held no mystery for her, and there was no way she was going to do *that* with *them*. On the other hand, that handsome and virile bricklayer, with the swaggering walk and the burning glance which stripped her naked in the street and reduced her legs to jelly, was no good either. Laura was not ruled by class distinction, but she had heard him speak, seen him lurch from the public houses at closing time, and she knew that while their bodies might make glorious contact, their minds were a million miles apart.

A great surge of loneliness engulfed her. There was no one to whom she could talk, except her father, and she had to hide from him any unhappiness she might feel. Valiantly Laura fought against her depression. She was tired and she always felt depressed when she was tired. She had her father and they adored each other and she must be grateful for that. But – and here the doubts returned – he had been looking so tired and ill lately. She would speak to him again about going to the doctor. Because without him whatever would she do?

Matthew spent a brief time at Brightwell, but was soon back in town. The sun had lost its warmth and mellow September days drew into cool, misty nights. The Princess returned to her London home.

'I am giving a small party, Your Highness,' Matthew said formally when he called, 'for the select few who remain in town. Will you come?'

'Of course. Thank you.'

'I must warn you that the gathering will take place at a gambling club. It will be a private party, of course. I am hiring the entire establishment for the evening. My family will be present – my niece Julia is fond of a small wager.'

'I am not easily shocked, Sir Matthew.'

'It will be rather different from the entertainments in Berlin.' He smiled confidently. 'You do not need to join in the games of chance if they offend you – or if your finances are a trifle strained.'

Katherine's eyes flashed. 'I shall not be offended and my finances are in perfect order. A little game of roulette will be highly diverting.'

'I hoped you would think so.'

As Matthew had intended, Katherine's guilty conscience was alert to the innuendo that she might have money problems. She calculated that she could afford to lose £500 but no more, and there was always the hope that she might win. Her spirits rose on a tide of optimism as she dressed in a superb golden gown, its velvet folds revealing the deep cleavage between her breasts. Tonight she disdained the pearls; the smooth apricot bloom on her skin was ornament enough. She packed £500 in banknotes into a small velvet bag and gloated over the possibility of returning with £5,000.

The gaming-room was decorated with taste and elegance, giving the appearance of a private house rather than a casino. Huge banks of chrysanthemums softened the walls and Katherine found her reflection snatched by a dozen mirrors and tossed like an echo down the room. The atmosphere was intimate. She found that she knew everyone present and Matthew's niece seemed particularly friendly tonight. Katherine blossomed and lowered her guard. She believed that Matthew had admitted her to a charmed circle beyond the requirements and conventions of society. She responded with genuine warmth, suddenly and painfully aware of her total lack of family and friends.

She would have been less happy if she could have overheard the conversation which took place earlier.

'Julia, I want you to be nice to her,' Matthew asked.

'For heaven's sake, Matthew, I really can't stand the woman.'

'I will get that bloody bitch into bed if it is the last thing I do. And I am getting close, very close.'

'She will probably be the biggest disappointment of your life, and frankly it would be no more than you deserve.'

'She will not be a disappointment. That one will explode with the biggest bang since the Battle of Waterloo, once I get my hands on her. Come on, Julia, be a sport! I am your darling uncle, remember? And I will give you a generous donation for your new school.'

'Your persuasive powers are irresistible, as usual. All right, I will pretend to be welcoming her into the bosom of the family. But by God, Matthew, if you do marry her, I'll make sure you suffer for it for the rest of your life.'

'There is not the slightest danger of that, never fear.'

So Julia was charming to her, Lord Nicholas hung on her every word, Matthew personally ensured that her champagne glass was constantly filled and asked her opinion of President Kruger's latest moves. Princess Katherine Raminska basked and glowed in the approbation and attention she knew to be rightfully hers and became more and more certain that she had captured Matthew's love.

'Kate, Kate,' he whispered, 'you are the most captivating creation that the Lord ever made. Never has there been such a devastating combination of beauty and brains. You have quite bewitched me.'

The combination of the champagne and his sexuality lifted her to the crest of a wave which carried her with reckless confidence to the roulette table. Matthew sat opposite her and Julia, Alfred and Nicholas settled in their places, albeit with rather puzzled expressions, while the table filled up with other guests.

The game began.

Katherine started cautiously with £20 on the black. And won. Matthew had wagered £50 on the red and lost with a careless wave of his hand.

Then he placed another £50 on the red and drew sensuously on a cigar as he waited for her move.

He made her feel marvellously alive, her heightened senses aware of every sound and smell and touch. She saw the blond hairs gleaming on his beautiful hands, felt the silky embrace of the soft velvet against her skin, the tantalising touch of the dark curls at the nape of her neck. She felt totally female from head to toe. Leaning forward so that he could receive the full impact of her décolletage, she placed £50 on the black, won again and flashed him a triumphant smile.

Without taking his eyes off her, he placed £50 on the red and another £50 on number 9. She followed immediately with black and, defiantly, 13. Matthew won with both stakes. His eyes dared her to continue.

There was a hush around the table as the contest between them became apparent to the onlookers. The champagne circulated while Matthew and the Princess, two magnificent animals on the prowl, pushed each other to higher and higher stakes. Her £500 was soon gone.

'Do you wish to stop now, Your Highness?' he asked when he saw her hesitation.

Katherine observed the arrogant tilt of his head, the challenge on his face and the amusement which lurked in the depths of his blue eyes.

'Certainly not! But I have run short of ready cash. Will you accept an IOU?'

'Of course. How could you doubt it?'

When Matthew eventually called a halt, Katherine had lost £10,000.

Somehow she maintained an outward calm and an indifferent air as she said her farewells and quietly slipped away.

When all the guests had gone, Matthew twirled Julia round the room. 'Now it can only be a matter of time before I claim my reward!'

She held out for a month. Until her creditors would wait no longer. Then she sat once more at her desk, staring at another sheaf of unpaid bills and surveying her options.

There were other men who would marry her, she must not forget that. Katherine flipped through a mental list of available suitors and shuddered. She would have been better off with Prince Raminska than with any of them. To marry any of them would be merely to exchange one gilded cage for another – only this time the gilding would be more gilt than gold.

There was not another man like *him* – she must have him, whatever the consequences. With a dull sense of finality, Katherine realised that it was meant to be, that it had always been intended. He was her fate, he had manoeuvred her into a corner and she acknowledged his superiority with a wry smile.

A package lay on the desk beside the pile of accounts. It had arrived the day after the roulette game: a fabulous ruby and diamond necklace and a pair of pendant earrings. His message was plain. Katherine had prevaricated – she had not returned the jewels, but neither had she worn them. Now she picked up the package and rose, throwing back her head defiantly as she ran her pink tongue over her lips. If she must capitulate, she was damn well going to enjoy it.

Matthew was sitting in the library at Park Lane. It had been a tiring day, but when she was announced at ten in the evening his body leaped into vibrant life.

'Do not disturb us,' he told his butler, 'under any circumstances.'

He stood with his back to the blazing fire as she entered. The door closed behind her and she leaned against it. Wordlessly they stared as if seeing each other for the first time, waiting for the magic to envelop them.

She was darkly glowing and sensuous, wrapped in a sable coat which matched her hair, her throat and the deep cleavage of her breasts bare but for the shining jewels at her neck. Her hair was dressed high in smooth gleaming coils and caught at the back with combs which clasped every tendril in place. The high cap of hair emphasised the oval of her face, the size of the huge brown eyes and the length of her slender neck. The combination of glossy hair, peach-bloom skin and luxurious fur produced an impression of deep velvet against which the jewelled necklace and long pendants at her ears swung and sparkled.

She was the epitome of sensual perfection. Matthew longed to touch her but stood unable to move as she crossed the room to stand a short distance from him. Her hands moved with studied deliberation to the folds of her cloak and she opened it as if performing some ancient rite. As the fur swung back and fell in a tumbled heap to the floor, so the study in black was replaced by a burst of colour as Katherine's ruby-red silk dress glowed in the soft light of the muted lamp and the flickering flames of the fire.

Matthew took an involuntary step towards her, desire rising in him and flooding through his veins as he began to absorb the reality of her presence. For months he had waited for this moment, planned it, schemed for it. Now they were alone and there was no mistaking her surrender. The jewels she wore conveyed the message that she had come here so that he could take her and he still believed she wanted him as much as he wanted her.

The thin straps of her gown flared into two narrow strips of material which joined the skirt at the waist but which barely covered her breasts. The magnificent mounds of those breasts pushed hard against the silk, the nipples and areolae clearly outlined. The skirt was full, but it clung to her hips and thighs as though a mysterious friction existed between silk and skin. Behind them the fire sent up a shower of sparks and the dark lady became a vivid, vibrant being. The sexual current ran strong between them but still they stood, hands hanging limply at their sides, savouring the anticipation of what was to come.

At last Matthew moved. He stepped behind her, covering the high pointed breasts with his hands, rubbing and kneading them through the silk. Katherine pressed her body back against his, her breasts arching forward into his clasp. Then she turned towards him and they fell upon each other ravenously, mouths welded together as feverishly he tore aside the red silk at her bosom and his fingernails dug into her naked flesh.

Still they did not speak but uttered only inarticulate groans. Matthew stooped over her to kiss her breasts, the rosy nipples hardening and stiffening under his caress, then gathered up the long skirt and slid his hands up the slender legs to the silkiness of her thighs. Katherine tensed as she waited for him to discover that she was wearing no undergarments and heard him gasp as his touch embraced the rounded smoothness of her buttocks. Then she sought his mouth again, kissing him violently as his hand explored and his fingers probed the soft wetness between her legs.

Finally he ripped the dress from her and gazed for a moment spellbound at her beauty. She stood proudly before him, knowing that he would not find a flaw. Never had she so enjoyed the admiration in a man's eyes, eyes which told her what she already knew – that she was even lovelier without her clothes.

Frantically she helped him to remove his clothes. Deftly she unbuttoned his shirt and when his torso was bare rubbed the softness of her jutting breasts against his muscular chest. Then Matthew felt her hands lightly clasping his erection through the material of his trousers and with indescribable pleasure felt the coolness of her fingers groping through his clothes. Katherine teased him, first caressing his inner thighs before moving with tantalising slowness to his penis. As she touched him their mouths fused together in a fresh upsurge of passion.

Swiftly Matthew shed the rest of his clothes and pulled her down on to the sable cloak which lay on the hearthrug. With a feather touch his fingers wandered down her shapely shoulders and slender hands and arms, over the twin mountains of her breasts, the curve of her hips and the flatness of her stomach and the long supple silkiness of her legs – to rest at last on the swelling mound with its triangle of dark curls. Against her nakedness the diamonds and rubies flashed their own fire as they caught the light from the flames in the hearth and Katherine trembled as Matthew's lips followed the erotic path his hands had already discovered. Her longing was unbearable. Each moment was exquisite but silently she urged him to hurry, to hasten the moment when he would part her legs and satisfy the aching, tugging, pulling void inside her.

When his cool hard lips and soft beard reached the dark fuzz he roughly pulled her legs apart and began kissing her there, licking and flicking with his tongue in the musky sweetness so that Katherine spasmed into an unexpected and involuntary orgasm her hips gyrating rhythmically as though he was already inside her. Then lifting her legs and wrapping them round his neck, he thrust into her with a violence she almost feared would tear her apart.

He seemed to fill her completely, driving ever deeper inside her and sending pulsating waves of delight through her body as she clung closer and closer to him, digging her fingers into his firm buttocks as she tried to draw him nearer still. She came again and again, shaking helplessly as the convulsions wracked her, her muscles contracting and squeezing him tightly. Matthew seemed tireless and Katherine was about to cry out for mercy when at last she felt the quickening of his pace and heard the strangled moan as he climaxed.

At last he rolled away and they lay panting, bodies slippery with sweat. Katherine closed her eyes in the peaceful afterglow. Then Matthew spoke for the first time.

'Send me the bills,' he said.

CHAPTER NINE

January 26 1899 was Laura's twenty-third birthday and by coincidence she had a day off from work. Only four girls had come to school, two of them looking seedy as though succumbing to the current epidemics of scarlet fever and influenza. Having suffered from these illnesses herself as a child, Laura could sympathise but still felt excited at the prospect of some free time.

'There is a meeting I must attend,' Julia announced. 'What will you do, Laura?'

'I think I might give myself a treat,' said Laura shyly, not wanting to mention her birthday, 'and go to the West End to look at the shops.'

'Not my idea of fun,' remarked Julia drily, 'but each to his own, I suppose. Would you like a lift in my car? Alfred is away, foxhunting in Gloucestershire, so I have the use of the Daimler. It is ironic that this morning's meeting is part of my Anti-Blood Sports Campaign. Never mind, I shall convert Alfred eventually, even if I have to emulate Lysistrata.'

'I would love a ride in the car, if you are quite sure it isn't any trouble.'

'No trouble at all. I can drop you in Knightsbridge by Harrods.'

'Oh, I wasn't thinking of going into . . .' Laura faltered, '. . . but thank you, that will be fine.'

'Come on, then. It isn't raining, thank goodness. No doubt these motor-car manufacturers will produce enclosed vehicles one day, but at the moment one is exposed to the elements. Have you ridden in a car before?'

Laura shook her head.

'I thought not.' Julia eyed Laura's brown felt hat and brown cloth coat. 'You should be warm enough, but tie your scarf over your hat or it will blow off.'

Meekly Laura obeyed and followed Julia into the street where a curious crowd had collected round the car, kept at bay by the haughty stare of the chauffeur. He assisted Julia into the luxuriously padded front seat, leaving Laura to scramble unceremoniously into the spartan accommodation at the rear which was little more than a bench with a small back-rest.

'It's a Coventry Daimler,' Julia threw over her shoulder, adding vaguely, 'with four cylinders. Whatever that means.'

The engine sputtered into life and the crowd jumped back nervously. Then they were off, with the noise roaring in Laura's ears and the cold winter breeze stinging her face. She pushed the spectacles further up her nose to protect her eyes and cowered behind the driver to gain protection from the wind, but she was loving every minute, revelling in the experience of travelling by such a new mode of transport and in the status it bestowed. Cars were still the playthings of the fortunate few and it seemed that everyone turned to stare; cab-drivers shook their whips as horses shied at the noise, small boys pointed with excitement and Laura had to suppress a giggle as she saw one old man cross himself as they rattled past. She knew that no one was looking at her, conscious of what a dowdy brown sparrow she appeared compared with Julia's fur-clad opulence, but she basked blissfully in the reflected glory and thought how her father would laugh when she told him.

All too soon they were approaching the West End.

'Do you mind if we go to Park Lane first?' shouted Julia, trying to make herself heard above the general cacophony of sound. 'There is a call I must make. You can walk across the Park to Knightsbridge if you like.'

'I'm in no hurry,' Laura shouted back, only too happy to prolong the journey.

The Daimler stopped outside an enormous mansion and quiet was restored to Laura's eardrums.

'Good,' Julia announced, 'he's at home; that's his carriage in front of us. Ah, here he comes now and – oh Lord – in a foul mood again by the look of it.'

The most magnificent man Laura had ever seen was striding down the steps, his handsome brow creased in a frown and his lips compressed. His black frock coat was open, showing the high starched collar of the white shirt, a grey silk tie, dove-grey waistcoat and black-and-grey striped trousers. He wore a shiny black top hat and his cane was tucked under his arm as he angrily pulled on a pair of pale grey leather gloves. When he saw Julia he stopped in his tracks and, still glaring, walked across to them.

'What the hell do you want, Julia?'

'Oh, how charming! I never knew anybody else who could make one feel so welcome! What has upset you this morning, Matthew, or shouldn't I ask?'

'That bloody nanny will have to go – I've just told her so!'

'Matthew, that's the *third* nanny you've had for Miranda in as many years. What on earth do they do wrong?'

'I will not have a pack of silly women telling me how to bring up my daughter! If I have to hear again what is or is not "suitable for a young lady" I will take a horse-whip to the silly bitch. Miranda is not a "young lady", she is my daughter, and I will make sure she is brought up to be something better than a mere ornament to some weak-chinned lordling's drawing-room. These nannies are all the same – damn difficult, the lot of 'em.'

'Of course, it couldn't possibly be *you* who is being difficult?' said Julia sweetly.

Matthew glowered at her. 'What are you doing here, Julia? Or perhaps it would be quicker to ask how much do you want?'

'Much quicker,' agreed Julia breezily. 'A hundred should do it.'

'What is it for this time?'

'Sewing materials for the school. We're managing to sell a fair proportion of our output, but we're not covering our costs. You see, we have to pay the girls when an item they have made is sold. It's the only reason some mothers will allow the girls to come to school in the first place – isn't that right, Laura?'

Laura started as if she had been shot. Mesmerised by the deep voice and bright blue eyes, she was in a trancelike state. Here at last was the perfect combination of body and mind which she had come to believe was non-existent. And it was far, far above her reach.

'Oh, yes. Absolutely right,' she managed to gulp, shrinking back further into the corner of the seat and acutely aware of her ghastly hat and scarf and even ghastlier spectacles.

Sir Matthew Bright, however, did not so much as glance her way.

'You seem to think I am made of money,' he grumbled to Julia.

'So you are!'

'I didn't make money just to give it away,' he retorted. 'Oh well, I suppose I can spare a hundred if it will keep you quiet for a bit.' His face cleared suddenly and he broke into a boyish chuckle. 'By God, Julia, if Edward does as well as you in *his* chosen career, he'll win the bloody VC!'

But the sunshine which had broken through his cloudy expression was fleeting and disappeared completely as a carriage drew up and a lady alighted.

'Damn!' he said intensely. 'Damn the woman!'

'I hate to say that I told you so, Uncle Matthew,' said Julia loftily, 'but the fact remains that I did!'

'Mind your own business!' Matthew growled and stalked off to confront the new arrival. Laura felt a catch in her throat as she looked at her: that face and hair; those furs and jewels; how must it feel to look like that? She had a vivid mental picture of herself as she must appear now in the brown coat, down-at-heel shoes, hideous hat and spectacles, and she gazed at the two splendid creatures who were ascending the steps to Sir Matthew's front door and felt there was no justice in the world.

'I'll get out here,' she said suddenly, the joy gone from the day, unable to revel any longer in her dreams of grandeur in the motor car, 'and walk across the Park.'

'As you like.'

'Lady Julia,' Laura stood beside the car gazing up into Julia's face, 'who is she?'

'The bewitching beauty? Why, the Princess herself.' Julia gave a short laugh. 'Princess Raminska – a very good friend of my uncle. And the chief reason for his ill-temper.'

Julia drove off and Laura walked slowly into Hyde Park. She no longer wished to gaze at the shops; the only thing she wanted to do was to go home, to crawl back into her refuge and lick her wounds. She knew that it was not the title or the face, hair, furs and jewels that she envied. It was what they attracted: Matthew.

She envied the Princess her possession of 'Diamond Bright'.

Laura travelled straight home by bus and it was as well she did. Robert Bruce was waiting for her and by his face she knew that he brought bad news.

Julia was wrong. The Princess was not the chief cause of Matthew's ill-temper, although she was a contributory factor. Matthew had been irritable and sensitive since the previous March.

It was then that he had heard that Woolf Joel had been murdered in Johannesburg, and that a Baron Von Veltheim had been charged with the shooting. When he first received this news, Matthew broke out in a cold sweat. Terrified in case his association with Von Veltheim should become known, he searched his mind over and over again for any links which could be made between them. Did Von Veltheim know Matthew's name and if so, would he mention it? Did he know Connor's name? If he did, could any link be found between Connor and Matthew?

He was highly nervous as he waited for the case to come to court in the Transvaal. The trial lasted nine days and they were nine of the most unpleasant days of Matthew's life. Even if his name were to be mentioned, he reasoned, there could not possibly be proof of any connection. But mud sticks – and if Connor was called to give evidence and started talking of IDB and the old days, the mud could turn into a quicksand. As the days passed Matthew's fear became mixed with anger. To think that he was enduring all this anxiety and loss of sleep over something he didn't do! He had never intended that anyone should be hurt, let alone killed. Now there were two faces gone forever from the Board of the Diamond Company.

Von Veltheim pleaded self-defence and a tangled story of blackmail and political plots was aired in court. Matthew held his breath when he read that Von Veltheim claimed to have been introduced to Barney Barnato by a mutual friend in the smoke-room of the Hotel Metropole in the summer of 1896. And released that breath in a long hissing sigh when Von Veltheim refused to name that friend and the man never appeared in court.

Most of Matthew's acquaintances in London dismissed the

story of a Barnato plot to overthrow the Kruger regime as unadulterated nonsense, and were inclined to believe that Von Veltheim had been trying to extort money from the Joels and had turned nasty when the money was not forthcoming. The jury of Transvaal burghers, however, did accept the story and, with it, the plea of self-defence. It took the jury only three minutes to find Von Veltheim not guilty, but President Kruger immediately deported him from the Transvaal as a public danger.

Apparently Matthew was in the clear, but it was taking a long time to overcome his sensitivity to any mention of Barney's death, Joel's murder, vacancies on the Board, or his own position in the Company which undoubtedly had been strengthened by both untimely deaths. And all because Connor had come to him with a bait labelled 'political plot' and because Barnato and the Joels had been mixed up in the affairs of the Transvaal government. More than ever, Matthew determined to avoid such traps.

It was unfortunate, therefore, that the Princess chose that period to mount her campaign to increase her influence in government circles and even more unfortunate that she expected Matthew to aid and abet her.

'Where were you last night?'

Matthew shut the library door behind them and resignedly peeled off the pale grey gloves. It was beginning to look as though he would never reach his office today.

'Out,' he replied shortly.

'Out? *Out*? I invited you to dinner.'

'Correction. You *summoned* me to dinner. You should have realised by now that that attitude is most unwise.'

'It was extremely embarrassing,' Katherine raged. 'I had invited some very important people – two Cabinet ministers, the editor of *The Times* and several high-ranking officials from the Colonial Office. I expected you to be there!'

'If I needed another reason for my absence, you have now provided it,' said Matthew as he sat down at his desk, withdrew a cheque book from the top drawer and began writing a cheque to Julia for £100. 'You know how I loathe your political soirées. I loathe everything about your manoeuvrings and meddling in world affairs. I have forbidden you to indulge in such activities under my roof; I cannot prevent you from doing so under your own roof, but I can damn well stop paying for them.'

Katherine went white. 'You can't do that!'

'Don't ever use the word "can't" to me. It is not in my vocabulary.' He leaned back in his chair and stared at her. 'This has been coming for a long time, Katherine, so you need not look so stricken. I have warned you repeatedly about your extravagance and told you that I will not finance your pathetic ambitions.'

'But I have outstanding bills.'

'I gave you a cheque last month which would have kept any reasonable woman for a year.'

'I am not reasonable. I am *royal*,' she flashed.

'More a pauper than a princess,' he said caustically.

'Matthew, you must help. I thought you loved me!'

'You know perfectly well that love was never part of our arrangement.' Matthew stood up with lazy grace and smiled at her sardonically. 'You have overstepped the mark, Katherine. When I made you my mistress fifteen months ago I wanted you in my bed, not in my hair or on my back.'

'How dare you refer to me as your mistress? You forget who I am!'

'There is little chance of that,' he retorted. 'If you are so ashamed of the description, why does the whole of London know about it? Certainly it was not I who boasted of my conquest. It was you who spread word of our relationship in order to boost your position in society and to gain credit from every supplier in the town.'

The cheque book was still lying on the desk. Matthew tore off Julia's payment, swiftly wrote out another and handed it to Katherine.

'Here you are, Princess. That is positively my last contribution to the bottomless pit of your extravagance and inflated ego.'

Katherine longed to tear up the offending piece of paper and fling the scraps in his mocking face. However, she had a practical streak in her nature and merely tucked the cheque into her bag. Changing her tactics, she then swayed towards him and raised trembling eager lips to his.

Matthew took a step backwards. 'It's quite all right, Katherine, you don't have to earn the money now.'

'You are a devil,' she hissed, 'and I hope you go to hell where you belong.'

He laughed as he returned the cheque book to the desk drawer.

'The only place I intend to go to is the office. I'm late for an appointment. As usual, you have overstayed your welcome.'

'But, Matthew, what am I going to do?'

'Find yourself another rich lover. Or,' and he grinned, 'you could, of course, always sell your pearls.'

The strength seemed to seep from Katherine's legs and she subsided into a chair as he left the room. So he knew. He knew that she could not sell the pearls. For fifteen months she had slept with him and probably he had known all the time. It was how he had gained the advantage over her in the first place.

He would be aware, too, that it would not be easy to ensnare another rich lover, not in London anyway. Too many men knew of her relationship with Matthew. Too few would want 'Diamond Bright's' cast-off. There would be those who lusted after her beauty, but no one would take her seriously and form a lasting association. They would use her for their pleasure and then tire of her. Was that her future? To be passed from hand to hand down an endless string of Matthews?

How, she wondered, with her rank, beauty and intelligence, had she ever come to this?

But she knew how: Matthew!

He had dragged her from what should have been the pinnacle of her success down into this destitute gutter. Her feelings for him were a confused mixture of love and hate. She hated the power he wielded over her and the cold-blooded way he used her. She hated him for not loving her. But she still ached for the fleeting touch of his fingertips which could turn her to flame.

Katherine stood up and resolutely straightened her back. She was not finished yet, not by a long way. With a wary eye on the library door which Matthew had left open, she walked softly to the desk and took out the cheque book. Tearing off a handful of blank forms, she pushed them into her bag beside the cheque which Matthew had already given her and which also provided a useful specimen of his signature.

Talking of Katherine's pearls reminded Matthew of his own jewel collection. That night in the privacy of his room he opened the caskets and lifted the diamonds from the velvet-lined depths in which they had slept since Anne died. For a long time he sat with the necklace in his hand, turning it this way and that, the brilliance of the refracted light dazzling his eyes.

All this, and much more, would be Miranda's one day. Miranda, so beautiful and good, on whom his every hope was pinned. Miranda, his only child, who therefore must resemble him in every possible way, who must grow up strong and bright to take charge of her share of his diamond empire.

He would give her the necklace on her eighteenth birthday, he decided, and smiled with pleasure at the prospect. His fascination with diamonds seemed to deepen with the passing of the years. The gems mesmerised him, pulling him down into their blue-white hearts; ensnaring him forever, siren-like, in the toils of their entrancing beauty. But Matthew believed that his passion for diamonds was pure. He still had no conception of the darker world which lurked in their fiery depths, concealed by the radiance of their blinding light.

Anne could have told him. And she would have begged him not to give the necklace to Miranda and so pass on to her the burden of its curse. But Anne was dead and Miranda must brave the legacy of the Bright necklace unwarned and alone.

The Comtesse could have warned her. She understood the evil genius that diamonds and the desire for them released. But the Comtesse could help neither Miranda nor Matthew because she could not speak.

Paralysed, she lay imprisoned within the walls of her inert flesh: becoming a living corpse, since while her body faded her brain remained alert.

The pear-shaped diamond hung around her neck, as it had hung for so many years. She dwelled on it constantly and it gave her no peace. She dwelled on it because when she had made her will, before the final illness struck, she had bequeathed the stone to Matthew.

The Comtesse had loved Matthew, been hurt by him and been envious of his other women. Growing older and more bitter as the illness advanced, she remained convinced that the diamond was the root of her misfortune. Therefore she had willed it to Matthew knowingly, because while she was convinced that he was already ill-fated and under the diamonds' spell, she was also certain that he would give the diamond to the real love of his life.

Now, as death inexorably approached, the Comtesse regretted her vengeance. But there was nothing she could do. She could not speak or write or communicate her thoughts in any way at all. She could only lie motionless and contemplate the terrible influences she had unleashed on to Matthew's future wife.

CHAPTER TEN

A week after her birthday Laura sat alone in the kitchen of the small house in Princes Terrace. It had been the worst week of her life, during which she had been reduced to a state of stunned exhaustion. The funeral had taken place that morning but still she wore her black coat and bonnet. Her arms felt heavy and she was too tired to lift them to undo the fastenings of her clothes. Besides, the house was cold and she had no money to buy coal.

Mr Bruce had accompanied her to the hospital where they had taken her father. It was some sort of stroke or heart attack, they said, brought on by anxiety and overwork. He was alive but died two days later without regaining consciousness.

Everyone was very kind but Laura spurned all offers of help, welcoming the work and the funeral arrangements to fill the vacuum of her mind. Even the lonely, empty evenings were occupied with restless activity as she cleaned and polished the house from top to bottom. She felt oddly detached, as though she was standing outside herself and watching a stranger. This sense of unreality kept her grief at bay and enabled her to undertake each task mechanically and competently.

But now her father had been buried and she could no longer ignore the abyss which had opened at her feet. She had to face the fact that he was dead and that she had lost the only family and friend she had ever known. Moreover, she had to confront the problems which pressed in upon her – she had no money, could not afford the rent of this house and the school did not pay her enough to live on. The abyss yawned wider as Laura was jolted into the full realisation that she had no money, no home and no means of support. An unexpected rush of tears filled her eyes, but she blinked them back furiously. She had not cried for her father and she certainly would not cry from self-pity.

Consumed by a growing sense of panic, Laura continued to sit in the darkening gloom of the early February afternoon until she was roused by a knock at the front door. It was Julia. Flustered, Laura showed her into the front parlour. Automatically she went to light the lamp but suddenly remembered that she was not wearing her spectacles and so allowed the twilight to remain, relying on the shadows and the brim of her bonnet to hide her face. Certainly Julia showed no sign of noticing any difference in Laura's appearance.

'It's freezing in here,' shivered Julia, who had been about to draw off her gloves but changed her mind as she tested the temperature.

'I'm sorry, Lady Julia, I didn't think of lighting the fire,' Laura lied, blushing with humiliation.

'Well, you had better think about it or else you will be ill. Don't light it for me, though, because I'm not stopping. I called to say how sorry I was to hear about your father's death and to ask you when you were coming back to the school.'

'Back to school?' Laura stalled.

'Yes.' Julia's tone was brisk and businesslike. 'Work is the best healer, you know.'

Laura took a deep breath. She had known ever since her father died what she had to do, but had baulked at admitting it, especially to herself.

'I'm afraid I shall not be able to return, Lady Julia. I have my living to earn. I know that you pay me as much as you can, but the wage will not be enough to support me.' She swallowed but carried on bravely, 'I must look for a residential post. As a governess.'

'How dreadful!' With a pang of guilt, Julia remembered how she had hated her own governess and what a misery the poor woman's life must have been. She also realised to what extent she relied on Laura at the school and how much she would miss the girl's calm competence. 'Have you no family with whom you could live?'

'None.'

'Good gracious!' To Julia relations were not the greatest blessing in the world and she frequently considered them more of a hindrance than a help. However, she conceded that it must be very strange and disconcerting to have none at all, especially in times of trouble. 'Not even an uncle?'

'No, I am afraid there is no one at all.'

'Talking of uncles gives me an idea.' Julia glanced at Laura's averted face and then shook her head vigorously. 'But no, it's quite out of the question. I wouldn't wish it on my worst enemy, let alone on you.'

'I would be very grateful for any suggestions you could make,' said Laura in a low voice. 'I was wondering if I dared ask you or Lady Jane for a letter of recommendation. It might help me to obtain a position.'

'Uncle Matthew is looking for someone. He has sacked the current nanny just as he threatened to do. You might be exactly what he needs.'

Laura's heart began to beat faster. 'But doesn't Sir Matthew need a nanny rather than a governess?'

'Most people would think so, as Miranda is only four and a half. But Matthew, as you will discover, is a law unto himself and has decided that nannies are superfluous. There are two nursery-maids to cater for Miranda's bodily needs and now he wishes to give attention to her mind. *His daughter*,' and Julia mimicked Matthew's customary emphasis on the words, 'is required to be intelligent and well-informed.'

Laura was seized with doubts. Resolutely pushing aside vivid memories of his magnetic attraction, she recollected that she had also witnessed his forceful style and towering personality. And, apart from the difficulties of dealing with him, Miranda must surely be the most spoiled and pampered little monster in Christendom? But it would certainly be a job and she was hardly in a position to pick and choose.

'I really do need the job, Lady Julia.'

'I will speak to him tonight, then either Jane or I will let you know tomorrow.'

It was Lady Jane who called the next day to announce that Laura was to present herself at Park Lane as soon as possible.

'For an interview?' Laura inquired.

'No, he has accepted our recommendation.' Jane hesitated. 'I think, though, that you should be prepared to treat it as a trial period of, say, three months. My brother-in-law can be an . . . exacting employer.'

Laura nodded, her mind whirling in a kaleidoscope of hopes and fears and sadness.

'I quite understand.' Slowly her gaze travelled around the sparsely-furnished parlour, lingering lovingly on old and familiar objects. 'Before I go, I must clear everything from the house.' Her breath caught in her throat as she visualised the final disintegration of the only home she had ever known.

'Laura, what an ordeal!' Jane eyed Laura's quivering shoulders. 'Look,' she said impulsively, 'Robert and I can do that for you if it would help. Just pack your clothes and anything else you wish to keep. I'm sure Robert will know someone who will clear the other items and he'll negotiate a good price for you – if you trust us, that is.'

'Of course I trust you.' Laura managed a tremulous smile. 'Besides, there isn't anything very valuable. The whole contents of the house won't fetch very much.'

'No,' agreed Jane gently, 'I'm afraid they won't. That's settled then. When will you go to Park Lane?'

'Tomorrow, I suppose.' Laura's heart turned somersaults, but there was no sense in postponing the evil day. 'Have you found someone to help at the school?'

'Not yet, but you are not to worry about that.'

'Maggie Green could take the sewing class for you. She's sixteen now and quite capable of teaching the other girls. There's no work at the factory at the moment, so her mother would let her stay if you paid her a bit extra.'

'What a good idea! I will speak to her about it.' Jane smiled wryly. 'I could certainly do with some help. As you're aware, Laura, Julia's enthusiasm for actually teaching the girls wore off a long time ago. Nowadays, there is always some meeting she *must* attend!' She rose to leave. 'Au revoir, Laura, and good luck. I really feel we are throwing you into the lion's den.'

Yes, thought Laura, he is rather like a lion with that thick mane of golden hair and the snarl upon his lips.

* * *

She sorted her clothes first, selecting those garments suitable for her new vocation and ruthlessly rejecting the rest. When she had finished it was a sombre pile of garments which lay on the bed – black, grey and brown, with only an occasional touch of white in a blouse or a collar to brighten the drabness. When they were packed, there was a little space left – enough, Laura estimated, for two more garments. For sentimental reasons she chose from the discarded pile a burgundy skirt and jacket which her father had always admired, and an emerald green dress which matched her eyes, made from a piece of taffeta she had found in the house and which she fancied might have belonged to her mother. She had never worn the green dress and it represented a small gesture of defiance, a spark of hope that life might not yet be over.

Then Laura wandered slowly through each room, straightening the curtains, plumping the cushions and tenderly touching every well-loved object. Each cracked cup or patchwork quilt held a memory and her set lips relaxed into a wistful smile as she contemplated the happy images they evoked. But when she had completed her tour of the house and returned to the kitchen, desolation swept over her again. This home had been an anchor for so long, holding her steady in the strong tides of life. Now she had to cut loose, leave the comforting haven of its walls and set forth alone on uncharted seas.

She could rescue so little from the ruins. After careful deliberation she chose a selection of her father's favourite books and, of course, the family Bible. To these she added a photograph of her father taken the previous year at school; a rag doll which had been a faithful friend of her childhood; and the small clock which had stood upon the kitchen shelf ticking off each minute of her life. It had been Laura's job to wind the clock each night ever since she was a little girl and she was seized with a sudden superstition that when the clock stopped, so would she. She wound it now and took it upstairs to stand upon the trunk which, with its load of books, was extremely heavy. She knew that she could not possibly carry her luggage and travel by omnibus to Park Lane, so she must hire a cab – hideous though the expense would be. However, there was another reason why she did not begrudge the cost. Laura was a great believer in keeping up appearances and making the right initial impression. It was important that she showed some semblance of gentility by arriving in a cab rather than as a pauper lugging her own cases along the street. To this end she had set aside her best coat and skirt of good quality dark green cloth which she hoped would boost her confidence as she mounted those imposing steps to that formidable front door. She tried not to remember that her employer and the household staff would realise she was impoverished by the very fact that she sought such a job.

Her packing completed, Laura lay down to pass her last night under the roof of her old home. She slep fitfully and was glad when it was time to get up. She had no appetite, but made a pot of tea and sat in the kitchen, staring out at the grey February day. It was raining steadily, that soft soaking English rain which shows no sign of ceasing and can be infinitely depressing. Laura's spirits sank lower and she felt as if the worries of the world were pressing on her shoulders.

Then it occurred to her that it might not be considered genteel to arrive in the morning. Mid-afternoon might be a more suitable time. She went into the rain to find a cab and asked the driver to collect her at two-thirty. Back at the house she dragged the trunk and valises down the stairs into the hall and returned to shivering contemplation of the overcast sky through the rest of that cold interminable morning.

At two o'clock she meticulously washed up the teapot and cup, put on her hat and coat and began pacing the floor in the front room, watching for the cab. By two-thirty she was so tense and strung-up that she greeted the vehicle's arrival with an almost hysterical relief which quite overcame the painful parting she had anticipated. She was out of the house, the luggage stowed away and the front door pulled shut behind her before she had time to think, and set off down the street without a last look at the dear familiar façade of her home. Dry-eyed and resolute, Laura fixed her mind on Park Lane and the future.

The mansion looked even larger and the steps steeper than she remembered. The cab-driver carried her bags to the porch and Laura rewarded him with a flash of gratitude in her lovely eyes and a handsome tip. He refused the money with a gruff kindness and a look of sympathy which indicated he understood her circumstances and this brought Laura closer to tears than she had been all day. When he drove off, she donned her spectacles and marched up the steps with a back as straight as a ramrod. To her satisfaction the door opened before she knocked and she knew that her arrival in the cab had been noticed. However, the butler's stare was frosty.

'I am Miss Vaughan,' Laura announced with considerably more confidence and hauteur than she was feeling. 'I am expected.'

'The staff entrance is at the back,' and he began to close the door.

'I am the governess,' snapped Laura. 'We do not use the staff entrance.'

She was by no means sure of her ground on this point, but wished to make it clear from the start that she was not to be browbeaten.

The butler, presumably conceding her right to use the front entrance, opened the door sufficiently for her to pass through and beckoned a footman to fetch the luggage.

'Please let Sir Matthew know that I have arrived.'

'Sir Matthew is not at home. I will advise him as soon as he returns.' The butler, whose name was Parker, turned to the footman. 'Miss Vaughan is to be in the guest room adjacent to the nursery.'

Laura walked through the vast marble hall, heading boldly for the main staircase. Governesses did not use the back stairs either – at least, this one did not. She could not restrain a gasp of surprise as the footman opened the door to her room. She had been expecting bare floorboards or threadbare carpets, dingy hangings and dilapidated furniture. The reality was a neat, bright room with chintz curtains and bedspread in gold and yellow. The bed looked supremely comfortable and there was an ample wardrobe and chest of drawers and even a writing table. The overwhelming impression was one of cosiness and warmth.

'How beautifully warm it is,' she exclaimed, aware that the heating had been noticeable since she entered the house, and eyeing the radiator curiously.

'I'll say that for him,' the footman replied, setting down the cases, 'he's not stingy.'

'He certainly is not,' Laura agreed, realising that she had been chilled to the bone all day. 'What a pleasant room! Was it used by the former nanny?'

'No.' The footman's manner was somewhat terse. 'She had a room in the nursery wing next door.'

'Who looks after Miss Miranda at night?'

'There are two nursery-maids and one of them is always within call.'

The man's tone was distant. He disapproves of the nanny being dismissed and replaced with a governess, thought Laura, as he left the room. Which doubtless means the entire household staff disapprove, so there is a lot of prejudice to overcome and there will be difficulties with the nursery-maids. Undoubtedly the path ahead was fraught with hazards, but it was impossible to be totally miserable in such a pretty room. Warmer in body and spirit, Laura began to unpack. She was interrupted by a knock at the door and the entry of a small maid carrying a tray.

'Mr Parker said as how you might like a cup of tea, miss, after your journey.'

'Thank you very much.'

Before Laura could say more, the girl had given her an intensely curious look and hurried away. Looking me over, Laura said to her reflection, in order to tell the others. At this moment the maid and the footman are doubtless regaling the servants' hall with a full description of this poor dowdy person who is such a failure in life that she has to be a governess. Because a governess is always reckoned to be a failure, and that is because no one *chooses* such a position but is forced into it. Nannies are fat, pink and happy and dispense security and good cheer, while a governess is thin, pale and miserable and struggles to thrust learning down unwilling throats. Somehow, Laura reflected, she had to be a satisfactory combination of the two.

Her unpacking long since completed and the tea-tray having been collected by the same maid, darkness had fallen and the lamps had been lit but still Laura received no summons to Sir Matthew. She waited patiently but with growing anxiety that she had been forgotten. Several times she nearly ventured out into the passage to go downstairs in search of Parker, but on each occasion her courage failed her. Eventually she could bear the suspense no longer. She opened the door and walked along the corridor to the head of the stairs.

Below her, chandeliers blazed with light and two gorgeously gowned ladies walked through the hall, while a hum of conversation and spurts of well-bred laughter came from the reception rooms. Laura retreated quickly and ventured in the opposite direction towards the back stairs. Here the noise was louder and more raucous but equally redolent of a happy and companionable atmosphere. Desolately, she walked back to the nursery where a gleam of light showed under the closed door. She was standing hesitantly outside, trying to decide whether or not to knock, when the maid appeared carrying a large tray. Feeling extremely foolish, Laura ducked into her own room but was sure her hesitation and uncertaintly had been noticed and would be duly reported.

The supper-tray was placed on the desk. When Laura lifted the covers she gasped. The food was superb: a bowl of soup, a fish entrée, a large plate of roast chicken and vegetables with a delicious sauce, and fruit jelly piled high with whipped cream. This was, she surmised, the same meal now being served to Sir Matthew and his guests. Whatever else she might be, she was not likely to be cold or hungry under his roof.

But she was lonely. As she sat in her room with her solitary tray the waves of laughter from all parts of the house seemed to batter tauntingly against her ears, emphasising her position in limbo a no-man's-land between the upstairs and downstairs worlds of the great houses. Still she fought against the tears which burned against her eyelids and she forced herself to eat something, fearing that to send back an untouched tray would offend Cook.

Afterwards she placed the tray outside the door and prepared for bed. Only when the light was out did she permit the tears of grief and loneliness to flow in the kindly dark and finally sobbed herself into exhausted sleep.

'Sir Matthew will see you now, miss.'

Laura smoothed her grey skirt, patted the unbecoming coil of hair and followed the maid to the library. It occurred to her that it was ironic that she had spent so much time making herself unattractive for the interview while ladies such as the Princess would adorn themselves for his pleasure. She still preferred to hide behind her disguise in the belief that voluptuous, green-eyed governesses were unlikely to keep their jobs.

However, as she entered the library Laura's first impression was not of the man who waited for her but of the beauty of the room and its contents. She stared spellbound at the magnificent proportions of the long library, its crimson velvet draperies and deep armchairs and, above all, at the seemingly endless rows of gleaming, leather-bound books. She was seized with exultation and an intense yearning to read every single volume and realised for the first time that while her father had left her no money he had given her a more valuable bequest – a genuine love of learning.

'I have never seen so many books!' she exclaimed impulsively. 'Sir Matthew, may I read them? I would only take one at a time and return it to its place so quickly!'

She turned towards the man who stood with his back to the fire and immediately wished the floor would open up and swallow her. He towered over her, his expression fierce and unsmiling, the force of his dominant personality reducing her to reluctant submission. Laura cringed inwardly as she waited for furious rage or biting sarcasm to put her in her place.

'Certainly, if you wish.'

Laura gaped at his ready agreement and at the unexpected courtesy in his rich, deep voice.

'In fact, it would be an excellent thing,' Matthew continued. 'To date, the books have served merely as decoration. I do not think a single volume has been removed from a shelf – except for occasional dusting, I presume – since the house was occupied. We are not an intellectual family!' He smiled, and his face was suddenly that of a young man. 'Feel free, Miss Vaughan, to use the library at any time.'

'Thank you very much.'

'The more knowledge you acquire, the more you may impart to my daughter. How do you intend to start her education, Miss Vaughan?'

Laura took a deep breath. This was a question she had anticipated and she had prepared her answer carefully.

'A great deal depends, Sir Matthew, on the nature and ability of your daughter. I have not yet had the opportunity to meet her and therefore I have formed no opinion. Most probably, we will begin with a little reading and writing, progress to some elementary mathematics and then to history. It is really much too early to be specific.'

Matthew nodded but did not interrupt.

'In addition, I will attempt to broaden her general knowledge. For instance, whereas a nanny took her for a walk in the park chiefly for fresh air and exercise, I will ensure that she also learns the names of the trees, birds and flowers.'

He nodded again. 'Do you feel qualified, Miss Vaughan, to take Miranda's education beyond the elementary stage?'

For the second time in two days Laura exuded a confidence which she was far from feeling. 'Yes, I do. My father was a Classics master so I have a smattering of Latin, although my Greek was never good. I also have an excellent knowledge of literature and history and a good grasp of mathematics. I speak a little French and German, but there will be ample time for me to improve my own knowledge of these subjects before teaching Miranda. Also, while Miranda will not need to know dressmaking such as I taught the girls at Lady Julia's school, I can show her how to embroider.' Laura hesitated and decided to be frank. 'However, I must admit to one area of weakness. While I feel able to help Miranda to acquire an appreciation of music and drawing, I do not feel qualified to actually instruct her in those arts.'

'That will not be necessary. Drawing-room accomplishments are not a priority, but should Miranda show a talent for either music or art, suitable masters can be engaged. I am much more interested in the development of Miranda's mind. Incidentally, part of her education will include a thorough knowledge of the diamond industry, but I will undertake that myself.'

'May I inquire, Sir Matthew, if any guidelines have been laid down as to the division of responsibility between myself and the nursery staff?' Laura hoped that she had phrased the question with sufficient delicacy.

The gaze of his blue eyes was penetrating. 'No. I have every confidence, Miss Vaughan, in your ability to produce a satisfactory compromise and to establish a happy working relationship with the nursery-maids.'

In other words, Laura interpreted, it was a test. And if she failed to solve the problem, there would be an indelible black mark against her name.

The eyes continued to bore into her relentlessly.

'One more question, Miss Vaughan, before Miranda arrives. What do you consider to be the most important aspect of education?'

Laura looked at him steadily. 'Stimulation of the mind. A good teacher should be able to convey her own fascination with a subject in a way which will arouse the pupil's interest. This leads to curiosity and a desire to know more – a state of mind which does not end when schooldays are over. Such stimulation, Sir Matthew, is far more beneficial in my opinion than cramming a head with facts and figures.'

His contemplation of her had become more thoughtful and there was a significant pause before he replied.

'A very good answer, Miss Vaughan, and one with which I concur.'

Laura had no time to assimilate the compliment because Sir Matthew pulled a bell and the door opened to admit a maid and a small girl with a speed which indicated they had been waiting outside. Again Laura braced herself for the ordeal, for the meeting with the spoiled and petted light of Sir Matthew's life.

He held out his arms and the child ran to him. While they were playing, Laura took a good look at her charge. Miranda was a carbon copy of her father. She was big for her age and sturdily built, with a mass of tawny gold hair and Matthew's bright blue eyes. Obviously she adored her father. She radiated joy at the attention he was giving her, but the game did not last for long and apprehension filled the little face as she was led towards Laura.

'Miranda, this is Miss Vaughan, the governess who will be giving you lessons and looking after you instead of Nanny.' Suddenly he saw the maid standing by the door. 'That will be all, Hetty. Miss Vaughan will bring Miranda to the nursery when we have finished.'

Hetty shot Laura a venomous look and departed, her back rigid with disapproval.

'Say how-do-you-do, Miranda,' Matthew ordered.

'How do you do, Miss V . . .' The little girl's voice trailed away, obviously uncertain of the name.

'Hello, Miranda.' Laura smiled warmly and hoped she did not appear too intimidating. Perhaps when she and Miranda were alone, she could shed the spectacles.

'You will do exactly as Miss Vaughan tells you.'

Surely, Laura thought, his tone was more authoritative and formidable than was necessary with such a small child and his face was stern and serious. This was not the indulgent father she had expected.

'Yes, Papa,' said Miranda obediently.

'And you will learn your lessons well and each day you will tell me what you have learned.'

Great heavens! Laura's eyes widened in horror. She hoped that this edict would soon be forgotten, both for her sake and Miranda's.

'Yes, Papa.'

The child's voice was little more than a whisper. Her head was bent, but Laura could see the frightened look on her face.

'And you, Miss Vaughan, will tell me truthfully whether or not she has been a good girl.'

'Yes, Sir Matthew,' said Laura with a distinct lack of enthusiasm.

'I must go now.' He lifted Miranda and kissed her on the cheek.

'Will I see you tonight, Papa?'

'I don't know yet. I have a busy day and then I have to go out. But I will try. You know how I like to see you and that I always try.'

'Yes, Papa.'

This time the monotonous repetition held echoes of sadness.

'Go with Miss Vaughan, now.'

'Come, Miranda.' Laura smiled encouragingly and held out her hand. She would not have been surprised if the gesture had been ignored, but Miranda walked obediently to her side and slipped a small hand into hers.

As they climbed the stairs, Laura said, 'I don't think we will do any lessons today, Miranda. I think we should spend the day getting to know each other.'

Most children would have whooped for joy, but Miranda only looked worried. 'Papa said he would ask me what I have learned. He will be angry if I have nothing to tell him.'

'But you will learn something,' Laura said lightly. 'You can tell him what you have learned about me. How old are you, Miranda?'

'Four and a half. Nearly four and three-quarters.'

'I would have thought,' said Laura, with great feeling, 'that you were a great deal older.'

They reached the nursery door and Laura hesitated. On the other side lurked Hetty and her colleague, guarding their territory like Scylla and Charybdis. Laura felt that she must establish contact with Miranda before she did battle with the 'enemy', so she guided Miranda to the door of her golden bedroom.

'This is my room, Miranda. Right next to the nursery. You can come here whenever you like. Can you reach the door handle? Good girl!'

There was not a lot to interest a little girl, but the rag doll was an instant success.

'I expect you have a lot of toys of your own.'

'A few, but I am only allowed to play with them at certain times. And they're not nearly as nice as this.' Miranda stared enviously at the homely features and faded dress of the home-made doll.

It was on the tip of Laura's tongue to tell Miranda that she could keep the doll and take it to bed with her at night. But in the nick of time she realised that the doll would then pass into Hetty's care and that its presence in her own room could be both an attraction and an incentive.

'You can come here and play with it as often as you like.'

'Thank you, Miss V . . .'

'We had better decide what you should call me. You can't call me Nanny because I'm not a nanny. And I don't think you should call me Governess because that sounds horrid. Vaughan is a silly name, so I think you should call me by my first name: Laura.'

'Laura,' Miranda repeated.

'It is a bit unusual and your father might not like it, but we will see.'

Miranda nodded contentedly. Laura realised that this was a

most biddable child. The only discipline required was the slightest suggestion that 'Papa might not like it.'

'Laura, will you stay longer than the nannies?'

Laura's heart lurched. She saw with startling clarity how little security the child possessed. Her father flashed in and out of her life like a magnificent meteor, but Miranda never knew when he would appear or how long he would stay. Moreover, his expectations of his daughter were very high and woe betide her if she fell short of them. Nannies came and went – how many had Lady Julia said? Three in three years? Contrary to every expectation, this was no spoiled and pampered child of a fabulously rich magnate. Miranda did not get what *she* wanted. She got what *Matthew* wanted.

Would she stay longer than the nannies? Laura was essentially an honest person and she wanted to say that the length of her tenure depended almost entirely on the whims of Sir Matthew Bright. But the appeal in the little girl's eyes was so great, the need in the little body so intense that Laura sank to her knees and hugged Miranda close.

'Yes, I am staying for a very long time. Probably forever and ever.'

CHAPTER ELEVEN

The lamps and the crimson draperies cast a rosy glow, the fire blazed in the hearth and Laura lingered in the library as she selected a book to read. It was late and she should have returned to her own quarters, but she loved this room so much that she prolonged her visit. In the fortnight during which she had been resident at Park Lane, she had crept in here several times, after unobtrusively ascertaining that Sir Matthew was not at home.

It had been a busy two weeks. She was building a happy relationship with Miranda and, after a stormy start, had achieved an amicable relationship with the nursery-maids. Laura took charge of Miranda during the day and ate breakfast and luncheon in the nursery, but handed the child into Hetty's care after tea. She had won the point over taking meals in the nursery by emphasising the extra work her separate tray of superior food caused the kitchen staff. However, she had deemed it tactful to stay away from the nursery in the evenings and continued to partake of her lonely supper in her room. With free evenings, but no company and nowhere to go, it was little wonder that she was rapidly devouring Matthew's books.

Luxuriating in the choice of titles upon the shelves as some women might revel in the colours of rich silks, Laura was roused from her reverie by the sound of the door opening. With horror, she heard Matthew's voice and worse still, he was not alone. Laura stood motionless, screened from their sight by the tall bookshelves, unsure whether she should declare her presence or stay where she was in the hope that they would soon go away.

'There is not the slightest use denying it, Katherine. I know damn well it was you!'

'You cannot know any such thing because it is not true.'

'Normally your beauty is your greatest asset, but on this occasion it served you ill. The clerk who cashed the cheque described you perfectly.'

Katherine gave up. 'Did he? What a pity! Still, it does not prove I took the other cheques.'

'For God's sake, don't be ridiculous. Of course you took them and forged my signature on all of them. What I cannot understand is how you imagined you would get away with it.'

'Matthew, I needed the money so desperately! I have nothing, and there is no one I can turn to.'

'You should have thought of that before you divorced your husband. Perhaps you should consider going back to him – if he would have you, which is doubtful.'

'The workhouse would be preferable to life with that man,' she hissed dramatically.

'Fine words, Katherine!' said Matthew drily. 'But I fancy you might find the reality rather different. Of course, you could always work.'

'Work? You seem to forget, Matthew, that I am a royal princess.'

'Not royal enough, Katherine, and we are moving into a time when a full bank balance means more than an empty title. However, I concede that your job opportunities are limited. With your looks, you had best seek a husband.'

'There is only one husband I want.' Katherine moved closer and stared up at him with burning eyes. 'What a team we would make, Matthew! We are both beautiful and intelligent. With your money and my political flair, we could rule the world.'

Matthew burst out laughing. 'Me? Marry you? Are you out of your mind?'

Katherine flinched before his scorn but she pressed on desperately. 'You are naturally angry because I forged the cheques. But Matthew, I did need the money and also I wanted to bring to your attention how much I needed it. I thought . . .'

'You thought that I might marry you in order to avoid a scandal,' interrupted Matthew. 'How little you know me, Katherine! Never, at any stage of our relationship, did I consider marrying you.'

Her face was white and hurt. 'Why not? What is wrong with me?'

'A man wants you in bed, not at the altar.'

'Yet I could make a good wife to the right man.'

'Then you must carry on looking, Princess, because you have not found him yet.'

'How hurtful you are,' she said softly. 'And to think that I came here to warn you.'

'Warn me of what?'

'I have a premonition that within six months an attempt will be made on your life.'

'Really, Katherine, what nonsense!' scoffed Matthew.

Her eyes were dark, strange pools in the perfect oval of her face and her expression was remote and mysterious.

'I have the second sight. It is a characteristic of my family, and I am certain that what I say is true. Someone will try to kill you. I wanted to give you this,' she held out a thick heavy medallion. 'It is a talisman given to my uncle by the gipsies. He was a soldier and it kept him safe through all his campaigns.'

'Superstitious rubbish!'

'Take it!' Katherine pushed the medallion into the breast pocket of his coat.

'You are merely trying to divert attention from the fact that you forged the cheques.'

'What do you intend to do about it?'

'I will strike a bargain with you. I will let the matter drop – *if* you promise to go away and stay out of my life.'

'No!'

'It is *over*, Katherine. Finished. I don't want to see you again.'

'Ah, but I want to see you.' Katherine's voice was low and tense. 'At first I made a calculated decision to marry you because you possessed all the attributes I sought. My relationship with you has undergone many changes since then, but I am left now with the inescapable knowledge that I have reached the final stage. To my infinite regret, I have fallen in love with you.'

'I suggest you fall out again – fast!'

'Impossible! So I will not agree to your bargain. I must go on seeing you, and I will never give up hope. Somehow I will make you marry me.'

Matthew smiled but there was no real humour in his eyes. 'Then you will pay for the forgeries in another way.' He gripped her tightly by the shoulders.

'You're hurting me,' she protested.

'By the time I am finished, I guarantee that your love for me will have been put to a severe test.'

He pushed her against the sofa and began pulling off her clothes, fastening his mouth to her breasts and biting hard with his strong white teeth.

'You're hurting me!' she cried again.

'Surely a few bruises on your fair flesh are preferable to the stain on your lily-white reputation if I were to sue over the cheques.' Now he was taking off his own clothes and smiling devilishly. 'Tonight I am going to work off a few of my fantasies on you, and somehow I don't think you are going to like it.'

'Someone might come in.'

'No one has ever come in before and I see no reason why they should start now. Bend over.'

'*What!*'

'You heard me.'

Laura was still standing, transfixed with horror, behind the bookshelves. She was petrified at the thought of being discovered and in terror of making the smallest noise. When she realised what Matthew was doing, her face flamed and instinctively she closed her eyes. However, since she was hidden from view the sounds were more penetrating and pervasive than the sights. She covered her ears, but no matter how much pressure she applied it was impossible to shut out the noise. From time to time she had to relax her arms and the full force of the scene burst upon her. She could hear the Princess's groans and cries, but whether they were caused by pain or pleasure she could not tell. Matthew made not a sound – only the slap of flesh against flesh advertised his continued presence.

'No, no more, please . . . I cannot take any more,' the Princess was begging. And then a shriek: 'My pearls! You have broken my pearls.'

Laura opened her eyes and was appalled to see several pearls rolling over the floor towards her.

'Your valuable necklace, Princess! What a shame,' Matthew mocked.

'It is valuable. It is!'

I must do something, said Laura to herself. They are bound to look for the pearls.

The door to the winter garden was situated on the far wall, and Laura calculated that it should be beyond the view of the couple by the hearth. Cautiously she craned her head round the shelves and gauged the distance to the door – she should be able to cover it in about six strides, but at the very first step she took there was a crunching sound which froze her in her tracks.

'What was that?' the Princess gasped.

There was a pause while Matthew listened. 'Nothing,' he said eventually. 'Probably the furniture creaking.'

Laura had been holding her breath and now she let it out in a soft sigh of relief. She lifted her skirt to see what had caused the noise and, moving her foot, saw that she had stepped on a pearl. It had been squashed on the polished floor and automatically she bent to pick up the pieces, so that she would leave no evidence of her presence. Reaching the door, she placed shaking fingers on the handle and slowly began turning it, praying that the mechanism was smooth and well-oiled. To her immense relief it opened silently and she slipped into the welcome darkness and silence of the winter garden.

She was trembling violently, but managed to stagger to a chair before her legs collapsed under her. Eventually the shivering and shaking stopped and she was able to assess the situation more calmly. She had to admit that so far her thoughts had been solely for herself and revolved around her fear of discovery. Even now, in her sanctuary, she was unable to feel much sympathy for the Princess who seemed to have behaved most foolishly and, indeed, dishonestly. What Laura did feel was relief at her own escape; surprise that life was not invariably smooth and happy for those with rank and beauty – why, even the Princess's pearls were false; and an overwhelming and totally ridiculous happiness that Sir Matthew Bright was not intending to remarry.

* * *

'We shall spend Easter at Brightwell,' Matthew informed Laura a few weeks later. 'Philip will join us there.'

'Who is Philip?'

'My son, of course.'

'Your *son*?' Laura's eyes widened in astonishment.

'Yes.' Matthew was impatient. 'Why so surprised, Miss Vaughan?'

'I had assumed that Miranda was an only child.' Laura's indignation boiled over. 'And I do find it surprising, Sir Matthew, that no one – absolutely no one – has mentioned his existence. Not you, nor Miranda nor Hetty, not even Lady Julia or Lady Jane when they spoke to me about working here.'

'There is no reason why Philip should have been discussed. He will soon be fourteen and is in his first year at Eton. He rarely comes to London and has little contact with the staff or his sister.'

Or with you either, thought Laura.

'Originally,' continued Matthew, 'it was not my intention that you should have responsibility for him. Philip is a difficult boy and I considered you would be fully occupied with Miranda. However you are a sensible woman, Miss Vaughan, and perhaps your influence on Philip may be beneficial.'

He nodded his head curtly in dismissal.

And that, reflected Laura, is about the nearest thing to a compliment which I am likely to receive from him.

Brightwell was looking beautiful when they arrived, clothed in the full glory of an English spring. Laura loved it immediately, just as she had come to love the Park Lane house. She responded instinctively to the exquisite works of art around her and to the natural beauty of the grounds. Sometimes it seemed unreal that she, Laura Vaughan, born and bred in lower-middle-class London, should be privileged to live in such surroundings. At other times she was only too well aware of her precarious position and cold fear gripped her heart at the prospect of ejection from the Bright household, in which case she would not only have to fend for herself again but also to adjust to her old environment or worse.

Philip soon arrived from nearby Eton and Laura was relieved to find that the boy had his own niche in the life of the country house. He showed no surprise at finding a new face in the nursery and no resentment at the fact that his old nanny had been retired. His self-reliance was remarkable and, Laura thought, unhealthy. She tried to encourage more contact between brother and sister, but neither child seemed to welcome the idea and the age gap between them was too great to give them much in common.

On the third day after Philip's arrival, Laura discovered that it was not only his self-reliance which was unhealthy when he rushed from the tea-table and vomited violently in the bathroom. Inquiries revealed that he also had a headache and a sore throat. Laura felt his burning forehead, ordered him to bed and summoned the doctor. Two days later a faint rash appeared on his neck and chest and in the armpits and groin.

'Scarlet fever,' groaned Laura. 'He must have caught it at school. I hope to goodness he has not given it to Miranda.'

Miranda and the nursery-maids were removed to other quarters while Laura, who had had scarlet fever as a child and was therefore considered immune to another attack, nursed the sick boy. He had reached the stage of 'strawberry tongue' when it become evident that Miranda's isolation had been in vain. It was when she went down with the illness that Laura's nightmare really began, because Miranda's case was far more severe than her brother's. In addition to the more common symptoms, the little girl developed abscesses in the ears which caused excruciating earache and the child screamed and sobbed with pain. For Laura it was three weeks of hell as she tried to cope with the demands of the children, plus the moods and concern of Sir Matthew, while struggling to keep going with the minimum of sleep.

It was a pale and noticeably thinner trio which later sat on the terrace in the balmy spring sunshine. Laura was tucking rugs more firmly round the convalescents.

'You're very much better now, Philip,' she said brightly, 'and you should try to start doing a little more. Your strength needs building up before you go back to school.'

'There's nothing I feel like doing,' he said listlessly.

'Oh, come on Philip, there are lots of things to do. Why not go down to the stables to see your father's lovely horses? He has a colt in training for the Derby, I believe, and there must be lots of horses for you to ride yourself.'

'I am not very fond of horses.'

'What are you fond of?' There must be something which interested this lonely, withdrawn boy.

'Motor cars. But Papa doesn't allow me in the Daimler.'

'I'm sure you must be mistaken there. Why, a ride in the car would be the very thing to bring some colour to your cheeks.'

'I am not mistaken,' said Philip obstinately.

'Here comes your father now. If I ask him, I am sure he will agree.'

'Don't ask him!' Philip's voice was so vehement that Laura looked at him in surprise. 'I don't want any favours from *him*!'

The boy stared sullenly at the garden as his father strode across the terrace and bent to kiss Miranda. After talking to the child for a few minutes, but without taking any notice of Philip, Matthew beckoned Laura aside.

'I must return to London, Miss Vaughan. I have neglected my business interests for too long. We shall leave tomorrow.'

'*We?*'

'Naturally Miranda will accompany me, which means that you will come too.'

'Sir Matthew, that is quite impossible.'

'Nothing is impossible, Miss Vaughan, particularly to me,' thundered Matthew at his most intimidating.

Laura drew herself up to her full height of five feet, five inches and glared into his furious face. 'You must see, Sir Matthew, that Miranda needs plenty of country air and sunshine. She is still far from well and is not likely to find such fresh air in the heart of London. Besides, Philip needs me here too.'

'Philip must go back to school.'

'Don't be ridiculous.' Laura was quite forgetting to whom she was speaking. 'It will be several weeks before we can even consider his return to Eton.'

'I will be the judge of that!'

'Not in this instance, Sir Matthew. *Both* your children need to stay here in the country in order to recover their strength.'

They stood glaring defiantly at each other.

Minanda's welfare was the deciding factor. She was all the world to Matthew, perfect in every way. The high standards he set for her behaviour and education were intended to ensure that her mind should be as flawless as her body.

'Very well, but make sure that Philip does not pass on some other disease to Miranda.'

'You cannot possibly blame Philip for Miranda's illness,' exclaimed Laura incredulously. 'If it was anyone's fault it was mine, for encouraging more contact between them. Your son and daughter are strangers to each other, Sir Matthew, and that cannot be a good thing.'

Matthew turned away without another word and returned to the house. Laura's heart sank. She had won the day, but it was probably at the expense of her job. She walked back to the children and stood behind Miranda's chair.

'Look at that lovely bird!' she said. 'Do you know what it is?'

'Of course. It's a woodpecker,' Philip replied.

'Good. Can you see it, Miranda? It's the green woodpecker and rather difficult to see against the grass.'

Miranda still did not reply.

'Miranda, you're not paying attention,' scolded Laura. She crouched beside the chair and pointed to the bird. 'Over there. Look!'

The little girl followed the direction of Laura's finger and smiled. 'Pretty bird,' she said.

'The green woodpecker. Look at its red crown and when it flies you can see it has a yellow bottom.'

Miranda smiled again. What a good girl she was, Laura thought with a rush of affection. Always so obedient and eager to please. But she seemed pathetically pale and withdrawn after her illness and Laura racked her brains for ways to amuse the child.

There was a noticeable easing in the atmosphere after Matthew left. Philip relaxed and became a most pleasant companion. A bond had been forged between them in the sick-room and Laura tried conscientiously to treat both children equally and to show no favouritism to Miranda, although the girl was recovering more slowly from her illness. Miranda missed her father for the first few days, but she too sensed that his absence lessened the pressure upon her. For the first time in their lives Philip and Miranda were having a holiday together in their own home with someone who loved and understood them.

For Laura the new freedom meant the opportunity to do her best for the children without constantly looking over her shoulder to watch Sir Matthew's reaction. Also, she abandoned her 'disguise' temporarily and indulged herself by dressing her hair becomingly. It was pleasant to look in the mirror and see a familiar face again.

One of the first things Laura did was to speak to the driver of Sir Matthew's Daimler.

'Why doesn't he use it in London?' she asked.

'I don't know, Miss Vaughan. Absolute waste it is, keeping it here. I never take the car out except to go to the station to meet the London train.'

'The doctor has ordered that Master Philip and Miss Miranda should have plenty of fresh air after their illness,' Laura continued guilelessly. 'And I was thinking that a drive in the car would be ideal.'

'Sir Matthew never did seem to want Master Philip in the car,' said the chauffeur doubtfully.

'Didn't he? Oh dear, then I suppose I must order the pony and trap after all.'

'Wait a minute.' The chauffeur was obviously torn between his desire to drive his beloved Daimler and his respect for his employer's wishes. 'I gathered it was some sort of punishment for the young fellow, but it's more than two years ago now. I expect Sir Matthew has forgotten all about it.'

Laura treated him to a glance of gratitude from her emerald eyes, and within the hour she and the two children were bowling through the Berkshire countryside. An overjoyed Philip sat in front beside the driver, directing a barrage of questions at him and displaying such an unusual knowledge of the subject that they became fast friends. Miranda had ridden in the car fairly frequently, but never before had it seemed such fun.

The outings became a regular feature of each day and soon restored the roses to the cheeks of the convalescents. Laura was surprised, therefore, to receive a message one morning that the car would not be available because the chauffeur had to meet the Paddington train at Reading station.

'Never mind!' she comforted the disappointed children. 'We will go for a walk instead. Perhaps we can go for a drive this afternoon.'

It was a glorious day with a fresh breeze which whipped Laura's skirts as she walked. She was thoroughly tired of her drab governess garb and had decided to welcome spring by donning her favourite burgundy skirt and short fitted coat with a fresh white blouse. They set off towards the lake, where they searched for wild flowers and tried to see how many they could name. Philip was a changed boy, laughing and joking and touchingly patient with Miranda who seemed slow to learn and stumbled over the names of the flowers.

'We must hurry now or we shall be late for lunch,' said Laura in mock horror. 'Come on, we'll run. Philip, take Miranda's other hand.'

Laughing, they ran across the lawns towards the rose garden. The wind and the exercise loosened the coil of Laura's hair so that it tumbled down her back. Hand-in-hand the trio raced round the hedge, only to stop abruptly in their tracks as they were suddenly confronted by two people strolling in the rose garden.

'Lady Julia . . .' said Laura faintly.

Julia said nothing, but stared in blank amazement at the group before her, Laura could feel a crimson tide washing over her face, its intensity increased by a very odd look in the eyes of Lady Julia's companion.

Laura and the children made a charming picture: Philip, slim and tall for his age with Anne's silver-gilt hair and violet eyes: Miranda, who possessed Matthew's tawny gold colouring and an angelic face; and Laura herself, hair blowing in the breeze, vivid emerald eyes sparkling and the curves of her figure accentuated by the burgundy suit; all three of them smiling and laughing, exuding an aura of artless innocence and happiness.

'My apologies, Lady Julia. I did not know you were expected.'

'Evidently.' Julia found her voice at last. 'It was a sudden decision. I wished to see how the invalids were progressing and how you were liking the job. It seems my interest was misplaced and unnecessary.'

Laura was so startled by the acidity in Lady Julia's voice that she could think of no suitable reply and the embarrassing silence was finally broken by Lady Julia's companion.

'Aren't you going to introduce me, Julia?' he asked.

Julia fixed him with a furious look and said in strangled tones: 'Laura, my brother Charles, the Earl of Highclere. Charles, you know perfectly well that Miss Vaughan is the *governess*.'

'Hello, Laura.'

The message in his eyes was unmistakable. His burning glance was raking every part of her and mentally stripping the clothes from her body. She did not answer him, but unconsciously gripped Miranda's hand a little tighter.

'I must take the children indoors. We will see you after lunch, Lady Julia.'

'Let's all lunch together,' suggested Charles easily. 'Julia and I can't stay long. We're en route to Highclere and must catch the afternoon train to Newbury.'

Laura's heart sank, but she could tell that the expression on the Earl's face had not escaped the notice of his sister. Lady Julia would certainly veto the suggestion, she thought. To her surprise, however, Lady Julia's gaze rested thoughtfully on her brother before returning to Laura's flushed face.

'An excellent idea,' she said.

The meal was torture for Laura. Neither of the children seemed pleased to see their cousins, Philip had reverted to his former sullen self and although Miranda smiled prettily and politely she seemed loth to join in the conversation. Laura's tentative questions about Lady Jane and the school received monosyllabic replies from Julia and only the Earl ate heartily.

'Miranda, it's time for your afternoon rest,' Laura said as she helped her climb down from the table. Philip was already sidling through the door.

'I have a letter to write,' announced Julia. 'It will take me half an hour or so.' She gave her brother a conspiratorial smile and left the room.

Charles looked utterly astonished, but quickly made the most of his opportunity and said, 'I'll come with you, Laura. We can have a little chat while Miranda sleeps.'

'I don't think . . .' Laura began, but Charles had picked up Miranda and was carrying her towards the stairs.

How unfortunate that it was Hetty's day off, thought Laura as she took as long as possible over putting Miranda to bed, and found numerous other small jobs to do. But she could not avoid him forever. He shut Miranda's bedroom door and trapped her against the wall of the nursery, his hands flat against the wall-paper and his body pressing close to hers. She could smell the wine on his breath and tried to turn her face aside.

'Pretending to be shy!' he leered. 'You women are all the same! But I don't mind, I enjoy the chase.'

'I am not pretending, sir. Please let me go.'

'You don't fool me, Miss Laura. No one with a body like yours and eyes that flash green fire can possibly be so innocent.'

I will never leave my room again without those damned spectacles, vowed Laura.

'This scene is ridiculous,' she said with an effort at calmness. 'Please let me go and we will say no more about it.'

'It was not conversation that I had in mind.'

'Someone might come in,' and Laura stifled an hysterical laugh as she suddenly recalled hearing those very words in the library at Park Lane. She stared resolutely into the face which was only inches away from hers. One could see a resemblance to Sir Matthew but the features were coarser and ruddier, with an arrogance born more of rank and privilege than the self-confidence which was part of Sir Matthew's irresistible attraction.

'For reasons best known to herself, my sister has blessed our union and there is no one else who can do anything to stop it.'

His hands dropped from the wall and one arm encircled her roughly while the fingers of the other hand tore at the buttons of her jacket and blouse and plunged inside to encircle her breast. Laura fought and squirmed to escape him, but he was tall and broad and strong and he held her easily, laughing delightedly at her efforts. She realised that her resistance was arousing him all the more. Then his wet lips were on hers and although she twisted and turned desperately in his grip, Laura realised that if he intended to rape her there was nothing she could do about it.

She was summoning her remaining strength for one last rally when she heard the door open, there was a loud yell and the Earl's grip on her suddenly relaxed. As Laura ducked past him and headed for the freedom of the corridor, she saw the furious figure of Philip pummelling the Earl in the back. With fists flailing and face livid with rage, he was shouting, 'You shan't hurt her, you shan't!' He clung tenaciously to his cousin's coat and although Charles took vicious swipes behind him it was like watching a bear try to swat a gnat. There was a loud rending sound as the Earl's jacket seams tore apart.

'Blast you!' shouted Charles, but Philip did not flag. He came at his cousin again, pounding his fists against his chest.

The noise brought Julia to the door; she eyed the combatants and Laura's dishevelled state and frowned.

'You disappoint me, Laura,' she said coldly. 'I had thought you maintained better control over the children than this.'

'It wasn't her fault,' yelled Philip, who was breathing heavily from his exertions. 'Charles was hurting her.'

'Perhaps,' returned Julia, 'Laura wanted him to . . . hurt her.'

'She didn't, she was shouting for help.'

'Yes,' said Laura firmly, 'I most certainly was.'

'I'm sure you must have misunderstood my brother's intentions, Laura,' said Julia smoothly. 'You must allow him to rectify the matter. We were saying earlier, weren't we, Charles, that it would be a splendid plan for Laura and Miranda to spend some time at Highclere.'

Charles cast another look of astonishment at Julia but nodded enthusiastically. 'Marvellous idea! Miss Laura and I need an opportunity to improve our acquaintance.' He glared at Philip. 'But he's not invited.'

'Oh no,' agreed Julia, 'we don't want Philip.'

'Philip will be returning to school next week,' said Laura icily. 'And Sir Matthew wishes Miranda and me to return to London.'

'I will speak to him about it. Charles, go downstairs and find someone to mend that coat. Tell them it was torn in a game with the children.'

After he had gone, Julia turned to Laura. How often had Matthew seen her like this, she wondered – the tumbled hair in glorious profusion, green eyes flashing in the lovely face and that full bosom rising and falling with the intensity of her emotions. Well, Matthew would not want her after Charles had used her! The venom rose in Julia again and she spat out her parting thrust:

'You must forgive my brother, Laura. He has a penchant for *lower-class* girls.'

She swept out of the room and Laura closed the door, leaning against it thankfully as the customary peace of the nursery returned.

'I hate her,' said Philip abruptly. 'She called me a coward once. I'll never forgive her for that.'

Laura saw that he was trembling. She wondered if she ought to invent some story about the scene between herself and the Earl, but Philip was nearly fourteen and she was sure he knew very well what his cousin had tried to do.

'Thank you for protecting me, Philip,' she said, and she opened her arms. He flew into them but as he buried his head against her breast, felt her soft cheek against his hair and inhaled the sweet scent of her, Philip was prey to a surge of emotions which he had only dreamed about until now.

Matthew did not permit his daughter to visit Highclere. Julia's entreaties were apparently in vain and Laura breathed more easily. It was necessary, however, to tread carefully at Park Lane for Matthew's moods were volatile and his temper short. The reason for his irritation was known to everyone: he had tired of the Princess Raminska but she would not let him go. As spring burgeoned into early summer, it seemed that Matthew could not set foot outside his door without being accosted by her. She was present at every function he attended, talked to him loudly and excitedly on political affairs as if politics was the cause of their estrangement, and could even be observed laying siege to his home and his office. The gossip columns were in their element and gleefully reported the progress of the quarrel without actually mentioning names.

'No one takes any notice of this sort of rubbish,' said Matthew to Nicholas disdainfully, tossing the newspaper to one side.

Unfortunately for Matthew, however, someone was taking notice and the Princess received a visit from a man called Connor.

The name had an immediate effect on Matthew and Katherine smiled triumphantly.

'Come outside,' he said and preceded her to the terrace of the Amblesides' London home, away from the crowded ballroom.

'IDB, Matthew,' Katherine taunted, shaking her head sadly. 'I would never have thought it of you. I always believed you to be a man of subtlety.'

'Connor was the IDB merchant, not me. What else did he tell you?'

'About your involvement with Barnato and Woolf Joel in a plot to overthrow the Transvaal government. Why, Matthew, did you waste so much breath in telling me you were not interested in politics? You never succeeded in convincing me and now I have proof.'

'Proof! You don't have any proof. Connor's story is a tissue of lies.'

'True or false, it makes a very interesting story.'

'A story which you are hoping I don't wish to have spread abroad?'

'Of course.'

'What is the price of your silence?'

'I had hoped that you would marry me.' Katherine watched his face and sighed as she saw his murderous expression. 'Alternatively, I will settle for cash . . . a considerable amount of cash.'

'Why doesn't Connor do his own blackmailing?'

'He said that you would squash him like an insect beneath your feet. *I* am a more formidable proposition.'

'The answer is still no.'

'How foolish of you, Matthew.'

'On the contrary, it is you who are foolish. I would never give in to blackmail demands, even if the allegations were true. If you spread false rumours about me I will sue you for blackmail and for forging cheques in my name – *and* I will notify the police that you claimed insurance money on the so-called theft of your fake jewellery.'

Matthew strode into the house, called his carriage and went

home. He was far more worried about this development than his attitude to the Princess indicated. He still feared that his acquisition of additional power and prestige in the Diamond Company, as a result of the deaths of Barnato and Joel, might be seen as sufficient reason for him to have engineered their murder. Proof most certainly would not be forthcoming, but in the City of London even the lightest coating of mud sticks firmly and smothers reputations without trace.

'That woman is driving me mad with her incessant attention. She pesters me morning, noon and night.'

Matthew was pacing the floor of the library while Nicholas relaxed in one of the deep armchairs.

'I must get away for a while – far away, to let her cool down. When I return, either she will leave me alone or I will feel in better shape to deal with her. I am going to South Africa.'

Nicholas sat bolt upright and gripped the arms of his chair.

'Please, Matthew, not South Africa. Anywhere but there.'

'Why not? There is some business to be settled in Kimberley; I had intended to send someone else, but it would be an excellent thing if I saw to it myself.'

'You cannot go away now,' said Nicholas, floudering for obstacles to put in Matthew's path. 'The children need you here.'

'Philip can spend the summer holidays at Brightwell, Desborough or Highclere. Naturally, Miranda will come with us.'

'*Us?*'

'The trip will do you good. We haven't been out of England for ages.'

'I will travel with you anywhere, at any time, you know that. But it is out of the question that you should take Miranda. War clouds are gathering.'

'Miss Vaughan will accompany us. She is an extremely competent and sensible young woman and I have formed a considerable respect for her. She will take good care of Miranda. As for war clouds, I don't think they will come to anything. Kruger is bluffing – he'll never dare to take on the British army.'

'I hope you're right. But there is a school of opinion which believes he is stupid or fanatical enough to try.'

'If it's any comfort to you, Kimberley is a long way from Pretoria. We will not travel north if it looks as though there may be trouble.'

'Matt, I hate to mention this because you were so jolly cross last time I spoke of it. But don't forget the warning John Court gave you.'

'Warning? What warning?'

'This chap, Danie Steyn or whatever his name is, who wants to kill you.'

'Oh, *that*! Don't be such an old woman, Nicky. How can you possibly expect me to take such nonsense seriously? I'm going and that's final.'

Part Four

KIMBERLEY
OCTOBER 1899–FEBRUARY 1900

CHAPTER ONE

It was the second week of October and to Laura the heat of Kimberley was stifling and enervating. She rested in the shade on the stoep while Miranda had her afternoon nap, dozing limply. Roused by the sound of footsteps, she looked up to see Nicholas puffing towards her.

'I hope I'm not disturbing you,' he said, plumping down in a chair beside her. 'I thought I would find you here.'

Laura smiled at him. She had become fond of Lord Nicholas during the months they had travelled together. He was unfailingly courteous and pleasant, never too lofty to take notice of a humble governess and always pointing out places of interest and concerning himself with her comfort. 'The garden gives me much pleasure,' she said. 'It is by far the loveliest in Kimberley.'

'This garden was the work of my sister.' Nicholas's eyes rested reminiscently on the lawns as he visualised Anne walking there. 'I was surprised to find how well it had been looked after in the years since she left.'

'It provides a haven of peace for Miranda and me because in truth, Lord Nicholas, there is nowhere else to go. Once one has seen the diamond mine, one has seen everything Kimberley has to offer. And for me, one visit to the mine is enough!'

Laura shuddered at the memory of their sightseeing trip. Underground mining was in progress at Kimberley and operations were dominated by a huge steel headgear which stood starkly against the sky. Matthew had explained that a main shaft had been sunk adjacent to the diamond pipe. A system of tunnels linked the shaft with the diamond-bearing ground and in these tunnels the miners toiled, loading the blueground into skips which were hauled to the surface.

'Would you care to go down and take a closer look?' Matthew

had inquired casually, pointing at a small truck which apparently operated in the same shaft as the skips.

Laura's throat went dry as she imagined plunging into the blackness, to go hundreds of feet below ground into the hot labyrinths among the mass of workmen, in a flimsy vehicle which looked remarkably like an open coffin. The claustrophobia caused her throat to constrict and, unable to speak, she shook her head in answer to Matthew's invitation.

Laura disliked the mines; she disliked the noise and the heat and the dirt and dust. The end product, that small shining pebble, did not seem worth the trouble. But perhaps, Laura told herself wryly, her feelings were coloured by the indisputable fact that she was very unlikely ever to own a diamond.

'Matthew,' Lord Nicholas was saying, 'was disappointed that Miranda did not take more interest.'

'She's only five,' exclaimed Laura. 'It's hardly likely that a little girl of that age would be the least interested in all that machinery.'

'I hope she falls victim to its fatal fascination when she's older, for her sake. Matthew is dead set on both Miranda and Philip going into the business.'

'So that is why she has to be well-educated! It's an unusual step, to prepare a girl for such a career.'

'Matthew is an unusual sort of fellow.'

Laura did not reply. The mention of Philip's name had taken the smile from her face.

'Every day I hope for a letter from Philip,' she said slowly, 'but it never comes. Has he written to his father?'

'I don't know, but I very much doubt it.'

'He was terribly upset when we came to South Africa without him. I went to see him at school and tried to explain what his father had said – that the journey here was too long to be undertaken in the school holidays – but I could tell Philip didn't believe it. He thinks we just didn't want him. He said: "I was so looking forward to the summer holidays. I thought we could have fun together like we did before. I might have known you would side with Papa and Miranda against me. I thought you were different, but you're just like all the others." He gave me a look of pure hatred and walked away and I never felt more guilty and miserable in my life.'

'Don't worry about it.' Nicholas patted her hand comfortingly and trotted out the standard family phrase: 'Philip is difficult.'

'He *isn't* difficult! Nobody has ever cared for him enough to get to know him. I have nightmares thinking about him spending those summer holidays alone. We must make it up to him at Christmas. I do hope we won't be staying in Kimberley much longer.'

Nicholas gave one of his awkward coughs. 'That's actually why I wanted to speak to you,' he said apologetically. 'We might in fact be in for a prolonged stay.'

'Why?'

'The Boers have delivered an ultimatum.'

'Does that mean we are at war?'

'Not *quite*,' said Nicholas, 'but almost. Let me explain what has been happening. You will remember, no doubt, the Jameson Raid which was sparked off by the grievances of the so-called *uitlanders* in the Transvaal. Last year the *uitlanders* sent a petition to Queen Victoria, setting out these grievances and asking for British support. In the meantime, Lord Alfred Milner had been appointed Governor of the Cape and he strongly supported the case for British intervention. President Steyn of the Free State, fearing war between the two groups, arranged a meeting in Bloemfontein between Kruger and Milner, but the talks were a failure. Kruger would not grant the franchise to British subjects in the Transvaal and nothing less than equal rights would satisfy Milner.'

'They sound extremely uncompromising people.'

'Exactly so, Miss Vaughan,' agreed Nicholas. 'While I have the greatest respect for Lord Milner, it does appear that he is quite the wrong person to be dealing with the Transvaal President. They will never see eye to eye. Anyway, Milner persuaded the British government to send troops to South Africa and they have been arriving at the Cape in recent months. The build-up of these forces has been interpreted by the Transvaal and the Orange Free State as a threat to their independence.'

'So the Free State has allied itself with the Transvaal?'

'I am afraid so. Two days ago, on 9 October, an ultimatum was presented to Britain – either we withdraw the troops or a state of war will exist between us.'

'What do you think Britain will say?'

'I can't see us acceding to such an impertinent demand, can you?'

Speculation was ended when Matthew strode across the verandah towards them; a rejuvenated Matthew, with a spring in his step and blue eyes sparkling in a face tanned by the African sun.

'It's war!' he shouted. 'We have refused to meet the Boers' terms.'

'Hurrah!' cried Nicholas. 'We'll show 'em.'

'It won't come anywhere near here, will it?' asked Laura, trying not to sound alarmed.

'Yes,' said Matthew, 'I'm afraid it will.'

'I did come to tell you.' Nicholas sounded apologetic again. 'Rumour says that we may be besieged.'

'*Besieged!*' Laura stared from one to the other incredulously. 'Isn't there time for us to get away?'

'The railway line is still open,' Matthew said. 'Incidentally, Nicky, there's a message from Rhodes – he's on his way! However, Miss Vaughan, we shall not be leaving.'

It must be all a bad dream, Laura said to herself. This cannot possibly be happening to me.

'Why shall we not be leaving?' She faced Matthew resolutely.

'Don't you want to be a heroine, Miss Vaughan?' countered Matthew.

'It is not a question of what I want. I happen to think that Miranda is too young to be a heroine!'

'There is no real danger, I assure you. And to answer your question, I will not leave here for three reasons. First, no bloody Boer is going to push me around. Second, I am a Director of the Diamond Company and it is my duty to set an example and assume responsibility for our employees. Third, and most important, I am staying for the same reason Cecil Rhodes is travelling here. This is *our* town, Miss Vaughan. We built it. I came here when this was bare veld with a rocky hill sticking up out of it – a hill we called Colesberg Kopje. I grubbed in the dirt with my bare hands to find the diamonds which have made the city famous. I worked in the heat and dust, I beat off the flies and the claim-jumpers. Kimberley is part of me and anyone who tries to take it has to reckon with me first!'

Matthew went to his room and slumped into a chair, closing his eyes. Already he was regretting his spontaneous outburst. He must be feeling the heat more than he realised; or else he was a trifle overwrought. This morning's mail – probably the last delivery they would receive if the rumours were true – had brought a packet from London. Looking at the writing and the registration, Matthew had laughed and joked that Reynolds was 'sending coals to Newcastle'. It was indeed a diamond, but the sight of it had brought pain to Matthew's heart as he gazed upon the well-remembered pear-shaped drop. The Comtesse de Gravigny was dead and had bequeathed the diamond to Matthew. And Reynolds wished to resign his position in Matthew's service.

This was the end of an era; Matthew felt it most strongly. Ever since he had arrived in Kimberley he had been living in the past. Not even the more recent past – his thoughts were not of Anne or Victoria or the consolidation of the mines. No, his mind was focused on the beginning of his adventures, thirty years ago, when he had first dreamed of El Dorado. He saw again the open veld covered only by scrub and thorn bushes, the thousands of men scrambling like ants in their claims; heard once more the shouts of joy as treasure was unearthed.

As he held the Comtesse's diamond in his hand, Matthew knew that Kimberley was his fate and it was right and proper that he should be here at its moment of crisis. That spark of goodness which the Comtesse had divined so many years ago, flickered and then began to burn more brightly.

On Saturday 14 October Laura hitched up her skirts and followed Matthew and Nicholas up the gentle slope of a debris dump on the outskirts of the town. Around the city were a number of these dumps, formed by the 'tailings' of mud left after the blueground had been washed for diamonds, which were to be used as look-out posts and defensive positions. The tallest point in the town, the steel headgear of the Kimberley mine, would form a conning tower and another lookout post had been set up at the Reservoir.

'I can't see any enemy,' said Laura, rather disappointed. She had adapted to the idea of being besieged surprisingly swiftly and was infected by the general air of excitement pervading the town.

'They're there all right. They seem to be massing in the vicinity of Scholtz's Nek, about ten miles south of here.'

'Will they come any closer?'

'Yes, but no nearer than three or four miles. The terrain is too flat and open to afford them cover from our guns.'

'How many guns do we have?'

Matthew laughed shortly. 'Only twelve – but I hope the Boers don't know that! And to anticipate your next question, Colonel Kekewich, the garrison commander, has about four thousand men at his disposal, comprising troops from the North Lancashire Regiment, the Kimberley Regiment and the Town Guard which is a civilian militia made up of every shop-boy, clerk and artisan who can tote a rifle. There is also a contingent of Cape Police.'

'Four thousand doesn't sound very many,' said Laura doubtfully, squinting through her spectacles at the ugly town which sprawled in ungainly fashion for miles in each direction.

'It's not a great many,' agreed Matthew. 'We are evacuating the outlying farms and homesteads and bringing the people into the city, but even so there will be about thirteen miles of border to protect and a population within the city of approximately forty-five thousand. But don't worry, Miss Vaughan. We only have to hold out for a short while until reinforcements arrive.'

'What will the Boers do first?'

'Break our communications, if they can. We're expecting them to start today. I have a feeling that Rhodes came in on the last train we are likely to see for a while. And the Boers will cut the telegraph wires as well, of course.'

'I don't understand why they should besiege Kimberley. Is it the diamonds they want?'

Matthew shook his head. 'No, I don't think so, although there would be enormous prestige in capturing a town as famous as Kimberley. But that is not their main objective in this case. Other Boer commandos are heading for Dundee and Ladysmith in Natal, and Mafeking to our north. Those towns are garrisoned and we think the Boers are trying to neutralise the British forces stationed here before reinforcements can arrive.'

'That sounds like clever tactics.'

'I'm not quite so sure.' Matthew frowned. 'It isn't the sort of thing the Boer is good at. We saw in the previous war of 1880–1881 that the Boer is a brilliant horseman and an excellent sharp-shooter. His great advantage is his knowledge of the terrain and his mobility over that terrain, coupled with an uncanny ability to merge with the landscape and fire crippling volleys at solid ranks of British infantry. Now, what is he doing here?' Matthew pointed into the distance. 'He is tying himself down behind rigid defences and heavy guns. And think of the number of men needed to encircle Kimberley, Mafeking and Ladysmith all at the same time! In addition, he needs other forces to take on the Relief Columns which will march to our aid. Damn it, Miss Vaughan, the entire white population of both Boer republics only numbers about 300,000. I do not understand the Boers' tactics and I certainly do not understand how they can remotely expect to win this war.'

'Then why are they fighting?'

'Don't ask me. Go out there and ask one of them.'

'I cannot even see why *we* are fighting. Oh, I know about the ultimatum, but surely Great Britain is powerful enough to ignore it?'

'It is more a matter of Great Britain wanting to remain great,' said Matthew soberly. 'There is a lot of competition these days, both in Europe and here in Africa, with envious countries eyeing our colonies and our trade. We have to prove that we are not to be ordered about by a twopenny-halfpenny republic like the Transvaal and that, on the contrary, such recalcitrance will be dealt with swiftly and sharply.'

'I do hope that no one gets hurt in the process.'

'Are you afraid of being hit by a shell, Miss Vaughan?'

'Actually, Sir Matthew, I am much more afraid of not having enough to eat.'

Matthew took her arm and pointed towards the city. 'That area over there is called Kenilworth and I promise you it is swarming with oxen. Have no fear, you will not starve.'

'It would be rather a tragedy if the Boers shelled the cattle. We would have fresh meat galore for a few days and then it would go bad.'

'I don't think there is any need to worry about that. Now, over there is Rhodes's house. He's already furious with Colonel Kekewich and is setting up a rival headquarters. Have you seen Rhodes, Miss Vaughan?'

'Yes, but only from a distance. I thought he looked ill. His hair is grey and his face is purple and puffy.'

Matthew chuckled. 'You would never think he is three years younger than me, would you? His birthday is the same day as poor old Barney's and Barney was two years younger than me.' His face clouded for a moment, then he cheered up again. 'I shall outlive the lot of them. They let themselves go to seed.'

No one could accuse Sir Matthew of letting himself go, thought Laura. He looked about thirty-five with his fair hair untouched by grey and a look of boyish glee on his face at the siege arrangements going on around him. He had appeared this morning in cotton shirt, corduroys and polished high boots and he looked tough and hard and ready for action.

'I must go now. Miranda is getting on very well with the native nanny, but she likes me there when she wakes up. Sir Matthew, one last question: how long do you think the siege will last?'

'Oh, a couple of weeks – three at the most.'

'So we could still be home for Christmas?'

'Easily.'

'Thank goodness! I really couldn't bear to disappoint Philip again.'

As she left, Nicholas spoke for the first time.

'First-class woman, that. But you know, Matt, I can't understand why she hides behind those awful spectacles and that ghastly bun. She'd be a fine-looking woman without 'em.'

'Would she? I hadn't noticed,' said Matthew absently, his mind patently elsewhere. 'Nicky, she's got a point about the cattle. It would be a disaster if our friends killed the lot at one fell swoop. We must build a refrigeration plant.'

'Easier said than done, old chap.'

'Not at all. The Company workshop can do it. They manufacture and repair all the mining machinery and it would be a matter of simplicity for them to turn their hands to more military pursuits. Let's go and see Rhodes – he's already busy with a signalling mechanism.'

'You're enjoying yourself.'

'I certainly am! This is going to be the most stimulating three weeks of my life.'

Danie Steyn gulped the hot strong coffee and made himself more comfortable on his blanket on the hard ground. He watched the leisurely arrival of the Free State commandos – a steady stream of horsemen, guns, cattle and wagons grouping into a series of camps and forming a rough ring which eventually would encircle Kimberley. In a few days' time another line would be made, well forward of the camps: a line of redoubts and guns, placed between two to three miles from the city wherever the terrain offered natural shelter and out of range of the British cannon. But now the scene was relaxed and happy, more like a picnic than a preparation for war, as the burghers greeted family and old friends. Danie smiled. There was no hurry; they would be here for a long time.

For weeks, while Kruger delayed his ultimatum until the spring grass provided fodder for horses and cattle, Pretoria had been a military camp. Since the Jameson Raid, Kruger had prepared for war and had imported guns, rifles and ammunition from France and Germany. Now the Transvaal hills echoed with the crack of rifles as the burghers practised with their Mauser carbines. Their bandoliers were stuffed with ammunition and their saddlebags were packed. Not for the Boers the problems of lumbering supply routes. They travelled light on their horses, with a flask of brandy and a bundle of dried meat or 'biltong'; their fresh meat was driven before them on the hoof. When the call to war came, they were ready.

Like all male burghers aged between sixteen and sixty, Danie had been called up for military service. But like all his compatriots he could choose where, with whom and for how long he served. Danie had chosen to come south with a band of his neighbours who had links with the Free State. Although he bivouacked with them now, his ties with them were tenuous. Danie was not only on commando but was acting as a war correspondent for *De Volksstem*. He would go wherever there was a story and he had maintained that the capture of Cecil Rhodes in Kimberley would be very good news indeed. However, he had told no one of the real reason for his presence here – that he knew Matthew Bright, with his daughter and brother-in-law, was inside the beleaguered city.

The men were shouting joyfully that already the first blow of the war had been struck and that the British forces in Mafeking, commanded by Baden-Powell, had been isolated. Momentarily Danie's mind moved from Kimberley to the larger theatre of war. In his heart he disliked the siege strategy, but had supported it for his own personal reasons. Moreover, he had urged war on his people for so long that he could not now quibble over tactics.

Danie did not know whether or not his people could win the war; they would certainly be heavily outnumbered in the long term. The Boers had mustered about sixty thousand men and at the moment enjoyed numerical superiority over the British. But British reinforcements would soon arrive, and then the balance would be reversed. Danie experienced a growing sense of urgency and agitation to get on with the job before the odds against the Boers lengthened. The siege strategy demanded time and patience and did not utilise the great strengths of the Boer forces. And Danie was only too well aware of their greatest weakness – lack of discipline. No burgher could be ordered to do anything against his will and, since he could return home whenever he wanted, no commander ever knew how many men would turn up for battle.

But win or lose, Danie was satisfied that *his* objectives would be realised. His chief aim was the unification of the Boer people. A significant step had already been taken in that direction with the alliance of the Transvaal and the Free State in this war. Since the Jameson Raid the Cape Boers had been increasingly sympathetic. As soon as Transvaalers and Free Staters began dying in a hail of British bullets, their Cape and Natal kinsmen would rise in rebellion.

Danie's second objective was personal. He took a swig of brandy from his flask and stared across the veld towards the Diamond City. Many men would die in this war, but it gave him a unique opportunity to claim his own victim.

CHAPTER TWO

'Your three weeks is up,' Laura said to Matthew, 'but the siege has not been lifted.'

It was the afternoon of Sunday 5 November and they had brought Miranda to the Public Gardens. After a dust storm the previous day, the sun shone from a cloudless sky and the Gardens were thronged with people. The atmosphere was carefree, the Boers were chaffed, and the crowd awaited with anticipation a concert by the combined bands of the Kimberley and Lancashire Regiments.

'It seems that our original estimate may have been a trifle optimistic,' Matthew admitted.

'Just a trifle,' agreed Laura sarcastically. 'Yesterday the Boers displayed what can only be described as ominous energy: digging trenches, erecting forts and generally making themselves comfortable. They seem to believe our submission is inevitable.'

'Commandant Wessels demanded the surrender of the city yesterday. He was told to take it – if he could!'

'So I heard. I also heard that the bombardment of Kimberley would be the painful alternative to refusal. How many guns do they have?'

'Their shells are falling short,' said Matthew defensively, but under Laura's relentless stare, he admitted reluctantly, 'The garrison have confirmed four enemy guns so far, but are sure the Boers will bring up more.'

'Then,' said Laura, 'we shall have to hope that the Boers' aim does not improve.'

She looked about her with pleasure, at the finery of the ladies and at the musicians assembling on the bandstand.

'The concert is about to begin,' she told Miranda. 'Thank

goodness the Boers are such devout people that they refuse to fight on Sundays.'

Laura spoke too soon, however, for at that moment the fiendish banshee wail of the mine-hooters shattered the peace of the afternoon, announcing activity in the Boer encampments. The noise was awe-inspiring and weird and Laura covered her ears while Matthew snatched Miranda into his arms and they all began running.

'I hate that noise,' panted Laura to Nicholas. 'It sounds like the cries of the unburied dead.'

They ran past huge posters proclaiming Martial Law and, in accordance with the provisions of that Law, headed straight home. Members of the Town Guard were hurrying to the Town Hall, from which they marched to the redoubts in orderly squads of four with grim, stern faces. The bandsmen laid aside their flutes for more deadly instruments and prepared to give the Boer as much music as he cared to face. It was a magnificent dissolution, rapidly accomplished.

'And, of course, it is all for nothing,' said Matthew as he set down Miranda in the safety of the house. 'As usual, there will be no attack. Wessels is a wag.'

'It is too bad of him to spoil the concert,' complained Laura resentfully. 'Poor Miranda! Are you very disappointed, darling?'

'No, I don't mind that but I am hungry, Laura. Please can I have some cake?'

Laura sighed. The little eyes were so wistful and Miranda was not a child who made frequent demands. It was heart-breaking to refuse. 'I'm sorry, but you know that we are not allowed to make cakes or pastries,' she said gently. 'There is not enough flour. When the Relief Column comes, you shall have the biggest cake you have ever seen.'

'Will they come tomorrow?'

'You had better ask your Papa,' said Laura impishly and with a degree of familiarity which would have been unthinkable at Park Lane. The unusual conditions under which they lived in this comparatively small house had broken down many of the barriers between the governess and her employers, and already Laura was acting more as housekeeper than governess. She ordered the meals, looked after the rations and organised the servants. The enforced economy of food and fuel made it practical for her to share Matthew's meals while the native servants ate in their own quarters. Matthew and Nicholas accepted her presence at their dining-table without question and it was distinctly to their credit, Laura felt, that they never made her feel *de trop*.

Another old thing about the past three weeks, she thought as she went to the kitchen to order tea, was that the ghastly shriek of the hooters aroused anger and resentment rather than fear. She wanted to giggle as she recalled the frantic scramble from the Gardens this afternoon. At this stage, the Siege of Kimberley definitely contained an element of farce.

In the kitchen, Laura instructed the cook to make tea while she took a large key from her bag and unlocked the larder. She disliked keeping the food under such strict control, but Sir Matthew insisted that it was absolutely necessary or else the servants would pilfer eveything in sight. The larder was well-stocked, but Laura only lifted down a jar of jam and took a slab of butter from the cold stone shelf. Cutting a loaf of bread into thick slices, she then carried the tray into the drawing-room.

'That awful bread,' groaned Nicholas as he saw the humble repast. 'It might well be an army loaf – it's as khaki in colour as their uniforms.'

'It doesn't taste too bad,' said Laura bracingly, 'and you must agree it's extremely sustaining. The colour is rather brown because each loaf must now consist of three parts meal to one part flour, from which I deduce we have a great deal of the former and very little of the latter.'

'That damn Colonel Kekewich and his Proclamations,' grumbled Nicholas, taking the tea-cup Laura handed to him. 'The meat ration is an insult – a mere half-pound per person per day. The man is a high-handed vegetarian!'

'Jam or butter, Sir Matthew?' asked Laura pointedly.

'Good God, woman, now you're going too far!' said Matthew violently. 'I'll have *both*. There's plenty of food in that larder and you know it.'

'Our larder is full because during the first few days of the siege the grocers put up their prices so much that only the very rich could afford to stockpile,' snapped Laura. 'And you brought home what looked like the contents of an entire shop. Plus the fact that we can obtain fresh vegetables from the Diamond Company's garden when all the produce is supposed to go to the hospital.'

'Nobody will miss those few vegetables,' said Matthew sulkily, spreading jam on his bread without the butter. 'Besides, what's the use of having a lot of money and being a director of the Diamond Company if one cannot enjoy a few privileges?' He brightened suddenly. 'I'm doing it for Miranda,' he said virtuously.

'I'm delighted that Miranda is not going without necessities. However, I do feel that we must join the rest of the populace in foregoing luxuries. The stocks in our larder and in the shops are likely to dwindle all too rapidly. The Colonel is right in imposing restrictions. We have no idea how long the food will have to last.'

'It won't have to last much longer if Rhodes has anything to do with it.' The thought of Rhodes overcame Matthew's ill-humour and brought a smile to his lips. 'He is sending irate signals, demanding immediate relief for the city.'

Rhodes had set up a powerful searchlight which had a brilliant beam and also revolved to illumine the surrounding countryside. Thus a surprise visit from the Boers at night was out of the question. However, he also used the searchlight to send morse code messages at night, while the military had a heliograph system for use during the day.

'Rhodes is absolutely hopping mad that no help has arrived,' Matthew went on. 'He came rushing up from Cape Town to do his bit for Kimberley, with the best of intentions, but the whole inconvenient episode has gone on far longer than he anticipated. I think he is beginning to wish he hadn't come here.'

'I think there are a great many other people who wish he hadn't come,' observed Nicholas. 'They think the Boers want Rhodes more than they want Kimberley itself. What about you, Matt? Don't you wish we had left before all this started?'

'Not on your life. It's a wonderful experience. I'm even prepared to confess that I hope it continues a bit longer. Being besieged is rather like being at sea – ordinary life with its mundane problems seems remote and unimportant. Here our problems are new and exciting and in a strange way I don't relish the prospect of taking up everyday responsibilities again.'

Neither do I, thought Laura, with a sudden shock of realisation. It was so pleasant sitting here, dispensing tea and talking to Sir Matthew and Lord Nicholas almost as though they were equals. In some ways they were – the Colonel's rationing measures had no respect for class. The curfew affected everyone equally, too. Laura no longer had to put a brave face on her omission from Kimberley's social events for the very good reason that a nine o'clock curfew and a dearth of refreshments prevented any such gatherings from taking place. Yes, it would be hard for her to return to her old subservient position and to go for days without seeing Matthew. Her eyes slid involuntarily to where he sat, the fashionable Sir Matthew Bright of Park Lane, munching a slice of second-rate bread and jam and seeming strangely at home in these humble circumstances. He had taken on the colour of Kimberley and blended with the background in a way which Laura and Nicholas had not managed to achieve. This is how he must have been when he was young, she thought – quick, vibrant and alive and eager to seize every opportunity.

However, she concealed her feelings with an acid retort. 'There have been five deaths already,' she said, 'and there will be more casualties if the siege continues. Miranda, time for bed now.'

'Do I have to wash tonight?' Miranda asked.

Laura laughed. The Boers had cut the water supply and although the Reservoir was about half-full, drought remained an appalling possibility and water had to be used with great circumspection.

'No, you washed this morning and that will have to do for today.' And as Miranda beamed, she murmured, 'There's always a bright side to everything, isn't there!' She only wished she could find a silver lining for herself.

Another week went by and Laura still had the same sensation of waiting for something to happen. Of the British forces there was still no sign. The Boers continued to fire at the city, but the shells fell short. The enemy placed a big gun on Wimbleton Ridge which was three to four miles away and out of range of the garrison's cannon, although the British seven-pounders regularly sounded a warning that the enemy artillery should not try to come too close. A few projectiles reached the town, but they were 'dead' missiles and did not explode. The souvenir hunters were out in force.

There was considerable elation in the town at the failure of the Boer as a gunner and the belief was entertained that his stock of ammunition would soon be blown to the winds. It was on the Saturday of this fourth week of the Siege that the mood changed and the joke went sour.

The city was startled from its slumbers at an early hour by the booming of artillery and a succession of explosions. The shells whistled and whizzed overhead and burst on contact with a loud crash. Witticisms about the Boers being unacquainted with the mysteries of a fuse, jokes asserting that they knew as little about 'timing' a shell as they did about discipline, or that they had 'forgotten the powder', no longer seemed amusing. They had remembered the powder this time; its odour was everywhere. Then, as consternation reigned, came the news that a woman had been killed in the Dutoitspan Road.

The British retaliated, but the bombardment was resumed in the afternoon. When peace finally fell over the town at six in the evening, Laura was still stunned by the news of the civilian casualty. The place where the victim – a poor washerwoman – had died was horrifyingly close to the Bright home. For the first time Laura whispered to herself that the victim might have been Miranda or Matthew or Nicholas and she wondered if it would be one of them next time.

The days dragged on in the stifling heat, under intermittent bombardment. Laura struggled to keep Miranda occupied and did her best to stretch the food rations, but boredom and ennui were her worst enemies. Nicholas strolled about the town, chatting to all and sundry, and making sure he returned to the house in good time for meals. Matthew was consumed with frustrated energy. He longed to seize a rifle and a horse and blast his way through the Boer lines. Since this was impossible, he embarked on a whirlwind of activity. With Rhodes, he set the Diamond Company workshop to manufacturing shells from mining explosives, each shell engraved 'With compliments from C.J.R.' Then he tackled the problem of the thirteen thousand natives who, since the mines closed, had lolled indolently about the town, drinking heavily and looting abandoned homes. At Matthew's suggestion, the most expert looters were recruited to loot from the enemy instead – a series of night raids on the Boer cattle were organised. Other men were employed at road-making. with Rhodes and Matthew personally putting up two thousand pounds a week.

But these civic activities were insufficient to satisfy Matthew's restless spirit. The mood of Kimberley had changed from joviality to frustration. The novelty of being besieged had worn off and like the rest of the populace, Matthew stared south and willed the Relief Column to arrive.

A heavy hailstorm was pelting Danie's tent, so heavy that the canvas seemed likely to be ripped open by the huge missiles. Danie listened morosely to the clatter of the storm and, like Matthew a couple of miles away, cursed the stalemate in the Kimberley Siege.

'You are not trying hard enough,' he had accused Wessels. 'All you do is send letters demanding surrender. We outnumber their fighting men by at least two to one. We must storm the city.'

'The ground is too open,' Wessels replied obstinately. 'We would lose too many men under the garrison's heavy fire. No, Danie, we must starve them out.'

'It's taking too long! As well as our forces here, we have ten thousand men immobilised at Ladysmith and seven thousand sitting outside Mafeking. British reinforcements are pouring into the Cape and we are losing the initiative in this war.'

'My orders are to take Kimberley.' Wessel's chin set stubbornly. 'And I will carry out those orders with the minimum loss of life.'

So they sat here, day after miserable day, firing pot-shots at the city while those bastards sneaked out at night to pinch Boer cattle and further delay the day when Kimberley's food supplies would be exhausted. Except for the gunners, military duties were virtually non-existent and confined to the occasional fatigue party for fetching supplies. The majority of the burghers had been home at least once to supervise their farms and see their families. Some had returned with wives and children, which increased the lack of discipline and the spirit of inactivity. Sentry duty was neglected, particularly at night when that damned searchlight lit up the countryside for miles around. Now the men were falling ill with dysentery and typhoid fever and the doctor – a Scotsman who had been 'commandeered' – maintained that he had insufficient medicines.

'We can ask the doctors in Kimberley for medicines,' said the doctor calmly.

His captors stared at him in astonishment.

'They would never help us,' said one man.

'The British are a humane people,' the Scotsman insisted. 'It is worth a try.'

'Well, I will not be the one who asks,' said another burgher.

Danie's mind was working quickly. 'The doctor's right. We owe it to our sick comrades to make the attempt. I will go. As a war correspondent, I can claim to be a non-combatant and there might be a doctor there whom I remember from the old days, although,' and Danie smiled, 'I hear Dr Jameson is at Ladysmith. If the British refuse us aid, I will write a piece for *De Volksstem* which will stir the hardest-hearted Cape Boer and raise him in rebellion.'

The doctor shot him a look of intense dislike. 'I am sure you will, Mr Steyn. I will make out a list of my requirements.'

The only aspect of the expedition which stuck in Danie's throat was the necessity of carrying a pole flying a white flag of truce. This smacked of surrender and he hoped it was not an experience which would have to be repeated. However, the flag had the desired effect. Danie waited for a lull in the firing and then rode out across the plain; the British guns remained silent as their look-outs saw his white flag. He was conducted to the Town Hall, where a reception committee of military personnel, the Mayor and city councillors and Diamond Company Directors awaited him. Eagerly Danie's eyes swept round the group, but the only face he recognised was that of Rhodes; and as he saw the sick, ageing figure of the 'Colossus', Danie smiled. With luck the siege was shortening Rhodes's days and, with even more luck, Matthew Bright was in bad shape too.

Danie handed a letter to Colonel Kekewich from Commandant Wessels, demanding that Boer families in the city be allowed to leave. It was not the first such request, but the families in question had obstinately refused to leave Kimberley.

'We cannot believe they wish to stay here to be fired on by their own people. We believe you are restraining them.'

'Is it likely, Mr Steyn,' said Kekewich wearily, 'that in the present circumstances I wish to feed more mouths than is absolutely necessary? The simple fact of the matter is that they do not wish to wander homeless in the veld; nor do they want to join your camp where they might obtain less to eat than they do here or run the danger of being attacked by us and by the Relief Column.'

Danie was about to contest the existence of any Relief Column but, in view of his next request, he curbed his tongue. He produced the doctor's list of medicines.

'And he also requests that one of your doctors come to help him with the patients.'

A ripple of laughter spread round the room.

'You've certainly got a cheek!' exclaimed Kekewich. 'I see that your doctor is a Scotsman. I will not refuse the medicines, but as you have already commandeered one doctor, I cannot see my way to lend you another!'

Danie sat down and waited for the medicines to be made up. That was not all he awaited – he kept his eyes fixed on the door and eventually his patience was rewarded when Matthew strode in to see this nonchalant envoy who had made impudent requests for aid with so little humility.

Their eyes met and they stared at each other silently.

A great rage engulfed Danie as he looked again on the man he hated most in the world. He would have known him anywhere, because it seemed that he had hardly changed. Danie knew that Matthew was forty-nine years old, but standing there in his well-remembered casual clothes and high boots, his fair hair flaming in the sun which filtered through the windows, he looked not a day over thirty-five. And filled with hate and chagrin, Danie vowed that Matthew Bright would not reach fifty.

Matthew turned on his heel and left the room. This was neither the place nor the time to continue an old personal quarrel, not with the Mayor and councillors and his fellow directors looking on. But the menace in Danie's grey-green eyes disturbed him briefly. Perhaps there was something in that message Court had originally sent him? Then Matthew mentally shook himself and told himself not to be ridiculous. He would be believing in Katherine's second sight next! Anyway, Danie was in no position to carry out any threats while the siege lasted.

Outside he met Nicholas with Laura and Miranda.

'I know him,' he said abruptly. 'It's Danie Steyn.'

'Not the same man who . . .!' Nicholas was horrified.

'The same.'

At that moment Danie left the building to run the gauntlet of the curious populace. Automatically his eyes swivelled towards Matthew and then his gaze dropped to Miranda who was clutching her father's hand tightly. Danie stared at the little girl intently as if engraving her face on his memory and then he rode away.

His mission completed, Danie decided he could bear the inactivity no longer. He knew that General de La Rey was moving south to prepare a welcome for the British forces which had left Cape Town en route to Kimberley. Of all the Boers, De La Rey and his Lichtenburg commando were the doughtiest fighters and the shrewdest tacticians. The action should be interesting and after all, Matthew Bright was not going anywhere; he would still be here when Danie returned.

Danie packed his saddlebag, mounted his roan mare and headed south.

On 23 November, two days after Danie left the Boer camp, a native came into Kimberley with the news that a Relief Column was on the way. His tale was greeted with scepticism and caution – the Africans had not earned a reputation for accuracy and truthfulness – but the story was a good one and people were anxious to believe it.

The next morning Matthew raced into the house brandishing a copy of the *Diamond Fields Advertiser*. 'Listen to this!' he shouted. ' "We are authorised to state that a strong force has left Orange River and is moving forward to the relief of Kimberley." '

Seizing Miranda's hand, he ran back into the street and, with Laura and Nicholas in hot pursuit, hurried to the town. The joy was universal. In only a few days apparently the column would be arriving. Kimberley was free! The siege was over! 'God Save the Queen!' rang out from ten thousand loyal throats and Colonel Kekewich was praised to the skies. Baden-Powell at Mafeking was promised help. The Relief Column was toasted, not wisely but too well. The crowd were generous in their forgiveness of the Boers, but it was clear they must all be captured; in the interests of the campaign, it was not expedient that even one should escape. Where should they be housed? The jail was not large enough. With what was to be an exquisite irony, the mines were selected as the Boers' place of imprisonment.

Laura had a lump in her throat and she tried to blink back the tears of joy which stung her eyes. She turned to smile at Lord Nicholas, whose comforting bulk was close beside her.

'Well done, Laura! Happy days,' he said, in that delightfully inconsequential way of his and to Laura's astonishment he leaned over and kissed her on the cheek.

She was still reeling from the shock when Matthew tossed Miranda into the air, catching her safely and hugging her close, then his left arm suddenly encircled Laura's shoulder.

'Yes, well done, Laura, and you too, Miranda. You have been a little heroine, haven't you!' and he smiled into his daughter's adoring eyes. 'You have both been heroines,' he added softly.

She stood motionless within the circle of his arm, feeling the hard grip of his hand against her shoulder, and for a moment the world stood still. This has to be, she thought dazedly, the happiest day of my life.

At two o'clock on the morning of 23 November, the Honourable Edward Harcourt-Bright was riding into battle. A subaltern in the 9th Lancers, he was approximately fifty miles from Kimberley and approaching a little-known dorp called Belmont.

Everything had happened very fast and nothing was as he had expected. In a few short weeks he had been gazetted, loaded on to a troopship at Southampton and off-loaded again at Cape Town, and attached to the squadron of the 9th Lancers which formed part of Lord Methuen's relieving force. Edward had discovered that there was no glory attached to having attended the Staff College and that on the contrary its graduates were treated with derision and suspicion by their fellow officers. Lord Methuen did not seem to follow any of the traditions and rules and regulations which Edward had so painstakingly absorbed. There was not even a smart uniform. Lord Methuen insisted that everything must be khaki. The very buttons on one's tunic even had to be painted khaki, likewise anything else which would reflect light. All insignia were removed and an officer must be indistinguishable from his men – apparently, Boer snipers had an irritating habit of picking off the officers first in order to throw the ranks into leaderless confusion. Helmets were out of fashion and Boer-type slouch hats were *de rigeur*.

The force had travelled by train from Cape Town to the Orange River, where they halted for several days. The 9th Lancers were ordered to reconnoitre the country ahead. Edward stared with awe at the vast expanse of the Great Karoo. Surely the family stories of Uncle Matthew's walk to Kimberley must be pure legend. No one could *walk* across that rolling desolate plain! It was grand riding country, though, and at first Edward revelled in the open air and the burning sun.

Reconnoitring duties were very hard work. It was becoming increasingly clear that the War Office had seriously misjudged the composition of the troops sent to South Africa. Lord Methuen's force numbered ten thousand men, of whom only nine hundred were cavalry: the 9th Lancers, the Rimington Guides and some Mounted Infantry. Obviously the mounted troops comprised far too small a proportion of the total force considering the distances to be covered, the nature of the terrain and the devastating mobility of the enemy.

The Lancers reported that a force of about two thousand Boers was encamped on the hills at Belmont, nineteen miles up the railway line from the Orange River. On the night of 20 November tents were struck. This was more like it, thought Edward, as excitement spread, songs were sung round the camp fires and the troops slept under the stars.

A point two miles south of Belmont was reached on the afternoon of the second day's march and Methuen completed his plans, hampered by the absence of a good map, by ironstone boulders which threw out compass readings and by Boer sharpshooting which prevented further reconnaissance.

The force attacked in the chill darkness of the early morning. The infantry wheeled to the right and the Rimington Guides also headed east to cover their right flank. Edward and the 9th Lancers rode north, to the west and parallel with the railway line, to take up a position beyond Belmont where they could cut off any Boer retreat. The Lancers moved quietly, surprise being the essence of this dawn attack, the horses' hooves muffled in the long dry grass. There was an eerie silence as they took up their positions. The sky began to lighten and they strained their ears for the sound of a shot – the infantry attack was late.

Then it commenced and a burst of flame along the ridge was followed by the spatter of rifle fire. 'Boers!' said Edward's nearest neighbour. 'The Scots Guards are catching it.'

In fact it was the Grenadiers who were taking the worst of the assault but Edward had no way of knowing this. He was only aware of the confused cacophony of rifle fire and artillery, of bugles blowing and even the occasional skirl of the pipes. But they were winning. Messages reaching them from Lord Methuen were encouraging. Stiff and cold, with horses dropping from fatigue and lack of water, the Lancers waited for the vital message. It came early. At only 7.30 am, Methuen sent urgent orders for them to move forward and cut off the Boer retreat.

Action at last! Edward's heart pounded as they crossed the railway line and headed north-west in pursuit of the fleeing figures on their sturdy ponies. But to his enormous chagrin, the Lancers failed in their task. Their horses were too exhausted from the rigorous reconnaissance work they had undertaken, and there were far too few of them. A Boer turned round and thumbed his nose at the British before riding off as jauntily as if his people had been victorious, while all Edward could do was glare at the retreating backs in sheer frustration.

However, although they had not been able to follow up, it had nevertheless been a stirring victory. Morale soared: in three hours they had shifted the Boers from a position the enemy had expected to occupy for three weeks.

Now the road to Kimberley lay straight before them.

Edward's elation returned. 'Hold on, Uncle Matthew, it won't be long now!' he thought.

CHAPTER THREE

Danie had found De La Rey at Modder River, a pleasant place about twenty miles from Kimberley which was used by the townsfolk as a holiday resort. The north bank of the river was covered in trees and shrubs, with scattered houses, an hotel and the railway station.

Boer morale was low after the rebuff at Belmont and loss of a similar encounter at Graspan two days later. However, De La Rey was confident that the tide could be stemmed and had prepared a surprise for the British. Instead of deploying the Boer forces on the crests of the kopjes, De La Rey placed them in trenches on the south bank of the river.

Early on November 28 Danie watched the British infantry move forward into the trap which was waiting for them. He wished they still wore the scarlet tunics of old instead of the dull khaki which made them more difficult to see. However, they were more visible than the Boers – Danie knew that not a burgher could be seen, so perfect was their art of concealment in natural and man-made cover. There was one good thing, though – the British were mounting their usual frontal attack, advancing across the veld towards the south bank of the river and intending to ford the Modder.

Any moment now the commandos would open fire. The British would be thinking that the Boers were not there but they were, they were. Now! The air was split by rifle fire and by the boom of a pom-pom gun firing at the British right flank. To a man they fell to the ground and frantically sought cover.

The noise of the battle drummed in Edward's ears. The shock of that sudden salvo of enemy fire had been like a punch in the chest, freezing him into momentary immobility and causing his heart to miss a beat. Somehow the impact was not lessened by the fact that he himself was out of the firing line. He had to endure the agony of worrying about his countrymen, while powerless to help them.

The Lancers were not taking part in the battle. To their fury and frustration they had spent the day in idle isolation on the right flank, away from the chaos and carnage along the river. The sun scorched down, bringing a burning thirst to add to the tension. Everyone was hungry, for the orders to march had been sudden and there had been no time for breakfast. The British ate no lunch that day either and some went without supper. If it was like this for him, thought Edward as he tried to brush off the flies, it must be infinitely worse for the poor sods under fire.

They told us the Boers hate cold steel, he said to himself bitterly as the day wore on. The infantry ought to be running towards the enemy with fixed bayonets. And where is the cavalry charge I dreamed of? Why are we not riding across the veld at full gallop, with lances poised and sabres swinging?

But the valour of the British infantry won the day. The fact that this was their third battle within a week did not diminish their grit and determination. The next morning Methuen's force crossed the Modder in silence: the Boers had gone and taken their guns with them. As Edward rode through the beautiful summer morning, his head whirled in the confusion of conclusions he drew from the events of the previous day. He decided that the most important lesson to be learned from the Battle of Modder River was 'never do what the enemy expects you to do'.

Edward sat a little straighter and more proudly in the saddle. It was such a lovely day, they were victorious and he was still here, unscathed. Next time they would trounce the Boer once and for all, and remove the last obstacle to the Relief of Kimberley. Because no one had the slightest doubt that the Boers and their guns were gathering in the veld to meet them again.

Meanwhile, the mood of the beleaguered city remained jubilant and everyone was convinced that it was the last week of the siege. On Monday 27 November, the directors of the Diamond Company had been due to gather for their annual meeting but it was postponed until Thursday so that the dividend declared could be cabled to shareholders throughout the world. The wires, everyone was agreed, were bound to be in flashing order by Thursday.

The predominant and all-absorbing subject of discussion was the Relief Column. The searchlight continued to flash Rhodes's impatient demands for release and cheers rang through the town when a response came at last: an answering gleam from Modder River.

Rumours of the fighting there had spread through Kimberley at the beginning of December, and for the next ten days the people strained their eyes to the south in daily – almost hourly – expectation of the Column's arrival. Excitement was tempered with anxiety. What could be taking them so long?

Funerals had to take place, the saddest being that of an officer and twenty-four of his men who had been killed in a sortie against the besieging Boers. The enemy did not seem to realise that their cause was lost; they strengthened their trenches and continued to shell the town, aiming in particular at the searchlight which was sending its violet-coloured messages south to Modder River.

Matthew was furious because the Diamond Company directors had been forced to postpone their meeting yet again. Laura was worried about food.

'Hardly any fruit or vegetables are available,' she told Nicholas. 'Small potatoes are 4½d each. Cabbages are a dream, cauliflowers merely a memory and onions are 'off'. A few wizened carrots are all that the market can offer – small, cadaverous, brick-coloured things, no bigger than a cork. Eggs are 1/1d *each*. It's not quite so bad for us, at least we have enough money to buy what we can. But what about the poor people who cannot afford such prices?'

'I know.' Nicholas looked distressed. 'We have been subsidising the Refugee Committee who are caring for the destitute and have created a fund for those families who have lost their breadwinner, but we cannot give money to everyone. Besides, there is not enough food to go round.'

'And the beef is all neck,' said Laura, warming to her theme. 'Everyone says so. But we are supposed to be eating oxen, not giraffes! Again, we're lucky. In view of Sir Matthew's status, the butcher puts our ration to one side for me to collect at leisure, although,' she added scrupulously, 'I have instructed him to give us only our fair share and no more. But some people are breaking curfew in order to go out at five in the morning to make sure they obtain their ration.'

'It's that mealie-pap stuff I can't stand.' Nicholas sighed, wistful with memories of the gourmet meals to which he had been accustomed. He was sure that not all the directors of the Diamond Company were living on siege rations to the same extent as the Bright household, but he had long since learned not to challenge Laura on the subject. 'Horrible, tasteless porridge, that's all it is. How the natives live on it, I'll never know.'

'It's filling,' said Laura grimly. 'But what is keeping back the Column, Lord Nicholas? I am so afraid we will run out of food before they come.'

Nicholas could not suggest the reason, but on Monday 11 December they finally heard the unmistakable boom of British artillery. They ran helter-skelter for the debris dumps on the Reservoir whence they could see shells bursting at Spytfontein. Excitement mounted as something strange was seen in the sky.

'What on earth is that?' asked Laura, watching in fascination as the weird object floated up to heaven.

'A reconnaissance balloon,' said Matthew. 'The balloonist uses a telephone to communicate with army officers on the ground.'

'They're coming,' said Laura. 'This time they really are coming!'

In the afternoon a football match was played between the Lancashire Regiment and the Town Guard but further south a more serious contest was taking place.

Methuen's force had rested at Modder River Station, while six miles away the Boers held the Spytfontein and Magersfontein range between the Upper Modder River and the Kimberley Road. On the night of 10 December, the orders came. The crux of the plan was a night march by the newly-arrived Highland Brigade. They set off half an hour after midnight in a wild storm with lashing rain, a chilly wind and crashes of thunder, the only illumination coming from flashes of lightning and the faint beam of the Kimberley searchlight.

The 9th Lancers were assigned to the right flank with the King's Own Yorkshire Light Infantry, to hold the gap between the Magersfontein Ridge and the river. As dawn broke, the sound of a single rifle-shot split the air and before Edward's astonished gaze the hills seemed to burst into tiers of flame as bullets rained down on the Highlanders.

It was the beginning of a day which would live in Edward's memory forever, no matter how hard he tried to forget. Indelibly etched in his memory was the sight of that sheet of flame on the hillside, and the spectacle of the dead and wounded; the noise of the guns like a great roar in his ears, and the singing of the bullets, the babble of commands. First he was shivering in wet clothes and then scorching in the heat and wishing he was wet again. Hot, thirsty, hungry and confused.

The Lancers were forced to withdraw from their early position and to dismount in order to seek shelter from the invisible enemy. Two squadrons and a machine gun were ordered forward to the north-eastern section and it was there, nine hours after the dawn attack, that Edward saw a sight he hoped never to see again – men of the Highland Brigade running for all they were worth, while their General lay dead on the battlefield. The Lancers tried to rally those who came near them, but it was no use: the kilted Scotsmen had had enough.

Edward was one of the lucky ones. As darkness fell he returned to his bivouac, but others lay out all night under what shelter they could find. Silently, in the bright moonlight, ambulances combed the battlefield for the wounded.

Fighting was not resumed the following afternoon when the truce ended. An orderly, unhurried and dignified retreat was carried out before dusk. The casualties were not large, but the loss of face was mortifying. After the Battle of Magersfontein the Relief Column turned its back on Kimberley and returned to Modder River. It was to be nearly two months before it moved forward again.

'Do you know what I have missed most of all?' Laura's eyes grew dreamy. 'Hot water. Lots and lots of hot water, in which to bathe and wash my hair. Without water in which to wash one feels dirty anyway, but this heat and dust make it intolerable.'

'I've missed the letters,' said Nicholas. 'I long for news of home, don't you?'

'I am afraid that there is no one who would write to me,' Laura confessed sadly. 'I was so hoping to hear from Philip. Lord Nicholas, I am so worried about him: what sort of Christmas will he have?'

'One of the family will look after him.' Nicholas's tone was robustly reassuring. 'Julia, probably.'

Laura remembered the venom in Philip's voice as he avowed his hatred of his cousin, but thought it tactful to remain silent on the matter. 'What do you think Sir Matthew has missed most?'

'The Stock Exchange quotations, I expect.'

Laura laughed. 'Thank heaven it is nearly over. How we shall appreciate all the little things we previously took so much for granted.'

But the days passed and there was still no news. Laura began to worry. That a battle had taken place on 11 December was a fact – they had listened for hours to the booming of the artillery. If the outcome were being kept from them, it must mean that something was wrong. So, gradually, Kimberley became permeated with pessimism. There was no sudden shock announcement, but a gradual acceptance that Methuen had been checked. On Monday 18 December rumour became fact but strangely enough, although the world was ringing with criticism of Methuen, Kimberley blamed nobody: Lord Methuen was a hero who had only failed at the last fence. All the same, that Monday was a miserable day as the people resigned themselves to further captivity and mourned the brave soldiers who had died in attempting their rescue.

Valiantly Laura set her mind to plans for Christmas. The store cupboard was nearly empty but a few little treats were left – tinned meat and fish; biscuits and jam; raisins which she could add to the mealie-meal to make a pudding; and sweets for Miranda. Laura divided the hoard into three: one portion for themselves, one for the servants and one for the troops in the military camps in town. She knew that Sir Matthew could acquire tobacco and wine and she would ask him to supply some to the troops as well. One chicken remained in the run outside which would serve for their Christmas dinner. As for the shops, the predominant feature of window displays was starch. Evidently the water shortage was seriously affecting the cleanliness of Kimberley's linen.

Typhoid fever broke out in the Light Horse camp and scurvy was playing havoc with the native population. Then came news of the British defeats at Colenso in Natal and Stormberg in the Cape. 'Black week' spread gloom throughout the Empire, but nowhere was the depression deeper than in the besieged towns under the African sun.

Laura reached her lowest ebb on Christmas Eve. The heat of the day was excruciating; it literally took her breath away. There was no air, no breeze and the thermometer registered 107°F in the shade. She did not even want to eat. Miranda was fretful, too hot to work or play or sleep. Rain, prayed Laura, please let it rain! A dust storm intervened by way of compromise – hot, choking and blinding, nevertheless it brought a breeze. Thunder and lightning made their appearance but still the rain hesitated, as if it knew there was little left in Kimberley to soak. Then during the night it came down in torrents, drumming on the roof with the noise of a thousand cannon. Laura peeped into the nursery, worried that the noise would disturb Miranda but the child was sleeping peacefully in the cooler atmosphere. It was odd, thought Laura as she returned to her own room, that not even the loudest thunder or gunfire upset the child. A horrible suspicion was beginning to form in her mind, but she dared not speak to Sir Matthew about it just now. He had worries enough.

She did not climb straight back into bed but stood by the window, staring out at the torrential downpour. Water! Masses of it pouring from the sky, and it was not rationed. After the unbearable heat of the day, Laura felt stickier and dirtier than ever. Dare she . . .? The house was dark and silent and everyone was asleep. Swiftly she shed her nightgown and, wrapping a towel round her, crept to the garden door.

Leaving the towel in the dry porch, she stepped naked into the rain, glorying in the stinging stream of water that cascaded over her flesh. The thunder still rolled overhead, but Laura lifted her face to the storm and shook her hair loose to soak and stream in the downpour. The water ran in rivers over her body and she rubbed her hands hard over her skin as if soaping herself, trying to rub out the dirt and sweat that she felt ingrained in every pore. She was thinner than before, but her breasts still jutted proudly and the slimness suited her shapely limbs.

She turned towards the house and threw back her head for the last time, running her fingers through her long hair. Lightning flashed again and suddenly illuminated a figure standing in the porch.

Laura froze, instinctively crossing her arms to cover her breasts. She stood still and waited, but at the next lightning flash the figure was still there. It could only be him – anyone else, even if they had been watching her, would have slipped away as she approached.

'You had better come in, Miss Vaughan,' he said in a low voice, 'before you melt.'

Flaming with shame and fury, Laura stepped into the porch and he handed her the towel.

'That was not fair!' she said angrily, wrapping the towel hastily around her glistening flesh.

'No, it was not,' he agreed and in the darkness she saw the gleam of his white teeth. 'But it was infinitely enjoyable.'

There was a huskiness in his voice that she had not heard before and he was standing very close. Laura's heart was thudding uncomfortably and her stomach was twisting in a most peculiar way. Time seemed to hang suspended, but then he moved abruptly as if tearing himself away.

'Good night,' he said and disappeared into the house.

With a strange emptiness inside her which she refused to recognise as disappointment, Laura went to bed. But she lay sleepless for a long time. How, she asked herself, could she face him in the morning?

By contrast to the previous day, Christmas Day was wonderful; cool and delicious, with shifting, hustling clouds instead of that glaring azure sky. Laura rose and dressed in her usual everyday clothes, determined to act as if nothing had happened.

Christmas presents for Miranda were the household's first concern. Laura avoided Sir Matthew's eye, but was touched by Nicholas's warm greeting and the gentle pressure of his hand as he wished her the compliments of the season. Each of them had a parcel for the little girl. There was a doll from Matthew, a gorgeous creation which it must have taken all his influence to secure. The drapers' shops had not been entirely denuded of their stock and Laura had acquired a length of blue silk which she had fashioned into a dress for the child, putting her sewing talent and the long empty evenings to good use. Nicholas gave Miranda a gold locket.

'You can put a lock of my hair into it,' he joked to her.

'Yes, I should like to do that.' Miranda's big blue eyes gazed seriously at her uncle. 'And some of Papa's. And yours, too, Laura.'

'Oh, I don't think you want mine,' exclaimed Laura 'Just the family would be more suitable.'

'I do want yours. You are family,' Miranda insisted.

'Of course she is. Come on, Miss Vaughan,' Matthew spoke to her for the first time that day. 'I don't trust Miranda with a pair of scissors, so you shall have the honour of cutting our hair.'

Laura went first to Nicholas and, with difficulty, selected a lock of hair which would not unduly denude his balding head. As she approached Matthew she found her hands were shaking. She was consumed with an overwhelming desire to caress that thick mane of hair and she touched it gingerly as if it were red hot. As she bent over him, his eyes met hers with an unfathomable expression. Flushing, she backed away and handed the shorn lock to Miranda.

'Now it's your turn, Miss Vaughan,' he said lazily.

Her hand flew to the bun at the back of her neck. He was surely teasing her? She would *not* undo her hair in the drawing-room, especially after last night.

'I shall cut mine in the nursery. Miranda, shall we put on your new dress and the locket? You can wear them today because it's Christmas.'

'One moment, Laura. I . . . have a little present for you.' Nicholas fumbled in his pocket and handed her a small package with a nervous smile.

'For me!' This was the last thing Laura had expected. 'You remembered *me*!'

'Open it,' he urged.

It was a brooch, a delicate graceful spray blazing with diamonds. Speechless, Laura looked from the brooch to Nicholas and back again. Matthew rose from his chair and walked to the window, apparently losing interest in the proceedings.

'Diamonds,' Laura said at last. 'Diamonds for me? Lord Nicholas, it is far too beautiful a present. I am only the governess.'

'Not to me.' His face went purple with embarrassment. 'You've been splendid, Laura. We brought you here and incarcerated you in the Diamond City. Least we can do is give you a memento, what?'

'It's exquisite,' she said softly. 'It's the most lovely thing I have ever seen. And I think you are the nicest, kindest man I have ever known. Thank you!'

Tears blinded her eyes and impulsively she leaned forward and kissed Nicholas on the cheek. Then she fled and had a good cry in the nursery, explaining to a bewildered Miranda that she was crying because she was happy, while in truth she was crying simply because someone had been so kind and thoughtful.

She cut a lock of her hair and together she and Miranda twisted the three strands into a plait: Laura's dark lock in sharp contrast to the bright gold of Matthew's and the fading yellow-grey of Nicholas. In her new blue dress, the locket shining at her neck and the doll clasped firmly in her arms, Miranda was in heaven.

'You ought to dress up, too, since it's Christmas.' She looked inquiringly at Laura. 'Have you got a party dress?'

Laura started to say 'No' but remembered the emerald green taffeta, as yet unworn. She went to her closet and removed the dress, shaking out its shining folds.

'It's lovely,' cried Miranda. 'Please put it on.'

Hesitantly, Laura complied.

'I really don't think I can wear it, Miranda.' She stared at her reflection in the mirror. The heart-shaped neckline was cut too low and the expanse of white flesh gleamed against the rich fabric.

'It looks nice. And you could wear your new brooch.'

Laura pinned the diamond spray to her shoulder. When she had made this dress, she had never dreamed of wearing it with such an ornament.

'No, I can't.' Laura used her last line of defence. 'Papa wouldn't like it.'

But for once the ultimate deterrent did not work.

'*I* like it,' said Miranda firmly, and she dragged Laura along the passage to the drawing-room where Matthew was alone.

'Papa, see how pretty Laura looks!'

He turned and stared at her for a long time. Laura felt faint. Then he smiled at Miranda.

'Yes, darling. She looks very pretty indeed. Now, please tell Uncle Nicholas that there is a glass of sherry waiting for him.'

Obediently Miranda trotted away.

Matthew walked towards her. 'Very pretty indeed,' he said again, 'particularly when one knows what is underneath.'

Laura flinched and tried to turn away but he laid a restraining hand on her arm.

'The brooch is lovely,' he went on. 'I am sorry, Miss Vaughan, that I did not think to buy you a Christmas present. You are right, Nicholas *is* the nicest and kindest man in the world.'

He was staring at her intently, then, releasing her arm his hands moved to the nape of her neck and expertly unpinned her hair. It fell free in luxuriant ripples, gleaming after its wash in the rain. Finally he lifted the spectacles from her nose and peered through them.

'Plain glass,' he commented. 'How interesting.'

Calmly he dropped them on the carpet and stood on them, grinding them into fragments with his heel. As Laura started to protest, he placed a hand under her chin and tilted her face to his.

'Laura,' he murmured softly, but let go of her swiftly as Nicholas and Miranda entered the room. 'See, Nicky, what magic your diamonds have wrought!' He handed a glass of sherry to the stunned Nicholas and the blushing Laura. 'I don't normally care much for Christmas, but this year I find myself visualising

Brightwell and Park Lane, Desborough and Highclere, and remembering snow and ice and frost and the traditional trimmings of the festive season. So there are three toasts we must drink today. The first, as always, is to the Queen. The second is "Happy Christmas". And the third is "Absent Friends".'

They drank and, laughing, Matthew bent down to give Miranda a sip from his glass. I don't have any absent friends, thought Laura. All my happiness is here, tied to the three people in this room. May God protect them and keep them safe.

CHAPTER FOUR

'I have our permits,' announced Laura triumphantly. 'You should have seen the Town Hall, Lord Nicholas. It was crammed to the roof with people shoving and jostling for a small but very precious piece of paper.'

'It was extremely good of you to endure that, on behalf of us all.'

'Well, I daresay I am more accustomed to lining up than you are.' Laura handed him a slip of paper. 'There you are, Lord Nicholas. You can eat for another week. After that the permit expires and we have to go through the whole rigmarole again.'

'I see that it entitles the holder to purchase the "regulation" quantity of provisions for one week.' Nicholas stared at it gloomily. 'What are the "regulations" at the moment, Laura? I have quite lost track of our esteemed colonel's proclamations.'

'Bread is limited to 14oz per day. The sugar ration has been reduced. Tea and coffee are rationed. There is no milk whatsoever. Eggs are two shillings each. And,' Laura hesitated to give the bad news, 'the meat ration has now been halved. Four ounces per adult and two ounces per child per day.'

Nicholas groaned. 'I *dream* of a steak. I drool and *slaver* for a steak! And now they are about to issue us with . . .' He stopped.

'Horsemeat!' said Laura grimly. 'The rumours are all over town. You knew, didn't you? You might have warned me! The whole of Kimberley is appalled and disgusted. It has caused more consternation than anything else which has happened since the beginning of the siege.'

'We are short of meat,' said Nicholas gently, 'and the horses are starving for lack of fodder. The cavalry or "fighting" horses are given priority for hay and straw, but there is nothing to give the other animals.'

'I know.' Laura tried to swallow the lump in her throat. 'It is pitiful to see their protruding ribs and forlorn looks. The horse is such a noble animal and eating it seems almost as bad as cannibalism. And there are still cattle in the fields at Kenilworth.'

'As you said many weeks ago in connection with the stores in the larder, we do not know how long they must last.'

Laura sat down beside him and looked at him earnestly. 'You and Sir Matthew know more than you are telling. Even bad news is better than none.'

'Ladysmith and Mafeking are holding out – we are not alone in our tribulations! But it is true that the Relief Column is stuck at Modder River.'

'But not for long, surely? We can hear them firing from here. Every day we can hear the sound of the guns.'

'The Battle of Magersfontein was a severe blow. Reinforcements are absolutely essential. While he waits, Methuen is pinning down a considerable force of Boers and preventing them from fighting elsewhere. And don't forget, Laura, that Lord Roberts is on his way to take up the position of Commander-in-Chief. Old "Bobs" will surely have us out of here in no time.'

'But in the meantime we must eat horses.' Laura shuddered.

'Damn Matthew and his bright ideas and his obstinacy and his sudden affectation of principles,' said Nicholas with uncharacteristic violence. 'It is quite iniquitous that you should have been subjected to this.' He took hold of her hand. 'And yet,' he said wistfully, 'if it had not been for the siege and these weeks of unusual conditions, I might never have come to know you.'

Laura could think of nothing to say in response and they were sitting silently, hand in hand, when Matthew burst into the room. He took one look at them and disappeared as abruptly as he had arrived.

It was a week later, as Laura sat with Nicholas in the drawing-room, that Matthew sprang his surprise.

'I have something to show you,' he announced. 'You must come to the Company workshops right away – unless you have something better to do.'

'Of course I have nothing better to do.' Laura laid down her book gratefully. 'I must have read every book in Kimberley at least six times.'

'That was not what I meant,' Matthew said enigmatically.

With an air of suppressed excitement, he led them into the workshop. Evidently Nicholas was privy to the secret, for he wandered off and began to talk to the men but Laura gasped in surprise.

'A gun! The biggest I've ever seen. Where did it come from?'

'We made it,' said Matthew proudly. 'Here, in the Diamond Company workshops, out of material in store.'

'That's incredible. But is it safe?' Laura eyed the monster doubtfully. 'And will it work?'

'Of course it will work.' Matthew's tone was indignant. 'It was made by George Labram, an American engineer from Detroit who works for the Company. It's constructed from steel shafting. Now the Boers are in for a pounding,' and he slapped the cannon's great barrel affectionately.

Laura was filled with relief. So this was why she had hardly seen him for the past week – she had begun to worry that she might have offended him in some way. 'It ought to have a name.'

'It has already been christened. The Boer big guns are known as "Long Toms". It seemed appropriate to call our gun "Long Cecil".'

'What a wonderful boost to morale! You would not believe, Sir Matthew, how upset everyone is over the horsemeat. Things were bad enough when the ration was half horse and half meat – because no one will recognise horseflesh as *meat* – but now that the proportions are four-fifths horse to one-fifth ox, some people are refusing to eat meat of any kind.'

Matthew shrugged impatiently. 'We cannot afford to be so fussy. Let them go hungry if they wish.'

'The health of the town will suffer,' Laura pointed out, 'but there is a remedy. I was speaking to Captain Tyson and discussing the possibility of setting up a soup kitchen. He is willing to make the soup, from ox meat only. It would be sold at threepence a pint, on an allocation of one pint per adult in exchange for one meat coupon. The soup should be extremely nourishing, excellent value and economical to make. Captain Tyson thinks he could persuade Colonel Kekewich to allow the soup to be thickened with mealie-meal, but I did have to promise something in exchange.'

'I'm quite sure you did,' said Matthew sarcastically. 'Whatever will Nicholas say?'

Laura did not understand his innuendo and merely looked puzzled. 'It does not affect Lord Nicholas in any way. I promised that I would ask you if the Company could spare some vegetables for the soup from its garden.'

'I expect so. I'll ask Rhodes.'

'And I promised that we would set an example and drink the soup ourselves.'

'If you insist.'

'I'm afraid that's not all.' Laura took a deep breath. 'I said that you would help to serve the soup, on the first day anyway, as a kind of guarantee of its excellence and flavour.'

'You expect *me* to stand behind a counter and ladle out pints of soup to the masses?'

'Yes. Please!'

'You are sure you don't want me to peel the potatoes or cut up the meat?'

'That won't be necessary.'

'I am vastly relieved to hear it. All right, Miss Vaughan, tell me where and when to report and I will be there.' His expression lightened for a moment. He took a small bag from his pocket and drew out a beautiful pear-shaped diamond. 'I was right,' he said, gazing at the gem thoughtfully. 'The wheel has come full circle. How many years is it since I ate a meal costing threepence?'

He replaced the diamond in his pocket and looked at Laura. 'You seem to be widening your circle of acquaintances,' he commented.

'I meet a lot of people in the food and permit queues,' answered Laura, 'and naturally we talk to each other to pass the time. There is one very interesting thing that I have noticed.'

'What's that?'

'Not once have I ever heard *anyone* advocate surrender!'

'Long Cecil', everyone felt, was an unqualified success. After a few teething troubles it had driven the Boers from their intermediate station a couple of miles away and aimed a series of C.J.R.'s 'compliments' at the Kamfers Dam *laager*. The performance of the gun, combined with the long period without casualties, greatly increased the people's sense of security. Talk of George Labram's skill was on everyone's lips. Indeed, the feeling in Kimberley was growing that there should be less reliance on a Column coming in and more belief in their own ability to blast a way out.

This new-found confidence was shattered on the night of Wednesday 24 January.

Laura was woken in the middle of the night by a sound which at first she thought was thunder. She lay still in the darkness, listening. Then she realised that it was not thunder but the booming of cannon and it was followed by the hissing and bursting of shells. And those shells were exploding in rapid succession in the very streets of the city.

Without even thinking to put on a robe over her nightgown, Laura ran out of the front door into the drive. The night was alive with the sound of the bombardment and the alarmed shouts of the populace. Before her horrified gaze a shell whistled over her head and landed on the roof of the house opposite. There was a loud blast as the roof caved in.

Suddenly she was seized from behind and strong arms carried her back inside the house. Matthew set her down and shook her hard.

'I didn't think I would need to tell *you* to stay in the house,' he said angrily. 'I thought you had some sense.'

Laura felt dazed. The shock attack in the blackness of the early morning lacked reality. 'What's happening?'

'The Boers are firing every gun they've got. Well, nearly every gun.'

'What do you mean, nearly?'

'We believe they've brought up a Long Tom. And German officers to use it. Which probably explains why their aim and range have suddenly improved.'

'But they're not using the big gun yet?'

'No.'

'How will we know when they do?'

'We shall know all right,' he said grimly.

'Miranda.' Laura's whirling thoughts steadied at last. 'I must go to her.'

'She is sleeping soundly, I'm glad to say.'

I'm not glad, Laura wanted to say. His statement only confirmed her worst fears. No one should be able to sleep through this infernal racket.

'Nicholas has gone to calm the servants. I'm going to see if they need any help at the house across the road. Now stay here.'

He vanished into the hell outside. Laura stood with her nose pressed to the window until she saw him running back up the drive and her life could start again. Then she saw the expression on his face.

'Dead!' His voice was a strangled mixture of grief and fury. 'Those bastards killed that young girl. How old was she? About seventeen? Killed as she lay in her own bed! By God, those bastards will pay for this!'

Laura felt the colour drain from her face as she steadied herself against the back of the chair. 'In her own bed! Miranda might be next! Where can we go?'

'We're staying right here, there is nowhere else we can go.' He walked across and gripped her arm tightly, staring fiercely into her eyes. 'Nothing is going to happen to us. You must believe that, Laura. We are *survivors*!'

'I do believe that,' gulped Laura. 'Yes, I do, honestly.'

'Good. Now, what we need is a drink. Thank the Lord I had the sense and the money to lay in a good cellar while stocks lasted. Fetch Nicholas while I pour.'

Laura fetched Miranda as well, the child hardly stirring as Laura carried her into the drawing-room and tucked her up in a blanket on the sofa.

Matthew handed her a glass of whisky. Laura drank the unaccustomed liquid, pulling a face at the strange taste and feeling the warmth settling her uneasy stomach.

'What are we going to do?' asked Nicholas a trifle plaintively.

'There is no point in going back to bed. We haven't a hope of sleeping. Do you play poker, Laura?'

'No.'

'Well, now is as good a time as any to learn.'

The fusillade ceased at 8 am and while Matthew and Nicholas sallied forth to inspect the damage, Laura dressed herself and Miranda and organised some breakfast. She stood, aghast, as the bombardment resumed before either Nicholas or Matthew had returned.

About five minutes later Nicholas hurtled through the door, clutching the battered remains of his hat to his chest.

'My hat! Look at my hat! Bastards shot it off.'

'Nicholas, you might have been killed!'

'Well, I wasn't.' He looked proudly at his hat. 'I'm keeping this The family at home will never believe it.'

'Where's Matthew?'

'He went into town. Don't worry, he'll find shelter somewhere.'

'Oh, I'm not really worried. I am sure he can look after himself.'

But she worried for nine hours. The bombardment continued, shell after shell whistling through the air, and still Matthew did not return. Only at dusk did peace prevail and bring him home.

'Where have you been?' wailed Laura.

'It's been a rather hectic day. I'm sorry I couldn't get back home, but I knew Nicholas would look after you.'

'We cowered on the floor of the drawing-room most of the time,' confessed Laura. 'Are there many people hurt?'

'Surprisingly few really. Some broken limbs, but no more deaths. The Public Library has been hit and at least five churches – ironically, the worst damaged was the Dutch Reformed! And many houses and shops have suffered. The men on duty at the redoubts are growing restive because the shells are passing clean over them and falling onto their families in town.'

'I'll get something to eat. You must find Nicholas, he wants to tell you about his hat!'

The respite was only brief. At nine in the evening the Boer guns opened up again and Kimberley underwent a second night of hell. Laura was too tired to stay up but lay in bed with Miranda asleep beside her and tried to rest, watching the hours tick away on her faithful old clock which stood on the bedside table. But the longer the raid went on, the more the strain intensified and one nocturnal shell brought as much terror as did ten during daylight.

Dawn, however, brought no abatement in the attack. Shells showered on to every part of the town and a woman and her six-year-old child were killed as they sat at breakfast. The Boers allowed forty-five minutes for lunch and began firing again at two o'clock. First came the boom, then the warning whistle, next the boom of a second gun almost before the bursting crash of the first shell had proclaimed its contact with the earth. The guns were fired at long range and 10–15 seconds had to elapse before anybody could be sure that his turn had not come. Had a closer range been feasible, the bombardment might have been more destructive but the suspense would have been less harrowing. The shells fell thickly all afternoon and then stopped at six o'clock.

They had not used the 'Long Tom'.

'It's been nearly forty-eight hours.' Laura was so tired she could hardly speak. 'Please, please, let them leave us alone tonight!'

'The casualties have been extraordinarily few,' said Nicholas, 'but the possibilities of the situation remain awesome.'

'I am going to bed tonight and I am going to sleep, no matter what they do,' Laura vowed. 'And tomorrow we must dig some sort of shelter. We cannot endure this experience again.'

To their astonishment the night was peaceful and they awoke refreshed to a quiet day. They gathered on the smooth lawns and chose a site, then Matthew set the servants to work with picks and shovels to excavate a dug-out.

When it was finished, it was a somewhat damp and dismal pit. It was not at all well-ventilated, but the atmosphere outside so reeked of smoke and powder that it did not seem to make much difference. As Laura helped to cover it with sacks of earth she admitted to herself that such a shelter did not offer much security although it might be splinter-proof. Matthew and Nicholas were exaggerating the protection it offered, she knew, but their motives were kind.

It was disagreeably suggestive of a grave, however, and Laura felt the claustrophobia smothering her again.

Suddenly she remembered that today was her birthday.

'Poor Anne,' Nicholas was murmuring. 'She was so proud of her beautiful garden.'

'This is no time for sentiment,' said Matthew sharply. 'Do you think Anne would begrudge a few yards of turf and the odd rose-bush when Miranda's life is at stake?'

Laura's heart turned a somersault. It was the first time Matthew had admitted the possibility.

CHAPTER FIVE

'Another balloon,' said Laura listlessly. 'At least Methuen is still there. Do you remember, Nicholas, how happy we were when we saw the first reconnaissance balloon and heard the sound of the Column's guns? That was nearly two months ago. What a mockery it turned out to be.'

'We must look on the bright side, Laura. That frightful forty-eight-hour bombardment has not been repeated and your soup kitchen is flourishing.'

'The quality of the soup has been deteriorating day by day,' Laura sighed in despair. 'Condiments are no longer available and the mealie-meal has been withheld, so the soup is thinner and less seasoned. And I am very much afraid that horsemeat is being used.'

'The soup has become an absolute necessity,' Nicholas asserted firmly. 'And what's more the people enjoy it.'

'Only because they are so very hungry.' Laura's voice wavered. 'I heard that kittens are fetching five shillings and sixpence on the black market.' She paused and made a visible effort to conquer her distress. 'I'm afraid I have destroyed more of your sister's garden. A new scheme for vegetable growing has been started and I have joined in. Miranda and I have planted some seeds and at the current rate of progress of the Relief Column I have little doubt we will be here to enjoy the crop.'

'What would we do without you, Laura?' As had become their habit, they were sitting on the stoep in the early afternoon while Miranda slept and Matthew was busy elsewhere. Nicholas transferred his gaze from his sister's garden to Laura's face. 'In fact, doing without you is not something I care to contemplate. Either during or after this siege.'

'I shall still be around,' laughed Laura, 'unless Sir Matthew terminates my employment.'

'You can't be a governess all your life. Don't you ever want to marry?'

'I did at one time,' she said reflectively, 'but I have grown very fond of Miranda and could not bear to leave her. Besides, I don't think you realise how difficult it is for penniless females to find a husband.'

'Is money the only problem?' he asked eagerly. 'You don't have to worry about money, I've simply pots of it.'

'I don't understand,' said a perplexed Laura, 'how your money would help.'

Nicholas was clearing his throat and mopping his brow with a handkerchief. 'Fact is, I wondered if you'd care to marry me.'

'M . . . m . . . marry you!' stammered Laura. The declaration came as such a complete shock that she was thunderstruck and gaped at him foolishly.

'I am not surprised you don't think much of the idea,' said Nicholas humbly. 'I know I'm not much of a catch. Old enough to be your father.'

'Not much of a catch!' Laura shook her head in amazement. 'Lord Nicholas, you are far, far above me! Why, you could pick a bride from the cream of London society.'

'Yes,' he agreed honestly, 'but I never met one I wanted to marry. Pretty enough, most of them, plenty of money and of good family, but I always felt they'd turn out to be like their mamas – pushy and interfering, never leaving me alone. Now, you are much prettier than any of them, and intelligent too, and you've been an absolute brick during this siege. It's more than that, though,' he paused and coughed. 'You make me feel so comfortable and happy,' he said awkwardly. 'I like being with you and no one ever made me feel like that before.'

'You are the dearest, sweetest man,' whispered Laura. She would truly have liked to make him happy, but she could not believe that a marriage between them could ever be. She had never contemplated such a relationship. He *was* old enough to be her father, but then so was Matthew. The difference was that Nicholas was a fatherly or avuncular figure while Matthew was . . . not.

Nicholas gazed at her with beseeching eyes, waiting for her answer.

'I am tremendously flattered, Lord Nicholas, but I am afraid that perhaps you are being influenced by our very extraordinary circumstances. You are likely to feel quite different when we return to England and resume our normal lives.'

'No, I won't,' he maintained stoutly.

'There is an enormous gap between our social positions,' she reminded him gently. 'You are the son of a Duke, while I am a governess. Your family and friends might well be horrified at such a *mésalliance*.'

'Matthew likes you and his is the only opinion that matters to me. Please say yes, Laura,' he pleaded wistfully. 'Or don't you care for me at all?'

'I *like* you very much,' Laura said, with utter sincerity. 'But I do feel it would be a mistake to commit ourselves now. Your proposal is the greatest compliment I have ever received, or am ever likely to receive. I do suggest, however, that we ought to wait to see how we feel when we return home.'

With that Nicholas had to be content. Laura had not wanted to hurt him, but his disappointment was plain to see. The atmosphere seemed strained, Laura thought fretfully, and their relaxed companionship had been spoiled. Or perhaps it was the insufferable heat and the strange quiet which hung over Kimberley like the calm before a storm, that made her feel uneasy.

Without warning, the storm broke.

A boom rang through the oppressive air. It struck a deep unearthly chord which was followed by the whizzing whine of a shell and – after an aeon of unnerving suspense had passed – the most fearful crash.

No such sound had been heard in Kimberley before. Laura and Nicholas sat perfectly still in their chairs and looked at each other. The Boer big gun had been brought up at last and Laura knew that the crisis had come.

Frantically she rushed into the house which was empty but for Miranda in her bed. The servants had already sought shelter. Laura bundled the child into her clothes, pushed the doll into her arms and hurried her across the lawn to the shelter. Nicholas heaved the sacks of earth across the opening above their heads, leaving several small apertures for air and light.

'It's not too bad,' said Laura with relief. 'In fact the air is surprisingly cool and there is just enough light for us to see a little of each other. Can you see me, Miranda?'

The little girl did not reply.

'I asked you if you could see me, Miranda.'

Still there was no response.

'Are you all right?' Laura shouted into her ear.

'Yes, thank you,' she said in a perfectly normal voice.

'You must answer Laura at once when she speaks to you,' admonished Nicholas.

'She's such a good girl,' murmured Laura, ruffling the bright golden hair. 'She would answer if she could, wouldn't you, darling?'

The dug-out was more sound-proof than the house, the sacks of earth absorbing a good proportion of the noise of the bombardment. Laura felt rather than heard the bursting of the shells and could hardly hear the boom of the cannon. But in a way she found the tension harder to bear and found she was keeping her eyes fixed on the 'roof', expecting a shell to burst through at any moment. She tried not to worry about Matthew, but was intensely relieved when at about six o'clock light appeared above and his face peered down at them.

'You can come out now. They seem to have stopped for the moment.'

Laura handed Miranda up to him and scrambled out. She stared at him in horror.

'You're hurt!'

His face was scratched and bleeding and his shirt was torn.

'It's nothing,' he said tersely. 'The shells are digging holes in the Market Square and sending up showers of pebbles, which are flying through the air like buckshot and doing more damage than the shell itself.'

'Are there any casualties?'

'Injuries but no fatalities.'

'We are firing back, aren't we?' asked Laura anxiously. 'Can "Long Cecil" reach their big gun?'

'Not a chance,' Matthew replied. ' "Long Tom" has a range of ten thousand yards. That's nearly six miles! Not even Labram's masterpiece can touch it. But, yes, we are firing back – out of defiance, if nothing else.'

'Are the shells very big?'

'Let's just say that the missiles we've become accustomed to are corks by comparison.'

The bombardment began again the next day at four in the afternoon and lasted until six. On this occasion Matthew joined them underground and somehow the shelter seemed to shrink as his large frame filled the space. But, oh, how comforting and reassuring was his presence. He clasped Miranda in his arms and told them stories of his early days in Kimberley which had them all entranced. Wedged up against him in the darkness, acutely aware of the nearness of his body and grateful for the occasional comforting pressure of Nicholas's hand, Laura did not notice the passage of time. She climbed out of the shelter at dusk, laughing and happy – only to feel instant guilt and fear at the sight of the fires blazing in the city against the backdrop of the darkening sky. And they learned later that 'Long Tom' had claimed its first victim.

The third day was worse still. Beginning at six in the morning, the firing continued unceasingly until nightfall. All day long the death-dealing shells swept like a hurricane through the city – terrorising, killing, lacerating, maiming – greatly surpassing previous bombardments in intensity. Matthew made occasional forays for news and Nicholas dashed into the house to fetch food and water on several occasions. The first bulletin brought news of the death of a woman and her infant child who were struck down as they emerged from their shelter for a breath of air. With undiminished fury the bombardment continued, battering down walls and gables and filling hearts with a longing for vengeance. For the first time since the siege began nearly four months ago, all business in the town was suspended.

Late on this tragic Friday the sensational news, the worst news of all, spread through the town. George Labram had been killed by a shell at the Grand Hotel. Matthew sat in the drawing-room with his head buried in his hands, unheeding the continued fury of the Boer attack. It seemed incredible, so improbable and astounding that Labram of all people should be a victim; that he who had achieved greatness by building the big gun, the famous 'Long Cecil', should be dead. The irony was bitter indeed.

Contrary to expectations, the ferocious assault was not resumed on the Saturday morning. Kimberley drew breath, prepared to bury its dead and complained vociferously about the Boers and the town's own garrison with impartiality. When four in the afternoon came and went but brought no resumption of firing from the Boer guns, Laura decided that it would be safe to venture into the street. They were badly in need of supplies.

'Can't I go?' asked Nicholas.

'Thank you, but it will be much quicker and easier if I go myself. It will be a matter of discovering which stores are open, and all the shopkeepers know me now.'

'I'll walk with you,' said Matthew unexpectedly. 'Nicholas, will you look after Miranda? I must find out what arrangements are being made for Labram's funeral.'

Alone with him for the first time in days, Laura felt a shyness creeping over her as he strode beside her in silence and she struggled desperately for something to say.

'Lord Methuen's guns are audible in the distance, like faint, sympathetic coughs. Will they be able to hear the Boer bombardment?' she ventured.

'Yes. They will know exactly what's happening here and will be moving heaven and earth to reach us in time.'

'Suppose,' said Laura slowly, 'that they do not reach us in time? This is our crisis hour, isn't it? The Boers held back their big gun until they were sure we were so short of food that this extra suffering would be the last straw. Now they intend to continue shelling until we surrender or until they can take the town by force?'

'Yes.'

'Suppose they do take the town by force. What will happen?'

He smiled. 'Your classical education is encouraging your imagination to run riot. You can discount the colourful and lurid scenes that allegedly took place after the fall of Troy, Miss Vaughan. The Boer is extremely unlikely to rape and pillage – well, a little looting perhaps. You are British but you are also white and the Boers do not harm white women.'

'Yet they have killed several with their shells.'

'They would have preferred to kill British soldiers.'

'So Miranda would be safe if the city fell?'

'Absolutely safe. I trust, Miss Vaughan, that you are not advocating surrender?'

'Surrender? Never! The Queen's flag flies over Kimberley and they shall never drag it in the dust!'

They had reached the main street but to Laura's consternation the town was nearly empty of people.

'I don't think any of the stores are open,' she said in disappointment. 'I was hoping that at least I could buy bread. Perhaps . . .'

The words died on her lips and they both stood frozen to the ground as the air was shattered by the boom of the big gun. Exposed in the middle of the street, Laura felt as if her feet were literally nailed down and while she longed to run for cover she could not move. The weird hissing of the shell was growing louder and louder, and she was gripped by the conviction that it was heading straight for her.

Then she felt herself being lifted, carried to the side of the road and dumped unceremoniously on the ground. There was a crash like thunder as the shell burst and the air was filled with smoke and dust, the acrid smell of powder and flying fragments. Laura was not sure whether she had been carried by the blast or by Matthew – she only knew that she was sandwiched between the hard ground and his equally hard body as he shielded her from harm. She lay with her head buried against his shoulder, amazed that in the midst of danger such happiness was possible. As the noise abated he relaxed his hold slightly and moved his head so that he could look into her face. The smoke swirled about them as they stared into each other's eyes and then Laura was aware only of his lips as she felt herself drawn helplessly towards them. As his mouth pressed against hers, Laura parted her lips and his tongue plunged into her and his arms tightened convulsively. She seemed to spin through space as their mouths fused into one whole and her body was consumed with an anguished emptiness and a yearning to blend more closely with his.

But he tore himself away, jumped up and pulled her to her feet.

'I'm sorry,' he said stiffly. He was shaken by his longing for her. But she belonged to Nicholas and the last thing Matthew would ever do was hurt Nicholas.

'Why?' Her hair had come undone and she pushed back the thick waves from her face.

'I imagine that in any social strata it is not done to kiss one's best friend's girl.'

'I'm not . . .' Laura began. Then she noticed a movement across the road. 'That bakery is open!' she exclaimed.

Matthew was dusting himself down self-consciously as if suddenly aware that someone might have seen Sir Matthew Bright kissing the governess on the dusty ground of the main street in broad daylight.

'You're going home,' he said. 'Listen, the cannon is booming again.'

'There is no point in escaping the shells in order to die of starvation,' Laura pointed out.

She bought the bread and they ran back the way they had come, the insistent clangour of the bombardment ringing in their ears. It was a long walk at any time but today the journey seemed endless as Laura, weakened by lack of normal exercise and insufficient food, struggled to keep up with him.

'Take the bread and go on ahead!' she panted.

'Do you really think I would leave you out here alone?' and he took her hand and dragged her forward.

As they reached the house the firing stopped but the dreaded note of 'Long Tom' rang out again at eight in the evening just as Laura was setting the bread and a pot of weak tea on the table. They had reached the garden when the shell burst nearby, engulfing them in a roar so terrible that Miranda cried out and clapped her hands over her ears. She continued to cry when they were settled in the shelter and refused to stop even when Matthew took her in his arms and tried to comfort her.

'My dolly,' she sobbed. 'I left her in the house and she might get hurt.'

'I will fetch her for you,' Matthew promised reassuringly.

'No, you stay with the child, I'll go.' Nicholas made an opening in the roof just big enough for him to crawl through. 'I will only be a minute.'

The gap in the 'roof' of the dug-out was not large, but it was surprising how much of the noise and tumult of the bombardment it let in.

'They're really peppering our part of town tonight,' Matthew commented. Suddenly he chuckled. 'For some reason I'm thinking of the family. I can imagine that they will be having to forcibly restrain Julia from sailing out here and charging the Boers with her umbrella.'

Laura was listening for the thud of Nicholas's returning footsteps, but what she did hear was less reassuring. The whine of an approaching shell grew deafening, seeming to pass within inches of their heads with a scream that pierced Laura's skull and caused Miranda to howl again. It burst with a gigantic roar and the ground shuddered as though rocked by an earthquake. The night above them turned into day.

'The house has been hit. Nicky!' Matthew placed Miranda on the rough floor and leaped out of the shelter.

Laura followed him, just in time to see his dark silhouette outlined against a wall of flame as he disappeared into the burning house. The fire was blazing fiercely at the living-room end of the building. If Nicholas was in the nursery, he could be unharmed but if he had been approaching the garden door . . . and now Matthew . . .

With a gasp of relief she saw a figure emerge from the inferno and ran forwards. Matthew was carrying something over his shoulder and one side of his shirt was alight. Hurriedly Laura tore off her petticoats and as Matthew heaved his burden to the ground she flung the wad of material over his shoulder and arm and forced him to roll on the earth to extinguish the flames.

He pushed her away, kneeling beside his friend. 'Never mind me. Nicky! Are you all right? Nicky, answer me! For God's sake, *answer me*!'

Laura bent over the motionless figure which lay spreadeagled on the ground. As the burning house lit up the night sky she could see the fearful wound on Nicholas's forehead and a sob rose in her throat. Cold dread gripped her as she slowly and fearfully felt for his heartbeat.

There was none.

With infinite sadness and sympathy, she raised her eyes to Matthew's tortured face, bathed in the unearthly glow of the flames.

'He is dead, Matthew. I am so sorry.'

'No.' Matthew shook his head violently. 'He can't be. Not Nicky, I don't believe it.' He began slapping Nicholas's face gently and shaking his limp form. 'Come on, Nicky. Come on, old chap. You'll be all right.'

Fresh sounds from the other side of the house indicated the arrival of the fire brigade.

Laura crouched beside Matthew and tried to pull him away.

'Nicholas is dead, Matthew. There is nothing you can do for him now. You must think of your own safety.'

Then she saw something on the grass: Miranda's doll. Nicholas must have tucked it under his coat and it had been carried to safety. With all her strength she pulled Matthew away and thrust the doll into his hands.

'Miranda needs you. She is all alone in the shelter, crying and afraid. Now take the doll and go to her!'

Stunned, he stumbled to the shelter and disappeared into its murky depths. Bracing herself, Laura tugged Nicholas's body further away from the house. Then, dodging falling debris, she ran round to the front drive to ask the fire brigade to send for a doctor. She watched as they expended precious water extinguishing the flames and when the drawing-room and dining-room had been reduced to sodden, smoking rubble, she returned to the garden.

Miranda was asleep in her father's arms now, clutching the doll tightly. Laura could not see his face but his anguish was almost tangible.

'Does your arm hurt?'

'I feel nothing,' he said.

Laura sat down, desperately wanting to comfort him but not daring to intrude upon his grief. They sat in silence and after a while Laura tentatively placed a hand on his. He clutched it fiercely and she moved closer. So they remained until at midnight the guns ceased and some semblance of peace fell on the battered town and its people.

As soon as they emerged from the shelter Matthew lurched to the body on the ground while Laura peered cautiously at the house. It was a low, rambling building and the fire brigade had maintained that the remaining structure should be safe. Carefully Laura carried Miranda through the ruins into the passage leading to the bedrooms. There was a horrible smell, but nothing had been touched. Laura went to her own room and laid the still sleeping child on the bed. Then she returned to Matthew.

'We must carry him inside,' she said in her most practical voice. 'You take his shoulders and I will carry his feet.'

Tenderly, as though the slightest movement might hurt him, they carried Nicholas to his room. They were arranging him on the bed when the doctor arrived. Laura lit a lamp and gasped in horror at the sight of the raw red flesh of Matthew's burned left arm and shoulder. The doctor dressed the wound and handed Matthew a sleeping draught which he swallowed without a word and then went to bed. The doctor offered some to Laura.

She was tempted to accept. She was so tired and grief-stricken that sleep seemed like an elixir of heaven.

'No.' She shook her head. 'One of us must be alert in case the guns start again.'

'It's after midnight, it's Sunday.'

'Sir Matthew or Miranda might need something.' Laura smiled wearily. 'The Boers keep us as short of sleep as they do of every other commodity.'

After the doctor had departed, Laura lay down beside Miranda. She turned her head to see the time on the clock beside her bed – and her heart missed a beat. Her faithful old clock had stopped. The blast of the shell had knocked it over and shattered the glass face. Frantically Laura shook and banged it in an effort to start it ticking again, but in vain. With trembling hands she laid it face downwards on the table and lay, rigid and tense, in the darkness. In addition to all her other problems she must now contend with her old superstition that when the clock stopped, so would she.

CHAPTER SIX

Matthew awoke from his drugged sleep, groped through the jumbled images in his confused mind, and then remembered . . . The pain twisted within him and he closed his eyes and buried his face in the pillow. The loss of Nicholas left an aching hollow inside him which he felt would never be filled.

A horrible guilt began to permeate his being. *He* had persuaded Nicholas to come to Kimberley and *he* had insisted on staying. Matthew contemplated the ghastly possibility that the death of Nicholas was partly his fault. And into his mind swam the images of all the other people he had hurt.

Then the plump pleasant face of Nicholas filled Matthew's inner eye and with it came a kind of calm. Matthew was sure that the steadfast quality of their friendship had been shared and had been of equal importance to both of them. Nicholas surely knew that Matthew would never knowingly harm him. That absolution renewed Matthew's strength. To lay the ghosts of the dead, he must ensure the safety of the living: Miranda and Laura must survive.

Matthew dressed, struggling impatiently with his wounded arm, and hurried from the house. He went to make the funeral arrangements and to call an emergency meeting of Diamond Company directors, then he returned to tell Laura that Nicholas would be buried at dusk that day while the Sunday truce lasted. All over town, defences were being strengthened and men were even excavating the debris heaps to convert them into shelters.

'The Company has made a suggestion concerning the safety of the women and children and Kekewich has accepted our offer. This afternoon you and Miranda will take refuge in the Mine.'

Laura felt as if hands were clasping her throat, tightening, squeezing the air out of her.

'The tunnels afford excellent shelter,' Matthew continued. 'Even if a shell should fall into the open pit of the Mines, it would not penetrate the underground chambers.'

I can't, thought Laura wildly, I simply can't.

'I'd rather stay with you,' she burst out.

'I won't be here; I'll be busy. As a director of the Mine, I'm partly responsible for the safety of its inhabitants.'

'With one arm?' She pointed to the bandages. 'What can you do with one arm?'

'Plenty. And I can use the injured arm in an emergency. Is something the matter, Laura? You look as white as a sheet.'

I'm afraid, she wanted to say. I am horribly, terribly afraid of plunging into that black hole, to be incarcerated with thousands of others around me. I'm afraid of dying down there, in flames or in panic, gasping for air and unable to escape. But if I tell him, she thought, he will worry that I am incapable of looking after Miranda.

'I'm upset about Nicholas, that's all.'

'My poor Laura.' He came to her, tilting her face to his with his good right hand. 'In my grief at my own loss, I had forgotten yours. Try to remember that he loved you and that the one thing we can do for him now is to keep you safe.'

'I was not as close to him as you seemed to think. He asked me to marry him, but I would never have accepted.' Laura looked at Matthew steadily, while a feeling of wonderful relief swept through him at her words. 'I did not think of Nicholas in those terms. But he was such a good friend to me in the short time I knew him, that I can well understand your feelings at losing a lifetime's companion.'

'He reminded me of Anne,' said Matthew slowly. 'Or did Anne remind me of him? I am never quite sure which way round it was or which love was the greater. I only know that I will feel his loss more and more, and not less and less, as each day passes. Now,' he was determined to be practical, 'will you take Miranda into the Mine?'

'Is it the safest place for her?'

'Undoubtedly.'

'Then we will go.'

'Good, and on this occasion you will please allow me to use my influence to gain you an advantage. There may not be enough room for all the women and children, so I shall arrange for you to be one of the first.'

Laura opened her mouth to protest but he seized her arm and shook her roughly.

'I dug that hole, Laura! Thirty years ago I came here and scratched in that ground with my bare hands! Now that hole is going to keep my daughter safe. And you, too.'

'All right.' She hesitated. 'But Nicholas's funeral . . .' she said.

He nodded. 'I'm very sorry, but you won't be able to come. It would have been difficult anyway, because I would not want Miranda there. Don't worry, I shall not be alone. The Directors and many others will attend.'

'Say a prayer for him from me,' she whispered and her eyes filled with tears.

'I will,' he promised.

At four o'clock he escorted them to the headgear of the Kimberley Mine. Laura had packed a bundle of bedding and clothes and they carried a basket of provisions and crockery. A long procession of similarly laden people was wending its way through the streets and a large crowd had gathered at the entrance to the Mine. As Matthew forced a path through to the front, Laura took heart from the many frightened faces among the women. Apparently she was not the only one who viewed the descent with alarm.

The truck was standing ready at the shaft entrance but Laura averted her eyes from it.

'The tunnels were inspected this morning,' Matthew informed her. 'Some are very damp, but I have instructed that you shall be taken to the driest part.'

'What will you do?'

'I shall stay here to supervise the lowering of the "lift", except for a break to attend the funeral. I estimate it will take all evening to move this crowd, because the truck can only carry eight people at a time and some travellers have brought a great deal of baggage! If there isn't room for everyone, the rest will go to the caverns in the debris dumps. We must try to have everyone safely stowed by midnight in case the Boers open fire.'

'Where will you sleep? Not at the house, surely?'

'I'll stay with Rhodes, his house has become a civilian headquarters. I will lock up the jewellery and other valuables in the Company safe. There is one thing I must mention though,' and he drew her to one side and looked at her seriously. 'It is possible that I may end up like Nicholas,' he said quietly. 'If that happens, you must go straight to Rhodes or one of the other Directors. They will look after you and Miranda and give you money for the journey home. Do you understand?'

She nodded, unable to speak.

'Good! Now it's time to put you in the lift. We must start moving people underground soon or we shall never be through by midnight.'

Five other women and a girl of about ten were already settled in the vehicle. It looked horribly similar to a tumbril on its way to the guillotine. Matthew kissed Miranda and lifted her in with his one good arm while Laura settled in her seat. When their baggage had been added, the truck was full. His hand passed lightly over Miranda's curls and then squeezed Laura's shoulder.

'Take care of her for me,' he whispered. 'There is no one else in the world but you to whom I would entrust her. Take care of her, and of yourself.'

Before Laura could reply he gave the signal. There was a screech as the machinery began to turn and then the truck was moving, sliding down the track into the darkness, and the sunshine faded away. Laura put her arm round Miranda's shoulders and closed her eyes, feeling the motion of the vehicle but preferring not to dwell on the distance they were plummeting. Hot humid air rushed past her face and stirred her hair while Laura sat rigid, tense and terrified, as the truck plunged hundreds of feet into the sweltering gloom.

At last they squeaked to a standstill and Laura opened her eyes to see that they had arrived in a large oblong chamber into which various tunnels converged. A group of mine employees was waiting for them and as the truck ascended for its next load, one of the men lifted a lamp and led them down the main passage. It was lined with timber, dripping wet and festooned with fungus. The bobbing lantern cast an eerie light and the only sound in the still dank air was the hollow ring of their footsteps. Behind them several other men were carrying their bundles of possessions and the need for this additional assistance became apparent when their guide stopped beside a hole in the wall. Laura could see the shadowy outline of poles set in the rock to form a series of steps which disappeared from view up the 'chimney', and she was absorbing the shock realisation that they must ascend this 'ladder' when the first man climbed up out of sight. Laura stared at Miranda in alarm: she was much too small to manage for herself. But she need not have worried, for a giant of a man detached himself from the bundles of bedding, swung Miranda and her precious doll gently into his arms and carried her effortlessly to the upper level. When it was Laura's turn, she gritted her teeth and resolutely set herself to climb. A lantern at the top of the chimney lit the ladder and she hauled herself up some twenty feet, gasping for breath from the effort and the hot, heavy air.

She found herself in a cavern about ten feet long by six feet wide and the height of a small man.

'The climb is worth it, ladies,' one of the men declared. 'This is the driest part of the Mine. You will be more comfortable here than in the tunnels.'

'It doesn't seem right that we should be privileged,' Laura protested, but the man shrugged. 'Someone has to have the best accommodation; it might as well be you.'

After depositing their belongings on the floor of the cave, the men departed to meet their next batch of visitors. However, they left behind a lamp which cast a comforting glow. Several women produced candles, but had been warned not to burn them too long because oxygen would be in short supply.

They busied themselves with spreading blankets and arranging their belongings. Happily the young girl took an immediate interest in Miranda and the two of them were soon playing with their dolls. Laura discovered that two of the ladies were married to directors of the Company and the others to senior employees. They were pleasant and sensible and as a babble of noise permeated the cavern from the tunnels, Laura began to feel reluctantly grateful for Matthew's insistence on this one mark of privilege. The comparative privacy of the cavern and the compatibility of her companions would make the ordeal easier to bear.

Already she was losing track of time and although the Mine was in an uproar it was impossible to hear any murmur from the outside world. It seemed as though hours passed before a jug of cold water was passed up to them and then some tea arrived and a bucket for their '. . . ablutions', as the man phrased it with all the delicacy he could muster.

As they ate a portion of their precious provisions and drank the tea, Laura began to appreciate the enormity of the task facing the employees of the Diamond Company in provisioning and caring for the thousands of women and children who now depended on them. She wondered what Matthew was doing and, imagining the sad cortège winding its way to the cemetery, said a silent prayer for Nicholas.

Another man then appeared. 'Eleven o'clock, ladies, and the directors have declared Kimberley Mine "house full".' He lowered the lamp a little so that there was just enough light to see the opening of the chimney in the floor. 'Try to sleep if you can. If you need anything, I'll be on duty at the junction of the tunnel below and the main shaft.'

Miranda was already fast asleep. How kind everyone is, thought Laura drowsily, how very kind. And as comparative silence fell over the labyrinth, she dozed and then slept.

Monday morning passed with dreadful slowness in thirsty, hungry boredom. Packed closely together in the confined space of the caverns and tunnels, the women suffered from the heat and humidity of the poorly-ventilated passages. Their clothes were soon soaked in moisture and sweat and their hair hung limply in damp tendrils. It became too much of an effort to move and they sprawled, exhausted, on their blankets. However, the majority did find sufficient energy to talk and the chatter of the thousands of women and children reached a deafening crescendo.

Like all women everywhere, they worried most about the safety of their menfolk. It was awful to be down here with no notion of what was happening up above. Eventually news arrived that the bombardment of the town had begun at seven. Laura longed to go to the surface to keep in touch with developments at first hand and to stand in the open air. To see the sun and the sky seemed the most wonderful dream in the world at this moment. But she knew her ordeal had only just begun and that she must wait.

They were assured that the Boer guns had claimed no victims. But Matthew did not come.

He arrived on Tuesday, however, Laura's heart leaping with joy at the sight of his golden head appearing through the floor of the cave as he hauled himself up the 'pole-road'. He hugged Miranda and gave an eager audience the latest news.

The streets were apparently deserted; the whole machinery of man's life and work was at a stop. A stillness, weird and uncanny, hovered like a pall over the Diamond City. The bombardment had begun again and shells were crashing on to vacated houses. The noise of the fusillade echoed strangely through the empty thoroughfares and Kimberley seemed like a ghost town assaulted by demons.

'The noise couldn't be worse than it is down here,' declared Laura. 'The babble never stops: babies crying, children screaming, women shouting. The subdued roar of the machinery is always in the background and in the tunnel below the women are quarrelling about space and accusing each other of pilfering utensils. We're lucky here, though,' and she smiled at her companions. 'We're away from the worst of it.'

'Cheer up. I have a little present for you.'

He handed her a basket. Eagerly she lifted the cloth and let out a cry of surprise.

'*Grapes!* I don't believe it. Grapes on the one hundred and eleventh day of the siege! It must be a mirage.'

'They are real enough, I assure you. A present from Rhodes. He has been cultivating them most carefully these many months. Don't look so anguished, Laura. There are not enough grapes for everyone, but I do promise that you are not the only lucky ones.'

Laura looked at them reverently. 'We are sitting in the heart of a diamond mine, but right now these grapes are more precious than gems.'

Wednesday was 14 February, St Valentine's Day, and the 'Valentines' were delivered by early post. But, the joke went through the catacombs, the intended recipents had happily changed their addresses and were not at home. Rumours began to circulate that the balloon had been sighted again, that the Boers were perturbed and that an air of violent agitation was conspicuous in the portion of the cordon nearest to Modder River. These rumours were treated with suspicion. Too many hopes had been raised too often on previous occasions.

But the day wore on and the rumours grew. Rhodes's house had been hit. Laura held her breath. But no, it was only his bakehouse. Laura lived again. Persistently the whispers were passed on that the Boers were evacuating their positions and that a sortie had been made by the Kimberley militia.

Again Laura longed to go above ground and discover the truth. She was afraid, however, that even if she was able to secure a ride in the lift she would never find the courage to descend again into these dismal, smelly, damp and noisy passages. Besides, she could not leave Miranda and yet dared not risk Matthew's wrath by removing her from the safety of the Mine.

Miranda had quickly tired of the other girl's company and clung to Laura's side throughout the long empty days. Always a quiet child, she seemed more withdrawn than ever, confused and frightened by the strangeness of their surroundings. Patiently Laura tried to comfort the child, but an ache of anguish and concern gripped her as she became more and more convinced of the reason for Miranda's isolation.

That night Laura found it impossible to sleep. She tossed restlessly, haunted by the loss of her clock and by the terrible stories she had read about other sieges. The Siege of Lucknow, she recalled, had lasted one hundred and forty-two days, a month longer than their own incarceration. Four days she had been in the Mine; four months under siege. Nicholas was dead; Matthew injured and in danger from cannon; she and Miranda dirty, hungry, tired and risking asphyxiation. How much more could the human spirit endure? Just how much longer could Kimberley hold out?

* * *

In the early morning of Sunday II February, as Matthew and Laura laid Nicholas's body on his bed, Edward saddled his horse and prepared to leave the camps at Modder River. The reinforced army was intending to outflank the Boer positions at Magersfontein in a desperate attempt to reach Kimberley.

The responsibility for the relief of Kimberley was to lie with the cavalry, under the command of Colonel French. Once the army had outflanked the chief Boer positions, the cavalry must break through any remaining opposition and gallop on to the Diamond City while the infantry – led by Field Marshal Lord Roberts and Major-General Lord Kitchener of Khartoum – marched east to the Free State to continue the campaign.

Edward and his companions were keyed-up and tingling for action after long weeks of waiting. They rode swiftly and purposefully and then waited, consumed with impatience, for the plodding infantry to catch up. Apart from some minor setbacks, all went well for the first two days but Tuesday the 13th was a gruelling, gruesome experience. The cavalry advance began late, when the heat of the day was already making itself felt. Their orders were to cross the Modder, but reaching the river involved a journey of twenty-five miles across the seared, waterless veld. During the river crossing only three men were wounded by marauding bands of Boers, but forty horses died from heat exhaustion and five hundred could go no farther. Sweating, tired and drained, Edward tried to conceal his emotion but he found it harrowing to hear the pistol shots as the farriers slaughtered the beautiful beasts.

Wednesday the 14th was a day of frustration as the cavalry waited for the rest of the army to reach the Modder. They had to hold the river crossing for the infantry, but they chafed at the delay, longing to embark on the next stage of the operation – the dash to Kimberley. Colonel French spent the day surveying the terrain ahead, estimating the strength of the enemy and finalising his plan. At eight o'clock on the morning of 15 February the last of the infantry crossed the Modder. The cavalry was now free to ride to the aid of the beleaguered city.

When French's plan was revealed, a tremor of anticipation ran through the division. It was a plan of daring and panache which would show the British cavalry at its very best.

The Boers were holding two positions north of the Modder: a line of kopjes on the east and a long ridge which stretched towards the principal Boer encampments in the west. Between the ridge and the kopjes was a long valley which had to be, French maintained, the weakest point in the enemy line. 'Remember,' said the Colonel, 'that our job is not to engage the Boer in battle. We do not want to fight him, or kill him, or capture him – not this time. Our task is to break through his line and ride into the open country beyond to the relief of Kimberley.'

And in every man's mind there was a picture of the classic cavalry charge up that long sweeping valley, and there was not a man amongst them who did not wish to be in the van of that glorious gallop.

Please, prayed Edward, let it be us! Let the Lancers avenge the mortification and humiliation of their impotence in the other battles of this campaign!

The division moved off at nine-thirty on the morning of Thursday 15 February to the shouts and cheers of the infantry who had gathered to watch the stirring procession of eight thousand men mounted on their big Walers. The horses' hooves threw up a great dust cloud as the column clattered and jangled its way forward. Edward's hopes were high. Gordon's Brigade, which included the 9th Lancers, led the procession and they were first to emerge from cover and enter the open ground between the river and the valley. Immediately they appeared the Boer rifles and artillery opened fire, but French had his reply ready. Fifty-six British guns blasted the Boer positions and soon the hills were covered in smoke and flying debris.

French then issued his final orders. The ridge to the west of the valley appeared to be more weakly held than the kopjes to the east. Therefore the cavalry charge would be off-centre, swerving to the left to hug the ridge's lower levels. And Edward's heart sang. Gordon's Brigade was ordered to take the far ridge 'at a fast gallop'. The other Brigades would follow, covered by fire from the Royal Horse Artillery which would race for the ridge at the last moment.

Edward's heart was pounding and his throat was dry. He felt no fear of death or injury but was terribly afraid of disgracing himself in some way. This was his first real taste of battle, and suddenly he worried that his nerve might break.

He took up his position near the front of the regiment. They were deployed in extended order, with about six or seven yards between each man. Twenty yards behind them, the 12th Lancers were in similar array. A command rang out: swords scraped from their scabbards while lances – nine feet of steel-tipped bamboo – were lowered to the 'engage' position. Edward steadied his big black horse and waited for Gordon's signal. Charge! And they were off, the wind singing in their ears, hooves drumming on the hard dry ground, an awe-inspiring death-machine sweeping down the valley on an irresistible tide of exhilaration and determination. Never had Edward experienced such a glorious sensation, never had he felt more at one with his steed, as they hurtled on through the thick cloud of dust with the crash of gunfire echoing from the hills and an occasional Boer bullet whining past his head.

He was riding on the extreme left, closest to the slopes of the ridge, and he judged that the time had come to extend his flank. He spurred further to the left and now he could see the Boers running from the valley for cover on the hill. He saw one fleeing figure trampled beneath the pounding hooves and then glimpsed another scrambling out of their path. Without hesitation Edward wheeled and charged straight for the man. His victim sensed him coming and turned, a look of frozen terror on his face, as Edward bore down on him. He seemed about to raise his rifle, but it was too late. Edward's huge horse ate up the ground between them and his lethal lance was ready for the blow. He speared the Boer clean through the chest, the impact lifting the man from the ground before he dropped into a crumpled heap. Edward reined in his snorting, blowing horse and pulled his lance free. As blood gushed from the gaping wound, he struck again and again to make sure that this was one Boer who would trouble them no more. Then he plunged back into the dust cloud of horsemen, his dripping lance again dipped at the engage as the inexorable wave of horses and flashing steel swept through the Boer line and into the open plain.

As they rested and re-formed, Edward remained buoyed up with euphoria and relief. He had passed his first test and taken part in a charge which fulfilled and even surpassed his wildest dreams. Now only the thin cordon of the investing Boers separated them from Kimberley.

On that Thursday morning, Laura realised she could stand the Mine no longer. She and Miranda had to see daylight and breathe fresh air before they lost their health and their minds. She hung on until afternoon in the hope that Matthew would come, but when he did not appear she decided to risk his anger. Inquiries revealed that the morning's bombardment had ceased and, by rather ostentatious mention of Sir Matthew's name, she obtained assistance in conveying Miranda to the tunnel below and the promise of a ride in the lift. A life of privilege, she reflected wryly, was something to which one could easily become accustomed.

The sunshine on her face felt warm and wonderful, but it took a while for her eyes to adjust to the dazzling light after the gloom of the caverns. Her limbs were stiff and weak from lack of exercise and she stumbled as she guided Miranda's wobbling steps from the Mine.

Laura saw only one other woman in the street, but men were hurrying about briskly enough, clearing up the trail of damage left by the Boer guns. A man passed her, smiled broadly and shouted: 'Heard the news? The Column's coming.'

Laura looked at him suspiciously. She had heard that so many times before!

Further down the road, another passer-by cried out the same tidings and Laura glared. What sort of fool did they think she was? She would believe no more rumours. She walked on, enjoying the fresh air and the sky above her head and always hoping for a glimpse of Matthew. She passed a group of badly-damaged buildings and fear stabbed her, jolting her from that brief sunny contentment. Perhaps Matthew had been hurt, or killed, and no one had told her.

Excited knots of people were standing in the street, discussing the rumours. Laura was informed by one group that a huge body of cavalry was approaching.

'I shall believe it when I see it for myself,' she said firmly.

But the tales grew more insistent and confident as she reached the centre of town. People were scaling every vantage point and staring eagerly to the south. 'I can see them! I can see them!' she heard someone shout. She lifted her eyes to the mine headgear where the men in the conning tower were cheering frantically, waving handkerchiefs and pointing to the south. For the first time her doubts were transformed into wild hope.

'They *are* coming. Miranda, we must try to see them. Do you think you can climb up that debris heap? Come on, I'll help you.'

Holding tightly to Miranda's hand, she ran to the hillock and joined the throng of people who were scrambling to the top. And then she saw it for herself: the massive dust cloud advancing rapidly across the veld towards them. Suddenly she could not stop the tears from spilling down her cheeks and she gave way to the pent-up emotions of those four weary months. But once the first rush of tears was gone, she was seized with a fierce exultant joy. The column on the plain was coming closer. She could see the figures of the horsemen now. The crowd around her began to cheer and shout and Laura found herself being hugged and kissed by complete strangers who had suspiciously moist eyes. From every verandah, window, debris heap and redoubt, the roars of welcome were sent across the veld. People were scrambling down again, in order to be first in the streets to greet their deliverers, but Laura remained where she was for a little longer. She wanted to imprint this moment on her memory forever – the magnificent sight of eight thousand British cavalry galloping to their rescue.

When she and Miranda reached the street again, Laura's one thought was to find Matthew. She discovered, however, that she had no choice of direction. A surging mass of people propelled her relentlessly towards the road along which the cavalry were entering the city. The advance guard, exhausted and travel-stained, were already being swamped by the delirious crowd who were trying to shake their hands, slap them on the backs and pull the very buttons from their tunics. The news had spread to the mines and apparently the lift was working overtime in transporting the ladies to the surface because there was an increasingly large number of women to be seen. Laura fought her way through the joyous groups of laughing, whistling, singing, crying, dancing people until she reached the Kimberley Club. She could see Rhodes at the entrance in his distinctive white flannels and then, with a great surge of relief, she saw Matthew. He was still wearing the same filthy shirt, grubby breeches and high boots and with a pang of tenderness she recalled the immaculate figure which had descended the Park Lane steps only a year ago when she had seen him for the first time.

'There's Papa!' she told Miranda triumphantly. 'It's all over, darling. The Siege is raised. Now we can go home.'

Summoning all her strength she put her shoulders to the crowd and barged a way through. She emerged just as Matthew was embracing a young cavalry officer and paused, not liking to intrude.

'There they are!' said Matthew.

Edward turned and gazed at them. He was utterly exhausted and drained. He had ridden for hours under the blazing African sun and taken part in one of the greatest cavalry charges in British military history. He had killed his first Boer. And a moment ago he had learned that his Uncle Nicholas was dead. But now a kind of peace came over him as he saw the reason why he and his companions were here.

Their dresses were torn and dirty, stained with damp and hanging loosely on their thin bodies. Their faces were pale but streaked with dust and grime and their hair a tousled mass of forlorn limp curls. Yet they stood straight and unbowed, the dark girl with the steadfast eyes and serene expression and his little cousin with her solemn face and Edward's heart ached when he thought of all they had endured.

Above them the Queen's Flag flew bravely in the breeze, as it had done throughout the Siege, and Edward knew that the valiant men and horses who had fallen along the way had not died in vain.

CHAPTER SEVEN

'Damn!'

Explosively Matthew threw the paper on to the table and stalked to the door.

'The siege is ended,' he muttered bitterly, 'but our other problems return to plague us.'

Furtively Laura glanced at the page he had been reading. He had seized the Cape Town newspapers with such eagerness after these months of deprivation that it must be something really serious to upset him so. Her eye fell on a short paragraph which stated that the Governor of the Cape had entertained Princess Raminska to luncheon in Cape Town. The Princess, thought Laura, did not give up easily and perhaps Matthew might feel differently about her now. The months in Kimberley must make him yearn for the sight of that lovely face and tempting body.

Her spirits sank. Now that Edward and the army had left Kimberley to continue the campaign, she was finding the transition to normal life even more difficult than she had anticipated. Mechanically she continued packing the picnic basket. Fresh white bread! Laura handled it reverently, vowing that never again would she take it for granted. She glanced at her clock, now happily restored to full working order, and saw that it was time to go.

'There! We're ready.'

She smiled at Miranda, who was watching the proceedings with wide-eyed amazement.

'Are we really having a picnic, Laura? Just you, me and Papa?'

'It is a special treat because you've been such a good girl. Papa has even managed to borrow a pony and trap to take us out of town.'

Matthew returned, wearing one of his London jackets over his shirt and breeches. He had donned the jacket reluctantly, for the last time he wore it there had been that tempestuous scene with Katherine when he challenged her about the cheques and he fancied the garment still reeked of her perfume. But the sky looked threatening and, out of what was now a very limited wardrobe, this coat offered the best protection against the elements.

'It's looking a bit like rain. Are you sure you want to go today?' he asked.

'Oh yes! Miranda would be so disappointed if we didn't go and the cooler weather will be better for the pony.'

As they climbed into the cart, Laura noticed a rifle wedged behind the driving seat.

'Why do you need a gun?' she exclaimed in alarm. 'I thought you said it was safe to go out.'

'It's safe for us but not for a rabbit or buck which might provide our dinner.'

Laura sighed with relief. 'So all the Boers really have gone.'

'The garrison made another inspection yesterday and they are sure no pockets of resistance remain. A lone Boer could be hiding out, of course, but there's no earthly reason why he should.'

Danie lay on his stomach in the shelter of the rock-strewn kopje and watched the road.

He had decamped with his companions when the cavalry column arrived, knowing they could offer no effective resistance to such a show of British strength. On the 16th, the day after Kimberley was relieved, the Boers managed to evacuate 'Long Tom' and they had wreaked considerable havoc among the cavalry horses that day. But Danie declined to follow the commandos to their new position at Paardeberg. He had a private matter to settle in Kimberley first.

He had lain hidden here for several days. Knowing the terrain intimately, it had been simple to dodge the British patrols. He watched the activity round the town; the repair of the railway line was nearly complete and soon trains would reach Kimberley again. Doubtless Matthew would be one of the first to leave.

Danie began to feel anxious – surely he must come out of the city soon? He stared into the distance, willing Matthew to appear.

Matthew let the pony choose its own pace and it ambled along at a steady trot. Laura stole a sideways glance at his absorbed profile. His slouch hat was pulled down over his blue eyes which glittered brightly in his bronzed face. He seemed loose and relaxed, content to hold the pony's reins and drive in quiet anonymity through the stark grandeur of this remote land.

But in a few short weeks from now he would become 'Diamond Bright' again and be driven in the comfort of his splendid carriage or the Daimler. He would be busy with his business affairs once more and, instead of picnics in the veld, would eat his customary gourmet meals in the magnificence of his dining-room, while she sat upstairs with her solitary tray. She was the governess and she must never forget it. She had tried to explain to Nicholas how different everything would be when they went home, and now she must swallow this unpalatable truth herself.

And she had to tell him about Miranda. Apparently he had noticed nothing. But he loved his daughter so much! How and when could she break the news to him?

'I think we've come far enough. We can stop over there, on the slopes of that kopje.'

Matthew turned the pony from the road and they bumped over the uneven ground for half a mile or so. The sun was shining weakly from behind hazy cloud and the only sound was the rattle of the trap. Everything around them, every stone and each blade of grass seemed extraordinarily vivid and clearly defined. Laura gazed at the landscape intently. She felt that this might be her last perfect day and she wanted to remember every detail. How peaceful it was after the disturbance and danger of the siege. Then she looked at Matthew again. At least he was safe. Nothing could touch him now – she was so grateful for that.

Danie watched the cart coming closer, hardly daring to hope. Then he saw the tall, slouch-hatted figure and recognised the little girl whom he had seen holding Matthew's hand outside the Kimberley Town Hall. He smiled exultantly. The war was going badly, indeed it might be lost, but the Lord was blessing Danie's private conflict.

He picked up his rifle and, leaping and creeping noiselessly over the boulders, worked his way round to a vantage point above the spot where they had stopped.

Laura cleared away the crumbs and handed Miranda one of the big red apples which had recently arrived from the orchards of the southern Cape. Miranda bit sharply into the apple's sweet flesh and wandered off to look for flowers and rabbits.

'Have you heard from Philip?' Laura asked hesitantly.

Matthew shook his head.

'Perhaps his letters are still delayed at the Cape,' Laura suggested doubtfully.

'Perhaps,' said Matthew drily, 'he has not written.'

'Edward told me that Philip spent the last holidays at Desborough. I do hope we can be home for Easter.' Laura sighed as she remembered holding a similar conversation with Nicholas about spending Christmas in England.

'We should be able to leave Kimberley within the next few days. The railway is nearly ready. And I take it you will not object if I use my influence to secure a passage on the first mailship to leave the Cape?'

'No, I shall not object,' said Laura seriously, even though she was sure he was laughing at her. 'But I thought you might want to stop in Cape Town for a while.'

'Why on earth should I do that?'

'I thought . . . the Princess . . .' Laura floundered.

'She's the last person I want to see! Nothing but a cheap adventuress. No, on second thoughts she isn't even cheap, as my bank balance will testify! Princess indeed,' he snorted, 'the woman's a fake.'

'Like her pearls,' said Laura absently.

'What?'

'I stepped on one and it squashed . . .' she broke off, horrified at the implications of what she had said.

Matthew was lying on the blanket next to where she sat, but now he raised himself on one elbow and gazed into her face.

'You stepped on one,' he repeated slowly. 'There is only one time and place when you could have stepped on one of Katherine's pearls. You were there! My God, Laura Vaughan, you were there!'

Laura's face was beetroot red as she stared steadfastly over his head. 'I didn't intend to be there, honestly I didn't,' she whispered at last.

He sat up so that his face was level with hers and she waited for the storm of his wrath to break over her.

'You were there. And what a scene you witnessed.' He began to laugh. 'What a shock to a young lady's delicate sensibilities!' He leaned closer to her, the smile fading from his lips and his eyes darkening. 'But you're made of stronger stuff, aren't you, Laura! I've already had one brief, tantalising taste of the response of which you're capable.'

His lips were coming nearer and Laura was about to abandon herself to their irresistible attraction when suddenly she looked around.

'Where's Miranda?' she gasped.

Miranda had not seen a rabbit but she had found a butterfly. It was a beautiful creature with orange and black wings and it flew gently up the hillside. Still chewing her apple, Miranda trotted after it.

Danie watched her and then his gaze returned to Matthew. The dark-haired woman obstructed his view and he wished that Matthew would stand up. The little girl was scrambling up the shallow slope of the kopje now, heading in his direction. She presented a possibility, a distinct possibility. Her life or her father's – Matthew would have no choice. Danie knew that he must kill Matthew now – while the deed could be counted an act of war, not an act of murder. This would be his only chance.

'There she is!' Matthew pointed to the small figure in the blue dress higher up the hill.

Laura jumped to her feet. 'She mustn't wander so far on her own. She might fall.'

Matthew rose and stood beside her. 'Miranda! Come back!

Damn it, there are all sorts of gullies and crevasses in these hills. She could break her neck. *Miranda!*'

'She can't hear you,' said Laura in a strangled voice.

'What do you mean?'

Laura swallowed and took a deep breath. 'She's deaf.'

He was facing the hillside, but he turned his head slightly to look at her with a puzzled look of disbelief and horror. Just as he was opening his mouth to speak a shot rang out. Everything seemed to happen in slow motion for Laura as she saw his hand move to his chest before he pitched sideways, striking his head on the wheel of the trap.

At the same instant Miranda screamed.

Laura stood helplessly, horribly torn as she struggled to choose between them. Then, with a last anguished look at Matthew's inert body, she ran up the slope of the kopje. There was no sign of Miranda and it was no use calling her name. Suddenly a man stepped out from behind a rock, a rifle in his hand.

'Where is she?' Laura gasped. 'What have you done to her?'

The man pointed to the rocks lining the brow of the hill. His eyes were shining with a strange excitement, lingering on her bosom and the curve of her hips. Laura ran forward and then stopped abruptly as she realised that this part of the kopje fell away in a steep, jagged incline. The ground under her feet was unsteady, loosened by recent rains or, judging by wheel tracks across the surface, by Boer artillery dragged to the siege of Kimberley.

Miranda was clinging to rocky outcrop about fifty feet down. She was gazing up at Laura with a white, terrified face, but she was alive.

Beneath the narrow ledge which supported her was a sheer drop into the valley below.

'I tried to warn her, but she didn't listen,' the man said. He was breathing heavily and Laura felt his hand on her waist.

'She's deaf,' said Laura again.

The man lowered his eyes and released her. Suddenly he looked troubled.

She moved closer to the edge and sent a shower of loose earth and pebbles hurtling into the void. Her mind was working frantically. How could she climb down to Miranda and carry her to safety? She turned to the man beside her.

'You must help me,' she implored. 'Please, you must help me! She's only a child – you cannot let her die.'

Danie gazed at the huddled figure on the ledge and then he surveyed the cliff face. He laid down the rifle.

'I cannot climb straight down to her. There is too much danger of slipping and also I would send an avalanche of stones into her face.'

'So you will help me?'

'I will climb down here.' Danie pointed to the escarpment to their left which had a more gradual slope. 'Then I will cut sideways across the steep face to the ledge. From here it seems as if there are enough footholds. You must tell the child not to move.'

'I can't. She will not hear me.'

'Of course not. I forgot.' He frowned. 'How will I tell her what to do when I reach her?'

'She isn't completely deaf, she will hear if you shout loudly into her ear. Or, if you can speak straight into her face, I think she watches the movements of one's lips. Fortunately she is an extremely intelligent child. If you can only indicate clearly what you want her to do, she will understand very quickly.'

Danie nodded, stripping off his hat, bandolier and jacket and piling them on the ground next to the rifle. He was short, but his body was hard and tough and his arms were strong.

'It will be more difficult if she is hurt,' he warned.

And then he was gone, his dark head disappearing from view over the side of the cliff. Laura stayed where Miranda could see her, hoping her presence would be reassuring; trying to pin the child to the rock face by her very strength of will; trying not to think of Matthew.

The man was about thirty feet down now and beginning to move diagonally across the cliff face towards the ledge, sending showers of stones and debris plummeting harmlessly into the depths. The cascade was hypnotising and Laura could envisage only too easily a bright golden head tumbling down the same path.

He was climbing with speed and agility but, Laura reminded

herself, this was the easy part. Miranda turned her head and watched him approach. She was crouching against the cliff, her hands clinging to the rough earth and a meagre tuft of grass. The ledge was too narrow and sloping to enable the man to stand upon it and lift her, and Laura waited with thudding heart to see how he would prise her loose.

Then he was there, leaning across the ledge and shouting loudly into Miranda's face. His bellow reached Laura above.

'Are you hurt?'

Miranda shook her head and Laura let out a sobbing sigh of thankfulness.

'Take hold of my hands.' His voice was calm and reassuring.

He lowered himself into a sitting position on the edge of the ledge and leaned backwards, reaching his hands over his shoulders behind his head. Laura held her breath. Would Miranda be able to let go of the cliff and reach outwards to touch him?

The child hesitated while Danie waited, poised perilously on the brink of the abyss. Then slowly Miranda inched towards him and reached out one hand. Danie gripped it firmly and Miranda let go with her other hand and pushed it into his clasp. Carefully Danie pulled her a few more inches until he could wrap her arms around his neck. Instinctively the child clasped her hands tightly together under his chin.

'*Goeie meisie!*' murmured Danie. 'Good girl.'

He reached for a handhold on the cliff face beside him, chose his foothold and then levered himself up and out into space. He wavered as Miranda's weight pulled him backwards, but his strength and determination triumphed and cautiously he moved back the way he had come.

Miranda was hanging on to his back like a monkey. Laura wondered how much strength there must be in his arms to support both their weights and prevent them from tipping backwards into the valley. And how much strength remained in Miranda's little arms, thin and wasted after the ordeal of the siege?

At last Danie reached the edge of the cliff and started up the more gradual slope which enabled him to lean forward and achieve a better angle for his body. As he heaved himself and his burden on to the flat brow of the kopje, Laura ran to take his hand and help pull them clear of the edge.

And then, and only then, did Miranda begin to cry.

After comforting her and ensuring that she was unhurt, Laura tried to lift her but found that her own limbs were shaking too much to support the child's weight.

'I'll take her,' offered Danie gruffly, swinging her into his arms and setting off down the hill.

They rounded the bend and Laura felt something between a scream and a sob rising in her throat. Matthew was still lying where she had left him, limp and motionless on the grass.

'Why did you kill him?'

'We had an old score to settle,' Danie answered.

He carried Miranda to the trap and sat her gently in the back. Laura bent over Matthew and let out a small scream of surprise and joy as he opened his eyes and tried to sit up.

'You're alive!'

'Of course I'm alive,' Matthew muttered irritably. His gaze fell on Danie. 'I should have known! I must confess I had forgotten all about you.'

Danie's eyes spat hatred. Automatically he reached for his rifle but remembered he had left it on top of the kopje. He took a step towards Matthew, but quickly Laura sprang for the rifle which lay on the front seat of the trap. She levelled it at him.

'I shall always be grateful to you for saving Miranda, but if you take one more step towards Matthew I will kill you.'

Laura had no notion how to fire a rifle but Danie did not know that. He was accustomed to Boer women who were brought up with guns and often fired as straight and true as their menfolk.

'You always manage to escape,' he said bitterly to Matthew, 'but I would swear I hit you in the chest.'

Weakly Matthew fumbled in his breast-pocket and extracted a thick heavy medallion. Embedded in it was a bullet.

'It seems as if I own Katherine an apology,' he murmured incredulously, 'and a debt of gratitude. Her stupid talisman has remained here, forgotten, since she pushed it into my pocket all those months ago. I am sorry to disappoint you, Danie, but the only damage is a lump the size of a hen's egg where I hit my head on the cart and knocked myself out.'

'Willem often used to tell me that I owed my life to you,' Danie said. 'Now we are equal on that score. I brought your daughter up the cliff face, just as you carried me from the claim pit. But there is still Alida's death between us and the knowledge of what the British have done to our country.'

'It isn't only your country,' said Matthew. 'If it belongs to any one particular people, it belongs to the natives.'

'Even if I cannot kill you, I will continue the fight against you. If it is not settled in our lifetime, then it will be carried into the next generation.' Danie's eyes rested on Miranda. 'We Boers are a patient people. It may take years, but the Steyns will beat the Brights and the Boers will oust the British from this land. We will even gain control of your beloved diamond mine in the end.'

He turned to go, but paused to look at Laura.

'Who are you?'

'Only the child's governess.'

'Stay away from him.' Danie jerked his head in Matthew's direction. 'He will destroy you as he destroys every woman and every man who comes into his path.'

He strode up the kopje and vanished from their sight.

'Do you think he'll come back?' asked Laura anxiously. 'He has a rifle up there.'

'So I gathered but, no, I don't think he will return.' Matthew rose shakily to his feet, still holding the medallion. 'Katherine and her second sight! Damn it, it's mere superstitious rubbish. I was born lucky, that's all.'

'I thought you were dead.'

'And were you sorry?'

'Yes, of course.'

'Well, that is one good thing to come out of the day's events.' His legs gave way and he sat hurriedly on the grass. 'My head is spinning! But things are coming back to me slowly. What was Danie saying about Miranda and the cliff face?'

Laura explained.

Matthew shivered and sat silent for a while. 'He is right,' he said at last. 'That old debt has been expunged and we start the next round on more equal terms. But wait . . . you were saying something else before Danie fired at me.'

'I was saying that Miranda is deaf.'

'You can't be serious. She hears me! And she speaks in an entirely normal voice.'

'It is a recent development. She learned to speak when her hearing was normal. She hears if you shout and I believe she follows the movement of your lips.'

'How would she know to do that?'

'She doesn't do it consciously, in fact I don't believe she realises her hearing is impaired. I only knew for certain myself when we were in the shelter and she was so frightened – frightened because it was too dark for her to see our lips and to 'hear' what we were saying. She must have felt very isolated and alone.'

'It can't be true,' Matthew said, his eyes making an anguished appeal. 'Not Miranda! She is so perfect! And I had such hopes for her.'

'I see no reason why it should make any difference,' Laura maintained stoutly. 'We will take her to a doctor as soon as we reach London. It might only be a temporary problem, but we shouldn't count too much on that.'

'But why? How did it happen?'

Laura opened her mouth to say that it was caused by the scarlet fever and those dreadful ear infections. But in the nick of time she remembered how angry Matthew had been with Philip for passing on the disease to his little sister. If Matthew suspected that Philip was the indirect cause of Miranda's deafness, the consequences could be too terrible for them all.

'I think it was the shelling,' she invented desperately. 'Do you remember one particularly loud bang the night Nicholas was killed? Miranda clapped her hands to her ears and cried out in a way she had not done before.'

'Yes, I do remember.' Matthew's face was haunted. 'So the shelling hurt Miranda, as well as Nicky.' The sadness twisted his heart and he closed his eyes in pain.

Laura could not know that by absolving Philip she had passed the burden of guilt to Matthew.

'Talking of Nicky reminds me that I still have his presents in safe keeping. Weren't you worried about your brooch? I'm surprised you were willing to let it out of your sight.'

'It means a great deal to me because it was a gift from Nicholas, but its value has been purely sentimental in recent weeks. One cannot eat diamonds, unfortunately.'

He laughed but then grew serious again. He took her face in his hands and stared at her intently.

'Laura,' he said softly, 'will you marry me?'

His gaze was hypnotic but she battled against the wave of exhilaration and happiness which engulfed her, struggling to be sensible. She started to say that it could never be, that what was heaven in Kimberley could turn to hell in Park Lane . . .

But he placed a finger on her lips. 'You must,' he said, his voice low and insistent. 'I love you. And I'm not very good at taking "No" for an answer.'

And then he was kissing her, ruthlessly and very thoroughly, and when at last he let her go Laura knew that anything, anything at all, was preferable to the sheer impossibility of living without him.

'Marry me before we leave Kimberley,' Matthew was murmuring against her hair.

Laura nodded and from his pocket he withdrew that small leather bag.

'I don't have an engagement ring for you yet, but I can give you this.'

Slowly he withdrew the exquisite pear-shaped drop on its slender gold chain. The gem reflected the light of the African sky into a dazzling spectrum of radiant colour and, as Matthew clasped the diamond round Laura's neck, its beauty seemed symbolic of the brilliance of their many-faceted future together.

THE VEGAS LEGACY

OVID DEMARIS

Bestselling author of THE LAST MAFIOSO

Ruthless multi-billionaire Rufus Boutwell made his fortune in the wild days of the Nevada gold rush. He bought up land and politicians, then promoted gambling and prostitution for his own profit – while trumpeting the virtues of personal freedom. Now, as head of Nevada Consolidated Mines, he is about to launch the mightiest political coup of his long career which will make or break him forever. . . .

From the barren sands of the Nevada desert to the razzamatazz of a Vegas-style Republican convention, THE VEGAS LEGACY is a whirlwind-paced saga of greed, drugs, sex, ambition and corruption . . . in the blockbusting tradition of Harold Robbins and Mario Puzo.

GENERAL FICTION 0 7221 30163 £2.50

The greatest storyteller since Harold Robbins

GRAHAM MASTERTON

MAIDEN VOYAGE

The year is 1924 – the year of dizzy flappers, champagne baths and wild parties in the purple dawn. It is also the year of the maiden voyage of a fabulous Transatlantic luxury liner, the SS *Arcadia* – and a first for sparkling Catriona Keys, transformed overnight from carefree partygoer to powerful head of giant Keys Shipping. Enter young Mark Beeney, handsome but dangerous American shipping magnate, who is about to launch a daring takeover bid for Keys Shipping – and for Catriona's heart. As the champagne bubbles above decks, Keys Shipping is about to sail into troubled waters . . .

MAIDEN VOYAGE is an enthralling saga of destiny and decadence, passion and power – a wonderful epic recreation of the glamour and excitement of a bygone age.

GENERAL FICTION 0 7221 6028 3 £2.50